The suprem...
of the Ninet...

〰 Lev T̶o̶l̶s̶t̶o̶y̶, born a member of the Russian nobility, became one of its sharpest critics. His novels, WAR AND PEACE, ANNA KARENINA, RESURRECTION, and his later moralistic writings put him squarely in the camp of social reform that swept across Europe in the nineteenth century. Despite Tolstoy's bitter attacks on the Russian social system, his prestige was so enormous that even the Tsar did not dare to challenge him. In his lifetime, Tolstoy became the center of a group of disciples that extended as far as the shores of America. His literary and philosophical genius exerts its influence on each successive generation.

About this edition:

〰 The abridgment of Tolstoy's monumental classic is based upon the Maude translation, the only one authorized by Tolstoy. It has been prepared by Ernest J. Simmons, the distinguished American teacher and critic who is noted for his highly popular biographies and critical studies of Pushkin, Tolstoy, Dostoevsky, and Chekhov, as well as many other critical works and essays in American literary journals. He is justly considered the leading authority in the Western world on Tolstoy and his works.

WAR
AND
PEACE

Lev Tolstoy

The authorized translation by
Louise and Aylmer Maude

Abridged, Edited and with an Introduction
by Ernest J. Simmons

WSP

WASHINGTON SQUARE PRESS, INC. • NEW YORK

WAR AND PEACE

A *Washington Square Press* edition

1st printing.....................August, 1963
4th printing.........................May, 1967

A new edition of a distinguished literary work now made available in an inexpensive, well-designed format

L

Published by
Washington Square Press, Inc., 630 Fifth Avenue, New York, N.Y.

WASHINGTON SQUARE PRESS editions are distributed in the U.S. by Simon & Schuster, Inc., 630 Fifth Avenue, New York, N.Y. 10020 and in Canada by Simon & Schuster of Canada, Ltd., Richmond Hill, Ontario, Canada.

INTRODUCTION

In this effort to abridge Tolstoy's *War and Peace,* I was more than once reminded of an incident in the life of Chekhov who so firmly believed that to write with talent meant to write with brevity. For he undertook to abridge a Russian translation of Dumas' *Count of Monte Cristo,* not solely for money, but also because he was convinced that he could improve the novel by cutting it. He bled it so drastically, he wrote the publisher, that the novel looked like a person who has suffered from typhoid fever. An artist friend, observing Chekhov at this task, drew an amusing caricature in which he represented Dumas weeping copious tears as he stood behind Chekhov's chair and watched him slashing away at *The Count of Monte Cristo.*

I hasten to add that no abridgment of *War and Peace* can possibly improve it, and that any such attempt is an infinitely more hazardous act of literary violence than Chekhov's in the case of *The Count of Monte Cristo,* an undertaking which, incidentally, he wisely abandoned. It may be fairly argued, however, that an abridgment of *War and Peace* may find some justification in terms of the extreme length of the book as well as in the more controversial field of aesthetics. For Tolstoy is trying to do two things in his novel: to create one of the most enchanting stories of war and peace ever written, involving the variegated experiences of five families between 1805–1820 and of hundreds of other characters drawn from the aristocracy, the gentry and the peasantry; and secondly, to propound elaborate and dubious theories of his own about the philosophy of history, the purpose of war and the true essence of human greatness. Though Tolstoy labors to weave the threads of his theorizing into the fascinating tapestry portraying the lives of his imaginary men and women, it cannot be said that he is altogether successful. These essentially digressive elements interrupt the smooth flow of the narrative and undermine the novel's artistic unity. They add hundreds of pages to the book, and though these sections are often astutely argued and intellectually interesting, many critics agree that they create an obstacle to the average reader's appreciation of *War and Peace*.

Later, Tolstoy himself appears to have suspected that he had committed an artistic mistake in introducing into the novel his own personal views on purely theoretical matters, for he wrote a friend:

> The aim of an artist is not to resolve a question irrefutably, but to compel one to love life in all its manifestations, and these are inexhaustible. If I were told that I could write a novel in which I could indisputably establish as true my point of view on all social questions, I would not dedicate two hours to such a work; but if I were told that what I wrote would be read twenty years from now by those who are children today, and that they would laugh over it and fall in love with the life in it, then I would dedicate all my existence and all my powers to it.

Much of the cutting in the present abridgment is directed to the many pages devoted to Tolstoy's theories on the philosophy of history. But an effort has been made to retain their substance, especially when they are integrated with the views of leading characters such as Prince Andrew and Pierre. In addition, as in the case of all substantial deletions, very brief summaries of the omitted passages have been introduced into the appropriate places in the text, in order to alert the reader to such omissions and also to keep the total story line intact.

In a novel that runs to over half a million words, however, much more than these theorizing passages had to be dropped in coping with the space limitations of a popular paperback edition. Here selection imposes a heavy burden on any abridger who happens to have a literary conscience. After all, he is dealing with a world-famous masterpiece of fiction. The problem is not only to retain the leading characters, the important secondary ones and all the significant events that shaped the course of their lives, but also an adequate representation of Tolstoy's magnificent descriptive powers, his illuminating background material and particularly the philosophical flavor of his mind that imparts a peculiarly Tolstoyan intellectual quality to all his fiction. Such an effort has been made in this abridgment, but only the reader can gauge the measure of its success.

I am fully aware that the purist rejects any tampering with an artistic work, and in truth I have some sympathy with this point of view. Carried to its logical conclusion, of course, such an attitude should also require that *War and Peace* be read only in the original Russian, for artistic values are patently lost in translation no matter how perfect the rendering may be.

Nevertheless, we are compelled to adapt ourselves to this atomic world of ours, so radically different from that relatively leisurely one of the 1860's when *War and Peace* first appeared. In our rocket age, travel has become unbelievably swift, communications almost instantaneous and the quantitative production of what entertains and informs man absolutely staggering. The tempo of our lives has quickened so that it is little wonder, in the face of a mountainous outpouring of printed matter, that digests of articles, magazines, newspapers and books have today become commonplace. Over the years I have talked to hundreds of students to whom I have assigned *War and Peace* in my classes, and I have discovered that most of them, while expressing ecstatic admiration for the work, have rarely read all of it, and complain of what they regard as its excessive length. If this is the reaction of busy students of literature, what of the hundreds of thousands of busier amateur lovers of literature in the workaday world who all their lives have heard about *War and Peace* but have been frightened away from a book of more than half a millions words in length. Hence, there is the likely possibility that a shortened, inexpensive paperback edition would attract them to a famous literary classic which they might otherwise never read. None of this is offered as a justification for an abridgment of *War and Peace*, but at any rate it is a justifiable excuse.

The translation used in this edition is that of Louise and Aylmer Maude. Of the several English renderings of *War and Peace*, there can be no doubt that this is by far the best. The Maudes spent years in Russia, and had virtually a native command of the language. Aylmer Maude, who knew Tolstoy well, was for a time one of his disciples, and had a profound knowledge of the man and his writings—advantages which enabled him, as far as was possible for a non-Russian, to capture and duplicate the nuances of Tolstoy's thought and language. Further, Maude possessed to a high degree those essential attributes of the expert translator—refined literary taste and a sense of the fitness of things in English style.

Many major writers since Tolstoy have gone on record saying that *War and Peace* is the greatest novel ever written. And countless readers have never ceased to be amazed at the extraordinary richness of the life in it. Tolstoy seems to have exhausted all human experience in portraying the multitude of characters that crowd its pages. Yet nothing appears to be contrived or invented. Life in the exact sense of the word is lived in *War and Peace* with a fullness and convincingness that would be the despair of imitators. The transformation of reality into art may have been achieved with equal skill in other great novels, such as Stendhal's *The Red and the Black* and Flaubert's *Madame Bovary,* but in no novel is so much reality transformed into art as in *War and Peace.*

Something of this overwhelming impression of God's plenty is necessarily sacrificed in any extensive abridgment. In the words of the poet, however, though much is taken, much abides. And what abides will provide the reader with an authentic and delightful experience of having come in contact with supreme literary art. Indeed, this experience may move him, in a less hurried period of life, to read the full-length novel, *War and Peace*—a hoped-for achievement on the part of this conscience-stricken abridger, who has suffered a recurring nightmare in which Lev Tolstoy, standing by his desk, sadly watched the dreadful red pencil eliminating page after page of his masterpiece.

Ernest J. Simmons
Dublin, N. H.
March, 1963

SUGGESTED FURTHER READING

Principal Literary Works*

Major Novels
War and Peace (1865–69)
Anna Karenina (1875–78)
Resurrection (1899)

Shorter Novels
Childhood, Boyhood, Youth (1852, 1854, 1857)
Two Hussars (1856)
Family Happiness (1859)
The Cossacks (1863)
Polikushka (1863)
The Death of Ivan Ilych (1886)
The Kreutzer Sonata (1889)
Master and Man (1893)
Father Sergius (1898)
Hadji Murad (posthumous, 1911)
The Devil (posthumous, 1911)

Short Stories
The Raid (1852)
The Wood-Felling (1855)
The Snowstorm (1856)
Lucerne (1857)
Albert (1858)
Three Deaths (1859)
God Sees the Truth, but Waits (1872)
What Men Live By (1881)
Where Love Is, God Is (1885)
Ivan the Fool (1885)

* First Russian publication dates

Evil Allures, but Good Endures (1885)
Strider: The Story of a Horse (1886)
Walk in the Light While There Is Light (1893)
Three Questions (1903)
Memoirs of a Madman (posthumous, 1911)

Plays

The Power of Darkness (1886)
The Fruits of Enlightenment (1889)
The Light Shines in Darkness (posthumous, 1911)
The Live Corpse (posthumous, 1911)

Principal Critical, Religious, Philosophical Works

A Confession (1879)
What I Believe (1884)
The Kingdom of God Is Within You (1893)
Christianity and Patriotism (1894)
What Is Art? (1898)
What Then Must We Do? (1902)

Selected Biographical and Critical Works on Tolstoy

Christian, R. F. *Tolstoy's War and Peace*. London: Oxford University Press, 1962.

Maude, Aylmer. *The Life of Tolstoy*. 2 vols. London: Constable & Co., 1908–10.

Noyes, George. *Tolstoy*. New York: Duffield & Co., 1918.

Simmons, Ernest J. *Leo Tolstoy*. 2 vols. New York: Vintage Books, Inc. (pap), 1961.

Steiner, George. *Tolstoy or Dostoevsky*. New York: Alfred A. Knopf, Inc., 1959.

Tolstoy, Alexandra. *Tolstoy, A Life of My Father*. New York: Harper & Row, 1953.

WAR
AND
PEACE

1805

❚━━❚❙━━❙❚━━❙❚━━━❚❙━━❙❚━━❚

BOOK ONE

1

"Well, Prince, so Genoa and Lucca are now just family estates of the Bonapartes. But I warn you, if you don't tell me that this means war, if you still try to defend the infamies and horrors perpetrated by that Antichrist—I really believe he is Antichrist—I will have nothing more to do with you and you are no longer my friend, no longer my 'faithful slave,' as you call yourself! But how do you do? I see I have frightened you—sit down and tell me all the news."

It was in July, 1805, and the speaker was the well-known Anna Pávlovna Schérer, maid of honor and favorite of the Empress Márya Fëdorovna. With these words she greeted Prince Vasíli Kurágin, a man of high rank and importance, who was the first to arrive at her reception.

"Heavens! what a virulent attack!" replied the prince, not in the least disconcerted by this reception. He went up to Anna Pávlovna, kissed her hand, presenting to her his bald, scented, and shining head, and complacently seated himself on the sofa.

"First of all, dear friend, tell me how you are. Set your friend's mind at rest," said he without altering his tone, beneath the politeness and affected sympathy of which indifference and even irony could be discerned.

"Can one be well while suffering morally? Can one be calm in times like these if one has any feeling?" said Anna Pávlovna. "You are staying the whole evening, I hope?"

"And the fête at the English ambassador's? Today is Wednesday. I must put in an appearance there," said the prince. "My daughter is coming for me to take me there."

"Well, and what has been decided about Novosíltsev's dispatch? You know everything."

"What can one say about it?" replied the prince in a cold, listless tone. "What has been decided? They have decided that Bonaparte has burnt his boats, and I believe that we are ready to burn ours."

Prince Vasíli always spoke languidly, like an actor repeating a stale part. Anna Pávlovna Schérer on the contrary, despite her forty years, overflowed with animation and impulsiveness.

In the midst of a conversation on political matters Anna Pávlovna burst out:

"Oh, don't speak to me of Austria. Perhaps I don't understand things, but Austria never has wished, and does not wish, for war. She is betraying us! Russia alone must save Europe. Our gracious sovereign recognizes his high vocation and will be true to it. That is the one thing I have faith in! Our good and wonderful sovereign has to perform the noblest role on earth, and he is so virtuous and noble that God will not forsake him. Prussia has always declared that Bonaparte is invincible and that all Europe is powerless before him."

She suddenly paused, smiling at her own impetuosity.

"I think," said the prince with a smile, "that if you had been sent instead of our dear Wintzingerode you would have captured the King of Prussia's consent by assault. You are so eloquent. Will you give me a cup of tea?"

"In a moment. À propos," she added, becoming calm again, "I am expecting two very interesting men tonight, le Vicomte de Mortemart, who is connected with the Montmorencys through the Rohans, one of the best French families. He is one of the genuine *émigrés*, the good ones. And also the Abbé Morio. Do you know that profound thinker? He has been received by the Emperor. Had you heard?"

"I shall be delighted to meet them," said the prince. "But tell me," he added with studied carelessness as if it had only just occurred to him, though the question he was about to ask was the chief motive of his visit, "is it true that the Dowager Empress wants Baron Funke to be appointed first secretary at Vienna? The baron by all accounts is a poor creature."

Prince Vasíli wished to obtain this post for his son, but others were trying through the Dowager Empress Márya Fëdorovna to secure it for the baron.

Anna Pávlovna almost closed her eyes to indicate that neither she nor anyone else had a right to criticize what the Empress desired or was pleased with.

"Baron Funke has been recommended to the Dowager Empress by her sister," was all she said, in a dry and mournful tone.

The prince was silent and looked indifferent. But, with the womanly and courtierlike quickness and tact habitual to her, Anna Pávlovna wished both to rebuke him (for daring to speak as he had done of a man recommended to the Empress) and at the same time to console him, so she said:

"Now about your family. Do you know that since your daughter came out everyone has been enraptured by her? They say she is amazingly beautiful."

The prince bowed to signify his respect and gratitude.

"I often think," she continued after a short pause, drawing nearer to the prince and smiling amiably at him as if to show that political and social topics were ended and the time had come for intimate conversation—"I often think how unfairly sometimes the joys of life are distributed. Why has fate given you two such splendid children? I don't speak of Anatole, your youngest. I don't like him."

"What would you have me do?" he said at last. "You know I did all a father could for their education, and they have both turned out fools. Hippolyte is at least a quiet fool, but Anatole is an active one. That is the only difference between them."

"And why are children born to such men as you? If you were not a father there would be nothing I could reproach you with," said Anna Pávlovna, looking up pensively.

"Have you never thought of marrying your prodigal son, Anatole?" she asked. "They say old maids have a mania for matchmaking, and though I don't feel that weakness in myself as yet, I know a little person who is very unhappy with her father. She is a relation of yours, Princess Mary Bolkónskaya."

Prince Vasíli did not reply though, with the quickness of memory and perception befitting a man of the world, he indicated by a movement of the head that he was considering this information.

"Do you know," he said at last, evidently unable to check the sad current of his thoughts, "that Anatole is costing me forty thousand rubles a year? And," he went on after a pause, "what will it be in five years, if he goes on like this?" Presently he added: "That's what we fathers have to put up with. . . . Is this princess of yours rich?"

"Her father is very rich and stingy. He lives in the country. He is the well-known Prince Bolkónski who had to retire from the army under the late Emperor, and was nicknamed 'the King of Prussia.' He is very clever but eccentric, and a bore. The poor girl is very unhappy. She has a brother; I think you know him, he married Lise Meinen lately. He is an aide-de-camp of Kutúzov's and will be here tonight."

"Listen, dear Annette," said the prince, suddenly taking Anna Pávlovna's hand and for some reason drawing it downwards. "Arrange that affair for me and I shall always be your most devoted slave—*slafe* with an *f*, as a village elder of mine writes in his reports. She is rich and of good family and that's all I want."

"*Attendez*," said Anna Pávlovna, reflecting, "I'll speak to Lise, young Bolkónski's wife, this very evening, and perhaps the thing can be arranged. It shall be on your family's behalf that I'll start my apprenticeship as old maid."

Anna Pávlovna's drawing room was gradually filling. The highest Petersburg society was assembled there: people differing widely in age and character but alike in the social circle to which they belonged. Prince Vasíli's daughter, the beautiful Hélène, came to take her father to the ambassador's entertainment; she wore a ball dress and her badge as maid of honor. The youthful little Princess Bolkónskaya was also there. She had been married during the previous winter, and being pregnant did not go to any large gatherings, but only to small receptions. Prince Vasíli's son, Hippolyte, had come with Mortemart, whom he introduced. The Abbé Morio and many others had also come.

The young Princess Bolkónskaya had brought some work in a gold-embroidered velvet bag. Her pretty little upper lip, on which a delicate dark down was just perceptible, was too short for her teeth, but it lifted all the more sweetly, and was especially charming when she occasionally drew it down to meet the lower lip. As is always the case with a thoroughly attractive woman, her defect—the shortness of her upper lip and her half-open mouth—seemed to be her own special and peculiar form of beauty. Everyone brightened at the sight of this pretty young woman, so soon to become a mother, so full of life and health, and carrying her burden so lightly.

"I have brought my work," said she in French, displaying her bag and addressing all present. "Mind, Annette, I hope you have not played a wicked trick on me," she added, turning to her hostess. "You wrote that it was to be quite a small reception, and just see how badly I am dressed." And she spread out her arms to show her short-waisted, lace-trimmed, dainty gray dress, girdled with a broad ribbon just below the breast.

"*Soyez tranquille, Lise,* you will always be prettier than anyone else," replied Anna Pávlovna.

"You know," said the princess in the same tone of voice and still in French, turning to a general, "my husband is deserting me? He is going to get himself killed. Tell me what this wretched war is for?" she added, addressing Prince Vasíli, and without waiting for an answer she turned to speak to his daughter, the beautiful Hélène.

One of the next arrivals was a stout, heavily built young man with close-cropped hair, spectacles, the light-colored breeches fashionable at that time, a very high ruffle, and a brown dress coat. This stout young man was an illegitimate son of Count Bezúkhov, a well-known grandee of Catherine's time who now lay dying in Moscow. The young man had not yet entered either the military or civil service, as he had only just returned from abroad where he had been educated, and this was his first appearance in society. Anna Pávlovna greeted him with the nod she accorded to the lowest hierarchy in her drawing room. But in spite of this lowest-grade greeting, a look of anxiety and fear, as at the sight of something too large and unsuited to the place, came over her face when she saw Pierre enter. Though he was certainly rather bigger than the other men in the room, her anxiety could only have reference to the clever though shy, but observant and natural, expression which distinguished him from everyone else in that drawing room.

Pierre had been educated abroad, and this reception at Anna Pávlovna's was the first he had attended in Russia. He knew that all the intellectual lights of Petersburg were gathered there and, like a child in a toyshop, did not know which way to look, afraid of missing any clever conversation that was to be heard. Seeing the self-confident and refined expression on the faces of those present he was always expecting to hear something very profound. At last he came up to Morio. Here the conversation seemed interesting and he stood waiting for an opportunity to express his own views, as young people are fond of doing.

Anna Pávlovna's reception was in full swing. The spindles hummed steadily and ceaselessly on all sides. The whole company had settled into three groups. One, chiefly masculine, had formed round the abbé. Another, of young people, was grouped round the beautiful Princess Hélène, Prince Vasíli's daughter, and the little Princess Bolkónskaya, very pretty and rosy, though rather too plump for her age. The third group was gathered round Mortemart and Anna Pávlovna.

The vicomte was a nice-looking young man with soft features and polished manners, who evidently considered himself a celebrity but out of politeness modestly placed himself at the disposal of the circle in which he found himself. The group about Mortemart immediately began discussing the murder of the Duc d'Enghien. The vicomte said that the Duc d'Enghien had perished by his own magnanimity, and that there were particular reasons for Bonaparte's hatred of him.

"Ah, yes! Do tell us all about it, Vicomte," said Anna Pávlovna.

The vicomte bowed and smiled courteously in token of his willingness to comply. Anna Pávlovna arranged a group round him, inviting everyone to listen to his tale.

The vicomte wished to begin his story and gave a subtle smile.

"Come over here, Hélène, dear," said Anna Pávlovna to the beautiful young princess who was sitting some way off, the center of another group.

The princess smiled. She rose with the same unchanging smile with which she had first entered the room—the smile of a perfectly beautiful woman. With a slight rustle of her white dress trimmed with moss and ivy, with a gleam of white shoulders, glossy hair, and sparkling diamonds, she passed between the men who made way for her, not looking at any of them but smiling on all, as if graciously allowing each the privilege of admiring her beautiful figure and shapely shoulders, back, and bosom—which in the fashion of those days were very much exposed—and she seemed to bring the glamour of a ballroom with her as she moved toward Anna Pávlovna. Hélène was so lovely that not only did she not show any trace of coquetry, but on the contrary she even appeared shy of her unquestionable and all too victorious beauty. She seemed to wish, but to be unable, to diminish its effect.

"How lovely!" said everyone who saw her; and the vicomte lifted his shoulders and dropped his eyes as if startled by something extraordinary when she took her seat opposite and beamed upon him also with her unchanging smile.

"Madame, I doubt my ability before such an audience," said he, smilingly inclining his head.

The princess rested her bare round arm on a little table and considered a reply unnecessary. She smilingly waited. All the time the story was being told she sat upright, glancing now at her beautiful round arm, altered in shape by its pressure on the table, now at her still more beautiful bosom, on which she readjusted a diamond necklace. From time to time she smoothed the folds of her dress, and whenever the story produced an effect she glanced at Anna Pávlovna, at once adopted just the expression she saw on the maid of honor's face, and again relapsed into her radiant smile.

The little princess had also left the tea table and followed Hélène.

"Wait a moment, I'll get my work. . . . Now then, what are you thinking of?" she went on, turning to Prince Hippolyte. "Fetch me my workbag."

There was a general movement as the princess, smiling and talking merrily to everyone at once, sat down and gaily arranged herself in her seat.

"Now I am all right," she said, and asking the vicomte to begin, she took up her work.

Prince Hippolyte, having brought the workbag, joined the circle and moving a chair close to hers seated himself beside her.

Le charmant Hippolyte was surprising by his extraordinary resemblance to his beautiful sister, but yet more by the fact that in spite of this resemblance he was exceedingly ugly. His features were like his sister's, but while in her case everything was lit up by a joyous, self-satisfied, youthful, and constant smile of animation, and by the wonderful classic beauty of her figure, his face on the contrary was dulled by imbecility and a constant expression of sullen self-confidence, while his body was thin and weak. His eyes, nose, and mouth all seemed puckered into a vacant, wearied grimace, and his arms and legs always fell into unnatural positions.

The story was very pretty and interesting, especially at the point where the rivals suddenly recognized one another; and the ladies looked agitated.

"Charming!" said Anna Pávlovna with an inquiring glance at the little princess.

"Charming!" whispered the little princess, sticking the needle into her work as if to testify that the interest and fascination of the story prevented her from going on with it.

The vicomte appreciated this silent praise and smiling gratefully prepared to continue, but just then Anna Pávlovna, who had kept a watchful eye on the young man who so alarmed her, noticed that he was talking too loudly and vehemently with the abbé, so she hurried to the rescue. Pierre had managed to start a conversation with the abbé about the balance of power, and the latter, evidently interested by the young man's simple-minded eagerness, was explaining his pet theory. Both were talking and listening too eagerly and too naturally, which was why Anna Pávlovna disapproved.

Not letting the abbé and Pierre escape, Anna Pávlovna, the more conveniently to keep them under observation, brought them into the larger circle.

Just then another visitor entered the drawing room: Prince Andrew Bolkónski, the little princess' husband. He was a very handsome young man, of medium height, with firm, clear-cut features. Everything about him, from his weary, bored expression to his quiet, measured step, offered a most striking contrast to his lively little wife. It was evident that he not only knew everyone in the drawing room, but had found them to be so tiresome that it wearied him to look at or listen to them. And among all these faces that he found so tedious, none seemed to bore him so much as that of his pretty wife. He turned away from her with a grimace that distorted his handsome face, kissed Anna Pávlovna's hand, and screwing up his eyes scanned the whole company.

"You are off to the war, Prince?" said Anna Pávlovna.

"General Kutúzov," said Bolkónski, speaking French and stressing the last syllable of the general's name like a Frenchman, "has been pleased to take me as an aide-de-camp. . . ."

"And Lise, your wife?"

"She will go to the country."

"Are you not ashamed to deprive us of your charming wife?"

"*André*," said his wife, addressing her husband in the same coquettish manner in which she spoke to other men, "the vicomte has been telling us such a tale."

Prince Andrew screwed up his eyes and turned away. Pierre, who from the moment Prince Andrew entered the room had watched him with glad, affectionate eyes, now came up and took his arm. Before he looked round Prince Andrew frowned again, expressing his annoyance with whoever was touching his arm, but when he saw Pierre's beaming face he gave him an unexpectedly kind and pleasant smile.

"There now! . . . So you, too, are in the great world?" said he to Pierre.

"I knew you would be here," replied Pierre. "I will come to supper with you. May I?" he added in a low voice so as not to disturb the vicomte who was continuing his story.

"No, impossible!" said Prince Andrew, laughing and pressing Pierre's hand to show that there was no need to ask the question. He wished to say something more, but at that moment Prince Vasíli and his daughter got up to go and the two young men rose to let them pass.

"You must excuse me, dear Vicomte," said Prince Vasíli to the Frenchman, holding him down by the sleeve in a friendly way to prevent his rising. "This unfortunate fete at the ambassador's deprives me of a pleasure, and obliges me to interrupt you. I am very sorry to leave your enchanting party," said he, turning to Anna Pávlovna.

His daughter, Princess Hélène, passed between the chairs, lightly holding up the folds of her dress, and the smile shone still more radiantly on her beautiful face. Pierre gazed at her with rapturous, almost frightened, eyes as she passed him.

"Very lovely," said Prince Andrew.

"Very," said Pierre.

In passing, Prince Vasíli seized Pierre's hand and said to Anna Pávlovna: "Educate this bear for me! He has been staying with me a whole month and this is the first time I have seen him in society. Nothing is so necessary for a young man as the society of clever women."

As Prince Vasíli is about to leave, he is detained by an old family friend, Princess Anna Mikháylovna Drubetskáya, who persuades him to use his influence to get her son Borís transferred to the Guards. Pierre, in an argument with the vicomte, defends the greatness of Napoleon.

2

Having thanked Anna Pávlovna for her charming soirée, the guests began to take their leave.

Pierre was ungainly. Stout, about the average height, broad, with huge red hands; he did not know, as the saying is, how to enter a drawing room and still less how to leave one; that is, how to say something particularly agreeable before going away. Besides this he was absent-minded. When he rose to go, he took up instead of his own, the general's three-cornered hat, and held it, pulling at the plume, till the general asked him to restore it. All his absent-mindedness and inability to enter a room and converse in it was, however, redeemed by his kindly, simple, and modest expression. Anna Pávlovna turned toward him and, with a Christian mildness that expressed forgiveness of his indiscretion, nodded and said: "I hope to see you again, but I also hope you will change your opinions, my dear Monsieur Pierre."

Prince Andrew had gone out into the hall, and, turning his shoulders to the footman who was helping him on with his cloak, listened indifferently to his wife's chatter with Prince Hippolyte who had also come into the hall. Prince Hippolyte stood close to the pretty, pregnant princess, and stared fixedly at her through his eyeglass.

"Go in, Annette, or you will catch cold," said the little princess, taking leave of Anna Pávlovna. "It is settled," she added in a low voice.

Anna Pávlovna had already managed to speak to Lise about the match she contemplated between Anatole and the little princess' sister-in-law.

"I rely on you, my dear," said Anna Pávlovna, also in a low tone. "Write to her and let me know how her father looks at the matter. *Au revoir!*"—and she left the hall.

Prince Hippolyte approached the little princess and, bending his face close to her, began to whisper something.

Still smiling, she gracefully moved away, turning and glancing at her husband. Prince Andrew's eyes were closed, so weary and sleepy did he seem.

"Are you ready?" he asked his wife, looking past her.

The princess, picking up her dress, was taking her seat in the dark carriage, her husband was adjusting his saber; Prince Hippolyte, under pretense of helping, was in everyone's way.

"Allow me, sir," said Prince Andrew in Russian in a cold, disagreeable tone to Prince Hippolyte, who was blocking his path.

"I am expecting you, Pierre," said the same voice, but gently and affectionately.

The postilion started, the carriage wheels rattled. Prince Hippolyte laughed spasmodically as he stood in the porch waiting for the vicomte whom he had promised to take home.

Pierre reaching the house first went into Prince Andrew's study like one quite at home, and from habit immediately lay down on the sofa.

"What have you done to Mlle. Schérer? She will be quite ill now," said Prince Andrew, as he entered the study, rubbing his small white hands.

Pierre turned his whole body, making the sofa creak. He lifted his eager face to Prince Andrew, smiled, and waved his hand.

"One can't everywhere say all one thinks, *mon cher*. Well, have you at last decided on anything? Are you going to be a guardsman or a diplomatist?" asked Prince Andrew after a momentary silence.

Pierre at the age of ten had been sent abroad with an abbé as tutor, and had remained away till he was twenty. When he returned to Moscow his father dismissed the abbé and said to the young man, "Now go to Petersburg, look round, and choose your profession. I will agree to anything. Here is a letter to Prince Vasíli, and here is money. Write to me all about it, and I will help you in everything." Pierre had already been choosing a career for three months, and had not decided on anything. It was about this choice that Prince Andrew was speaking. Pierre rubbed his forehead.

"No, I have not; but this is what I have been thinking and wanted to tell you. There is a war now against Napoleon. If it were a war for freedom I could understand it and should be the first to enter the army; but to help England and Austria against the greatest man in the world is not right."

Prince Andrew only shrugged his shoulders at Pierre's childish words. He put on the air of one who finds it impossible to reply to such nonsense, but it would in fact have been difficult to give any other answer than the one Prince Andrew gave to this naïve question.

"If no one fought except on his own conviction, there would be no wars," he said.

"And that would be splendid," said Pierre.

Prince Andrew smiled ironically.

"Very likely it would be splendid, but it will never come about. . . ."

"Well, why are you going to the war?" asked Pierre.

"What for? I don't know. I must. Besides that I am going . . ." He paused. "I am going because the life I am leading here does not suit me!"

The rustle of a woman's dress was heard in the next room. Prince Andrew shook himself as if waking up, and his face assumed the look it had had in Anna Pávlovna's drawing room. Pierre removed his feet from the sofa. The princess came in. She had changed her gown for a house dress as fresh and elegant as the other. Prince Andrew rose and politely placed a chair for her.

"How is it," she began, as usual in French, settling down briskly and fussily in the easy chair, "how is it Annette never got married? How stupid you men all are not to have married her! Excuse me for saying so, but you have no sense about women. What an argumentative fellow you are, Monsieur Pierre!"

"And I am still arguing with your husband. I can't understand why he wants to go to the war," replied Pierre, addressing the princess with none of the embarrassment so commonly shown by young men in their intercourse with young women.

The princess started. Evidently Pierre's words touched her to the quick.

"Ah, that is just what I tell him!" said she. "I don't understand it; I don't in the least understand why men can't live without wars."

Pierre looked at his friend and, noticing that he did not like the conversation, gave no reply.

"When are you starting?" he asked.

"Oh, don't speak of his going, don't! I won't hear it spoken of," said the princess in the same petulantly playful tone in which she had spoken to Hippolyte in the drawing room and which was so plainly ill-suited to the family circle of which Pierre was almost a member. "Today when I remembered that all these delightful associations must be broken off . . . and then you know, André . . ." (she looked significantly at her husband) "I'm afraid, I'm afraid!" she whispered, and a shudder ran down her back.

Her husband looked at her as if surprised to notice that someone besides Pierre and himself was in the room, and addressed her in a tone of frigid politeness.

"What is it you are afraid of, Lise? I don't understand," said he.

"There, what egotists men all are: all, all egotists! Just for a whim of his own, goodness only knows why, he leaves me and locks me up alone in the country."

"With my father and sister, remember," said Prince Andrew gently.

"Alone all the same, without *my* friends. . . . And he expects me not to be afraid."

"I still can't understand what you are afraid of," said Prince Andrew slowly, not taking his eyes off his wife.

The princess blushed, and raised her arms with a gesture of despair.

"No, Andrew, I must say you have changed. Oh, how you have . . ."

"Your doctor tells you to go to bed earlier," said Prince Andrew. "You had better go."

The princess said nothing, but suddenly her short downy lip quivered. Prince Andrew rose, shrugged his shoulders, and walked about the room.

Pierre looked over his spectacles with naïve surprise, now at him and now at her, moved as if about to rise too, but changed his mind.

"Why should I mind Monsieur Pierre being here?" exclaimed the little princess suddenly, her pretty face all at once distorted by a tearful grimace. "I have long wanted to ask you, Andrew, why you have changed so to me? What have I done to you? You are going to the war and have no pity for me. Why is it?"

"Lise!" was all Prince Andrew said. But that one word expressed an entreaty, a threat, and above all conviction that she would herself regret her words. But she went hurriedly:

"You treat me like an invalid or a child. I see it all! Did you behave like that six months ago?"

"Lise, I beg you to desist," said Prince Andrew still more emphatically.

Pierre, who had been growing more and more agitated as he listened to all this, rose and approached the princess. He seemed unable to bear the sight of tears and was ready to cry himself.

"Calm yourself, Princess! It seems so to you because . . . I assure you I myself have experienced . . . and so . . . because . . . No, excuse me! An outsider is out of place here . . . No, don't distress yourself . . . Good-by!"

Prince Andrew caught him by the hand.

"No, wait, Pierre! The princess is too kind to wish to deprive me of the pleasure of spending the evening with you."

"No, he thinks only of himself," muttered the princess without restraining her angry tears.

"Lise!" said Prince Andrew dryly, raising his voice to the pitch which indicates that patience is exhausted.

Suddenly the angry, squirrel-like expression of the princess' pretty face changed into a winning and piteous look of fear.

Her beautiful eyes glanced askance at her husband's face, and her own assumed the timid, deprecating expression of a dog when it rapidly but feebly wags its drooping tail.

"*Mon Dieu, mon Dieu!*" she muttered, and lifting her dress with one hand she went up to her husband and kissed him on the forehead.

"Good night, Lise," said he, rising and courteously kissing her hand as he would have done to a stranger.

The friends were silent. Neither cared to begin talking. Pierre continually glanced at Prince Andrew; Prince Andrew rubbed his forehead with his small hand.

"Let us go and have supper," he said with a sigh, going to the door.

They entered the elegant, newly decorated, and luxurious dining room. Halfway through supper Prince Andrew leaned his elbows on the table and, with a look of nervous agitation such as Pierre had never before seen on his face, began to talk—as one who has long had something on his mind and suddenly determines to speak out.

"Never, never marry, my dear fellow! That's my advice: never marry till you can say to yourself that you have done all you are capable of, and until you have ceased to love the woman of your choice and have seen her plainly as she is, or else you will make a cruel and irrevocable mistake. Marry when you are old and good for nothing—or all that is good and noble in you will be lost. It will all be wasted on trifles. Yes! Yes! Yes! Don't look at me with such surprise. If you marry expecting anything from yourself in the future, you will feel at every step that for you all is ended, all is closed except the drawing room, where you will be ranged side by side with a court lackey and an idiot! . . . But what's the good? . . ." and he waved his arm.

Pierre took off his spectacles, which made his face seem different and the good-natured expression still more apparent, and gazed at his friend in amazement.

"My wife," continued Prince Andrew, "is an excellent woman, one of those rare women with whom a man's honor is safe; but, O God, what would I not give now to be un-married! You are the first and only one to whom I mention this, because I like you."

As he said this Prince Andrew was less than ever like that Bolkónski who had lolled in Anna Pávlovna's easy chairs and with half-closed eyes had uttered French phrases between his teeth.

"You don't understand why I say this," he continued, "but it is the whole story of life . . . I am now going to the war, the greatest war there ever was, and I know nothing and am fit for nothing."

"It seems funny to me," said Pierre, "that *you, you* should consider yourself incapable and your life a spoiled life. You have everything before you, everything. And you . . ."

He did not finish his sentence, but his tone showed how highly he thought of his friend and how much he expected of him in the future.

"How can he talk like that?" thought Pierre. He considered his friend a model of perfection because Prince Andrew possessed in the highest degree just the very qualities Pierre lacked, and which might be best described as strength of will. Pierre was always astonished at Prince Andrew's calm manner of treating everybody, his extraordinary memory, his extensive reading (he had read everything, knew everything, and had an opinion about everything), but above all at his capacity for work and study. And if Pierre was often struck by Andrew's lack of capacity for philosophical meditation (to which he himself was particularly addicted), he regarded even this not as a defect but as a sign of strength.

"My part is played out," said Prince Andrew. "What's the use of talking about me? Let us talk about you," he added after a silence, smiling at his reassuring thoughts.

That smile was immediately reflected on Pierre's face.

"But what is there to say about me?" said Pierre, his face relaxing into a careless, merry smile. "What am I? An illegitimate son!" He suddenly blushed crimson, and it was plain that he had made a great effort to say this. "Without a name and without means . . . And it really . . . " But he did not say what "it really" was. "For the present I am free and am all right. Only I haven't the least idea what I am to do; I wanted to consult you seriously."

Prince Andrew looked kindly at him, yet his glance—friendly and affectionate as it was—expressed a sense of his own superiority.

"I am fond of you, especially as you are the one live man among our whole set. Yes, you're all right! Choose what you will; it's all the same. You'll be all right anywhere. But look here: give up visiting those Kurágins and leading that sort of life. It suits you so badly—all this debauchery, dissipation, and the rest of it!"

"What would you have, my dear fellow?" answered Pierre, shrugging his shoulders. "Women, my dear fellow; women!"

"I don't understand it," replied Prince Andrew. "Women who are *comme il faut*, that's a different matter; but the Kurágins' set of women, 'women and wine,' I don't understand!"

Pierre was staying at Prince Vasíli Kurágin's and sharing the dissipated life of his son Anatole, the son whom they were planning to reform by marrying him to Prince Andrew's sister.

"Do you know?" said Pierre, as if suddenly struck by a happy thought, "seriously, I have long been thinking of it. . . . Leading such a life I can't decide or think properly about anything. One's head aches, and one spends all one's money. He asked me for tonight, but I won't go."

"You give me your word of honor not to go?"

"On my honor!"

3

Pierre goes to Kurágin's, gets drunk, watches Dólokhov —Kurágin's roommate, officer of the Semënov regiment, a gambler and duelist—win a wager by drinking a bottle of rum while sitting on the outside ledge of a three-story window without holding on.

4

Prince Vasíli kept the promise he had given to Princess Drubetskáya who had spoken to him on behalf of her only son Borís on the evening of Anna Pávlovna's soirée. Soon after Anna Pávlovna's reception Anna Mikháylovna returned to Moscow and went straight to her rich relations, the

Rostóvs, with whom she stayed when in the town and where her darling Bóry [Borís], who had only just entered a regiment of the line and was being at once transferred to the Guards as a cornet, had been educated from childhood and lived for years at a time.

It was St. Natalia's day and the name day of two of the Rostóvs—the mother and the youngest daughter—both named Nataly. Ever since the morning, carriages with six horses had been coming and going continually, bringing visitors to the Countess Rostóva's big house on the Povarskáya, so well known to all Moscow. The countess herself and her handsome eldest daughter were in the drawing room with the visitors who came to congratulate, and who constantly succeeded one another in relays.

The countess was a woman of about forty-five, with a thin Oriental type of face, evidently worn out with childbearing—she had had twelve. A languor of motion and speech, resulting from weakness, gave her a distinguished air which inspired respect. The count met the guests and saw them off, inviting them all to dinner.

"I am very, very grateful to you, *mon cher,*" or *"ma chère"* —he called everyone without exception and without the slightest variation in his tone, "my dear," whether they were above or below him in rank—"I thank you for myself and for our two dear ones whose name day we are keeping. But mind you come to dinner or I shall be offended, *ma chère!* On behalf of the whole family I beg you to come, *mon cher!"* These words he repeated to everyone without exception or variation, and with the same expression on his full, cheerful, clean-shaven face, the same firm pressure of the hand and the same quick, repeated bows.

"Márya Lvóvna Karágina and her daughter!" announced the countess' gigantic footman in his bass voice, entering the drawing room. The countess reflected a moment and took a pinch from a gold snuffbox with her husband's portrait on it.

"I'm quite worn out by these callers. However, I'll see her and no more. She is so affected. Ask her in," she said to the footman in a sad voice, as if saying: "Very well, finish me off."

A tall, stout, and proud-looking woman, with a round-faced smiling daughter, entered the drawing room, their dresses rustling.

The conversation was on the chief topic of the day: the illness of the wealthy and celebrated beau of Catherine's day, Count Bezúkhov, and about his illegitimate son Pierre, the one who had behaved so improperly at Anna Pávlovna's reception.

"I am so sorry for the poor count," said the visitor. "He is in such bad health, and now this vexation about his son is enough to kill him!"

"What is that?" asked the countess as if she did not know what the visitor alluded to, though she had already heard about the cause of Count Bezúkhov's distress some fifteen times.

"That's what comes of a modern education," exclaimed the visitor. "It seems that while he was abroad this young man was allowed to do as he liked, and now in Petersburg I hear he has been doing such terrible things that he has been expelled by the police."

"You don't say so!" replied the countess.

"He chose his friends badly," interposed Anna Mikháylovna. "Prince Vasíli's son, he, and a certain Dólokhov have, it is said, been up to heaven only knows what! And they have had to suffer for it. Dólokhov has been degraded to the ranks and Bezúkhov's son sent back to Moscow. Anatole Kurágin's father managed somehow to get his son's affair hushed up, but even he was ordered out of Petersburg."

"But what have they been up to?" asked the countess.

"They are regular brigands, especially Dólokhov," replied the visitor. "He is a son of Márya Ivánovna Dólokhova, such a worthy woman, but there, just fancy! Those three got hold of a bear somewhere, put it in a carriage, and set off with it to visit some actresses! The police tried to interfere, and what did the young men do? They tied a policeman and the bear back to back and put the bear into the Moyka Canal. And there was the bear swimming about with the policeman on his back!"

"What a nice figure the policeman must have cut, my dear!" shouted the count, dying with laughter.

Princess Anna Mikháylovna intervened in the conversation,

evidently wishing to show her connections and knowledge of what went on in society.

"The fact of the matter is," said she significantly, and also in a half whisper, "everyone knows Count Cyril's reputation. . . . He has lost count of his children, but this Pierre was his favorite."

"How handsome the old man still was only a year ago!" remarked the countess. "I have never seen a handsomer man."

"He is very much altered now," said Anna Mikháylovna. "Well, as I was saying, Prince Vasíli is the next heir through his wife, but the count is very fond of Pierre . . . no one knows who will inherit his immense fortune, Pierre or Prince Vasíli. Forty thousand serfs and millions of rubles!"

"Prince Vasíli arrived in Moscow yesterday. I hear he has come on some inspection business," remarked the visitor.

"Yes, but between ourselves," said the princess, "that is a pretext. The fact is he has come to see Count Cyril Vladímirovich, hearing how ill he is."

"But do you know, my dear, that was a capital joke," said the count; and seeing that the elder visitor was not listening, he turned to the young ladies. "I can just imagine what a funny figure that policeman cut!"

And as he waved his arms to impersonate the policeman, his portly form again shook with a deep ringing laugh, the laugh of one who always eats well and, in particular, drinks well. "So do come and dine with us!" he said.

5

Silence ensued. The countess looked at her callers, smiling affably, but not concealing the fact that she would not be distressed if they now rose and took their leave. The visitor's daughter was already smoothing down her dress with an inquiring look at her mother, when suddenly from the next room were heard the footsteps of boys and girls running to the door and the noise of a chair falling over, and a girl of thirteen, hiding something in the folds of her short muslin frock, darted in and stopped short in the middle of the room. It was evident that she had not intended her flight to bring her so far. Behind her in the doorway appeared a student with a crimson coat collar, an officer of the Guards, a girl of fifteen, and a plump rosy-faced boy in a short jacket.

The count jumped up and, swaying from side to side, spread his arms wide and threw them round the little girl who had run in.

"Ah, here she is!" he exclaimed laughing. "My pet, whose name day it is. My dear pet!"

"*Ma chère*, there is a time for everything," said the countess with feigned severity. "You spoil her, Ilyá," she added, turning to her husband.

"How do you do, my dear? I wish you many happy returns of your name day," said the visitor. "What a charming child," she added, addressing the mother.

This black-eyed, wide-mouthed girl, not pretty but full of life—with childish bare shoulders which after her run heaved and shook her bodice, with black curls tossed backward, thin bare arms, little legs in lace-frilled drawers, and feet in low slippers—was just at that charming age when a girl is no longer a child, though the child is not yet a young woman. Escaping from her father she ran to hide her flushed face in the lace of her mother's mantilla—not paying the least attention to her severe remark—and began to laugh. She laughed, and in fragmentary sentences tried to explain about a doll which she produced from the folds of her frock.

"Do you see? . . . My doll . . . Mimi . . .You see . . ." was all Natásha managed to utter (to her everything seemed funny). She leaned against her mother and burst into such a loud, ringing fit of laughter that even the prim visitor could not help joining in.

"Now then, go away and take your monstrosity with you," said the mother, pushing away her daughter with pretended sternness, and turning to the visitor she added: "She is my youngest girl."

Natásha, raising her face for a moment from her mother's mantilla, glanced up at her through tears of laughter, and again hid her face.

The visitor, compelled to look on at this family scene, thought it necessary to take some part in it.

"Tell me, my dear," said she to Natásha, "is Mimi a relation of yours? A daughter, I suppose?"

Natásha did not like the visitor's tone of condescension to childish things. She did not reply, but looked at her seriously.

Meanwhile the younger generation: Borís, the officer, Anna Mikháylovna's son; Nicholas, the undergraduate, the count's eldest son; Sónya, the count's fifteen-year-old niece, and little Pétya, his youngest boy, had all settled down in the drawing room and were obviously trying to restrain within the bounds of decorum the excitement and mirth that shone in all their faces.

The two young men, the student and the officer, friends from childhood, were of the same age and both handsome fellows, though not alike. Borís was tall and fair, and his calm and handsome face had regular, delicate features. Nicholas was short with curly hair and an open expression. Dark hairs were already showing on his upper lip, and his whole face expressed impetuosity and enthusiasm. Nicholas blushed when he entered the drawing room. He evidently tried to find something to say, but failed. Borís on the contrary at once found his footing, and related quietly and humorously how he had known that doll Mimi when she was still quite a young lady, before her nose was broken; how she had aged during the five years he had known her, and how her head had cracked right across the skull. Having said this he glanced at Natásha. She turned away from him and glanced at her younger brother, who was screwing up his eyes and shaking with suppressed laughter, and unable to control herself any longer, she jumped up and rushed from the room as fast as her nimble little feet would carry her. Borís did not laugh.

Borís quietly left the room and went in search of Natásha. The plump boy ran after them angrily, as if vexed that their program had been disturbed.

The only young people remaining in the drawing room, not counting the young lady visitor and the countess' eldest daughter (who was four years older than her sister and behaved already like a grown-up person), were Nicholas and Sónya, the niece. Sónya was a slender little brunette with a tender look in her eyes which were veiled by long lashes, thick black plaits coiling twice round her head, and a tawny tint in her complexion and especially in the color of her slender but graceful and muscular arms and neck. By the grace of her movements, by the softness and flexibility of her small limbs, and by a certain coyness and reserve of manner, she reminded one of a pretty, half-grown kitten which promises to become a beautiful little cat. She evidently considered it proper to show an interest in the general conversation by smiling, but in spite of herself her eyes under their thick long lashes watched her cousin who was going to join the army, with such passionate girlish adoration that her smile could not for a single instant impose upon anyone, and it was clear that the kitten had settled down only to spring up with more energy and again play with her cousin as soon as they too could, like Natásha and Borís, escape from the drawing room.

"Ah yes, my dear," said the count, addressing the visitor and pointing to Nicholas, "his friend Borís has become an officer, and so for friendship's sake he is leaving the university and me, his old father, and entering the military service, my dear."

"It's not at all from friendship," declared Nicholas, flaring up and turning away as if from a shameful aspersion. "It is not from friendship at all; I simply feel that the army is my vocation."

The little kitten, feasting her eyes on him, seemed ready at any moment to start her gambols again and display her kittenish nature.

"All right, all right!" said the old count. "He always flares up! This Bonaparte has turned all their heads; they all think of how he rose from an ensign and became Emperor. Well, well, God grant it," he added, not noticing his visitor's sarcastic smile.

The elders began talking about Bonaparte. Julie Karágina turned to young Rostóv.

"What a pity you weren't at the Arkhárovs' on Thursday. It was so dull without you," said she, giving him a tender smile.

The young man, flattered, sat down nearer to her with a coquettish smile, and engaged the smiling Julie in a confidential conversation without at all noticing that his involuntary smile had stabbed the heart of Sónya, who blushed and smiled unnaturally. In the midst of his talk he glanced round at her. She gave him a passionately angry glance, and hardly able to restrain her tears and maintain the artificial smile on her lips, she got up and left the room. All Nicholas' animation vanished. He waited for the first pause in the conversation, and then with a distressed face left the room to find Sónya.

"How plainly all these young people wear their hearts on their sleeves!" said Anna Mikháylovna, pointing to Nicholas as he went out.

"What a charming creature your younger girl is," said the visitor; "a little volcano!"

"And she's in love with Borís already. Just fancy!" said the countess with a gentle smile, looking at Borís' mother . . . "Perhaps I spoil her, but really that seems the best plan. With her elder sister I was stricter."

"Yes, I was brought up quite differently," remarked the handsome elder daughter, Countess Véra, with a smile.

But the smile did not enhance Véra's beauty as smiles generally do; on the contrary it gave her an unnatural, and therefore unpleasant, expression. Véra was good-looking, not at all stupid, quick at learning, was well brought up, and had a pleasant voice; what she said was true and appropriate, yet, strange to say, everyone—the visitors and countess alike —turned to look at her as if wondering why she had said it, and they all felt awkward.

"People are always too clever with their eldest children and try to make something exceptional of them," said the visitor.

"What's the good of denying it, my dear? Our dear countess was too clever with Véra," said the count. "Well, what of that? She's turned out splendidly all the same," he added, winking at Véra.

The guests got up and took their leave, promising to return to dinner.

"What manners! I thought they would never go," said the countess, when she had seen her guests out.

When Natásha ran out of the drawing room she only went as far as the conservatory. There she paused and stood listening to the conversation in the drawing room, waiting for Borís to come out. She was already growing impatient, and stamped her foot, ready to cry at his not coming at once, when she heard the young man's discreet steps approaching neither quickly nor slowly. At this Natásha dashed swiftly among the flower tubs and hid there.

Borís paused in the middle of the room, looked round, brushed a little dust from the sleeve of his uniform, and going up to a mirror examined his handsome face. Natásha, very still, peered out from her ambush, waiting to see what he would do. He stood a little while before the glass, smiled, and walked toward the other door. Natásha was about to call him but changed her mind. "Let him look for me," thought she. Hardly had Borís gone than Sónya, flushed, in tears, and muttering angrily, came in at the other door. Natásha checked her first impulse to run out to her, and remained in her hiding place, watching—as under an invisible cap—to see what went on in the world. She was experiencing a new and peculiar pleasure. Sónya, muttering to herself, kept looking round toward the drawingroom door. It opened and Nicholas came in.

"Sónya, what is the matter with you? How can you?" said he, running up to her.

"It's nothing, nothing; leave me alone!" sobbed Sónya.

"Ah, I know what it is."

"Well, if you do, so much the better, and you can go back to her!"

"Só-o-onya! Look here! How can you torture me and yourself like that, for a mere fancy?" said Nicholas taking her hand.

Sónya did not pull it away, and left off crying. Natásha, not stirring and scarcely breathing, watched from her ambush with sparkling eyes. "What will happen now?" thought she.

"Sónya! What is anyone in the world to me? You alone are everything!" said Nicholas. "And I will prove it to you."

"I don't like you to talk like that."

"Well, then, I won't; only forgive me, Sónya!" He drew her to him and kissed her.

"Oh, how nice," thought Natásha; and when Sónya and

Nicholas had gone out of the conservatory she followed and called Borís to her.

"Borís, come here," said she with a sly and significant look. "I have something to tell you. Here, here!" and she led him into the conservatory to the place among the tubs where she had been hiding.

Borís followed her, smiling.

"What is the *something?*" asked he.

She grew confused, glanced round, and, seeing the doll she had thrown down on one of the tubs, picked it up.

"Kiss the doll," said she.

Borís looked attentively and kindly at her eager face, but did not reply.

"Don't you want to? Well, then, come here," said she, and went further in among the plants and threw down the doll. "Closer, closer!" she whispered.

She caught the young officer by his cuffs, and a look of solemnity and fear appeared on her flushed face.

"And me? Would you like to kiss me?" she whispered almost inaudibly, glancing up at him from under her brows, smiling, and almost crying from excitement.

Borís blushed.

"How funny you are!" he said, bending down to her and blushing still more, but he waited and did nothing.

Suddenly she jumped up onto a tub to be higher than he, embraced him so that both her slender bare arms clasped him above his neck, and, tossing back her hair, kissed him full on the lips.

Then she slipped down among the flowerpots on the other side of the tubs and stood, hanging her head.

"Natásha," he said, "you know that I love you, but . . ."

"You are in love with me?" Natásha broke in.

"Yes, I am, but please don't let us do like that. . . . In another four years . . . then I will ask for your hand."

Natásha considered.

"Thirteen, fourteen, fifteen, sixteen," she counted on her slender little fingers. "All right! Then it's settled?"

A smile of joy and satisfaction lit up her eager face.

"Settled!" replied Borís.

"Forever?" said the little girl. "Till death itself?"

She took his arm and with a happy face went with him into the adjoining sitting room.

Véra joins Borís and Sónya, Nicholas and Natásha in the sitting room and spitefully scolds them. Meanwhile, Countess Rostóva and Anna Mikháylovna converse in the drawing room.

"Ah, my dear," said the countess, "my life is not all roses either. Don't I know that at the rate we are living our means won't last long? It's all the Club and his easygoing nature. Even in the country do we get any rest? Theatricals, hunting, and heaven knows what besides! But don't let's talk about me; tell me how you managed everything. I often wonder at you, Annette—how at your age you can rush off alone in a carriage to Moscow, to Petersburg, to those ministers and great people, and know how to deal with them all! It's quite astonishing. How did you get things settled? I couldn't possibly do it."

"Ah, my love," answered Anna Mikháylovna, "God grant you never know what it is to be left a widow without means and with a son you love to distraction! . . . I need five hundred rubles, and have only one twenty-five-ruble note. I am in such a state. . . . My only hope now is in Count Cyril Vladímirovich Bezúkhov. If he will not assist his godson—you know he is Bóry's godfather—and allow him something for his maintenance, all my trouble will have been thrown away. . . . I shall not be able to equip him."

The countess' eyes filled with tears and she pondered in silence.

"I often think, though, perhaps it's a sin," said the princess, "that here lives Count Cyril Vladímirovich Bezúkhov so rich, all alone . . . that tremendous fortune . . . and what is his life worth? It's a burden to him, and Bóry's life is only just beginning. . . ."

"Surely he will leave something to Borís," said the countess.

"Heaven only knows, my dear! These rich grandees are so selfish. Still, I will take Borís and go to see him at once, and I shall speak to him straight out. Let people think what they will of me, it's really all the same to me when my son's fate is at stake." The princess rose. "It's now two o'clock and you dine at four. There will just be time."

"Are you going to Count Cyril Vladímirovich, my dear?" said the count coming out from the dining hall into the anteroom, and he added: "If he is better, ask Pierre to dine with us."

6-7

In Sections 6 and 7, Anna Mikháylovna forces her way into the dying Count Bezúkhov's room to plead the cause of her son Borís, who assures Pierre that he and his mother want nothing from his father. Borís tenders Pierre the invitation of the Rostóvs to dinner.

8

After Anna Mikháylovna had driven off with her son to visit Count Cyril Vladímirovich Bezúkhov, Countess Rostóva sat for a long time all alone applying her handkerchief to her eyes. At last she rang.

"Ask the count to come to me."

The count came waddling in to see his wife with a rather guilty look as usual.

"Well, little countess? What a *sauté* of game *au madère* we are to have, my dear! I tasted it."

He sat down by his wife, his elbows on his knees and his hands ruffling his gray hair.

"What are your commands, little countess?"

"You see, my dear . . . What's that mess?" she said, pointing to his waistcoat. "It's the *sauté*, most likely," she added with a smile. "Well, you see, Count, I want some money."

Her face became sad.

"Oh, little countess!" . . . and the count began bustling to get out his pocketbook.

"I want a great deal, Count! I want five hundred rubles," and taking out her cambric handkerchief she began wiping her husband's waistcoat.

"Yes, immediately, immediately! Hey, who's there?" he

called out in a tone only used by persons who are certain that those they call will rush to obey the summons. "Send Dmítri to me!"

Dmítri, a man of good family who had been brought up in the count's house and now managed all his affairs, stepped softly into the room.

"This is what I want, my dear fellow," said the count to the deferential young man who had entered. "Bring me . . ." he reflected a moment, "yes, bring me seven hundred rubles, yes! But mind, don't bring me such tattered and dirty notes as last time, but nice clean ones for the countess."

"Yes, Dmítri, clean ones, please," said the countess, sighing deeply.

"When would you like them, your excellency?" asked Dmítri. "Allow me to inform you . . . But, don't be uneasy," he added, noticing that the count was beginning to breathe heavily and quickly which was always a sign of approaching anger. "I was forgetting . . . Do you wish it brought at once?"

"Yes, yes; just so! Bring it. Give it to the countess."

"Ah, money, Count, money! How much sorrow it causes in the world," said the countess. "But I am in great need of this sum."

"You, my little countess, are a notorious spendthrift," said the count, and having kissed his wife's hand he went back to his study.

When Anna Mikháylovna returned from Count Bezúkhov's the money, all in clean notes, was lying ready under a handkerchief on the countess' little table, and Anna Mikháylovna noticed that something was agitating her.

"Well, my dear?" asked the countess.

"Oh, what a terrible state he is in! One would not know him, he is so ill! I was only there a few moments and hardly said a word . . ."

"Annette, for heaven's sake don't refuse me," the countess began, with a blush that looked very strange on her thin, dignified, elderly face, and she took the money from under the handkerchief.

Anna Mikháylovna instantly guessed her intention and stooped to be ready to embrace the countess at the appropriate moment.

"This is for Borís from me, for his outfit."

Anna Mikháylovna was already embracing her and weeping. The countess wept too. They wept because they were friends, and because they were kindhearted, and because they —friends from childhood—had to think about such a base thing as money, and because their youth was over. . . . But those tears were pleasant to them both.

9

Countess Rostóva, with her daughters and a large number of guests, was already seated in the drawing room. The count took the gentlemen into his study and showed them his choice collection of Turkish pipes. From time to time he went out to ask: "Hasn't she come yet?" They were expecting Márya Dmítrievna Akhrosímova, known in society as *le terrible dragon*, a lady distinguished not for wealth or rank, but for common sense and frank plainness of speech.

In the count's room, which was full of tobacco smoke, they talked of the war that had been announced in a manifesto, and about the recruiting. None of them had yet seen the manifesto, but they all knew it had appeared. The count sat on the sofa between two guests who were smoking and talking. He neither smoked nor talked, but bending his head first to one side and then to the other watched the smokers with evident pleasure and listened to the conversation of his two neighbors, whom he egged on against each other.

Lieutenant Berg argues with Shinshín on the financial advantages of serving in the Guards over the cavalry.

Pierre had come just at dinnertime and was sitting awkwardly in the middle of the drawing room on the first chair he had come across, blocking the way for everyone. The countess tried to make him talk, but he went on naïvely looking around through his spectacles as if in search of somebody and answered all her questions in monosyllables. He was in the way and was the only one who did not notice the fact. Most of the guests, knowing of the affair with the bear, looked with curiosity at this big, stout, quiet man, wondering how such a clumsy, modest fellow could have played such a prank on a policeman.

The countess exchanged glances with Anna Mikháylovna. The latter understood that she was being asked to entertain this young man, and sitting down beside him she began to speak about his father; but he answered her, as he had the countess, only in monosyllables. The other guests were all conversing with one another. "The Razumóvskis . . . It was charming . . . You are very kind . . . Countess Apráksina . . ." was heard on all sides. The countess rose and went into the ballroom.

"Márya Dmítrievna?" came her voice from there.

"Herself," came the answer in a rough voice, and Márya Dmítrievna entered the room.

All the unmarried ladies and even the married ones except the very oldest rose. Márya Dmítrievna paused at the door. Tall and stout, holding high her fifty-year-old head with its gray curls, she stood surveying the guests, and leisurely arranged her wide sleeves as if rolling them up. Márya Dmítrievna always spoke in Russian.

"Health and happiness to her whose name day we are keeping and to her children," she said, in her loud, full-toned voice which drowned all others. "Well, you old sinner," she went on, turning to the count who was kissing her hand, "you're feeling dull in Moscow, I daresay? Nowhere to hunt with your dogs? But what is to be done, old man? Just see how these nestlings are growing up," and she pointed to the girls. "You must look for husbands for them whether you like it or not. . . .

"Well," said she, "how's my Cossack?" (Márya Dmítrievna always called Natásha a Cossack) and she stroked the child's arm as she came up fearless and gay to kiss her hand. "I know she's a scamp of a girl, but I like her."

She took a pair of pear-shaped ruby earrings from her huge reticule and, having given them to the rosy Natásha, who beamed with the pleasure of her saint's-day fete, turned away at once.

"Well, I suppose it is time we were at table?" said Márya Dmítrievna.

The count went in first with Márya Dmítrievna, the countess followed on the arm of a colonel of hussars, a man of importance to them because Nicholas was to go with him to the regiment; then came Anna Mikháylovna with Shinshín. Berg gave his arm to Véra. The smiling Julie Karágina went in with Nicholas. After them other couples followed, filling the whole dining hall, and last of all the children, tutors, and governesses followed singly. The footmen began moving about, chairs scraped, the band struck up in the gallery, and the guests settled down in their places. Then the strains of the count's household band were replaced by the clatter of knives and forks, the voices of visitors, and the soft steps of the footmen. Berg with tender smiles was saying to Véra that love is not an earthly but a heavenly feeling. Borís was telling his new friend Pierre who the guests were and exchanging glances with Natásha, who was sitting opposite. Pierre spoke little but examined the new faces, and ate a great deal. Of the two soups he chose turtle with savory patties and went on to the game without omitting a single dish or one of the wines. Natásha, who sat opposite, was looking at Borís as girls of thirteen look at the boy they are in love with and have just kissed for the first time. Sometimes that same look fell on Pierre, and that funny lively little girl's look made him inclined to laugh without knowing why.

Nicholas sat at some distance from Sónya, beside Julie Karágina, to whom he was again talking with the same involuntary smile. Sónya wore a company smile but was evidently tormented by jealousy; now she turned pale, now blushed and strained every nerve to overhear what Nicholas and Julie were saying to one another.

At the men's end of the table the talk grew more and more animated. The colonel told them that the declaration of war had already appeared in Petersburg and that a copy, which he had himself seen, had that day been forwarded by courier to the commander in chief.

"And why the deuce are we going to fight Bonaparte?" remarked Shinshín. "He has stopped Austria's cackle and I fear it will be our turn next."

"What are you making such a noise about over there?" Márya Dmítrievna's deep voice suddenly inquired from the other end of the table. "What are you thumping the table for?" she demanded of the hussar, "and why are you exciting yourself? Do you think the French are here?"

Once more the conversations concentrated, the ladies' at the one end and the men's at the other.

"You won't ask," Natásha's little brother was saying; "I know you won't ask!"

"I will," replied Natásha.

Her face suddenly flushed with reckless and joyous resolution. She half rose, by a glance inviting Pierre, who sat opposite, to listen to what was coming, and turning to her mother:

"Mamma!" rang out the clear contralto notes of her childish voice, audible the whole length of the table.

"What is it?" asked the countess, startled; but seeing by her daughter's face that it was only mischief, she shook a finger at her sternly with a threatening and forbidding movement of her head.

The conversation was hushed.

"Mamma! What sweets are we going to have?" and Natásha's voice sounded still more firm and resolute.

The countess tried to frown, but could not. Márya Dmítrievna shook her fat finger.

"Cossack!" she said threateningly.

Most of the guests, uncertain how to regard this sally, looked at the elders.

"You had better take care!" said the countess.

"Mamma! What sweets are we going to have?" Natásha again cried boldly, with saucy gaiety, confident that her prank would be taken in good part.

Sónya and fat little Pétya doubled up with laughter.

"You see! I *have* asked," whispered Natásha to her little brother and to Pierre, glancing at him again.

"Ice pudding, but you won't get any," said Márya Dmítrievna.

Natásha saw there was nothing to be afraid of and so she braved even Márya Dmítrievna.

"Márya Dmítrievna! What kind of ice pudding? I don't like ice cream."

"Carrot ices."

"No! What kind, Márya Dmítrievna? What kind?" she almost screamed; "I want to know!"

Márya Dmítrievna and the countess burst out laughing, and all the guests joined in. Everyone laughed, not at Márya Dmítrievna's answer but at the incredible boldness and smartness of this little girl who had dared to treat Márya Dmítrievna in this fashion.

Natásha only desisted when she had been told that there would be pineapple ice. Before the ices, champagne was served round. The band again struck up, the count and countess kissed, and the guests, leaving their seats, went up to "congratulate" the countess, and reached across the table to clink glasses with the count, with the children, and with one another.

10

The card tables were drawn out, sets made up for boston, and the count's visitors settled themselves, some in the two drawing rooms, some in the sitting room, some in the library.

The count, holding his cards fanwise, kept himself with difficulty from dropping into his usual after-dinner nap, and laughed at everything. The young people, at the countess' instigation, gathered round the clavichord and harp. Julie by general request played first. After she had played a little air with variations on the harp, she joined the other young ladies in begging Natásha and Nicholas, who were noted for their musical talent, to sing something. Natásha, who was treated as though she were grown up, was evidently very proud of this but at the same time felt shy.

"What shall we sing?" she said.

"'The Brook,'" suggested Nicholas.

"Well, then, let's be quick. Borís, come here," said Natásha. "But where is Sónya?"

She looked round and seeing that her friend was not in the room ran to look for her.

Running into Sónya's room and not finding her there, Natásha ran to the nursery, but Sónya was not there either. Natásha concluded that she must be on the chest in the passage. The chest in the passage was the place of mourning for the younger female generation in the Rostóv household. And there in fact was Sónya lying face downward on Nurse's dirty feather bed on the top of the chest, crumpling her gauzy pink dress under her, hiding her face with her slender fingers, and sobbing so convulsively that her bare little shoulders shook. Natásha's face, which had been so radiantly happy all that saint's day, suddenly changed: her eyes became fixed, and then a shiver passed down her broad neck and the corners of her mouth drooped.

"Sónya! What is it? What is the matter? . . . Oo . . . Oo . . . Oo . . . !" And Natásha's large mouth widened, making her look quite ugly, and she began to wail like a baby without knowing why, except that Sónya was crying. Sónya tried to lift her head to answer but could not, and hid her face still deeper in the bed. Natásha wept, sitting on the blue-striped feather bed and hugging her friend. With an effort Sónya sat up and began wiping her eyes and explaining.

"Nicholas is going away in a week's time, his . . . papers . . . have come . . . he told me himself . . . but still I should not cry," and she showed a paper she held in her hand—with the verses Nicholas had written, "still, I should not cry, but you can't . . . no one can understand . . . what a soul he has!"

And she began to cry again because he had such a noble soul.

"It's all very well for you . . . I am not envious . . . I love you and Borís also," she went on, gaining a little strength; "he is nice . . . there are no difficulties in your way. . . . But Nicholas is my cousin . . . one would have to . . . the Metropolitan himself . . . and even then it can't be done. And besides, if she tells Mamma" (Sónya looked upon the countess as her mother and called her so) "that I am spoiling Nicholas' career and am heartless and ungrateful, while truly . . . God is my witness," and she made the sign of the cross, "I love her so much, and all of you, only Véra . . . And what for? What have I done to her? I am so grateful to you that I would willingly sacrifice everything, only I have nothing. . . ."

Sónya could not continue, and again hid her face in her hands and in the feather bed. Natásha began consoling her, but her face showed that she understood all the gravity of her friend's trouble.

"Sónya," she suddenly exclaimed, as if she had guessed the true reason of her friend's sorrow, "I'm sure Véra has said something to you since dinner? Hasn't she?"

"Yes, these verses Nicholas wrote himself and I copied some others, and she found them on my table and said she'd show them to Mamma, and that I was ungrateful, and that Mamma would never allow him to marry me, but that he'll marry Julie. You see how he's been with her all day . . . Natásha, what have I done to deserve it? . . ."

And again she began to sob, more bitterly than before. Natásha lifted her up, hugged her, and, smiling through her tears, began comforting her.

"Sónya, don't believe her, darling! Don't believe her! Do you remember how we and Nicholas, all three of us, talked in the sitting room after supper? Why, we settled how everything was to be. I don't quite remember how, but don't you remember that it could all be arranged and how nice it all was? There's Uncle Shinshín's brother has married his first cousin. And we are only second cousins, you know. And Borís says it is quite possible. You know I have told him all about it. And he is so clever and so good!" said Natásha. "Don't you cry, Sónya, dear love, darling Sónya!" and she kissed her and laughed. "Véra's spiteful; never mind her! And all will come right and she won't say anything to Mamma. Nicholas will tell her himself, and he doesn't care at all for Julie."

Natásha kissed her on the hair.

Sónya sat up. The little kitten brightened, its eyes shone, and it seemed ready to lift its tail, jump down on its soft paws, and begin playing with the ball of worsted as a kitten should.

"Do you think so? . . . Really? Truly?" she said, quickly smoothing her frock and hair.

"Really, truly!" answered Natásha, pushing in a crisp lock that had strayed from under her friend's plaits.

Both laughed.

"Well, let's go and sing 'The Brook.'"

"Come along!"

"Do you know, that fat Pierre who sat opposite me is so funny!" said Natásha, stopping suddenly. "I feel so happy!"

And she set off at a run along the passage.

Sónya, shaking off some down which clung to her and tucking away the verses in the bosom of her dress close to her bony little chest, ran after Natásha down the passage into the sitting room with flushed face and light, joyous steps. At the visitors' request the young people sang the quartette, "The Brook," with which everyone was delighted. Then Nicholas sang a song he had just learned.

He had not finished the last verse before the young people began to get ready to dance in the large hall, and the sound of the feet and the coughing of the musicians were heard from the gallery.

Pierre was sitting in the drawing room where Shinshín had engaged him, as a man recently returned from abroad, in a political conversation in which several others joined but which bored Pierre. When the music began Natásha came in and walking straight up to Pierre said, laughing and blushing:

"Mamma told me to ask you to join the dancers."

"I am afraid of mixing the figures," Pierre replied; "but if you will be my teacher . . ." And lowering his big arm he offered it to the slender little girl.

While the couples were arranging themselves and the musicians tuning up, Pierre sat down with his little partner. Natásha was perfectly happy; she was dancing with a *grown-up* man, who had been *abroad*. She was sitting in a conspicuous place and talking to him like a grown-up lady. She had a fan in her hand that one of the ladies had given her to hold. Assuming quite the pose of a society woman (heaven knows when and where she had learned it) she talked with her partner, fanning herself and smiling over the fan.

"Dear, dear! Just look at her!" exclaimed the countess as she crossed the ballroom, pointing to Natásha.

Natásha blushed and laughed.

"Well, really, Mamma! Why should you? What is there to be surprised at?"

Count Rostóv does a special dance with Márya Dmítrievna, and all the company applaud.

11-12-13

In Sections 11, 12, and 13, relatives of the dying Count Bezúkhov, Catiche and Prince Vasíli, conspire to deprive Pierre of his inheritance. Anna Mikháylovna, still seeking favors for her son Borís, accompanies Pierre to the death-bed of the count, and ruins the plans of the conspirators.

14

At Bald Hills, Prince Nicholas Andréevich
Bolkónski's estate, the arrival of young Prince Andrew and his
wife was daily expected, but this expectation did not upset the
regular routine of life in the old prince's household. General
in Chief Prince Nicholas Andréevich (nicknamed in society,
"the King of Prussia") ever since the Emperor Paul had exiled
him to his country estate had lived there continuously with his
daughter, Princess Mary, and her companion, Mademoiselle
Bourienne. Though in the new reign he was free to return to
the capitals, he still continued to live in the country, remarking
that anyone who wanted to see him could come the hundred
miles from Moscow to Bald Hills, while he himself needed no
one and nothing. He used to say that there are only two
sources of human vice—idleness and superstition, and only
two virtues—activity and intelligence. He himself undertook
his daughter's education, and to develop these two cardinal
virtues in her gave her lessons in algebra and geometry till she
was twenty, and arranged her life so that her whole time was
occupied. He was himself always occupied: writing his memoirs, solving problems in higher mathematics, turning snuffboxes on a lathe, working in the garden, or superintending the
building that was always going on at his estate. As regularity
is a prime condition facilitating activity, regularity in his
household was carried to the highest point of exactitude. He
always came to table under precisely the same conditions, and
not only at the same hour but at the same minute. With those
about him, from his daughter to his serfs, the prince was sharp
and invariably exacting, so that without being a hardhearted
man he inspired such fear and respect as few hardhearted men
would have aroused. Although he was in retirement and had
now no influence in political affairs, every high official appointed to the province in which the prince's estate lay considered it his duty to visit him and waited in the lofty antechamber just as the architect, gardener, or Princess Mary did, till
the prince appeared punctually at the appointed hour.

On the morning of the day that the young couple were to
arrive, Princess Mary entered the antechamber as usual at the

time appointed for the morning greeting, crossing herself with trepidation and repeating a silent prayer. Every morning she came in like that, and every morning she prayed that the daily interview might pass off well.

An old powdered manservant who was sitting in the ante-chamber rose quietly and said in a whisper: "Please walk in."

Through the door came the regular hum of a lathe. The princess timidly opened the door which moved noiselessly and easily. She paused at the entrance. The prince was working at the lathe and after glancing round continued his work.

The enormous study was full of things evidently in constant use. The large table covered with books and plans, the tall glass-fronted bookcases with keys in the locks, the high desk for writing while standing up, on which lay an open exercise book, and the lathe with tools laid ready to hand and shavings scattered around—all indicated continuous, varied, and order-ly activity. After a few more turns of the lathe he removed his foot from the pedal, wiped his chisel, dropped it into a leather pouch attached to the lathe, and, approaching the table, sum-moned his daughter. He never gave his children a blessing, so he simply held out his bristly cheek (as yet unshaven) and, regarding her tenderly and attentively, said severely:

"Quite well? All right then, sit down." He took the exercise book containing lessons in geometry written by himself and drew up a chair with his foot.

"For tomorrow!" said he, quickly finding the page and mak-ing a scratch from one paragraph to another with his hard nail.

The princess bent over the exercise book on the table.

"Wait a bit, here's a letter for you," said the old man sud-denly, taking a letter addressed in a woman's hand from a bag hanging above the table, onto which he threw it.

At the sight of the letter red patches showed themselves on the princess' face. She took it quickly and bent her head over it.

"From Héloïse?" asked the prince with a cold smile that showed his still sound, yellowish teeth.

"Yes, it's from Julie," replied the princess with a timid glance and a timid smile.

"I'll let two more letters pass, but the third I'll read," said the prince sternly; "I'm afraid you write much nonsense. I'll read the third!"

"Read this if you like, Father," said the princess, blushing still more and holding out the letter.

"The third, I said the third!" cried the prince abruptly, pushing the letter away, and leaning his elbows on the table he drew toward him the exercise book containing geometrical figures.

"Well, madam," he began, stooping over the book close to his daughter and placing an arm on the back of the chair on which she sat, so that she felt herself surrounded on all sides by the acrid scent of old age and tobacco, which she had known so long. "Now, madam, these triangles are equal; please note that the angle ABC . . ."

The princess looked in a scared way at her father's eyes glittering close to her; the red patches on her face came and went, and it was plain that she understood nothing and was so frightened that her fear would prevent her understanding any of her father's future explanations, however clear they might be.

The princess gave a wrong answer.

"Well now, isn't she a fool!" shouted the prince, pushing the book aside and turning sharply away; but rising immediately, he paced up and down, lightly touched his daughter's hair and sat down again.

He drew up his chair and continued to explain.

"This won't do, Princess; it won't do," said he, when Princess Mary, having taken and closed the exercise book with the next day's lesson, was about to leave: "Mathematics are most important, madam! I don't want to have you like our silly ladies. Get used to it and you'll like it," and he patted her cheek. "It will drive all the nonsense out of your head."

He patted her on the shoulder and himself closed the door after her.

Princess Mary went back to her room with the sad, scared expression that rarely left her and which made her plain, sickly face yet plainer. She put down the geometry book and eagerly broke the seal of her letter. It was from her most intimate friend from childhood; that same Julie Karágina who had been at the Rostóvs' name-day party.

Julie wrote in French:

"Dear and precious Friend, How terrible and frightful a thing is separation! Though I tell myself that half my life and half my happiness are wrapped up in you, and that in spite of the distance separating us our hearts are united by indissoluble bonds, my heart rebels against fate and in spite of the pleasures and distractions around me I cannot overcome a certain secret sorrow that has been in my heart ever since we parted. Why are we not together as we were last summer, in your big study, on the blue sofa, the confidential sofa? Why cannot I now, as three months ago, draw fresh moral strength from your look, so gentle, calm, and penetrating, a look I loved so well and seem to see before me as I write?"

Having read thus far, Princess Mary sighed and glanced into the mirror which stood on her right. It reflected a weak, ungraceful figure and thin face. Her eyes, always sad, now looked with particular hopelessness at her reflection in the glass. "She flatters me," thought the princess, turning away and continuing to read. But Julie did not flatter her friend; the princess' eyes—large, deep and luminous (it seemed as if at times there radiated from them shafts of warm light)—were so beautiful that very often in spite of the plainness of her face they gave her an attraction more powerful than that of beauty. But the princess never saw the beautiful expression of her own eyes—the look they had when she was not thinking of herself. As with everyone, her face assumed a forced unnatural expression as soon as she looked in a glass. She went on reading:

"All Moscow talks of nothing but war. One of my two brothers is already abroad, the other is with the Guards, who are starting on their march to the frontier. Our dear Emperor has left Petersburg and it is thought intends to expose his precious person to the chances of war. God grant that the Corsican monster who is destroying the peace of Europe may be overthrown by the angel whom it has pleased the Almighty, in His goodness, to give us as sovereign! To say nothing of my brothers, this war has deprived me of one of the associations nearest my heart. I mean young Nicholas Rostóv, who with his enthusiasm could not bear to remain inactive and has left the university to join the army. I will confess to you, dear Mary, that in spite of his extreme youth his departure for the army was a great grief to me. This young man, of whom I spoke to you last summer, is so noble-minded and full of that real youthfulness which one seldom finds nowadays among our old men of twenty and, particularly, he is so frank and has so much heart. He is so pure and poetic that my relations with him, transient as they were, have been one of the sweetest comforts to my poor heart, which has already suffered so much . . . but enough of this! The chief news, about which all Moscow gossips, is the death of old Count Bezúkhov, and his inheritance. Fancy! The three princesses have received very little, Prince Vasíli nothing, and it is Monsieur Pierre who has inherited all the property and has besides been recognized as legitimate; so that he is now Count Bezúkhov and possessor of the finest fortune in Russia. It is rumored that Prince Vasíli played a very despicable part in this affair and that he returned to Petersburg quite crestfallen.

"I confess I understand very little about all these matters of wills and inheritance; but I do know that since this young man, whom we all used to know as plain Monsieur Pierre, has become Count Bezúkhov and the owner of one of the largest fortunes in Russia, I am much amused to watch the change in the tone and manners of the mammas burdened by marriageable daughters, and of the young ladies themselves, toward him, though, between you and me, he always seemed to me a poor sort of fellow . . . À *propos* of marriages: do you know that a while ago that *universal auntie* Anna Mikháylovna told me, under the seal of strict secrecy, of a plan of marriage for you. It is neither more nor less than with Prince Vasíli's son Anatole, whom they wish to reform by marrying him to someone rich and *distinguée,* and it is on you that his relations' choice has fallen. I don't know what you will think of it, but I consider it my duty to let you know of it. He is said to be very handsome and a terrible scapegrace. That is all I have been able to find out about him.

"But enough of gossip. I am at the end of my second sheet of paper, and Mamma has sent for me to go and dine at the Apráksins'. . . . Adieu! Give my respects to monsieur your father and my compliments to Mademoiselle Bourienne. I embrace you as I love you.

JULIE"

The princess pondered awhile with a thoughtful smile and her luminous eyes lit up so that her face was entirely transformed. Then she suddenly rose and with her heavy tread went up to the table. She took a sheet of paper and her hand moved rapidly over it. This is the reply she wrote, also in French:

"Dear and precious Friend, Your letter of the 13th has given me great delight. So you still love me, my romantic Julie? Separation, of which you say so much that is bad, does not seem to have had its usual effect on you. You complain of our separation. What then should I say, if I *dared* complain, I who am deprived of all who are dear to me? Ah, if we had not religion to console us life would be very sad. Why do you suppose that I should look severely on your affection for that young man? On such matters I am only severe with myself. I understand such feelings in others, and if never having felt them I cannot approve of them, neither do I condemn them. Only it seems to me that Christian love, love of one's neighbor, love of one's enemy, is worthier, sweeter, and better than the feelings which the beautiful eyes of a young man can inspire in a romantic and loving young girl like yourself. . . .

"I cannot agree with you about Pierre, whom I knew as a child. He always seemed to me to have an excellent heart, and that is the quality I value most in people. . . .

"My father has not spoken to me of a suitor, but has only told me that he has received a letter and is expecting a visit from Prince Vasíli. In regard to this project of marriage for me, I will tell you, dear sweet friend, that I look on marriage as a divine institution to which we must conform. However painful it may be to me, should the Almighty ever lay the duties of wife and mother upon me I shall try to perform them as faithfully as I can, without disquieting myself by examining my feelings toward him whom He may give me for husband.

"I have had a letter from my brother, who announces his speedy arrival at Bald Hills with his wife. This pleasure will be but a brief one, however, for he will leave us again to take part in this unhappy war into which we have been drawn, God knows how or why. Not only where you are—at the heart of affairs and of the world— is the talk all of war, even here amid fieldwork and the calm of nature—which townsfolk consider characteristic of the country—rumors of war are heard and painfully felt. My father talks of nothing but marches and counter-marches, things of which I understand nothing; and the day before yesterday during my daily walk through the village I witnessed a heartrending scene. . . .

"Adieu, dear and kind friend; may our divine Saviour and His most Holy Mother keep you in their holy and all-powerful care!

MARY"

The princess glanced at her watch and, seeing that she was five minutes late in starting her practice on the clavichord, went into the sitting room with a look of alarm. Between twelve and two o'clock, as the day was mapped out, the prince rested and the princess played the clavichord.

15

The gray-haired valet was sitting drowsily listening to the snoring of the prince, who was in his large study. From the far side of the house through the closed doors came the sound of difficult passages—twenty times repeated—of a sonata by Dussek.

Just then a closed carriage and another with a hood drove up to the porch. Prince Andrew got out of the carriage, helped his little wife to alight, and let her pass into the house before him. Old Tíkhon, wearing a wig, put his head out of the door of the antechamber, reported in a whisper that the prince was sleeping, and hastily closed the door. Tíkhon knew that nei-ther the son's arrival nor any other unusual event must be allowed to disturb the appointed order of the day. Prince Andrew apparently knew this as well as Tíkhon; he looked at his watch as if to ascertain whether father's habits had changed since he was at home last, and, having assured himself that they had not, he turned to his wife.

"He will get up in twenty minutes. Let us go across to Mary's room," he said.

The little princess had grown stouter during this time, but her eyes and her short, downy, smiling lip lifted when she began to speak just as merrily and prettily as ever.

"Why, this is a palace!" she said to her husband, looking around with the expression with which people compliment their host at a ball. "Let's come, quick, quick!" And with a glance round, she smiled at Tíkhon, at her husband, and at the footman who accompanied them.

"Is that Mary practicing? Let's go quietly and take her by surprise."

Prince Andrew followed her with a courteous but sad expression.

"You've grown older, Tíkhon," he said in passing to the old man, who kissed his hand.

Before they reached the room from which the sounds of the clavichord came, the pretty, fair-haired Frenchwoman, Mademoiselle Bourienne, rushed out apparently beside herself with delight.

"Ah! what joy for the princess!" exclaimed she: "At last! I must let her know."

"No, no, please not . . . You are Mademoiselle Bourienne," said the little princess, kissing her. "I know you already through my sister-in-law's friendship for you. She was not expecting us?"

They went up to the door of the sitting room from which came the sound of the oft-repeated passage of the sonata. Prince Andrew stopped and made a grimace, as if expecting something unpleasant.

The little princess entered the room. The passage broke off in the middle, a cry was heard, then Princess Mary's heavy tread and the sound of kissing. When Prince Andrew went in the two princesses, who had only met once before for a short time at his wedding, were in each other's arms warmly pressing their lips to whatever place they happened to touch.

Mademoiselle Bourienne stood near them pressing her hand to her heart, with a beatific smile and obviously equally ready to cry or to laugh. Prince Andrew shrugged his shoulders and frowned, as lovers of music do when they hear a false note. The two women let go of one another, and then, as if afraid of being too late, seized each other's hands, kissing them and pulling them away, and again began kissing each other on the face, and then to Prince Andrew's surprise both began to cry and kissed again. Mademoiselle Bourienne also began to cry. Prince Andrew evidently felt ill at ease, but to the two women it seemed quite natural that they should cry, and apparently it never entered their heads that it could have been otherwise at this meeting.

"Ah! my dear! . . . Ah! Mary! . . ." they suddenly exclaimed, and then laughed. "I dreamed last night . . ."—"You were not expecting us? . . ."—"Ah! Mary, you have got thinner! . . ." "And you have grown stouter! . . ."

"I knew the princess at once," put in Mademoiselle Bourienne.

"And I had no idea! . . ." exclaimed Princess Mary. "Ah, Andrew, I did not see you."

Prince Andrew and his sister, hand in hand, kissed one another, and he told her she was still the same crybaby as ever. Princess Mary had turned toward her brother, and through her tears the loving, warm, gentle look of her large luminous eyes, very beautiful at that moment, rested on Prince Andrew's face.

The little princess talked incessantly, her short, downy upper lip continually and rapidly touching her rosy nether lip when necessary and drawing up again next moment when her face broke into a smile of glittering teeth and sparkling eyes. Princess Mary was still looking silently at her brother and her beautiful eyes were full of love and sadness. It was plain that she was following a train of thought independent of her sister-in-law's words. In the midst of a description of the last Petersburg fete she addressed her brother:

"So you are really going to the war, Andrew?" she said sighing.

Lise sighed too.

"Yes, and even tomorrow," replied her brother.

"He is leaving me here; God knows why, when he might have had promotion . . ."

Princess Mary did not listen to the end, but continuing her train of thought turned to her sister-in-law with a tender glance at her figure.

"Is it certain?" she said.

The face of the little princess changed. She sighed and said: "Yes, quite certain. Ah! it is very dreadful . . ."

Her lip descended. She brought her face close to her sister-in-law's and unexpectedly again began to cry.

"She needs rest," said Prince Andrew with a frown. "Don't you, Lise? Take her to your room and I'll go to Father. How is he? Just the same?"

When the twenty minutes had elapsed and the time had come for the old prince to get up, Tíkhon came to call the young prince to his father. The old man made a departure from his usual routine in honor of his son's arrival: he gave orders to admit him to his apartments while he dressed for dinner. The old prince always dressed in old-fashioned style, wearing an antique coat and powdered hair; and when Prince Andrew entered his father's dressing room (not with the contemptuous look and manner he wore in drawing rooms, but with the animated face with which he talked to Pierre), the old man was sitting on a large leather-covered chair, wrapped in a powdering mantle, entrusting his head to Tíkhon.

"Ah! here's the warrior! Wants to vanquish Bonaparte?" said the old man, shaking his powdered head as much as the tail, which Tíkhon was holding fast to plait, would allow.

"You at least must tackle him properly, or else if he goes on like this he'll soon have us, too, for his subjects! How are you?" And he held out his cheek.

The old man was in a good temper after his nap before dinner. Prince Andrew went up and kissed his father on the spot indicated to him. He made no reply on his father's favorite topic—making fun of the military men of the day, and more particularly of Bonaparte.

"Yes, Father, I have come to you and brought my wife who is pregnant," said Prince Andrew, following every movement of his father's face with an eager and respectful look. "How is your health?"

"Only fools and rakes fall ill, my boy. You know me: I am

busy from morning till night and abstemious, so of course I am well."

"Thank God," said his son smiling.

"God has nothing to do with it! Well, go on," he continued, returning to his hobby; "tell me how the Germans have taught you to fight Bonaparte by this new science you call 'strategy.'"

Prince Andrew smiled.

"Give me time to collect my wits, Father," said he, with a smile that showed that his father's foibles did not prevent his son from loving and honoring him. "Why, I have not yet had time to settle down!"

"Nonsense, nonsense!" cried the old man, shaking his pigtail to see whether it was firmly plaited, and grasping his son by the hand. "The house for your wife is ready. Princess Mary will take her there and show her over, and they'll talk nineteen to the dozen. That's their woman's way! I am glad to have her. Sit down and talk. About Mikhelson's army I understand—Tolstóy's too . . . a simultaneous expedition."

Prince Andrew, seeing that his father insisted, began—at first reluctantly, but gradually with more and more animation, and from habit changing unconsciously from Russian to French as he went on—to explain the plan of operation for the coming campaign.

"Well, you've told me nothing new," and the old man repeated, meditatively and rapidly:

"*Dieu sait quand reviendra.* Go to the dining room."

At the appointed hour the prince, powdered and shaven, entered the dining room where his daughter-in-law, Princess Mary, and Mademoiselle Bourienne were already awaiting him.

In the dining room, which like all the rooms in the house was exceedingly lofty, the members of the household and the footmen—one behind each chair—stood waiting for the prince to enter.

The prince walked in quickly and jauntily as was his wont, as if intentionally contrasting the briskness of his manners with the strict formality of his house. At that moment the great clock struck two and another with a shrill tone joined in from the drawing room. The prince stood still; his lively glittering eyes from under their thick, bushy eyebrows sternly scanned all present and rested on the little princess. She felt, as courtiers do when the Tsar enters, the sensation of fear and respect which the old man inspired in all around him. He stroked her hair and then patted her awkwardly on the back of her neck.

"I'm glad, glad, to see you," he said, looking attentively into her eyes and then quickly went to his place and sat down.

He indicated a place beside him to his daughter-in-law. A footman moved the chair for her.

"Ho, ho!" said the old man, casting his eyes on her rounded figure. "You've been in a hurry. That's bad!"

He laughed in his usual dry, cold, unpleasant way, with his lips only and not with his eyes.

"You must walk, walk as much as possible, as much as possible," he said.

The little princess did not, or did not wish to, hear his words. She was silent and seemed confused. The prince asked her about her father, and she began to smile and talk. He asked about mutual acquaintances, and she became still more animated and chattered away giving him greetings from variour people and relating the town gossip.

And the conversation again turned on the war, on Bonaparte, and the generals and statesmen of the day. The old prince seemed convinced not only that all the men of the day were mere babies who did not know the A B C of war or of politics, and that Bonaparte was an insignificant little Frenchy, successful only because there were no longer any Potëmkins or Suvórovs left to oppose him; but he was also convinced that there were no political difficulties in Europe and no real war, but only a sort of puppet show at which the men of the day were playing, pretending to do something real. Prince Andrew gaily bore with his father's ridicule of the new men, and drew him on and listened to him with evident pleasure.

"The past always seems good," said he, "but did not Suvórov himself fall into a trap Moreau set him, and from which he did not know how to escape?"

"Who told you that? Who?" cried the prince. "Suvórov!" And he jerked away his plate, which Tíkhon briskly caught.

And the prince began explaining all the blunders which, according to him, Bonaparte had made in his campaigns and even in politics. His son made no rejoinder, but it was evident that whatever arguments were presented he was as little able as his father to change his opinion. He listened, refraining from a reply, and involuntarily wondered how this old man, living alone in the country for so many years, could know and discuss so minutely and acutely all the recent European military and political events.

"You think I'm an old man and don't understand the present state of affairs?" concluded his father. "But it troubles me. I don't sleep at night. Come now, where has this great commander of yours shown his skill?" he concluded.

"That would take too long to tell," answered the son.

"Well, then go off to your Bonaparte! Mademoiselle Bourienne, here's another admirer of that powder-monkey emperor of yours," he exclaimed in excellent French.

"You know, Prince, I am not a Bonapartist!"

"*Dieu sait quand reviendra*" . . . hummed the prince out of tune and, with a laugh still more so, he quitted the table.

The little princess during the whole discussion and the rest of the dinner sat silent, glancing with a frightened look now at her father-in-law and now at Princess Mary. When they left the table she took her sister-in-law's arm and drew her into another room.

"What a clever man your father is," said she; "perhaps that is why I am afraid of him."

"Oh, he is so kind!" answered Princess Mary.

16

Prince Andrew was to leave next evening. The old prince, not altering his routine, retired as usual after dinner. The little princess was in her sister-in-law's room. Prince Andrew in a traveling coat without epaulettes had been packing with his valet in the rooms assigned to him. After inspecting the carriage himself and seeing the trunks put in, he ordered the horses to be harnessed.

When starting on a journey or changing their mode of life, men capable of reflection are generally in a serious frame of mind. Did he fear going to the war, or was he sad at leaving his wife?—perhaps both, but evidently he did not wish to be seen in that mood, for hearing footsteps in the passage he hurriedly unclasped his hands, stopped at a table as if tying the cover of the small box, and assumed his usual tranquil and impenetrable expression. It was the heavy tread of Princess Mary that he heard.

"I hear you have given orders to harness," she cried, panting (she had apparently been running), "and I did so wish to have another talk with you alone! God knows how long we may again be parted. You are not angry with me for coming? You have changed so, Andrúsha," she added, as if to explain such a question.

She smiled as she uttered his pet name, "Andrúsha." It was obviously strange to her to think that this stern handsome man should be Andrúsha—the slender mischievous boy who had been her playfellow in childhood.

"And where is Lise?" he asked, answering her question only by a smile.

"She was so tired that she has fallen asleep on the sofa in my room. Oh, Andrew! What a treasure of a wife you have," said she, sitting down on the sofa, facing her brother. "She is quite a child: such a dear, merry child. I have grown so fond of her."

Prince Andrew was silent, but the princess noticed the ironical and contemptuous look that showed itself on his face.

"One must be indulgent to little weaknesses; who is free from them, Andrew? Don't forget that she has grown up and been educated in society, and so her position now is not a rosy one."

Prince Andrew smiled as he looked at his sister, as we smile at those we think we thoroughly understand.

"You live in the country and don't think the life terrible," he replied.

"I . . . that's different. Why speak of me? I don't want any other life, and can't, for I know no other. But think, Andrew: for a young society woman to be buried in the country during the best years of her life, all alone—for Papa is always busy, and I . . . well, you know what poor resources I have for entertaining a woman used to the best society. There is only Mademoiselle Bourienne. . . ."

"I don't like your Mademoiselle Bourienne at all," said Prince Andrew.

"No? She is very nice and kind and, above all, she's much to be pitied. She has no one, no one. To tell the truth, I don't need her, and she's even in my way. You know I always was a savage, and now am even more so. I like being alone. . . . Father likes her very much."

"To be quite frank, Mary, I expect Father's character sometimes makes things trying for you, doesn't it?" Prince Andrew asked suddenly.

Princess Mary was first surprised and then aghast at this question.

"For me? For me? . . . Trying for me! . . ." said she.

"He always was rather harsh; and now I should think he's getting very trying," said Prince Andrew, apparently speaking lightly of their father in order to puzzle or test his sister.

"You are good in every way, Andrew, but you have a kind of intellectual pride," said the princess, following the train of her own thoughts rather than the trend of the conversation—"and that's a great sin. How can one judge Father? But even if one might, what feeling except veneration could such a man as my father evoke? And I am so contented and happy with him. I only wish you were all as happy as I am."

Her brother shook his head incredulously.

"As I was saying to you, Andrew, be kind and generous as you always used to be. Don't judge Lise harshly," she began. "She is so sweet, so good-natured, and her position now is a very hard one."

"I do not think I have complained of my wife to you, Másha, or blamed her. Why do you say all this to me?"

Red patches appeared on Princess Mary's face and she was silent as if she felt guilty.

"I have said nothing to you, but you have already been talked to. And I am sorry for that," he went on.

The patches grew deeper on her forehead, neck, and cheeks. She tried to say something but could not. Her brother had guessed right: the little princess had been crying after dinner and had spoken of her forebodings about her confinement, and of how she dreaded it, and had complained of her fate, her father-in-law, and her husband. After crying she had fallen asleep. Prince Andrew felt sorry for his sister.

"Know this, Másha: I can't reproach, have not reproached, and never shall reproach *my wife* with anything, and I cannot reproach myself with anything in regard to her; and that always will be so in whatever circumstances I may be placed. But if you want to know the truth . . . if you want to know whether I am happy? No! Is she happy? No! But why this is so I don't know. . . ."

As he said this he rose, went to his sister, and, stooping, kissed her forehead. His fine eyes lit up with a thoughtful, kindly, and unaccustomed brightness, but he was looking not at his sister but over her head toward the darkness of the open doorway.

"Let us go to her, I must say good-by. Or—go and wake her, and I'll come in a moment. Petrúshka!" he called to his valet: "Come here, take these away. Put this on the seat and this to the right."

Princess Mary rose and moved to the door, then stopped and said: "Andrew, if you had faith you would have turned to God and asked him to give you the love you do not feel, and your prayer would have been answered."

"Well, may be!" said Prince Andrew. "Go, Másha; I'll come immediately."

He entered the room softly. The little princess, plump and rosy, was sitting in an easy chair with her work in her hands, talking incessantly, repeating Petersburg reminiscences and even phrases. Prince Andrew came up, stroked her hair, and asked if she felt rested after their journey. She answered him and continued her chatter.

Prince Andrew had been called to his father's study as the latter wished to say good-by to him alone. All were waiting for them to come out.

When Prince Andrew entered the study the old man in his old-age spectacles and white dressing gown, in which he received no one but his son, sat at the table writing. He glanced round.

"Going?" And he went on writing.

"I've come to say good-by."

"Kiss me here," and he touched his cheek: "Thanks, thanks!"

"What do you thank me for?"

"For not dilly-dallying and not hanging to a woman's apron strings. The Service before everything. Thanks, thanks!" And he went on writing, so that his quill spluttered and squeaked. "If you have anything to say, say it. These two things can be done together," he added.

"About my wife . . . I am ashamed as it is to leave her on your hands. . . ."

"Why talk nonsense? Say what you want."

"When her confinement is due, send to Moscow for an *accoucheur*. . . . Let him be here. . . ."

The old prince stopped writing and, as if not understanding, fixed his stern eyes on his son.

"I know that no one can help if nature does not do her work," said Prince Andrew, evidently confused. "I know that out of a million cases only one goes wrong, but it is her fancy and mine. They have been telling her things. She has had a dream and is frightened."

"Hm . . . Hm . . ." muttered the old prince to himself, finishing what he was writing. "I'll do it."

He signed with a flourish and suddenly turning to his son began to laugh.

"It's a bad business, eh?"

"What is bad, Father?"

"The wife!" said the old prince, briefly and significantly.

"I don't understand!" said Prince Andrew.

"No, it can't be helped, lad," said the prince. "They're all like that; one can't unmarry. Don't be afraid; I won't tell anyone, but you know it yourself."

He seized his son by the hand with small bony fingers, shook it, looked straight into his son's face with keen eyes which seemed to see through him, and again laughed his frigid laugh.

"Listen!" said he; "don't worry about your wife: what can be done shall be. Now listen! Give this letter to Michael Ilariónovich. I have written that he should make use of you in proper places and not keep you long as an adjutant: a bad position! Tell him I remember and like him. Write and tell me how he receives you. If he is all right—serve him. Nicholas Bolkónski's son need not serve under anyone if he is in disfavor."

He spoke so rapidly that he did not finish half his words, but his son was accustomed to understand him.

"Well, now, good-by!" He gave his son his hand to kiss, and embraced him. "Remember this, Prince Andrew, if they kill you it will hurt me, your old father . . ." he paused unexpectedly, and then in a querulous voice suddenly shrieked: "but if I hear that you have not behaved like a son of Nicholas Bolkónski, I shall be ashamed!"

"You need not have said that to me, Father," said the son with a smile.

The old man was silent.

"I also wanted to ask you," continued Prince Andrew, "if I'm killed and if I have a son, do not let him be taken away from you—as I said yesterday . . . let him grow up with you. . . . Please."

"Not let the wife have him?" said the old man, and laughed.

They stood silent, facing one another. The old man's sharp eyes were fixed straight on his son's. Something twitched in the lower part of the old prince's face.

"We've said good-by. Go!" he suddenly shouted in a loud, angry voice, opening his door.

"What is it? What?" asked both princesses when they saw for a moment at the door Prince Andrew and the figure of the old man in a white dressing gown, spectacled and wigless, shouting in an angry voice.

Prince Andrew sighed and made no reply.

"Well!" he said, turning to his wife.

And this "Well!" sounded coldly ironic, as if he were saying: "Now go through your performance."

"Andrew, already!" said the little princess, turning pale and looking with dismay at her husband.

He embraced her. She screamed and fell unconscious on his shoulder.

He cautiously released the shoulder she leaned on, looked into her face, and carefully placed her in an easy chair.

"Adieu, Mary," said he gently to his sister, taking her by the hand and kissing her, and then he left the room with rapid steps.

The little princess lay in the armchair, Mademoiselle Bourienne chafing her temples. Princess Mary, supporting her sister-in-law, still looked with her beautiful eyes full of tears at the door through which Prince Andrew had gone and made the sign of the cross in his direction. From the study, like pistol shots, came the frequent sound of the old man angrily blowing his nose. Hardly had Prince Andrew gone when the study door opened quickly and the stern figure of the old man in the white dressing gown looked out.

"Gone? That's all right!" said he; and looking angrily at the unconscious little princess, he shook his head reprovingly and slammed the door.

1805

■──■■──■■■──■■■──■■■──■

BOOK TWO

1

In October, 1805, a Russian army was occupying the villages and towns of the Archduchy of Austria, and yet other regiments freshly arriving from Russia were settling near the fortress of Braunau and burdening the inhabitants on whom they were quartered. Braunau was the headquarters of the commander in chief, Kutúzov.

On October 11, 1805, one of the infantry regiments that had just reached Braunau had halted half a mile from the town, waiting to be inspected by the commander in chief.

The commander of the regiment was an elderly, choleric, stout, and thick-set general with grizzled eyebrows and whiskers, and wider from chest to back than across the shoulders.

A member of the Hofkriegsrath from Vienna had come to Kutúzov the day before with proposals and demands for him to join up with the army of the Archduke Ferdinand and Mack, and Kutúzov, not considering this junction advisable, meant, among other arguments in support of his view, to show the Austrian general the wretched state in which the troops arrived from Russia. With this object he intended to meet the regiment; so the worse the condition it was in, the better pleased the commander in chief would be.

The regimental commander walked with his jerky steps to the front of the regiment and examined it from a distance.

"Whatever is this? This!" he shouted and stood still. "Commander of the third company!"

The missing officer appeared from behind his company and, though he was a middle-aged man and not in the habit of running, trotted awkwardly stumbling on his toes toward

57

the general. The captain's face showed the uneasiness of a schoolboy who is told to repeat a lesson he has not learned. Spots appeared on his nose, the redness of which was evidently due to intemperance, and his mouth twitched nervously. The general looked the captain up and down as he came up panting, slackening his pace as he approached.

"You will soon be dressing your men in petticoats! What is this?" shouted the regimental commander, thrusting forward his jaw and pointing at a soldier in the ranks of the third company in a greatcoat of bluish cloth, which contrasted with the others.

"Your excellency, it's the officer Dólokhov, who has been reduced to the ranks," said the captain softly.

"Well? Has he been degraded into a field marshal, or into a soldier? If a soldier, he should be dressed in regulation uniform like the others."

"Your excellency, you gave him leave yourself, on the march."

"Gave him leave? Leave? That's just like you young men," said the regimental commander cooling down a little. "Leave indeed. . . . One says a word to you and you . . . What?" he added with renewed irritation, "I beg you to dress your men decently."

And the commander, turning to look at the adjutant, directed his jerky steps down the line. He was evidently pleased at his own display of anger and walking up to the regiment wished to find a further excuse for wrath. Having snapped at an officer for an unpolished badge, at another because his line was not straight, he reached the third company.

"H-o-o-w are you standing? Where's your leg? Your leg?" shouted the commander with a tone of suffering in his voice, while there were still five men between him and Dólokhov with his bluish-gray uniform.

Dólokhov slowly straightened his bent knee, looking straight with his clear, insolent eyes in the general's face.

"Why a blue coat? Off with it . . . Sergeant major! Change his coat . . . the ras . . ." he did not finish.

"General, I must obey orders, but I am not bound to endure . . ." Dólokhov hurriedly interrupted.

"No talking in the ranks! . . . No talking, no talking!"

"Not bound to endure insults," Dólokhov concluded in loud, ringing tones.

The eyes of the general and the soldier met. The general became silent, angrily pulling down his tight scarf.

"I request you to have the goodness to change your coat," he said as he turned away.

"He's coming!" shouted the signaler at that moment.

"Att-ention!" shouted the regimental commander in a soul-shaking voice which expressed joy for himself, severity for the regiment, and welcome for the approaching chief.

Along the broad country road, edged on both sides by trees, came a high, light-blue Viennese *calèche* slightly creaking on its springs and drawn by six horses at a smart trot. Behind the *calèche* galloped the suite and a convoy of Croats. Beside Kutúzov sat an Austrian general, in a white uniform that looked strange among the Russian black ones. The *calèche* stopped in front of the regiment. Kutúzov and the Austrian general were talking in low voices and Kutúzov smiled slightly as treading heavily he stepped down from the carriage just as if those two thousand men breathlessly gazing at him and the regimental commander did not exist.

Kutúzov walked through the ranks, sometimes stopping to say a few friendly words to officers he had known in the Turkish war, sometimes also to the soldiers. Looking at their boots he several times shook his head sadly, pointing them out to the Austrian general with an expression which seemed to say that he was not blaming anyone, but could not help noticing what a bad state of things it was. The regimental commander ran forward on each such occasion, fearing to miss a single word of the commander in chief's regarding the regiment. Behind Kutúzov, at a distance that allowed every softly spoken word to be heard, followed some twenty men of his suite. These gentlemen talked among themselves and sometimes laughed. Nearest of all to the commander in chief walked a handsome adjutant. This was Prince Bolkónski. Beside him was his comrade Nesvítski, a tall staff officer, extremely stout, with a kindly, smiling, handsome face and moist eyes.

Kutúzov walked slowly and languidly past thousands of eyes which were starting from their sockets to watch their chief. On reaching the third company he suddenly stopped. His suite, not having expected this, involuntarily came closer to him.

"Ah, Timókhin!" said he, recognizing the red-nosed captain who had been reprimanded on account of the blue great-coat.

The third company was the last, and Kutúzov pondered, apparently trying to recollect something. Prince Andrew stepped forward from among the suite and said softly in French:

"You told me to remind you of the officer Dólokhov, reduced to the ranks in this regiment."

"Where is Dólokhov?" asked Kutúzov.

Dólokhov, who had already changed into a soldier's gray greatcoat, did not wait to be called. The shapely figure of the fair-haired soldier, with his clear blue eyes, stepped forward from the ranks, went up to the commander in chief, and presented arms.

"Have you a complaint to make?" Kutúzov asked with a slight frown.

"This is Dólokhov," said Prince Andrew.

"Ah!" said Kutúzov. "I hope this will be a lesson to you. Do your duty. The Emperor is gracious, and I shan't forget you if you deserve well."

The clear blue eyes looked at the commander in chief just as boldly as they had looked at the regimental commander, seeming by their expression to tear open the veil of convention that separates a commander in chief so widely from a private.

"One thing I ask of your excellency," Dólokhov said in his firm, ringing, deliberate voice. "I ask an opportunity to atone for my fault and prove my devotion to His Majesty the Emperor and to Russia!"

The regiment broke up into companies, which went to their appointed quarters near Braunau, where they hoped to receive boots and clothes and to rest after their hard marches.

"You won't bear me a grudge, Prokhór Ignátych?" said the regimental commander, overtaking the third company on its way to its quarters and riding up to Captain Timókhin who was walking in front. (The regimental commander's face now that the inspection was happily over beamed with irrepressible delight.)

"Don't mention it, General, as if I'd be so bold!" replied the captain, his nose growing redder as he gave a smile which showed where two front teeth were missing that had been knocked out by the butt end of a gun at Ismail.

"And tell Mr. Dólokhov that I won't forget him—he may be quite easy. And tell me, please—I've been meaning to ask—how is he behaving himself, and in general . . ."

"As far as the service goes he is quite punctilious, your excellency; but his character . . ." said Timókhin.

"And what about his character?" asked the regimental commander.

"It's different on different days," answered the captain. "One day he is sensible, well educated, and good-natured, and the next he's a wild beast. . . . In Poland, if you please, he nearly killed a Jew."

The cheerful mood of their officers after the inspection infected the soldiers. The company marched on gaily. The soldiers' voices could be heard on every side.

"And they said Kutúzov was blind of one eye?"

"And so he is! Quite blind!"

"No, friend, he is sharper-eyed than you are. Boots and leg bands . . . he noticed everything . . ."

"Singers to the front!" came the captain's order.

And from the different ranks some twenty men ran to the front. A drummer, their leader, turned round facing the singers, and flourishing his arm, began a long-drawn-out soldiers' song.

The soldiers, swinging their arms and keeping time spontaneously, marched with long steps. Behind the company the sound of wheels, the creaking of springs, and the tramp of horses' hoofs were heard. Kutúzov and his suite were returning to the town. The commander in chief made a sign that the men should continue to march at ease, and he and all his suite showed pleasure at the sound of the singing and the sight of a dancing soldier and the gay and smartly marching men. In the second file from the right flank, beside which the carriage passed the company, a blue-eyed soldier involuntarily attracted notice. It was Dólokhov marching with particular grace and boldness in time to the song and looking at those driving past as if he pitied all who were not at that moment marching with the company. The hussar cornet Zherkóv of Kutúzov's suite, fell back from the carriage and rode up to Dólokhov.

Hussar cornet Zherkóv had at one time, in Petersburg, belonged to the wild set led by Dólokhov. Zherkóv had met Dólokhov abroad as a private and had not seen fit to recognize him. But now that Kutúzov had spoken to the gentleman ranker, he addressed him with the cordiality of an old friend.

"My dear fellow, how are you?" said he through the singing, making his horse keep pace with the company.

"How am I?" Dólokhov answered coldly. "I am as you see."

The lively song gave a special flavor to the tone of free and easy gaiety with which Zherkóv spoke, and to the intentional coldness of Dólokhov's reply.

"And how do you get on with the officers?" inquired Zherkóv.

"All right. They are good fellows. And how have you wriggled onto the staff?"

"I was attached; I'm on duty."

Both were silent.

"Is it true that the Austrians have been beaten?" asked Dólokhov.

"The devil only knows! They say so."

"I'm glad," answered Dólokhov briefly and clearly, as the song demanded.

"I say, come round some evening and we'll have a game of faro!" said Zherkóv.

"Why, have you too much money?"

"Do come."

"I can't. I've sworn not to. I won't drink and won't play till I get reinstated."

"Well, that's only till the first engagement."

"We shall see."

They were again silent.

"Come if you need anything. One can at least be of use on the staff . . ."

Dólokhov smiled. "Don't trouble. If I want anything, I won't beg—I'll take it!"

"Well, never mind; I only . . ."
"And I only . . ."
"Good-by."
"Good health . . ."

2

Though not much time had passed since Prince Andrew had left Russia, he had changed greatly during that period. In the expression of his face, in his movements, in his walk, scarcely a trace was left of his former affected languor and indolence. He now looked like a man who has no time to think of the impression he makes on others, but is occupied with agreeable and interesting work. His face expressed more satisfaction with himself and those around him, his smile and glance were brighter and more attractive.

Kutúzov, whom he had overtaken in Poland, had received him very kindly, promised not to forget him, distinguished him above the other adjutants, and had taken him to Vienna and given him the more serious commissions. From Vienna Kutúzov wrote to his old comrade, Prince Andrew's father:

"Your son bids fair to become an officer distinguished by his industry, firmness, and expedition. I consider myself fortunate to have such a subordinate by me."

On Kutúzov's staff, among his fellow officers and in the army generally, Prince Andrew had, as he had had in Petersburg society, two quite opposite reputations. Some, a minority, acknowledged him to be different from themselves and from everyone else, expected great things of him, listened to him, admired, and imitated him, and with them Prince Andrew was natural and pleasant. Others, the majority, disliked him and considered him conceited, cold, and disagreeable. But among these people Prince Andrew knew how to take his stand so that they respected and even feared him.

While the Russians are being urged to join forces with the Austrians, under General Mack at Ulm, this commander arrives at Kutúzov's Braunau headquarters to announce the total defeat of his army by the French.

Prince Andrew was one of those rare staff officers whose chief interest lay in the general progress of the war. When he saw Mack and heard the details of his disaster he understood that half the campaign was lost, understood all the difficulties of the Russian army's position, and vividly imagined what awaited it and the part he would have to play. Involuntarily he felt a joyful agitation at the thought of the humiliation of arrogant Austria and that in a week's time he might, perhaps, see and take part in the first Russian encounter with the French since Suvórov met them. He feared that Bonaparte's genius might outweigh all the courage of the Russian troops, and at the same time could not admit the idea of his hero being disgraced.

Excited and irritated by these thoughts Prince Andrew went toward his room to write to his father, to whom he wrote every day. In the corridor he met Nesvítski, with whom he shared a room, and the wag Zherkóv; they were as usual laughing.

"Why are you so glum?" asked Nesvítski noticing Prince Andrew's pale face and glittering eyes.

"There's nothing to be gay about," answered Bolkónski.

Just as Prince Andrew met Nesvítski and Zherkóv, there came toward them from the other end of the corridor, Strauch, an Austrian general who was on Kutúzov's staff in charge of the provisioning of the Russian army.

"I have the honor to congratulate you. General Mack has arrived, quite well, only a little bruised just here," Zherkóv added, pointing with a beaming smile to his head.

The general frowned, turned away, and went on.

"*Gott, wie naiv* [Good God, what simplicity]!" said he angrily, after he had gone a few steps.

Nesvítski with a laugh threw his arms round Prince Andrew, but Bolkónski, turning still paler, pushed him away with an angry look and turned to Zherkóv. The nervous irritation aroused by the appearance of Mack, the news of his defeat, and the thought of what lay before the Russian army found vent in anger at Zherkóv's untimely jest.

"If you, sir, choose to make a *buffoon* of yourself," he said sharply, with a slight trembling of the lower jaw, "I can't prevent your doing so; but I warn you that if you *dare* to play the fool in my presence, I will teach you to behave yourself."

"What's the matter? I only congratulated them," said Zherkóv.

"I am not jesting with you; please be silent!" cried Bolkónski, and taking Nesvítski's arm he left Zherkóv, who did not know what to say.

"Come, what's the matter, old fellow?" said Nesvítski trying to soothe him.

"What's the matter?" exclaimed Prince Andrew standing still in his excitement. "Don't you understand that either we are officers serving our Tsar and our country, rejoicing in the successes and grieving at the misfortunes of our common cause, or we are merely lackeys who care nothing for their master's business. Forty thousand men massacred and the army of our allies destroyed, and you find that a cause for jesting. It is all very well for that good-for-nothing fellow of whom you have made a friend, but not for you, not for you. Only a *hobbledehoy* could amuse himself in this way," he added—having noticed that Zherkóv could still hear him.

He waited a moment to see whether the cornet would answer, but he turned and went out of the corridor.

3

The Pavlograd Hussars were stationed two miles from Braunau. The squadron in which Nicholas Rostóv served as a cadet was quartered in the German village of Salzeneck. The best quarters in the village were assigned to cavalry-captain Denísov, the squadron commander, known throughout the whole cavalry division as Váska Denísov. Cadet Rostóv, ever since he had overtaken the regiment in Poland, had lived with the squadron commander.

Denísov, who had been losing at cards all night, had not yet come home when Rostóv rode back early in the morning from a foraging expedition. Rostóv in his cadet uniform, with a jerk to his horse, rode up to the porch, swung his leg over the saddle with a supple youthful movement, stood for a moment in the stirrup as if loath to part from his horse, and at last sprang down and called to his orderly.

"Ah, Bondarénko, dear friend!" said he to the hussar who rushed up headlong to the horse. "Walk him up and down, my dear fellow," he continued, with that gay brotherly cordiality which goodhearted young people show to everyone when they are happy.

"What about your master?" he asked Lavrúshka, Denísov's orderly, whom all the regiment knew for a rogue.

"Hasn't been in since the evening. Must have been losing," answered Lavrúshka. "Will you have coffee?"

"Yes, bring some."

Ten minutes later Lavrúshka brought the coffee. "He's coming!" said he. "Now for trouble!" Rostóv looked out of the window and saw Denísov coming home. Denísov was a small man with a red face, sparkling black eyes, and black tousled mustache and hair. He wore an unfastened cloak, wide breeches hanging down in creases, and a crumpled shako on the back of his head. He came up to the porch gloomily, hanging his head.

"Ah, you're up already," said Denísov, entering the room.

"Long ago," answered Rostóv, "I have already been for the hay, and have seen Fräulein Mathilde."

"Weally! And I've been losing, bwother. I lost yesterday like a damned fool!" cried Denísov, not pronouncing his r's. "Such ill luck! Such ill luck. As soon as you left, it began and went on. Hullo there! Tea!"

Then he remained silent for a while, and all at once looked cheerfully with his glittering, black eyes at Rostóv.

"If at least we had some women here; but there's nothing foh one to do but dwink. If we could only get to fighting soon. Hullo, who's there?" he said, turning to the door as he heard a tread of heavy boots and the clinking of spurs that came to a stop, and a respectful cough.

"The squadron quartermaster!" said Lavrúshka.

Denísov's face puckered still more.

"Wetched!" he muttered, throwing down a purse with some gold in it. "Wostó, deah fellow, just see how much there is left and shove the purse undah the pillow," he said, and went out to the quartermaster.

Rostóv took the money and, mechanically arranging the old and new coins in separate piles, began counting them.

"Ah! Telyánin! How d'ye do? They plucked me last night," came Denísov's voice from the next room.

"Where? At Bykov's, at the rat's . . . I knew it," replied a piping voice, and Lieutenant Telyánin, a small officer of the same squadron, entered the room.

Rostóv thrust the purse under the pillow and shook the damp little hand which was offered him. Telyánin for some reason had been transferred from the Guards just before this campaign. He behaved very well in the regiment but was not liked; Rostóv especially detested him and was unable to overcome or conceal his groundless antipathy to the man.

"Well, young cavalryman, how is my Rook behaving?" he asked. (Rook was a young horse Telyánin had sold to Rostóv.)

"Oh, he's all right, a good horse," answered Rostóv, though the horse for which he had paid seven hundred rubles was not worth half that sum. "He's begun to go a little lame on the left foreleg," he added.

"The hoof's cracked! That's nothing. I'll teach you what to do and show you what kind of rivet to use."

"Then I'll have it brought round," said Rostóv wishing to avoid Telyánin, and he went out to give the order.

In the passage Denísov, with a pipe, was squatting on the threshold facing the quartermaster who was reporting to him. On seeing Rostóv, Denísov screwed up his face and pointing over his shoulder with his thumb to the room where Telyánin was sitting, he frowned and gave a shudder of disgust.

"Ugh! I don't like that fellow," he said, regardless of the quartermaster's presence.

Rostóv shrugged his shoulders as much as to say: "Nor do I, but what's one to do?" and, having given his order, he returned to Telyánin.

Telyánin was sitting in the same indolent pose in which Rostóv had left him, rubbing his small white hands.

"Have you told them to bring the horse?" asked Telyánin, getting up and looking carelessly about him.

"I have."

"Let us go ourselves. I only came round to ask Denísov about yesterday's order."

They went through the porch and into the stable. The lieutenant explained how to rivet the hoof and went away to his own quarters.

When Rostóv went back there was a bottle of vodka and a sausage on the table. Denísov was sitting there scratching with his pen on a sheet of paper. He looked gloomily in Rostóv's face and said: "I am witing to her."

He leaned his elbows on the table with his pen in his hand and, evidently glad of a chance to say quicker in words what he wanted to write, told Rostóv the contents of his letter.

"You see, my fwiend," he said, "we sleep when we don't love. We are childwen of the dust . . . but one falls in love and one is a God, one is pua' as on the fihst day of cweation . . . Who's that now? Send him to the devil, I'm busy!" he shouted to Lavrúshka, who went up to him not in the least abashed.

"Who should it be? You yourself told him to come. It's the quartermaster for the money."

Denísov frowned and was about to shout some reply but stopped.

"Wetched business," he muttered to himself. "How much is left in the puhse?" he asked, turning to Rostóv.

"Seven new and three old imperials."

"Oh, it's wetched! Well, what are you standing there for, you sca'-cwow? Call the quahtehmasteh," he shouted to Lavrúshka.

"Please, Denísov, let me lend you some: I have some, you know," said Rostóv, blushing.

"Don't like bowwowing from my own fellows, I don't," growled Denísov.

And Denísov went to the bed to get the purse from under the pillow.

"Where have you put it, Wostóv?"

"Under the lower pillow."

"It's not there."

Denísov threw both pillows on the floor. The purse was not there.

"That's a miwacle."

"Wait, haven't you dropped it?" said Rostóv, picking up the pillows one at a time and shaking them.

He pulled off the quilt and shook it. The purse was not there.

"Dear me, can I have forgotten? No, I remember thinking that you kept it under your head like a treasure," said Rostóv. "I put it just here. Where is it?" he asked, turning to Lavrúshka.

"I haven't been in the room. It must be where you put it."

"But it isn't? . . ."

"You're always like that; you thwow a thing down anywhere and forget it. Feel in your pockets."

"No, if I hadn't thought of it being a treasure," said Rostóv, "but I remember putting it there."

Lavrúshka turned all the bedding over, looked under the bed and under the table, searched everywhere, and stood still in the middle of the room. Denísov silently watched Lavrúshka's movements, and when the latter threw up his arms in surprise saying it was nowhere to be found Denísov glanced at Rostóv.

"Wostóv, you've not been playing schoolboy twicks. . . ."

Rostóv felt Denísov's gaze fixed on him, raised his eyes, and instantly dropped them again. All the blood which had seemed congested somewhere below his throat rushed to his face and eyes. He could not draw breath.

"And there hasn't been anyone in the room except the lieutenant and yourselves. It must be here somewhere," said Lavrúshka.

"Now then, you devil's puppet, look alive and hunt for it!" shouted Denísov, suddenly, turning purple and rushing at the man with a threatening gesture. "If the purse isn't found I'll flog you, I'll flog you all."

Rostóv, his eyes avoiding Denísov, began buttoning his coat, buckled on his saber, and put on his cap.

"I must have that purse, I tell you," shouted Denísov, shaking his orderly by the shoulders and knocking him against the wall.

"Denísov, let him alone, I know who has taken it," said Rostóv, going toward the door without raising his eyes.

Denísov paused, thought a moment, and, evidently understanding what Rostóv hinted at, seized his arm.

"Nonsense!" he cried, and the veins on his forehead and neck stood out like cords. "You are mad, I tell you. I won't allow it. The purse is here! I'll flay this scoundwel alive, and it will be found."

"I know who has taken it," repeated Rostóv in an unsteady voice, and went to the door.

"And I tell you, don't you dahe to do it!" shouted Denísov, rushing at the cadet to restrain him.

But Rostóv pulled away his arm and, with as much anger as

though Denísov were his worst enemy, firmly fixed his eyes directly on his face.

"Do you understand what you're saying?" he said in a trembling voice. "There was no one else in the room except myself. So that if it is not so, then . . ."

He could not finish, and ran out of the room.

"Ah, may the devil take you and evewybody," were the last words Rostóv heard.

Rostóv went to Telyánin's quarters.

"The master is not in, he's gone to headquarters," said Telyánin's orderly.

The headquarters were situated two miles away from Salzeneck, and Rostóv, without returning home, took a horse and rode there. There was an inn in the village which the officers frequented. Rostóv rode up to it and saw Telyánin's horse at the porch.

In the second room of the inn the lieutenant was sitting over a dish of sausages and a bottle of wine.

"Ah, you've come here too, young man!" he said, smiling and raising his eyebrows.

"Yes," said Rostóv as if it cost him a great deal to utter the word; and he sat down at the nearest table.

Both were silent. There were two Germans and a Russian officer in the room. No one spoke and the only sounds heard were the clatter of knives and the munching of the lieutenant.

When Telyánin had finished his lunch he took out of his pocket a double purse and, drawing its rings aside with his small, white, turned-up fingers, drew out a gold imperial, and lifting his eyebrows gave it to the waiter.

"Please be quick," he said.

The coin was a new one. Rostóv rose and went up to Telyánin.

"Allow me to look at your purse," he said in a low, almost inaudible, voice.

With shifting eyes but eyebrows still raised, Telyánin handed him the purse.

"Yes, it's a nice purse. Yes, yes," he said, growing suddenly pale, and added, "Look at it, young man."

Rostóv took the purse in his hand, examined it and the money in it, and looked at Telyánin. The lieutenant was looking about in his usual way and suddenly seemed to grow very merry.

"If we get to Vienna I'll get rid of it there but in these wretched little towns there's nowhere to spend it," said he. "Well, let me have it, young man, I'm going."

Rostóv did not speak.

"And you? Are you going to have lunch too? They feed you quite decently here," continued Telyánin. "Now then, let me have it."

He stretched out his hand to take hold of the purse. Rostóv let go of it. Telyánin took the purse and began carelessly slipping it into the pocket of his riding breeches.

"Well, young man?" he said with a sigh, and from under his lifted brows he glanced into Rostóv's eyes.

Some flash as of an electric spark shot from Telyánin's eyes to Rostóv's and back, and back again and again in an instant.

"Come here," said Rostóv, catching hold of Telyánin's arm and almost dragging him to the window. "That money is Denísov's; you took it . . ." he whispered just above Telyánin's ear.

"What? What? How dare you? What?" said Telyánin.

But these words came like a piteous, despairing cry and an entreaty for pardon. As soon as Rostóv heard them, an enormous load of doubt fell from him. He was glad, and at the same instant began to pity the miserable man who stood before him, but the task he had begun had to be completed.

"Heaven only knows what the people here may imagine," muttered Telyánin, taking up his cap and moving toward a small empty room. "We must have an explanation . . ."

"I know it and shall prove it," said Rostóv.

"I . . ."

Every muscle of Telyánin's pale, terrified face began to quiver, his eyes still shifted from side to side but with a downward look not rising to Rostóv's face, and his sobs were audible.

"Count! . . . Don't ruin a young fellow . . . here is this wretched money, take it . . ." He threw it on the table. "I have an old father and mother! . . ."

Rostóv took the money, avoiding Telyánin's eyes, and went out of the room without a word. But at the door he stopped and then retraced his steps. "O God," he said with tears in his eyes, "how could you do it?"

"Count . . ." said Telyánin drawing nearer to him.

"Don't touch me," said Rostóv, drawing back. "If you need it, take the money," and he threw the purse to him and ran out of the inn.

4

That same evening there was an animated discussion among the squadron's officers in Denísov's quarters.

"And I tell you, Rostóv, that you must apologize to the colonel!" said a tall, grizzly-haired staff captain, with enormous mustaches and many wrinkles on his large features, to Rostóv who was crimson with excitement.

The staff captain, Kírsten, had twice been reduced to the ranks for affairs of honor and had twice regained his commission.

"I will allow no one to call me a liar!" cried Rostóv. "He told me I lied, and I told him he lied. And there it rests. He may keep me on duty every day, or may place me under arrest, but no one can make me apologize, because if he, as commander of this regiment, thinks it beneath his dignity to give me satisfaction, then . . ."

"You just wait a moment, my dear fellow, and listen," interrupted the staff captain in his deep bass, calmly stroking his long mustache. "You tell the colonel in the presence of other officers that an officer has stolen . . ."

"I'm not to blame that the conversation began in the presence of other officers. Perhaps I ought not to have spoken before them, but I am not a diplomatist. That's why I joined the hussars, thinking that here one would not need finesse; and he tells me that I am lying—so let him give me satisfaction . . ."

"That's all right. No one thinks you a coward, but that's not the point. Ask Denísov whether it is not out of the question for a cadet to demand satisfaction of his regimental commander?"

Denísov sat gloomily biting his mustache and listening to the conversation, evidently with no wish to take part in it. He answered the staff captain's question by a disapproving shake of his head.

"You speak to the colonel about this nasty business before other officers," continued the staff captain, "and Bogdánich" (the colonel was called Bogdánich) "shuts you up."

"He did not shut me up, he said I was telling an untruth."

"Well, have it so, and you talked a lot of nonsense to him and must apologize."

"Not on any account!" exclaimed Rostóv.

"You value your own pride and don't wish to apologize," continued the staff captain, "but we old fellows, who have grown up in and, God willing, are going to die in the regiment, we prize the honor of the regiment, and Bogdánich knows it. Oh, we do prize it, old fellow! And all this is not right, it's not right! You may take offense or not but I always stick to mother truth. It's not right!"

And the staff captain rose and turned away from Rostóv.

"That's twue, devil take it!" shouted Denísov, jumping up. "Now then, Wostóv, now then!"

Just then Zherkóv entered the room.

"What brings you here?" cried the officers turning to the newcomer.

"We're to go into action, gentlemen! Mack has surrendered with his whole army."

"It's not true!"

"I've seen him myself!"

"What? Saw the real Mack? With hands and feet?"

"Into action! Into action! Bring him a bottle for such news! But how did you come here?"

"I've been sent back to the regiment all on account of that devil, Mack. An Austrian general complained of me. I congratulated him on Mack's arrival . . . What's the matter, Rostóv? You look as if you'd just come out of a hot bath."

"Oh, my dear fellow, we're in such a stew here these last two days."

The regimental adjutant came in and confirmed the news brought by Zherkóv. They were under orders to advance next day.

"We're going into action, gentlemen!"

"Well, thank God! We've been sitting here too long!"

5

After Mack's defeat, Kutúzov falls back toward Vienna. His forces cross the river Enns on October 23, and the Pávlograd hussars burn the bridge in the face of the fire of the French advance guard under Murat. Cadet Nicholas Rostóv participates in this engagement and feels that he acted in a cowardly fashion.

6

Pursued by the French army of a hundred thousand men under the command of Bonaparte, encountering a population that was unfriendly to it, losing confidence in its allies, suffering from shortness of supplies, and compelled to act under conditions of war unlike anything that had been foreseen, the Russian army of thirty-five thousand men commanded by Kutúzov was hurriedly retreating along the Danube, stopping where overtaken by the enemy and fighting rearguard actions only as far as necessary to enable it to retreat without losing its heavy equipment.

On the twenty-eighth of October Kutúzov with his army crossed to the left bank of the Danube and took up a position for the first time with the river between himself and the main body of the French. On the thirtieth he attacked Mortier's division, which was on the left bank, and broke it up. In this action for the first time trophies were taken: banners, cannon, and two enemy generals. For the first time, after a fortnight's retreat, the Russian troops had halted and after a fight had not only held the field but had repulsed the French. Throughout the whole army and at headquarters most joyful though erroneous rumors were rife of the imaginary approach of columns from Russia, of some victory gained by the Austrians, and of the retreat of the frightened Bonaparte.

Prince Andrew during the battle had been in attendance on the Austrian General Schmidt, who was killed in the action. His horse had been wounded under him and his own arm slightly grazed by a bullet. As a mark of the commander in chief's special favor he was sent with the news of this victory to the Austrian court, now no longer at Vienna (which was threatened by the French) but at Brünn. To be so sent meant not only a reward but an important step toward promotion.

The night was dark but starry, the road showed black in the snow that had fallen the previous day—the day of the battle. Reviewing his impressions of the recent battle, picturing pleasantly to himself the impression his news of a victory would create, or recalling the sendoff given him by the commander in chief and his fellow officers, Prince Andrew was galloping along in a post chaise enjoying the feelings of a man who has at length begun to attain a long-desired happiness. As soon as he closed his eyes his ears seemed filled with the rattle of the wheels and the sensation of victory.

It was already quite dark when Prince Andrew rattled over the paved streets of Brünn and found himself surrounded by high buildings, the lights of shops, houses, and street lamps, fine carriages, and all that atmosphere of a large and active town which is always so attractive to a soldier after camp life. Despite his rapid journey and sleepless night, Prince Andrew when he drove up to the palace felt even more vigorous and alert than he had done the day before. Only his eyes gleamed feverishly and his thoughts followed one another with extraordinary clearness and rapidity. He again vividly recalled the details of the battle, no longer dim, but definite and in the concise form in which he imagined himself stating them to the Emperor Francis. He vividly imagined the casual questions that might be put to him and the answers he would give. He expected to be at once presented to the Emperor.

The adjutant on duty, meeting Prince Andrew, asked him to wait, and went in to the Minister of War. Five minutes later he returned and bowing with particular courtesy ushered Prince Andrew before him along a corridor to the cabinet where the Minister of War was at work. The adjutant by his elaborate courtesy appeared to wish to ward off any attempt at familiarity on the part of the Russian messenger.

Prince Andrew's joyous feeling was considerably weakened as he approached the door of the minister's room. He felt offended, and without his noticing it the feeling of offense immediately turned into one of disdain which was quite uncalled for. This feeling of disdain was heightened when he saw the minister seated at a large table reading some papers and making pencil notes on them, and for the first two or three minutes taking no notice of his arrival. A wax candle stood at each side of the minister's bent bald head with its gray temples. He went on reading to the end, without raising his eyes at the opening of the door and the sound of footsteps.

"Take this and deliver it," said he to his adjutant, handing him the papers and still taking no notice of the special messenger.

Prince Andrew felt that either the actions of Kutúzov's army interested the Minister of War less than any of the other matters he was concerned with, or he wanted to give the Russian special messenger that impression. "But that is a matter of perfect indifference to me," he thought. The minister drew the remaining papers together, arranged them evenly, and then raised his head. He had an intellectual and distinctive head, but the instant he turned to Prince Andrew the firm, intelligent expression on his face changed in a way evidently deliberate and habitual to him. His face took on the stupid artificial smile (which does not even attempt to hide its artificiality) of a man who is continually receiving many petitioners one after another.

"From General Field Marshal Kutúzov?" he asked. "I hope it is good news? There has been an encounter with Mortier? A victory? It was high time!"

He took the dispatch which was addressed to him and began to read it with a mournful expression.

"Oh, my God! My God! Schmidt!" he exclaimed in German. "What a calamity! What a calamity!"

Having glanced through the dispatch he laid it on the table and looked at Prince Andrew, evidently considering something.

"Ah, what a calamity! You say the affair was decisive? But Mortier is not captured." Again he pondered. "I am very glad you have brought good news, though Schmidt's death is a heavy price to pay for the victory. His Majesty will no doubt wish to see you, but not today. I thank you! You must have a rest. Be at the levee tomorrow after the parade. However, I will let you know."

When Prince Andrew left the palace he felt that all the interest and happiness the victory had afforded him had been now left in the indifferent hands of the Minister of War and the polite adjutant. The whole tenor of his thoughts instantaneously changed; the battle seemed the memory of a remote event long past.

7

Prince Andrew stayed at Brünn with Bilíbin, a Russian acquaintance of his in the diplomatic service.

"Ah, my dear prince! I could not have a more welcome visitor," said Bilíbin as he came out to meet Prince Andrew. "Franz, put the prince's things in my bedroom," said he to the servant who was ushering Bolkónski in. "So you're a messenger of victory, eh? Splendid! And I am sitting here ill, as you see."

After washing and dressing, Prince Andrew came into the diplomat's luxurious study and sat down to the dinner prepared for him. Bilíbin settled down comfortably beside the fire.

Bilíbin was a man of thirty-five, a bachelor, and of the same circle as Prince Andrew. They had known each other previously in Petersburg, but had become more intimate when Prince Andrew was in Vienna with Kutúzov. Just as Prince Andrew was a young man who gave promise of rising high in the military profession, so to even greater extent Bilíbin gave promise of rising in his diplomatic career.

Bilíbin liked conversation as he liked work, only when it could be made elegantly witty. In society he always awaited an opportunity to say something striking and took part in a conversation only when that was possible.

"Well, now tell me about your exploits," said he.

Bolkónski, very modestly without once mentioning himself, described the engagement and his reception by the Minister of War.

"They received me and my news as one receives a dog in a game of skittles," said he in conclusion.

Bilíbin smiled and the wrinkles on his face disappeared.

"Why didn't you capture one, just one, marshal for us?"

"Because not everything happens as one expects or with the smoothness of a parade. We had expected, as I told you, to get at their rear by seven in the morning but had not reached it by five in the afternoon."

"And why didn't you do it at seven in the morning? You ought to have been there at seven in the morning," returned Bilíbin with a smile. "You ought to have been there at seven in the morning."

"It is now my turn to ask you 'why?' *mon cher*," said Bolkónski. "I confess I do not understand: perhaps there are diplomatic subtleties here beyond my feeble intelligence, but I can't make it out. Mack loses a whole army, the Archduke Ferdinand and the Archduke Karl give no signs of life and make blunder after blunder. Kutúzov alone at last gains a real victory, destroying the spell of the invincibility of the French, and the Minister of War does not even care to hear the details."

"That's just it, my dear fellow. You see it's *hurrah* for the Tsar, for Russia, for the Orthodox Greek faith! All that is beautiful, but what do we, I mean the Austrian court, care for your victories? . . . Besides, suppose you did gain a brilliant victory, if even the Archduke Karl gained a victory, what effect would that have on the general course of events? It's too late now when Vienna is occupied by the French army!"

"What? Occupied? Vienna occupied?"

"Not only occupied, but Bonaparte is at Schönbrunn, and the count, our dear Count Vrbna, goes to him for orders."

"Really I don't care about that, I don't care at all," said Prince Andrew, beginning to understand that his news of the battle before Krems was really of small importance in view of such events as the fall of Austria's capital.

"But still this does not mean that the campaign is over," said Prince Andrew.

"Well, I think it is. The bigwigs here think so too, but they daren't say so. . . . The only question is what will come of the meeting between the Emperor Alexander and the King of Prussia in Berlin? If Prussia joins the Allies, Austria's hand will be forced and there will be war."

"What an extraordinary genius!" Prince Andrew suddenly exclaimed, clenching his small hand and striking the table with it, "and what luck the man has!

"But joking apart," said Prince Andrew, "do you really think the campaign is over?"

"This is what I think. Austria has been made a fool of, and she is not used to it. She will retaliate. . . . And therefore—this is between ourselves—I instinctively feel that we are being deceived, my instinct tells me of negotiations with France and projects for peace, a secret peace concluded separately."

"Impossible!" cried Prince Andrew. "That would be too base."

"If we live we shall see," replied Bilíbin, his face again becoming smooth as a sign that the conversation was at an end.

When Prince Andrew reached the room prepared for him and lay down in a clean shirt on the feather bed with its warmed and fragrant pillows, he felt that the battle of which he had brought tidings was far, far away from him. The alliance with Prussia, Austria's treachery, Bonaparte's new triumph, tomorrow's levee and parade, and the audience with the Emperor Francis occupied his thoughts.

8

The next day a group of friends from the diplomatic corps gather at Bilíbin's to greet Prince Andrew. They make fun of Hippolyte Kurágin. Prince Andrew announces he must leave for his audience with the Austrian Emperor.

9

At the levee Prince Andrew stood among the Austrian officers as he had been told to, and the Emperor Francis merely looked fixedly into his face and just nodded to him with his long head. But after it was over, the adjutant he had seen the previous day ceremoniously informed Bolkónski that the Emperor desired to give him an audience. The Emperor Francis received him standing in the middle of the room. Before the conversation began Prince Andrew was struck by the fact that the Emperor seemed confused and blushed as if not knowing what to say.

"Tell me, when did the battle begin?" he asked hurriedly.

Prince Andrew replied. Then followed other questions just

as simple: "Was Kutúzov well? When had he left Krems?" and so on. The Emperor spoke as if his sole aim were to put a given number of questions—the answers to these questions, as was only too evident, did not interest him.

"At what o'clock did the battle begin?" asked the Emperor.

"I cannot inform Your Majesty at what o'clock the battle began at the front, but at Dürrenstein, where I was, our attack began after five in the afternoon," replied Bolkónski growing more animated and expecting that he would have a chance to give a reliable account, which he had ready in his mind, of all he knew and had seen. But the Emperor smiled and interrupted him.

"How many miles?"

"From where to where, Your Majesty?"

"From Dürrenstein to Krems."

"Three and a half miles, Your Majesty."

"The French have abandoned the left bank?"

"According to the scouts the last of them crossed on rafts during the night."

"Is there sufficient forage in Krems?"

"Forage has not been supplied to the extent . . ."

The Emperor interrupted him.

"At what o'clock was General Schmidt killed?"

"At seven o'clock, I believe."

"At seven o'clock? It's very sad, very sad!"

The Emperor thanked Prince Andrew and bowed. Prince Andrew withdrew and was immediately surrounded by courtiers on all sides. Everywhere he saw friendly looks and heard friendly words. Yesterday's adjutant reproached him for not having stayed at the palace, and offered him his own house. The Minister of War came up and congratulated him on the Maria Theresa Order of the third grade, which the Emperor was conferring on him. The Empress' chamberlain invited him to see Her Majesty. The archduchess also wished to see him. He did not know whom to answer, and for a few seconds collected his thoughts. Then the Russian ambassador took him by the shoulder, led him to the window, and began to talk to him.

Contrary to Bilíbin's forecast the news he had brought was joyfully received. A thanksgiving service was arranged, Kutúzov was awarded the Grand Cross of Maria Theresa, and the whole army received rewards. Bolkónski was invited everywhere, and had to spend the whole morning calling on the principal Austrian dignitaries. Between four and five in the afternoon, having made all his calls, he was returning to Bilíbin's house thinking out a letter to his father about the battle and his visit to Brünn. At the door he found a vehicle half full of luggage. Franz, Bilíbin's man, was dragging a portmanteau with some difficulty out of the front door.

"What is it?" he asked.

"Oh, your excellency!" said Franz, with difficulty rolling the portmanteau into the vehicle, "we are to move on still farther. The scoundrel is again at our heels!"

"Eh? What?" asked Prince Andrew.

Bilíbin came out to meet him. His usually calm face showed excitement.

"There now! Confess that this is delightful," said he. "This affair of the Thabor Bridge, at Vienna. . . . They have crossed without striking a blow!"

Prince Andrew could not understand.

"But where do you come from not to know what every coachman in the town knows?"

"I come from the archduchess'. I heard nothing there."

"And you didn't see that everybody is packing up?"

"I did not . . . What is it all about?" inquired Prince Andrew impatiently.

"What's it all about? Why, the French have crossed the bridge that Auersperg was defending, and the bridge was not blown up: so Murat is now rushing along the road to Brünn and will be here in a day or two."

"What? Here? But why did they not blow up the bridge, if it was mined?"

"That is what I ask you. No one, not even Bonaparte, knows why."

Bolkónski shrugged his shoulders.

"But if the bridge is crossed it means that the army too is lost? It will be cut off," said he.

"Where are you off to?" he said suddenly to Prince Andrew who had risen and was going toward his room.

"I am going away."

"Where to?"

"To the army."

"But you meant to stay another two days?"

"But now I am off at once."

And Prince Andrew after giving directions about his departure went to his room.

"Do you know, *mon cher*," said Bilíbin following him, "I have been thinking about you. Why are you going?"

And in proof of the conclusiveness of his opinion all the wrinkles vanished from his face.

Prince Andrew looked inquiringly at him and gave no reply.

"Why are you going? I know you think it your duty to gallop back to the army now that it is in danger. I understand that. *Mon cher*, it is heroism!"

"Not at all," said Prince Andrew.

"But as you are a philosopher, be a consistent one, look at the other side of the question and you will see that your duty, on the contrary, is to take care of yourself. Leave it to those who are no longer fit for anything else. . . . You have not been ordered to return and have not been dismissed from here; therefore, you can stay and go with us wherever our ill-luck takes us. They say we are going to Olmütz, and Olmütz is a very decent town. You and I will travel comfortably in my *calèche*."

"Do stop joking, Bilíbin," cried Bolkónski.

"I am speaking sincerely as a friend! Consider! Where and why are you going, when you might remain here? You are faced by one of two things," and the skin over his left temple puckered, "either you will not reach your regiment before peace is concluded, or you will share defeat and disgrace with Kutúzov's whole army."

And Bilíbin unwrinkled his temple, feeling that the dilemma was insoluble.

"I cannot argue about it," replied Prince Andrew coldly, but he thought: "I am going to save the army."

"My dear fellow, you are a hero!" said Bilíbin.

10

That same night, having taken leave of the Minister of War, Bolkónski set off to rejoin the army, not knowing where he would find it and fearing to be captured by the French on the way to Krems.

Near Hetzelsdorf Prince Andrew struck the highroad along which the Russian army was moving with great haste and in the greatest disorder. The road was so obstructed with carts that it was impossible to get by in a carriage. Prince Andrew took a horse and a Cossack from a Cossack commander, and hungry and weary, making his way past the baggage wagons, rode in search of the commander in chief and of his own luggage. Very sinister reports of the position of the army reached him as he went along, and the appearance of the troops in their disorderly flight confirmed these rumors.

Prince Andrew . . . galloped on to the village where he was told that the commander in chief was. On reaching the village he dismounted and went to the nearest house, intending to rest if but for a moment, eat something, and try to sort out the stinging and tormenting thoughts that confused his mind. "This is a mob of scoundrels and not an army," he was thinking as he went up to the window of the first house, when a familiar voice called him by name.

He turned round. Nesvítski's handsome face looked out of the little window. Nesvítski, moving his moist lips as he chewed something, and flourishing his arm, called him to enter.

"Bolkónski! Bolkónski . . . Don't you hear? Eh? Come quick . . ." he shouted.

Entering the house, Prince Andrew saw Nesvítski and another adjutant having something to eat. They hastily turned round to him asking if he had any news. On their familiar faces he read agitation and alarm. This was particularly noticeable on Nesvítski's usually laughing countenance.

"Where is the commander in chief?" asked Bolkónski.

"Here, in that house," answered the adjutant.

"Well, is it true that it's peace and capitulation?" asked Nesvítski.

"I was going to ask you. I know nothing except that it was all I could do to get here."

"And we, my dear boy! It's terrible! I was wrong to laugh at Mack, we're getting it still worse," said Nesvítski. "But sit down and have something to eat."

"You won't be able to find either your baggage or anything else now, Prince. And God only knows where your man Peter is," said the other adjutant.

"Where are headquarters?"

"We are to spend the night in Znaim."

"What is the commander in chief doing here?" he asked.

"I can't make out at all," said Nesvítski.

"Well, all I can make out is that everything is abominable, abominable, quite abominable!" said Prince Andrew, and he went off to the house where the commander in chief was.

Passing by Kutúzov's carriage and the exhausted saddle horses of his suite, with their Cossacks who were talking loudly together, Prince Andrew entered the passage. Kutúzov himself, he was told, was in the house with Prince Bagratión and Weyrother. Weyrother was the Austrian general who had succeeded Schmidt.

Through the door came the sounds of Kutúzov's voice, excited and dissatisfied, interrupted by another, an unfamiliar voice.

Prince Andrew moved toward the door from whence voices were heard. Just as he was going to open it the sounds ceased, the door opened, and Kutúzov with his eagle nose and puffy face appeared in the doorway. Prince Andrew stood right in front of Kutúzov but the expression of the commander in chief's one sound eye showed him to be so preoccupied with thoughts and anxieties as to be oblivious of his presence. He looked straight at his adjutant's face without recognizing him.

Bagratión, a gaunt middle-aged man of medium height with a firm, impassive face of Oriental type, came out after the commander in chief.

"I have the honor to present myself," repeated Prince Andrew rather loudly, handing Kutúzov an envelope.

"Ah, from Vienna? Very good. Later, later!"

Kutúzov went out into the porch with Bagratión.

"Well, good-by, Prince," said he to Bagratión. "My blessing, and may Christ be with you in your great endeavor!"

His face suddenly softened and tears came into his eyes. With his left hand he drew Bagratión toward him, and with his right, on which he wore a ring, he made the sign of the cross over him with a gesture evidently habitual, offering his puffy cheek, but Bagratión kissed him on the neck instead.

"Christ be with you!" Kutúzov repeated and went toward his carriage. "Get in with me," said he to Bolkónski.

"Your excellency, I should like to be of use here. Allow me to remain with Prince Bagratión's detachment."

"Get in," said Kutúzov, and noticing that Bolkónski still delayed, he added: "I need good officers myself, need them myself!"

They got into the carriage and drove for a few miles in silence.

"There is still much, much before us," he said, as if with an old man's penetration he understood all that was passing in Bolkónski's mind. "If a tenth part of his detachment returns I shall thank God," he added as if speaking to himself.

Prince Andrew glanced at Kutúzov's face only a foot distant from him and involuntarily noticed the carefully washed seams of the scar near his temple, where an Ismail bullet had pierced his skull, and the empty eye socket. "Yes, he has a right to speak so calmly of those men's death," thought Bolkónski.

"That is why I beg to be sent to that detachment," he said.

Kutúzov did not reply. He seemed to have forgotten what he had been saying, and sat plunged in thought. Five minutes later, gently swaying on the soft springs of the carriage, he turned to Prince Andrew. There was not a trace of agitation on his face. With delicate irony he questioned Prince Andrew about the details of his interview with the Emperor, about the remarks he had heard at court concerning the Krems affair, and about some ladies they both knew.

Bagratión is sent with a small advance guard to delay the enemy at Hollabrünn and cover the retreat of Kutúzov's main force from Krems to Znaim. When Murat confronts Bagratión at Hollabrünn with his advanced detachment, he thinks it is the whole Russian army and tries to trick it by a truce until his main force arrives. Napoleon at Schönbrunn guesses the real situation and dispatches an adjutant to Murat with orders to attack.

11

Between three and four o'clock in the afternoon Prince Andrew, who had persisted in his request to Kutúzov, arrived at Grunth and reported himself to Bagratión.

Bonaparte's adjutant had not yet reached Murat's detachment and the battle had not yet begun. In Bagratión's detachment no one knew anything of the general position of affairs. They talked of peace but did not believe in its possibility; others talked of a battle but also disbelieved in the nearness of an engagement. Bagratión, knowing Bolkónski to be a favorite and trusted adjutant, received him with distinction and special marks of favor, explaining to him that there would probably be an engagement that day or the next, and giving him full liberty to remain with him during the battle or to join the rearguard and have an eye on the order of retreat, "which is also very important."

"However, there will hardly be an engagement today," said Bagratión as if to reassure Prince Andrew.

"If he is one of the ordinary little staff dandies sent to earn a medal he can get his reward just as well in the rearguard, but if he wishes to stay with me, let him . . . he'll be of use here if he's a brave officer," thought Bagratión. Prince Andrew, without replying, asked the prince's permission to ride round the position to see the disposition of the forces, so as to know his bearings should he be sent to execute an order. The officer on duty, a handsome, elegantly dressed man with a diamond ring on his forefinger, who was fond of speaking French though he spoke it badly, offered to conduct Prince Andrew.

On all sides they saw rain-soaked officers with dejected faces who seemed to be seeking something, and soldiers dragging doors, benches, and fencing from the village.

"There now, Prince! We can't stop those fellows," said the staff officer pointing to the soldiers. "The officers don't keep them in hand. And there," he pointed to a sutler's tent, "they crowd in and sit. This morning I turned them all out and now look, it's full again. I must go there, Prince, and scare them a bit. It won't take a moment."

"Yes, let's go in and I will get myself a roll and some cheese," said Prince Andrew who had not yet had time to eat anything.

They dismounted and entered the tent. Several officers, with flushed and weary faces, were sitting at the table eating and drinking.

"Now what does this mean, gentlemen?" said the staff officer, in the reproachful tone of a man who has repeated the same thing more than once. "You know it won't do to leave your posts like this. The prince gave orders that no one should leave his post. Now you, Captain," and he turned to a thin, dirty little artillery officer who without his boots (he had given them to the canteen keeper to dry), in only his stockings, rose when they entered, smiling not altogether comfortably.

"Well, aren't you ashamed of yourself, Captain Túshin?" he continued. "One would think that as an artillery officer you would set a good example, yet here you are without your boots! The alarm will be sounded and you'll be in a pretty position without your boots!" (The staff officer smiled.) "Kindly return to your posts, gentlemen, all of you, all!" he added in a tone of command.

Prince Andrew smiled involuntarily as he looked at the artillery officer Túshin, who silent and smiling, shifting from one stockinged foot to the other, glanced inquiringly with his large, intelligent, kindly eyes from Prince Andrew to the staff officer.

The staff officer and Prince Andrew mounted their horses and rode on.

Having ridden beyond the village, continually meeting and overtaking soldiers and officers of various regiments, they saw on their left some entrenchments being thrown up, the freshly dug clay of which showed up red. Several battalions of soldiers, in their shirt sleeves despite the cold wind, swarmed in these earthworks like a host of white ants; spadefuls of red clay were continually being thrown up from behind the bank by unseen hands.

They rode up the opposite hill. From there the French could already be seen. Prince Andrew stopped and began examining the position.

"That's our battery," said the staff officer indicating the highest point. "It's in charge of the queer fellow we saw without his boots. You can see everything from there; let's go there, Prince."

"Thank you very much, I will go on alone," said Prince Andrew, wishing to rid himself of this staff officer's company, "please don't trouble yourself further."

The staff officer remained behind and Prince Andrew rode on alone.

The farther forward and nearer the enemy he went, the

more orderly and cheerful were the troops. Soldiers scattered over the whole place were dragging logs and brushwood and were building shelters with merry chatter and laughter; around the fires sat others, dressed and undressed, drying their shirts and leg bands or mending boots or overcoats and crowding round the boilers and porridge cookers. In one company dinner was ready, and the soldiers were gazing eagerly at the steaming boiler, waiting till the sample, which a quartermaster sergeant was carrying in a wooden bowl to an officer who sat on a log before his shelter, had been tasted.

Prince Andrew, having reached the front line, rode along it. Our front line and that of the enemy were far apart on the right and left flanks, but in the center where the men with a flag of truce had passed that morning, the lines were so near together that the men could see one another's faces and speak to one another. Besides the soldiers who formed the picket line on either side, there were many curious onlookers who, jesting and laughing, stared at their strange foreign enemies.

Since early morning—despite an injunction not to approach the picket line—the officers had been unable to keep sightseers away. The soldiers forming the picket line, like showmen exhibiting a curiosity, no longer looked at the French but paid attention to the sightseers and grew weary waiting to be relieved. Prince Andrew halted to have a look at the French.

"Look! Look there!" one soldier was saying to another, pointing to a Russian musketeer who had gone up to the picket line with an officer and was rapidly and excitedly talking to a French grenadier. "Hark to him jabbering! Fine, isn't it? It's all the Frenchy can do to keep up with him. There now, Sídorov!"

"Wait a bit and listen. It's fine!" answered Sídorov, who was considered an adept at French.

The soldier to whom the laughers referred was Dólokhov. Prince Andrew recognized him and stopped to listen to what he was saying. Dólokhov had come from the left flank where their regiment was stationed, with his captain.

"Now then, go on, go on!" incited the officer, bending forward and trying not to lose a word of the speech which was incomprehensible to him. "More, please: more! What's he saying?"

Dólokhov did not answer the captain; he had been drawn

into a hot dispute with the French grenadier. They were naturally talking about the campaign. The Frenchman, confusing the Austrians with the Russians, was trying to prove that the Russians had surrendered and had fled all the way from Ulm, while Dólokhov maintained that the Russians had not surrendered but had beaten the French.

"We have orders to drive you off here, and we shall drive you off," said Dólokhov.

And Dólokhov swore at him in coarse soldier's Russian and shouldering his musket walked away.

"Let us go, Iván Lukích," he said to the captain.

"Ah, that's the way to talk French," said the picket soldiers. "Now, Sídorov, you have a try!"

Sídorov, turning to the French, winked, and began to jabber meaningless sounds very fast: "*Kari, mala, tafa, safi, muter, Kaská,*" he said, trying to give an expressive intonation to his voice.

"Ho! ho! ho! Ha! ha! ha! ha! Ouh! ouh!" came peals of such healthy and good-humored laughter from the soldiers that it infected the French involuntarily, so much so that the only thing left to do seemed to be to unload the muskets, explode the ammunition, and all return home as quickly as possible.

But the guns remained loaded, the loopholes in blockhouses and entrenchments looked out just as menacingly, and the unlimbered cannon confronted one another as before.

12

Having ridden round the whole line from right flank to left, Prince Andrew made his way up to the battery from which the staff officer had told him the whole field could be seen. Here he dismounted, and stopped beside the farthest of the four unlimbered cannon. To the left, not far from the farthest cannon, was a small, newly constructed wattle shed from which came the sound of officers' voices in eager conversation.

It was true that a view over nearly the whole Russian position and the greater part of the enemy's opened out from this battery. Just facing it, on the crest of the opposite hill, the village of Schön Grabern could be seen, and in

three places to left and right the French troops amid the
smoke of their campfires, the greater part of whom were
evidently in the village itself and behind the hill. In the
center, where Túshin's battery stood and from which Prince
Andrew was surveying the position, was the easiest and most
direct descent and ascent to the brook separating us from
Schön Grabern. On the left our troops were close to a copse,
in which smoked the bonfires of our infantry who were felling
wood. The French line was wider than ours, and it was
plain that they could easily outflank us on both sides. Behind
our position was a steep and deep dip, making it difficult
for artillery and cavalry to retire. Prince Andrew took out
his notebook and, leaning on the cannon, sketched a plan of
the position. He made some notes on two points, intending
to mention them to Bagratión. Suddenly, however, he was
struck by a voice coming from the shed, and its tone was so
sincere that he could not but listen.

"No, friend," said a pleasant and, as it seemed to Prince
Andrew, a familiar voice, "what I say is that if it were
possible to know what is beyond death, none of us would
be afraid of it. That's so, friend."

Another, a younger voice, interrupted him: "Afraid or not,
you can't escape it anyhow."

"All the same, one is afraid! Oh, you clever people," said
a third manly voice interrupting them both. "Of course you
artillery men are very wise, because you can take everything
along with you—vodka and snacks."

And the owner of the manly voice, evidently an infantry
officer, laughed.

"Yes, one is afraid," continued the first speaker, he of the
familiar voice. "One is afraid of the unknown, that's what it
is. Whatever we may say about the soul going to the sky . . .
we know there is no sky but only an atmosphere."

The manly voice again interrupted the artillery officer.

"Well, stand us some of your herb vodka, Túshin," it said.

"Why," thought Prince Andrew, "that's the captain who
stood up in the sutler's hut without his boots." He recognized
the agreeable, philosophizing voice with pleasure.

"Some herb vodka? Certainly!" said Túshin. "But still,
to conceive a future life . . ."

He did not finish. Just then there was a whistle in the air;

nearer and nearer, faster and louder, louder and faster, a cannon ball, as if it had not finished saying what was necessary, thudded into the ground near the shed with superhuman force, throwing up a mass of earth. The ground seemed to groan at the terrible impact.

And immediately Túshin, with a short pipe in the corner of his mouth and his kind, intelligent face rather pale, rushed out of the shed followed by the owner of the manly voice, a dashing infantry officer who hurried off to his company, buttoning up his coat as he ran.

13

Mounting his horse again Prince Andrew lingered with the battery, looking at the puff from the gun that had sent the ball. The smoke of the first shot had not yet dispersed before another puff appeared, followed by a report. The battle had begun! Prince Andrew turned his horse and galloped back to find Prince Bagratión.

Lemarrois had just arrived at a gallop with Bonaparte's stern letter, and Murat, humiliated and anxious to expiate his fault, had at once moved his forces to attack the center and outflank both the Russian wings, hoping before evening and before the arrival of the Emperor to crush the contemptible detachment that stood before him.

"It has begun. Here it is!" thought Prince Andrew, feeling the blood rush to his heart.

Before he had reached the embankments that were being thrown up, he saw, in the light of the dull autumn evening, mounted men coming toward him. The foremost, wearing a Cossack cloak and lambskin cap and riding a white horse, was Prince Bagratión. Prince Andrew stopped, waiting for him to come up; Prince Bagratión reined in his horse and recognizing Prince Andrew nodded to him. He still looked ahead while Prince Andrew told him what he had seen.

The feeling, "It has begun! Here it is!" was seen even on Prince Bagratión's hard brown face with its half-closed, dull, sleepy eyes. Prince Andrew gazed with anxious curiosity at that impassive face and wished he could tell what, if anything, this man was thinking and feeling at that moment. "Is there anything at all behind that impassive face?" Prince Andrew asked himself as he looked. Prince Bagratión bent his head in sign of agreement with what Prince Andrew told him, and said, "Very good!" in a tone that seemed to imply that everything that took place and was reported to him was exactly what he had foreseen. Prince Andrew, out of breath with his rapid ride, spoke quickly. Prince Bagratión, uttering his words with an Oriental accent, spoke particularly slowly, as if to impress the fact that there was no need to hurry. However, he put his horse to a trot in the direction of Túshin's battery. Prince Andrew followed with the suite.

"Whose company?" asked Prince Bagratión of an artillery-man standing by the ammunition wagon.

"Captain Túshin's, your excellency!" shouted the red-haired, freckled gunner in a merry voice, standing to attention.

"Yes, yes," muttered Bagratión as if considering something, and he rode past the limbers to the farthest cannon.

As he approached, a ringing shot issued from it deafening him and his suite, and in the smoke that suddenly surrounded the gun they could see the gunners who had seized it strain-ing to roll it quickly back to its former position. A huge, broad-shouldered gunner, Number One, holding a mop, his legs far apart, sprang to the wheel; while Number Two with a trembling hand placed a charge in the cannon's mouth. The short, round-shouldered Captain Túshin, stumbling over the tail of the gun carriage, moved forward and, not noticing the general, looked out shading his eyes with his small hand.

"Lift it two lines more and it will be just right," cried he in a feeble voice to which he tried to impart a dashing note, ill suited to his weak figure. "Number Two!" he squeaked. "Fire, Medvédev!"

Bagratión called to him, and Túshin, raising three fingers to his cap with a bashful and awkward gesture not at all like a military salute but like a priest's benediction, approached the general. "Very good!" said Bagratión in reply to the officer's report, and began deliberately to examine the whole battlefield extended before him. The French had advanced nearest on our right. Below the height on which the Kiev regiment was stationed, in the hollow where the rivulet flowed, the soul-stirring rolling and crackling of musketry was heard, and much farther to the right beyond the dragoons, the officer of the suite pointed out to Bagratión a French column that was outflanking us. To the left the horizon was bounded by the adjacent wood. Prince Bagratión ordered two battalions from the center to be sent to reinforce the right flank. The officer of the suite ventured to remark to the prince that if these battalions went away, the guns would remain without support. Prince Bagratión turned to the officer and with his dull eyes looked at him in silence. It seemed to Prince Andrew that the officer's remark was just and that really no answer could be made to it.

About Túshin and the battalion that had been in support of his battery all was forgotten. Prince Andrew listened attentively to Bagratión's colloquies with the commanding officers and the orders he gave them and, to his surprise, found that no orders were really given, but that Prince Bagratión tried to make it appear that everything done by necessity, by accident, or by the will of subordinate commanders was done, if not by his direct command, at least in accord with his intentions. Prince Andrew noticed, however, that though what happened was due to chance and was independent of the commander's will, owing to the tact Bagratión showed, his presence was very valuable. Officers who approached him with disturbed countenances became calm; soldiers and officers greeted him gaily, grew more cheerful in his presence, and were evidently anxious to display their courage before him.

14

Inspired by Bagratión's courage on the field, the Sixth Chasseurs successfully stem the advance of a French column.

The attack of the Sixth Chasseurs secured the retreat of our right flank. In the center Túshin's forgotten battery, which had managed to set fire to the Schön Grabern village, delayed the French advance. The French were putting out the fire which the wind was spreading, and thus gave us time to retreat. The retirement of the center to the other side of the dip in the ground at the rear was hurried and noisy, but the different companies did not get mixed. But our left—which consisted of the Azóv and Podólsk infantry and the Pávlograd hussars—was simultaneously attacked and outflanked by superior French forces under Lannes and was thrown into confusion.

The squadron in which Rostóv was serving had scarcely time to mount before it was halted facing the enemy. Again, as at the Enns bridge, there was nothing between the squadron and the enemy, and again that terrible dividing line of uncertainty and fear—resembling the line separating the living from the dead—lay between them. All were conscious of this unseen line, and the question whether they would cross it or not, and how they would cross it, agitated them all.

The colonel rode to the front, angrily gave some reply to questions put to him by the officers, and, like a man desperately insisting on having his own way, gave an order. No one said anything definite, but the rumor of an attack spread through the squadron. The command to form up rang out and the sabers whizzed as they were drawn from their scabbards. Still no one moved. The troops of the left flank, infantry and hussars alike, felt that the commander did not himself know what to do, and this irresolution communicated itself to the men.

"If only they would be quick!" thought Rostóv, feeling that at last the time had come to experience the joy of an attack of which he had so often heard from his fellow hussars.

"Fo'ward, with God, lads!" rang out Denísov's voice. "At a twot fo'ward!"

The horses' croups began to sway in the front line. Rook pulled at the reins and started of his own accord.

Before him, on the right, Rostóv saw the front lines of his hussars and still farther ahead a dark line which he could not see distinctly but took to be the enemy. Shots could be heard, but some way off.

"Faster!" came the word of command, and Rostóv felt Rook's flanks drooping as he broke into a gallop.

"Hur-a-a-a-ah!" came a roar of voices. "Let anyone come my way now," thought Rostóv driving his spurs into Rook and letting him go at a full gallop so that he outstripped the others. Ahead, the enemy was already visible. Suddenly something like a birch broom seemed to sweep over the squadron.

Rostóv raised his saber, ready to strike, but at that instant the trooper Nikítenko, who was galloping ahead, shot away from him, and Rostóv felt as in a dream that he continued to be carried forward with unnatural speed but yet he stayed on the same spot. From behind him Bondarchúk, an hussar he knew, jolted against him and looked angrily at him. Bondarchúk's horse swerved and galloped past.

"How is it I am not moving? I have fallen, I am killed!" Rostóv asked and answered at the same instant. He was alone in the middle of a field. Instead of the moving horses and hussars' backs, he saw nothing before him but the motionless earth and the stubble around him. There was warm blood under his arm. "No, I am wounded and the horse is killed."

Having disentangled his leg, he rose. "Where, on which side, was now the line that had so sharply divided the two armies?" he asked himself and could not answer. "Can something bad have happened to me?" he wondered as he got up: and at that moment he felt that something superfluous was hanging on his benumbed left arm. The wrist felt as if it were not his. He examined his hand carefully, vainly trying to find blood on it. "Ah, here are people coming," he thought joyfully, seeing some men running toward him. "They will help me!" In front came a man wearing a strange shako and a blue cloak, swarthy, sunburned, and with a hooked nose. Then came two more, and many more running behind. One of them said something strange, not in Russian. In among the hindmost of these men wearing similar shakos was a Russian hussar. He was being held by the arms and his horse was being led behind him.

"It must be one of ours, a prisoner. Yes. Can it be that they will take me too? Who are these men?" thought Rostóv, scarcely believing his eyes. "Can they be French?" He looked at the approaching Frenchmen, and though but a moment before he had been galloping to get at them and hack them to pieces, their proximity now seemed so awful that he could not believe his eyes. "Who are they? Why are they running? Can they be coming at me? And why? To kill me? *Me* whom everyone is so fond of?" He remembered his mother's love for him, and his family's, and his friends', and the enemy's intention to kill him seemed impossible. "But perhaps they may do it!" He seized his pistol and, instead of firing it, flung it at the Frenchmen and ran with all his might toward the bushes. He did not now run with the feeling of doubt and conflict with which he had trodden the Enns bridge, but with the feeling of a hare fleeing from the hounds. One single sentiment, that of fear for his young and happy life, possessed his whole being. Rapidly leaping the furrows, he fled across the field with the impetuosity he used to show at catchplay, now and then turning his good-natured, pale, young face to look back. A shudder of terror went through him: "No, better not look," he thought, but having reached the bushes he glanced round once more. The French had fallen behind, and just as he looked round the first man changed his run to a walk and, turning, shouted something loudly to a comrade farther back. Rostóv paused. "No, there's some mistake," thought he. "They can't have wanted to kill me." But at the same time, his left arm felt as heavy as if a seventy-pound weight were tied to it. He could run no more. The Frenchman also stopped and took aim. Rostóv closed his eyes and stooped down. One bullet and then another whistled past him. He mustered his last remaining strength, took hold of his left hand with his right, and reached the bushes. Behind these were some Russian sharpshooters.

15

The infantry regiments that had been caught unawares in the outskirts of the wood ran out of it, the different companies getting mixed, and retreated as a disorderly crowd. One soldier, in his fear, uttered the senseless cry, "Cut off!" that is so terrible in battle, and that word infected the whole crowd with a feeling of panic.

"Surrounded! Cut off! We're lost!" shouted the fugitives.

The general had a fit of coughing as a result of shouting and of the powder smoke and stopped in despair. Everything seemed lost. But at that moment the French who were attacking, suddenly and without any apparent reason, ran back and disappeared from the outskirts, and Russian sharpshooters showed themselves in the copse. It was Timókhin's company, which alone had maintained its order in the wood and, having lain in ambush in a ditch, now attacked the French unexpectedly. Timókhin, armed only with a sword, had rushed at the enemy with such a desperate cry and such mad, drunken determination that, taken by surprise, the French had thrown down their muskets and run. Dólokhov, running beside Timókhin, killed a Frenchman at close quarters and was the first to seize the surrendering French officer by his collar. Our fugitives returned, the battalions re-formed, and the French who had nearly cut our left flank in half were for the moment repulsed. Our reserve units were able to join up, and the fight was at an end. The regimental commander and Major Ekonómov had stopped beside a bridge, letting the retreating companies pass by them, when a soldier came up and took hold of the commander's stirrup, almost leaning against him. The man was wearing a bluish coat of broadcloth, he had no knapsack or cap, his head was bandaged, and over his shoulder a French munition pouch was slung. He had an officer's sword in his hand. The soldier was pale, his blue eyes looked impudently into the commander's face, and his lips were smiling. Though the commander was occupied in giving instructions to Major Ekonómov, he could not help taking notice of the soldier.

"Your excellency, here are two trophies," said Dólokhov, pointing to the French sword and pouch. "I have taken an officer prisoner. I stopped the company." Dólokhov breathed heavily from weariness and spoke in abrupt sentences. "The whole company can bear witness. I beg you will remember this, your excellency!"

"All right, all right," replied the commander, and turned to Major Ekonómov.

But Dólokhov did not go away; he untied the hankerchief around his head, pulled it off, and showed the blood congealed on his hair.

"A bayonet wound. I remained at the front. Remember, your excellency!"

Túshin's battery had been forgotten and only at the very end of the action did Prince Bagratión, still hearing the cannonade in the center, send his orderly staff officer, and later Prince Andrew also, to order the battery to retire as quickly as possible. When the supports attached to Túshin's battery had been moved away in the middle of the action by someone's order, the battery had continued firing and was only not captured by the French because the enemy could not surmise that anyone could have the effrontery to continue firing from four quite undefended guns. On the contrary, the energetic action of that battery led the French to suppose that here—in the center—the main Russian forces were concentrated. Twice they had attempted to attack this point, but on each occasion had been driven back by grapeshot from the four isolated guns on the hillock.

Soon after Prince Bagratión had left him, Túshin had succeeded in setting fire to Schön Grabern.

"Look at them scurrying! It's burning! Just see the smoke! Fine! Grand! Look at the smoke, the smoke!" exclaimed the artillerymen, brightening up. The French columns that had advanced beyond the village went back; but as though in revenge for this failure, the enemy placed ten guns to the right of the village and began firing them at Túshin's battery.

In their childlike glee, aroused by the fire and their luck in successfully cannonading the French, our artillerymen only noticed this battery when two balls, and then four more, fell among our guns, one knocking over two horses and another tearing off a munition-wagon driver's leg. Their spirits once roused were, however, not diminished, but only changed character. The horses were replaced by others from a reserve gun carriage, the wounded were carried away, and the four guns were turned against the ten-gun battery. Túshin's companion officer had been killed at the beginning of the engagement and within an hour seventeen of the forty men of the guns' crews had been disabled, but the artillerymen were still as merry and lively as ever. Twice they noticed the French appearing below them, and then they fired grapeshot at them.

Little Túshin, moving feebly and awkwardly, kept telling his orderly to "refill my pipe for that one!" and then, scattering sparks from it, ran forward shading his eyes with his small hand to look at the French.

"Smack at 'em, lads!" he kept saying, seizing the guns by the wheels and working the screws himself.

Owing to the terrible uproar and the necessity for concentration and activity, Túshin did not experience the slightest unpleasant sense of fear, and the thought that he might be killed or badly wounded never occurred to him. On the contrary, he became more and more elated. It seemed to him that it was a very long time ago, almost a day, since he had first seen the enemy and fired the first shot, and that the corner of the field he stood on was well-known and familiar ground. Though he thought of everything, considered everything, and did everything the best of officers could do in his position, he was in a state akin to feverish delirium or drunkenness.

"Come along, our Matvévna!" he said to himself. "Matvévna" [daughter of Matthew] was the name his fancy gave to the farthest gun of the battery, which was large and of an old pattern. The French swarming round their guns seemed to him like ants.

He imagined himself as an enormously tall, powerful man who was throwing cannon balls at the French with both hands.

"Now then, Matvévna, dear old lady, don't let me down!" he was saying as he moved from the gun, when a strange, unfamiliar voice called above his head: "Captain Túshin! Captain!"

Túshin turned round in dismay. It was the staff officer who had turned him out of the booth at Grunth. He was shouting in a gasping voice:

"Are you mad? You have twice been ordered to retreat, and you . . ."

"Why are they down on me?" thought Túshin, looking in alarm at his superior.

"I . . . don't . . ." he muttered, holding up two fingers to his cap. "I . . ."

But the staff officer did not finish what he wanted to say. A cannon ball, flying close to him, caused him to duck and bend over his horse. He paused, and just as he was about to say something more, another ball stopped him. He turned his horse and galloped off.

"Retire! All to retire!" he shouted from a distance.

The soldiers laughed. A moment later, an adjutant arrived with the same order.

It was Prince Andrew. The first thing he saw on riding up to the space where Túshin's guns were stationed was an unharnessed horse with a broken leg, that lay screaming piteously beside the harnessed horses. Blood was gushing from its leg as from a spring. Among the limbers lay several dead men. One ball after another passed over as he approached and he felt a nervous shudder run down his spine. But the mere thought of being afraid roused him again. "I cannot be afraid," thought he, and dismounted slowly among the guns. He delivered the order and did not leave the battery. He decided to have the guns removed from their positions and withdrawn in his presence. Together with Túshin, stepping across the bodies and under a terrible fire from the French, he attended to the removal of the guns.

Prince Andrew said nothing to Túshin. They were both so busy as to seem not to notice one another. When having limbered up the only two cannon that remained uninjured out of the four, they began moving down the hill. Prince Andrew rode up to Túshin.

"Well, till we meet again . . ." he said, holding out his hand to Túshin.

"Good-by, my dear fellow," said Túshin. "Dear soul! Good-by, my dear fellow!" and for some unknown reason tears suddenly filled his eyes.

16

The wind had fallen and black clouds, merging with the powder smoke, hung low over the field of battle on the horizon. It was growing dark and the glow of two conflagrations was the more conspicuous. The cannonade was dying down, but the rattle of musketry behind and on the right sounded oftener and nearer. As soon as Túshin with his guns, continually driving round or coming upon wounded men, was out of range of fire and had descended into the dip, he was met by some of the staff, among them the staff officer and Zherkóv, who had been twice sent to Túshin's battery but had never reached it. Though the orders were to abandon the wounded, many of them dragged themselves after the troops and begged for seats on the gun carriages. At the foot of the hill, a pale hussar cadet, supporting one hand with the other, came up to Túshin and asked for a seat.

"Captain, for God's sake! I've hurt my arm," he said timidly. "For God's sake . . . I can't walk. For God's sake!"

It was plain that this cadet had already repeatedly asked for a lift and been refused. He asked in a hesitating, piteous voice.

"Tell them to give me a seat, for God's sake!"

"Give him a seat," said Túshin. "Lay a cloak for him to sit on, lad," he said, addressing his favorite soldier.

The cadet was Rostóv. With one hand he supported the other; he was pale and his jaw trembled, shivering feverishly. He was placed on "Matvévna."

"What, are you wounded, my lad?" said Túshin, approaching the gun on which Rostóv sat.

"No, it's a sprain."

Suddenly, near by on the right, shouting and firing were again heard. Flashes of shot gleamed in the darkness. This was the last French attack and was met by soldiers who had sheltered in the village houses.

The French had been repulsed for the last time. And again and again in the complete darkness Túshin's guns moved forward, surrounded by the humming infantry as by a frame.

In the darkness, it seemed as though a gloomy unseen river was flowing always in one direction, humming with whispers and talk and the sound of hoofs and wheels. The whole moving mass began pressing closer together and a report spread that they were ordered to halt; evidently those in front had halted. All remained where they were in the middle of the muddy road.

Fires were lighted and the talk became more audible. Captain Túshin, having given orders to his company, sent a soldier to find a dressing station or a doctor for the cadet, and sat down by a bonfire the soldiers had kindled on the road. Rostóv, too, dragged himself to the fire. From pain, cold, and damp, a feverish shivering shook his whole body. Drowsiness was irresistibly mastering him, but he was kept awake by an excruciating pain in his arm, for which he could find no satisfactory position. He kept closing his eyes and then again looking at the fire, which seemed to him dazzlingly red, and at the feeble, round-shouldered figure of Túshin who was sitting cross-legged like a Turk beside him. Túshin's large, kind, intelligent eyes were fixed with sympathy and commiseration on Rostóv, who saw that Túshin with his whole heart wished to help him but could not.

From all sides were heard the footsteps and talk of the infantry, who were walking, driving past, and settling down all around. The sound of voices, the tramping feet, the horses' hoofs moving in mud, the crackling of wood fires near and afar, merged into one tremulous rumble.

It was no longer, as before, a dark, unseen river flowing through the gloom, but a dark sea swelling and gradually subsiding after a storm. Rostóv looked at and listened listlessly to what passed before and around him. An infantryman came to the fire, squatted on his heels, held his hands to the blaze, and turned away his face.

"You don't mind, your honor?" he asked Túshin. "I've lost my company, your honor. I don't know where . . . such bad luck!"

"Your honor, you're wanted by the general. He is in the hut here," said a gunner, coming up to Túshin.

"Coming, friend."

Túshin rose and, buttoning his greatcoat and pulling it straight, walked away from the fire.

Not far from the artillery campfire, in a hut that had been prepared for him, Prince Bagratión sat at dinner, talking with some commanding officers who had gathered at his quarters. The little old man with the half-closed eyes was there greedily gnawing a mutton bone, and the general who had served blamelessly for twenty-two years, flushed by a glass of vodka and the dinner; and the staff officer with the signet ring, and Zherkóv, uneasily glancing at them all, and Prince Andrew, pale, with compressed lips and feverishly glittering eyes. Prince Bagratión was thanking the individual commanders and inquiring into details of the action and our losses. The general whose regiment had been inspected at Braunau was informing the prince that as soon as the action began he had withdrawn from the wood, mustered the men who were woodcutting, and, allowing the French to pass him, had made a bayonet charge with two battalions and had broken up the French troops.

"When I saw, your excellency, that their first battalion was disorganized, I stopped in the road and thought: 'I'll let them come on and will meet them with the fire of the whole battalion'—and that's what I did."

The general had so wished to do this and was so sorry he had not managed to do it that it seemed to him as if it had really happened. Perhaps it might really have been so? Could one possibly make out amid all that confusion what did or did not happen?

"By the way, your excellency, I should inform you," he continued—remembering Dólokhov's conversation with Kutúzov and his last interview with the gentleman-ranker—"that Private Dólokhov, who was reduced to the ranks, took a French officer prisoner in my presence and particularly distinguished himself."

Prince Bagratión turned to the old colonel: "Gentlemen, I thank you all; all arms have behaved heroically: infantry, cavalry, and artillery. How was it that two guns were abandoned in the center?" he inquired, searching with his eyes for someone. (Prince Bagratión did not ask about the guns on the left flank; he knew that all the guns there had been abandoned at the very beginning of the action.) "I think I sent you?" he added, turning to the staff officer on duty.

"One was damaged," answered the staff officer, "and the other I can't understand. I was there all the time giving orders and had only just left. . . . It is true that it was hot there," he added, modestly.

Someone mentioned that Captain Túshin was bivouacking close to the village and had already been sent for.

"Oh, but you were there?" said Prince Bagratión, addressing Prince Andrew.

"Of course, we only just missed one another," said the staff officer, with a smile to Bolkónski.

"I had not the pleasure of seeing you," said Prince Andrew, coldly and abruptly.

All were silent. Túshin appeared at the threshold and made his way timidly from behind the backs of the generals. As he stepped past the generals in the crowded hut, feeling embarrassed as he always was by the sight of his superiors, he did not notice the staff of the banner and stumbled over it. Several of those present laughed.

"How was it a gun was abandoned?" asked Bagratión, frowning, not so much at the captain as at those who were laughing, among whom Zherkóv laughed loudest.

Only now, when he was confronted by the stern authorities, did his guilt and the disgrace of having lost two guns and yet remaining alive present themselves to Túshin in all their horror. He had been so excited that he had not thought about it until that moment. The officers' laughter confused him still more. He stood before Bagratión with his lower jaw trembling and was hardly able to mutter: "I don't know . . . your excellency . . . I had no men . . . your excellency."

"You might have taken some from the covering troops."

Túshin did not say that there were no covering troops, though that was perfectly true. He was afraid of getting some other officer into trouble, and silently fixed his eyes on Bagratión as a schoolboy who has blundered looks at an examiner.

The silence lasted some time. Prince Bagratión, apparently not wishing to be severe, found nothing to say; the others did not venture to intervene. Prince Andrew looked at Túshin from under his brows and his fingers twitched nervously.

"Your excellency!" Prince Andrew broke the silence with his abrupt voice, "you were pleased to send me to Captain Túshin's battery. I went there and found two thirds of the men and horses knocked out, two guns smashed, and no supports at all."

Prince Bagratión and Túshin looked with equal intentness at Bolkónski, who spoke with suppressed agitation.

"And, if your excellency will allow me to express my opinion," he continued, "we owe today's success chiefly to the action of that battery and the heroic endurance of Captain Túshin and his company," and without awaiting a reply, Prince Andrew rose and left the table.

Prince Bagratión looked at Túshin, evidently reluctant to show distrust in Bolkónski's emphatic opinion yet not feeling able fully to credit it, bent his head, and told Túshin that he could go. Prince Andrew went out with him.

"Thank you; you saved me, my dear fellow!" said Túshin.

Prince Andrew gave him a look, but said nothing and went away. He felt sad and depressed. It was all so strange, so unlike what he had hoped.

"Who are they? Why are they here? What do they want? And when will all this end?" thought Rostóv, looking at the changing shadows before him. The pain in his arm became more and more intense. Irresistible drowsiness overpowered him, red rings danced before his eyes, and the impression of those voices and faces and a sense of loneliness merged with the physical pain. It was they, these soldiers—wounded and unwounded—it was they who were crushing, weighing down, and twisting the sinews and scorching the flesh of his sprained arm and shoulder. To rid himself of them, he closed his eyes.

For a moment he dozed, but in that short interval innumerable things appeared to him in a dream: his mother and her large white hand, Sónya's thin little shoulders, Natásha's eyes and laughter, Denísov with his voice and mustache, and Telyánin and all that affair with Telyánin and Bogdánich.

He opened his eyes and looked up. The black canopy of night hung less than a yard above the glow of the charcoal. Flakes of falling snow were fluttering in that light. Túshin had not returned, the doctor had not come.

"Nobody wants me!" thought Rostóv. "There is no one to help me or pity me. Yet I was once at home, strong, happy, and loved." He sighed and, doing so, groaned involuntarily.

He looked at the snowflakes fluttering above the fire and remembered a Russian winter at his warm, bright home, his fluffy fur coat, his quickly gliding sleigh, his healthy body, and all the affection and care of his family. "And why did I come here?" he wondered.

Next day the French army did not renew their attack, and the remnant of Bagratión's detachment was reunited to Kutúzov's army.

1805

BOOK THREE

1

Prince Vasíli was not a man who deliberately thought out his plans. Still less did he think of injuring anyone for his own advantage. He was merely a man of the world who had got on and to whom getting on had become a habit. Nor did he say to himself: "Pierre is a rich man, I must entice him to marry my daughter and lend me the forty thousand rubles I need."

He had Pierre at hand in Moscow and procured for him an appointment as Gentleman of the Bedchamber, and insisted on the young man accompanying him to Petersburg and staying at his house.

Pierre, on unexpectedly becoming Count Bezúkhov and a rich man, felt himself after his recent loneliness and freedom from cares so beset and preoccupied that only in bed was he able to be by himself. These different people—businessmen, relations, and acquaintances alike—were all disposed to treat the young heir in the most friendly and flattering manner: they were all evidently firmly convinced of Pierre's noble qualities.

It seemed so natural to Pierre that everyone should like him, and it would have seemed so unnatural had anyone disliked him, that he could not but believe in the sincerity of those around him.

More than anyone else, Prince Vasíli took possession of Pierre's affairs and of Pierre himself in those early days. From the death of Count Bezúkhov he did not let go his hold of the lad.

In Petersburg, as in Moscow, Pierre found the same atmosphere of gentleness and affection. He could not refuse the post, or rather the rank (for he did nothing), that Prince Vasíli had procured for him, and acquaintances, invitations, and social occupations were so numerous that, even more than in Moscow, he felt a sense of bewilderment, bustle, and continual expectation of some good, always in front of him but never attained.

In the beginning of the winter of 1805-6 Pierre received one of Anna Pávlovna's usual pink notes with an invitation to which was added: "You will find the beautiful Hélène here, whom it is always delightful to see."

When he read that sentence, Pierre felt for the first time that some link which other people recognized had grown up between himself and Hélène, and that thought both alarmed him, as if some obligation were being imposed on him which he could not fulfill, and pleased him as an entertaining supposition.

Anna Pávlovna's "At Home" was like the former one. She received Pierre with a shade of melancholy, evidently relating to the young man's recent loss by the death of Count Bezúkhov. She touched his sleeve with her finger, saying:

"Wait a bit, I have something in view for you this evening." (She glanced at Hélène and smiled at her.) "My dear Hélène, be charitable to my poor aunt who adores you. Go and keep her company for ten minutes. And that it will not be too dull, here is the dear count who will not refuse to accompany you."

The old aunt received the two young people in her corner. She was just speaking of a collection of snuffboxes that had belonged to Pierre's father, Count Bezúkhov, and showed them her own box. Princess Hélène asked to see the portrait of the aunt's husband on the box lid.

"That is probably the work of Vinesse," said Pierre, mentioning a celebrated miniaturist, and he leaned over the table to take the snuffbox while trying to hear what was being said at the other table.

He half rose, meaning to go round, but the aunt handed him the snuffbox, passing it across Hélène's back. Hélène stooped forward to make room, and looked round with a smile. She was, as always at evening parties, wearing a dress such as was then fashionable, cut very low at front and back. Her bust, which had always seemed like marble to Pierre, was so close to him that his shortsighted eyes could not but perceive the living charm of her neck and shoulders, so near to his lips that he need only have bent his head a little to have touched them. He was conscious of the warmth of her body, the scent of perfume, and the creaking of her corset as she moved. He did not see her marble beauty forming a complete whole with her dress, but all the charm of her body only covered by her garments. And having once seen this he could not help being aware of it, just as we cannot renew an illusion we have once seen through.

"So you have never noticed before how beautiful I am?" Hélène seemed to say. "You had not noticed that I am a woman? Yes, I am a woman who may belong to anyone—to you too," said her glance. And at that moment Pierre felt that Hélène not only could, but must be his wife, and that it could not be otherwise.

He knew this at that moment as surely as if he had been standing at the altar with her. How and when this would be he did not know, he did not even know if it would be a good thing (he even felt, he knew not why, that it would be a bad thing), but he knew it would happen.

When he got home he could not sleep for a long time for thinking of what had happened. What had happened? Nothing. He had merely understood that the woman he had known as a child, of whom when her beauty was mentioned he had said absent-mindedly: "Yes, she's good-looking," he had understood that this woman might belong to him.

"But she's stupid. I have myself said she is stupid," he thought. "There is something nasty, something wrong, in the feeling she excites in me. I have been told that her brother Anatole was in love with her and she with him, that there was quite a scandal and that that's why he was sent away. Hippolyte is her brother . . . Prince Vasíli is her father . . . It's bad. . . ." he reflected, but while he was thinking this (the reflection was still incomplete), he caught himself smiling and was conscious that another line of thought had sprung up, and while thinking of her worthlessness he was also dreaming of how she would be his wife, how she would love him and become quite different, and how all he had thought and heard of her might be false.

In November, 1805, Prince Vasíli had to go on a tour of inspection in four different provinces. He had arranged this for himself so as to visit his neglected estates at the same time and pick up his son Anatole where his regiment was stationed, and take him to visit Prince Nicholas Bolkónski in order to arrange a match for him with the daughter of that rich old man. But before leaving home and undertaking these new affairs, Prince Vasíli had to settle matters with Pierre, who, it is true, had latterly spent whole days at home, that is, in Prince Vasíli's house where he was staying, and had been absurd, excited, and foolish in Hélène's presence (as a lover should be), but had not yet proposed to her.

"This is all very fine, but things must be settled," said Prince Vasíli to himself, with a sorrowful sigh, one morning, feeling that Pierre who was under such obligations to him ("But never mind that") was not behaving very well in this matter. "Youth, frivolity . . . well, God be with him," thought he, relishing his own goodness of heart, "but it must be brought to a head. The day after tomorrow will be Lëlya's° name day. I will invite two or three people, and if he does not understand what he ought to do then it will be my affair —yes, my affair. I am her father."

On Hélène's name day, a small party of just their own people—as his wife said—met for supper at Prince Vasíli's. All these friends and relations had been given to understand that the fate of the young girl would be decided that evening. The visitors were seated at supper.

Everybody laughed a great deal. At the head of the table, where the honored guests sat, everyone seemed to be in high spirits and under the influence of a variety of exciting sensations. Only Pierre and Hélène sat silently side by side almost at the bottom of the table, a suppressed smile brightening both their faces.

Pierre felt that he was the center of it all, and this both pleased and embarrassed him. He was like a man entirely absorbed in some occupation. He did not see, hear, or understand anything clearly. Only now and then detached ideas and impressions from the world of reality shot unexpectedly through his mind.

"So it is all finished!" he thought. "And how has it all hap-

° Lëlya, a pet name for Hélène.—A.M.

pened? How quickly! Now I know that not because of her alone, nor of myself alone, but because of everyone, *it* must inevitably come about. They are all expecting *it*, they are so sure that it will happen that I cannot, I cannot, disappoint them. But how will it be? I do not know, but it will certainly happen!" thought Pierre, glancing at those dazzling shoulders close to his eyes.

After supper Pierre with his partner followed the others into the drawing room. The guests began to disperse, some without taking leave of Hélène. Some, as if unwilling to distract her from an important occupation, came up to her for a moment and made haste to go away, refusing to let her see them off.

While the guests were taking their leave, Pierre remained for a long time alone with Hélène in the little drawing room where they were sitting. He had often before, during the last six weeks, remained alone with her, but had never spoken to her of love. Now he felt that it was inevitable, but he could not make up his mind to take the final step. He felt ashamed; he felt that he was occupying someone else's place here beside Hélène. "This happiness is not for you," some inner voice whispered to him. "This happiness is for those who have not in them what there is in you."

Prince Vasíli came up to Pierre with languid footsteps. Pierre rose and said it was getting late. Prince Vasíli gave him a look of stern inquiry, as though what Pierre had just said was so strange that one could not take it in. But then the expression of severity changed, and he drew Pierre's hand downwards, made him sit down, and smiled affectionately.

"Well, Lëlya?" he asked, turning instantly to his daughter and addressing her with the careless tone of habitual tenderness natural to parents who have petted their children from babyhood, but which Prince Vasíli had only acquired by imitating other parents.

And he again turned to Pierre.

Pierre smiled. Prince Vasíli suddenly muttered something and went away. It seemed to Pierre that even the prince was disconcerted. The sight of the discomposure of that old man of the world touched Pierre: he looked at Hélène and she too seemed disconcerted, and her look seemed to say: "Well, it is your own fault."

When Prince Vasíli returned to the drawing room, the princess, his wife, was talking in low tones about Pierre.

"Aline," he said to his wife, "go and see what they are about."

The princess went up to the door, passed by it with a dignified and indifferent air, and glanced into the little drawing room. Pierre and Hélène still sat talking just as before.

"Still the same," she said to her husband.

Prince Vasíli frowned, twisting his mouth, his cheeks quivered and his face assumed the coarse, unpleasant expression peculiar to him. Shaking himself, he rose, threw back his head, and with resolute steps went past the ladies into the little drawing room. With quick steps he went joyfully up to Pierre. His face was so unusually triumphant that Pierre rose in alarm on seeing it.

"Thank God!" said Prince Vasíli. "My wife has told me everything!"—(He put one arm around Pierre and the other around his daughter.)—"My dear boy . . . Lëlya . . . I am very pleased." (His voice trembled.) "I loved your father . . . and she will make you a good wife . . . God bless you! . . "

He embraced his daughter, and then again Pierre, and kissed him with his malodorous mouth. Tears actually moistened his cheeks.

"Princess, come here!" he shouted.

The old princess came in and also wept. Pierre was kissed, and he kissed the beautiful Hélène's hand several times. After a while they were left alone again.

"All this had to be and could not be otherwise," thought Pierre, "so it is useless to ask whether it is good or bad. It is good because it's definite and one is rid of the old tormenting doubt." Pierre held the hand of his betrothed in silence, looking at her beautiful bosom as it rose and fell.

"Hélène!" he said aloud and paused.

"Something special is always said in such cases," he thought, but could not remember what it was that people say. He looked at her face. She drew nearer to him. Her face flushed.

"Oh, take those off . . . those . . ." she said, pointing to his spectacles.

Pierre took them off, and his eyes, besides the strange look eyes have from which spectacles have just been removed, had also a frightened and inquiring look. He was about to stoop over her hand and kiss it, but with a rapid, almost brutal movement of her head, she intercepted his lips and met them with her own. Her face struck Pierre, by its altered, unpleasantly excited expression.

"It is too late now, it's done; besides I love her," thought Pierre.

"*Je vous aime!*" he said, remembering what has to be said at such moments: but his words sounded so weak that he felt ashamed of himself.

Six weeks later he was married, and settled in Count Bezúkhov's large, newly furnished Petersburg house, the happy possessor, as people said, of a wife who was a celebrated beauty and of millions of money.

2

Prince Vasíli and his son Anatole arrive at Bald Hills with the intention of offering marriage to Princess Mary. Her father suspects the sincerity of the handsome but unscrupulous Anatole. Lise and Mlle. Bourienne attempt to improve Mary's appearance; her feelings alternate between hopefulness and fear.

3

When Princess Mary came down, Prince Vasíli and his son were already in the drawing room, talking to the little princess and Mademoiselle Bourienne. When she entered with her heavy step, treading on her heels, the gentlemen and Mademoiselle Bourienne rose and the little princess, indicating her to the gentlemen, said: "*Voilá Marie!*" Princess Mary saw them all and saw them in detail. She saw Prince Vasíli's face, serious for an instant at the sight of her, but immediately smiling again, and the little princess curiously noting the impression "Marie" produced on the visitors. And she saw Mademoiselle Bourienne, with her ribbon and pretty face, and her unusually animated look which was fixed on *him*, but *him* she could not see, she only saw something large, brilliant, and handsome moving toward her as she entered the room. Then Anatole came up to her. She still could not see him. She only felt a soft hand taking hers firmly, and she touched with her lips a white forehead, over which was beautiful light-brown hair smelling of pomade. When she looked up at him she was struck by his beauty. Anatole was not quick-witted, nor ready or eloquent in conversation, but he had the faculty, so invaluable in society, of composure and imperturbable self-possession. Besides this, in his behavior to women Anatole had a manner which particularly inspires in them curiosity, awe, and even love— a supercilious consciousness of his own superiority. The princess felt this, and as if wishing to show him that she did not even dare expect to interest him, she turned to his father. The conversation was general and animated, thanks to Princess Lise's voice and little downy lip that lifted over her white teeth.

When Paris was mentioned, Mademoiselle Bourienne for her part seized the opportunity of joining in the general current of recollections.

She took the liberty of inquiring whether it was long since Anatole had left Paris and how he had liked that city. Anatole answered the Frenchwoman very readily and, looking at her with a smile, talked to her about her native land. When he saw the pretty little Bourienne, Anatole came to the conclusion that he would not find Bald Hills dull either. "Not at all bad!" he thought, examining her, "not at all bad, that little companion! I hope she will bring her along with her when we're married, *la petite est gentille* [the little one is charming]."

The old prince dressed leisurely in his study, frowning and considering what he was to do. The coming of these visitors annoyed him. "What are Prince Vasíli and that son of his to me? Prince Vasíli is a shallow braggart and his son, no doubt, is a fine specimen," he grumbled to himself. What angered him was that the coming of these visitors revived in his mind an unsettled question he always tried to stifle, one about which he always deceived himself. The question was whether he could ever bring himself to part from his daughter and give her to a husband. "And why should she marry?" he thought. "To be unhappy for certain. There's Lise, married to Andrew—a better husband one would think could hardly be found nowadays—but is she contented with her lot? And who would marry Marie for love? Plain and awkward! They'll take her for her connections and wealth. . . . Well, I've nothing against it," the prince said to himself, "but he must be worthy of her. And that is what we shall see."

He entered the drawing room with his usual alert step, glancing rapidly round the company. He noticed the change in the little princess' dress, Mademoiselle Bourienne's ribbon, Princess Mary's unbecoming coiffure, Mademoiselle Bourienne's and Anatole's smiles, and the loneliness of his daughter amid the general conversation. "Got herself up like a fool!" he thought, looking irritably at her. "She is shameless, and he ignores her!"

Prince Bolkónski sat down in his usual place in the corner of the sofa and, drawing up an armchair for Prince Vasíli, pointed to it and began questioning him about political affairs and news. He seemed to listen attentively to what Prince Vasíli said, but kept glancing at Princess Mary.

"And so they are writing from Potsdam already?" he said, repeating Prince Vasíli's last words. Then rising, he suddenly went up to his daughter.

"Is it for visitors you've got yourself up like that, eh?" said he. "Fine, very fine! You have done up your hair in this new way for the visitors, and before the visitors I tell you that in future you are never to dare to change your way of dress without my consent."

"It was my fault, *mon père*," interceded the little princess, with a blush.

"*You* must do as you please," said Prince Bolkónski, bowing to his daughter-in-law, "but she need not make a fool of herself, she's plain enough as it is."

And he sat down again, paying no more attention to his daughter, who was reduced to tears.

"Now you, young prince, what's your name?" said Prince Bolkónski, turning to Anatole, "come here, let us talk and get acquainted."

"Now the fun begins," thought Anatole, sitting down with a smile beside the old prince.

"Well, my dear boy, I hear you've been educated abroad, not taught to read and write by the deacon, like your father and me. Now tell me, my dear boy, are you serving in the

Horse Guards?" asked the old man, scrutinizing Anatole closely and intently.

"No, I have been transferred to the line," said Anatole, hardly able to restrain his laughter.

"Ah! That's a good thing. So, my dear boy, you wish to serve the Tsar and the country? It is wartime. Such a fine fellow must serve. Well, are you off to the front?"

"No, Prince, our regiment has gone to the front, but I am attached . . . what is it I am attached to, Papa?" said Anatole, turning to his father with a laugh.

"A splendid soldier, splendid! 'What am I attached to!' Ha, ha, ha!" laughed Prince Bolkónski, and Anatole laughed still louder. Suddenly Prince Bolkónski frowned.

"You may go," he said to Anatole.

"And so you've had him educated abroad, Prince Vasíli, haven't you?" said the old prince to Prince Vasíli.

"I have done my best for him, and I can assure you the education there is much better than ours."

As soon as they were alone together, Prince Vasíli announced his hopes and wishes to the old prince.

"Well, do you think I shall prevent her, that I can't part from her?" said the old prince angrily. "What an idea! I'm ready for it tomorrow! Only let me tell you, I want to know my son-in-law better. You know my principles—everything aboveboard! I will ask her tomorrow in your presence; if she is willing, then he can stay on. He can stay and I'll see." The old prince snorted. "Let her marry, it's all the same to me!"

As always happens when women lead lonely lives for any length of time without male society, on Anatole's appearance all the three women of Prince Bolkónski's household felt that their life had not been real till then.

Princess Mary grew quite unconscious of her face and coiffure. The handsome open face of the man who might perhaps be her husband absorbed all her attention.

"But am I not too cold with him?" thought the princess. "I try to be reserved because in the depth of my soul I feel too near to him already, but then he cannot know what I think of him and may imagine that I do not like him."

And Princess Mary tried, but could not manage, to be

cordial to her new guest. "Poor girl, she's devilish ugly!" thought Anatole.

Mademoiselle Bourienne, also roused to great excitement by Anatole's arrival, thought in another way. It was not calculation that guided her (she did not even for a moment consider what she should do), but all this had long been familiar to her, and now that Anatole had appeared it just grouped itself around him and she wished and tried to please him as much as possible.

The little princess, like an old war horse that hears the trumpet, unconsciously and quite forgetting her condition, prepared for the familiar gallop of coquetry, without any ulterior motive or any struggle, but with naïve and light-hearted gaiety.

Although in female society Anatole usually assumed the role of a man tired of being run after by women, his vanity was flattered by the spectacle of his power over these three women. Besides that, he was beginning to feel for the pretty and provocative Mademoiselle Bourienne that passionate animal feeling which was apt to master him with great suddenness and prompt him to the coarsest and most reckless actions.

4

They all separated, but, except Anatole who fell asleep as soon as he got into bed, all kept awake a long time that night.

"Is he really to be my husband, this stranger who is so kind—yes, kind, that is the chief thing," thought Princess Mary; and fear, which she had seldom experienced, came upon her.

Mademoiselle Bourienne walked up and down the conservatory for a long time that evening, vainly expecting someone, now smiling at someone, now working herself up to tears with the imaginary words of her *pauvre mère* rebuking her for her fall.

The old prince did not sleep either. He felt as though he had been insulted through his daughter. The insult was the more pointed because it concerned not himself but another, his daughter, whom he loved more than himself.

The old prince knew that if he told his daughter she was making a mistake and that Anatole meant to flirt with Mademoiselle Bourienne, Princess Mary's self-esteem would be wounded and his point (not to be parted from her) would be gained, so pacifying himself with this thought, he called Tíkhon and began to undress.

Though no words had passed between Anatole and Mademoiselle Bourienne, they understood that they had much to say to one another in private and so they had been seeking an opportunity since morning to meet one another alone. When Princess Mary went to her father's room at the usual hour, Mademoiselle Bourienne and Anatole met in the conservatory.

Princess Mary went to the door of the study with special trepidation. It seemed to her that not only did everybody know that her fate would be decided that day, but that they also knew what she thought about it.

The old prince was very affectionate and careful in his treatment of his daughter that morning.

He came to the point at once, treating her ceremoniously.

"I have had a proposition made me concerning you," he said with an unnatural smile. "I expect you have guessed that Prince Vasíli has not come and brought his pupil with him" (for some reason Prince Bolkónski referred to Anatole as a "pupil") "for the sake of my beautiful eyes. Last night a proposition was made me on your account and, as you know my principles, I refer it to you."

"How am I to understand you, *mon père?*" said the princess, growing pale and then blushing.

"How understand me!" cried her father angrily. "Prince Vasíli finds you to his taste as a daughter-in-law and makes a proposal to you on his pupil's behalf. That's how it's to be understood! 'How understand it'! . . . And I ask you!"

"I do not know what you think, Father," whispered the princess.

"I? I? What of me? Leave me out of the question. I'm not going to get married. What about *you?* That's what I want to know."

The princess saw that her father regarded the matter with

disapproval, but at that moment the thought occurred to her that her fate would be decided now or never. She lowered her eyes so as not to see the gaze under which she felt that she could not think, but would only be able to submit from habit, and she said: "I wish only to do your will, but if I had to express my own desire . . ." She had no time to finish. The old prince interrupted her.

"That's admirable!" he shouted. "He will take you with your dowry and take Mademoiselle Bourienne into the bargain. She'll be the wife, while you . . ."

The prince stopped. He saw the effect these words had produced on his daughter. She lowered her head and was ready to burst into tears.

"Now then, now then, I'm only joking!" he said. "Remember this, Princess, I hold to the principle that a maiden has a full right to choose. I give you freedom. Only remember that your life's happiness depends on your decision. Never mind me!"

"But I do not know, Father!"

"There's no need to talk! He receives his orders and will marry you or anybody; but you are free to choose. . . . Go to your room, think it over, and come back in an hour and tell me in his presence: yes or no."

Her fate was decided and happily decided. But what her father had said about Mademoiselle Bourienne was dreadful. It was untrue to be sure, but still it was terrible, and she could not help thinking of it. She was going straight on through the conservatory, neither seeing nor hearing anything, when suddenly the well-known whispering of Mademoiselle Bourienne aroused her. She raised her eyes, and two steps away saw Anatole embracing the Frenchwoman and whispering something to her. With a horrified expression on his handsome face, Anatole looked at Princess Mary, but did not at once take his arm from the waist of Mademoiselle Bourienne who had not yet seen her.

"Who's that? Why? Wait a moment!" Anatole's face seemed to say. Princess Mary looked at them in silence. She could not understand it. At last Mademoiselle Bourienne gave a scream and ran away. Anatole bowed to Princess Mary with a gay smile, as if inviting her to join in a laugh at this strange incident, and then shrugging his shoulders went to the door that led to his own apartments.

An hour later, Tíkhon came to call Princess Mary to the old prince; he added that Prince Vasíli was also there. When Tíkhon came to her Princess Mary was sitting on the sofa in her room, holding the weeping Mademoiselle Bourienne in her arms and gently stroking her hair. The princess' beautiful eyes with all their former calm radiance were looking with tender affection and pity at Mademoiselle Bourienne's pretty face.

Prince Vasíli, with one leg thrown high over the other and a snuffbox in his hand, was sitting there with a smile of deep emotion on his face, as if stirred to his heart's core and himself regretting and laughing at his own sensibility, when Princess Mary entered. He hurriedly took a pinch of snuff.

"Ah, my dear, my dear!" he began, rising and taking her by both hands. Then, sighing, he added: "My son's fate is in your hands. Decide, my dear, good, gentle Marie, whom I have always loved as a daughter!"

He drew back and a real tear appeared in his eye.

"Fr . . . fr . . ." snorted Prince Bolkónski. "The prince is making a proposition to you in his pupil's—I mean, his son's —name. Do you wish or not to be Prince Anatole Kurágin's wife? Reply: yes or no," he shouted, "and then I shall reserve the right to state my opinion also."

"My desire is never to leave you, Father, never to separate my life from yours. I don't wish to marry," she answered positively, glancing at Prince Vasíli and at her father with her beautiful eyes.

"Humbug! Nonsense! Humbug, humbug, humbug!" cried Prince Bolkónski, frowning and taking his daughter's hand; he did not kiss her, but only bending his forehead to hers just touched it, and pressed her hand so that she winced and uttered a cry.

"Well, so that's finished, my dear fellow! I am very glad to have seen you. Very glad! Go back to your rooms, Princess. Go!" said the old prince. "Very, very glad to have seen you," repeated he, embracing Prince Vasíli.

"My vocation is a different one," thought Princess Mary. "My vocation is to be happy with another kind of happiness, the happiness of love and self-sacrifice. And cost what it may,

I will arrange poor Amélie's happiness, she loves him so passionately, and so passionately repents. I will do all I can to arrange the match between them. If he is not rich I will give her the means; I will ask my father and Andrew. I shall be so happy when she is his wife. She is so unfortunate, a stranger, alone, helpless! And, oh God, how passionately she must love him if she could so far forget herself! Perhaps I might have done the same! . . ." thought Princess Mary.

5

It was long since the Rostóvs had news of Nicholas. Not till midwinter was the count at last handed a letter addressed in his son's handwriting. On receiving it, he ran on tiptoe to his study in alarm and haste, trying to escape notice, closed the door, and began to read the letter.

Anna Mikháylovna, who always knew everything that passed in the house, on hearing of the arrival of the letter went softly into the room and found the count with it in his hand, sobbing and laughing at the same time.

Anna Mikháylovna, though her circumstances had improved, was still living with the Rostóvs.

"My dear friend?" said she, in a tone of pathetic inquiry, prepared to sympathize in any way.

The count sobbed yet more.

"Nikólenka . . . a letter . . . wa . . . a . . . s . . . wounded . . . my darling boy . . . the countess . . . promoted to be an officer . . . thank God . . . Now tell the little countess!"

Anna Mikháylovna sat down beside him, with her own handkerchief wiped the tears from his eyes and from the letter, then having dried her own eyes she comforted the count, and decided that at dinner and till teatime she would prepare the countess, and after tea, with God's help, would inform her.

At dinner Anna Mikháylovna talked the whole time about the war news and about Nikólenka, twice asked when the last letter had been received from him, though she knew that already, and remarked that they might very likely be getting a letter from him that day. Each time that these hints began to make the countess anxious and she glanced uneasily at the count and at Anna Mikháylovna, the latter very adroitly turned the conversation to insignificant matters. Natásha, who, of the whole family, was the most gifted with a capacity to feel any shades of intonation, look, and expression, pricked up her ears from the beginning of the meal and was certain that there was some secret between her father and Anna Mikháylovna, that it had something to do with her brother, and that Anna Mikháylovna was preparing them for it. Bold as she was, Natásha, who knew how sensitive her mother was to anything relating to Nikólenka, did not venture to ask any questions at dinner, but she was too excited to eat anything and kept wriggling about on her chair regardless of her governess' remarks. After dinner, she rushed headlong after Anna Mikháylovna and, dashing at her, flung herself on her neck as soon as she overtook her in the sitting room.

"Auntie, darling, do tell me what it is!"

"Nothing, my dear."

"No, dearest, sweet one, honey, I won't give up—I know you know something."

Anna Mikháylovna shook her head.

"You are a little slyboots," she said.

"A letter from Nikólenka! I'm sure of it!" exclaimed Natásha, reading confirmation in Anna Mikháylovna's face.

"But for God's sake, be careful, you know how it may affect your mamma."

"I will, I will, only tell me! You won't? Then I will go and tell at once."

Anna Mikháylovna, in a few words, told her the contents of the letter, on condition that she should tell no one.

"No, on my true word of honor," said Natásha, crossing herself, "I won't tell anyone!" and she ran off at once to Sónya.

"Nikólenka . . . wounded . . . a letter," she announced in gleeful triumph.

"Nicholas!" was all Sónya said, instantly turning white.

Natásha, seeing the impression the news of her brother's wound produced on Sónya, felt for the first time the sorrowful side of the news.

She rushed to Sónya, hugged her, and began to cry.

"A little wound, but he has been made an officer; he is well now, he wrote himself," said she through her tears.

"There now! It's true that all you women are crybabies," remarked Pétya, pacing the room with large, resolute strides. "Now I'm very glad, very glad indeed, that my brother has distinguished himself so. You are all blubberers and understand nothing."

Natásha smiled through her tears.

"You haven't read the letter?" asked Sónya.

"No, but she said that it was all over and that he's now an officer."

"Thank God!" said Sónya, crossing herself. "But perhaps she deceived you. Let us go to Mamma."

Pétya paced the room in silence for a time.

"If I'd been in Nikólenka's place I would have killed even more of those Frenchmen," he said. "What nasty brutes they are! I'd have killed so many that there'd have been a heap of them."

"Hold your tongue, Pétya, what a goose you are!"

"I'm not a goose, but they are who cry about trifles," said Pétya.

"Do you remember him?" Natásha suddenly asked, after a moment's silence.

Sónya smiled.

"Do I remember *Nicholas?*"

"No, Sónya, but do you remember so that you remember him perfectly, remember everything?" said Natásha, with an expressive gesture, evidently wishing to give her words a very definite meaning. "I remember Nikólenka too, I remember him well," she said. "But I don't remember Borís. I don't remember him a bit."

"What! You don't remember Borís?" asked Sónya in surprise.

"It's not that I don't remember—I know what he is like, but not as I remember Nikólenka. Him—I just shut my eyes and remember, but Borís . . . No!" (She shut her eyes.) "No! there's nothing at all."

"Oh, Natásha!" said Sónya, looking ecstatically and earnestly at her friend as if she did not consider her worthy to hear what she meant to say and as if she were saying it to someone else, with whom joking was out of the question, "I am in love with your brother once for all and, whatever may happen to him or to me, shall never cease to love him as long as I live."

Natásha looked at Sónya with wondering and inquisitive eyes, and said nothing. She felt that Sónya was speaking the truth, that there was such love as Sónya was speaking of. But Natásha had not yet felt anything like it. She believed it could be, but did not understand it.

"Shall you write to him?" she asked.

Sónya became thoughtful. The question of how to write to *Nicholas,* and whether she ought to write, tormented her. Now that he was already an officer and a wounded hero, would it be right to remind him of herself and, as it might seem, of the obligations to her he had taken on himself?

"I don't know. I think if he writes, I will write too," she said, blushing.

"And you won't feel ashamed to write to him?"

Sónya smiled.

"No."

"And I should be ashamed to write to Borís. I'm not going to."

"Why should you be ashamed?"

"Well, I don't know. It's awkward and would make me ashamed."

"And I know why she'd be ashamed," said Pétya, offended by Natásha's previous remark. "It's because she was in love with that fat one in spectacles" (that was how Pétya described his namesake, the new Count Bezúkhov) "and now she's in love with that singer" (he meant Natásha's Italian singing master), "that's why she's ashamed!"

"Pétya, you're a stupid!" said Natásha.

"Not more stupid than you, madam," said the nine-year-old Pétya, with the air of an old brigadier.

The countess had been prepared by Anna Mikháylovna's hints at dinner. On retiring to her own room, she sat in an armchair, her eyes fixed on a miniature portrait of her son on the lid of a snuffbox, while the tears kept coming into her eyes. Anna Mikháylovna, with the letter, came on tiptoe to the countess' door and paused.

"Don't come in," she said to the old count who was following her. "Come later." And she went in, closing the door behind her.

The count put his ear to the keyhole and listened.

At first he heard the sound of indifferent voices, then Anna Mikháylovna's voice alone in a long speech, then a cry, then silence, then both voices together with glad intonations, and then footsteps. Anna Mikháylovna opened the door. Her face wore the proud expression of a surgeon who has just performed a difficult operation and admits the public to appreciate his skill.

"It is done!" she said to the count, pointing triumphantly to the countess, who sat holding in one hand the snuffbox with its portrait and in the other the letter, and pressing them alternately to her lips.

When she saw the count, she stretched out her arms to him, embraced his bald head, over which she again looked at the letter and the portrait, and in order to press them again to her lips, she slightly pushed away the bald head. Véra, Natásha, Sónya, and Pétya now entered the room, and the reading of the letter began. After a brief description of the campaign and the two battles in which he had taken part, and his promotion, Nicholas said that he kissed his father's and mother's hands asking for their blessing, and that he kissed Véra, Natásha, and Pétya. Besides that, he sent greetings to Monsieur Schelling, Madame Schoss, and his old nurse, and asked them to kiss for him "dear Sónya, whom he loved and thought of just the same as ever." When she heard this Sónya blushed so that tears came into her eyes and, unable to bear the looks turned upon her, ran away into the dancing hall, whirled round it at full speed with her dress puffed out like a balloon, and, flushed and smiling, plumped down on the floor. The countess was crying.

"Why are you crying, Mamma?" asked Véra. "From all he says one should be glad and not cry."

This was quite true, but the count, the countess, and Natásha looked at her reproachfully. "And who is it she takes after?" thought the countess.

Nicholas' letter was read over hundreds of times, and those who were considered worthy to hear it had to come to the countess, for she did not let it out of her hands.

"What a *style*! How charmingly he describes!" said she, reading the descriptive part of the letter. "And what a soul! Not a word about himself. . . . Not a word! About some

Denísov or other, though he himself, I dare say, is braver than any of them. He says nothing about his sufferings. What a heart! How like him it is! And how he has remembered everybody! Not forgetting anyone. I always said when he was only so high—I always said . . ."

For more than a week preparations were being made, rough drafts of letters to Nicholas from all the household were written and copied out, while under the supervision of the countess and the solicitude of the count, money and all things necessary for the uniform and equipment of the newly commissioned officer were collected. Anna Mikháylovna, practical woman that she was, had even managed by favor with army authorities to secure advantageous means of communication for herself and her son. She had opportunities of sending her letters to the Grand Duke Constantine Pávlovich, who commanded the Guards. And so it was decided to send the letters and money by the Grand Duke's courier to Borís and Borís was to forward them to Nicholas. The letters were from the old count, the countess, Pétya, Véra, Natásha, and Sónya, and finally there were six thousand rubles for his outfit and various other things the old count sent to his son.

6

Nicholas Rostóv, with Kutúzov's army at Olmütz, hears from Borís Drubetskóy, stationed ten miles away with the newly arrived Guards, that he has money and letters for him. Nicholas, affecting the swagger of an old campaigner, rides to the billet of Borís and Berg. As he is giving them an exaggerated account of his exploits, Prince Andrew enters to see Borís whom Pierre has recommended to him.

In the middle of his story, just as he was saying: "You cannot imagine what a strange frenzy one experiences during an attack," Prince Andrew, whom Borís was expecting, entered the room. Having been sent with papers from Kutúzov to the Tsarévich, he looked in on Borís, hoping to find him alone. When he came in and saw an hussar of the line recounting his military exploits (Prince Andrew could not endure that sort of man), he gave Borís a pleasant smile, frowned as with half-closed eyes he looked at Rostóv, bowed slightly and wearily, and sat down languidly on the sofa: he felt it unpleasant to have dropped in on bad company. Rostóv flushed up on noticing this, but he did not care, this was a mere stranger. Glancing, however, at Borís, he saw that he too seemed ashamed of the hussar of the line.

In spite of Prince Andrew's disagreeable, ironical tone, in spite of the contempt with which Rostóv, from his *fighting* army point of view, regarded all these little adjutants on the staff, of whom the newcomer was evidently one, Rostóv felt confused, blushed, and became silent. Borís inquired what news there might be on the staff, and what, without indiscretion, one might ask about our plans.

"We shall probably advance," replied Bolkónski, evidently reluctant to say more in the presence of a stranger.

Berg took the opportunity to ask, with great politeness, whether, as was rumored, the allowance of forage money to captains of companies would be doubled. To this Prince Andrew answered with a smile that he could give no opinion on such an important government order, and Berg laughed gaily.

"As to your business," Prince Andrew continued, addressing Borís, "we will talk of it later" (and he looked round at Rostóv). "Come to me after the review and we will do what is possible."

And, having glanced round the room, Prince Andrew turned to Rostóv, whose state of unconquerable childish embarrassment now changing to anger he did not condescend to notice, and said: "I think you were talking of the Schön Grabern affair? Were you there?"

"I was there," said Rostóv angrily, as if intending to insult the aide-de-camp.

Bolkónski noticed the hussar's state of mind, and it amused him. With a slightly contemptuous smile, he said: "Yes, there are many stories now told about that affair!"

"Yes, stories!" repeated Rostóv loudly, looking with eyes suddenly grown furious, now at Borís, now at Bolkónski. "Yes, many stories! But our stories are the stories of men who have been under the enemy's fire! *Our* stories have some weight, not like the stories of those fellows on the staff who get rewards without doing anything!"

"Of whom you imagine me to be one?" said Prince Andrew, with a quiet and particularly amiable smile.

A strange feeling of exasperation and yet of respect for this man's self-possession mingled at that moment in Rostóv's soul.

"I am not talking about you," he said, "I don't know you and, frankly, I don't want to. I am speaking of the staff in general."

"And I will tell you this," Prince Andrew interrupted in a tone of quiet authority, "you wish to insult me, and I am ready to agree with you that it would be very easy to do so if you haven't sufficient self-respect, but admit that the time and place are very badly chosen. In a day or two we shall all have to take part in a greater and more serious duel, and besides, Drubetskóy, who says he is an old friend of yours, is not at all to blame that my face has the misfortune to displease you. However," he added rising, "you know my name and where to find me, but don't forget that I do not regard either myself or you as having been at all insulted, and as a man older than you, my advice is to let the matter drop. Well then, on Friday after the review I shall expect you, Drubetskóy. *Au revoir!*" exclaimed Prince Andrew, and with a bow to them both he went out.

Only when Prince Andrew was gone did Rostóv think of what he ought to have said. And he was still more angry at having omitted to say it. He ordered his horse at once and, coldly taking leave of Borís, rode home. Should he go to headquarters next day and challenge that affected adjutant, or really let the matter drop, was the question that worried him all the way. He thought angrily of the pleasure he would have at seeing the fright of that small and frail but proud man when covered by his pistol, and then he felt with surprise that of all the men he knew there was none he would so much like to have for a friend as that very adjutant whom he so hated.

7

The Russian and Austrian Emperors review the allied army before Olmütz. Nicholas Rostóv, in the ranks of the Pávlograd hussars, is ecstatic over the majestic appearance and words of his Emperor, Alexander I.

8

The day after the review, Borís, in his best uniform and with his comrade Berg's best wishes for success, rode to Olmütz to see Bolkónski, wishing to profit by his friendliness and obtain for himself the best post he could—preferably that of adjutant to some important personage, a position in the army which seemed to him most attractive.

He did not find Prince Andrew in Olmütz that day, but the appearance of the town where the headquarters and the diplomatic corps were stationed and the two Emperors were living with their suites, households, and courts only strengthened his desire to belong to that higher world.

He knew no one, and despite his smart Guardsman's uniform, all these exalted personages passing in the streets in their elegant carriages with their plumes, ribbons, and medals, both courtiers and military men, seemed so immeasurably above him, an insignificant officer of the Guards, that they not only did not wish to, but simply could not, be aware of his existence. In spite of this, or rather because of it, next day, November 15, after dinner he again went to Olmütz and, entering the house occupied by Kutúzov, asked for Bolkónski.

When he entered, Prince Andrew, his eyes drooping contemptuously (with that peculiar expression of polite weariness which plainly says, "If it were not my duty I would not talk to you for a moment"), was listening to an old Russian general with decorations, who stood very erect, almost on tiptoe, with a soldier's obsequious expression on his purple face, reporting something.

"Very well, then, be so good as to wait," said Prince Andrew to the general, in Russian, speaking with the French intonation he affected when he wished to speak contemptuously, and noticing Borís, Prince Andrew, paying no more heed to the general who ran after him imploring him to hear something more, nodded and turned to him with a cheerful smile.

At that moment Borís clearly realized what he had before surmised, that in the army, besides the subordination and discipline prescribed in the military code, which he and the others knew in the regiment, there was another, more important, subordination, which made this tight-laced, purple-faced

general wait respectfully while Captain Prince Andrew, for
his own pleasure, chose to chat with Lieutenant Drubetskóy.
More than ever was Borís resolved to serve in future not according to the written code, but under this unwritten law. He
felt now that merely by having been recommended to Prince
Andrew he had already risen above the general who at the
front had the power to annihilate him, a lieutenant of the
Guards. Prince Andrew came up to him and took his hand.

"Well, my dear fellow, so you still want to be an adjutant?
I have been thinking about you."

"Yes, I was thinking"—for some reason Borís could not help
blushing—"of asking the commander in chief. He has had a
letter from Prince Kurágin about me. I only wanted to ask because I fear the Guards won't be in action," he added as if in
apology.

"You see, my dear fellow, I have been thinking about you,"
said Prince Andrew. "It's no use your going to the commander
in chief. He would say a lot of pleasant things, ask you to dinner" ("That would not be bad as regards the unwritten code,"
thought Borís), "but nothing more would come of it. There
will soon be a battalion of us aides-de-camp and adjutants!
But this is what we'll do: I have a good friend, an adjutant
general and an excellent fellow, Prince Dolgorúkov; and
though you may not know it, the fact is that now Kutúzov
with his staff and all of us count for nothing. Everything is
now centered round the Emperor. So we will go to Dolgorúkov; I have to go there anyhow and I have already spoken to
him about you. We shall see whether he cannot attach you to
himself or find a place for you somewhere nearer the sun."

Prince Andrew always became specially keen when he had
to guide a young man and help him to worldly success. Under
cover of obtaining help of this kind for another, which from
pride he would never accept for himself, he kept in touch with
the circle which conferred success and which attracted him.
He very readily took up Borís' cause and went with him to
Dolgorúkov.

It was late in the evening when they entered the palace at
Olmütz occupied by the Emperors and their retinues.

That same day a council of war had been held in which all
the members of the Hofkriegsrath and both Emperors took
part. At that council, contrary to the views of the old generals

Kutúzov and Prince Schwartzenberg, it had been decided to advance immediately and give battle to Bonaparte. The council of war was just over when Prince Andrew accompanied by Borís arrived at the palace to find Dolgorúkov.

Dolgorúkov, one of the warmest advocates of an attack, had just returned from the council, tired and exhausted but eager and proud of the victory that had been gained. Prince Andrew introduced his protégé, but Prince Dolgorúkov politely and firmly pressing his hand said nothing to Borís and, evidently unable to suppress the thoughts which were uppermost in his mind at that moment, addressed Prince Andrew in French.

"Ah, my dear fellow, what a battle we have gained! God grant that the one that will result from it will be as victorious!"

"So the attack is definitely resolved on?" asked Bolkónski.

"And do you know, my dear fellow, it seems to me that Bonaparte has decidedly lost his bearings; you know that a letter was received from him today for the Emperor." Dolgorúkov smiled significantly.

"Is that so? And what did he say?" inquired Bolkónski.

"What can he say? Tra-di-ri-di-ra and so on . . . merely to gain time. I tell you he is in our hands, that's certain!"

"Delightful!" said Bolkónski. "But I have come to you, Prince, as a petitioner on behalf of this young man. You see . . ." but before Prince Andrew could finish, an aide-de-camp came in to summon Dolgorúkov to the Emperor.

"Oh, what a nuisance," said Dolgorúkov, getting up hurriedly and pressing the hands of Prince Andrew and Borís. "You know I should be very glad to do all in my power both for you and for this dear young man." Again he pressed the hand of the latter with an expression of good-natured, sincere, and animated levity. "But you see . . . another time!"

Next day, the army began its campaign, and up to the very battle of Austerlitz, Borís was unable to see either Prince Andrew or Dolgorúkov again and remained for a while with the Ismáylov regiment.

9

Failure of the Pávlograd hussars to participate in the small victorious action at Wischau depresses Nicholas

Rostóv, but the unexpected appearance of Emperor Alexander turns his gloom into delight.

10

At daybreak on the seventeenth, a French officer who had come with a flag of truce, demanding an audience with the Russian Emperor, was brought into Wischau from our outposts. This officer was Savary. The Emperor had only just fallen asleep and so Savary had to wait. At midday he was admitted to the Emperor, and an hour later he rode off with Prince Dolgorúkov to the advance post of the French army.

Toward evening Dolgorúkov came back, went straight to the Tsar, and remained alone with him for a long time.

On the eighteenth and nineteenth of November, the army advanced two days' march and the enemy's outposts after a brief interchange of shots retreated. In the highest army circles from midday on the nineteenth, a great, excitedly bustling activity began which lasted till the morning of the twentieth, when the memorable battle of Austerlitz was fought.

Prince Andrew was on duty that day and in constant attendance on the commander in chief.

At six in the evening, Kutúzov went to the Emperor's headquarters and after staying but a short time with the Tsar went to see the grand marshal of the court, Count Tolstóy.

Bolkónski took the opportunity to go in to get some details of the coming action from Dolgorúkov. He felt that Kutúzov was upset and dissatisfied about something and that at headquarters they were dissatisfied with him, and also that at the Emperor's headquarters everyone adopted toward him the tone of men who know something others do not know: he therefore wished to speak to Dolgorúkov.

"Well, how d'you do, my dear fellow?" said Dolgorúkov, who was sitting at tea with Bilíbin. "The fete is for tomorrow. How is your old fellow? Out of sorts?"

"I won't say he is out of sorts, but I fancy he would like to be heard."

"But they heard him at the council of war and will hear him when he talks sense, but to temporize and wait for something now when Bonaparte fears nothing so much as a general battle is impossible."

"Yes, you have seen him?" said Prince Andrew. "Well, what is Bonaparte like? How did he impress you?"

"Yes, I saw him, and am convinced that he fears nothing so much as a general engagement," repeated Dolgorúkov, evidently prizing this general conclusion which he had arrived at from his interview with Napoleon. "If he weren't afraid of a battle why did he ask for that interview? Why negotiate, and above all why retreat, when to retreat is so contrary to his method of conducting war? Believe me, he is afraid, afraid of a general battle. His hour has come! Mark my words!"

"But in what position are we going to attack him? I have been at the outposts today and it is impossible to say where his chief forces are situated," said Prince Andrew.

He wished to explain to Dolgorúkov a plan of attack he had himself formed.

"Oh, that is all the same," Dolgorúkov said quickly, and getting up he spread a map on the table. "All eventualities have been foreseen. If he is standing before Brünn . . ."

"There will be a council of war at Kutúzov's tonight, though; you can say all this there," remarked Dolgorúkov.

"I will do so," said Prince Andrew, moving away from the map.

"However, I think General Kutúzov has come out," he said. "I wish you good luck and success, gentlemen!" he added and went out after shaking hands with Dolgorúkov and Bilíbin.

On the way home, Prince Andrew could not refrain from asking Kutúzov, who was sitting silently beside him, what he thought of tomorrow's battle.

Kutúzov looked sternly at his adjutant and, after a pause, replied: "I think the battle will be lost, and so I told Count Tolstóy and asked him to tell the Emperor. What do you think he replied? 'But, my dear general, I am engaged with rice and cutlets, look after military matters yourself!' Yes . . . That was the answer I got!"

At the council of war, the Austrian Chief of Staff, Weyrother, explains his complicated battle plan which already has the approval of the Russian and Austrian Emperors. Kutúzov, who is opposed to the plan, sleeps through most of the meeting.

The council of war, at which Prince Andrew had not been able to express his opinion as he had hoped to, left on him a vague and uneasy impression. Whether Dolgorúkov and Weyrother, or Kutúzov, Langeron, and the others who did not approve of the plan of attack, were right—he did not know. "But was it really not possible for Kutúzov to state his views plainly to the Emperor? Is it possible that on account of court and personal considerations tens of thousands of lives, and my life, *my* life," he thought, "must be risked?

"Yes, it is very likely that I shall be killed tomorrow," he thought. And suddenly, at this thought of death, a whole series of most distant, most intimate, memories rose in his imagination: he remembered his last parting from his father and his wife; he remembered the days when he first loved her. He thought of her pregnancy and felt sorry for her and for himself, and in a nervously emotional and softened mood he went out of the hut in which he was billeted with Nesvítski and began to walk up and down before it.

The night was foggy and through the fog the moonlight gleamed mysteriously. "Yes, tomorrow, tomorrow!" he thought. "Tomorrow everything may be over for me! All these memories will be no more, none of them will have any meaning for me. Tomorrow perhaps, even certainly, I have a presentiment that for the first time I shall have to show all I can do." And his fancy pictured the battle, its loss, the concentration of fighting at one point, and the hesitation of all the commanders. And then that happy moment, that Toulon for which he had so long waited, presents itself to him at last. He firmly and clearly expresses his opinion to Kutúzov, to Weyrother, and to the Emperors. All are struck by the justness of his views, but no one undertakes to carry them out, so he takes a regiment, a division—stipulates that no one is to interfere with his arrangements—leads his division to the decisive point, and gains the victory alone. "But death and suffering?" suggested another voice. Prince Andrew, however, did not answer that voice and went on dreaming of his triumphs. The dispositions for the next battle are planned by him alone. Nominally he is only an adjutant on Kutúzov's staff, but he does everything alone. The next battle is won by him alone. Kutúzov is removed and he is appointed . . . "Well and then?" asked the other voice. "If before that you are not ten times wounded, killed, or betrayed, well . . . what then? . . ." "Well then," Prince Andrew answered himself, "I don't know what will happen and don't want to know, and can't, but if I want this —want glory, want to be known to men, want to be loved by them, it is not my fault that I want it and want nothing but that and live only for that. Yes, for that alone! I shall never tell anyone, but oh God! what am I to do if I love nothing but fame and men's esteem? Death, wounds, the loss of family—I fear nothing. And precious and dear as many persons are to me—father, sister, wife—those dearest to me—yet dreadful and unnatural as it seems, I would give them all at once for a moment of glory, of triumph over men, of love from men I don't know and never shall know, for the love of these men here," he thought, as he listened to voices in Kutúzov's courtyard.

"All the same, I love and value nothing but triumph over them all, I value this mystic power and glory that is floating here above me in this mist!"

12

That same night, Rostóv was with a platoon on skirmishing duty in front of Bagratión's detachment. His hussars were placed along the line in couples and he himself rode along the line trying to master the sleepiness that kept coming over him. An enormous space, with our army's campfires dimly glowing in the fog, could be seen behind him; in front of him was misty darkness. His eyes kept closing, and in his fancy appeared—now the Emperor, now Denísov, and now Moscow memories. "Why not? . . . It might easily happen," thought Rostóv, "that the Emperor will meet me and give me an order as he would to any other officer; he'll say: 'Go and find out what's there.' There are many stories of his getting to know an officer in just such a chance way and attaching him to himself! What if he gave me a place near him? Oh, how I would guard him, how I would tell him the truth, how I would unmask his deceivers!"

"Keep to the right, your honor, there are bushes here," came the voice of an hussar, past whom Rostóv was riding in the act of falling asleep. Rostóv lifted his head that had sunk almost to his horse's mane and pulled up beside the hussar. He was succumbing to irresistible, youthful, childish drowsiness. "But what was I thinking? I mustn't forget. How shall I speak to the Emperor? No, that's not it—that's tomorrow. Oh yes! Natásha . . . sabretache . . . saber them . . . That's right!" And his head once more sank to his horse's neck. All at once it seemed to him that he was being fired at. "What? What? What? . . . Cut them down! What? . . ." said Rostóv, waking up. At the moment he opened his eyes he heard in front of him, where the enemy was, the long-drawn shouts of thousands of voices. His horse and the horse of the hussar near him pricked their ears at these shouts. Over there, where the shouting came from, a fire flared up and went out again, then another, and all along the French line on the hill fires flared up and the shouting grew louder and louder.

Rostóv no longer wanted to sleep. The gay triumphant shouting of the enemy army had a stimulating effect on him. *"Vive l'Empereur! l'Empereur!"* he now heard distinctly.

"Your honor, the generals!" said the sergeant, riding up to Rostóv.

Rostóv, still looking round toward the fires and the shouts, rode with the sergeant to meet some mounted men who were riding along the line. One was on a white horse. Prince Bagratión and Prince Dolgorúkov with their adjutants had come to witness the curious phenomenon of the lights and shouts in the enemy's camp. Rostóv rode up to Bagratión, reported to him, and then joined the adjutants listening to what the generals were saying.

"Believe me," said Prince Dolgorúkov, addressing Bagratión, "it is nothing but a trick! He has retreated and ordered the rearguard to kindle fires and make a noise to deceive us."

"Hardly," said Bagratión. "I saw them this evening on that knoll; if they had retreated they would have withdrawn from that too. . . . Officer!" said Bagratión to Rostóv, "are the enemy's skirmishers still there?"

"They were there this evening, but now I don't know, your excellency. Shall I go with some of my hussars to see?" replied Rostóv.

Bagratión stopped and, before replying, tried to see Rostóv's face in the mist.

"Well, go and see," he said, after a pause.

"Yes, sir."

Rostóv spurred his horse, called to Sergeant Fédchenko and two other hussars, told them to follow him, and trotted downhill in the direction from which the shouting came. He felt both frightened and pleased to be riding alone with three hussars into that mysterious and dangerous misty distance where no one had been before him. "Follow me!" said he, crossed the road, and began riding up the hill at a gallop toward the point where the French pickets had been standing that evening.

"Your honor, there he is!" cried one of the hussars behind him. And before Rostóv had time to make out what the black thing was that had suddenly appeared in the fog, there was a flash, followed by a report, and a bullet whizzing high up in the mist with a plaintive sound passed out of hearing. Another musket missed fire but flashed in the pan. Rostóv turned his horse and galloped back. Four more reports followed at intervals, and the bullets passed somewhere in the fog singing in different tones. Rostóv reined in his horse, whose spirits had risen, like his own, at the firing, and went back at a footpace. "Well, some more! Some more!" a merry voice was saying in his soul. But no more shots came.

Only when approaching Bagratión did Rostóv let his horse gallop again, and with his hand at the salute rode up to the general.

Dolgorúkov was still insisting that the French had retreated and had only lit fires to deceive us.

"What does that prove?" he was saying as Rostóv rode up. "They might retreat and leave the pickets."

"It's plain that they have not all gone yet, Prince," said Bagratión. "Wait till tomorrow morning, we'll find out everything tomorrow."

"The picket is still on the hill, your excellency, just where it was in the evening," reported Rostóv, stooping forward with his hand at the salute and unable to repress the smile of delight induced by his ride and especially by the sound of the bullets.

"Very good, very good," said Bagratión. "Thank you, officer."

"Your excellency," said Rostóv, "may I ask a favor?"

"What is it?"

"Tomorrow our squadron is to be in reserve. May I ask to be attached to the first squadron?"

"What's your name?"

"Count Rostóv."

"Oh, very well, you may stay in attendance on me."

"Count Ilyá Rostóv's son?" asked Dolgorúkov.

But Rostóv did not reply.

"Then I may reckon on it, your excellency?"

"I will give the order."

"Tomorrow very likely I may be sent with some message to the Emperor," thought Rostóv. "Thank God!"

The fires and shouting in the enemy's army were occasioned by the fact that while Napoleon's proclamation was being read to the troops the Emperor himself rode round his bivouacs. The soldiers, on seeing him, lit wisps of straw and ran after him, shouting, "*Vive l'Empereur!*"

13

At five in the morning it was still quite dark. The troops of the center, the reserves, and Bagratión's right flank had not yet moved, but on the left flank the columns of infantry, cavalry, and artillery, which were to be the first to descend the heights to attack the French right flank and drive it into the Bohemian mountains according to plan, were already up and astir. The smoke of the campfires, into which they were throwing everything superfluous, made the eyes smart. It was cold and dark. The adjutants and battalion and regimental commanders mounted, crossed themselves, gave final instructions, orders, and commissions to the baggage men who remained behind, and the monotonous tramp of thousands of feet resounded. The column moved forward without knowing where and unable, from the masses around them, the smoke and the increasing fog, to see either the place they were leaving or that to which they were going.

Though none of the column commanders rode up to the ranks or talked to the men, the troops marched gaily, as they always do when going into action, especially to an attack. But when they had marched for about an hour in the dense fog, the greater part of the men had to halt and an unpleasant consciousness of some dislocation and blunder spread through the ranks. How such a consciousness is communicated is very difficult to define, but it certainly is communicated very surely, and flows rapidly, imperceptibly, and irrepressibly, as water does in a creek.

"Why have we stopped? Is the way blocked? Or have we already come up against the French?"

"No, one can't hear them. They'd be firing if we had."

"They were in a hurry enough to start us, and now here we stand in the middle of a field without rhyme or reason. It's all those damned Germans' muddling! What stupid devils!"

The cause of the confusion was that while the Austrian cavalry was moving toward our left flank, the higher command found that our center was too far separated from our right flank and the cavalry were all ordered to turn back to the right. Several thousand cavalry crossed in front of the infantry, who had to wait.

It was nine o'clock in the morning. The fog lay unbroken like a sea down below, but higher up at the village of Schlappanitz where Napoleon stood with his marshals around him, it was quite light. Napoleon, in the blue cloak which he had worn on his Italian campaign, sat on his small gray Arab horse a little in front of his marshals. Not a single muscle of his face —which in those days was still thin—moved. His gleaming eyes were fixed intently on one spot. His predictions were being justified. Part of the Russian force had already descended into the valley toward the ponds and lakes and part were leaving these Pratzen Heights which he intended to attack and regarded as the key to the position. From information he had received the evening before, from the sound of wheels and footsteps heard by the outposts during the night, by the disorderly movement of the Russian columns, and from all indications, he saw clearly that the allies believed him to be far away in front of them, and that the columns moving near Pratzen constituted the center of the Russian army, and that that center was already sufficiently weakened to be successfully attacked. But still he did not begin the engagement.

Today was a great day for him—the anniversary of his coronation. Before dawn he had slept for a few hours, and refreshed, vigorous, and in good spirits, he mounted his horse and rode out into the field in that happy mood in which everything seems possible and everything succeeds. He sat motionless, looking at the heights visible above the mist, and his cold face wore that special look of confident, self-complacent happiness that one sees on the face of a boy happily in love. The marshals stood behind him not venturing to distract his attention. He looked now at the Pratzen Heights, now at the sun floating up out of the mist.

When the sun had entirely emerged from the fog, and fields and mist were aglow with dazzling light—as if he had only awaited this to begin the action—he drew the glove from his shapely white hand, made a sign with it to the marshals, and ordered the action to begin. The marshals, accompanied by adjutants, galloped off in different directions, and a few minutes later the chief forces of the French army moved rapidly toward those Pratzen Heights which were being more and more denuded by Russian troops moving down the valley to their left.

At eight o'clock Kutúzov rode to Pratzen at the head of the fourth column. He greeted the men of the foremost regiment and gave them the order to march, thereby indicating that he intended to lead that column himself. When he had reached the village of Pratzen he halted. Prince Andrew was behind, among the immense number forming the commander in chief's suite. He was in a state of suppressed excitement and irritation, though controlledly calm as a man is at the approach of a long-awaited moment. How it would come about he did not know, but he felt sure it would do so. The locality and the position of our troops were known to him as far as they could be known to anyone in our army. His own strategic plan, which obviously could not now be carried out, was forgotten. Now, entering into Weyrother's plan, Prince Andrew considered possible contingencies and formed new projects such as might call for his rapidity of perception and decision.

That morning Kutúzov seemed worn and irritable. The infantry passing before him came to a halt without any command being given, apparently obstructed by something in front.

"Do order them to form into battalion columns and go round the village!" he said angrily to a general who had ridden up. "Don't you understand, your excellency, my dear sir, that you must not defile through narrow village streets when we are marching against the enemy?"

"I intend to re-form them beyond the village, your excellency," answered the general.

Kutúzov laughed bitterly.

"You'll make a fine thing of it, deploying in sight of the enemy! Very fine!"

"The enemy is still far away, your excellency. According to the dispositions . . ."

"The dispositions!" exclaimed Kutúzov bitterly. "Who told you that? . . . Kindly do as you are ordered."

"Yes, sir."

Just then at a distance behind Kutúzov was heard the sound of regiments saluting, and this sound rapidly came nearer along the whole extended line of the advancing Russian columns. Evidently the person they were greeting was riding quickly. When the soldiers of the regiment in front of which Kutúzov was standing began to shout, he rode a little to one side and looked round with a frown. Along the road from Pratzen galloped what looked like a squadron of horsemen in various uniforms. Two of them rode side by side in front, at full gallop. One in a black uniform with white plumes in his hat rode a bobtailed chestnut horse, the other who was in a white uniform rode a black one. These were the two Emperors followed by their suites. Kutúzov, affecting the manners of an old soldier at the front, gave the command "Attention!" and rode up to the Emperors with a salute. His whole appearance and manner were suddenly transformed. He put on the air of a subordinate who obeys without reasoning. With an affectation of respect which evidently struck Alexander unpleasantly, he rode up and saluted.

"Why aren't you beginning, Michael Ilariónovich?" said the Emperor Alexander hurriedly to Kutúzov, glancing courteously at the same time at the Emperor Francis.

"I am waiting, Your Majesty," answered Kutúzov, bending forward respectfully.

The Emperor, frowning slightly, bent his ear forward as if he had not quite heard.

"Waiting, Your Majesty," repeated Kutúzov. (Prince Andrew noted that Kutúzov's upper lip twitched unnaturally as he said the word "waiting.") "Not all the columns have formed up yet, Your Majesty."

"You know, Michael Ilariónovich, we are not on the Empress' Field where a parade does not begin till all the troops are assembled," said the Tsar with another glance at the Emperor Francis, as if inviting him if not to join in at least to listen to what he was saying. But the Emperor Francis continued to look about him and did not listen.

"That is just why I do not begin, sire," said Kutúzov in a resounding voice, apparently to preclude the possibility of not being heard, and again something in his face twitched—"That is just why I do not begin, sire, because we are not on parade and not on the Empress' Field," said he clearly and distinctly.

In the Emperor's suite all exchanged rapid looks that expressed dissatisfaction and reproach. "Old though he may be, he should not, he certainly should not speak like that," their glances seemed to say.

The Tsar looked intently and observantly into Kutúzov's eye waiting to hear whether he would say anything more. But Kutúzov, with respectfully bowed head, seemed also to be waiting. The silence lasted for about a minute.

"However, if you command it, Your Majesty," said Kutúzov, lifting his head and again assuming his former tone of a dull, unreasoning, but submissive general.

He touched his horse and having called Milorádovich, the commander of the column, gave him the order to advance.

Kutúzov accompanied by his adjutants rode at a walking pace behind the carabineers.

The fog had begun to clear and enemy troops were already dimly visible about a mile and a half off on the opposite heights. Down below, on the left, the firing became more distinct. Kutúzov had stopped and was speaking to an Austrian general. Prince Andrew, who was a little behind and looking at them, turned to an adjutant to ask him for a field glass.

"Look, look!" said this adjutant, looking not at the troops in the distance, but down the hill before him. "It's the French!"

The two generals and the adjutant took hold of the field glass, trying to snatch it from one another. The expression on all their faces suddenly changed to one of horror. The French were supposed to be a mile and a half away, but had suddenly and unexpectedly appeared just in front of us.

"It's the enemy? . . . No! . . . Yes, see it is! . . . for certain. . . . But how is that?" said different voices.

With the naked eye Prince Andrew saw below them to the right, not more than five hundred paces from where Kutúzov was standing, a dense French column.

"Here it is! The decisive moment has arrived. My turn has come," thought Prince Andrew, and striking his horse he rode up to Kutúzov.

But at that very instant a cloud of smoke spread all round, firing was heard quite close at hand, and a voice of naïve terror barely two steps from Prince Andrew shouted, "Brothers! All's lost!" And at this voice, as if at a command, everyone began to run.

Confused and ever-increasing crowds were running back to where five minutes before the troops had passed the Emperors. Not only would it have been difficult to stop that crowd, it was even impossible not to be carried back with it oneself. Bolkónski only tried not to lose touch with it, and looked around bewildered and unable to grasp what was happening in front of him. Nesvítski with an angry face, red and unlike himself, was shouting to Kutúzov that if he did not ride away at once he would certainly be taken prisoner. Kutúzov remained in the same place and without answering drew out a handkerchief. Blood was flowing from his cheek. Prince Andrew forced his way to him.

"You are wounded?" he asked, hardly able to master the trembling of his lower jaw.

"The wound is not here, it is there!" said Kutúzov, pressing the handkerchief to his wounded cheek and pointing to the fleeing soldiers. "Stop them!" he shouted, and at the same moment, probably realizing that it was impossible to stop them, spurred his horse and rode to the right.

Having forced his way out of the crowd of fugitives, Prince Andrew, trying to keep near Kutúzov, saw on the slope of the hill amid the smoke a Russian battery that was still firing and Frenchmen running toward it. Higher up stood some Russian infantry, neither moving forward to protect the battery nor backward with the fleeing crowd. A mounted general separated himself from the infantry and approached Kutúzov. Of Kutúzov's suite only four remained. They were all pale and exchanged looks in silence.

"Stop those wretches!" gasped Kutúzov to the regimental commander, pointing to the flying soldiers; but at that instant, as if to punish him for those words, bullets flew hissing across the regiment and across Kutúzov's suite like a flock of little birds.

The French had attacked the battery and, seeing Kutúzov, were firing at him. After this volley the regimental commander clutched at his leg; several soldiers fell, and a second lieutenant who was holding the flag let it fall from his hands. It swayed and fell, but caught on the muskets of the nearest soldiers. The soldiers started firing without orders.

"Oh! Oh! Oh!" groaned Kutúzov despairingly and looked around. . . . "Bolkónski!" he whispered, his voice trembling from a consciousness of the feebleness of age, "Bolkónski!" he whispered, pointing to the disordered battalion and at the enemy, "what's that?"

But before he had finished speaking, Prince Andrew, feeling tears of shame and anger choking him, had already leapt from his horse and run to the standard.

"Forward, lads!" he shouted in a voice piercing as a child's.

"Here it is!" thought he, seizing the staff of the standard and hearing with pleasure the whistle of bullets evidently aimed at him. Several soldiers fell.

"Hurrah!" shouted Prince Andrew, and, scarcely able to hold up the heavy standard, he ran forward with full confidence that the whole battalion would follow him.

And really he only ran a few steps alone. One soldier moved and then another and soon the whole battalion ran forward shouting "Hurrah!" and overtook him. A sergeant of the battalion ran up and took the flag that was swaying from its weight in Prince Andrew's hands, but he was immediately killed. Prince Andrew again seized the standard and, dragging it by the staff, ran on with the battalion.

"What's this? Am I falling? My legs are giving way," thought he, and fell on his back. He opened his eyes. Above him there was now nothing but the sky—the lofty sky, not clear yet still immeasurably lofty, with gray clouds gliding slowly across it. "How quiet, peaceful, and solemn; not at all as I ran," thought Prince Andrew—"not as we ran, shouting and fighting . . . how differently do those clouds glide across that lofty infinite sky! How was it I did not see that lofty sky before? And how happy I am to have found it at last! Yes! All is vanity, all falsehood, except that infinite sky. There is nothing, nothing, but that. But even it does not exist, there is nothing but quiet and peace. Thank God! . . ."

Bagratión, commanding the Russian right flank and unwilling to accept responsibility for ordering his troops to attack, sends his adjutant Nicholas Rostóv to the commander in chief for instructions. Bagratión realizes that Rostóv will hardly be able to return, if at all, before evening.

Rostóv had been ordered to look for Kutúzov and the Emperor near the village of Pratzen. But neither they nor a single commanding officer were there, only disorganized crowds of troops of various kinds. He urged on his already weary horse to get quickly past these crowds, but the farther he went the more disorganized they were. The highroad on which he had come out was thronged with *calèches*, carriages of all sorts, and Russian and Austrian soldiers of all arms, some wounded and some not. This whole mass droned and jostled in confusion under the dismal influence of cannon balls flying from the French batteries stationed on the Pratzen Heights.

"Where is the Emperor? Where is Kutúzov?" Rostóv kept asking everyone he could stop, but got no answer from anyone.

In the village of Hosjeradek there were Russian troops retiring from the field of battle, who though still in some confusion were less disordered. The French cannon did not reach there and the musketry fire sounded far away. Here everyone clearly saw and said that the battle was lost. No one whom Rostóv asked could tell him where the Emperor or Kutúzov was. One officer told Rostóv that he had seen someone from headquarters behind the village to the left, and thither Rostóv rode, not hoping to find anyone but merely to ease his conscience. When he had ridden about two miles and had passed the last of the Russian troops, he saw, near a kitchen garden with a ditch round it, two men on horseback facing the ditch. One with a white plume in his hat seemed familiar to Rostóv; the other on a beautiful chestnut horse (which Rostóv fancied he had seen before) rode up to the ditch, struck his horse with his spurs, and giving it the rein leaped lightly over. Only a little earth crumbled from the bank under the horse's hind hoofs. Turning the horse sharply, he again jumped the ditch, and deferentially addressed the horseman with the white plumes, evidently suggesting that he should do the same. The rider, whose figure seemed familiar to Rostóv and involuntarily riveted his attention, made a gesture of refusal with his head and hand and by that gesture Rostóv instantly recognized his lamented and adored monarch.

But as a youth in love trembles, is unnerved, and dares not utter the thoughts he has dreamed of for nights, but looks around for help or a chance of delay and flight when the longed-for moment comes and he is alone with *her*, so Rostóv, now that he had attained what he had longed for more than anything else in the world, did not know how to approach the Emperor, and a thousand reasons occurred to him why it would be inconvenient, unseemly, and impossible to do so.

"What! It is as if I were glad of a chance to take advantage of his being alone and despondent! A strange face may seem unpleasant or painful to him at this moment of sorrow; besides, what can I say to him now, when my heart fails me and my mouth feels dry at the mere sight of him?" Not one of the innumerable speeches addressed to the Emperor that he had composed in his imagination could he now recall. Those speeches were intended for quite other conditions, they were for the most part to be spoken at a moment of victory and triumph, generally when he was dying of wounds and the sovereign had thanked him for heroic deeds, and while dying he expressed the love his actions had proved.

"Besides how can I ask the Emperor for his instructions for

the right flank now that it is nearly four o'clock and the battle is lost? No, certainly I must not approach him, I must not intrude on his reflections. Better die a thousand times than risk receiving an unkind look or bad opinion from him," Rostóv decided; and sorrowfully and with a heart full of despair he rode away, continually looking back at the Tsar, who still remained in the same attitude of indecision.

Before five in the evening the battle had been lost at all points. More than a hundred cannon were already in the hands of the French.

After five o'clock it was only at the Augesd dam that a hot cannonade (delivered by the French alone) was still to be heard from numerous batteries ranged on the slopes of the Pratzen Heights, directed at our retreating forces.

In the rearguard, Dokhtúrov and others rallying some battalions kept up a musketry fire at the French cavalry that was pursuing our troops. It was growing dusk. On the narrow Augesd dam amid the wagons and the cannon, under the horses' hoofs and between the wagon wheels, men disfigured by fear of death now crowded together, crushing one another, dying, stepping over the dying and killing one another, only to move on a few steps and be killed themselves in the same way.

Every ten seconds a cannon ball flew compressing the air around, or a shell burst in the midst of that dense throng, killing some and splashing with blood those near them.

Dólokhov—now an officer—wounded in the arm, and on foot, with the regimental commander on horseback and some ten men of his company, represented all that was left of that whole regiment. Impelled by the crowd, they had got wedged in at the approach to the dam and, jammed in on all sides, had stopped because a horse in front had fallen under a cannon and the crowd was dragging it out. A cannon ball killed someone behind them, another fell in front and splashed Dólokhov with blood. The crowd, pushing forward desperately, squeezed together, moved a few steps, and again stopped.

"Move on a hundred yards and we are certainly saved, remain here another two minutes and it is certain death," thought each one.

Dólokhov who was in the midst of the crowd forced his way

to the edge of the dam, throwing two soldiers off their feet, and ran onto the slippery ice that covered the millpool.

"Turn this way!" he shouted, jumping over the ice which creaked under him; "turn this way!" he shouted to those with the gun. "It bears! . . ."

The ice bore him but it swayed and creaked, and it was plain that it would give way not only under a cannon or a crowd, but very soon even under his weight alone. The men looked at him and pressed to the bank, hesitating to step onto the ice. The general on horseback at the entrance to the dam raised his hand and opened his mouth to address Dólokhov. Suddenly a cannon ball hissed so low above the crowd that everyone ducked. It flopped into something moist, and the general fell from his horse in a pool of blood. Nobody gave him a look or thought of raising him.

"Get onto the ice, over the ice! Go on! Turn! Don't you hear? Go on!" innumerable voices suddenly shouted after the ball had struck the general, the men themselves not knowing what, or why, they were shouting.

Still the cannon balls continued regularly to whistle and flop onto the ice and into the water and oftenest of all among the crowd that covered the dam, the pond, and the bank.

On the Pratzen Heights, where he had fallen with the flagstaff in his hand, lay Prince Andrew Bolkónski bleeding profusely and unconsciously uttering a gentle, piteous, and childlike moan.

Toward evening he ceased moaning and became quite still. He did not know how long his unconsciousness lasted. Suddenly he again felt that he was alive and suffering from a burning, lacerating pain in his head.

"Where is it, that lofty sky that I did not know till now, but saw today?" was his first thought. "And I did not know this suffering either," he thought. "Yes, I did not know anything, anything at all till now. But where am I?"

He listened and heard the sound of approaching horses, and voices speaking French. He opened his eyes. Above him again was the same lofty sky with clouds that had risen and were floating still higher, and between them gleamed blue infinity. He did not turn his head and did not see those who, judging by the sound of hoofs and voices, had ridden up and stopped near him.

It was Napoleon accompanied by two aides-de-camp. Bonaparte riding over the battlefield had given final orders to strengthen the batteries firing at the Augesd dam and was looking at the killed and wounded left on the field.

"Fine men!" remarked Napoleon, looking at a dead Russian grenadier, who, with his face buried in the ground and a blackened nape, lay on his stomach with an already stiffened arm flung wide.

"The ammunition for the guns in position is exhausted, Your Majesty," said an adjutant who had come from the batteries that were firing at Augesd.

"Have some brought from the reserve," said Napoleon, and having gone on a few steps he stopped before Prince Andrew, who lay on his back with the flagstaff that had been dropped beside him. (The flag had already been taken by the French as a trophy.)

"That's a fine death!" said Napoleon as he gazed at Bolkónski.

Prince Andrew understood that this was said of him and that it was Napoleon who said it. He heard the speaker addressed as *Sire*. But he heard the words as he might have heard the buzzing of a fly. Not only did they not interest him, but he took no notice of them and at once forgot them. His head was burning, he felt himself bleeding to death, and he saw above him the remote, lofty, and everlasting sky. He knew it was Napoleon—his hero—but at that moment Napoleon seemed to him such a small, insignificant creature compared with what was passing now between himself and that lofty infinite sky with the clouds flying over it. At that moment it meant nothing to him who might be standing over him, or what was said of him; he was only glad that people were standing near him and only wished that they would help him and bring him back to life, which seemed to him so beautiful now that he had today learned to understand it so differently. He collected all his strength, to stir and utter a sound. He feebly moved his leg and uttered a weak, sickly groan which aroused his own pity.

"Ah! He is alive," said Napoleon. "Lift this young man up and carry him to the dressing station."

Having said this, Napoleon rode on to meet Marshal Lannes, who, hat in hand, rode up smiling to the Emperor to congratulate him on the victory.

Prince Andrew remembered nothing more: he lost consciousness from the terrible pain of being lifted onto the stretcher, the jolting while being moved, and the probing of his wound at the dressing station. He did not regain consciousness till late in the day, when with other wounded and captured Russian officers he was carried to the hospital. During this transfer he felt a little stronger and was able to look about him and even speak.

The first words he heard on coming to his senses were those of a French convoy officer, who said rapidly: "We must halt here: the Emperor will pass here immediately; it will please him to see these gentlemen prisoners."

Bonaparte, having come up at a gallop, stopped his horse.

"Which is the senior?" he asked, on seeing the prisoners.

They named the colonel, Prince Repnín.

"You are the commander of the Emperor Alexander's regiment of Horse Guards?" asked Napoleon.

"I commanded a squadron," replied Repnín.

"Your regiment fulfilled its duty honorably," said Napoleon.

"The praise of a great commander is a soldier's highest reward," said Repnín.

"I bestow it with pleasure," said Napoleon.

Prince Andrew, who had also been brought forward before the Emperor's eyes to complete the show of prisoners, could not fail to attract his attention. Napoleon apparently remembered seeing him on the battlefield and, addressing him, again used the epithet "young man" that was connected in his memory with Prince Andrew.

"Well, and you, young man," said he. "How do you feel, *mon brave?*"

Though five minutes before, Prince Andrew had been able to say a few words to the soldiers who were carrying him, now with his eyes fixed straight on Napoleon, he was silent. . . . So insignificant at that moment seemed to him all the interests that engrossed Napoleon, so mean did his hero himself with his paltry vanity and joy in victory appear, compared to the lofty, equitable, and kindly sky which he had seen and understood, that he could not answer him.

Everything seemed so futile and insignificant in comparison with the stern and solemn train of thought that weakness from loss of blood, suffering, and the nearness of death aroused in him. Looking into Napoleon's eyes Prince Andrew thought of the insignificance of greatness, the unimportance of life which no one could understand, and the still greater unimportance of death, the meaning of which no one alive could understand or explain.

The Emperor without waiting for an answer turned away and said to one of the officers as he went: "Have these gentlemen attended to and taken to my bivouac; let my doctor, Larrey, examine their wounds. *Au revoir*, Prince Repnín!" and he spurred his horse and galloped away.

His face shone with self-satisfaction and pleasure.

The soldiers who had carried Prince Andrew had noticed and taken the little gold icon Princess Mary had hung round her brother's neck, but seeing the favor the Emperor showed the prisoners, they now hastened to return the holy image.

Prince Andrew did not see how and by whom it was replaced, but the little icon with its thin gold chain suddenly appeared upon his chest outside his uniform.

"It would be good," thought Prince Andrew, glancing at the icon his sister had hung round his neck with such emotion and reverence, "it would be good if everything were as clear and simple as it seems to Mary. How good it would be to know where to seek for help in this life, and what to expect after it beyond the grave! How happy and calm I should be if I could now say: 'Lord, have mercy on me!' . . . But to whom should I say that? Either to a Power indefinable, incomprehensible, which I not only cannot address but which I cannot even express in words—the Great All or Nothing—" said he to himself, "or to that God who has been sewn into this amulet by Mary! There is nothing certain, nothing at all except the unimportance of everything I understand, and the greatness of something incomprehensible but all-important."

The stretchers moved on. At every jolt he again felt unendurable pain; his feverishness increased and he grew delirious. Visions of his father, wife, sister, and future son, and the tenderness he had felt the night before the battle, the figure of the insignificant little Napoleon, and above all this the lofty sky, formed the chief subjects of his delirious fancies.

The quiet home life and peaceful happiness of Bald Hills presented itself to him. He was already enjoying that happiness when that little Napoleon had suddenly appeared with his unsympathizing look of short-sighted delight at the misery of others, and doubts and torments had followed, and only the heavens promised peace. Toward morning all these dreams melted and merged into the chaos and darkness of unconsciousness and oblivion, which in the opinion of Napoleon's doctor, Larrey, was much more likely to end in death than in convalescence.

"He is a nervous, bilious subject," said Larrey, "and will not recover."

And Prince Andrew, with others fatally wounded, was left to the care of the inhabitants of the district.

1806

<hr/>

BOOK FOUR

1

Early in the year 1806 Nicholas Rostóv
returned home on leave. Denísov was going home to Vorónezh and Rostóv persuaded him to travel with him as far
as Moscow and to stay with him there. Meeting a comrade
at the last post station but one before Moscow, Denísov had
drunk three bottles of wine with him and, despite the jolting
ruts across the snow-covered road, did not once wake up on
the way to Moscow, but lay at the bottom of the sleigh
beside Rostóv, who grew more and more impatient the
nearer they got to Moscow.

At last the sleigh bore to the right, drew up at an entrance,
and Rostóv saw overhead the old familiar cornice with a bit
of plaster broken off, the porch, and the post by the side of
the pavement. He sprang out before the sleigh stopped, and
ran into the hall.

Rostóv, who had completely forgotten Denísov, not wishing anyone to forestall him, threw off his fur coat and ran
tiptoe through the large dark ballroom. All was the same:
there were the same old card tables and the same chandelier
with a cover over it; but someone had already seen the
young master, and, before he had reached the drawing room,
something flew out from a side door like a tornado and began
hugging and kissing him. Another and yet another creature
of the same kind sprang from a second door and a third;
more hugging, more kissing, more outcries, and tears of
joy. He could not distinguish which was Papa, which Natásha, and which Pétya. Everyone shouted, talked, and kissed
him at the same time. Only his mother was not there, he
noticed that.

"And I did not know . . . Nicholas . . . My darling! . . ."

"Here he is . . . our own . . . Kólya [Nicholas], dear fellow . . . How he has changed! . . . Where are the candles? . . . Tea! . . ."

"And me, kiss me!"

"Dearest . . . and me!"

Sónya, Natásha, Pétya, Anna Mikháylovna, Véra, and the old count were all hugging him, and the serfs, men and maids, flocked into the room, exclaiming and oh-ing and ah-ing.

Pétya, clinging to his legs, kept shouting, "And me too!"

Natásha, after she had pulled him down toward her and covered his face with kisses, holding him tight by the skirt of his coat, sprang away and pranced up and down in one place like a goat and shrieked piercingly.

All around were loving eyes glistening with tears of joy, and all around were lips seeking a kiss.

Sónya too, all rosy red, clung to his arm, radiant with bliss, looked eagerly toward his eyes, waiting for the look for which she longed. Sónya now was sixteen and she was very pretty, especially at this moment of happy, rapturous excitement. She gazed at him, not taking her eyes off him, and smiling and holding her breath. He gave her a grateful look, but was still expectant and looking for someone. The old countess had not yet come. But now steps were heard at the door, steps so rapid that they could hardly be his mother's.

Yet it was she, dressed in a new gown which he did not know, made since he had left. All the others let him go, and he ran to her. When they met, she fell on his breast, sobbing. She could not lift her face, but only pressed it to the cold braiding of his hussar's jacket. Denísov, who had come into the room unnoticed by anyone, stood there and wiped his eyes at the sight.

"Vasíli Denísov, your son's friend," he said, introducing himself to the count, who was looking inquiringly at him.

"You are most welcome! I know, I know," said the count, kissing and embracing Denísov. "Nicholas wrote us . . . Natásha, Véra, look! Here is Denísov!"

The same happy, rapturous faces turned to the shaggy figure of Denísov.

"Darling Denísov!" screamed Natásha, beside herself with

rapture, springing to him, putting her arms round him, and kissing him. This escapade made everybody feel confused. Denísov blushed too, but smiled and, taking Natásha's hand, kissed it.

Rostóv was very happy in the love they showed him; but the first moment of meeting had been so beatific that his present joy seemed insufficient, and he kept expecting something more, more and yet more.

Next morning, after the fatigues of their journey, the travelers slept till ten o'clock.

"Hallo, Gwíshka—my pipe!" came Vasíli Denísov's husky voice. "Wostóv, get up!"

Rostóv, rubbing his eyes that seemed glued together, raised his disheveled head from the hot pillow.

"Why, is it late?"

"Late! It is nearly ten o'clock," answered Natásha's voice. A rustle of starched petticoats and the whispering and laughter of girl's voices came from the adjoining room.

"Nicholas! Get up!" Natásha's voice was again heard at the door.

"Directly!"

"Nicholas! Come out in your dressing gown!" said Natásha's voice.

Rostóv hurriedly put something on his feet, drew on his dressing gown, and went out. Natásha had put on one spurred boot and was just getting her foot into the other. Sónya, when he came in, was twirling round and was about to expand her dresses into a balloon and sit down. They were dressed alike, in new pale-blue frocks, and were both fresh, rosy, and bright. Sónya ran away, but Natásha, taking her brother's arm, led him into the sitting room, where they began talking.

"Oh, how nice, how splendid!" she said to everything.

Rostóv felt that, under the influence of the warm rays of love, that childlike smile which had not once appeared on his face since he left home now for the first time after eighteen months again brightened his soul and face.

"No, but listen," she said, "now you are quite a man, aren't you? I'm awfully glad you're my brother." She touched his mustache. "I want to know what you men are like. Are you the same as we? No?"

"Why did Sónya run away?" asked Rostóv.

"Ah, yes! That's a whole long story!"

She pulled up her muslin sleeve and showed him a red scar on her long, slender, delicate arm, high above the elbow on that part that is covered even by a ball dress.

"I burned this to prove my love for her. I just heated a ruler in the fire and pressed it there!"

Sitting on the sofa with the little cushions on its arms, in what used to be his old schoolroom, and looking into Natásha's wildly bright eyes, Rostóv re-entered that world of home and childhood which had no meaning for anyone else, but gave him some of the best joys of his life; and the burning of an arm with a ruler as a proof of love did not seem to him senseless, he understood and was not surprised at it.

"Well, and is that all?" he asked.

"We are such friends, such friends! All that ruler business was just nonsense, but we are friends forever. She, if she loves anyone, does it for life, but I don't understand that, I forget quickly."

"Well, what then?"

"Well, she loves me and you like that."

Natásha suddenly flushed.

"Why, you remember before you went away? . . . Well, she says you are to forget all that. . . . She says: 'I shall love him always, but let him be free.' Isn't that lovely and noble! Yes, very noble? Isn't it?" asked Natásha, so seriously and excitedly that it was evident that what she was now saying she had talked of before, with tears.

Rostóv became thoughtful.

"I never go back on my word," he said. "Besides, Sónya is so charming that only a fool would renounce such happiness."

"No, no!" cried Natásha, "she and I have already talked it over. We knew you'd say so. But it won't do, because you see, if you say that—if you consider yourself bound by your promise—it will seem as if she had not meant it seriously. It makes it as if you were marrying her because you must, and that wouldn't do at all."

Rostóv saw that it had been well considered by them. Sónya had already struck him by her beauty on the preceding day. Today, when he had caught a glimpse of her, she seemed still more lovely. She was a charming girl of sixteen, evidently passionately in love with him (he did not doubt that for an instant). Why should he not love her now, and even marry her, Rostóv thought, but just now there were so many other pleasures and interests before him! "Yes, they have taken a wise decision," he thought, "I must remain free."

"Well then, that's excellent," said he. "We'll talk it over later on. Oh, how glad I am to have you! Well, and are you still true to Borís?" he continued.

"Oh, what nonsense!" cried Natásha, laughing. "I don't think about him or anyone else, and I don't want anything of the kind."

"Dear me!" said Rostóv.

"But that's all rubbish," Natásha chattered on. "And is Denísov nice?" she asked.

"Yes, indeed!"

"Well then, be quick. We'll all have breakfast together."

And Natásha rose and went out of the room on tiptoe, like a ballet dancer, but smiling as only happy girls of fifteen can smile. When Rostóv met Sónya in the drawing room, he reddened. He did not know how to behave with her. The evening before, in the first happy moment of meeting, they had kissed each other, but today they felt it could not be done; he felt that everybody, including his mother and sisters, was looking inquiringly at him and watching to see how he would behave with her. Her looks asked him to forgive her for having dared, by Natásha's intermediacy, to remind him of his promise, and then thanked him for his love. His looks thanked her for offering him his freedom and told her that one way or another he would never cease to love her, for that would be impossible.

"How strange it is," said Véra, selecting a moment when all were silent, "that Sónya and Nicholas now meet like . . . strangers."

Véra's remark was correct, as her remarks always were, but, like most of her observations, it made everyone feel uncomfortable, not only Sónya, Nicholas, and Natásha, but even the old countess, who—dreading this love affair which might hinder Nicholas from making a brilliant match—blushed like a girl.

Denísov, to Rostóv's surprise, appeared in the drawing room with pomaded hair, perfumed, and in a new uniform, looking just as smart as he made himself when going into battle, and he was more amiable to the ladies and gentlemen than Rostóv had ever expected to see him.

2

On his return to Moscow from the army, Nicholas Rostóv was welcomed by his home circle as the best of sons, a hero, and their darling Nikólenka; by his relations as a charming, attractive, and polite young man; by his acquaintances as a handsome lieutenant of hussars, a good dancer, and one of the best matches in the city.

During Rostóv's short stay in Moscow, before rejoining the army, he did not draw closer to Sónya, but rather drifted away from her. She was very pretty and sweet, and evidently deeply in love with him, but he was at the period of youth when there seems so much to do that there is *no time* for that sort of thing and a young man fears to bind himself and prizes his freedom which he needs for so many other things. When he thought of Sónya, during this stay in Moscow, he said to himself, "Ah, there will be, and there are, many more such girls somewhere whom I do not yet know. There will be time enough to think about love when I want to, but now I have no time." Besides, it seemed to him that the society of women was rather derogatory to his manhood. He went to balls and into ladies' society with an affectation of doing so against his will. The races, the English Club, sprees with Denísov, and visits to a certain house—that was another matter and quite the thing for a dashing young hussar!

Old Count Ilyá Rostóv is selected to arrange a large dinner in honor of Bagratión at the English Club. As he is asking his son to request certain delicacies from Pierre Bezúkhov's hothouses, Anna Mikháylovna Dru-

betskáya, who is still living with the Rostóvs, enters the room.

Though she came upon the count in his dressing gown every day, he invariably became confused and begged her to excuse his costume.

"No matter at all, my dear count," she said, meekly closing her eyes. "But I'll go to Bezúkhov's myself. Pierre has arrived, and now we shall get anything we want from his hothouses. I have to see him in any case. He has forwarded me a letter from Borís. Thank God, Borís is now on the staff."

The count was delighted at Anna Mikháylovna's taking upon herself one of his commissions and ordered the small closed carriage for her.

"Tell Bezúkhov to come. I'll put his name down. Is his wife with him?" he asked.

Anna Mikháylovna turned up her eyes, and profound sadness was depicted on her face.

"Ah, my dear friend, he is very unfortunate," she said. "If what we hear is true, it is dreadful. How little we dreamed of such a thing when we were rejoicing at his happiness! And such a lofty angelic soul as young Bezúkhov! Yes, I pity him from my heart, and shall try to give him what consolation I can."

"Wh-what is the matter?" asked both the young and old Rostóv.

Anna Mikháylovna sighed deeply.

"Dólokhov, Mary Ivánovna's son," she said in a mysterious whisper, "has compromised her completely, they say. Pierre took him up, invited him to his house in Petersburg, and now . . . she has come here and that daredevil after her!" said Anna Mikháylovna, wishing to show her sympathy for Pierre, but by involuntary intonations and a half smile betraying her sympathy for the "daredevil," as she called Dólokhov. "They say Pierre is quite broken by his misfortune."

"Dear, dear! But still tell him to come to the Club—it will all blow over. It will be a tremendous banquet."

Next day, the third of March, soon after one o'clock, two hundred and fifty members of the English Club and fifty guests were awaiting the guest of honor and hero of the Austrian campaign, Prince Bagratión, to dinner.

3

Bagratión is presented a gift, and a cantata is sung in his honor at the dinner. Toasts are drunk. Count Ilyá is radiant over the success of the dinner and the fact that Bagratión remembers his son. Among those present are Nicholas, Pierre, Denísov, and Dólokhov.

4

Pierre sat opposite Dólokhov and Nicholas Rostóv. As usual, he ate and drank much, and eagerly. But those who knew him intimately noticed that some great change had come over him that day. His face was depressed and gloomy. He seemed to see and hear nothing of what was going on around him and to be absorbed by some depressing and unsolved problem.

The unsolved problem that tormented him was caused by hints given by the princess, his cousin, at Moscow, concerning Dólokhov's intimacy with his wife, and by an anonymous letter he had received that morning, which in the mean jocular way common to anonymous letters said that he saw badly through his spectacles, but that his wife's connection with Dólokhov was a secret to no one but himself. Pierre absolutely disbelieved both the princess' hints and the letter, but he feared now to look at Dólokhov, who was sitting opposite him. Every time he chanced to meet Dólokhov's handsome insolent eyes, Pierre felt something terrible and monstrous rising in his soul and turned quickly away. Involuntarily recalling his wife's past and her relations with Dólokhov, Pierre saw clearly that what was said in the letter might be true, or might at least seem to be true had it not referred to *his wife*. He involuntarily remembered how Dólokhov, who had fully recovered his former position after the campaign, had returned to Petersburg and come to him. Availing himself of his friendly relations with Pierre as a boon companion, Dólokhov had come straight to his house, and Pierre had put him up and lent him money.

"Yes, he is a bully," thought Pierre, "to kill a man means nothing to him. It must seem to him that everyone is afraid of him, and that must please him. He must think that I, too, am afraid of him—and in fact I am afraid of him," he thought, and again he felt something terrible and monstrous rising in his soul. Dólokhov, Denísov, and Rostóv were now sitting opposite Pierre and seemed very gay. Rostóv was talking merrily to his two friends, one of whom was a dashing hussar and the other a notorious duelist and rake, and every now and then he glanced ironically at Pierre, whose preoccupied, absent-minded, and massive figure was a very noticeable one at the dinner. Rostóv looked inimically at Pierre, first because Pierre appeared to his hussar eyes as a rich civilian, the husband of a beauty, and in a word—an old woman; and secondly because Pierre in his preoccupation and absent-mindedness had not recognized Rostóv and had not responded to his greeting. When the Emperor's health was drunk, Pierre, lost in thought, did not rise or lift his glass.

"What are you about?" shouted Rostóv, looking at him in an ecstasy of exasperation. "Don't you hear it's His Majesty the Emperor's health?"

Pierre sighed, rose submissively, emptied his glass, and, waiting till all were seated again, turned with his kindly smile to Rostóv.

"Why, I didn't recognize you!" he said. But Rostóv was otherwise engaged; he was shouting "Hurrah!"

"Why don't you renew the acquaintance?" said Dólokhov to Rostóv.

"Confound him, he's a fool!" said Rostóv.

"One should make up to the husbands of pretty women," said Denísov.

Pierre did not catch what they were saying, but knew they were talking about him. He reddened and turned away.

"Well, now to the health of handsome women!" said Dólokhov, and with a serious expression, but with a smile lurking at the corners of his mouth, he turned with his glass to Pierre.

"Here's to the health of lovely women, Peterkin—and their lovers!" he added.

Pierre, with downcast eyes, drank out of his glass without looking at Dólokhov or answering him. The footman, who was distributing leaflets with Kutúzov's cantata, laid one before Pierre as one of the principal guests. He was just going to take it when Dólokhov, leaning across, snatched it from his hand and began reading it. Pierre looked at Dólokhov and his eyes dropped, the something terrible and monstrous that had tormented him all dinnertime rose and took possession of him. He leaned his whole massive body across the table.

"How dare you take it?" he shouted.

Hearing that cry and seeing to whom it was addressed, Nesvítski and the neighbor on his right quickly turned in alarm to Bezúkhov.

"Don't! Don't! What are you about?" whispered their frightened voices.

Dólokhov looked at Pierre with clear, mirthful, cruel eyes, and that smile of his which seemed to say, "Ah! This is what I like!"

"You shan't have it!" he said distinctly.

Pale, with quivering lips, Pierre snatched the copy.

"You . . . ! you . . . scoundrel! I challenge you!" he ejaculated, and, pushing back his chair, he rose from the table.

At the very instant he did this and uttered those words, Pierre felt that the question of his wife's guilt which had been tormenting him the whole day was finally and indubitably answered in the affirmative. He hated her and was forever sundered from her. Despite Denísov's request that he would take no part in the matter, Rostóv agreed to be Dólokhov's second, and after dinner he discussed the arrangements for the duel with Nesvítski, Bezúkhov's second. Pierre went home, but Rostóv with Dólokhov and Denísov stayed on at the Club till late, listening to the gypsies and other singers.

Next day, at eight in the morning, Pierre and Nesvítski drove to the Sokólniki forest and found Dólokhov, Denísov, and Rostóv already there. Pierre had the air of a man preoccupied with considerations which had no connection with the matter in hand. He was entirely absorbed by two considerations: his wife's guilt, of which after his sleepless night he had not the slightest doubt, and the guiltlessness of Dólokhov, who had no reason to preserve the honor of a man who was nothing to him. . . .

When all was ready, the sabers stuck in the snow to mark

the barriers, and the pistols loaded, Nesvítski went up to Pierre.

"I should not be doing my duty, Count," he said in timid tones, "and should not justify your confidence and the honor you have done me in choosing me for your second, if at this grave, this very grave, moment I did not tell you the whole truth. I think there is no sufficient ground for this affair, or for blood to be shed over it. . . . You were not right, not quite in the right, you were impetuous . . ."

"Oh yes, it is horribly stupid," said Pierre.

"Then allow me to express your regrets, and I am sure your opponent will accept them," said Nesvítski.

"No! What is there to talk about?" said Pierre. "It's all the same. . . . Is everything ready?" he added. "Only tell me where to go and where to shoot," he said with an unnaturally gentle smile.

He took the pistol in his hand and began asking about the working of the trigger, as he had not before held a pistol in his hand—a fact that he did not wish to confess.

"Oh yes, like that, I know, I only forgot," said he.

"No apologies, none whatever," said Dólokhov to Denísov (who on his side had been attempting a reconciliation), and he also went up to the appointed place.

5

"Well, begin!" said Dólokhov.

"All right," said Pierre, still smiling in the same way. A feeling of dread was in the air. It was evident that the affair so lightly begun could no longer be averted but was taking its course independently of men's will.

Denísov first went to the barrier and announced: "As the adve'sawies have wefused a weconciliation, please pwoceed. Take your pistols, and at the word thwee begin to advance.

"O-ne! T-wo! Thwee!" he shouted angrily and stepped aside.

The combatants advanced along the trodden tracks, nearer and nearer to one another, beginning to see one another through the mist. They had the right to fire when they liked as they approached the barrier. Dólokhov walked slowly without raising his pistol, looking intently with his bright, sparkling blue eyes into his antagonist's face. His mouth wore its usual semblance of a smile.

"So I can fire when I like!" said Pierre, and at the word "three," he went quickly forward, missing the trodden path and stepping into the deep snow. He held the pistol in his right hand at arm's length, apparently afraid of shooting himself with it. His left hand he held carefully back, because he wished to support his right hand with it and knew he must not do so. Having advanced six paces and strayed off the track into the snow, Pierre looked down at his feet, then quickly glanced at Dólokhov and, bending his finger as he had been shown, fired. Not at all expecting so loud a report, Pierre shuddered at the sound and then, smiling at his own sensations, stood still. The smoke, rendered denser by the mist, prevented him from seeing anything for an instant, but there was no second report as he had expected. He only heard Dólokhov's hurried steps, and his figure came in view through the smoke. He was pressing one hand to his left side, while the other clutched his drooping pistol. His face was pale. Rostóv ran toward him and said something.

"No-o-o!" muttered Dólokhov through his teeth, "no, it's not over." And after stumbling a few staggering steps right up to the saber, he sank on the snow beside it. His left hand was bloody; he wiped it on his coat and supported himself with it. His frowning face was pallid and quivered.

"Plea . . ." began Dólokhov, but could not at first pronounce the word.

"Please," he uttered with an effort.

Pierre, hardly restraining his sobs, began running toward Dólokhov and was about to cross the space between the barriers, when Dólokhov cried:

"To your barrier!" and Pierre, grasping what was meant, stopped by his saber. Only ten paces divided them. Dólokhov lowered his head to the snow, greedily bit at it, again raised his head, adjusted himself, drew in his legs and sat up, seeking a firm center of gravity. He sucked and swallowed the cold snow, his lips quivered, but his eyes, still smiling, glittered with effort and exasperation as he mustered his remaining strength. He raised his pistol and aimed.

"Sideways! Cover yourself with your pistol!" ejaculated Nesvítski.

"Cover yourself!" even Denísov cried to his adversary.

Pierre, with a gentle smile of pity and remorse, his arms and legs helplessly spread out, stood with his broad chest directly facing Dólokhov and looked sorrowfully at him. Denísov, Rostóv, and Nesvítski closed their eyes. At the same instant they heard a report and Dólokhov's angry cry.

"Missed!" shouted Dólokhov, and he lay helplessly, face downwards on the snow.

Pierre clutched his temples, and turning round went into the forest, trampling through the deep snow, and muttering incoherent words:

"Folly . . . folly! Death . . . lies . . ." he repeated, puckering his face.

Nesvítski stopped him and took him home.

Rostóv and Denísov drove away with the wounded Dólokhov.

The latter lay silent in the sleigh with closed eyes and did not answer a word to the questions addressed to him. But on entering Moscow he suddenly came to and, lifting his head with an effort, took Rostóv, who was sitting beside him, by the hand. Rostóv was struck by the totally altered and unexpectedly rapturous and tender expression on Dólokhov's face.

"Well? How do you feel?" he asked.

"Bad! But it's not that, my friend—" said Dólokhov with a gasping voice. "Where are we? In Moscow, I know. I don't matter, but I have killed her, killed . . . She won't get over it! She won't survive. . . ."

"Who?" asked Rostóv.

"My mother! My mother, my angel, my adored angel mother," and Dólokhov pressed Rostóv's hand and burst into tears.

When he had become a little quieter, he explained to Rostóv that he was living with his mother, who, if she saw him dying, would not survive it. He implored Rostóv to go on and prepare her.

Rostóv went on ahead to do what was asked, and to his great surprise learned that Dólokhov the brawler, Dólokhov the bully, lived in Moscow with an old mother and a hunch-back sister, and was the most affectionate of sons and brothers.

6

Pierre had of late rarely seen his wife alone. The night after the duel he did not go to his bedroom but, as he often did, remained in his father's room, that huge room in which Count Bezúkhov had died.

Such a storm of feelings, thoughts, and memories suddenly arose within him that he could not fall asleep, nor even remain in one place, but had to jump up and pace the room with rapid steps.

"But in what was I to blame?" he asked. "In marrying her without loving her; in deceiving yourself and her." And he vividly recalled that moment after supper at Prince Vasíli's, when he spoke those words he had found so difficult to utter: "I love you." "It all comes from that! Even then I felt it," he thought. "I felt then that it was not so, that I had no right to do it. And so it turns out.

"Anatole used to come to borrow money from her and used to kiss her naked shoulders. She did not give him the money, but let herself be kissed. Her father in jest tried to rouse her jealousy, and she replied with a calm smile that she was not so stupid as to be jealous: 'Let him do what he pleases,' she used to say of me. One day I asked her if she felt any symptoms of pregnancy. She laughed contemptuously and said she was not a fool to want to have children, and that she was not going to have any children by *me*."

Then he recalled the coarseness and bluntness of her thoughts and the vulgarity of the expressions that were natural to her, though she had been brought up in the most aristocratic circles.

In the night he called his valet and told him to pack up to go to Petersburg. He could not imagine how he could speak to her now. He resolved to go away next day and leave a letter informing her of his intention to part from her forever.

Next morning when the valet came into the room with his

coffee, Pierre was lying asleep on the ottoman with an open book in his hand.

He woke up and looked round for a while with a startled expression, unable to realize where he was.

"The countess told me to inquire whether your excellency was at home," said the valet.

But before Pierre could decide what answer he would send, the countess herself in a white satin dressing gown embroidered with silver and with simply dressed hair (two immense plaits twice round her lovely head like a coronet) entered the room, calm and majestic, except that there was a wrathful wrinkle on her rather prominent marble brow.

"Well, what's this now? What have you been up to now, I should like to know?" she asked sternly.

"I? What have I . . . ?" stammered Pierre.

"So it seems you're a hero, eh? Come now, what was this duel about? What is it meant to prove? What? I ask you."

Pierre turned over heavily on the ottoman and opened his mouth, but could not reply.

"If you won't answer, I'll tell you . . ." Hélène went on. "You believe everything you're told. You were told . . ." Hélène laughed, "that Dólokhov was my lover. . . . What does this duel prove? That you're a fool, but everybody knew that. What will be the result? That I shall be the laughingstock of all Moscow, that everyone will say that you, drunk and not knowing what you were about, challenged a man you are jealous of without cause." Hélène raised her voice and became more and more excited, "A man who's a better man than you in every way . . ."

"Hm . . . Hm . . . !" growled Pierre, frowning without looking at her, and not moving a muscle.

"And how could you believe he was my lover? Why? Because I like his company? If you were cleverer and more agreeable, I should prefer yours."

"Don't speak to me . . . I beg you," muttered Pierre hoarsely.

"Why shouldn't I speak? I can speak as I like, and I tell you plainly that there are not many wives with husbands such as you who would not have taken lovers, but I have not done so," said she.

Pierre wished to say something, looked at her with eyes whose strange expression she did not understand, and lay down again. He was suffering physically at that moment, there was a weight on his chest and he could not breathe. He knew that he must do something to put an end to this suffering, but what he wanted to do was too terrible.

"We had better separate," he muttered in a broken voice.

"Separate? Very well, but only if you give me a fortune," said Hélène. "Separate! That's a thing to frighten me with!"

Pierre leaped up from the sofa and rushed staggering toward her.

"I'll kill you!" he shouted, and seizing the marble top of a table with a strength he had never before felt, he made a step toward her brandishing the slab.

Hélène's face became terrible, she shrieked and sprang aside. His father's nature showed itself in Pierre. He felt the fascination and delight of frenzy. He flung down the slab, broke it, and swooping down on her with outstretched hands shouted, "Get out!" in such a terrible voice that the whole house heard it with horror. God knows what he would have done at that moment had Hélène not fled from the room.

A week later Pierre gave his wife full power to control all his estates in Great Russia, which formed the larger part of his property, and left for Petersburg alone.

7

Two months had elapsed since the news of the battle of Austerlitz and the loss of Prince Andrew had reached Bald Hills, and in spite of the letters sent through the embassy and all the searches made, his body had not been found nor was he on the list of prisoners. A week after the gazette report of the battle of Austerlitz came a letter from Kutúzov informing the prince of the fate that had befallen his son.

"Your son," wrote Kutúzov, "fell before my eyes, a standard in his hand and at the head of a regiment—he fell as a hero, worthy of his father and his fatherland. To the great regret of myself and of the whole army it is still uncertain whether he is alive or not."

When Princess Mary went to him at the usual hour he was working at his lathe and, as usual, did not look round at her.

"Ah, Princess Mary!" he said suddenly in an unnatural voice, throwing down his chisel. (The wheel continued to revolve by its own impetus, and Princess Mary long remembered the dying creak of that wheel, which merged in her memory with what followed.)

"Father! Andrew!"—said the ungraceful, awkward princess with such an indescribable charm of sorrow and self-forgetfulness that her father could not bear her look but turned away with a sob.

"Bad news! He's not among the prisoners nor among the killed! Kutúzov writes . . ." and he screamed as piercingly as if he wished to drive the princess away by that scream . . . "Killed!"

The princess did not fall down or faint. She was already pale, but on hearing these words her face changed and something brightened in her beautiful, radiant eyes. It was as if joy—a supreme joy apart from the joys and sorrows of this world—overflowed the great grief within her. She forgot all fear of her father, went up to him, took his hand, and drawing him down put her arm round his thin, scraggy neck.

"Father," she said, "do not turn away from me, let us weep together."

"Scoundrels! Blackguards!" shrieked the old man, turning his face away from her. "Destroying the army, destroying the men! And why? Go, go and tell Lise."

When Princess Mary returned from her father, the little princess sat working and looked up with that curious expression of inner, happy calm peculiar to pregnant women. It was evident that her eyes did not see Princess Mary but were looking within . . . into herself . . . at something joyful and mysterious taking place within her.

Several times in the course of the morning Princess Mary began trying to prepare her sister-in-law, and every time began to cry. Unobservant as was the little princess, these tears, the cause of which she did not understand, agitated her.

She said nothing but looked about uneasily as if in search of something.

"Has anything come from Andrew?" she asked.

"No, you know it's too soon for news. But my father is anxious and I feel afraid."

"So there's nothing?"

"Nothing," answered Princess Mary, looking firmly with her radiant eyes at her sister-in-law.

She had determined not to tell her and persuaded her father to hide the terrible news from her till after her confinement, which was expected within a few days.

8

On the evening of Lise's confinement, Princess Mary is worried over the delayed arrival of the doctor from Moscow. With him, to everyone's delight, comes Prince Andrew. His unexpected appearance is explained by the failure of his letter to reach Bald Hills.

9

The little princess lay supported by pillows, with a white cap on her head (the pains had just left her). Strands of her black hair lay round her inflamed and perspiring cheeks, her charming rosy mouth with its downy lip was open and she was smiling joyfully. Prince Andrew entered and paused facing her at the foot of the sofa on which she was lying. Her glittering eyes, filled with childlike fear and excitement, rested on him without changing their expression. "I love you all and have done no harm to anyone; why must I suffer so? Help me!" her look seemed to say. She saw her husband, but did not realize the significance of his appearance before her now. Prince Andrew went round the sofa and kissed her forehead.

"My darling!" he said—a word he had never used to her before. "God is merciful. . . ."

She looked at him inquiringly and with childlike reproach.

"I expected help from you and I get none, none from you

either!" said her eyes. She was not surprised at his having come; she did not realize that he had come. His coming had nothing to do with her sufferings or with their relief. The pangs began again and Mary Bogdánovna advised Prince Andrew to leave the room.

The doctor entered. Prince Andrew went out and, meeting Princess Mary, again joined her. They began talking in whispers, but their talk broke off at every moment. They waited and listened.

Prince Andrew went again to his wife and sat waiting in the room next to hers. A woman came from the bedroom with a frightened face and became confused when she saw Prince Andrew.

He began pacing the room. The screaming ceased, and a few more seconds went by. Then suddenly a terrible shriek— it could not be hers, she could not scream like that—came from the bedroom. Prince Andrew ran to the door; the scream ceased and he heard the wail of an infant.

Then suddenly he realized the joyful significance of that wail; tears choked him, and leaning his elbows on the window sill he began to cry, sobbing like a child. The door opened. The doctor with his shirt sleeves tucked up, without a coat, pale and with a trembling jaw, came out of the room. Prince Andrew turned to him, but the doctor gave him a bewildered look and passed by without a word. A woman rushed out and seeing Prince Andrew stopped, hesitating on the threshold. He went into his wife's room. She was lying dead, in the same position he had seen her in five minutes before and, despite the fixed eyes and the pallor of the cheeks, the same expression was on her charming childlike face with its upper lip covered with tiny black hair.

"I love you all, and have done no harm to anyone; and what have you done to me?"—said her charming, pathetic, dead face.

Two hours later Prince Andrew, stepping softly, went into his father's room. The old man already knew everything. He was standing close to the door and as soon as it opened his rough old arms closed like a vise round his son's neck, and without a word he began to sob like a child.

Three days later the little princess was buried, and Prince Andrew went up the steps to where the coffin stood, to give her the farewell kiss. And there in the coffin was the same face, though with closed eyes. "Ah, what have you done to me?" it still seemed to say, and Prince Andrew felt that something gave way in his soul and that he was guilty of a sin he could neither remedy nor forget. He could not weep. The old man too came up and kissed the waxen little hands that lay quietly crossed one on the other on her breast, and to him, too, her face seemed to say: "Ah, what have you done to me, and why?" And at the sight the old man turned angrily away.

Another five days passed, and then the young Prince Nicholas Andréevich was baptized. The wet nurse supported the coverlet with her chin, while the priest with a goose feather anointed the boy's little red and wrinkled soles and palms.

His grandfather, who was his godfather, trembling and afraid of dropping him, carried the infant round the battered tin font and handed him over to the godmother, Princess Mary. Prince Andrew sat in another room, faint with fear lest the baby should be drowned in the font, and awaited the termination of the ceremony.

10

Rostóv's share in Dólokhov's duel with Bezúkhov was hushed up by the efforts of the old count, and instead of being degraded to the ranks as he expected he was appointed an adjutant to the governor general of Moscow. As a result he could not go to the country with the rest of the family, but was kept all summer in Moscow by his new duties. Dólokhov recovered, and Rostóv became very friendly with him during his convalescence. Dólokhov lay ill at his mother's who loved him passionately and tenderly, and old Mary Ivánovna, who had grown fond of Rostóv for his friendship to her Fédya, often talked to him about her son.

"Yes, Count," she would say, "he is too noble and pure-souled for our present, depraved world."

Dólokhov himself during his convalescence spoke to Rostóv in a way no one would have expected of him.

"I know people consider me a bad man!" he said. "Let them! I don't care a straw about anyone but those I love; but those I love, I love so that I would give my life for them, and the others I'd throttle if they stood in my way . . . I have not yet met that divine purity and devotion I look for in women. If I found such a one I'd give my life for her! . . . But you don't understand it."

"Oh, yes, I quite understand," answered Rostóv, who was under his new friend's influence.

In the autumn the Rostóvs returned to Moscow. Early in the winter Denísov also came back and stayed with them. The first half of the winter of 1806, which Nicholas Rostóv spent in Moscow, was one of the happiest, merriest times for him and the whole family. Nicholas brought many young men to his parents' house. Véra was a handsome girl of twenty; Sónya a girl of sixteen with all the charm of an opening flower; Natásha, half grown up and half child, was now childishly amusing, now girlishly enchanting.

Among the young men introduced by Rostóv, one of the first was Dólokhov, whom everyone in the house liked except Natásha. She almost quarreled with her brother about him. She insisted that he was a bad man, and that in the duel with Bezúkhov, Pierre was right and Dólokhov wrong, and further that he was disagreeable and unnatural.

"There's nothing for me to understand," she cried out with resolute self-will, "he is wicked and heartless. . . . But Denísov . . ."

"Oh, Denísov is quite different," replied Nicholas, implying that even Denísov was nothing compared to Dólokhov—"you must understand what a soul there is in Dólokhov, you should see him with his mother. What a heart!"

"Well, I don't know about that, but I am uncomfortable with him. And do you know he has fallen in love with Sónya?"

"What nonsense. . . ."

"I'm certain of it; you'll see."

Natásha's prediction proved true. Dólokhov, who did not usually care for the society of ladies, began to come often to the house, and the question for whose sake he came (though no one spoke of it) was soon settled. He came because of Sónya. And Sónya, though she would never have dared to say so, knew it and blushed scarlet every time Dólokhov appeared.

It was evident that this strange, strong man was under the irresistible influence of the dark, graceful girl who loved another.

Rostóv noticed something new in Dólokhov's relations with Sónya, but he did not explain to himself what these new relations were.

In the autumn of 1806 everybody had again begun talking of the war with Napoleon with even greater warmth than the year before. For the Rostóv family the whole interest of these preparations for war lay in the fact that Nicholas would not hear of remaining in Moscow, and only awaited the termination of Denísov's furlough after Christmas to return with him to their regiment. His approaching departure did not prevent his amusing himself, but rather gave zest to his pleasures. He spent the greater part of his time away from home, at dinners, parties, and balls.

11

On the third day after Christmas Nicholas dined at home, a thing he had rarely done of late. It was a grand farewell dinner, as he and Denísov were leaving to join their regiment after Epiphany. About twenty people were present, including Dólokhov and Denísov.

Nicholas, having as usual exhausted two pairs of horses, without visiting all the places he meant to go to and where he had been invited, returned home just before dinner. As soon as he entered he noticed and felt the tension of the amorous air in the house, and also noticed a curious embarrassment among some of those present. Sónya, Dólokhov, and the old countess were especially disturbed, and to a lesser degree Natásha. On that same evening there was to be one of the balls that Iogel (the dancing master) gave for his pupils during the holidays.

"Nicholas, will you come to Iogel's? Please do!" said

Natásha. "He asked you, and Vasíli Dmítrich [Denísov] is also going."

"Where would I not go at the countess' command!" said Denísov, who at the Rostóvs' had jocularly assumed the role of Natásha's knight. "I'm even weady to dance the *pas de châle*."

"If I have time," answered Nicholas. "But I promised the Arkhárovs; they have a party."

"And you?" he asked Dólokhov, but as soon as he had asked the question he noticed that it should not have been put.

"There is something up," thought Nicholas, and he was further confirmed in this conclusion by the fact that Dólokhov left immediately after dinner. He called Natásha and asked her what was the matter.

"And I was looking for you," said Natásha running out to him. "I told you, but you would not believe it," she said triumphantly. "He has proposed to Sónya!"

Little as Nicholas had occupied himself with Sónya of late, something seemed to give way within him at this news. He tried to say, "That's capital; of course she'll forget her childish promises and accept the offer," but before he had time to say it Natásha began again.

"And fancy! she refused him quite definitely!" adding, after a pause, "she told him she loved another."

"Yes, my Sónya could not have done otherwise!" thought Nicholas.

"Much as Mamma pressed her, she refused, and I know she won't change once she has said . . ."

"And Mamma pressed her!" said Nicholas reproachfully.

"Yes," said Natásha. "Do you know, Nicholas—don't be angry—but I know you will not marry her. I know, heaven knows how, but I know for certain that you won't marry her."

"Now you don't know that at all!" said Nicholas. "But I must talk to her. What a darling Sónya is!" he added with a smile.

"Ah, she is indeed a darling! I'll send her to you."

A minute later Sónya came in with a frightened, guilty, and scared look. Nicholas went up to her and kissed her hand. This was the first time since his return that they had talked alone and about their love.

"Sophie," he began, timidly at first and then more and more boldly, "if you wish to refuse one who is not only a brilliant and advantageous match but a splendid, noble fellow . . . he is my friend . . ."

Sónya interrupted him.

"I have already refused," she said hurriedly.

"If you are refusing for my sake, I am afraid that I . . ."

Sónya again interrupted. She gave him an imploring, frightened look.

"Nicholas, don't tell me that!" she said.

"No, but I must. It may be arrogant of me, but still it is best to say it. If you refuse him on my account, I must tell you the whole truth. I love you, and I think I love you more than anyone else. . . ."

"That is enough for me," said Sónya, blushing.

"No, but I have been in love a thousand times and shall fall in love again, though for no one have I such a feeling of friendship, confidence, and love as I have for you. Then I am young. Mamma does not wish it. In a word, I make no promise. And I beg you to consider Dólokhov's offer," he said, articulating his friend's name with difficulty.

"Don't say that to me! I want nothing. I love you as a brother and always shall, and I want nothing more."

"You are an angel: I am not worthy of you, but I am afraid of misleading you."

And Nicholas again kissed her hand.

12

Nicholas dances with Sónya at Iogel's ball, and Denísov amazes all by his original interpretation of a mazurka with Natásha.

13

For two days after that Rostóv did not see
Dólokhov at his own or at Dólokhov's home: on the third
day he received a note from him:

"As I do not intend to be at your house again for reasons
you know of, and am going to rejoin my regiment, I am
giving a farewell supper tonight to my friends—come to the
English Hotel."

About ten o'clock Rostóv went to the English Hotel straight
from the theater, where he had been with his family and
Denísov. He was at once shown to the best room, which
Dólokhov had taken for that evening. Some twenty men
were gathered round a table at which Dólokhov sat between
two candles. On the table was a pile of gold and paper
money, and he was keeping the bank. Rostóv had not seen
him since his proposal and Sónya's refusal and felt uncomfortable at the thought of how they would meet.

Dólokhov's clear, cold glance met Rostóv as soon as he
entered the door, as though he had long expected him.

"It's a long time since we met," he said. "Thanks for
coming. I'll just finish dealing, and then Ilyúshka will come
with his chorus."

*Nicholas, though he had promised his father not to
ask for more money until May, is drawn into the card
game and constantly loses to the sharper Dólokhov
who is determined to win forty-three thousand rubles
because forty-three was the sum of his and Sónya's
joint ages.*

"You owe forty-three thousand, Count," said Dólokhov,
and stretching himself he rose from the table. "One does get
tired sitting so long," he added.

"Yes, I'm tired too," said Rostóv.

Dólokhov cut him short, as if to remind him that it was
not for him to jest.

"When am I to receive the money, Count?"

Rostóv, flushing, drew Dólokhov into the next room.

"I cannot pay it all immediately. Will you take an I.O.U.?" he said.

"I say, Rostóv," said Dólokhov clearly, smiling and looking Nicholas straight in the eyes, "you know the saying, 'Lucky in love, unlucky at cards.' Your cousin is in love with you, I know."

"Oh, it's terrible to feel oneself so in this man's power," thought Rostóv. He knew what a shock he would inflict on his father and mother by the news of this loss, he knew what a relief it would be to escape it all, and felt that Dólokhov knew that he could save him from all this shame and sorrow, but wanted now to play with him as a cat does with a mouse.

"Your cousin . . ." Dólokhov started to say, but Nicholas interrupted him.

"My cousin has nothing to do with this and it's not necessary to mention her!" he exclaimed fiercely.

"Then when am I to have it?"

"Tomorrow," replied Rostóv and left the room.

14

To say "tomorrow" and keep up a dignified tone was not difficult, but to go home alone, see his sisters, brother, mother, and father, confess and ask for money he had no right to after giving his word of honor, was terrible.

At home, they had not yet gone to bed. The young people, after returning from the theater, had had supper and were grouped round the clavichord. As soon as Nicholas entered, he was enfolded in that poetic atmosphere of love which pervaded the Rostóv household that winter and, now after Dólokhov's proposal and Iogel's ball, seemed to have grown thicker round Sónya and Natásha as the air does before a thunderstorm. Sónya and Natásha, in the light-blue dresses they had worn at the theater, looking pretty and conscious of it, were standing by the clavichord, happy and smiling. Véra was playing chess with Shinshín in the drawing room. The old countess, waiting for the return of her husband and son, sat playing patience with the old gentlewoman who lived in their house. Denísov, with sparkling eyes and ruffled hair, sat at the clavichord striking chords with his short fingers, his legs thrown back and his eyes rolling as he sang, with his small, husky, but true voice, some verses called "Enchantress," which he had composed, and to which he was trying to fit music.

He was singing in passionate tones, gazing with his sparkling black-agate eyes at the frightened and happy Natásha.

"Ah, and here's Nicholas!" cried Natásha, running up to him.

"Is Papa at home?" he asked.

"I am so glad you've come!" said Natásha, without answering him. "We *are* enjoying ourselves! Vasíli Dmítrich is staying a day longer for my sake! Did you know?"

"No, Papa is not back yet," said Sónya.

"Nicholas, have you come? Come here, dear!" called the old countess from the drawing room.

Nicholas went to her, kissed her hand, and sitting down silently at her table began to watch her hands arranging the cards. From the dancing room, they still heard the laughter and merry voices trying to persuade Natásha to sing.

"All wight! All wight!" shouted Denísov. "It's no good making excuses now! It's your turn to sing the ba'cawolla— I entweat you!"

"Everything's the same with them. They know nothing about it! Where am I to go?" thought Nicholas, and went again into the dancing room where the clavichord stood.

Sónya was sitting at the clavichord, playing the prelude to Denísov's favorite barcarolle. Natásha was preparing to sing. Denísov was looking at her with enraptured eyes.

"My God, I'm a ruined and dishonored man! A bullet through my brain is the only thing left me—not singing!" his thoughts ran on. "Go away? But where to? It's all one— let them sing!"

Natásha took the first note, her throat swelled, her chest rose, her eyes became serious.

Natásha, that winter, had for the first time begun to sing seriously, mainly because Denísov so delighted in her singing. While that untrained voice, with its incorrect breathing and labored transitions, was sounding, even the connoisseurs said nothing, but only delighted in it and wished to hear it again. In her voice there was a virginal freshness, an un-consciousness of her own powers, and an as yet untrained velvety softness, which so mingled with her lack of art in singing that it seemed as if nothing in that voice could be altered without spoiling it.

"What is this?" thought Nicholas, listening to her with widely opened eyes. "What has happened to her? How she is singing today! . . . Now then, Natásha, now then, dearest! Now then, darling! How will she take that *si?* She's taken it! Thank God!" And without noticing that he was singing, to strengthen the *si* he sung a second, a third below the high note. "Ah, God! How fine! Did I really take it? How for-tunate!" he thought.

Oh, how that chord vibrated, and how moved was some-thing that was finest in Rostóv's soul! And this something was apart from everything else in the world and above everything in the world. "What were losses, and Dólokhov, and words of honor?. . . All nonsense! One might kill and rob and yet be happy. . . ."

15

It was long since Rostóv had felt such en-joyment from music as he did that day. But no sooner had Natásha finished her barcarolle than reality again presented itself. He got up without saying a word and went down-stairs to his own room. A quarter of an hour later the old count came in from his Club, cheerful and contented. Nicho-las, hearing him drive up, went to meet him.

"Well—had a good time?" said the old count, smiling gaily and proudly at his son.

Nicholas tried to say "Yes," but could not: and he nearly burst into sobs. The count was lighting his pipe and did not notice his son's condition.

"Ah, it can't be avoided!" thought Nicholas, for the first and last time. And suddenly, in the most casual tone, which made him feel ashamed of himself, he said, as if merely asking his father to let him have the carriage to drive to town:

"Papa, I have come on a matter of business. I was nearly forgetting. I need some money."

"Dear me!" said his father, who was in a specially good humor. "I told you it would not be enough. How much?"

"Very much," said Nicholas flushing, and with a stupid careless smile, for which he was long unable to forgive himself, "I have lost a little, I mean a good deal, a great deal—forty-three thousand."

"What! To whom? . . . Nonsense!" cried the count, suddenly reddening with an apoplectic flush over neck and nape as old people do.

"I promised to pay tomorrow," said Nicholas.

"Well! . . ." said the old count, spreading out his arms and sinking helplessly on the sofa.

"It can't be helped! It happens to everyone!" said the son, with a bold, free, and easy tone, while in his soul he regarded himself as a worthless scoundrel whose whole life could not atone for his crime.

"Yes, yes," his father muttered, "it will be difficult, I fear, difficult to raise . . . happens to everybody! Yes, who has not done it?"

And with a furtive glance at his son's face, the count went out of the room. . . . Nicholas had been prepared for resistance, but had not at all expected this.

"Papa! Pa-pa!" he called after him, sobbing, "forgive me!" And seizing his father's hand, he pressed it to his lips and burst into tears.

While father and son were having their explanation, the mother and daughter were having one not less important. Natásha came running to her mother, quite excited.

"Mamma! . . . Mamma! . . . He has made me . . ."

"Made what?"

"Made, made me an offer, Mamma! Mamma!" she exclaimed.

The countess did not believe her ears. Denísov had proposed. To whom? To this chit of a girl, Natásha, who not so long ago was playing with dolls and who was still having lessons.

"Don't, Natásha! What nonsense!" she said, hoping it was a joke.

"Nonsense, indeed! I am telling you the fact," said Natásha

indignantly. "I come to ask you what to do, and you call it 'nonsense!' "

"If it is true that Monsieur Denísov has made you a proposal, tell him he is a fool, that's all!"

"No, he's not a fool!" replied Natásha indignantly and seriously.

"Well then, what do you want? You're all in love nowadays. Well, if you are in love, marry him!" said the countess, with a laugh of annoyance. "Good luck to you!"

"No, Mamma, I'm not in love with him, I suppose I'm not in love with him."

"Well then, tell him so."

"Mamma, are you cross? Don't be cross, dear! Is it my fault?"

"No, but what is it, my dear? Do you want me to go and tell him?" said the countess smiling.

"No, I will do it myself, only tell me what to say. It's all very well for you," said Natásha, with a responsive smile. "You should have seen how he said it! I know he did not mean to say it, but it came out accidentally."

"Well, all the same, you must refuse him."

"No, I mustn't. I am so sorry for him! He's so nice."

"Well then, accept his offer. It's high time for you to be married," answered the countess sharply and sarcastically.

"No, Mamma, but I'm so sorry for him. I don't know how I'm to say it."

"And there's nothing for you to say. I shall speak to him myself," said the countess, indignant that they should have dared to treat this little Natásha as grown up.

"No, not on any account! I will tell him myself, and you'll listen at the door," and Natásha ran across the drawing room to the dancing hall, where Denísov was sitting on the same chair by the clavichord with his face in his hands.

He jumped up at the sound of her light step.

"Nataly," he said, moving with rapid steps toward her, "decide my fate. It is in your hands."

"Vasíli Dmítrich, I'm so sorry for you! . . . No, but you are so nice . . . but it won't do . . . not that . . . but as a friend, I shall always love you."

Denísov bent over her hand and she heard strange sounds she did not understand. She kissed his rough curly black head. At this instant, they heard the quick rustle of the countess' dress. She came up to them.

"Vasíli Dmítrich, I thank you for the honor," she said, with an embarrassed voice, though it sounded severe to Denísov—"but my daughter is so young, and I thought that, as my son's friend, you would have addressed yourself first to me. In that case you would not have obliged me to give this refusal."

"Countess . . ." said Denísov, with downcast eyes and a guilty face. He tried to say more, but faltered.

Natásha could not remain calm, seeing him in such a plight. She began to sob aloud.

"Countess, I have done w'ong," Denísov went on in an unsteady voice, "but believe me, I so adore your daughter and all your family that I would give my life twice over . . ." He looked at the countess, and seeing her severe face said: "Well, good-by, Countess," and kissing her hand, he left the room with quick resolute strides, without looking at Natásha.

Next day Rostóv saw Denísov off. He did not wish to stay another day in Moscow.

After Denísov's departure, Rostóv spent another fortnight in Moscow, without going out of the house, waiting for the money his father could not at once raise, and he spent most of his time in the girls' room.

Sónya was more tender and devoted to him than ever. It was as if she wanted to show him that his losses were an achievement that made her love him all the more, but Nicholas now considered himself unworthy of her.

He filled the girls' albums with verses and music, and having at last sent Dólokhov the whole forty-three thousand rubles and received his receipt, he left at the end of November, without taking leave of any of his acquaintances, to overtake his regiment which was already in Poland.

1806-07

BOOK FIVE

1

After his interview with his wife Pierre left for Petersburg. At the Torzhók post station, either there were no horses or the postmaster would not supply them. Pierre was obliged to wait. Without undressing, he lay down on the leather sofa in front of a round table, put his big feet in their overboots on the table, and began to reflect.

"What is bad? What is good? What should one love and what hate? What does one live for? And what am I? What is life, and what is death? What power governs all?"

There was no answer to any of these questions, except one, and that not a logical answer and not at all a reply to them. The answer was: "You'll die and all will end. You'll die and know all, or cease asking." But dying was also dreadful.

Everything within and around him seemed confused, senseless, and repellent. Yet in this very repugnance to all his circumstances Pierre found a kind of tantalizing satisfaction.

"I make bold to ask your excellency to move a little for this gentleman," said the postmaster, entering the room followed by another traveler, also detained for lack of horses.

The newcomer was a short, large-boned, yellow-faced, wrinkled old man, with gray bushy eyebrows overhanging bright eyes of an indefinite grayish color.

Pierre took his feet off the table, stood up, and lay down on a bed that had been got ready for him, glancing now and then at the newcomer, who, with a gloomy and tired face, was wearily taking off his wraps with the aid of his servant, and not looking at Pierre. With a pair of felt boots on his thin bony legs, and keeping on a worn, nankeen-covered, sheepskin coat, the traveler sat down on the sofa, leaned back his big head with its broad temples and close-cropped hair, and looked at Bezúkhov. The stern, shrewd, and penetrating expression of that look struck Pierre.

The servant handed him a book which Pierre took to be a devotional work, and the traveler became absorbed in it. Pierre looked at him. All at once the stranger closed the book, putting in a marker, and again, leaning with his arms on the back of the sofa, sat in his former position with his eyes shut. Pierre looked at him and had not time to turn away when the old man, opening his eyes, fixed his steady and severe gaze straight on Pierre's face.

Pierre felt confused and wished to avoid that look, but the bright old eyes attracted him irresistibly.

"I have the pleasure of addressing Count Bezúkhov, if I am not mistaken," said the stranger in a deliberate and loud voice.

Pierre looked silently and inquiringly at him over his spectacles.

"I have heard of you, my dear sir," continued the stranger, "and of your misfortune." He seemed to emphasize the last word, as if to say—"Yes, misfortune! Call it what you please, I know that what happened to you in Moscow was a misfortune."—"I regret it very much, my dear sir."

Pierre flushed and, hurriedly putting his legs down from the bed, bent forward toward the old man with a forced and timid smile.

"I have not referred to this out of curiosity, my dear sir, but for greater reasons.

"You are unhappy, my dear sir," the stranger continued. "You are young and I am old. I should like to help you as far as lies in my power.

"But if for any reason you don't feel inclined to talk to me," said the old man, "say so, my dear sir." And he suddenly smiled, in an unexpected and tenderly paternal way.

"Oh no, not at all! On the contrary, I am very glad to make your acquaintance," said Pierre. And, glancing at the stranger's hands, he looked more closely at the ring, with its skull—a Masonic sign.

"Allow me to ask," he said, "are you a Mason?"

"Yes, I belong to the Brotherhood of the Freemasons," said the stranger, looking deeper and deeper into Pierre's eyes. "And in their name and my own I hold out a brotherly hand to you."

"I am afraid," said Pierre, smiling, and wavering between the confidence the personality of the Freemason inspired in him and his own habit of ridiculing the Masonic beliefs—"I am afraid I am very far from understanding—how am I to put it?—I am afraid my way of looking at the world is so opposed to yours that we shall not understand one another."

"I know your outlook," said the Mason, "and the view of life you mention, and which you think is the result of your own mental efforts, is the one held by the majority of people, and is the invariable fruit of pride, indolence, and ignorance. Forgive me, my dear sir, but if I had not known it I should not have addressed you. Your view of life is a regrettable delusion."

"Just as I may suppose you to be deluded," said Pierre, with a faint smile.

"I should never dare to say that I know the truth," said the Mason, whose words struck Pierre more and more by their precision and firmness. "No one can attain to truth by himself. Only by laying stone on stone with the co-operation of all, by the millions of generations from our forefather Adam to our own times, is that temple reared which is to be a worthy dwelling place of the Great God," he added, and closed his eyes.

"I ought to tell you that I do not believe . . . do not believe in God," said Pierre, regretfully and with an effort, feeling it essential to speak the whole truth.

The Mason looked intently at Pierre and smiled as a rich man with millions in hand might smile at a poor fellow who told him that he, poor man, had not the five rubles that would make him happy.

"Yes, you do not know Him, my dear sir," said the Mason. "You cannot know Him. You do not know Him and that is why you are unhappy."

"Yes, yes, I am unhappy," assented Pierre. "But what am I to do?"

"He exists, but to understand Him is hard," the Mason began again, looking not at Pierre but straight before him, and turning the leaves of his book with his old hands which from excitement he could not keep still. "If it were a man whose existence thou didst doubt I could bring him to thee, could take him by the hand and show him to thee. But how can I, an insignificant mortal, show His omnipotence, His infinity, and all His mercy to one who is blind, or who shuts his eyes that he may not see or understand Him and may not see or understand his own vileness and sinfulness?"

Pierre listened with swelling heart, gazing into the Mason's face with shining eyes, not interrupting or questioning him, but believing with his whole soul what the stranger said.

"He is not to be apprehended by reason, but by life," said the Mason.

"I do not understand," said Pierre, feeling with dismay doubts reawakening. He was afraid of any want of clearness, any weakness, in the Mason's arguments; he dreaded not to be able to believe in him. "I don't understand," he said, "how it is that the mind of man cannot attain the knowledge of which you speak."

"The highest wisdom is not founded on reason alone, not on those worldly sciences of physics, history, chemistry, and the like, into which intellectual knowledge is divided. The highest wisdom is one. The highest wisdom has but one science—the science of the whole—the science explaining the whole creation and man's place in it. To receive that science it is necessary to purify and renew one's inner self, and so before one can know, it is necessary to believe and to perfect one's self. And to attain this end, we have the light called conscience that God has implanted in our souls."

"Yes, yes," assented Pierre.

"Look then at thy inner self with the eyes of the spirit, and ask thyself whether thou art content with thyself. What hast thou attained relying on reason only? What art thou? You are young, you are rich, you are clever, you are well educated. And what have you done with all these good gifts? Are you content with yourself and with your life?"

"No, I hate my life," Pierre muttered, wincing.

"Thou hatest it. Then change it, purify thyself; and as thou art purified, thou wilt gain wisdom."

After these words, the Mason, as if tired by his long discourse, again leaned his arms on the back of the sofa and closed his eyes. Pierre looked at that aged, stern, motionless, almost lifeless face and moved his lips without uttering a sound.

The Mason cleared his throat huskily, as old men do, and called his servant.

"How about the horses?" he asked, without looking at Pierre.

"The exchange horses have just come," answered the servant. "Will you not rest here?"

"No, tell them to harness."

"Can he really be going away and leaving me alone without having told me all, and without promising to help me?" thought Pierre, rising with downcast head; and he began to pace the room, glancing occasionally at the Mason. "Yes, I never thought of it, but I have led a contemptible and profligate life, though I did not like it and did not want to," thought Pierre. "But this man knows the truth and, if he wished to, could disclose it to me."

"Where are you going to now, my dear sir?"

"I? . . . I'm going to Petersburg," answered Pierre, in a childlike, hesitating voice. "I thank you. I agree with all you have said. But do not suppose me to be so bad. With my whole soul I wish to be what you would have me be, but I have never had help from anyone. . . . But it is I, above all, who am to blame for everything. Help me, teach me, and perhaps I may . . ."

Pierre could not go on. He gulped and turned away.

The Mason remained silent for a long time, evidently considering.

"Help comes from God alone," he said, "but such measure of help as our Order can bestow it will render you, my dear sir. You are going to Petersburg. Hand this to Count Willarski" (he took out his notebook and wrote a few words on a large sheet of paper folded in four). "Allow me to give you a piece of advice. When you reach the capital, first of all devote some time to solitude and self-examination and do not resume your former way of life. And now I wish you a good journey, my dear sir," he added, seeing that his servant had entered ". . . and success."

The traveler was Joseph Alexéevich Bazdéev, as Pierre saw from the postmaster's book. Bazdéev was one of the best-known Freemasons and Martinists. Pierre did not go to bed or order horses but paced up and down the room, pondering over his vicious past, and with a rapturous sense of beginning anew pictured to himself the blissful, irreproachable, virtuous future that seemed to him so easy. It seemed to him that he had been vicious only because he had somehow forgotten how good it is to be virtuous. Not a trace of his former doubts remained in his soul. He firmly believed in the possibility of the brotherhood of men united in the aim of supporting one another in the path of virtue, and that is how Freemasonry presented itself to him.

2

At the conclusion of a lengthy ceremony inducting him into the Freemasons, Pierre joyfully feels that, in abiding by the prescriptions of the Order, he will leave behind him his former habits and lead a changed life.

3

The day after he had been received into the Lodge, Pierre was sitting at home reading a book and trying to fathom the significance of the Square, one side of which symbolized God, another moral things, a third physical things, and the fourth a combination of these. On the previous evening at the Lodge, he had heard that a rumor of his duel had reached the Emperor and that it would be wiser for him to leave Petersburg. Pierre proposed going to his estates in the south and there attending to the welfare of his serfs. He was joyfully planning this new life, when Prince Vasíli suddenly entered the room.

"My dear fellow, what have you been up to in Moscow? Why have you quarreled with Hélène, *mon cher?* You are under a delusion," said Prince Vasíli, as he entered.

Pierre was about to reply, but Prince Vasíli interrupted him.

"And why didn't you simply come straight to me as to a friend? I know all about it and understand it all," he said. "Remember, dear boy," and he drew Pierre's arm downwards, "it is simply a misunderstanding. I expect you feel it so yourself. Let us write her a letter at once, and she'll come here and all will be explained, or else, my dear boy, let me tell you it's quite likely you'll have to suffer for it."

Prince Vasíli gave Pierre a significant look.

"I know from reliable sources that the Dowager Empress is taking a keen interest in the whole affair. You know she is very gracious to Hélène."

Pierre tried several times to speak, but, on one hand, Prince Vasíli did not let him and, on the other, Pierre himself feared to begin to speak in the tone of decided refusal and disagreement in which he had firmly resolved to answer his father-in-law. Moreover, the words of the Masonic statutes, "be kindly and courteous," recurred to him.

"Now, dear boy," said Prince Vasíli playfully, "say 'yes,' and I'll write to her myself, and we will kill the fatted calf."

But before Prince Vasíli had finished his playful speech, Pierre, without looking at him, and with a kind of fury that made him like his father, muttered in a whisper:

"Prince, I did not ask you here. Go, please go." And he jumped up and opened the door for him.

"Go!" he repeated, amazed at himself and glad to see the look of confusion and fear that showed itself on Prince Vasíli's face.

"What's the matter with you? Are you ill?"

"Go!" the quivering voice repeated. And Prince Vasíli had to go without receiving any explanation.

A week later, Pierre, having taken leave of his new friends, the Masons, and leaving large sums of money with them for alms, went away to his estates. His new brethren gave him letters to the Kiev and Odessa Masons and promised to write to him and guide him in his new activity.

4

The duel between Pierre and Dólokhov was hushed up and, in spite of the Emperor's severity regarding duels at that time, neither the principals nor their seconds suffered for it. But the story of the duel, confirmed by Pierre's rupture with his wife, was the talk of society. Now he alone was blamed for what had happened, he was said to be insanely jealous and subject like his father to fits of bloodthirsty rage. And when after Pierre's departure Hélène returned to Petersburg, she was received by all her acquaintances not only cordially, but even with a shade of deference due to her misfortune.

Toward the end of 1806, when all the sad details of Napoleon's destruction of the Prussian army at Jena and Auerstadt and the surrender of most of the Prussian fortresses had been received, when our troops had already entered Prussia and our second war with Napoleon was beginning, Anna Pávlovna gave one of her soirées.

The novelty Anna Pávlovna was setting before her guests that evening was Borís Drubetskóy, who had just arrived as a special messenger from the Prussian army and was aide-de-camp to a very important personage.

When Borís, who was to be served up to the guests, entered the drawing room, almost all the company had assembled, and the conversation, guided by Anna Pávlovna, was about our diplomatic relations with Austria and the hope of an alliance with her.

Borís, grown more manly and looking fresh, rosy and self-possessed, entered the drawing room elegantly dressed in the uniform of an aide-de-camp and was duly conducted to pay his respects to the aunt and then brought back to the general circle.

Anna Pávlovna gave him her shriveled hand to kiss and introduced him to several persons whom he did not know, giving him a whispered description of each.

Thanks to Anna Mikháylovna's efforts, his own tastes, and the peculiarities of his reserved nature, Borís had managed during his service to place himself very advantageously. He was aide-de-camp to a very important personage, had been sent on a very important mission to Prussia, and had just returned from there as a special messenger. In consequence, his whole manner of life, all his relations with old friends, all his plans for his future, were completely altered. He was not rich, but would spend his last groat to be better dressed than others, and would rather deprive himself of many pleasures than allow himself to be seen in a shabby equipage or appear in the streets of Petersburg in an old uniform. He made friends with and sought the acquaintance of only those above him in position and who could therefore be of use to him. He liked Petersburg and despised Moscow. The remembrance of the Rostóvs' house and of his childish love for Natásha was unpleasant to him and he had not once been to see the Rostóvs since the day of his departure for the army. To be in Anna Pávlovna's drawing room he considered an important step up in the service, and he at once understood his role, letting his hostess make use of whatever interest he had to offer. He himself carefully scanned each face, appraising the possibilities of establishing intimacy with each of those present, and the advantages that might accrue. He took the seat indicated to him beside the fair Hélène and listened to the general conversation.

"Vienna considers the bases of the proposed treaty so unattainable that not even a continuity of most brilliant successes would secure them, and she doubts the means we have of gaining them. That is the actual phrase used by the Vienna cabinet," said the Danish chargé d'affaires.

After that Anna Pávlovna led up to the courage and firmness of the King of Prussia, in order to draw Borís into the conversation.

Borís listened attentively to each of the speakers, awaiting his turn, but managed meanwhile to look round repeatedly at his neighbor, the beautiful Hélène, whose eyes several times met those of the handsome young aide-de-camp with a smile.

Speaking of the position of Prussia, Anna Pávlovna very naturally asked Borís to tell them about his journey to Glogau and in what state he found the Prussian army. Borís, speaking with deliberation, told them in pure, correct French many interesting details about the armies and the court, carefully abstaining from expressing an opinion of his own about the facts he was recounting. For some time he engrossed the general attention, and Anna Pávlovna felt that the novelty she had served up was received with pleasure by all her visitors. The greatest attention of all to Borís' narrative was shown by Hélène.

"You absolutely must come and see me," she said in a tone that implied that, for certain considerations he could not know of, this was absolutely necessary.

"On Tuesday between eight and nine. It will give me great pleasure."

Borís promised to fulfill her wish and was about to begin a conversation with her, when Anna Pávlovna called him away on the pretext that her aunt wished to hear him.

"You know her husband, of course?" said Anna Pávlovna, closing her eyes and indicating Hélène with a sorrowful gesture. "Ah, she is such an unfortunate and charming woman! Don't mention him before her—please don't! It is too painful for her!"

5

When Boris and Anna Pávlovna returned to the others Prince Hippolyte had the ear of the company.

Bending forward in his armchair he said: "*Le Roi de Prusse!*" and having said this laughed. Everyone turned toward him.

Stupid as usual, Hippolyte fumbles a joke which he had heard at Vienna.

When everybody rose to go, Hélène who had spoken very little all the evening again turned to Borís, asking him in a tone of caressing significant command to come to her on Tuesday.

"It is of great importance to me," she said, turning with a smile toward Anna Pávlovna, and Anna Pávlovna, with the same sad smile with which she spoke of her exalted patroness, supported Hélène's wish.

But on Tuesday evening, having come to Hélène's splendid salon, Borís received no clear explanation of why it had been necessary for him to come. There were other guests and the countess talked little to him, and only as he kissed her hand on taking leave said unexpectedly and in a whisper, with a strangely unsmiling face: "Come to dinner tomorrow . . . in the evening. You must come . . . Come!"

During that stay in Petersburg, Borís became an intimate in the countess' house.

6

The war was flaming up and nearing the Russian frontier. Everywhere one heard curses on Bonaparte, "the enemy of mankind." Militiamen and recruits were being enrolled in the villages, and from the seat of war came contradictory news, false as usual and therefore variously interpreted.

The life of old Prince Bolkónski, Prince Andrew, and Princess Mary had greatly changed since 1805.

In 1806 the old prince was made one of the eight commanders in chief then appointed to supervise the enrollment decreed throughout Russia. He was continually traveling through the three provinces entrusted to him, was pedantic in the fulfillment of his duties, severe to cruelty with his subordinates, and went into everything down to the minutest details himself. Princess Mary had ceased taking lessons in mathematics from her father. The baby Prince Nicholas lived with his wet nurse and nurse Sávishna in the late princess' rooms and Princess Mary spent most of the day in the nursery, taking a mother's place to her little nephew as best she could.

Soon after Prince Andrew's return the old prince made over to him a large estate, Boguchárovo, about twenty-five miles from Bald Hills. Partly because of the depressing memories associated with Bald Hills, partly because Prince Andrew did not always feel equal to bearing with his father's peculiarities, and partly because he needed solitude, Prince Andrew made use of Boguchárovo, began building and spent most of his time there.

After the Austerlitz campaign Prince Andrew had firmly resolved not to continue his military service, and when the war recommenced and everybody had to serve, he took a post under his father in the recruitment so as to avoid active service.

On February 26, 1807, the old prince set off on one of his circuits. Prince Andrew remained at Bald Hills as usual during his father's absence. Little Nicholas had been unwell for four days. The coachman who had driven the old prince to town returned bringing papers and letters for Prince Andrew.

Not finding the young prince in his study the valet went with the letters to Princess Mary's apartments, but did not find him there. He was told that the prince had gone to the nursery.

"If you please, your excellency, Petrúsha has brought some papers," said one of the nursemaids to Prince Andrew who was sitting on a child's little chair while, frowning and with trembling hands, he poured drops from a medicine bottle into a wineglass half full of water.

"What is it?" he said crossly, and, his hand shaking unintentionally, he poured too many drops into the glass. He threw the mixture onto the floor and asked for some more water. The maid brought it.

"My dear," said Princess Mary, addressing her brother from beside the cot where she was standing, "better wait a bit . . . later . . ."

It was the second night that neither of them had slept, watching the boy who was in a high fever.

"Petrúsha has come with papers from your father," whispered the maid.

Prince Andrew went out.

"Devil take them!" he muttered, and after listening to the verbal instructions his father had sent and taking the correspondence and his father's letter, he returned to the nursery.

Prince Andrew went up to the child and felt him. He was burning hot.

"Andrew, don't!" said Princess Mary.

But he scowled at her angrily though also with suffering in his eyes, and stooped glass in hand over the infant.

"But I wish it," he said. "I beg you—give it him!"

Princess Mary shrugged her shoulders but took the glass submissively and calling the nurse began giving the medicine. The child screamed hoarsely. Prince Andrew winced and, clutching his head, went out and sat down on a sofa in the next room.

He still had all the letters in his hand. Opening them mechanically he began reading. The old prince, now and then using abbreviations, wrote in his large elongated hand on blue paper as follows:

"Have just this moment received by special messenger very joyful news—if it's not false. Bennigsen seems to have obtained a complete victory over Buonaparte at Eylau. In Petersburg everyone is rejoicing, and the rewards sent to the army are innumerable. Though he is a German—I congratulate him! I can't make out what the commander at Kórchevo—a certain Khandrikóv—is up to; till now the additional men and provisions have not arrived. Gallop off to him at once and say I'll have his head off if everything is not here in a week."

Prince Andrew sighed and broke the seal of another envelope. It was a closely written letter of two sheets from Bilíbin. He folded it up without reading it and reread his father's letter, ending with the words: "Gallop off to Kórchevo and carry out instructions!"

"No, pardon me, I won't go now till the child is better," thought he, going to the door and looking into the nursery.

Princess Mary was still standing by the cot, gently rocking the baby.

"Ah yes, and what else did he say that's unpleasant?" thought Prince Andrew, recalling his father's letter. "Yes, we have gained a victory over Bonaparte, just when I'm not serving. Yes, yes, he's always poking fun at me. . . . Ah, well! Let him!" And he began reading Bilíbin's letter which was written in French. He read without understanding half of it, read only to forget, if but for a moment, what he had too long been thinking of so painfully to the exclusion of all else.

7

Bilíbin's letter gives a picture of personal jealousy among the Russian commanders and of looting among their troops because of a lack of food.

At first Prince Andrew read with his eyes only, but after a while, in spite of himself (although he knew how far it was safe to trust Bilíbin), what he had read began to interest him more and more. When he had read thus far, he crumpled the letter up and threw it away. It was not what he had read that vexed him, but the fact that the life out there in which he had now no part could perturb him. He shut his eyes, rubbed his forehead as if to rid himself of all interest in what he had read, and listened to what was passing in the nursery. Suddenly he thought he heard a strange noise through the door. He was seized with alarm lest something should have happened to the child while he was reading the letter. He went on tiptoe to the nursery door and opened it.

Just as he went in he saw that the nurse was hiding something from him with a scared look and that Princess Mary was no longer by the cot.

As often happens after long sleeplessness and long anxiety, he was seized by an unreasoning panic—it occurred to him that the child was dead. All that he saw and heard seemed to confirm this terror.

"All is over," he thought, and a cold sweat broke out on his forehead. He went to the cot in confusion, sure that he would find it empty and that the nurse had been hiding the dead baby. He drew the curtain aside and for some time his frightened, restless eyes could not find the baby. At last he saw him: the rosy boy had tossed about till he lay across the bed with his head lower than the pillow, and was smacking his lips in his sleep and breathing evenly.

He was not dead, but evidently the crisis was over and he was convalescent. Prince Andrew longed to snatch up, to squeeze, to hold to his heart, this helpless little creature, but dared not do so. He stood over him, gazing at his head and at the little arms and legs which showed under the blanket. He heard a rustle behind him and a shadow appeared under the curtain of the cot. He did not look round, but still gazing at the infant's face listened to his regular breathing. The dark shadow was Princess Mary, who had come up to the cot with noiseless steps, lifted the curtain, and dropped it again behind her. Prince Andrew recognized her without looking and held out his hand to her. She pressed it.

Prince Andrew looked at his sister. In the dim shadow of the curtain her luminous eyes shone more brightly than usual from the tears of joy that were in them. She leaned over to her brother and kissed him, slightly catching the curtain of the cot. Each made the other a warning gesture and stood still in the dim light beneath the curtain as if not wishing to leave that seclusion where they three were shut off from all the world. Prince Andrew was the first to move away, ruffling his hair against the muslin of the curtain.

"Yes, this is the one thing left me now," he said with a sigh.

8

Soon after his admission to the Masonic Brotherhood, Pierre went to the Kiev province, where he had the greatest number of serfs, taking with him full directions which he had written down for his own guidance as to what he should do on his estates.

When he reached Kiev he sent for all his stewards to the head office and explained to them his intentions and wishes. He told them that steps would be taken immediately to free his serfs—and that till then they were not to be overburdened with labor, women while nursing their babies were not to be sent to work, assistance was to be given to the serfs, punishments were to be admonitory and not corporal, and hospitals, asylums, and schools were to be established on all the estates. Some of the stewards (there were semiliterate foremen among them) listened with alarm, supposing these words to mean that the young count was displeased with their management and embezzlement of money, some after their first fright were amused by Pierre's lisp and the new words they had not heard before, others simply enjoyed hearing how the master talked, while the cleverest among them, including the chief steward, understood from this speech how they could best handle the master for their own ends.

The chief steward expressed great sympathy with Pierre's intentions, but remarked that besides these changes it would be necessary to go into the general state of affairs which was far from satisfactory.

Despite Count Bezúkhov's enormous wealth, since he had come into an income which was said to amount to five hundred thousand rubles a year, Pierre felt himself far poorer than when his father had made him an allowance of ten thousand rubles.

Pierre had none of the practical persistence that would have enabled him to attend to the business himself and so he disliked it and only tried to pretend to the steward that he was attending to it. The steward for his part tried to pretend to the count that he considered these consultations very valuable for the proprietor and troublesome to himself.

In Kiev Pierre found some people he knew, and strangers hastened to make his acquaintance and joyfully welcomed the rich newcomer, the largest landowner of the province. Again whole days, weeks, and months of his life passed in as great a rush and were as much occupied with evening parties, dinners, lunches, and balls, giving him no time for reflection, as in Petersburg. Instead of the new life he had hoped to lead he still lived the old life, only in new surroundings.

Of the three precepts of Freemasonry Pierre realized that he did not fulfill the one which enjoined every Mason to set an example of moral life, and that of the seven virtues he lacked two—morality and the love of death. He consoled himself with the thought that he fulfilled another of the precepts —that of reforming the human race—and had other virtues— love of his neighbor, and especially generosity.

In the spring of 1807 he decided to return to Petersburg. On the way he intended to visit all his estates and see for himself how far his orders had been carried out and in what state were the serfs whom God had entrusted to his care and whom he intended to benefit.

The chief steward, who considered the young count's attempts almost insane—unprofitable to himself, to the count, and to the serfs—made some concessions.

The southern spring, the comfortable rapid traveling in a Vienna carriage, and the solitude of the road, all had a gladdening effect on Pierre. The estates he had not before visited were each more picturesque than the other; the serfs everywhere seemed thriving and touchingly grateful for the benefits conferred on them.

He did not know that the brick buildings, built to plan, were being built by serfs whose manorial labor was thus increased, though lessened on paper. He did not know that where the steward had shown him in the accounts that the serfs' payments had been diminished by a third, their obligatory manorial work had been increased by a half. And so Pierre was delighted with his visit to his estates and quite recovered the philanthropic mood in which he had left Petersburg, and wrote enthusiastic letters to his "brother-instructor" as he called the Grand Master.

"How easy it is, how little effort it needs, to do so much good," thought Pierre, "and how little attention we pay to it!"

The chief steward, a very stupid but cunning man who saw perfectly through the naïve and intelligent count and played with him as with a toy . . . pressed him still harder with proofs of the impossibility and above all the uselessness of freeing the serfs, who were quite happy as it was.

9

Returning from his journey through South Russia in the happiest state of mind, Pierre carried out an intention he had long had of visiting his friend Bolkónski, whom he had not seen for two years.

Boguchárovo lay in a flat uninteresting part of the country among fields and forests of fir and birch, which were partly cut down. The house lay behind a newly dug pond filled with water to the brink and with banks still bare of grass. Some domestic serfs Pierre met, in reply to inquiries as to where the prince lived, pointed out a small newly built lodge close to the pond.

Pierre went with rapid steps to the door and suddenly came face to face with Prince Andrew, who came out frowning and looking old. Pierre embraced him and lifting his spectacles kissed his friend on the cheek and looked at him closely.

"Well, I did not expect you, I am very glad," said Prince Andrew.

Pierre said nothing; he looked fixedly at his friend with surprise. He was struck by the change in him. His words were kindly and there was a smile on his lips and face, but his eyes were dull and lifeless and in spite of his evident wish to do so he could not give them a joyous and glad sparkle.

As is usually the case with people meeting after a prolonged separation, it was long before their conversation could settle on anything. Pierre began to feel that it was in bad taste to speak of his enthusiasms, dreams, and hopes of happiness or goodness, in Prince Andrew's presence.

Pierre began describing what he had done on his estates,

trying as far as possible to conceal his own part in the improvements that had been made. Prince Andrew several times prompted Pierre's story of what he had been doing, as though it were all an old-time story, and he listened not only without interest but even as if ashamed of what Pierre was telling him.

Pierre felt uncomfortable and even depressed in his friend's company and at last became silent.

"I'll tell you what, my dear fellow," said Prince Andrew, who evidently also felt depressed and constrained with his visitor, "I am only bivouacking here and have just come to look round. I am going back to my sister today. I will introduce you to her. But of course you know her already," he said, evidently trying to entertain a visitor with whom he now found nothing in common.

At dinner, conversation turned on Pierre's marriage.

"I was very much surprised when I heard of it," said Prince Andrew.

Pierre blushed, as he always did when it was mentioned, and said hurriedly: "I will tell you some time how it all happened. But you know it is all over, and forever."

"Forever?" said Prince Andrew. "Nothing's forever."

"But you know how it all ended, don't you? You heard of the duel?"

"And so you had to go through that too!"

"One thing I thank God for is that I did not kill the man," said Pierre.

"Why so?" asked Prince Andrew. "To kill a vicious dog is a very good thing really."

"No, to kill a man is bad—wrong."

"Why is it wrong?" urged Prince Andrew. "It is not given to man to know what is right and what is wrong. Men always did and always will err, and in nothing more than in what they consider right and wrong."

"What does harm to another is wrong," said Pierre, feeling with pleasure that for the first time since his arrival Prince Andrew was roused, had begun to talk, and wanted to express what had brought him to his present state.

"And who has told you what is bad for another man?" he asked.

"Bad! Bad!" exclaimed Pierre. "We all know what is bad for ourselves."

"Yes, we know that, but the harm I am conscious of in myself is something I cannot inflict on others," said Prince Andrew, growing more and more animated and evidently wishing to express his new outlook to Pierre. He spoke in French. "I only know two very real evils in life: remorse and illness. The only good is the absence of those evils. To live for myself avoiding those two evils is my whole philosophy now."

"And love of one's neighbor, and self-sacrifice?" began Pierre. "No, I can't agree with you! To live only so as not to do evil and not to have to repent is not enough. I lived like that, I lived for myself and ruined my life."

Prince Andrew looked silently at Pierre with an ironic smile.

"You lived for yourself and say you nearly ruined your life and only found happiness when you began living for others. I experienced just the reverse. I lived for glory— And after all what is glory? The same love of others, a desire to do something for them, a desire for their approval— So I lived for others, and not almost, but quite, ruined my life. And I have become calmer since I began to live only for myself."

"But what do you mean by living only for yourself?" asked Pierre, growing excited. "What about your son, your sister, and your father?"

"But that's just the same as myself—they are not *others*," explained Prince Andrew. "The others, one's neighbors, *le prochain*, as you and Princess Mary call it, are the chief source of all error and evil. *Le prochain*—your Kiev peasants to whom you want to do good."

And he looked at Pierre with a mocking, challenging expression. He evidently wished to draw him on.

"You are joking," replied Pierre, growing more and more excited. "What error or evil can there be in my wishing to do good, and even doing a little—though I did very little and did it very badly? What evil can there be in it if unfortunate people, our serfs, people like ourselves, were growing up and dying with no idea of God and truth beyond ceremonies and meaningless prayers and are now instructed in a comforting belief in future life, retribution, recompense, and consolation? What evil and error are there in it, if people were dying of disease without help while material assistance could so easily be rendered, and I supplied them with a doctor, a hospital, and an asylum for the aged? . . . And the main thing is," he continued, "that I know, and know for certain, that the enjoyment of doing this good is the only sure happiness in life."

"Yes, if you put it like that it's quite a different matter," said Prince Andrew. "I build a house and lay out a garden, and you build hospitals. The one and the other may serve as a pastime. But what's right and what's good must be judged by one who knows all, but not by us. Well, you want an argument," he added, "come on then."

They rose from the table and sat down in the entrance porch which served as a veranda.

"Come, let's argue then," said Prince Andrew. "You talk of schools," he went on, crooking a finger, "education and so forth; that is, you want to raise him" (pointing to a peasant who passed by them taking off his cap) "from his animal condition and awaken in him spiritual needs, while it seems to me that animal happiness is the only happiness possible, and that is just what you want to deprive him of. I envy him, but you want to make him what I am, without giving him my means. Then you say, 'lighten his toil.' But as I see it, physical labor is as essential to him, as much a condition of his existence, as mental activity is to you or me. You can't help thinking. I go to bed after two in the morning, thoughts come and I can't sleep but toss about till dawn, because I think and can't help thinking, just as he can't help plowing and mowing; if he didn't, he would go to the drink shop or fall ill. Just as I could not stand his terrible physical labor but should die of it in a week, so he could not stand my physical idleness, but would grow fat and die."

Prince Andrew expressed his ideas so clearly and distinctly that it was evident he had reflected on this subject more than once, and he spoke readily and rapidly like a man who has not talked for a long time. His glance became more animated as his conclusions became more hopeless.

"Oh, that is dreadful, dreadful!" said Pierre. "Why aren't you serving in the army?"

"After Austerlitz!" said Prince Andrew gloomily. "No, thank you very much! I have promised myself not to serve again in the active Russian army. And I won't—not even if Bonaparte were here at Smolénsk threatening Bald Hills—even then I wouldn't serve in the Russian army! Well, as I was saying," he continued, recovering his composure, "now there's this recruiting. My father is chief in command of the Third District, and my only way of avoiding active service is to serve under him."

Prince Andrew grew more and more animated. His eyes glittered feverishly while he tried to prove to Pierre that in his actions there was no desire to do good to his neighbor.

"There now, you wish to liberate your serfs," he continued; "that is a very good thing, but not for you—I don't suppose you ever had anyone flogged or sent to Siberia—and still less for your serfs. If they are beaten, flogged, or sent to Siberia, I don't suppose they are any the worse off. In Siberia they lead the same animal life, and the stripes on their bodies heal, and they are happy as before. But it is a good thing for proprietors who perish morally, bring remorse upon themselves, stifle this remorse and grow callous, as a result of being able to inflict punishments justly and unjustly. It is those people I pity, and for their sake I should like to liberate the serfs."

Prince Andrew spoke so earnestly that Pierre could not help thinking that these thoughts had been suggested to Prince Andrew by his father's case.

He did not reply.

"So that's what I'm sorry for—human dignity, peace of mind, purity, and not the serfs' backs and foreheads, which, beat and shave as you may, always remain the same backs and foreheads."

"No, no! A thousand times no! I shall never agree with you," said Pierre.

10

In the evening Andrew and Pierre got into the open carriage and drove to Bald Hills. Prince Andrew, glancing at Pierre, broke the silence now and then with remarks which showed that he was in a good temper.

Pierre remained gloomily silent, answering in monosyllables and apparently immersed in his own thoughts.

He was thinking that Prince Andrew was unhappy, had gone astray, did not see the true light, and that he, Pierre, ought to aid, enlighten, and raise him.

"No, but why do you think so?" Pierre suddenly began,

lowering his head and looking like a bull about to charge, "why do you think so? You should not think so."

"Think? What about?" asked Prince Andrew with surprise.

"About life, about man's destiny. It can't be so. I myself thought like that, and do you know what saved me? Freemasonry! No, don't smile. Freemasonry is not a religious ceremonial sect, as I thought it was: Freemasonry is the best expression of the best, the eternal, aspects of humanity."

And he began to explain Freemasonry as he understood it to Prince Andrew. He said that Freemasonry is the teaching of Christianity freed from the bonds of State and Church, a teaching of equality, brotherhood, and love.

Prince Andrew, looking straight in front of him, listened in silence to Pierre's words. More than once, when the noise of the wheels prevented his catching what Pierre said, he asked him to repeat it, and by the peculiar glow that came into Prince Andrew's eyes and by his silence, Pierre saw that his words were not in vain and that Prince Andrew would not interrupt him or laugh at what he said.

They reached a river that had overflowed its banks and which they had to cross by ferry.

Prince Andrew, leaning his arms on the raft railing, gazed silently at the flooding waters glittering in the setting sun.

"Well, what do you think about it?" Pierre asked. "Why are you silent?"

"What do I think about it? I am listening to you. It's all very well. . . . You say: join our brotherhood and we will show you the aim of life, the destiny of man, and the laws which govern the world. But who are *we?* Men. How is it you know everything? Why do I alone not see what you see? You see a reign of goodness and truth on earth, but I don't see it."

Pierre interrupted him.

"Do you believe in a future life?" he asked.

"A future life?" Prince Andrew repeated, but Pierre, giving him no time to reply, took the repetition for a denial, the more readily as he knew Prince Andrew's former atheistic convictions.

"You say you can't see a reign of goodness and truth on earth. Nor could I, and it cannot be seen if one looks on our life here as the end of everything. . . . Don't I feel in my soul that I am part of this vast harmonious whole? Don't I feel that I form one link, one step, between the lower and higher beings, in this vast harmonious multitude of beings in whom the Deity—the Supreme Power if you prefer the term—is manifest? . . . I feel that I cannot vanish, since nothing vanishes in this world, but that I shall always exist and always have existed. I feel that beyond me and above me there are spirits, and that in this world there is truth."

"Yes, that is Herder's theory," said Prince Andrew, "but it is not that which can convince me, dear friend—life and death are what convince. What convinces is when one sees a being dear to one, bound up with one's own life, before whom one was to blame and had hoped to make it right" (Prince Andrew's voice trembled and he turned away), "and suddenly that being is seized with pain, suffers, and ceases to exist. . . . Why? It cannot be that there is no answer. And I believe there is. . . . That's what convinces, that is what has convinced me," said Prince Andrew.

"Yes, yes, of course," said Pierre, "isn't that what I'm saying?"

"No. All I say is that it is not argument that convinces me of the necessity of a future life, but this: when you go hand in hand with someone and all at once that person vanishes *there, into nowhere,* and you yourself are left facing that abyss, and look in. And I have looked in. . . ."

"Well, that's it then! You know that there is a *there* and there is a *Someone? There* is the future life. The *Someone* is—God."

Prince Andrew did not reply. The carriage and horses had long since been taken off, onto the farther bank, and reharnessed. The sun had sunk half below the horizon and an evening frost was starring the puddles near the ferry, but Pierre and Andrew, to the astonishment of the footmen, coachmen, and ferrymen, still stood on the raft and talked.

"If there is a God and future life, there is truth and good, and man's highest happiness consists in striving to attain them. We must live, we must love, and we must believe that we live not only today on this scrap of earth, but have lived and shall live forever, there, in the Whole," said Pierre, and he pointed to the sky.

Prince Andrew stood leaning on the railing of the raft listening to Pierre, and he gazed with his eyes fixed on the red reflection of the sun gleaming on the blue waters. There was perfect stillness. Pierre became silent. The raft had long since stopped and only the waves of the current beat softly against it below. Prince Andrew felt as if the sound of the waves kept up a refrain to Pierre's words, whispering:

"It is true, believe it."

He sighed, and glanced with a radiant, childlike, tender look at Pierre's face, flushed and rapturous, but yet shy before his superior friend.

"Yes, if it only were so!" said Prince Andrew. "However, it is time to get on," he added, and, stepping off the raft, he looked up at the sky to which Pierre had pointed, and for the first time since Austerlitz saw that high, everlasting sky he had seen while lying on that battlefield; and something that had long been slumbering, something that was best within him, suddenly awoke, joyful and youthful, in his soul. It vanished as soon as he returned to the customary conditions of his life, but he knew that this feeling which he did not know how to develop existed within him. His meeting with Pierre formed an epoch in Prince Andrew's life. Though outwardly he continued to live in the same old way, inwardly he began a new life.

11

Pierre and Andrew at Bald Hills talk with some levity about miracles with "God's folk," the holy pilgrims whom Princess Mary protects and aids. Pierre, ashamed of his attitude, tries to placate one of the offended pilgrims.

12

The pilgrim woman was appeased. Prince Andrew went out of the room, and then, leaving "God's folk" to finish their tea, Princess Mary took Pierre into the drawing room.

"You are very kind," she said to him.

"Oh, I really did not mean to hurt her feelings. I understand them so well and have the greatest respect for them."

Princess Mary looked at him silently and smiled affectionately.

"I have known you a long time, you see, and am as fond of you as of a brother," she said. "How do you find Andrew?" she added hurriedly, not giving him time to reply to her affectionate words. "I am very anxious about him. His health was better in the winter, but last spring his wound reopened and the doctor said he ought to go away for a cure. And I am also very much afraid for him spiritually. He has not a character like us women who, when we suffer, can weep away our sorrows. He keeps it all within him. Today he is cheerful and in good spirits, but that is the effect of your visit—he is not often like that. If you could persuade him to go abroad. He needs activity, and this quiet regular life is very bad for him. Others don't notice it, but I see it."

Toward ten o'clock the menservants rushed to the front door, hearing the bells of the old prince's carriage approaching. Prince Andrew and Pierre also went out into the porch.

"Who's that?" asked the old prince, noticing Pierre as he got out of the carriage.

"Ah! Very glad! Kiss me," he said, having learned who the young stranger was.

The old prince was in a good temper and very gracious to Pierre.

Before supper, Prince Andrew, coming back to his father's study, found him disputing hotly with his visitor. Pierre was maintaining that a time would come when there would be no more wars. The old prince disputed it chaffingly, but without getting angry.

"Well, my boy," the old prince went on, addressing his son and patting Pierre on the shoulder. "A fine fellow—your friend—I like him! He stirs me up. Another says clever things and one doesn't care to listen, but this one talks rubbish yet stirs an old fellow up. Well, go! Get along! Perhaps I'll come and sit with you at supper. We'll have another dispute. Make friends with my little fool, Princess Mary," he shouted after Pierre, through the door.

Only now, on his visit to Bald Hills, did Pierre fully

realize the strength and charm of his friendship with Prince Andrew. That charm was not expressed so much in his relations with him as with all his family and with the household. With the stern old prince and the gentle, timid Princess Mary, though he had scarcely known them, Pierre at once felt like an old friend. They were all fond of him already.

The old prince came in to supper; this was evidently on Pierre's account. And during the two days of the young man's visit he was extremely kind to him and told him to visit them again.

When Pierre had gone and the members of the household met together, they began to express their opinions of him as people always do after a new acquaintance has left, but as seldom happens, no one said anything but what was good of him.

13

When returning from his leave, Rostóv felt, for the first time, how close was the bond that united him to Denísov and the whole regiment.

On approaching it, Rostóv felt as he had when approaching his home in Moscow. When he saw the first hussar with the unbuttoned uniform of his regiment, when he recognized red-haired Deméntyev and saw the picket ropes of the roan horses, when Lavrúshka gleefully shouted to his master, "The count has come!" and Denísov, who had been asleep on his bed, ran all disheveled out of the mud hut to embrace him, and the officers collected round to greet the new arrival, Rostóv experienced the same feeling as when his mother, his father, and his sister had embraced him, and tears of joy choked him so that he could not speak. The regiment was also a home, and as unalterably dear and precious as his parents' house.

Having once more entered into the definite conditions of this regimental life, Rostóv felt the joy and relief a tired man feels on lying down to rest. Life in the regiment, during this campaign, was all the pleasanter for him, because, after his loss to Dólokhov (for which, in spite of all his family's efforts to console him, he could not forgive himself), he had made up his mind to atone for his fault by serving, not as he had done before, but really well, and by being a perfectly first-rate comrade and officer—in a word, a splendid man altogether, a thing which seemed so difficult out *in the world*, but so possible in the regiment.

After his losses, he had determined to pay back his debt to his parents in five years. He received ten thousand rubles a year, but now resolved to take only two thousand and leave the rest to repay the debt to his parents.

Our army, after repeated retreats and advances and battles at Pultúsk and Preussisch-Eylau, was concentrated near Bartenstein. It was awaiting the Emperor's arrival and the beginning of a new campaign.

The Pávlograd regiment, belonging to that part of the army which had served in the 1805 campaign, had been recruiting up to strength in Russia, and arrived too late to take part in the first actions of the campaign. It had been neither at Pultúsk nor at Preussisch-Eylau and, when it joined the army in the field in the second half of the campaign, was attached to Plátov's division.

Plátov's division was acting independently of the main army. Several times parts of the Pávlograd regiment had exchanged shots with the enemy, had taken prisoners, and once had even captured Marshal Oudinot's carriages. In April the Pávlograds were stationed immovably for some weeks near a totally ruined and deserted German village.

A thaw had set in, it was muddy and cold, the ice on the river broke, and the roads became impassable. For days neither provisions for the men nor fodder for the horses had been issued. As no transports could arrive, the men dispersed about the abandoned and deserted villages, searching for potatoes, but found few even of these.

Everything had been eaten up and the inhabitants had all fled—if any remained, they were worse than beggars and nothing more could be taken from them; even the soldiers, usually pitiless enough, instead of taking anything from them, often gave them the last of their rations.

Rostóv lived, as before, with Denísov, and since their furlough they had become more friendly than ever. Denísov never spoke of Rostóv's family, but by the tender friendship his commander showed him, Rostóv felt that the elder hussar's luckless love for Natásha played a part in strengthening their friendship. Denísov evidently tried to expose Rostóv to danger as seldom as possible, and after an action greeted his safe return with evident joy. On one of his foraging expeditions, in a deserted and ruined village to which he had come in search of provisions, Rostóv found a family consisting of an old Pole and his daughter with an infant in arms. They were half clad, hungry, too weak to get away on foot and had no means of obtaining a conveyance. Rostóv brought them to his quarters, placed them in his own lodging, and kept them for some weeks while the old man was recovering. One of his comrades, talking of women, began chaffing Rostóv, saying that he was more wily than any of them and that it would not be a bad thing if he introduced to them the pretty Polish girl he had saved. Rostóv took the joke as an insult, flared up, and said such unpleasant things to the officer that it was all Denísov could do to prevent a duel. When the officer had gone away, Denísov, who did not himself know what Rostóv's relations with the Polish girl might be, began to upbraid him for his quickness of temper, and Rostóv replied:

"Say what you like. . . . She is like a sister to me, and I can't tell you how it offended me . . . because . . . well, for that reason. . . ."

Denísov patted him on the shoulder and began rapidly pacing the room without looking at Rostóv, as was his way at moments of deep feeling.

"Ah, what a mad bweed you Wostóvs are!" he muttered, and Rostóv noticed tears in his eyes.

14

Furious over the undernourished condition of his hussars, Denísov forcibly appropriates a transport of food consigned to the infantry and uses his fists when called to account for it by the commissariat. Threatened with a court-martial, he seeks escape in hospitalization after a slight leg wound in a skirmish with the French.

15

In June the battle of Friedland was fought, in which the Pávlograds did not take part, and after that an armistice was proclaimed. Rostóv, who felt his friend's absence very much, having no news of him since he left and feeling very anxious about his wound and the progress of his affairs, took advantage of the armistice to get leave to visit Denísov in the hospital.

The hospital was in a small Prussian town that had been twice devastated by Russian and French troops.

Directly Rostóv entered the door he was enveloped by a smell of putrefaction and hospital air. On the stairs he met a Russian army doctor smoking a cigar. The doctor was followed by a Russian assistant.

Rostóv explained that he wanted to see Major Denísov of the hussars, who was wounded.

"I don't know. I can't tell you, sir. Only think! I am alone in charge of three hospitals with more than four hundred patients!"

"Major Denísov," Rostóv said again. "He was wounded at Molliten."

"Dead, I fancy. Eh, Makéev?" queried the doctor, in a tone of indifference.

The assistant, however, did not confirm the doctor's words. Rostóv described Denísov's appearance.

"There was one like that," said the doctor, as if pleased. "That one is dead, I fancy. However, I'll look up our list. We had a list. Have you got it, Makéev?"

"Makár Alexéevich has the list," answered the assistant. "But if you'll step into the officers' wards you'll see for yourself," he added, turning to Rostóv.

"Ah, you'd better not go, sir," said the doctor, "or you may have to stay here yourself."

But Rostóv bowed himself away from the doctor and asked the assistant to show him the way.

Rostóv and the assistant went into the dark corridor. The smell was so strong there that Rostóv held his nose and had to pause and collect his strength before he could go on.

Glancing in at the door, Rostóv saw that the sick and wounded were lying on the floor on straw and overcoats.

"May I go in and look?"

"What is there to see?" said the assistant.

But, just because the assistant evidently did not want him to go in, Rostóv entered the soldiers' ward. The foul air, to which he had already begun to get used in the corridor, was still stronger here. It was a little different, more pungent, and one felt that this was where it originated.

In the long room, brightly lit up by the sun through the large windows, the sick and wounded lay in two rows with their heads to the walls, and leaving a passage in the middle. Most of them were unconscious and paid no attention to the newcomers. Just before him, almost across the middle of the passage on the bare floor, lay a sick man, probably a Cossack to judge by the cut of his hair. The man lay on his back, his huge arms and legs outstretched. His face was purple, his eyes were rolled back so that only the whites were seen, and on his bare legs and arms which were still red, the veins stood out like cords. He was knocking the back of his head against the floor, hoarsely uttering some word which he kept repeating. Rostóv listened and made out the word. It was "drink, drink, a drink!" Rostóv glanced round, looking for someone who would put this man back in his place and bring him water.

"Who looks after the sick here?" he asked the assistant.

Just then a commissariat soldier, a hospital orderly, came in from the next room, marching stiffly, and drew up in front of Rostóv.

"Good day, your honor!" he shouted, rolling his eyes at Rostóv and evidently mistaking him for one of the hospital authorities.

"Get him to his place and give him some water," said Rostóv, pointing to the Cossack.

"Yes, your honor," the soldier replied complacently, and rolling his eyes more than ever he drew himself up still straighter, but did not move.

"No, it's impossible to do anything here," thought Rostóv, lowering his eyes.

Going along the corridor, the assistant led Rostóv to the

officers' wards, consisting of three rooms, the doors of which stood open. There were beds in these rooms and the sick and wounded officers were lying or sitting on them. Some were walking about the rooms in hospital dressing gowns. The first person Rostóv met in the officers' ward was a thin little man with one arm, who was walking about the first room in a nightcap and hospital dressing gown, with a pipe between his teeth. Rostóv looked at him, trying to remember where he had seen him before.

"See where we've met again!" said the little man. "Túshin, Túshin, don't you remember, who gave you a lift at Schön Grabern? And I've had a bit cut off, you see . . ." he went on with a smile, pointing to the empty sleeve of his dressing gown. "Looking for Vasíli Dmítrich Denísov? My neighbor," he added, when he heard who Rostóv wanted. "Here, here," and Túshin led him into the next room, from whence came sounds of several laughing voices.

"How can they laugh, or even live at all here?" thought Rostóv, still aware of that smell of decomposing flesh that had been so strong in the soldiers' ward, and still seeming to see fixed on him those envious looks which had followed him out from both sides.

Denísov lay asleep on his bed with his head under the blanket, though it was nearly noon.

"Ah, Wostóv? How are you, how are you?" he called out, still in the same voice as in the regiment, but Rostóv noticed sadly that under this habitual ease and animation some new, sinister, hidden feeling showed itself in the expression of Denísov's face and the intonations of his voice.

His wound, though a slight one, had not yet healed even now, six weeks after he had been hit.

Rostóv even noticed that Denísov did not like to be reminded of the regiment, or in general of that other free life which was going on outside the hospital. He seemed to try to forget that old life and was only interested in the affair with the commissariat officers. On Rostóv's inquiry as to how the matter stood, he at once produced from under his pillow a paper he had received from the commission and the rough draft of his answer to it. He became animated when he began reading his paper and specially drew Rostóv's attention to the stinging rejoinders he made to his enemies. His hospital companions, who had gathered round Rostóv—a fresh arrival from the world outside—gradually began to disperse as soon as Denísov began reading his answer. Rostóv noticed by their faces that all those gentlemen had already heard that story more than once and were tired of it. Only the man who had the next bed, a stout Uhlan, continued to sit on his bed, gloomily frowning and smoking a pipe, and little one-armed Túshin still listened, shaking his head disapprovingly. In the middle of the reading, the Uhlan interrupted Denísov.

"But what I say is," he said, turning to Rostóv, "it would be best simply to petition the Emperor for pardon. They say great rewards will now be distributed, and surely a pardon would be granted. . . ."

"Me petition the Empewo'l!" exclaimed Denísov, in a voice to which he tried hard to give the old energy and fire, but which sounded like an expression of irritable impotence. "What for? If I were a wobber I would ask mercy, but I'm being court-martialed for bwinging wobbers to book. Let them twy me, I'm not afwaid of anyone. I've served the Tsar and my countwy honowably and have not stolen! And am I to be degwaded? . . . Listen, I'm w'iting to them stwaight. This is what I say: 'If I had wobbed the Tweasuwy . . .'"

"It's certainly well written," said Túshin, "but that's not the point, Vasíli Dmítrich," and he also turned to Rostóv. "One has to submit, and Vasíli Dmítrich doesn't want to. You know the auditor told you it was a bad business."

"Well, let it be bad," said Denísov.

"The auditor wrote out a petition for you," continued Túshin, "and you ought to sign it and ask this gentleman to take it. No doubt he" (indicating Rostóv) "has connections on the staff. You won't find a better opportunity."

"Haven't I said I'm not going to gwovel?" Denísov interrupted him, and went on reading his paper.

When the reading of Denísov's virulent reply, which took more than an hour, was over, Rostóv said nothing, and he spent the rest of the day in a most dejected state of mind amid Denísov's hospital comrades, who had gathered round him, telling them what he knew and listening to their stories. Denísov was moodily silent all the evening.

Late in the evening, when Rostóv was about to leave, he asked Denísov whether he had no commission for him.

"Yes, wait a bit," said Denísov, glancing round at the officers, and taking his papers from under his pillow he went to the window, where he had an inkpot, and sat down to write.

"It seems it's no use knocking one's head against a wall!" he said, coming from the window and giving Rostóv a large envelope. In it was the petition to the Emperor drawn up by the auditor, in which Denísov, without alluding to the offenses of the commissariat officials, simply asked for pardon.

"Hand it in. It seems . . ."

He did not finish, but gave a painfully unnatural smile.

16

Having returned to the regiment and told the commander the state of Denísov's affairs, Rostóv rode to Tilsit with the letter to the Emperor.

On the thirteenth of June the French and Russian Emperors arrived in Tilsit. Borís Drubetskóy had asked the important personage on whom he was in attendance to include him in the suite appointed for the stay at Tilsit.

Borís was among the few present at the Niemen on the day the two Emperors met. He saw the raft, decorated with monograms, saw Napoleon pass before the French Guards on the farther bank of the river, saw the pensive face of the Emperor Alexander as he sat in silence in a tavern on the bank of the Niemen awaiting Napoleon's arrival, saw both Emperors get into boats, and saw how Napoleon—reaching the raft first—stepped quickly forward to meet Alexander and held out his hand to him, and how they both retired into the pavilion. Since he had begun to move in the highest circles Borís had made it his habit to watch attentively all that went on around him and to note it down. He had not only become known, but people had grown accustomed to him and accepted him. Twice he had executed commissions to the Emperor himself, so that the latter knew his face, and all those at court, far from cold-shouldering him as at first when they considered him a newcomer, would now have been surprised had he been absent.

Borís lodged with another adjutant, the Polish Count Zhilínski. Zhilínski, a Pole brought up in Paris, was rich, and passionately fond of the French, and almost every day of the stay at Tilsit, French officers of the Guard and from French headquarters were dining and lunching with him and Borís.

On the evening of the twenty-fourth of June, Count Zhilínski arranged a supper for his French friends. The guest of honor was an aide-de-camp of Napoleon's, there were also several French officers of the Guard, and a page of Napoleon's, a young lad of an old aristocratic French family. That same day, Rostóv, profiting by the darkness to avoid being recognized in civilian dress, came to Tilsit and went to the lodging occupied by Borís and Zhilínski.

Rostóv, in common with the whole army from which he came, was far from having experienced the change of feeling toward Napoleon and the French—who from being foes had suddenly become friends—that had taken place at headquarters and in Borís. In the army, Bonaparte and the French were still regarded with mingled feelings of anger, contempt, and fear. Rostóv was therefore unpleasantly struck by the presence of French officers in Borís' lodging, dressed in uniforms he had been accustomed to see from quite a different point of view from the outposts of the flank. He stopped at the threshold and asked in Russian whether Drubetskóy lived there. Borís, hearing a strange voice in the anteroom, came out to meet him. An expression of annoyance showed itself for a moment on his face on first recognizing Rostóv.

"Ah, it's you? Very glad, very glad to see you," he said, however, coming toward him with a smile. But Rostóv had noticed his first impulse.

"I've come at a bad time I think. I should not have come, but I have business," he said coldly.

"Oh, come now! As if you could come at a wrong time!" said Borís, and he led him into the room where the supper table was laid and introduced him to his guests, explaining that he was not a civilian, but an hussar officer, and an old friend of his.

Rostóv had been out of humor from the moment he noticed

the look of dissatisfaction on Borís' face, and as always happens to those in a bad humor, it seemed to him that everyone regarded him with aversion and that he was in everybody's way. He really was in their way, for he alone took no part in the conversation which again became general. The looks the visitors cast on him seemed to say: "And what is he sitting here for?" He rose and went up to Borís.

"Anyhow, I'm in your way," he said in a low tone. "Come and talk over my business and I'll go away."

"Oh, no, not at all," said Borís. "But if you are tired, come and lie down in my room and have a rest."

"Yes, really . . ."

They went into the little room where Borís slept. Rostóv, without sitting down, began at once, irritably (as if Borís were to blame in some way) telling him about Denísov's affair, asking him whether, through his general, he could and would intercede with the Emperor on Denísov's behalf and get Denísov's petition handed in.

"I have heard of such cases and know that His Majesty is very severe in such affairs. I think it would be best not to bring it before the Emperor, but to apply to the commander of the corps. . . . But in general, I think . . ."

"So you don't want to do anything? Well then, say so!" Rostóv almost shouted, not looking Borís in the face.

Borís smiled.

"On the contrary, I will do what I can. Only I thought . . ."

At that moment Zhilínski's voice was heard calling Borís.

"Well then, go, go, go . . ." said Rostóv, and refusing supper and remaining alone in the little room, he walked up and down for a long time, hearing the lighthearted French conversation from the next room.

17

Rostóv had come to Tilsit on the day least suitable for a petition on Denísov's behalf. He could not himself go to the general in attendance as he was in mufti and had come to Tilsit without permission to do so, and Borís, even had he wished to, could not have done so on the following day. On that day, June 27, the preliminaries of peace were signed.

Rostóv felt so ill at ease and uncomfortable with Borís that, when the latter looked in after supper, he pretended to be asleep, and early next morning went away, avoiding Borís.

"Borís doesn't want to help me and I don't want to ask him. That's settled," thought Nicholas. "All is over between us, but I won't leave here without having done all I can for Denísov and certainly not without getting his letter to the Emperor. The Emperor! . . . He is here!" thought Rostóv, who had unconsciously returned to the house where Alexander lodged.

Saddled horses were standing before the house and the suite were assembling, evidently preparing for the Emperor to come out.

"I may see him at any moment," thought Rostóv. "If only I were to hand the letter direct to him and tell him all . . . could they really arrest me for my civilian clothes? Surely not! He would understand on whose side justice lies. He understands everything, knows everything. Who can be more just, more magnanimous than he? And even if they did arrest me for being here, what would it matter?" thought he, looking at an officer who was entering the house the Emperor occupied. "After all, people do go in. . . . It's all nonsense! I'll go in and hand the letter to the Emperor myself, so much the worse for Drubetskóy who drives me to it!" And suddenly with a determination he himself did not expect, Rostóv felt for the letter in his pocket and went straight to the house.

A broad staircase led straight up from the entry, and to the right he saw a closed door. Below, under the staircase, was a door leading to the lower floor.

"Whom do you want?" someone inquired.

"To hand in a letter, a petition, to His Majesty," said Nicholas, with a tremor in his voice.

"A petition? This way, to the officer on duty" (he was shown the door leading downstairs), "only it won't be accepted."

On hearing this indifferent voice, Rostóv grew frightened at what he was doing.

Cursing his temerity, his heart sinking at the thought of finding himself at any moment face to face with the Emperor and being put to shame and arrested in his presence, fully alive now to the impropriety of his conduct and repenting of it, Rostóv, with downcast eyes, was making his way out of the house through the brilliant suite when a familiar voice called him and a hand detained him.

"What are you doing here, sir, in civilian dress?" asked a deep voice.

It was a cavalry general who had obtained the Emperor's special favor during this campaign, and who had formerly commanded the division in which Rostóv was serving.

Rostóv, in dismay, began justifying himself, but seeing the kindly, jocular face of the general, he took him aside and in an excited voice told him the whole affair, asking him to intercede for Denísov, whom the general knew. Having heard Rostóv to the end, the general shook his head gravely.

"I'm sorry, sorry for that fine fellow. Give me the letter."

Hardly had Rostóv handed him the letter and finished explaining Denísov's case, when hasty steps and the jingling of spurs were heard on the stairs, and the general, leaving him, went to the porch. The gentlemen of the Emperor's suite ran down the stairs and went to their horses. Forgetting the danger of being recognized, Rostóv went close to the porch, together with some inquisitive civilians, and again, after two years, saw those features he adored: that same face and same look and step, and the same union of majesty and mildness. . . . And the feeling of enthusiasm and love for his sovereign rose again in Rostóv's soul in all its old force. In the uniform of the Preobrazhénsk regiment—white chamoisleather breeches and high boots—and wearing a star Rostóv did not know (it was that of the *Légion d'honneur*), the monarch came out into the porch, putting on his gloves and carrying his hat under his arm. He stopped and looked about him, brightening everything around by his glance. He spoke a few words to some of the generals, and recognizing the former commander of Rostóv's division, smiled and beckoned to him.

All the suite drew back and Rostóv saw the general talking for some time to the Emperor.

The Emperor said a few words to him and took a step

toward his horse. Again the crowd of members of the suite and street gazers (among whom was Rostóv) moved nearer to the Emperor. Stopping beside his horse, with his hand on the saddle, the Emperor turned to the cavalry general and said in a loud voice, evidently wishing to be heard by all:

"I cannot do it, General. I cannot, because the law is stronger than I," and he raised his foot to the stirrup.

The general bowed his head respectfully, and the monarch mounted and rode down the street at a gallop. Beside himself with enthusiasm, Rostóv ran after him with the crowd.

18

The Emperor rode to the square where, facing one another, a battalion of the Preobrazhénsk regiment stood on the right and a battalion of the French Guards in their bearskin caps on the left.

As the Tsar rode up to one flank of the battalions, which presented arms, another group of horsemen galloped up to the opposite flank, and at the head of them Rostóv recognized Napoleon. It could be no one else. He came at a gallop, wearing a small hat, a blue uniform open over a white vest, and the St. Andrew ribbon over his shoulder. He was riding a very fine thoroughbred gray Arab horse with a crimson gold-embroidered saddlecloth. On approaching Alexander he raised his hat, and as he did so, Rostóv, with his cavalryman's eye, could not help noticing that Napoleon did not sit well or firmly in the saddle. The battalions shouted "Hurrah!" and *"Vive l'Empereur!"* Napoleon said something to Alexander, and both Emperors dismounted and took each other's hands. Napoleon's face wore an unpleasant and artificial smile. Alexander was saying something affable to him.

In spite of the trampling of the French gendarmes' horses, which were pushing back the crowd, Rostóv kept his eyes on every movement of Alexander and Bonaparte. It struck him as a surprise that Alexander treated Bonaparte as an equal and that the latter was quite at ease with the Tsar, as if such relations with an Emperor were an everyday matter to him.

Napoleon publicly decorates a Russian soldier, Lázarev, with the Legion of Honor. After the ceremony the two emperors depart, and the Preobrazhénsk battalion and the French Guards sit down to a banquet together.

Borís, too, with his friend Zhilínski, came to see the Preobrazhénsk banquet. On his way back, he noticed Rostóv standing by the corner of a house.

"Rostóv! How d'you do? We missed one another," he said, and could not refrain from asking what was the matter, so strangely dismal and troubled was Rostóv's face.

"Nothing, nothing," replied Rostóv.

"You'll call round?"

"Yes, I will."

Rostóv stood at that corner for a long time, watching the feast from a distance. In his mind, a painful process was going on which he could not bring to a conclusion. Terrible doubts rose in his soul. Now he remembered Denísov with his changed expression, his submission, and the whole hospital, with arms and legs torn off and its dirt and disease. So vividly did he recall that hospital stench of dead flesh that he looked round to see where the smell came from. Next he thought of that self-satisfied Bonaparte, with his small white hand, who was now an Emperor, liked and respected by Alexander. Then why those severed arms and legs and those dead men? . . . Then again he thought of Lázarev rewarded and Denísov punished and unpardoned. He caught himself harboring such strange thoughts that he was frightened.

The smell of the food the Preobrazhénskis were eating and a sense of hunger recalled him from these reflections; he had to get something to eat before going away. He went to a hotel he had noticed that morning. There he found so many people, among them officers who, like himself, had come in civilian clothes, that he had difficulty in getting a dinner. Two officers of his own division joined him. The conversation naturally turned on the peace. The officers, his comrades, like most of the army, were dissatisfied with the peace concluded after the battle of Friedland. They said that had we held out a little longer Napoleon would have been done for, as his troops had neither provisions nor ammunition. Nicholas ate and drank (chiefly the latter) in silence. He finished a couple of bottles of wine by himself. The process in his mind went on tormenting him without reaching a conclusion. He feared to give way to his thoughts, yet could not get rid of them. Suddenly, on one of the officers' saying that it was humiliating to look at the French, Rostóv began shouting with uncalled-for wrath, and therefore much to the surprise of the officers:

"How can you judge what's best?" he cried, the blood suddenly rushing to his face. "How can you judge the Emperor's actions? What right have we to argue? We cannot comprehend either the Emperor's aims or his actions!"

"But I never said a word about the Emperor!" said the officer, justifying himself, and unable to understand Rostóv's outburst, except on the supposition that he was drunk.

But Rostóv did not listen to him.

"We are not diplomatic officials, we are soldiers and nothing more," he went on. "If we are ordered to die, we must die. If we're punished, it means that we have deserved it, it's not for us to judge. If the Emperor pleases to recognize Bonaparte as Emperor and to conclude an alliance with him, it means that that is the right thing to do. If once we begin judging and arguing about everything, nothing sacred will be left! That way we shall be saying there is no God—nothing!" shouted Nicholas, banging the table—very little to the point as it seemed to his listeners, but quite relevantly to the course of his own thoughts.

"Our business is to do our duty, to fight and not to think! That's all. . . ." said he.

"And to drink," said one of the officers, not wishing to quarrel.

"Yes, and to drink," assented Nicholas. "Hullo there! Another bottle!" he shouted.

1808-10

〓━━〓〓〓━━〓〓〓━━〓〓〓━━〓〓〓━━〓

BOOK SIX

1

In 1808 the Emperor Alexander went to Erfurt for a fresh interview with the Emperor Napoleon, and in the upper circles of Petersburg there was much talk of the grandeur of this important meeting.

Life meanwhile—real life, with its essential interests of health and sickness, toil and rest, and its intellectual interests in thought, science, poetry, music, love, friendship, hatred, and passions—went on as usual, independently of and apart from political friendship or enmity with Napoleon Bonaparte and from all the schemes of reconstruction.

Prince Andrew had spent two years continuously in the country.

All the plans Pierre had attempted on his estates—and constantly changing from one thing to another had never accomplished—were carried out by Prince Andrew without display and without perceptible difficulty.

He had in the highest degree a practical tenacity which Pierre lacked, and without fuss or strain on his part this set things going.

In the spring of 1809 he went to visit the Ryazán estates which had been inherited by his son, whose guardian he was.

Warmed by the spring sunshine he sat in the *calèche* looking at the new grass, the first leaves on the birches, and the first puffs of white spring clouds floating across the clear blue sky. He was not thinking of anything, but looked absent-mindedly and cheerfully from side to side.

At the edge of the road stood an oak. With its huge ungainly limbs sprawling unsymmetrically, and its gnarled hands and fingers, it stood an aged, stern, and scornful monster among the smiling birch trees.

"Spring, love, happiness!" this oak seemed to say. "Are you not weary of that stupid, meaningless, constantly repeated fraud."

As he passed through the forest Prince Andrew turned several times to look at that oak, as if expecting something from it.

"Yes, the oak is right, a thousand times right," thought Prince Andrew. "Let others—the young—yield afresh to that fraud, but we know life, our life is finished!"

Prince Andrew had to see the Marshal of the Nobility for the district in connection with the affairs of the Ryazán estate of which he was trustee. This Marshal was Count Ilyá Rostóv, and in the middle of May Prince Andrew went to visit him.

In 1809 Count Ilyá Rostóv was living at Otrádnoe just as he had done in former years, that is, entertaining almost the whole province with hunts, theatricals, dinners, and music. He was glad to see Prince Andrew, as he was to see any new visitor, and insisted on his staying the night.

During the dull day, in the course of which he was entertained by his elderly hosts and by the more important of the visitors (the old count's house was crowded on account of an approaching name day), Prince Andrew repeatedly glanced at Natásha, gay and laughing among the younger members of the company, and asked himself each time, "What is she thinking about? Why is she so glad?"

That night, alone in new surroundings, he was long unable to sleep. He got up and went to the window to open it. As soon as he opened the shutters the moonlight, as if it had been watching for this, burst into the room. He opened the casement. The night was fresh, bright, and very still. Prince Andrew leaned his elbows on the window ledge and his eyes rested on the sky.

His room was on the first floor. Those in the rooms above were also awake. He heard female voices overhead.

"Just once more," said a girlish voice above him which Prince Andrew recognized at once.

"But when are you coming to bed?" replied another voice.

"Sónya! Sónya!" he again heard the first speaker. "Oh, how

can you sleep? Only look how glorious it is! Ah, how glorious!
Do wake up, Sónya!" she said almost with tears in her voice.
"There never, never was such a lovely night before!"

Sónya made some reluctant reply.

"Do just come and see what a moon! . . . Oh, how lovely!
Come here. . . . Darling, sweetheart, come here! There, you
see? I feel like sitting down on my heels, putting my arms
around my knees like this, straining tight, as tight as possible,
and flying away! Like this. . . ."

"Take care, you'll fall out."

He heard the sound of a scuffle and Sónya's disapproving
voice: "It's past one o'clock."

"Oh, you only spoil things for me. All right, go, go!"

Again all was silent, but Prince Andrew knew she was still
sitting there. From time to time he heard a soft rustle and at
times a sigh.

"O God, O God! What does it mean?" she suddenly exclaimed. "To bed then, if it must be!" and she slammed the
casement.

"For her I might as well not exist!" thought Prince Andrew
while he listened to her voice, for some reason expecting yet
fearing that she might say something about him.

In his soul there suddenly arose such an unexpected turmoil
of youthful thoughts and hopes, contrary to the whole tenor
of his life, that unable to explain his condition to himself he
lay down and fell asleep at once.

Next morning, having taken leave of no one but the count,
and not waiting for the ladies to appear, Prince Andrew set off
for home.

It was already the beginning of June when on his return
journey he drove into the birch forest where the gnarled old
oak had made so strange and memorable an impression on
him.

"Yes, here in this forest was that oak with which I agreed,"
thought Prince Andrew. "But where is it?" he again wondered,
gazing at the left side of the road, and without recognizing it
he looked with admiration at the very oak he sought. The old
oak, quite transfigured, spreading out a canopy of sappy dark-
green foliage, stood rapt and slightly trembling in the rays of
the evening sun.

"Yes, it is the same oak," thought Prince Andrew, and all at once he was seized by an unreasoning springtime feeling of joy and renewal. All the best moments of his life suddenly rose to his memory. Austerlitz with the lofty heavens, his wife's dead reproachful face, Pierre at the ferry, that girl thrilled by the beauty of the night, and that night itself and the moon, and . . . all this rushed suddenly to his mind.

"No, life is not over at thirty-one!" Prince Andrew suddenly decided finally and decisively. "It is not enough for me to know what I have in me—everyone must know it: Pierre, and that young girl who wanted to fly away into the sky, everyone must know me, so that my life may not be lived for myself alone while others live so apart from it, but so that it may be reflected in them all, and they and I may live in harmony!"

On reaching home Prince Andrew decided to go to Petersburg that autumn and found all sorts of reasons for this decision. A whole series of sensible and logical considerations showing it to be essential for him to go to Petersburg, and even to re-enter the service, kept springing up in his mind. He could not now understand how he could ever even have doubted the necessity of taking an active share in life, just as a month before he had not understood how the idea of leaving the quiet country could ever enter his head. It now seemed clear to him that all his experience of life must be senselessly wasted unless he applied it to some kind of work and again played an active part in life.

2

In Petersburg Prince Andrew, with his new zeal to re-enter the service, offers a proposal for the reform of army regulations to the Minister of War, Count Aléxey Arak-chéev, who appoints him to the Committee of Army Regulations; and he meets and admires the Emperor's intimate adviser and reformist statesman, Count. M. M. Speránski, who makes him Chairman of a section of the committee for the revision of the laws.

3

Though Pierre works hard at Freemasonry, he cannot resist the temptations of his former life. He tends to ascribe his failure to the emphasis on externals in Russian Masonry, and he seeks wisdom from Masonic lodges abroad. But when he delivers a speech to his fellow Russian Masons on the necessity for action in order to obtain the victory of virtue over vice, he is denounced.

Again Pierre was overtaken by the depression he so dreaded. For three days after the delivery of his speech at the lodge he lay on a sofa at home receiving no one and going nowhere.

It was just then that he received a letter from his wife, who implored him to see her, telling him how grieved she was about him and how she wished to devote her whole life to him.

At the end of the letter she informed him that in a few days she would return to Petersburg from abroad.

Following this letter one of the Masonic Brothers whom Pierre respected less than the others forced his way in to see him and, turning the conversation upon Pierre's matrimonial affairs, by way of fraternal advice expressed the opinion that his severity to his wife was wrong and that he was neglecting one of the first rules of Freemasonry by not forgiving the penitent.

At the same time his mother-in-law, Prince Vasíli's wife, sent to him imploring him to come if only for a few minutes to discuss a most important matter. Pierre saw that there was a conspiracy against him and that they wanted to reunite him with his wife, and in the mood he then was, this was not even unpleasant to him.

"No one is right and no one is to blame; so she too is not to blame," he thought.

Without replying either to his wife or his mother-in-law, Pierre late one night prepared for a journey and started for Moscow to see Joseph Alexéevich. This is what he noted in his diary:

Moscow, 17th November

I have just returned from my benefactor, and hasten to write down what I have experienced. Joseph Alexéevich is living poorly and has for three years been suffering from a painful disease of the bladder. No one has ever heard him utter a groan or a word of complaint. From morning till late at night, except when he eats his very plain food, he is working at science. He received me graciously and made me sit down on the bed on which he lay. I told him everything as best I could, and told him what I had proposed to our Petersburg lodge, of the bad reception I had encountered, and of my rupture with the Brothers. Joseph Alexéevich, having remained silent and thoughtful for a good while, told me his view of the matter, which at once lit up for me my whole past and the future path I should follow. Joseph Alexéevich condemned my speech and my whole activity, and in the depth of my soul I agreed with him. Talking of my family affairs he said to me, "the chief duty of a true Mason, as I have told you, lies in perfecting himself." He advised me not to avoid intercourse with the Petersburg Brothers, but to take up only second grade posts in the lodge, to try, while diverting the Brothers from pride, to turn them toward the true path of self-knowledge and self-perfecting. Besides this he advised me for myself personally above all to keep a watch over myself, and to that end he gave me a notebook, the one I am now writing in and in which I will in future note down all my actions.

Petersburg, 23rd November

I am again living with my wife. My mother-in-law came to me in tears and said that Hélène was here and that she implored me to hear her; that she was innocent and unhappy at my desertion, and much more. I knew that if I once let myself see her I should not have strength to go on refusing what she wanted. In my perplexity I did not know whose aid and advice to seek. Had my benefactor been here he would have told me what to do. I went to my room and reread Joseph Alexéevich's letters and recalled my conversations with him, and deduced from it all that I ought not to refuse a suppliant, and ought to reach a helping hand to everyone—especially to one so closely bound to me—and that I must bear my cross. But if I forgive her for the sake of doing right, then let union with her have only a spiritual aim. That is what I decided, and what I wrote to Joseph Alexéevich. I told my wife that I begged her to forget the past, to forgive me whatever wrong I may have done her, and that I had nothing to forgive. It gave me joy to tell her this. She need not know how hard it was for me to see her again. I have settled on the upper floor of this big house and am experiencing a happy feeling of regeneration.

4

At that time, as always happens, the highest society that met at court and at the grand balls was divided into several circles, each with its own particular tone. The largest of these was the French circle of the Napoleonic alliance, the circle of Count Rumyántsev and Caulaincourt. In this group Hélène, as soon as she had settled in Petersburg with her husband, took a very prominent place.

Her success as a beautiful and elegant woman did not surprise Pierre, for she had become even handsomer than before. What did surprise him was that during these last two years his wife had succeeded in gaining the reputation of a charming woman, as witty as she was lovely. Pierre, who knew she was very stupid, sometimes attended, with a strange feeling of perplexity and fear, her evenings and dinner parties, where politics, poetry, and philosophy were discussed. But whether because stupidity was just what was needed to run such a salon, or because those who were deceived found pleasure in the deception, at any rate it remained unexposed and Hélène Bezúkhova's reputation as a lovely and clever woman became so firmly established that she could say the emptiest and stupidest things and yet everybody would go into raptures over every word of hers and look for a profound meaning in it of which she herself had no conception.

Pierre during the last two years, as a result of his continual absorption in abstract interests and his sincere contempt for all else, had acquired in his wife's circle, which did not interest him, that air of unconcern, indifference, and benevolence toward all, which cannot be acquired artificially and therefore inspires involuntary respect. But the general opinion concerning the queer husband of "the most distinguished woman in Petersburg" was so well established that no one took his freaks seriously.

Among the many young men who frequented her house every day, Borís Drubetskóy, who had already achieved great success in the service, was the most intimate friend of the Bezúkhov household since Hélène's return from Erfurt. Her smile for him was the same as for everybody, but sometimes that smile made Pierre uncomfortable. Toward him Borís behaved with a particularly dignified and sad deference. This shade of deference also disturbed Pierre. He had suffered so painfully three years before from the mortification to which his wife had subjected him that he now protected himself from the danger of its repetition, first by not being a husband to his wife, and secondly by not allowing himself to suspect.

In the eyes of the world Pierre was a great gentleman, the rather blind and absurd husband of a distinguished wife, a clever crank who did nothing but harmed nobody and was a first-rate, good-natured fellow. But a complex and difficult process of internal development was taking place all this time in Pierre's soul, revealing much to him and causing him many spiritual doubts and joys.

5

Pierre, who now serves on one of the government committees, tells in his diary of reading the Scriptures, and of his struggles against anger, lust, and worldliness. In inducting Borís Drubetskóy into the Masons, he experiences a feeling of hatred for him and condemns his insincerity in joining the movement for purely social reasons. Pierre also relates his dreams, symbolically involving his Masonic mentor Joseph Alexéevich.

6

The Rostóvs' monetary affairs had not improved during the two years they had spent in the country.

Though Nicholas Rostóv had kept firmly to his resolution and was still serving modestly in an obscure regiment, spending comparatively little, the way of life at Otrádnoe was such that the debts inevitably increased every year. The only resource obviously presenting itself to the old count was to apply for an official post, so he had come to Petersburg to look for one and also, as he said, to let the lassies enjoy themselves for the last time.

Soon after their arrival in Petersburg Berg proposed to Véra and was accepted.

Though some skeptics smiled when told of Berg's merits, it could not be denied that he was a painstaking and brave officer, on excellent terms with his superiors, and a moral young man with a brilliant career before him and an assured position in society.

Berg's proposal was at first received with a perplexity that was not flattering to him. At first it seemed strange that the son of an obscure Livonian gentleman should propose marriage to a Countess Rostóva; but Berg's chief characteristic was such a naïve and good-natured egotism that the Rostóvs involuntarily came to think it would be a good thing, since he himself was so firmly convinced that it was good, indeed excellent.

After the first feeling of perplexity aroused in the parents by Berg's proposal, the holiday tone of joyousness usual at such times took possession of the family, but the rejoicing was external and insincere. In the family's feeling toward this wedding a certain awkwardness and constraint were evident, as if they were ashamed of not having loved Véra sufficiently and of being so ready to get her off their hands. The old count felt this most. He would probably have been unable to state the cause of his embarrassment, but it resulted from the state of his affairs. He did not know at all how much he had, what his debts amounted to, or what dowry he could give Véra.

Berg had already been engaged a month, and only a week

remained before the wedding, but the count had not yet decided in his own mind the question of the dowry, nor spoken to his wife about it. At one time the count thought of giving her the Ryazán estate or of selling a forest, at another time of borrowing money on a note of hand. A few days before the wedding Berg entered the count's study early one morning and, with a pleasant smile, respectfully asked his future father-in-law to let him know what Véra's dowry would be.

"Because, consider, Count—if I allowed myself to marry now without having definite means to maintain my wife, I should be acting badly. . . ."

The conversation ended by the count, who wished to be generous and to avoid further importunity, saying that he would give a note of hand for eighty thousand rubles. Berg smiled meekly, kissed the count on the shoulder, and said that he was very grateful, but that it was impossible for him to arrange his new life without receiving thirty thousand in ready money. "Or at least twenty thousand, Count," he added, "and then a note of hand for only sixty thousand."

"Yes, yes, all right!" said the count hurriedly. "Only excuse me, my dear fellow, I'll give you twenty thousand and a note of hand for eighty thousand as well. Yes, yes! Kiss me."

7

Natásha was sixteen and it was the year 1809, the very year to which she had counted on her fingers with Borís after they had kissed four years ago. Since then she had not seen him. Before Sónya and her mother, if Borís happened to be mentioned, she spoke quite freely of that episode as of some childish, long-forgotten matter that was not worth mentioning. But in the secret depths of her soul the question whether her engagement to Borís was a jest or an important, binding promise tormented her.

Since Borís left Moscow in 1805 to join the army he had not seen the Rostóvs. He had been in Moscow several times, and had passed near Otrádnoe, but had never been to see them.

Anna Mikháylovna also had of late visited them less frequently, seemed to hold herself with particular dignity, and always spoke rapturously and gratefully of the merits of her son and the brilliant career on which he had entered. When the Rostóvs came to Petersburg Borís called on them.

He drove to their house in some agitation. The memory of Natásha was his most poetic recollection. But he went with the firm intention of letting her and her parents feel that the childish relations between himself and Natásha could not be binding either on her or on him. When he entered the Rostóvs' drawing room Natásha was in her own room. When she heard of his arrival she almost ran into the drawing room, flushed and beaming with a more than cordial smile.

Borís remembered Natásha in a short dress, with dark eyes shining from under her curls and boisterous, childish laughter, as he had known her four years before; and so he was taken aback when quite a different Natásha entered, and his face expressed rapturous astonishment. This expression on his face pleased Natásha.

"Well, do you recognize your little madcap playmate?" asked the countess.

Borís kissed Natásha's hand and said that he was astonished at the change in her.

"How handsome you have grown!"

"I should think so!" replied Natásha's laughing eyes.

Natásha sat down and, without joining in Borís' conversation with the countess, silently and minutely studied her childhood's suitor. He felt the weight of that resolute and affectionate scrutiny and glanced at her occasionally.

He did not stay more than ten minutes, then rose and took his leave. The same inquisitive, challenging, and rather mocking eyes still looked at him. After his first visit Borís said to himself that Natásha attracted him just as much as ever, but that he must not yield to that feeling, because to marry her, a girl almost without fortune, would mean ruin to his career, while to renew their former relations without intending to marry her would be dishonorable. Borís made up his mind to avoid meeting Natásha, but despite that resolution he called again a few days later and began calling often and spending whole days at the Rostóvs'. It seemed to him that he ought to have an explanation with Natásha and tell her that the old times must be forgotten, that in spite of everything . . . she could not be his wife, that he had no means, and they would never let her marry him. But he failed to do so and felt awkward about entering on such an explanation. He left off visiting Hélène and received reproachful notes from her every day, and yet he continued to spend whole days with the Rostóvs.

8

       One night when the old countess, in nightcap and dressing jacket, without her false curls, and with her poor little knob of hair showing under her white cotton cap, knelt sighing and groaning on a rug and bowing to the ground in prayer, her door creaked and Natásha, also in a dressing jacket with slippers on her bare feet and her hair in curlpapers, ran in. Seeing that her mother was still praying she ran on tiptoe to the bed and, rapidly slipping one little foot against the other, pushed off her slippers and jumped onto the bed. Natásha jumped on it, sank into the feather bed, rolled over to the wall, and began snuggling up the bedclothes as she settled down, raising her knees to her chin, kicking out and laughing almost inaudibly, now covering herself up head and all, and now peeping at her mother. The countess finished her prayers and came to the bed with a stern face, but seeing that Natásha's head was covered, she smiled in her kind, weak way.

"Now then, now then!" said she.

"Mamma, can we have a talk? Yes?" said Natásha. "Now, just one on your throat and another . . . that'll do!" And seizing her mother round the neck, she kissed her on the throat.

These visits of Natásha's at night before the count returned from his club were one of the greatest pleasures of both mother and daughter.

"What is it tonight?—But I have to tell you . . ."

Natásha put her hand on her mother's mouth.

"About Borís . . . I know," she said seriously; "that's what I have come about. Don't say it—I know. No, do tell me!" and she removed her hand. "Tell me, Mamma! He's nice?"

"Natásha, you are sixteen. At your age I was married. You say Borís is nice. He is very nice, and I love him like a son. But what then? . . . What are you thinking about? You have quite turned his head, I can see that. . . ."

Natásha was listening and considering.

"Well, what then?" said she.

"You have quite turned his head, and why? What do you want of him? You know you can't marry him."

"Why not?" said Natásha, without changing her position.

"Because he is young, because he is poor, because he is a relation . . . and because you yourself don't love him."

"How do you know?"

"I know. It is not right, darling!"

"But if I want to . . ." said Natásha.

"Leave off talking nonsense," said the countess.

"But if I want to . . ."

"It won't do, my love! Not everyone will understand this friendship dating from your childish days, and to see him so intimate with you may injure you in the eyes of other young men who visit us, and above all it torments him for nothing. He may already have found a suitable and wealthy match, and now he's half crazy."

"Crazy?" repeated Natásha.

"But this is what I'll do, Natásha, I'll have a talk with Borís. He need not come so often. . . ."

"Why not, if he likes to?"

"Because I know it will end in nothing. . . ."

"How can you know? No, Mamma, don't speak to him! What nonsense!" said Natásha in the tone of one being deprived of her property. "Well, I won't marry, but let him come if he enjoys it and I enjoy it." Natásha smiled and looked at her mother. "Not to marry, but just *so*," she added.

"How *so*, my pet?"

"Just *so*. There's no need for me to marry him. But . . . just *so*."

"Just *so*, just *so*," repeated the countess, and shaking all over, she went off into a good-humored, unexpected, elderly laugh.

"Don't laugh, stop!" cried Natásha. "You're shaking the whole bed! You're awfully like me, just such another giggler. . . . But, Mamma, is he very much in love? What do you think? Was anybody ever so much in love with you? And he's very nice, very, very nice. Only not quite my taste—he is so narrow, like the dining-room clock. . . . Don't you understand? Narrow, you know—gray, light gray . . ."

"What rubbish you're talking!" said the countess.

Natásha continued: "Don't you really understand? Nicholas would understand. . . . Bezúkhov, now, is blue, dark-blue and red, and he is square."

"You flirt with him too," said the countess, laughing.

"No, he is a Freemason, I have found out. He is fine, dark-blue and red. . . . How can I explain it to you?"

"Little countess!" the count's voice called from behind the door. "You're not asleep?" Natásha jumped up, snatched up her slippers, and ran barefoot to her own room.

She hummed a scrap from her favorite opera by Cherubini, threw herself on her bed, laughed at the pleasant thought that she would immediately fall asleep, called Dunyásha the maid to put out the candle, and before Dunyásha had left the room had already passed into yet another happier world of dreams, where everything was as light and beautiful as in reality, and even more so because it was different.

Next day the countess called Borís aside and had a talk with him, after which he ceased coming to the Rostóvs'.

9

On the thirty-first of December, New Year's Eve, 1809-10, an old grandee of Catherine's day was giving a ball and midnight supper. The diplomatic corps and the Emperor himself were to be present.

There had been many discussions and preparations for this ball in the Rostóv family, many fears that the invitation would not arrive, that the dresses would not be ready, or that something would not be arranged as it should be.

Márya Ignátevna Perónskaya, a thin and shallow maid of honor at the court of the Dowager Empress, who was a friend and relation of the countess and piloted the provincial Rostóvs in Petersburg high society, was to accompany them to the ball.

They were to call for her at her house in the Taurida Gardens at ten o'clock, but it was already five minutes to ten, and the girls were not yet dressed.

Natásha was going to her first grand ball. She had got up at eight that morning and had been in a fever of excitement and activity all day. All her powers since morning had been concentrated on ensuring that they all—she herself, Mamma, and Sónya—should be as well dressed as possible. Sónya and her mother put themselves entirely in her hands.

When her hair was done. Natásha, in her short petticoat from under which her dancing shoes showed, and her mother's dressing jacket, ran up to Sónya, scrutinized her, and then ran to her mother. Turning her mother's head this way and that, she fastened on the cap and, hurriedly kissing her gray hair, ran back to the maids who were turning up the hem of her skirt.

The cause of the delay was Natásha's skirt, which was too long. Two maids were turning up the hem and hurriedly biting off the ends of thread. A third with pins in her mouth was running about between the countess and Sónya, and a fourth held the whole of the gossamer garment up high on one uplifted hand.

"Mávra, quicker, darling!"

"Give me my thimble, Miss, from there . . ."

"Whenever will you be ready?" asked the count coming to the door. "Here is some scent. Perónskaya must be tired of waiting."

"What a beauty—a very queen!" said the nurse as she came to the door. "And Sónya! They are lovely!"

At a quarter past ten they at last got into their carriages and started. But they had still to call at the Taurida Gardens.

Natásha had not had a moment free since early morning and had not once had time to think of what lay before her.

She understood all that awaited her only when, after stepping over the red baize at the entrance, she entered the hall, took off her fur cloak, and, beside Sónya and in front of her mother, mounted the brightly illuminated stairs between the flowers. Only then did she remember how she must behave at a ball, and tried to assume the majestic air she considered indispensable for a girl on such an occasion. But, fortunately for her, she felt her eyes growing misty, she saw nothing clearly, her pulse beat a hundred to the minute, and the blood throbbed at her heart. She could not assume that pose, which would have made her ridiculous, and she moved on almost fainting from excitement and trying with all her might to conceal it. And this was the very attitude that became her best.

Natásha looked in the mirrors and could not distinguish her reflection from the others. All was blended into one brilliant procession. On entering the ballroom the regular hum of voices, footsteps, and greetings deafened Natásha, and the light and glitter dazzled her still more.

In the ballroom, guests stood crowding at the entrance doors awaiting the Emperor. The countess took up a position in one of the front rows of that crowd. Natásha heard and felt that several people were asking about her and looking at her. She realized that those noticing her liked her, and this observation helped to calm her.

Perónskaya was pointing out to the countess the most important people at the ball.

"That is the Dutch ambassador, do you see? That gray-haired man. Ah, here she is, the Queen of Petersburg, Countess Bezúkhova," said Perónskaya, indicating Hélène who had just entered. "How lovely! Beautiful and clever . . . they say Prince—— is quite mad about her. But see, those two, though not good-looking, are even more run after."

She pointed to a lady who was crossing the room followed by a very plain daughter.

"She is a splendid match, a millionairess," said Perónskaya. "And look, here come her suitors."

"That is Bezúkhova's brother, Anatole Kurágin," she said. "He's handsome, isn't he? I hear they will marry him to that rich girl. But your cousin, Drubetskóy, is also very attentive to her. They say she has millions. Oh yes, that's the French ambassador himself!" she replied to the countess' inquiry about Caulaincourt. "And that stout one in spectacles is the universal Freemason," she went on, indicating Pierre. "Put him beside his wife and he looks a regular buffoon!"

Pierre, swaying his stout body, advanced, making way through the crowd and nodding to right and left as casually and good-naturedly as if he were passing through a crowd at a fair. He pushed through, evidently looking for someone.

Natásha looked joyfully at the familiar face of Pierre, "the buffoon," as Perónskaya had called him, and knew he was looking for them, and for her in particular. He had promised to be at the ball and introduce partners to her.

But before he reached them Pierre stopped beside a very handsome, dark man of middle height, and in a white uniform, who stood by a window talking to a tall man wearing stars and a ribbon. Natásha at once recognized the shorter and younger man in the white uniform: it was Bolkónski, who seemed to her to have grown much younger, happier, and better-looking.

"There's someone else we know—Bolkónski, do you see, Mamma?" said Natásha, pointing out Prince Andrew. "You remember, he stayed a night with us at Otrádnoe."

"Oh, you know him?" said Perónskaya. "I can't bear him. He's too proud for anything. Takes after his father. And he's hand in glove with Speránski, writing some project or other. Just look how he treats the ladies! There's one talking to him and he has turned away," she said pointing at him. "I'd give it to him if he treated me as he does those ladies."

Suddenly everybody stirred, began talking, and pressed forward and then back, and between the two rows, which separated, the Emperor entered to the sounds of music that had immediately struck up. Behind him walked his host and hostess. He walked in rapidly, bowing to right and left is if anxious to get the first moments of the reception over. The band played the polonaise in vogue at that time. The men began to choose partners and take their places for the polonaise.

More than half the ladies already had partners and were taking up, or preparing to take up, their positions for the polonaise. Natásha felt that she would be left with her mother and Sónya among a minority of women who crowded near the wall, not having been invited to dance. She stood with her slender arms hanging down, her scarcely defined bosom rising and falling regularly, and with bated breath and glittering, frightened eyes gazed straight before her, evidently prepared for the height of joy or misery. She was not concerned about the Emperor or any of those great people whom Perónskaya was pointing out—she had but one thought: "Is it possible no one will ask me, that I shall not be among the first to dance? Is it possible that not one of all these men will notice me? They do not even seem to see me, or if they do they look as if they were saying, 'Ah, she's not the one I'm after, so it's not worth looking at her!' No, it's impossible," she thought. "They must know how I long to dance, how splendidly I dance, and how they would enjoy dancing with me."

The strains of the polonaise, which had continued for a considerable time, had begun to sound like a sad reminiscence in Natásha's ears. She wanted to cry. Prince Andrew with a lady passed by, evidently not recognizing them. The handsome Anatole was smilingly talking to a partner on his arm and looked at Natásha as one looks at a wall. Borís passed them twice and each time turned away. Berg and his wife, who were not dancing, came up to them.

At last the Emperor stopped beside his last partner (he had danced with three) and the music ceased. A worried aide-de-camp ran up to the Rostóvs requesting them to stand farther back, though as it was they were already close to the wall, and from the gallery resounded the distinct, precise, enticingly rhythmical strains of a waltz. An aide-de-camp, the Master of Ceremonies, went up to Countess Bezúkhova and asked her to dance. Natásha gazed at them and was ready to cry because it was not she who was dancing that first turn of the waltz.

Prince Andrew was watching the women who were breathlessly longing to be asked to dance.

Pierre came up to him and caught him by the arm.

"You always dance. I have a protégée, the young Rostóva, here. Ask her," he said.

He stepped forward in the direction Pierre indicated. The despairing, dejected expression of Natásha's face caught his eye. He recognized her, guessed her feelings, saw that it was her debut, remembered her conversation at the window, and with an expression of pleasure on his face approached Countess Rostóva.

"Allow me to introduce you to my daughter," said the countess, with heightened color.

"I have the pleasure of being already acquainted, if the countess remembers me," said Prince Andrew with a low and courteous bow quite belying Perónskaya's remarks about his rudeness, and approaching Natásha he held out his arm to grasp her waist before he had completed his invitation. He asked her to waltz. That tremulous expression on Natásha's face, prepared either for despair or rapture, suddenly brightened into a happy, grateful, childlike smile.

"I have long been waiting for you," that frightened happy little girl seemed to say by the smile that replaced the threatened tears, as she raised her hand to Prince Andrew's shoulder. They were the second couple to enter the circle. Prince Andrew was one of the best dancers of his day and Natásha danced exquisitely. Her little feet in their white satin dancing shoes did their work swiftly, lightly, and independently of herself, while her face beamed with ecstatic happiness. Her slender bare arms and neck were not beautiful—compared to Hélène's, her shoulders looked thin and her bosom undeveloped. But Hélène seemed, as it were, hardened by a varnish left by the thousands of looks that had scanned her person, while Natásha was like a girl exposed for the first time, who would have felt very much ashamed had she not been assured that this was absolutely necessary.

Prince Andrew liked dancing, and wishing to escape as quickly as possible from the political and clever talk which everyone addressed to him, wishing also to break up the circle of restraint he disliked, caused by the Emperor's presence, he danced, and had chosen Natásha because Pierre pointed her out to him and because she was the first pretty girl who caught his eye; but scarcely had he embraced that slender supple figure and felt her stirring so close to him and smiling so near him that the wine of her charm rose to his head, and he felt himself revived and rejuvenated when, after leaving her, he stood breathing deeply and watching the other dancers.

After Prince Andrew, Borís came up to ask Natásha for a dance, and then the aide-de-camp who had opened the ball, and several other young men, so that, flushed and happy, and passing on her superfluous partners to Sónya, she did not cease dancing all the evening. She noticed and saw nothing of what occupied everyone else. For one of the merry cotillions before supper Prince Andrew was again her partner. He reminded her of their first encounter in the Otrádnoe avenue, and how she had been unable to sleep that moonlight night, and told her how he had involuntarily overheard her. Natásha blushed at that recollection and tried to excuse herself, as if there had been something to be ashamed of in what Prince Andrew had overheard.

Like all men who have grown up in society, Prince Andrew liked meeting someone not of the conventional society stamp. And such was Natásha, with her surprise, her delight, her shyness, and even her mistakes in speaking French. With her he behaved with special care and tenderness, sitting beside her and talking of the simplest and most unimportant matters; he admired her shy grace. In the middle of the cotillion, having completed one of the figures, Natásha, still out of breath, was returning to her seat when another dancer chose her. She was tired and panting and evidently thought of declining, but immediately put her hand gaily on the man's shoulder, smiling at Prince Andrew.

When her partner left her Natásha ran across the room to choose two ladies for the figure.

"If she goes to her cousin first and then to another lady, she will be my wife," said Prince Andrew to himself quite to his own surprise, as he watched her. She did go first to her cousin.

"What rubbish sometimes enters one's head!" thought Prince Andrew, "but what is certain is that that girl is so charming, so original, that she won't be dancing here a month before she will be married. . . . Such as she are rare here," he thought, as Natásha readjusting a rose that was slipping on her bodice, settled herself beside him.

When the cotillion was over the old count in his blue coat came up to the dancers. He invited Prince Andrew to come and see them, and asked his daughter whether she was enjoying herself. Natásha did not answer at once but only looked up with a smile that said reproachfully: "How can you ask such a question?"

"I have never enjoyed myself so much before!" she said, and Prince Andrew noticed how her thin arms rose quickly as if to embrace her father and instantly dropped again. Natásha was happier than she had ever been in her life. She was at that height of bliss when one becomes completely kind and good and does not believe in the possibility of evil, unhappiness, or sorrow.

At that ball Pierre for the first time felt humiliated by the position his wife occupied in court circles. He was gloomy and absent-minded. A deep furrow ran across his forehead, and standing by a window he stared over his spectacles seeing no one.

On her way to supper Natásha passed him.

Pierre's gloomy, unhappy look struck her. She stopped in

front of him. She wished to help him, to bestow on him the superabundance of her own happiness.

"How delightful it is, Count!" said she. "Isn't it?"

Pierre smiled absent-mindedly, evidently not grasping what she said.

"Yes, I am very glad," he said.

"How can people be dissatisfied with anything?" thought Natásha. "Especially such a capital fellow as Bezúkhov!" In Natásha's eyes all the people at the ball alike were good, kind, and splendid people, loving one another; none of them capable of injuring another—and so they ought all to be happy.

10

Prince Andrew, under the subtle influence of his meeting with Natásha and also because of a deeper understanding of the personalities of Speránski and his henchmen, becomes disillusioned with his government work on reform legislation and yearns for the quiet life of his estate at Boguchárovo.

11

Next day Prince Andrew called at a few houses he had not visited before, and among them at the Rostóvs' with whom he had renewed acquaintance at the ball.

Natásha was one of the first to meet him. She and all the Rostóv family welcomed him as an old friend, simply and cordially. The old count's hospitality and good nature, which struck one especially in Petersburg as a pleasant surprise, were such that Prince Andrew could not refuse to stay for dinner. "Yes," he thought, "they are capital people, who of course have not the slightest idea what a treasure they possess in Natásha; but they are kindly folk and form the best possible setting for this strikingly poetic, charming girl, overflowing with life!"

After dinner Natásha, at Prince Andrew's request, went to the clavichord and began singing. Prince Andrew stood by a window talking to the ladies and listened to her. In the midst of a phrase he ceased speaking and suddenly felt tears choking him, a thing he had thought impossible for him. He looked at Natásha as she sang, and something new and joyful stirred in his soul. He felt happy and at the same time sad. He had absolutely nothing to weep about yet he was ready to weep. What about? His former love? The little princess? His disillusionments? . . . His hopes for the future? . . . Yes and no. The chief reason was a sudden, vivid sense of the terrible contrast between something infinitely great and illimitable within him and that limited and material something that he, and even she, was. This contrast weighed on and yet cheered him while she sang.

As soon as Natásha had finished she went up to him and asked how he liked her voice. She asked this and then became confused, feeling that she ought not to have asked it. He smiled, looking at her, and said he liked her singing as he liked everything she did.

Prince Andrew left the Rostóvs' late in the evening. He went to bed from habit, but soon realized that he could not sleep. Having lit his candle he sat up in bed, then got up, then lay down again not at all troubled by his sleeplessness: his soul was as fresh and joyful as if he had stepped out of a stuffy room into God's own fresh air. It did not enter his head that he was in love with Natásha; he was not thinking about her, but only picturing her to himself, and in consequence all life appeared in a new light. "Why do I strive, why do I toil in this narrow, confined frame, when life, all life with its joys, is open to me?" said he to himself. And for the first time for a very long while he began making happy plans for the future. He decided that he must attend to his son's education by finding a tutor and putting the boy in his charge, then he ought to retire from the service and go abroad, and see England, Switzerland, and Italy. "I must use my freedom while I feel so much strength and youth in me," he said to himself. "Pierre was right when he said one must believe in the possibility of happiness in order to be happy, and now I do believe in it. Let the dead bury their dead, but while one has life one must live and be happy!" thought he.

12

*In his social climbing, Berg and his wife Véra give a
small dinner party. The Rostóvs are present and also
Prince Andrew and Pierre. Pierre is struck by the curious
change that has come over Prince Andrew and Natásha.*

13

Next day, having been invited by the count,
Prince Andrew dined with the Rostóvs and spent the rest
of the day there.

In the evening, when Prince Andrew had left, the countess
went up to Natásha and whispered: "Well, what?"

"Mamma! For heaven's sake don't ask me anything now!
One can't talk about that," said Natásha.

But all the same that night Natásha, now agitated and now
frightened, lay a long time in her mother's bed gazing straight
before her. She told her how he had complimented her, how
he told her he was going abroad, asked her where they were
going to spend the summer, and then how he had asked her
about Borís.

"But such a . . . such a . . . never happened to me before!"
she said. "Only I feel afraid in his presence. I am always
afraid when I'm with him. What does that mean? Does it
mean that it's the real thing? Yes? Mamma, are you asleep?"

"No, my love; I am frightened myself," answered her
mother. "Now go!"

"All the same I shan't sleep. What silliness, to sleep! Mummy! Mummy! Such a thing never happened to me before,"
she said, surprised and alarmed at the feeling that she was
aware of in herself. "And could we ever have thought! . . ."

"What else did he say to you? What are those verses?
Read them . . ." said her mother, thoughtfully, referring to
some verses Prince Andrew had written in Natásha's album.

"Mamma, one need not to be ashamed of his being a
widower?"

"Don't, Natásha! Pray to God. 'Marriages are made in heaven,'" said her mother.

"Darling Mummy, how I love you! How happy I am!" cried Natásha, shedding tears of joy and excitement and embracing her mother.

At that very time Prince Andrew was sitting with Pierre and telling him of his love for Natásha and his firm resolve to make her his wife.

Prince Andrew, with a beaming ecstatic expression of renewed life on his face, paused in front of Pierre and, not noticing his sad look, smiled at him with the egotism of joy.

"Well, dear heart," said he, "I wanted to tell you about it yesterday and I have come to do so today. I never experienced anything like it before. I am in love, my friend!"

"With Natásha Rostóva, yes?" said he.

"Yes, yes! Who else should it be? I should never have believed it, but the feeling is stronger than I. Yesterday I tormented myself and suffered, but I would not exchange even that torment for anything in the world. I have not lived till now. At last I live, but I can't live without her! But can she love me? . . . I am too old for her. . . . Why don't you speak?"

"I? I? What did I tell you?" said Pierre suddenly, rising and beginning to pace up and down the room. "I always thought it. . . . That girl is such a treasure . . . she is a rare girl. . . . My dear friend, I entreat you, don't philosophize, don't doubt, marry, marry, marry. . . . And I am sure there will not be a happier man than you."

"But what of her?"

"She loves you."

"Don't talk rubbish . . ." said Prince Andrew, smiling and looking into Pierre's eyes.

"She does, I know," Pierre cried fiercely.

"I should not have believed anyone who told me that I was capable of such love," said Prince Andrew. "It is not at all the same feeling that I knew in the past. The whole world is now for me divided into two halves: one half is she, and there all is joy, hope, light: the other half is everything where she is not, and there all is gloom and darkness. . . ."

"Darkness and gloom," reiterated Pierre: "yes, yes, I understand that."

"I cannot help loving the light, it is not my fault. And I am very happy! You understand me? I know you are glad for my sake."

"Yes, yes," Pierre assented, looking at his friend with a touched and sad expression in his eyes. The brighter Prince Andrew's lot appeared to him, the gloomier seemed his own.

14

Prince Andrew needed his father's consent to his marriage, and to obtain this he started for the country next day.

His father received his son's communication with external composure, but inward wrath. He could not comprehend how anyone could wish to alter his life or introduce anything new into it, when his own life was already ending. "If only they would let me end my days as I want to," thought the old man, "then they might do as they please." With his son, however, he employed the diplomacy he reserved for important occasions and, adopting a quiet tone, discussed the whole matter.

In the first place the marriage was not a brilliant one as regards birth, wealth, or rank. Secondly, Prince Andrew was no longer as young as he had been and his health was poor (the old man laid special stress on this), while she was very young. Thirdly, he had a son whom it would be a pity to entrust to a chit of a girl. "Fourthly and finally," the father said, looking ironically at his son, "I beg you to put it off for a year: go abroad, take a cure, look out as you wanted to for a German tutor for Prince Nicholas. Then if your love or passion or obstinacy—as you please—is still as great, marry! And that's my last word on it. Mind, the last! . . ." concluded the prince, in a tone which showed that nothing would make him alter his decision.

Prince Andrew saw clearly that the old man hoped that his feelings, or his fiancée's, would not stand a year's test, or that he (the old prince himself) would die before then, and he decided to conform to his father's wish—to propose, and postpone the wedding for a year.

Three weeks after the last evening he had spent with the Rostóvs, Prince Andrew returned to Petersburg.

Next day after her talk with her mother Natásha expected Bolkónski all day, but he did not come. On the second and third day it was the same. Pierre did not come either and Natásha, not knowing that Prince Andrew had gone to see his father, could not explain his absence to herself.

Three weeks passed in this way. Natásha had no desire to go out anywhere and wandered from room to room like a shadow, idle and listless; she wept secretly at night and did not go to her mother in the evenings. She blushed continually and was irritable. It seemed to her that everybody knew about her disappointment and was laughing at her and pitying her. Strong as was her inward grief, this wound to her vanity intensified her misery.

In the hall the porch door opened, and someone asked, "At home?" and then footsteps were heard. Natásha was looking at the mirror, but did not see herself. She listened to the sounds in the hall. When she saw herself, her face was pale. It was *he*. She knew this for certain, though she hardly heard his voice through the closed doors.

Pale and agitated, Natásha ran into the drawing room. "Mamma! Bolkónski has come!" she said. "Mamma, it is awful, it is unbearable! I don't want . . . to be tormented! What am I to do? . . ."

Before the countess could answer, Prince Andrew entered the room with an agitated and serious face. As soon as he saw Natásha his face brightened. He kissed the countess' hand and Natásha's, and sat down beside the sofa.

"I have not been to see you all this time because I have been at my father's. I had to talk over a very important matter with him. I only got back last night," he said glancing at Natásha; "I want to have a talk with you, Countess," he added after a moment's pause.

The countess lowered her eyes, sighing deeply.

"Go, Natásha! I will call you," said the countess in a whisper.

Natásha glanced with frightened imploring eyes at Prince Andrew and at her mother and went out.

"I have come, Countess, to ask for your daughter's hand," said Prince Andrew.

The countess' face flushed hotly, but she said nothing. "Your offer . . ." she began at last sedately. He remained silent, looking into her eyes. "Your offer . . ." (she grew confused) "is agreeable to us, and . . . I accept your offer. I am glad. And my husband . . . I hope . . . but it will depend on her. . . ."

"I will speak to her when I have your consent. . . . Do you give it to me?" said Prince Andrew.

"Yes," replied the countess. She held out her hand to him, and with a mixed feeling of estrangement and tenderness pressed her lips to his forehead as he stooped to kiss her hand. She wished to love him as a son, but felt that to her he was a stranger and a terrifying man. "I am sure my husband will consent," said the countess, "but your father . . ."

"My father, to whom I have told my plans, has made it an express condition of his consent that the wedding is not to take place for a year. And I wished to tell you of that," said Prince Andrew.

"It is true that Natásha is still young, but—so long as that? . . ."

"It is unavoidable," said Prince Andrew with a sigh.

"I will send her to you," said the countess, and left the room.

"Well, Mamma? . . . Well? . . ."

"Go, go to him. He is asking for your hand," said the countess, coldly it seemed to Natásha. "Go . . . go," said the mother, sadly and reproachfully, with a deep sigh, as her daughter ran away.

Natásha never remembered how she entered the drawing room. When she came in and saw him she paused. "Is it possible that this stranger has now become *everything* to me?" she asked herself, and immediately answered, "Yes, everything! He alone is now dearer than everything in the world." Prince Andrew came up to her with downcast eyes.

"I have loved you from the very first moment I saw you. May I hope?"

He looked at her and was struck by the serious impassioned expression of her face. Her face said: "Why ask? Why doubt what you cannot but know. Why speak, when words cannot express what one feels?"

She drew near to him and stopped. He took her hand and kissed it.

"Do you love me?"

"Yes, yes!" Natásha murmured as if in vexation. Then she sighed loudly and, catching her breath more and more quickly, began to sob.

"What is it? What's the matter?"

"Oh, I am so happy!" she replied, smiled through her tears, bent over closer to him, paused for an instant as if asking herself whether she might, and then kissed him.

Prince Andrew held her hands, looked into her eyes, and did not find in his heart his former love for her. Something in him had suddenly changed; there was no longer the former poetic and mystic charm of desire, but there was pity for her feminine and childish weakness, fear at her devotion and trustfulness, and an oppressive yet joyful sense of the duty that now bound him to her forever. The present feeling, though not so bright and poetic as the former, was stronger and more serious.

"Did your mother tell you that it cannot be for a year?" asked Prince Andrew, still looking into her eyes.

"No," she replied, but she had not understood his question.

"Forgive me!" he said. "But you are so young, and I have already been through so much in life. I am afraid for you, you do not yet know yourself."

Natásha listened with concentrated attention, trying but failing to take in the meaning of his words.

"Hard as this year which delays my happiness will be," continued Prince Andrew, "it will give you time to be sure of yourself. I ask you to make me happy in a year, but you are free: our engagement shall remain a secret, and should you find that you do not love me, or should you come to love . . ." said Prince Andrew with an unnatural smile.

"Why do you say that?" Natásha interrupted him. "You know that from the very day you first came to Otrádnoe I have loved you," she cried, quite convinced that she spoke the truth.

"In a year you will learn to know yourself. . . ."

"A whole year!" Natásha repeated suddenly, only now

realizing that the marriage was to be postponed for a year.
"But why a year? Why a year? . . ."

Prince Andrew began to explain to her the reasons for this
delay. Natásha did not hear him.

"And can't it be helped?" she asked. Prince Andrew did
not reply, but his face expressed the impossibility of altering
that decision.

"It's awful! Oh, it's awful! awful!" Natásha suddenly cried,
and again burst into sobs. "I shall die, waiting a year: it's
impossible, it's awful!" She looked into her lover's face and
saw in it a look of commiseration and perplexity.

"No, no! I'll do anything!" she said, suddenly checking
her tears. "I am so happy."

The father and mother came into the room and gave the
betrothed couple their blessing.

From that day Prince Andrew began to frequent the Rostóvs' as Natásha's affianced lover.

15

        No betrothal ceremony took place and Na-
tásha's engagement to Bolkónski was not announced; Prince
Andrew insisted on that. He said that as he was responsible
for the delay he ought to bear the whole burden of it; that
he had given his word and bound himself forever, but that
he did not wish to bind Natásha and gave her perfect freedom. If after six months she felt that she did not love him
she would have full right to reject him. Naturally neither
Natásha nor her parents wished to hear of this, but Prince
Andrew was firm.

In the house that poetic dullness and quiet reigned which
always accompanies the presence of a betrothed couple.
Often when all sitting together everyone kept silent. Sometimes the others would get up and go away and the couple,
left alone, still remained silent. They rarely spoke of their
future life. Prince Andrew was afraid and ashamed to speak
of it. Natásha shared this as she did all his feelings, which
she constantly divined. Once she began questioning him
about his son. Prince Andrew blushed, as he often did now—

Natásha particularly liked it in him—and said that his son would not live with them.

"Why not?" asked Natásha in a frightened tone.

"I cannot take him away from his grandfather, and besides . . ."

"How I should have loved him!" said Natásha, immediately guessing his thought; "but I know you wish to avoid any pretext for finding fault with us."

Sometimes she fell into one of the mad, merry moods characteristic of her, and then she particularly loved to hear and see how Prince Andrew laughed. He seldom laughed, but when he did he abandoned himself entirely to his laughter, and after such a laugh she always felt nearer to him. Natásha would have been completely happy if the thought of the separation awaiting her and drawing near had not terrified her, just as the mere thought of it made him turn pale and cold.

On the eve of his departure from Petersburg Prince Andrew brought with him Pierre, who had not been to the Rostóvs' once since the ball. Pierre seemed disconcerted and embarrassed. He was talking to the countess, and Natásha sat down beside a little chess table with Sónya, thereby inviting Prince Andrew to come too. He did so.

"You have known Bezúkhov a long time?" he asked. "Do you like him?"

"Yes, he's a dear, but very absurd."

And as usual when speaking of Pierre, she began to tell anecdotes of his absent-mindedness, some of which had even been invented about him.

"Do you know I have entrusted him with our secret? I have known him from childhood. He has a heart of gold. I beg you, Natalie," Prince Andrew said with sudden seriousness—"I am going away and heaven knows what may happen. You may cease to . . . all right, I know I am not to say that. Only this, then: whatever may happen to you when I am not here . . ."

"What can happen?"

"Whatever trouble may come," Prince Andrew continued, "I beg you, Mademoiselle Sophie [Sónya], whatever may happen, to turn to him alone for advice and help! He is a most absent-minded and absurd fellow, but he has a heart of gold."

Neither her father, nor her mother, nor Sónya, nor Prince Andrew himself could have foreseen how the separation from her lover would act on Natásha. Flushed and agitated she went about the house all that day, dry-eyed, occupied with most trivial matters as if not understanding what awaited her. She did not even cry when, on taking leave, he kissed her hand for the last time. "Don't go!" she said in a tone that made him wonder whether he really ought not to stay and which he remembered long afterwards. Nor did she cry when he was gone; but for several days she sat in her room dry-eyed, taking no interest in anything and only saying now and then, "Oh, why did he go away?"

But a fortnight after his departure, to the surprise of those around her, she recovered from her mental sickness just as suddenly and became her old self again, but with a change in her moral physiognomy, as a child gets up after a long illness with a changed expression of face.

16

During that year after his son's departure, Prince Nicholas Bolkónski's health and temper became much worse. He grew still more irritable, and it was Princess Mary who generally bore the brunt of his frequent fits of unprovoked anger.

Soon after Prince Andrew had gone, Princess Mary wrote to her friend Julie Karágina in Petersburg, whom she had dreamed (as all girls dream) of marrying to her brother, and who was at the time in mourning for her own brother, killed in Turkey.

"Sorrow, it seems, is our common lot, my dear, tender friend Julie. Your loss is so terrible that I can only explain it to myself as a special providence of God who, loving you, wishes to try you and your excellent mother. Oh, my friend! Religion, and religion alone, can—I will not say comfort us—but save us from despair.

Our family life goes on in the old way except for my

brother Andrew's absence. He, as I wrote you before, has changed very much of late. After his sorrow he only this year quite recovered his spirits. He has again become as I used to know him when a child: kind, affectionate, with that heart of gold to which I know no equal. He has realized, it seems to me, that life is not over for him. But together with this mental change he had grown physically much weaker. He has become thinner and more nervous. I am anxious about him and glad he is taking this trip abroad which the doctors recommended long ago. I hope it will cure him. You write that in Petersburg he is spoken of as one of the most active, cultivated, and capable of the young men. Forgive my vanity as a relation, but I never doubted it. The good he has done to everybody here, from his peasants up to the gentry, is incalculable. On his arrival in Petersburg he received only his due. I always wonder at the way rumors fly from Petersburg to Moscow, especially such false ones as that you write about—I mean the report of my brother's betrothal to the little Rostóva. I do not think my brother will ever marry again, and certainly not her; and this is why: first, I know that though he rarely speaks about the wife he has lost, the grief of that loss has gone too deep in his heart for him ever to decide to give her a successor and our little angel a stepmother. Secondly because, as far as I know, that girl is not the kind of girl who could please Prince Andrew. I do not think he would choose her for a wife, and frankly I do not wish it. But I am running on too long and am at the end of my second sheet. Good-by, my dear friend. May God keep you in His holy and mighty care. My dear friend, Mademoiselle Bourienne, sends you kisses.

MARY."

17

In the middle of the summer Princess Mary received an unexpected letter from Prince Andrew in Switzerland in which he gave her strange and surprising news. He

informed her of his engagement to Natásha Rostóva. The
whole letter breathed loving rapture for his betrothed and
tender and confiding affection for his sister. He wrote that
he had never loved as he did now and that only now did he
understand and know what life was. "Besides," he wrote,
"the matter was not then so definitely settled as it is now.
My father then insisted on a delay of a year and now already
six months, half of that period, have passed, and my resolution is firmer than ever. If the doctors did not keep me here
at the spas I should be back in Russia, but as it is I have to
postpone my return for three months. You know me and my
relations with Father. I want nothing from him. I have been
and always shall be independent; but to go against his will
and arouse his anger, now that he may perhaps remain with
us such a short time, would destroy half my happiness. I am
now writing to him about the same question, and beg you
to choose a good moment to hand him the letter and to let
me know how he looks at the whole matter and whether
there is hope he may consent to reduce the term by four
months."

After long hesitations, doubts, and prayers, Princess Mary
gave the letter to her father. The next day the old prince said
to her quietly:

"Write and tell your brother to wait till I am dead. . . .
It won't be long—I shall soon set him free."

The princess was about to reply, but her father would
not let her speak and, raising his voice more and more, cried:

"Marry, marry, my boy! . . . A good family! . . . Clever
people, eh? Rich, eh? Yes, a nice stepmother little Nicholas
will have! Write and tell him that he may marry tomorrow
if he likes. She will be little Nicholas' stepmother and I'll
marry Bourienne!"

And latterly, to her surprise and bewilderment, Princess
Mary noticed that her father was really associating more and
more with the Frenchwoman. She wrote to Prince Andrew
about the reception of his letter, but comforted him with
hopes of reconciling their father to the idea.

1810-11

BOOK SEVEN

1

After three years away in the army, Nicholas Rostóv, who is not pleased with the news of his sister's engagement to Prince Andrew, reluctantly returns home at his mother's request in order to straighten out the family's critical financial situation.

After the rapture of meeting, and after that odd feeling of unsatisfied expectation—the feeling that "everything is just the same, so why did I hurry?"—Nicholas began to settle down in his old home world. His father and mother were much the same, only a little older. What was new in them was a certain uneasiness and occasional discord, which there used not to be, and which, as Nicholas soon found out, was due to the bad state of their affairs. Sónya was nearly twenty; she had stopped growing prettier and promised nothing more than she was already, but that was enough. She exhaled happiness and love from the time Nicholas returned, and the faithful, unalterable love of this girl had a gladdening effect on him. Pétya and Natásha surprised Nicholas most. Pétya was a big handsome boy of thirteen, merry, witty, and mischievous, with a voice that was already breaking. As for Natásha, for a long while Nicholas wondered and laughed whenever he looked at her.

"You're not the same at all," he said.

"How? Am I uglier?"

"On the contrary, but what dignity! A princess!" he whispered to her.

"Yes, yes, yes!" cried Natásha, joyfully.

She told him about her romance with Prince Andrew and of his visit to Otrádnoe and showed him his last letter.

"Well, are you glad?" Natásha asked. "I am so tranquil and happy now."

"Very glad," answered Nicholas. "He is an excellent fellow. . . . And are you very much in love?"

"How shall I put it?" replied Natásha. "I was in love with Borís, with my teacher, and with Denísov, but this is quite different. I feel at peace and settled. I know, that no better man than he exists, and I am calm and contented now. Not at all as before."

Nicholas expressed his disapproval of the postponement of the marriage for a year; but Natásha attacked her brother with exasperation, proving to him that it could not be otherwise, and that it would be a bad thing to enter a family against the father's will, and that she herself wished it so.

Her brother often wondered as he looked at her. She did not seem at all like a girl in love and parted from her affianced husband. She was even-tempered and calm and quite as cheerful as of old. It always seemed to him that there was something not quite right about this intended marriage.

2

Nicholas administers a drubbing to the thieving steward of the family estate and then wipes his hands of the matter.

3

The weather was already growing wintry and morning frosts congealed an earth saturated by autumn rains. The hounds of that ardent young sportsman Rostóv had not merely reached the hard winter condition, but were so jaded that at a meeting of the huntsmen it was decided to give them a three days' rest and then, on the sixteenth of September, to go on a distant expedition, starting from the oak grove where there was an undisturbed litter of wolf cubs.

"O-hoy!" came at that moment, that inimitable huntsman's

call which unites the deepest bass with the shrillest tenor, and round the corner came Daniel the head huntsman and head kennelman, a gray, wrinkled old man with hair cut straight over his forehead, Ukrainian fashion, a long bent whip in his hand, and that look of independence and scorn of everything that is only seen in huntsmen.

"It's a good day, eh? For a hunt and a gallop, eh?" asked Nicholas, scratching Mílka behind the ears.

Daniel did not answer, but winked instead.

Having finished his inquiries and extorted from Daniel an opinion that the hounds were fit (Daniel himself wished to go hunting), Nicholas ordered the horses to be saddled. But just as Daniel was about to go Natásha came in with rapid steps, not having done up her hair or finished dressing and with her old nurse's big shawl wrapped round her. Pétya ran in at the same time.

"You are going?" asked Natásha. "I knew you would! Sónya said you wouldn't go, but I knew that today is the sort of day when you couldn't help going."

"Yes, we are going," replied Nicholas reluctantly, for today, as he intended to hunt seriously, he did not want to take Natásha and Pétya. "We are going, but only wolf hunting: it would be dull for you."

"You know it is my greatest pleasure," said Natásha. "It's not fair; you are going by yourself, are having the horses saddled and said nothing to us about it."

" 'No barrier bars a Russian's path'—we'll go!" shouted Pétya.

"But you can't. Mamma said you mustn't," said Nicholas to Natásha.

"Yes, I'll go. I shall certainly go," said Natásha decisively. "Daniel, tell them to saddle for us, and Michael must come with my dogs," she added to the huntsman.

4

The old count, who had always kept up an enormous hunting establishment but had now handed it all completely over to his son's care, being in very good spirits on this fifteenth of September, prepared to go out with the others.

In an hour's time the whole hunting party was at the porch. Nicholas, with a stern and serious air which showed that now was no time for attending to trifles, went past Natásha and Pétya who were trying to tell him something.

They were taking fifty-four hounds, with six hunt attendants and whippers-in. Besides the family, there were eight borzoi kennelmen and more than forty borzois, so that, with the borzois on the leash belonging to members of the family, there were about a hundred and thirty dogs and twenty horsemen.

When they had gone a little less than a mile, five more riders with dogs appeared out of the mist, approaching the Rostóvs. In front rode a fresh-looking, handsome old man with a large gray mustache.

"Good morning, Uncle!" said Nicholas, when the old man drew near.

"That's it. Come on! . . . I was sure of it," began "Uncle." (He was a distant relative of the Rostóvs', a man of small means, and their neighbor.) "I knew you wouldn't be able to resist it and it's a good thing you're going."

"Uncle" looked round disapprovingly at Pétya and Natásha. He did not like to combine frivolity with the serious business of hunting.

"Good morning, Uncle! We are going too!" shouted Pétya.

"Good morning, good morning! But don't go overriding the hounds," said "Uncle" sternly.

"Well, nephew, you're going for a big wolf," said "Uncle." "Mind and don't let her slip!"

"That's as may happen," answered Rostóv. "Karáy, here!" he shouted, answering "Uncle's" remark by this call to his borzoi. Karáy was a shaggy old dog with a hanging jowl, famous for having tackled a big wolf unaided. They all took up their places.

The old count, knowing his son's ardor in the hunt, hurried so as not to be late, and the huntsmen had not yet reached their places when Count Ilyá Rostóv, cheerful, flushed, and with quivering cheeks, drove up with his black horses over the winter rye to the place reserved for him, where a wolf might come out.

After listening a few moments in silence, the count and his attendant, Simon, convinced themselves that the hounds had separated into two packs: the sound of the larger pack, eagerly giving tongue, began to die away in the distance, the other pack rushed by the wood past the count, and it was with this that Daniel's voice was heard calling *ulyulyu*. The sounds of both packs mingled and broke apart again, but both were becoming more distant.

The count and Simon galloped out of the wood and saw on their left a wolf which, softly swaying from side to side, was coming at a quiet lope farther to the left to the very place where they were standing. The angry borzois whined and getting free of the leash rushed past the horses' feet at the wolf.

The wolf paused, turned its heavy forehead toward the dogs awkwardly, like a man suffering from the quinsy, and, still slightly swaying from side to side, gave a couple of leaps and with a swish of its tail disappeared into the skirt of the wood. At the same instant, with a cry like a wail, first one hound, then another, and then another, sprang helter-skelter from the wood opposite and the whole pack rushed across the field toward the very spot where the wolf had disappeared. The hazel bushes parted behind the hounds and Daniel's chestnut horse appeared, dark with sweat. On its long back sat Daniel, hunched forward, capless, his disheveled gray hair hanging over his flushed, perspiring face.

"*Ulyulyulyu! ulyulyu! . . .*" he cried. When he caught sight of the count his eyes flashed lightning.

"Blast you!" he shouted, holding up his whip threateningly at the count.

"You've let the wolf go! . . . What sportsmen!" and as if scorning to say more to the frightened and shamefaced count, he lashed the heaving flanks of his sweating chestnut gelding with all the anger the count had aroused and flew off after the hounds.

5

Nicholas Rostóv meanwhile remained at his post, waiting for the wolf. By the way the hunt approached and receded, by the cries of the dogs whose notes were familiar to him, by the way the voices of the huntsmen approached, receded, and rose, he realized what was happening at the copse. He knew that young and old wolves were there, that the hounds had separated into two packs, that somewhere a wolf was being chased, and that something had gone wrong. He expected the wolf to come his way any moment.

"No, I shan't have such luck," thought Rostóv, "yet what wouldn't it be worth! It is not to be! Everywhere, at cards and in war, I am always unlucky."

Again he looked to the right and saw something running toward him across the deserted field. "No, it can't be!" thought Rostóv, taking a deep breath, as a man does at the coming of something long hoped for. The height of happiness was reached—and so simply, without warning, or noise, or display, that Rostóv could not believe his eyes and remained in doubt for over a second. The wolf ran forward and jumped heavily over a gully that lay in her path. She was an old animal with a gray back and big reddish belly. She ran without hurry, evidently feeling sure that no one saw her.

"*Ulyulyu!*" cried Nicholas, in a voice not his own, and of its own accord his good horse darted headlong downhill, leaping over gullies to head off the wolf, and the borzois passed it, running faster still.

"Karáy, *ulyulyu!* . . ." he shouted, looking round for the old borzoi who was now his only hope. Karáy, with all the strength age had left him, stretched himself to the utmost and, watching the wolf, galloped heavily aside to intercept it. A long, yellowish young borzoi, one Nicholas did not know, from another leash, rushed impetuously at the wolf from in front and almost knocked her over. But the wolf jumped up more quickly than anyone could have expected and, gnashing her teeth, flew at the yellowish borzoi, which, with a piercing yelp, fell with its head on the ground, bleeding from a gash in its side.

"Karáy? Old fellow! . . ." wailed Nicholas.

The old dog with its felted hair hanging from its thigh was within five paces of it. As if aware of her danger, the wolf turned her eyes on Karáy, tucked her tail yet further between her legs, and increased her speed. But here Nicholas only saw that something happened to Karáy—the borzoi was suddenly on the wolf, and they rolled together down into a gully just in front of them.

That instant, when Nicholas saw the wolf struggling in the gully with the dogs, while from under them could be seen her gray hair and outstretched hind leg and her frightened choking head, with her ears laid back (Karáy was pinning her by the throat), was the happiest moment of his life. With his hand on his saddlebow, he was ready to dismount and stab the wolf, when she suddenly thrust her head up from among that mass of dogs, and then her forepaws were on the edge of the gully. She clicked her teeth (Karáy no longer had her by the throat), leaped with a movement of her hind legs out of the gully, and having disengaged herself from the dogs with tail tucked in again, went forward. Karáy, his hair bristling, and probably bruised or wounded, climbed with difficulty out of the gully.

"Oh my God! Why?" Nicholas cried in despair.

Already, at the beginning of this chase, Daniel, hearing the *ulyulyuing,* had rushed out from the wood. He saw Karáy seize the wolf, and checked his horse, supposing the affair to be over. But when he saw that the horsemen did not dismount and that the wolf shook herself and ran for safety, Daniel set his chestnut galloping, not at the wolf but straight toward the wood, just as Karáy had run to cut the animal off.

Daniel galloped up silently, holding a naked dagger in his left hand and thrashing the laboring sides of his chestnut horse with his whip as if it were a flail.

Nicholas neither saw nor heard Daniel until the chestnut, breathing heavily, panted past him, and he heard the fall of a body and saw Daniel lying on the wolf's back among the dogs, trying to seize her by the ears. It was evident to the dogs, the hunters, and to the wolf herself that all was now over. The terrified wolf pressed back her ears and tried to rise, but the borzois stuck to her. Daniel rose a little, took a step, and with his whole weight, as if lying down to rest, fell on the wolf, seizing her by the ears. Nicholas was about to stab her, but Daniel whispered, "Don't! We'll gag her!" and, changing his position, set his foot on the wolf's neck. A stick was thrust between her jaws and she was fastened with a leash, as if bridled, her legs were bound together, and Daniel rolled her over once or twice from side to side.

6

After the wolf hunt, the old count leaves, but Natásha and Pétya remain. Nicholas is ready to quarrel with a neighbor Ilágin, whose huntsmen run down a fox on Rostóv land, but they make up. In a hare hunt "Uncle's" favorite dog surpasses those of Nicholas and Ilágin.

7

Toward evening Ilágin took leave of Nicholas, who found that they were so far from home that he accepted "Uncle's" offer that the hunting party should spend the night in his little village of Mikháylovna.

A huntsman was sent to Otrádnoe for a trap, while Nicholas rode with Natásha and Pétya to "Uncle's" house.

Some five male domestic serfs, big and little, rushed out to the front porch to meet their master. A score of women serfs, old and young, as well as children, popped out from the back entrance to have a look at the hunters who were arriving.

"Uncle" dismounted at the porch of his little wooden house which stood in the midst of an overgrown garden and, after a glance at his retainers, shouted authoritatively that the superfluous ones should take themselves off and that all necessary preparations should be made to receive the guests and the visitors.

"Uncle" asked his visitors to sit down and make themselves at home, and then went out of the room. Natásha, Nicholas, and Pétya took off their wraps and sat down on the sofa. Pétya, leaning on his elbow, fell asleep at once. Natásha and Nicholas were silent. Their faces glowed, they were hungry and very cheerful. They looked at one another (now that the hunt was over and they were in the house, Nicholas no longer considered it necessary to show his manly superiority over his sister), Natásha gave him a wink, and neither refrained long from bursting into a peal of ringing laughter even before they had a pretext ready to account for it.

After a while "Uncle" came in, in a Cossack coat, blue trousers, and small top boots. "Uncle" too was in high spirits and far from being offended by the brother's and sister's laughter (it could never enter his head that they might be laughing at his way of life) he himself joined in the merriment.

Soon after "Uncle's" reappearance the door was opened, evidently from the sound by a barefooted girl, and a stout, rosy, good-looking woman of about forty, with a double chin and full red lips, entered carrying a large loaded tray. "Here I am. I am she! Now do you understand 'Uncle'?" her expression said to Rostóv. How could one help understanding? Not only Nicholas, but even Natásha understood the meaning of his puckered brow and the happy complacent smile that slightly puckered his lips when Anísya Fëdorovna entered.

"Take this, little Lady-Countess!" she kept saying, as she offered Natásha first one thing and then another.

Natásha ate of everything and thought she had never seen or eaten such buttermilk cakes, such aromatic jam, such honey-and-nut sweets, or such a chicken anywhere. Anísya Fëdorovna left the room.

After supper, over their cherry brandy, Rostóv and "Uncle" talked of past and future hunts, while Natásha sat upright on the sofa and listened with sparkling eyes. She tried several times to wake Pétya that he might eat something, but he only muttered incoherent words without waking up. Natásha felt so lighthearted and happy in these novel surroundings that she only feared the trap would come for her too soon.

There was a rapid patter of bare feet, and an unseen hand opened the door into the huntsmen's room, from which came the clear sounds of a balaláyka on which someone, who was evidently a master of the art, was playing. Natásha had been listening to those strains for some time and now went out into the passage to hear better.

"That's Mítka, my coachman. . . . I have got him a good balaláyka. I'm fond of it," said "Uncle."

"How good! Really very good!" said Nicholas with some

unintentional superciliousness, as if ashamed to confess that the sounds pleased him very much.

"Very good?" said Natásha reproachfully, noticing her brother's tone. "Not 'very good'—it's simply delicious!"

"He doesn't play that part right!" said "Uncle" suddenly, with an energetic gesture. "Here he ought to burst out—that's it, come on!—ought to burst out."

"Do you play then?" asked Natásha.

"Uncle" did not answer, but smiled.

"Anísya, go and see if the strings of my guitar are all right. I haven't touched it for a long time. That's it—come on! I've given it up."

Anísya Fëdorovna, with her light step, willingly went to fulfill her errand and brought back the guitar.

Without looking at anyone, "Uncle" blew the dust off it and, tapping the case with his bony fingers, tuned the guitar and settled himself in his armchair. He took the guitar a little above the fingerboard, arching his left elbow with a somewhat theatrical gesture, and, with a wink at Anísya Fëdorovna, struck a single chord, pure and sonorous, and then quietly, smoothly, and confidently began playing in very slow time, not *My Lady*, but the well-known song: *Came a maiden down the street.*

"Lovely, lovely! Go on, Uncle, go on!" shouted Natásha as soon as he had finished. She jumped up and hugged and kissed him. "Nicholas, Nicholas!" she said, turning to her brother, as if asking him: "What is it moves me so?"

Nicholas too was greatly pleased by "Uncle's" playing.

"Go on, Uncle dear," Natásha wailed in an imploring tone as if her life depended on it.

"Uncle" rose, and it was as if there were two men in him: one of them smiled seriously at the merry fellow, while the merry fellow struck a naïve and precise attitude preparatory to a folk dance.

"Now then, niece!" he exclaimed, waving to Natásha the hand that had just struck a chord.

Natásha threw off the shawl from her shoulders, ran forward to face "Uncle," and setting her arms akimbo also made a motion with her shoulders and struck an attitude.

"Well, little countess; that's it—come on!" cried "Uncle," with a joyous laugh, having finished the dance. "Well done, niece! Now a fine young fellow must be found as husband for you. That's it—come on!"

"He's chosen already," said Nicholas smiling.

"Oh?" said "Uncle" in surprise, looking inquiringly at Natásha, who nodded her head with a happy smile.

"And such a one!" she said. But as soon as she had said it a new train of thoughts and feelings arose in her. "What did Nicholas' smile mean when he said 'chosen already'? Is he glad of it or not? It is as if he thought my Bolkónski would not approve of or understand our gaiety. But he would understand it all. Where is he now?" she thought, and her face suddenly became serious. But this lasted only a second. "Don't dare to think about it," she said to herself, and sat down again smilingly beside "Uncle," begging him to play something more.

After nine o'clock two traps and three mounted men, who had been sent to look for them, arrived to fetch Natásha and Pétya. The count and countess did not know where they were and were very anxious, said one of the men.

"What a darling Uncle is!" said Natásha, when they had come out onto the highroad.

"Yes," returned Nicholas. "You're not cold?"

"No. I'm quite, quite all right. I feel so comfortable!" answered Natásha, almost perplexed by her feelings.

What was passing in that receptive childlike soul that so eagerly caught and assimilated all the diverse impressions of life? How did they all find place in her?

"What were you thinking about just now, Nicholas?" inquired Natásha.

They were fond of asking one another that question.

"I?" said Nicholas, trying to remember. "Well, you see, first I thought that Rugáy, the red hound, was like Uncle, and that if he were a man he would always keep Uncle near him, if not for his riding, then for his manner. What a good fellow Uncle is! Don't you think so? . . . Well, and you?"

"I? Wait a bit, wait. . . . Yes, first I thought that we are driving along and imagining that we are going home, but that heaven knows where we are really going in the darkness, and that we shall arrive and suddenly find that we are

not in Otrádnoe, but in Fairyland. And then I thought . . .
No, nothing else."

"I know, I expect you thought of him," said Nicholas,
smiling as Natásha knew by the sound of his voice.

"No," said Natásha, though she had in reality been thinking about Prince Andrew at the same time as of the rest,
and of how he would have liked "Uncle." "And do you
know," she suddenly said, "I know that I shall never again
be as happy and tranquil as I am now."

"Rubbish, nonsense, humbug!" exclaimed Nicholas, and
he thought: "How charming this Natásha of mine is! I have
no other friend like her and never shall have. Why should
she marry? We might always drive about together!"

"What a darling this Nicholas of mine is!" thought Natásha.

8

Count Ilyá Rostóv had resigned the position
of Marshal of the Nobility because it involved him in too
much expense, but still his affairs did not improve. Natásha
and Nicholas often noticed their parents conferring together
anxiously and privately and heard suggestions of selling the
fine ancestral Rostóv house and estate near Moscow.

The countess, with her loving heart, felt that her children
were being ruined, and she tried to find means of remedying
the position. From her feminine point of view she could see
only one solution, namely, for Nicholas to marry a rich
heiress. This match was with Julie Karágina, the daughter of
excellent and virtuous parents, a girl the Rostóvs had known
from childhood, and who had now become a wealthy heiress
through the death of the last of her brothers.

Several times the countess, with tears in her eyes, told
her son that now both her daughters were settled, her only
wish was to see him married.

Nicholas guessed what his mother's remarks were leading
to and during one of these conversations induced her to
speak quite frankly. She told him that her only hope of
getting their affairs disentangled now lay in his marrying
Julie Karágina.

"But, Mamma, suppose I loved a girl who has no fortune, would you expect me to sacrifice my feelings and my honor for the sake of money?" he asked his mother, not realizing the cruelty of his question and only wishing to show his noble-mindedness.

But the countess did not want the question put like that: she did not want a sacrifice from her son, she herself wished to make a sacrifice for him.

"No, you have not understood me, don't let us talk about it," she replied, wiping away her tears.

"Maybe I do love a poor girl," said Nicholas to himself. "Am I to sacrifice my feelings and my honor for money? I wonder how Mamma could speak so to me. Because Sónya is poor I must not love her," he thought, "must not respond to her faithful, devoted love? Yet I should certainly be happier with her than with some doll-like Julie. I can always sacrifice my feelings for my family's welfare," he said to himself, "but I can't coerce my feelings. If I love Sónya, that feeling is for me stronger and higher than all else."

Nicholas did not go to Moscow, and the countess did not renew the conversation with him about marriage. She saw with sorrow, and sometimes with exasperation, symptoms of a growing attachment between her son and the portionless Sónya.

Nicholas was spending the last of his leave at home. A fourth letter had come from Prince Andrew, from Rome, in which he wrote that he would have been on his way back to Russia long ago had not his wound unexpectedly reopened in the warm climate, which obliged him to defer his return till the beginning of the new year. Natásha was still as much in love with her betrothed, found the same comfort in that love, and was still as ready to throw herself into all the pleasures of life as before; but at the end of the fourth month of their separation she began to have fits of depression which she could not master. She felt sorry for herself: sorry that she was being wasted all this time and of no use to anyone —while she felt herself so capable of loving and being loved.

Things were not cheerful in the Rostóvs' home.

9

On the third day of Christmas week, after the midday dinner, all the inmates of the house dispersed to various rooms. It was the dullest time of the day. The countess was playing patience. Natásha came into the room, went up to Sónya, glanced at what she was doing, and then went up to her mother and stood without speaking.

"Why are you wandering about like an outcast?" asked her mother. "What do you want?"

"*Him* . . . I want him . . . now, this minute! I want *him!*" said Natásha, with glittering eyes and no sign of a smile.

The countess lifted her head and looked attentively at her daughter.

"Don't look at me, Mamma! Don't look; I shall cry directly."

"Sit down with me a little," said the countess.

"Mamma, I want *him*. Why should I be wasted like this, Mamma?"

Her voice broke, tears gushed from her eyes, and she turned quickly to hide them and left the room.

She passed into the sitting room, stood there thinking awhile, and then went into the maids' room.

"O Lord, O Lord, it's always the same! Oh, where am I to go? What am I to do with myself?" And tapping with her heels, she ran quickly upstairs.

Her brother Pétya was upstairs too; with the man in attendance on him he was preparing fireworks to let off that night.

"Pétya! Pétya!" she called to him. "Carry me downstairs."

Pétya ran up and offered her his back. She jumped on it, putting her arms round his neck, and he pranced along with her.

Having as it were reviewed her kingdom, tested her power, and made sure that everyone was submissive, but that all the same it was dull, Natásha betook herself to the ballroom, picked up her guitar, sat down in a dark corner behind a bookcase, and began to run her fingers over the strings in the bass, picking out a passage she recalled from an opera she had heard in Petersburg with Prince Andrew.

Sónya passed to the pantry with a glass in her hand.

"Where were you going?" Natásha asked.

"To change the water in this glass. I am just finishing the design."

"You always find something to do, but I can't," said Natásha. "And where's Nicholas?"

"Asleep, I think."

"Sónya, go and wake him," said Natásha. "Tell him I want him to come and sing."

"Oh, if only Andrew would come quicker! I am so afraid it will never be! And, worst of all, I am growing old—that's the thing! There won't then be in me what there is now. But perhaps he'll come today, will come immediately. Perhaps he has come and is sitting in the drawing room. Perhaps he came yesterday and I have forgotten it." She rose, put down the guitar, and went to the drawing room.

All the domestic circle, tutors, governesses, and guests, were already at the tea table. The servants stood round the table —but Prince Andrew was not there and life was going on as before.

"Mamma!" she muttered, "give him to me, give him, Mamma, quickly, quickly!" and she again had difficulty in repressing her sobs.

She sat down at the table and listened to the conversation between the elders and Nicholas, who had also come to the table. "My God, my God! The same faces, the same talk, Papa holding his cup and blowing in the same way!" thought Natásha, feeling with horror a sense of repulsion rising up in her for the whole household, because they were always the same.

After tea, Nicholas, Sónya, and Natásha went to the sitting room, to their favorite corner where their most intimate talks always began.

10

A group of Rostóv serfs, dressed in outlandish costumes as Christmas mummers, break in on Natásha's

singing. Nicholas, Sónya, Pétya, and Natásha also dress
in costumes and decide to go with the mummers to call
on neighbors, the Melyukóvs. The whole company mer-
rily races over the snow in troika sleighs. Sónya feels
that her relations with Nicholas will be decided.

11

Pelagéya Danílovna Melyukóva, a broadly
built, energetic woman wearing spectacles, sat in the drawing
room in a loose dress, surrounded by her daughters whom
she was trying to keep from feeling dull.

Hussars, ladies, witches, clowns, and bears, after clearing
their throats and wiping the hoarfrost from their faces in
the vestibule, came into the ballroom where candles were
hurriedly lighted. The clown—Dimmler—and the lady—
Nicholas—started a dance. Surrounded by the screaming
children the mummers, covering their faces and disguising
their voices, bowed to their hostess and arranged themselves
about the room.

Natásha, the young Melyukóvs' favorite, disappeared with
them into the back rooms where a cork and various dressing
gowns and male garments were called for and received from
the footman by bare girlish arms from behind the door. Ten
minutes later, all the young Melyukóvs joined the mummers.

Pelagéya Danílovna, having given orders to clear the rooms
for the visitors and arranged about refreshments for the
gentry and the serfs, went about among the mummers without removing her spectacles, peering into their faces with
a suppressed smile and failing to recognize any of them.

"And who is this?" she asked her governess, peering into
the face of her own daughter dressed up as a Kazán-Tartar.
"I suppose it is one of the Rostóvs! Well, Mr. Hussar, and
what regiment do you serve in?" she asked Natásha. "Here,
hand some fruit jelly to the Turk!" she ordered the butler
who was handing things round. "That's not forbidden by his
law."

After Russian country dances and chorus dances, Pelagéya
Danílovna made the serfs and gentry join in one large circle:

a ring, a string, and a silver ruble were fetched and they all played games together.

"Now to tell one's fortune in the empty bathhouse is frightening!" said an old maid who lived with the Melyukóvs, during supper.

"Why?" said the eldest Melyukóv girl.

"You wouldn't go, it takes courage. . . ."

"I'll go," said Sónya.

Whether they were playing the ring and string game or the ruble game or talking as now, Nicholas did not leave Sónya's side, and gazed at her with quite new eyes. It seemed to him that it was only today, thanks to that burnt-cork mustache, that he had fully learned to know her. And really, that evening, Sónya was brighter, more animated, and prettier than Nicholas had ever seen her before.

"So that's what she is like; what a fool I have been!" he thought gazing at her sparkling eyes, and under the mustache a happy rapturous smile dimpled her cheeks, a smile he had never seen before.

"I'm not afraid of anything," said Sónya. "May I go at once?" She got up.

They told her where the barn was and how she should stand and listen, and they handed her a fur cloak. She threw this over her head and shoulders and glanced at Nicholas.

"What a darling that girl is!" thought he. "And what have I been thinking of till now?"

Sónya went out into the passage to go to the barn. Nicholas went hastily to the front porch, saying he felt too hot. The crowd of people really had made the house stuffy.

"I am a fool, a fool! what have I been waiting for?" thought Nicholas, and running out from the porch he went round the corner of the house and along the path that led to the back porch. He knew Sónya would pass that way. Halfway lay some snow-covered piles of firewood and across and along them a network of shadows from the bare old lime trees fell on the snow and on the path. This path led to the barn. His bosom seemed to inhale not air but the strength of eternal youth and gladness.

From the back porch came the sound of feet descending the steps, the bottom step upon which snow had fallen gave a ringing creak and he heard the voice of an old maidservant saying, "Straight, straight, along the path, Miss. Only, don't look back."

"I am not afraid," answered Sónya's voice, and along the path toward Nicholas came the crunching, whistling sound of Sónya's feet in her thin shoes.

Sónya came along, wrapped in her cloak. She was only a couple of paces away when she saw him, and to her too he was not the Nicholas she had known and always slightly feared. He was in a woman's dress, with tousled hair and a happy smile new to Sónya. She ran rapidly toward him.

"Quite different and yet the same," thought Nicholas, looking at her face all lit up by the moonlight. He slipped his arms under the cloak that covered her head, embraced her, pressed her to him, and kissed her on the lips that wore a mustache and had a smell of burnt cork. Sónya kissed him full on the lips, and disengaging her little hands pressed them to his cheeks.

"Sónya!" . . . "Nicholas!" . . . was all they said. They ran to the barn and then back again, re-entering, he by the front and she by the back porch.

12

On the way back Nicholas drove at a steady pace instead of racing and kept peering by that fantastic all-transforming light into Sónya's face and searching beneath the eyebrows and mustache for his former and his present Sónya from whom he had resolved never to be parted again.

"Sónya, is it well with *thee?*" he asked from time to time.

"Yes!" she replied. "And with *thee?*"

When halfway home Nicholas handed the reins to the coachman and ran for a moment to Natásha's sleigh and stood on its wing.

"Natásha!" he whispered in French, "do you know I have made up my mind about Sónya?"

"Have you told her?" asked Natásha, suddenly beaming all over with joy.

"Oh, how strange you are with that mustache and those eyebrows! . . . Natásha—are you glad?"

"I am so glad, so glad! I was beginning to be vexed with

you. I did not tell you, but you have been treating her badly. What a heart she has, Nicholas! I am horrid sometimes, but I was ashamed to be happy while Sónya was not," continued Natásha. "Now I am so glad! Well, run back to her."

"So you are glad and I have done right?"

"Oh, quite right! I had a quarrel with Mamma some time ago about it. Mamma said she was angling for you. How could she say such a thing! I nearly stormed at Mamma. I will never let anyone say anything bad of Sónya, for there is nothing but good in her."

"Then it's all right?" said Nicholas, again scrutinizing the expression of his sister's face to see if she was in earnest. Then he jumped down and, his boots scrunching the snow, ran back to his sleigh. The same happy, smiling Circassian, with mustache and beaming eyes looking up from under a sable hood, was still sitting there, and that Circassian was Sónya, and that Sónya was certainly his future happy and loving wife.

When they reached home and had told their mother how they had spent the evening at the Melyukóvs', the girls went to their bedroom. When they had undressed, but without washing off the cork mustaches, they sat a long time talking of their happiness. They talked of how they would live when they were married, how their husbands would be friends, and how happy they would be. On Natásha's table stood two looking glasses which Dunyásha had prepared beforehand.

"Only when will all that be? I am afraid never. . . . It would be too good!" said Natásha, rising and going to the looking glasses.

"Sit down, Natásha; perhaps you'll see him," said Sónya.

Natásha lit the candles, one on each side of one of the looking glasses, and sat down.

She sat a long time looking at the receding line of candles reflected in the glasses and expecting (from tales she had heard) to see a coffin, or *him*, Prince Andrew, in that last dim, indistinctly outlined square. But ready as she was to take the smallest speck for the image of a man or of a coffin, she saw nothing.

"Why is it others see things and I don't?" she said. "You sit down now, Sónya. You absolutely must, tonight! Do it for me. . . . Today I feel so frightened!"

Sónya sat down before the glasses, got the right position, and began looking.

"Oh, Natásha!" she cried.

"Did you see? Did you? What was it?" exclaimed Natásha, holding up the looking glass.

Sónya had not seen anything, she was just wanting to blink and to get up when she heard Natásha say, "Of course she will!" She did not wish to disappoint either Dunyásha or Natásha, but it was hard to sit still. She did not herself know how or why the exclamation escaped her when she covered her eyes.

"You saw him?" urged Natásha, seizing her hand.

"Yes. Wait a bit . . . I . . . saw him," Sónya could not help saying, not yet knowing whom Natásha meant by *him*, Nicholas or Prince Andrew.

"But why shouldn't I say I saw something? Others do see! Besides who can tell whether I saw anything or not?" flashed through Sónya's mind.

"Yes, I saw him," she said.

"How? Standing or lying?"

"No, I saw . . . At first there was nothing, then I saw him lying down."

"Andrew lying? Is he ill?" asked Natásha, her frightened eyes fixed on her friend.

"No, on the contrary, on the contrary! His face was cheerful, and he turned to me." And when saying this she herself fancied she had really seen what she described.

"Well, and then, Sónya? . . ."

"After that, I could not make out what there was; something blue and red. . . ."

"Sónya! When will he come back? When shall I see him! O, God, how afraid I am for him and for myself and about everything! . . ." Natásha began, and without replying to Sónya's words of comfort she got into bed, and long after her candle was out lay open-eyed and motionless, gazing at the moonlight through the frosty windowpanes.

13

Soon after the Christmas holidays Nicholas told his mother of his love for Sónya and of his firm resolve to marry her. The countess, who had long noticed what was going on between them and was expecting this declaration, listened to him in silence and then told her son that he might marry whom he pleased, but that neither she nor his father would give their blessing to such a marriage. Nicholas, for the first time, felt that his mother was displeased with him and that, despite her love for him, she would not give way. Coldly, without looking at her son, she sent for her husband and, when he came, tried briefly and coldly to inform him of the facts, in her son's presence, but unable to restrain herself she burst into tears of vexation and left the room. The old count began irresolutely to admonish Nicholas and beg him to abandon his purpose. Nicholas replied that he could not go back on his word, and his father, sighing and evidently disconcerted, very soon became silent and went in to the countess. In all his encounters with his son, the count was always conscious of his own guilt toward him for having wasted the family fortune, and so he could not be angry with him for refusing to marry an heiress and choosing the dowerless Sónya.

The father and mother did not speak of the matter to their son again, but a few days later the countess sent for Sónya and, with a cruelty neither of them expected, reproached her niece for trying to catch Nicholas and for ingratitude. Sónya listened silently with downcast eyes to the countess' cruel words, without understanding what was required of her. She was ready to sacrifice everything for her benefactors. Self-sacrifice was her most cherished idea; but in this case she could not see what she ought to sacrifice, or for whom. Nicholas felt the situation to be intolerable and went to have an explanation with his mother. He first implored her to forgive him and Sónya and consent to their marriage, then he threatened that if she molested Sónya he would at once marry her secretly.

The countess, with a coldness her son had never seen in

her before, replied that he was of age, that Prince Andrew was marrying without his father's consent, and he could do the same, but that she would never receive that *intriguer* as her daughter.

Exploding at the word *intriguer*, Nicholas, raising his voice, told his mother he had never expected her to try to force him to sell his feelings, but if that were so, he would say for the last time . . . But he had no time to utter the decisive word which the expression of his face caused his mother to await with terror, and which would perhaps have forever remained a cruel memory to them both. He had not time to say it, for Natásha, with a pale and set face, entered the room from the door at which she had been listening.

"Nicholas, you are talking nonsense! Be quiet, be quiet, be quiet, I tell you! . . ." she almost screamed, so as to drown his voice.

"Mamma darling, it's not at all so . . . my poor, sweet darling," she said to her mother, who conscious that they had been on the brink of a rupture gazed at her son with terror, but in the obstinacy and excitement of the conflict could not and would not give way.

"Nicholas, I'll explain to you. Go away! Listen, Mamma darling," said Natásha.

Her words were incoherent, but they attained the purpose at which she was aiming.

Natásha set to work to effect a reconciliation, and so far succeeded that Nicholas received a promise from his mother that Sónya should not be troubled, while he on his side promised not to undertake anything without his parents' knowledge.

Firmly resolved, after putting his affairs in order in the regiment, to retire from the army and return and marry Sónya, Nicholas, serious, sorrowful, and at variance with his parents, but, as it seemed to him, passionately in love, left at the beginning of January to rejoin his regiment.

After Nicholas had gone things in the Rostóv household were more depressing than ever, and the countess fell ill from mental agitation.

Sónya was unhappy at the separation from Nicholas and still more so on account of the hostile tone the countess could not help adopting toward her. The count was more perturbed than ever by the condition of his affairs, which called for some decisive action. Their town house and estate near Moscow had inevitably to be sold, and for this they had to go to Moscow. But the countess' health obliged them to delay their departure from day to day.

Natásha, who had borne the first period of separation from her betrothed lightly and even cheerfully, now grew more agitated and impatient every day. The thought that her best days, which she would have employed in loving him, were being vainly wasted, with no advantage to anyone, tormented her incessantly. His letters for the most part irritated her. It hurt her to think that while she lived only in the thought of him, he was living a real life, seeing new places and new people that interested him. The more interesting his letters were the more vexed she felt. Her letters to him, far from giving her any comfort, seemed to her a wearisome and artificial obligation.

There was still no improvement in the countess' health, but it was impossible to defer the journey to Moscow any longer. Natásha's trousseau had to be ordered and the house sold. Moreover, Prince Andrew was expected in Moscow, where old Prince Bolkónski was spending the winter, and Natásha felt sure he had already arrived.

So the countess remained in the country, and the count, taking Sónya and Natásha with him, went to Moscow at the end of January.

1811-12

BOOK EIGHT

1

After Prince Andrew's engagement to Natá-sha, Pierre without any apparent cause suddenly felt it impossible to go on living as before. Firmly convinced as he was of the truths revealed to him by his benefactor, and happy as he had been in perfecting his inner man, to which he had devoted himself with such ardor—all the zest of such a life vanished after the engagement of Andrew and Natásha and the death of Joseph Alexéevich, the news of which reached him almost at the same time. Only the skeleton of life remained: his house, a brilliant wife who now enjoyed the favors of a very important personage, acquaintance with all Petersburg, and his court service with its dull formalities. And this life suddenly seemed to Pierre unexpectedly loathsome. He ceased keeping a diary, avoided the company of the Brothers, began going to the Club again, drank a great deal, and came once more in touch with the bachelor sets, leading such a life that the Countess Hélène thought it necessary to speak severely to him about it. Pierre felt that she was right, and to avoid compromising her went away to Moscow.

In Moscow as soon as he entered his huge house in which the faded and fading princesses still lived, he felt himself at home in a quiet haven. In Moscow he felt at peace, at home, warm and dirty as in an old dressing gown.

For Moscow society Pierre was the nicest, kindest, most intellectual, merriest, and most magnanimous of cranks, a heedless, genial nobleman of the old Russian type. His purse was always empty because it was open to everyone.

Pierre no longer suffered moments of despair, hypochondria, and disgust with life, but the malady that had formerly found expression in such acute attacks was driven inwards and never left him for a moment. "What for? Why? What is going on in the world?" he would ask himself in perplexity several times a day, involuntarily beginning to reflect anew on the meaning of the phenomena of life; but knowing by experience that there were no answers to these questions he made haste to turn away from them, and took up a book, or hurried off to the Club or to Apollón Nikoláevich's, to exchange the gossip of the town.

He had the unfortunate capacity many men, especially Russians, have of seeing and believing in the possibility of goodness and truth, but of seeing the evil and falsehood of life too clearly to be able to take a serious part in it. Every sphere of work was connected, in his eyes, with evil and deception. Whatever he tried to be, whatever he engaged in, the evil and falsehood of it repulsed him and blocked every path of activity. Yet he had to live and to find occupation. It was too dreadful to be under the burden of these insoluble problems, so he abandoned himself to any distraction in order to forget them. He frequented every kind of society, drank much, bought pictures, engaged in building, and above all—read.

Sometimes he remembered how he had heard that soldiers in war when entrenched under the enemy's fire, if they have nothing to do, try hard to find some occupation the more easily to bear the danger. To Pierre all men seemed like those soldiers, seeking refuge from life: some in ambition, some in cards, some in framing laws, some in women, some in toys, some in horses, some in politics, some in sport, some in wine, and some in governmental affairs. "Nothing is trivial, and nothing is important, it's all the same—only to save oneself from it as best one can," thought Pierre. "Only not to see *it*, that dreadful *it!*"

2

At the beginning of winter Prince Nicholas Bolkónski and his daughter moved to Moscow. At that time enthusiasm for the Emperor Alexander's regime had weakened and a patriotic and anti-French tendency prevailed there, and this, together with his past and his intellect and his originality, at once made Prince Nicholas Bolkónski an object of particular respect to the Moscovites and the center of the Moscow opposition to the government

In Moscow Princess Mary had no one to talk to, no one to whom to confide her sorrow, and much sorrow fell to her lot just then. The time for Prince Andrew's return and marriage was approaching, but his request to her to prepare his father for it had not been carried out; in fact, it seemed as if matters were quite hopeless, for at every mention of the young Countess Rostóva the old prince (who apart from that was usually in a bad temper) lost control of himself. But what distressed the princess most of all was her father's irritability, which was always directed against her and had of late amounted to cruelty. Had he forced her to prostrate herself to the ground all night, had he beaten her or made her fetch wood or water, it would never have entered her mind to think her position hard; but this loving despot—the more cruel because he loved her and for that reason tormented himself and her—knew how not merely to hurt and humiliate her deliberately, but to show her that she was always to blame for everything. Of late he had exhibited a new trait that tormented Princess Mary more than anything else; this was his ever-increasing intimacy with Mademoiselle Bourienne.

One day in Moscow in Princess Mary's presence (she thought her father did it purposely when she was there) the old prince kissed Mademoiselle Bourienne's hand and, drawing her to him, embraced her affectionately. Princess Mary flushed and ran out of the room. A few minutes later Mademoiselle Bourienne came into Princess Mary's room smiling and making cheerful remarks in her agreeable voice. Princess Mary hastily wiped away her tears, went resolutely up to Mademoiselle Bourienne, and evidently unconscious of what she was doing began shouting in angry haste at the Frenchwoman, her voice breaking: "It's horrible, vile, inhuman, to take advantage of the weakness . . ." She did not finish. "Leave my room," she exclaimed, and burst into sobs.

Next day the prince did not say a word to his daughter, but she noticed that at dinner he gave orders that Mademoiselle Bourienne should be served first.

At such moments something like a pride of sacrifice

gathered in her soul. And suddenly that father whom she had judged would look for his spectacles in her presence, fumbling near them and not seeing them, or would forget something that had just occurred, or take a false step with his failing legs and turn to see if anyone had noticed his feebleness, or, worst of all, at dinner when there were no visitors to excite him would suddenly fall asleep, letting his napkin drop and his shaking head sink over his plate. "He is old and feeble, and I dare to condemn him" she thought at such moments, with a feeling of revulsion against herself.

3

Old Prince Bolkónski furiously blames his daughter for allowing the French physician Métivier to visit him, and insists they must think of parting. Among those at the Prince's dinner are Pierre, Borís Drubetskóy, whose social climbing continues, and Count Rostopchín, Governor General and Commander in Chief of Moscow and an extreme reactionary. He and the old prince approve the threatening rupture in the peaceful Russian-French relations.

4

Princess Mary turned with an absent-minded questioning look to Pierre, who hat in hand and with a smile on his face was the last of the guests to approach her after the old prince had gone out and they were left alone in the drawing room.

"May I stay a little longer?" he said, letting his stout body sink into an armchair beside her.

"Oh yes," she answered.

"Have you known that young man long, Princess?" he asked.

"Who?"

"Drubetskóy."

"No, not long. . . ."

"Do you like him?"

"Yes, he is an agreeable young man. . . . Why do you ask me that?" said Princess Mary, still thinking of that morning's conversation with her father.

"Because I have noticed that when a young man comes on leave from Petersburg to Moscow it is usually with the object of marrying an heiress. Would you marry him?"

"Oh, my God, Count, there are moments when I would marry anybody!" she cried suddenly to her own surprise and with tears in her voice. "Ah, how bitter it is to love someone near to you and to feel that . . ." she went on in a trembling voice, "that you can do nothing for him but grieve him, and to know that you cannot alter this. Then there is only one thing left—to go away, but where could I go?"

"What is wrong? What is it, Princess?"

But without finishing what she was saying, Princess Mary burst into tears.

"I don't know what is the matter with me today. Don't take any notice—forget what I have said!"

Pierre's gaiety vanished completely. He anxiously questioned the princess, asked her to speak out fully and confide her grief to him; but she only repeated that she begged him to forget what she had said, that she did not remember what she had said, and that she had no trouble except the one he knew of—that Prince Andrew's marriage threatened to cause a rupture between father and son.

"What is to be done? In a few months the year will be up. The thing is impossible . . . Tell me honestly the whole truth: what sort of girl is she, and what do you think of her?— The real truth, because you know Andrew is risking so much doing this against his father's will that I should like to know. . . ."

An undefined instinct told Pierre that these explanations, and repeated requests to be told the *whole truth*, expressed ill-will on the princess' part toward her future sister-in-law and a wish that he should disapprove of Andrew's choice; but in reply he said what he felt rather than what he thought.

"I really don't know what sort of girl she is; I can't analyze her at all. She is enchanting, but what makes her so I don't know. That is all one can say about her."

Princess Mary sighed, and the expression on her face said: "Yes, that's what I expected and feared."

"Ah, I so long to like her! Tell her so if you see her before I do."

"I hear they are expected very soon," said Pierre.

Princess Mary told Pierre of her plan to become intimate with her future sister-in-law as soon as the Rostóvs arrived and to try to accustom the old prince to her.

5

Borís, though he prefers the heiress Princess Mary, who is uninterested, woos her friend, the rich and unattractive Julie Karágina, prompted by his doting mother. His hesitancy because of her repulsiveness is cured by Anatole Kurágin's suit. Borís proposes and is joyfully accepted.

6

At the end of January old Count Rostóv went to Moscow with Natásha and Sónya. The countess was still unwell and unable to travel but it was impossible to wait for her recovery. Prince Andrew was expected in Moscow any day, the trousseau had to be ordered and the estate near Moscow had to be sold, besides which the opportunity of presenting his future daughter-in-law to old Prince Bolkónski while he was in Moscow could not be missed. The Rostóvs' Moscow house had not been heated that winter and, as they had come only for a short time and the countess was not with them, the count decided to stay with Márya Dmítrievna Akhrosímova, who had long been pressing her hospitality on them.

Late one evening the Rostóvs' four sleighs drove into Márya Dmítrievna's courtyard in the old Konyúsheny street. Márya Dmítrievna lived alone. She had already married off her daughter, and her sons were all in the service.

She held herself as erect, told everyone her opinion as candidly, loudly, and bluntly as ever, and her whole bearing seemed a reproach to others for any weakness, passion, or temptation—the possibility of which she did not admit.

She had not yet gone to bed when the Rostóvs arrived and the pulley of the hall door squeaked from the cold as it let in the Rostóvs and their servants. Márya Dmítrievna, with her spectacles hanging down on her nose and her head flung back, stood in the hall doorway looking with a stern, grim face at the new arrivals.

"I'm heartily glad you have come and are staying with me. It was high time," she said, giving Natásha a significant look. "The old man is here and his son's expected any day. You'll have to make his acquaintance. But we'll speak of that later on," she added, glancing at Sónya with a look that showed she did not want to speak of it in her presence.

Next morning Márya Dmítrievna took the young ladies to the Iberian shrine of the Mother of God and to Madame Suppert-Roguet, who was so afraid of Márya Dmítrievna that she always let her have costumes at a loss merely to get rid of her. Márya Dmítrievna ordered almost the whole trousseau. When they got home she turned everybody out of the room except Natásha, and then called her pet to her armchair.

"Well, now we'll talk. I congratulate you on your betrothed. You've hooked a fine fellow! I am glad for your sake and I've known him since he was so high." She held her hand a couple of feet from the ground. Natásha blushed happily. "I like him and all his family. Now listen! You know that old Prince Nicholas much dislikes his son's marrying. The old fellow's crotchety! Of course Prince Andrew is not a child and can shift without him, but it's not nice to enter a family against a father's will. One wants to do it peacefully and lovingly. You're a clever girl and you'll know how to manage. Be kind, and use your wits. Then all will be well."

Natásha remained silent, from shyness Márya Dmítrievna supposed, but really because she disliked anyone interfering in what touched her love of Prince Andrew, which seemed to her so apart from all human affairs that no one could understand it. She loved and knew Prince Andrew, he loved her only, and was to come one of these days and take her. She wanted nothing more.

7

Next day, by Márya Dmítrievna's advice, Count Rostóv took Natásha to call on Prince Nicholas Bolkónski. The count did not set out cheerfully on this visit, at heart he felt afraid. Natásha, on the other hand, having put on her best gown, was in the highest spirits. "They can't help liking me," she thought. "Everybody always has liked me, and I am so willing to do anything they wish, so ready to be fond of him —for being *his* father—and of her—for being *his* sister—that there is no reason for them not to like me. . . ."

When they had been announced a perturbation was noticeable among the servants. At last an old, cross-looking footman came and announced to the Rostóvs that the prince was not receiving, but that the princess begged them to walk up. The princess, looking excited and nervous, her face flushed in patches, ran in to meet the visitors, treading heavily, and vainly trying to appear cordial and at ease. From the first glance Princess Mary did not like Natásha. She thought her too fashionably dressed, frivolously gay and vain. She did not at all realize that before having seen her future sister-in-law she was prejudiced against her by involuntary envy of her beauty, youth, and happiness, as well as by jealousy of her brother's love for her. Apart from this insuperable antipathy to her, Princess Mary was agitated just then because on the Rostóvs' being announced, the old prince had shouted that he did not wish to see them, that Princess Mary might do so if she chose, but they were not to be admitted to him.

"There, my dear princess, I've brought you my songstress," said the count, bowing and looking round uneasily as if afraid the old prince might appear. "If you'll allow me to leave my Natásha in your hands for a quarter of an hour, Princess, I'll drive round to see Anna Semënovna, it's quite near in the Dogs' Square, and then I'll come back for her."

Despite the uneasy glances thrown at her by Princess Mary —who wished to have a tête-à-tête with Natásha—Mademoiselle Bourienne remained in the room and persistently talked about Moscow amusements and theaters. Natásha felt offended by the hesitation she had noticed in the anteroom, by her father's nervousness, and by the unnatural manner of the princess who—she thought—was making a favor of receiving her, and so everything displeased her. She did not like Princess Mary, whom she thought very plain, affected, and dry. Natásha suddenly shrank into herself and involuntarily assumed an offhand air which alienated Princess Mary still more. After five minutes of irksome, constrained conversation, they heard the sound of slippered feet rapidly approaching. Princess Mary looked frightened. The door opened and the old prince, in a dressing gown and a white nightcap, came in.

"Ah, madam!" he began. "Madam, Countess . . . Countess Rostóva, if I am not mistaken . . . I beg you to excuse me, to excuse me . . . I did not know, madam. God is my witness, I did not know you had honored us with a visit, and I came in such a costume only to see my daughter. I beg you to excuse me . . . God is my witness, I didn't know—" he repeated, stressing the word "God" so unnaturally and so unpleasantly that Princess Mary stood with downcast eyes not daring to look either at her father or at Natásha.

Nor did the latter, having risen and curtsied, know what to do. Mademoiselle Bourienne alone smiled agreeably.

"I beg you to excuse me, excuse me! God is my witness, I did not know," muttered the old man, and after looking Natásha over from head to foot he went out.

When the count returned, Natásha was impolitely pleased and hastened to get away: at that moment she hated the stiff, elderly princess, who could place her in such an embarrassing position and had spent half an hour with her without once mentioning Prince Andrew. "I couldn't begin talking about him in the presence of that Frenchwoman," thought Natásha. The same thought was meanwhile tormenting Princess Mary. She knew what she ought to have said to Natásha, but she had been unable to say it because Mademoiselle Bourienne was in the way, and because, without knowing why, she felt it very difficult to speak of the marriage. When the count was already leaving the room, Princess Mary went up hurriedly to Natásha, took her by the hand, and said with a deep sigh:

"Wait, I must . . ."

Natásha glanced at her ironically without knowing why.

"Dear Natalie," said Princess Mary, "I want you to know that I am glad my brother has found happiness. . . ."

She paused, feeling that she was not telling the truth. Natásha noticed this and guessed its reason.

"I think, Princess, it is not convenient to speak of that now," she said with external dignity and coldness, though she felt the tears choking her.

"What have I said and what have I done?" thought she, as soon as she was out of the room.

They waited a long time for Natásha to come to dinner that day. She sat in her room crying like a child, blowing her nose and sobbing. Sónya stood beside her, kissing her hair.

"Natásha, what is it about?" she asked. "What do they matter to you? It will all pass, Natásha."

"I can't tell you, I don't know. No one's to blame," said Natásha—"It's my fault. But it all hurts terribly. Oh, why doesn't he come? . . ."

8

That evening the Rostóvs went to the Opera, for which Márya Dmítrievna had taken a box.

Natásha did not want to go, but could not refuse Márya Dmítrievna's kind offer which was intended expressly for her. When she came ready dressed into the ballroom to await her father, and looking in the large mirror there saw that she was pretty, very pretty, she felt even more sad, but it was a sweet, tender sadness.

"O, God, if he were here now I would not behave as I did then, but differently. I would not be silly and afraid of things, I would simply embrace him, cling to him, and make him look at me with those searching inquiring eyes with which he has so often looked at me, and then I would make him laugh as he used to laugh. And his eyes—how I see those eyes!" thought Natásha. "And what do his father and sister matter to me? I love him alone, him, him, with that face and those eyes, with his smile, manly and yet childlike."

Having fallen into the line of carriages, the Rostóvs' carriage drove up to the theater, its wheels squeaking over the snow.

An attendant deferentially and quickly slipped before the ladies and opened the door of their box. Natásha, smoothing her gown, went in with Sónya and sat down, scanning the brilliant tiers of boxes opposite. A sensation she had not experienced for a long time—that of hundreds of eyes looking at her bare arms and neck—suddenly affected her both agreeably and disagreeably and called up a whole crowd of memories, desires, and emotions associated with that feeling.

The two remarkably pretty girls, Natásha and Sónya, with Count Rostóv who had not been seen in Moscow for a long time, attracted general attention. Moreover, everybody knew vaguely of Natásha's engagement to Prince Andrew, and knew that the Rostóvs had lived in the country ever since, and all looked with curiosity at a fiancée who was making one of the best matches in Russia.

Natásha's looks, as everyone told her, had improved in the country, and that evening thanks to her agitation she was particularly pretty. She struck those who saw her by her fullness of life and beauty, combined with her indifference to everything about her.

"The Karágins, Julie—and Borís with them. One can see at once that they're engaged . . ."

Behind them sat Anna Mikháylovna wearing a green headdress and with a happy look of resignation to the will of God on her face. Their box was pervaded by that atmosphere of an affianced couple which Natásha knew so well and liked so much. She turned away and suddenly remembered all that had been so humiliating in her morning's visit.

"What right has he not to wish to receive me into his family? Oh, better not think of it—not till he comes back!" she told herself, and began looking at the faces, some strange and some familiar, in the stalls. In the front, in the very center, leaning back against the orchestra rail, stood Dólokhov in a Persian dress, his curly hair brushed up into a huge shock.

The count, laughing, nudged the blushing Sónya and pointed to her former adorer.

"Do you recognize him?" said he. "And where has he sprung from?" he asked, turning to Shinshín. "Didn't he vanish somewhere?"

"He did," replied Shinshín. "He was in the Caucasus and ran away from there. They say he has been acting as minister to some ruling prince in Persia, where he killed the Shah's brother. Now all the Moscow ladies are mad about him! It's

'Dólokhov the Persian' that does it! We never hear a word but Dólokhov is mentioned. They swear by him, they offer him to you as they would a dish of choice sterlet. Dólokhov and Anatole Kurágin have turned all our ladies' heads."

A tall, beautiful woman with a mass of plaited hair and much exposed plump white shoulders and neck, round which she wore a double string of large pearls, entered the adjoining box rustling her heavy silk dress and took a long time settling into her place.

Natásha involuntarily gazed at that neck, those shoulders, and pearls and coiffure, and admired the beauty of the shoulders and the pearls. While Natásha was fixing her gaze on her for the second time the lady looked round and, meeting the count's eyes, nodded to him and smiled. She was the Countess Bezúkhova, Pierre's wife, and the count, who knew everyone in society, leaned over and spoke to her.

"Have you been here long, Countess?" he inquired. "I'll call, I'll call to kiss your hand. . . . Count Pierre never used to forget us. Is he here?"

"Yes, he meant to look in," answered Hélène, and glanced attentively at Natásha.

Count Rostóv resumed his seat.

"Handsome, isn't she?" he whispered to Natásha.

"Wonderful!" answered Natásha. "She's a woman one could easily fall in love with."

Just then the last chords of the overture were heard and the conductor tapped with his stick. Some latecomers took their seats in the stalls, and the curtain rose.

9

At a moment when all was quiet before the commencement of a song, a door leading to the stalls on the side nearest the Rostóvs' box creaked, and the steps of a belated arrival were heard. "There's Kurágin!" whispered Shinshín. Countess Bezúkhova turned smiling to the newcomer, and Natásha, following the direction of that look, saw an exceptionally handsome adjutant approaching their box with a self-assured yet courteous bearing. This was Anatole Kurágin whom she had seen and noticed long ago at the ball in Petersburg. He was now in an adjutant's uniform with one epaulet and a shoulder knot. He moved with a restrained swagger which would have been ridiculous had he not been so good-looking and had his handsome face not worn such an expression of good-humored complacency and gaiety. Though the performance was proceeding, he walked deliberately down the carpeted gangway, his sword and spurs slightly jingling and his handsome perfumed head held high. Having looked at Natásha he approached his sister, laid his well-gloved hand on the edge of her box, nodded to her, and leaning forward asked a question, with a motion toward Natásha.

"*Mais charmante!*" said he, evidently referring to Natásha, who did not exactly hear his words but understood them from the movement of his lips. Then he took his place in the first row of the stalls and sat down beside Dólokhov.

The first act was over. In the stalls everyone began moving about, going out and coming in.

Borís came to the Rostóvs' box, received their congratulations very simply, and raising his eyebrows with an absent-minded smile conveyed to Natásha and Sónya his fiancée's invitation to her wedding, and went away. Natásha with a gay, coquettish smile talked to him, and congratulated on his approaching wedding that same Borís with whom she had formerly been in love. In the state of intoxication she was in everything seemed simple and natural.

During the whole of that entr'acte Kurágin stood with Dólokhov in front of the orchestra partition, looking at the Rostóvs' box. Natásha knew he was talking about her and this afforded her pleasure. She even turned so that he should see her profile in what she thought was its most becoming aspect. Before the beginning of the second act Pierre appeared in the stalls. The Rostóvs had not seen him since their arrival. His face looked sad, and he had grown still stouter since Natásha last saw him. He passed up to the front rows, not noticing anyone. Anatole went up to him and began speaking to him, looking at and indicating the Rostóvs' box. On seeing Natásha Pierre grew animated and, hastily passing between the rows, came toward their box. When he got there he leaned on his elbows and, smiling, talked to her for a long time. While conversing with Pierre, Natásha heard a man's voice in Countess Bezúkhova's box and something told her it was Kurágin. She turned and their eyes met. Almost smiling, he gazed straight into her eyes with such an enraptured caressing look that it seemed strange to be so near him, to look at him like that, to be so sure he admired her, and not to be acquainted with him.

In the second act every time Natásha looked toward the stalls she saw Anatole Kurágin with an arm thrown across the back of his chair, staring at her. She was pleased to see that he was captivated by her and it did not occur to her that there was anything wrong in it.

When the second act was over Countess Bezúkhova rose, turned to the Rostóvs' box—her whole bosom completely exposed—beckoned the old count with a gloved finger, and paying no attention to those who had entered her box began talking to him with an amiable smile.

"Do make me acquainted with your charming daughters," said she. "The whole town is singing their praises and I don't even know them."

Natásha rose and curtsied to the splendid countess. She was so pleased by praise from this brilliant beauty that she blushed with pleasure.

Countess Bezúkhova quite deserved her reputation of being a fascinating woman. She could say what she did not think —especially what was flattering—quite simply and naturally.

"Dear count, you must let me look after your daughters! Though I am not staying here long this time—nor are you—I will try to amuse them. I have already heard much of you in Petersburg and wanted to get to know you," said she to Natásha with her stereotyped and lovely smile. To get better acquainted she asked that one of the young ladies should come into her box for the rest of the performance, and Natásha moved over to it.

10

During the entr'acte a whiff of cold air came into Hélène's box, the door opened, and Anatole entered, stooping and trying not to brush against anyone.

"Let me introduce my brother to you," said Hélène, her eyes shifting uneasily from Natásha to Anatole.

Natásha turned her pretty little head toward the elegant

young officer and smiled at him over her bare shoulder. Anatole, who was as handsome at close quarters as at a distance, sat down beside her and told her he had long wished to have this happiness—ever since the Narýshkins' ball in fact, at which he had had the well-remembered pleasure of seeing her. Kurágin was much more sensible and simple with women than among men. He talked boldly and naturally, and Natásha was strangely and agreeably struck by the fact that there was nothing formidable in this man about whom there was so much talk, but that on the contrary his smile was most naïve, cheerful, and good-natured.

"And do you know, Countess," he said, suddenly addressing her as an old, familiar acquaintance, "we are getting up a costume tournament; you ought to take part in it! It will be great fun. We shall all meet at the Karágins'! Please come! No! Really, eh?" said he.

While saying this he never removed his smiling eyes from her face, her neck, and her bare arms. Natásha knew for certain that he was enraptured by her. This pleased her, yet his presence made her feel constrained and oppressed. When she was not looking at him she felt that he was looking at her shoulders, and she involuntarily caught his eye so that he should look into hers rather than this. But looking into his eyes she was frightened, realizing that there was not that barrier of modesty she had always felt between herself and other men. She did not know how it was that within five minutes she had come to feel herself terribly near to this man. When she turned away she feared he might seize her from behind by her bare arm and kiss her on the neck. They spoke of most ordinary things, yet she felt that they were closer to one another than she had ever been to any man.

Natásha did not understand what he was saying any more than he did himself, but she felt that his incomprehensible words had an improper intention. She did not know what to say and turned away as if she had not heard his remark. But as soon as she had turned away she felt that he was there, behind, so close behind her.

"How is he now? Confused? Angry? Ought I to put it right?" she asked herself, and she could not refrain from turning round. She looked straight into his eyes, and his nearness, self-assurance, and the good-natured tenderness of his smile vanquished her. She smiled just as he was doing, gazing straight into his eyes. And again she felt with horror that no barrier lay between him and her.

The curtain rose again. Anatole left the box, serene and gay. Natásha went back to her father in the other box, now quite submissive to the world she found herself in.

As they were leaving the theater Anatole came up to them, called their carriage, and helped them in. As he was putting Natásha in he pressed her arm above the elbow. Agitated and flushed she turned round. He was looking at her with glittering eyes, smiling tenderly.

Only after she had reached home was Natásha able clearly to think over what had happened to her, and suddenly remembering Prince Andrew she was horrified, and at tea to which all had sat down after the opera, she gave a loud exclamation, flushed, and ran out of the room.

"O God! I am lost!" she said to herself. "How could I let him?" She sat for a long time hiding her flushed face in her hands trying to realize what had happened to her, but was unable either to understand what had happened or what she felt. Everything seemed dark, obscure, and terrible. "What is it? What was that terror I felt of him? What is this gnawing of conscience I am feeling now?" she thought.

"Am I spoiled for Andrew's love or not?" she asked herself, and with soothing irony replied: "What a fool I am to ask that! What did happen to me? Nothing! I have done nothing, I didn't lead him on at all. Nobody will know and I shall never see him again," she told herself. "So it is plain that nothing has happened and there is nothing to repent of, and Andrew can love me still. But why 'still'? O God, O God, why isn't he here?" Natásha quieted herself for a moment, but again some instinct told her that though all this was true, and though nothing had happened, yet the former purity of her love for Prince Andrew had perished.

11

Anatole Kurágin was staying in Moscow because his father had sent him away from Petersburg, where he had been spending twenty thousand rubles a year in cash, besides running up debts for as much more, which his creditors demanded from his father.

His father announced to him that he would now pay half his debts for the last time, but only on condition that he went to Moscow as adjutant to the commander in chief—a post his father had procured for him—and would at last try to make a good match there. He indicated to him Princess Mary and Julie Karágina.

Anatole consented and went to Moscow, where he put up at Pierre's house. Pierre received him unwillingly at first, but got used to him after a while, sometimes even accompanied him on his carousals, and gave him money under the guise of loans.

But he did not run after the unmarried girls, especially the rich heiresses who were most of them plain. There was a special reason for this, as he had got married two years before—a fact known only to his most intimate friends. At that time while with his regiment in Poland, a Polish landowner of small means had forced him to marry his daughter. Anatole had very soon abandoned his wife and, for a payment which he agreed to send to his father-in-law, had arranged to be free to pass himself off as a bachelor.

Dólokhov, who had reappeared that year in Moscow after his exile and his Persian adventures, and was leading a life of luxury, gambling, and dissipation, associated with his old Petersburg comrade Kurágin and made use of him for his own ends.

Natásha had made a strong impression on Kurágin. At supper after the opera he described to Dólokhov with the air of a connoisseur the attractions of her arms, shoulders, feet, and hair and expressed his intention of making love to her. Anatole had no notion and was incapable of considering what might come of such love-making, as he never had any notion of the outcome of any of his actions.

"She's first-rate, my dear fellow, but not for us," replied Dólokhov.

"I will tell my sister to ask her to dinner," said Anatole. "Eh?"

"You'd better wait till she's married. . . ."

"You know, I adore little girls, they lose their heads at once," pursued Anatole.

"You have been caught once already by a 'little girl,'" said Dólokhov who knew of Kurágin's marriage. "Take care!"

"Well, that can't happen twice! Eh?" said Anatole, with a good-humored laugh.

12

The day after the opera the Rostóvs went nowhere and nobody came to see them. Márya Dmítrievna talked to the count about something which they concealed from Natásha. Natásha guessed they were talking about the old prince and planning something, and this disquieted and offended her. She was expecting Prince Andrew any moment and twice that day sent a manservant to the Vozdvízhenka to ascertain whether he had come. He had not arrived. She continually fancied that either he would never come or that something would happen to her before he came.

On Sunday morning Márya Dmítrievna invited her visitors to Mass at her parish church—the Church of the Assumption built over the graves of victims of the plague.

After Mass, when they had finished their coffee in the dining room where the loose covers had been removed from the furniture, a servant announced that the carriage was ready, and Márya Dmítrievna rose with a stern air. She wore her holiday shawl, in which she paid calls, and announced that she was going to see Prince Nicholas Bolkónski to have an explanation with him about Natásha.

After she had gone, a dressmaker from Madame Suppert-Roguet waited on the Rostóvs, and Natásha, very glad of this diversion, having shut herself into a room adjoining the drawing room, occupied herself trying on the new dresses. Just as she had put on a bodice without sleeves and only tacked together, and was turning her head to see in the glass how the back fitted, she heard in the drawing room the animated sounds of her father's voice and another's—a woman's—that made her flush. It was Hélène. Natásha had not time to take off the bodice before the door opened and Countess Bezúkhova, dressed in a purple velvet gown with a high collar, came into the room beaming with good-humored amiable smiles.

"Oh, my enchantress!" she cried to the blushing Natásha. "Charming! No, this is really beyond anything, my dear count," said she to Count Rostóv who had followed her in. "How can you live in Moscow and go nowhere? No, I won't let you off! Mademoiselle George will recite at my house tonight and there'll be some people, and if you don't bring your lovely girls—who are prettier than Mademoiselle George—I won't know you! My husband is away in Tver or I would send him to fetch you. You must come. You positively must! Between eight and nine."

A smile of pleasure never left Natásha's face. She felt happy and as if she were blossoming under the praise of this dear Countess Bezúkhova who had formerly seemed to her so unapproachable and important and was now so kind to her. Natásha brightened up and felt almost in love with this woman, who was so beautiful and so kind. Hélène for her part was sincerely delighted with Natásha and wished to give her a good time.

As she was leaving the Rostóvs she called her protégée aside.

"My brother dined with me yesterday—we nearly died of laughter—he ate nothing and kept sighing for you, my charmer! He is madly, quite madly, in love with you, my dear."

Natásha blushed scarlet when she heard this.

"How she blushes, how she blushes, my pretty!" said Hélène. "You must certainly come. If you love somebody, my charmer, that is not a reason to shut yourself up. Even if you are engaged, I am sure your fiancé would wish you to go into society rather than be bored to death."

"So she knows I am engaged, and she and her husband Pierre—that good Pierre—have talked and laughed about this. So it's all right." And again, under Hélène's influence, what had seemed terrible now seemed simple and natural. "And she is such a *grande dame*, so kind, and evidently likes me so much. And why not enjoy myself?" thought Natásha, gazing at Hélène with wide-open, wondering eyes.

Márya Dmítrievna came back to dinner taciturn and serious, having evidently suffered a defeat at the old prince's. She was still too agitated by the encounter to be able to talk of the affair calmly. In answer to the count's inquiries she replied that things were all right and that she would tell about it next day. On hearing of Countess Bezúkhova's visit and the invitation for that evening, Márya Dmítrievna remarked:

"I don't care to have anything to do with Bezúkhova and don't advise you to; however, if you've promised—go. It will divert your thoughts," she added, addressing Natásha.

13

Count Rostóv took the girls to Countess Bezúkhova's. There were a good many people there, but nearly all strangers to Natásha. Count Rostóv was displeased to see that the company consisted almost entirely of men and women known for the freedom of their conduct. The count decided not to sit down to cards or let his girls out of his sight and to get away as soon as Mademoiselle George's performance was over.

Anatole was at the door, evidently on the lookout for the Rostóvs. Immediately after greeting the count he went up to Natásha and followed her. As soon as she saw him she was seized by the same feeling she had had at the opera—gratified vanity at his admiration of her and fear at the absence of a moral barrier between them.

Hélène welcomed Natásha delightedly and was loud in admiration of her beauty and her dress.

Mademoiselle George looked sternly and gloomily at the audience and began reciting some French verses describing her guilty love for her son. In some places she raised her voice, in others she whispered, lifting her head triumphantly; sometimes she paused and uttered hoarse sounds, rolling her eyes.

After giving several recitations, Mademoiselle George left, and Countess Bezúkhova asked her visitors into the ballroom. The count wished to go home, but Hélène entreated him not to spoil her improvised ball, and the Rostóvs stayed on. Anatole asked Natásha for a valse and as they danced he pressed her waist and hand and told her she was bewitching and that he loved her. During the *écossaise*, which she also danced with him, Anatole said nothing when they happened to be by themselves, but merely gazed at her. Natásha lifted her frightened eyes to him, but there was such confident tenderness in his affectionate look and smile that she could not, while looking at him, say what she had to say. She lowered her eyes.

"Don't say such things to me. I am betrothed and love another," she said rapidly. . . . She glanced at him.

Anatole was not upset or pained by what she had said.

"Don't speak to me of that! What can I do?" said he. "I tell you I am madly, madly, in love with you! Is it my fault that you are enchanting? . . . It's our turn to begin."

Natásha, animated and excited, looked about her with wide-open frightened eyes and seemed merrier than usual. She understood hardly anything that went on that evening. They danced the *écossaise* and the *Grossvater*. Her father asked her to come home, but she begged to remain. Wherever she went and whomever she was speaking to, she felt *his* eyes upon her. Later on she recalled how she had asked her father to let her go to the dressing room to rearrange her dress, that Hélène had followed her and spoken laughingly of her brother's love, and that she again met Anatole in the little sitting room. Hélène had disappeared leaving them alone, and Anatole had taken her hand and said in a tender voice:

"I cannot come to visit you but is it possible that I shall never see you? I love you madly. Can I never . . . ?" and, blocking her path, he brought his face close to hers.

His large, glittering, masculine eyes were so close to hers that she saw nothing but them.

"Natalie?" he whispered inquiringly while she felt her hands being painfully pressed. "Natalie?"

"I don't understand. I have nothing to say," her eyes replied.

Burning lips were pressed to hers, and at the same instant she felt herself released, and Hélène's footsteps and the rustle of her dress were heard in the room. Natásha looked round at her, and then, red and trembling, threw a frightened look of inquiry at Anatole and moved toward the door.

"One word, just one, for God's sake!" cried Anatole.

She paused. She so wanted a word from him that would explain to her what had happened and to which she could find no answer.

"Natalie, just a word, only one!" he kept repeating, evidently not knowing what to say—and he repeated it till Hélène came up to them.

Hélène returned with Natásha to the drawing room. The Rostóvs went away without staying for supper.

After reaching home Natásha did not sleep all night. She was tormented by the insoluble question whether she loved Anatole or Prince Andrew. She loved Prince Andrew—she remembered distinctly how deeply she loved him. But she also loved Anatole, of that there was no doubt. "Else how could all this have happened?" thought she. "If, after that, I could return his smile when saying good-by, if I was able to let it come to that, it means that I loved him from the first. It means that he is kind, noble, and splendid, and I could not help loving him. What am I to do if I love him and the other one too?" she asked herself, unable to find an answer to these terrible questions.

14

After breakfast, which was her best time, Márya Dmítrievna sat down in her armchair and called Natásha and the count to her.

"Well, friends, I have now thought the whole matter over and this is my advice," she began. "Yesterday, as you know, I went to see Prince Bolkónski. Well, I had a talk with him. . . . He took it into his head to begin shouting, but I am not one to be shouted down. I said what I had to say!"

"Well, and he?" asked the count.

"He? He's crazy . . . he did not want to listen. But what's the use of talking? As it is we have worn the poor girl out," said Márya Dmítrievna. "My advice to you is finish your business and go back home to Otrádnoe . . . and wait there."

"Oh, no!" exclaimed Natásha.

"Yes, go back," said Márya Dmítrievna, "and wait there. If your betrothed comes here now—there will be no avoiding a quarrel; but alone with the old man he will talk things over and then come on to you."

"That is perfectly true. And I am sorry I went to see him and took her," said the old count.

"No, why be sorry? Being here, you have to pay your respects. But if he won't—that's his affair," said Márya Dmítrievna, looking for something in her reticule.

Having found what she was looking for in the reticule she handed it to Natásha. It was a letter from Princess Mary.

Princess Mary wrote that she was in despair at the misunderstanding that had occurred between them. Whatever her father's feelings might be, she begged Natásha to believe that she could not help loving her as the one chosen by her brother, for whose happiness she was ready to sacrifice everything.

After reading the letter Natásha sat down at the writing table to answer it. "Dear Princess," she wrote in French quickly and mechanically, and then paused. What more could she write after all that had happened the evening before? "Yes, yes! All that has happened, and now all is changed," she thought as she sat with the letter she had begun before her. "Must I break off with him? Must I really? That's awful . . ." and to escape from these dreadful thoughts she went to Sónya and began sorting patterns with her.

After dinner Natásha went to her room and again took up Princess Mary's letter. "Can it be that it is all over?" she thought. "Can it be that all this has happened so quickly and has destroyed all that went before?" She recalled her love for Prince Andrew in all its former strength, and at the same time felt that she loved Kurágin. She vividly pictured herself as Prince Andrew's wife, and the scenes of happiness with him she had so often repeated in her imagination, and at the same time, aglow with excitement, recalled every detail of yesterday's interview with Anatole.

"Please, Miss!" whispered a maid entering the room with a mysterious air. "A man told me to give you this—" and she handed Natásha a letter.

"Only, for Christ's sake . . ." the girl went on, as Natásha, without thinking, mechanically broke the seal and read a love letter from Anatole, of which, without taking in a word, she understood only that it was a letter from him—from the man she loved. Yes, she loved him, or else how could that have happened which had happened? And how could she have a love letter from him in her hand?

With trembling hands Natásha held that passionate love letter which Dólokhov had composed for Anatole, and as she read it she found in it an echo of all that she herself imagined she was feeling.

"Since yesterday evening my fate has been sealed; to be loved by you or to die. There is no other way for me," the letter began. Then he went on to say that he knew her parents would not give her to him—for this there were secret reasons he could reveal only to her—but that if she loved him she need only say the word *yes,* and no human power could hinder their bliss. Love would conquer all. He would steal her away and carry her off to the ends of the earth.

"Yes, yes! I love him!" thought Natásha, reading the letter for the twentieth time and finding some peculiarly deep meaning in each word of it.

That evening Márya Dmítrievna was going to the Akhárovs' and proposed to take the girls with her. Natásha, pleading a headache, remained at home.

15

On returning late in the evening Sónya went to Natásha's room, and to her surprise found her still dressed and asleep on the sofa. Open on the table beside her lay Anatole's letter. Sónya picked it up and read it.

As she read she glanced at the sleeping Natásha, trying to find in her face an explanation of what she was reading, but did not find it. Her face was calm, gentle, and happy. Clutching her breast to keep herself from choking, Sónya, pale and trembling with fear and agitation, sat down in an armchair and burst into tears.

"How was it I noticed nothing? How could it go so far? Can she have left off loving Prince Andrew? And how could she let Kurágin go to such lengths? He is a deceiver and a villain, that's plain! What will Nicholas, dear noble Nicholas, do when he hears of it?"

Sónya wiped away her tears and went up to Natásha, again scanning her face.

"Natásha!" she said, just audibly.

Natásha awoke and saw Sónya.

"Ah, you're back?"

And with the decision and tenderness that often come at

the moment of awakening, she embraced her friend, but noticing Sónya's look of embarrassment, her own face expressed confusion and suspicion.

"Sónya, you've read that letter?" she demanded.

"Yes," answered Sónya softly.

Natásha smiled rapturously.

"No, Sónya, I can't any longer!" she said. "I can't hide it from you any longer. You know, we love one another! Sónya, darling, he writes . . . Sónya . . ."

Sónya stared open-eyed at Natásha, unable to believe her ears.

"And Bolkónski?" she asked.

"Ah, Sónya, if you only knew how happy I am!" cried Natásha. "You don't know what love is. . . ."

"But, Natásha, can *that* be all over?"

Natásha looked at Sónya with wide-open eyes as if she could not grasp the question.

"Well, then, are you refusing Prince Andrew?" said Sónya.

"Oh, you don't understand anything! Don't talk nonsense, just listen!" said Natásha, with momentary vexation.

"But I can't believe it," insisted Sónya. "I don't understand. How is it you have loved a man for a whole year and suddenly . . . Why, you have only seen him three times! Natásha, I don't believe you, you're joking! In three days to forget everything and so . . ."

"Three days?" said Natásha. "It seems to me I've loved him a hundred years. It seems to me that I have never loved anyone before. You can't understand it. . . . Sónya, wait a bit, sit here," and Natásha embraced and kissed her.

"I had heard that it happens like this, and you have heard it too, but it's only now that I feel such love. It's not the same as before. As soon as I saw him I felt he was my master and I his slave, and that I could not help loving him. Yes, his slave! Whatever he orders I shall do. You don't understand that. What can I do? What can I do, Sónya?" cried Natásha with a happy yet frightened expression.

"But think what you are doing," cried Sónya. "I can't leave it like this. This secret correspondence . . . How could you let him go so far?" she went on, with a horror and disgust she could hardly conceal.

"I told you that I have no will," Natásha replied. "Why can't you understand? I love him!"

"Then I won't let it come to that . . . I shall tell!" cried Sónya, bursting into tears.

"What do you mean? For God's sake . . . If you tell, you are my enemy!" declared Natásha. "You want me to be miserable, you want us to be separated. . . ."

When she saw Natásha's fright, Sónya shed tears of shame and pity for her friend.

"But what has happened between you?" she asked. "What has he said to you? Why doesn't he come to the house?"

Natásha did not answer her questions.

"For God's sake, Sónya, don't tell anyone, don't torture me," Natásha entreated. "Remember no one ought to interfere in such matters! I have confided in you. . . ."

"But why this secrecy? Why doesn't he come to the house?" asked Sónya. "Why doesn't he openly ask for your hand? You know Prince Andrew gave you complete freedom—if it is really so; but I don't believe it! Natásha, have you considered what these *secret reasons* can be?"

Natásha looked at Sónya with astonishment. Evidently this question presented itself to her mind for the first time and she did not know how to answer it.

"I don't know what the reasons are. But there must be reasons!"

Sónya sighed and shook her head incredulously.

"If there were reasons . . ." she began.

But Natásha, guessing her doubts, interrupted her in alarm.

"Sónya, one can't doubt him! One can't, one can't! Don't you understand?" she cried.

"Does he love you?"

"Does he love me?" Natásha repeated with a smile of pity at her friend's lack of comprehension. "Why, you have read his letter and you have seen him."

"But if he is dishonorable?"

"*He!* dishonorable? If you only knew!" exclaimed Natásha.

"If he is an honorable man he should either declare his intentions or cease seeing you; and if you won't do this, I will. I will write to him, and I will tell Papa!" said Sónya resolutely.

"But I can't live without him!" cried Natásha.

"Natásha, I don't understand you. And what are you saying! Think of your father and of Nicholas."

"I don't want anyone, I don't love anyone but him. How dare you say he is dishonorable? Don't you know that I love him?" screamed Natásha. "Go away, Sónya! I don't want to quarrel with you, but go, for God's sake go! You see how I am suffering!" Natásha cried angrily, in a voice of despair and repressed irritation. Sónya burst into sobs and ran from the room.

Natásha went to the table and without a moment's reflection wrote that answer to Princess Mary which she had been unable to write all the morning. In this letter she said briefly that all their misunderstandings were at an end; that availing herself of the magnanimity of Prince Andrew who when he went abroad had given her her freedom, she begged Princess Mary to forget everything and forgive her if she had been to blame toward her, but that she could not be his wife. At that moment this all seemed quite easy, simple, and clear to Natásha.

On Friday the Rostóvs were to return to the country, but on Wednesday the count went with the prospective purchaser to his estate near Moscow.

On the day the count left, Sónya and Natásha were invited to a big dinner party at the Karágins', and Márya Dmítrievna took them there. At that party Natásha again met Anatole, and Sónya noticed that she spoke to him, trying not to be overheard, and that all through dinner she was more agitated than ever. When they got home Natásha was the first to begin the explanation Sónya expected.

"Oh, Sónya, if you knew him as I do! He said . . . He asked me what I had promised Bolkónski. He was glad I was free to refuse him."

Sónya sighed sorrowfully.

"But you haven't refused Bolkónski?" said she.

"Perhaps I have. Perhaps all is over between me and Bolkónski. Why do you think so badly of me?"

"Natásha," said she, "you asked me not to speak to you, and I haven't spoken, but now you yourself have begun. I don't trust him, Natásha. Why this secrecy?"

"Again, again!" interrupted Natásha.

"Natásha, I am afraid for you!"

"Afraid of what?"

"I am afraid you're going to your ruin," said Sónya resolutely, and was herself horrified at what she had said.

Anger again showed in Natásha's face.

"And I'll go to my ruin, I will, as soon as possible! It's not your business! It won't be you, but I, who'll suffer. Leave me alone, leave me alone! I hate you!"

"Natásha!" moaned Sónya, aghast.

"I hate you, I hate you! You're my enemy forever!" And Natásha ran out of the room.

Natásha did not speak to Sónya again and avoided her. With the same expression of agitated surprise and guilt she went about the house, taking up now one occupation, now another, and at once abandoning them.

Hard as it was for Sónya, she watched her friend and did not let her out of her sight.

After tea Sónya noticed a housemaid at Natásha's door timidly waiting to let her pass. She let the girl go in, and then listening at the door learned that another letter had been delivered.

Then suddenly it became clear to Sónya that Natásha had some dreadful plan for that evening. Sónya knocked at her door. Natásha did not let her in.

"She will run away with him!" thought Sónya. "She is capable of anything." To tell Márya Dmítrievna who had such faith in Natásha seemed to Sónya terrible. "Well, anyway," thought Sónya as she stood in the dark passage, "now or never I must prove that I remember the family's goodness to me and that I love Nicholas. Yes! If I don't sleep for three nights I'll not leave this passage and will hold her back by force and not let the family be disgraced," thought she.

16

Dólokhov arranges a plan for Anatole to elope with Natásha, perform a mock marriage, and escape abroad with her.

17

Márya Dmítrievna learns of the elopement plan and prevents it.

18

Márya Dmítrievna, having found Sónya weeping in the corridor, made her confess everything, and intercepting the note to Natásha she read it and went into Natásha's room with it in her hand.

"You shameless good-for-nothing!" said she. "I won't hear a word."

Pushing back Natásha who looked at her with astonished but tearless eyes, she locked her in; and having given orders to the yard porter to admit the persons who would be coming that evening, but not to let them out again, and having told the footman to bring them up to her, she seated herself in the drawing room to await the abductors.

When Gabriel came to inform her that the men who had come had run away again, she rose frowning, and clasping her hands behind her paced through the rooms a long time considering what she should do. Toward midnight she went to Natásha's room fingering the key in her pocket. Sónya was sitting sobbing in the corridor. "Márya Dmítrievna, for God's sake let me in to her!" she pleaded, but Márya Dmítrievna unlocked the door and went in without giving her an answer. . . . "Disgusting, abominable . . . In my house . . . horrid girl, hussy! I'm only sorry for her father!" thought she, trying to restrain her wrath. "Hard as it may be, I'll tell them all to hold their tongues and will hide it from the count." She entered the room with resolute steps. Natásha was lying on the sofa, her head hidden in her hands, and she did not stir. She was in just the same position in which Márya Dmítrievna had left her.

"A nice girl! Very nice!" said Márya Dmítrievna. "Arranging meetings with lovers in my house! It's no use pretending: you listen when I speak to you!" And Márya Dmítrievna touched her arm. "Listen when I speak! You've disgraced yourself like the lowest of hussies. I'd treat you differently, but I'm sorry for your father, so I will conceal it."

Natásha did not change her position, but her whole body heaved with noiseless, convulsive sobs which choked her. Márya Dmítrievna glanced round at Sónya and seated herself on the sofa beside Natásha.

She put her large hand under Natásha's face and turned it toward her. Both Márya Dmítrievna and Sónya were amazed when they saw how Natásha looked. Her eyes were dry and glistening, her lips compressed, her cheeks sunken.

"Let me be! . . . What is it to me? . . . I shall die!" she muttered, wrenching herself from Márya Dmítrievna's hands with a vicious effort and sinking down again into her former position.

"Natalie!" said Márya Dmítrievna. "I wish for your good. Lie still, stay like that then, I won't touch you. But listen. I won't tell you how guilty you are. You know that yourself. But when your father comes back tomorrow—what am I to tell him? Eh?"

Again Natásha's body shook with sobs.

"Suppose he finds out, and your brother, and your betrothed?"

"I have no betrothed: I have refused him!" cried Natásha.

"That's all the same," continued Márya Dmítrievna. "If they hear of this will they let it pass? He, your father, I know him . . . if he challenges him to a duel will that be all right? Eh?"

"Oh, let me be! Why have you interfered at all? Why? Why? Who asked you to?" shouted Natásha, raising herself on the sofa and looking malignantly at Márya Dmítrievna.

"But what did you want?" cried Márya Dmítrievna, growing angry again. "Were you kept under lock and key? Who hindered his coming to the house? Why carry you off as if you were some gypsy singing girl? . . . Well, if he had carried you off . . . do you think they wouldn't have found him? Your father, or brother, or your betrothed? And he's a scoundrel, a wretch—that's a fact!"

"He is better than any of you!" exclaimed Natásha getting up. "If you hadn't interfered . . . Oh, my God! What is it all? What is it? Sónya, why? . . . Go away!"

"Well, let her sleep," said Márya Dmítrievna as she went out of the room.

Next day Count Rostóv returned from his estate near Moscow in time for lunch as he had promised. He was in very good spirits; the affair with the purchaser was going on satisfactorily, and there was nothing to keep him any longer in Moscow, away from the countess whom he missed. Márya Dmítrievna met him and told him that Natásha had been very unwell the day before and that they had sent for the doctor, but that she was better now. Natásha had not left her room that morning. With compressed and parched lips and dry fixed eyes, she sat at the window, uneasily watching the people who drove past and hurriedly glancing round at anyone who entered the room. She was evidently expecting news of him and that he would come or would write to her.

19

From the day his wife arrived in Moscow Pierre had been intending to go away somewhere, so as not to be near her. Soon after the Rostóvs came to Moscow the effect Natásha had on him made him hasten to carry out his intention. He went to Tver to see Joseph Alexéevich's widow, who had long since promised to hand over to him some papers of her deceased husband's.

When he returned to Moscow Pierre was handed a letter from Márya Dmítrievna asking him to come and see her on a matter of great importance relating to Andrew Bolkónski and his betrothed. Pierre had been avoiding Natásha because it seemed to him that his feeling for her was stronger than a married man's should be for his friend's fiancée. Yet some fate constantly threw them together.

"What has happened?" asked Pierre, entering Márya Dmítrievna's room.

"Fine doings!" answered Márya Dmítrievna. "For fifty-eight years have I lived in this world and never known anything so disgraceful!"

And having put him on his honor not to repeat anything she told him, Márya Dmítrievna informed him that Natásha had refused Prince Andrew without her parents' knowledge and that the cause of this was Anatole Kurágin into whose society Pierre's wife had thrown her and with whom Natásha had tried to elope during her father's absence, in order to be married secretly.

Pierre raised his shoulders and listened openmouthed to what was told him, scarcely able to believe his own ears. That Prince Andrew's deeply loved affianced wife—the same Natásha Rostóva who used to be so charming—should give up Bolkónski for that fool Anatole who was already secretly married (as Pierre knew), and should be so in love with him as to agree to run away with him, was something Pierre could not conceive and could not imagine.

He could not reconcile the charming impression he had of Natásha, whom he had known from a child, with this new conception of her baseness, folly, and cruelty. He thought of his wife. "They are all alike!" he said to himself, reflecting that he was not the only man unfortunate enough to be tied to a bad woman. But still he pitied Prince Andrew to the point of tears and sympathized with his wounded pride, and the more he pitied his friend the more did he think with contempt and even with disgust of that Natásha.

"But how get married?" said Pierre, in answer to Márya Dmítrievna. "He could not marry—he is married!"

"Things get worse from hour to hour!" ejaculated Márya Dmítrievna. "A nice youth! What a scoundrel! And she's expecting him—expecting him since yesterday. She must be told! Then at least she won't go on expecting him."

After hearing the details of Anatole's marriage from Pierre, and giving vent to her anger against Anatole in words of abuse, Márya Dmítrievna told Pierre why she had sent for him. She was afraid that the count or Bolkónski, who might arrive at any moment, if they knew of this affair (which she hoped to hide from them) might challenge Anatole to a duel, and she therefore asked Pierre to tell his brother-in-law in her name to leave Moscow and not dare to let her set eyes on him again. Pierre—only now realizing the danger to the old count, Nicholas, and Prince Andrew—promised to do as she wished. Having briefly and exactly explained her wishes to him, she let him go to the drawing room.

"Mind, the count knows nothing. Behave as if you know nothing either," she said. "And I will go and tell her it is

no use expecting him! And stay to dinner if you care to!"
she called after Pierre.

Pierre met the old count, who seemed nervous and upset.
That morning Natásha had told him that she had rejected
Bolkónski.

"Troubles, troubles, my dear fellow!" he said to Pierre. . .
"It's hard, Count, hard to manage daughters in their mother's
absence. . . ."

Sónya entered the room with an agitated face.

"Natásha is not quite well; she's in her room and would
like to see you. Márya Dmítrievna is with her and she too
asks you to come."

When Márya Dmítrievna told Natásha that Anatole was
married, Natásha did not wish to believe it and insisted on
having it confirmed by Pierre himself. Sónya told Pierre
this as she led him along the corridor to Natásha's room.

Natásha, pale and stern, was sitting beside Márya Dmítrievna, and her eyes, glittering feverishly, met Pierre with a
questioning look the moment he entered. She did not smile
or nod, but only gazed fixedly at him, and her look asked
only one thing: was he a friend, or like the others an enemy
in regard to Anatole? As for Pierre, he evidently did not
exist for her.

"He knows all about it," said Márya Dmítrievna pointing
to Pierre and addressing Natásha. "Let him tell you whether
I have told the truth."

Natásha looked from one to the other as a hunted and
wounded animal looks at the approaching dogs and sportsmen.

"Natálya Ilýnichna," Pierre began, dropping his eyes with
a feeling of pity for her and loathing for the thing he had to
do, "whether it is true or not should make no difference to
you, because . . ."

"Then it is not true that he's married!"

"Yes, it is true."

"Has he been married long?" she asked. "On your hon-
or? . . ."

Pierre gave his word of honor.

She was evidently unable to speak and made a sign with
her hands that they should leave her alone.

20

Pierre did not stay for dinner, but left the room and went away at once. He drove through the town seeking Anatole Kurágin, at the thought of whom now the blood rushed to his heart and he felt a difficulty in breathing.

Anatole, for whom Pierre was looking, dined that day with Dólokhov, consulting him as to how to remedy this unfortunate affair. It seemed to him essential to see Natásha. In the evening he drove to his sister's to discuss with her how to arrange a meeting. When Pierre returned home after vainly hunting all over Moscow, his valet informed him that Prince Anatole was with the countess. The countess' drawing room was full of guests.

Pierre without greeting his wife whom he had not seen since his return—at that moment she was more repulsive to him than ever—entered the drawing room and seeing Anatole went up to him.

"Ah, Pierre," said the countess going up to her husband. "You don't know what a plight our Anatole . . ."

She stopped, seeing in the forward thrust of her husband's head, in his glowing eyes and his resolute gait, the terrible indications of that rage and strength which she knew and had herself experienced after his duel with Dólokhov.

"Where you are, there is vice and evil!" said Pierre to his wife. "Anatole, come with me! I must speak to you," he added in French.

Anatole glanced round at his sister and rose submissively, ready to follow Pierre. Pierre, taking him by the arm, pulled him toward himself and was leading him from the room.

Having entered his study Pierre closed the door and addressed Anatole without looking at him.

"You promised Countess Rostóva to marry her and were about to elope with her, is that so?"

"Mon cher," answered Anatole (their whole conversation was in French), "I don't consider myself bound to answer questions put to me in that tone."

Pierre's face, already pale, became distorted by fury. He seized Anatole by the collar of his uniform with his big hand

312

and shook him from side to side till Anatole's face showed a sufficient degree of terror.

"When I tell you that I must talk to you! . . ." repeated Pierre.

"Come now, this is stupid. What?" said Anatole, fingering a button of his collar that had been wrenched loose with a bit of cloth.

"You're a scoundrel and a blackguard, and I don't know what deprives me from the pleasure of smashing your head with this!" said Pierre, expressing himself so artificially because he was talking French.

He took a heavy paperweight and lifted it threateningly, but at once put it back in its place.

"Did you promise to marry her?"

"I . . . I . . . I didn't think of it. I never promised, because . . ."

Pierre interrupted him.

"Have you any letters of hers? Any letters?" he said, moving toward Anatole.

Anatole glanced at him and immediately thrust his hand into his pocket and drew out his pocketbook.

Pierre took the letter Anatole handed him and, pushing aside a table that stood in his way, threw himself on the sofa.

"I shan't be violent, don't be afraid!" said Pierre in answer to a frightened gesture of Anatole's. "First, the letters," said he, as if repeating a lesson to himself. "Secondly," he continued after a short pause, again rising and again pacing the room, "tomorrow you must get out of Moscow."

"But how can I? . . ."

"Thirdly," Pierre continued without listening to him, "you must never breathe a word of what has passed between you and Countess Rostóva. I know I can't prevent your doing so, but if you have a spark of conscience . . ." Pierre paced the room several times in silence.

Anatole sat at a table frowning and biting his lips.

"After all, you must understand that besides your pleasure there is such a thing as other people's happiness and peace, and that you are ruining a whole life for the sake of amusing yourself."

Pierre paused and looked at Anatole no longer with an angry but with a questioning look.

"I don't know about that, eh?" said Anatole, growing more confident as Pierre mastered his wrath.

"Though it was tête-à-tête," Anatole continued, "still I can't . . ."

"Is it satisfaction you want?" said Pierre ironically.

"You could at least take back your words. What? If you want me to do as you wish, eh?"

"I take them back, I take them back!" said Pierre, "and I ask you to forgive me." Pierre involuntarily glanced at the loose button. "And if you require money for your journey . . ."

Anatole smiled. The expression of that base and cringing smile, which Pierre knew so well in his wife, revolted him.

"Oh, vile and heartless brood!" he exclaimed, and left the room.

Next day Anatole left for Petersburg.

21

Pierre drove to Márya Dmítrievna's to tell her of the fulfillment of her wish that Kurágin should be banished from Moscow. The whole house was in a state of alarm and commotion. Natásha was very ill, having, as Márya Dmítrievna told him in secret, poisoned herself the night after she had been told that Anatole was married, with some arsenic she had stealthily procured. After swallowing a little she had been so frightened that she woke Sónya and told her what she had done. The necessary antidotes had been administered in time and she was now out of danger, though still so weak that it was out of the question to move her to the country, and so the countess had been sent for. Pierre saw the distracted count, and Sónya, who had a tear-stained face, but he could not see Natásha.

Some days after Anatole's departure Pierre received a note from Prince Andrew, informing him of his arrival and asking him to come to see him.

As soon as he reached Moscow, Prince Andrew had received from his father Natásha's note to Princess Mary breaking off her engagement (Mademoiselle Bourienne had purloined it from Princess Mary and given it to the old prince), and he heard from him the story of Natásha's elopement, with additions.

Prince Andrew had arrived in the evening and Pierre came to see him next morning. Pierre expected to find Prince Andrew in almost the same state as Natásha and was therefore surprised on entering the drawing room to hear him in the study talking in a loud animated voice about some intrigue going on in Petersburg. The old prince's voice and another now and then interrupted him.

Pierre went into the study. Prince Andrew, greatly changed and plainly in better health, but with a fresh horizontal wrinkle between his brows, stood in civilian dress facing his father and Prince Meshchérski, warmly disputing and vigorously gesticulating. The conversation was about Speránski —the news of whose sudden exile and alleged treachery had just reached Moscow.

He paused at the sight of Pierre. His face quivered and immediately assumed a vindictive expression.

"Posterity will do him justice," he concluded, and at once turned to Pierre.

"Well, how are you? Still getting stouter?" he said with animation, but the new wrinkle in his forehead deepened. "Yes, I am well," he said in answer to Pierre's question, and smiled.

To Pierre that smile said plainly: "I am well, but my health is now of no use to anyone."

After a few words to Pierre about the awful roads from the Polish frontier, about people he had met in Switzerland who knew Pierre, and about M. Dessalles, whom he had brought from abroad to be his son's tutor, Prince Andrew again joined warmly in the conversation about Speránski which was still going on between the two old men.

Pierre now recognized in his friend a need with which he was only too familiar, to get excited and to have arguments about extraneous matters in order to stifle thoughts that were too oppressive and too intimate.

When Prince Meshchérski had left, Prince Andrew took Pierre's arm and asked him into the room that had been assigned him. A bed had been made up there, and some open portmanteaux and trunks stood about. Prince Andrew went to one and took out a small casket, from which he drew a packet wrapped in paper. He did it all silently and very quickly. He stood up and coughed. His face was gloomy and his lips compressed.

"Forgive me for troubling you. . . ."

Pierre saw that Prince Andrew was going to speak of Natásha, and his broad face expressed pity and sympathy. This expression irritated Prince Andrew, and in a determined, ringing, and unpleasant tone he continued:

"I have received a refusal from Countess Rostóva and have heard reports of your brother-in-law having sought her hand, or something of that kind. Is that true?"

"Both true and untrue," Pierre began; but Prince Andrew interrupted him.

"Here are her letters and her portrait," said he.

He took the packet from the table and handed it to Pierre.

"Give this to the countess . . . if you see her."

"She is very ill," said Pierre.

"Then she is here still?" said Prince Andrew. "And Prince Kurágin?" he added quickly.

"He left long ago. She has been at death's door."

"I much regret her illness," said Prince Andrew; and he smiled like his father, coldly, maliciously, and unpleasantly.

"So Monsieur Kurágin has not honored Countess Rostóva with his hand?" said Prince Andrew, and he snorted several times.

"He could not marry, for he was married already," said Pierre.

Prince Andrew laughed disagreeably, again reminding one of his father.

"And where is your brother-in-law now, if I may ask?" he said.

"He has gone to Peters . . . But I don't know," said Pierre.

"Well, it doesn't matter," said Prince Andrew. "Tell Countess Rostóva that she was and is perfectly free and that I wish her all that is good."

Pierre took the packet. Prince Andrew, as if trying to remember whether he had something more to say, or waiting to see if Pierre would say anything, looked fixedly at him.

"I say, do you remember our discussion in Petersburg?" asked Pierre, "about . . ."

"Yes," returned Prince Andrew hastily. "I said that a

fallen woman should be forgiven, but I didn't say I could forgive her. I can't."

"But can this be compared . . . ?" said Pierre.

Prince Andrew interrupted him and cried sharply: "Yes, ask her hand again, be magnanimous, and so on? . . . Yes, that would be very noble, but I am unable to follow in that gentleman's footsteps. If you wish to be my friend never speak to me of that . . . of all that! Well, good-by. So you'll give her the packet?"

Pierre left the room and went to the old prince and Princess Mary.

The old man seemed livelier than usual. Princess Mary was the same as always, but beneath her sympathy for her brother, Pierre noticed her satisfaction that the engagement had been broken off. Looking at them Pierre realized what contempt and animosity they all felt for the Rostóvs, and that it was impossible in their presence even to mention the name of her who could give up Prince Andrew for anyone else.

22

That same evening Pierre went to the Rostóv's to fulfill the commission entrusted to him. Natásha was in bed, the count at the Club, and Pierre, after giving the letters to Sónya, went to Márya Dmítrievna who was interested to know how Prince Andrew had taken the news. Ten minutes later Sónya came to Márya Dmítrievna.

"Natásha insists on seeing Count Peter Kirílovich," said she.

Natásha was standing in the middle of the drawing room, emaciated, with a pale set face, but not at all shamefaced as Pierre expected to find her. When he appeared at the door she grew flurried, evidently undecided whether to go to meet him or to wait till he came up.

Pierre hastened to her.

"Peter Kirílovich," she began rapidly, "Prince Bolkónski was your friend—is your friend," she corrected herself. (It seemed to her that everything that had once been must now be different.) "He told me once to apply to you . . ."

Pierre sniffed as he looked at her, but did not speak. Till then he had reproached her in his heart and tried to despise her, but he now felt so sorry for her that there was no room in his soul for reproach.

"He is here now: tell him . . . to for . . . forgive me!"

She stopped and breathed still more quickly, but did not shed tears.

"Yes . . . I will tell him," answered Pierre; "but . . ." He did not know what to say.

Natásha was evidently dismayed at the thought of what he might think she had meant.

"No, I know all is over," she said hurriedly. "No, that can never be. I'm only tormented by the wrong I have done him. Tell him only that I beg him to forgive, forgive, forgive me for everything. . . ."

She trembled all over and sat down on a chair.

A sense of pity he had never before known overflowed Pierre's heart.

"I will tell him, I will tell him everything once more," said Pierre. "But . . . I should like to know one thing. . . ."

"Know what?" Natásha's eyes asked.

"I should like to know, did you love . . ." Pierre did not know how to refer to Anatole and flushed at the thought of him—"did you love that bad man?"

"Don't call him bad!" said Natásha. "But I don't know, don't know at all. . . ."

She began to cry and a still greater sense of pity, tenderness, and love welled up in Pierre. He felt the tears trickle under his spectacles and hoped they would not be noticed.

"We won't speak of it any more, my dear," said Pierre, and his gentle, cordial tone suddenly seemed very strange to Natásha.

"We won't speak of it, my dear—I'll tell him everything; but one thing I beg of you, consider me your friend and if you want help, advice, or simply to open your heart to someone—not now, but when your mind is clearer—think of me!" He took her hand and kissed it. "I shall be happy if it's in my power . . ."

Pierre grew confused.

"Don't speak to me like that. I am not worth it!" exclaimed Natásha and turned to leave the room, but Pierre held her hand.

He knew he had something more to say to her. But when he said it he was amazed at his own words.

"Stop, stop! You have your whole life before you," said he to her.

"Before me? No! All is over for me," she replied with shame and self-abasement.

"All over?" he repeated. "If I were not myself, but the handsomest, cleverest, and best man in the world, and were free, I would this moment ask on my knees for your hand and your love!"

For the first time for many days Natásha wept tears of gratitude and tenderness, and glancing at Pierre she went out of the room.

Pierre too when she had gone almost ran into the anteroom, restraining tears of tenderness and joy that choked him, and without finding the sleeves of his fur cloak threw it on and got into his sleigh.

"Where to now, your excellency?" asked the coachman.

"Where to?" Pierre asked himself. "Where can I go now? Surely not to the Club or to pay calls?" All men seemed so pitiful, so poor, in comparison with this feeling of tenderness and love he experienced: in comparison with that softened, grateful, last look she had given him through her tears.

"Home!" said Pierre, and despite twenty-two degrees of frost Fahrenheit he threw open the bearskin cloak from his broad chest and inhaled the air with joy.

It was clear and frosty. Only looking up at the sky did Pierre cease to feel how sordid and humiliating were all mundane things compared with the heights to which his soul had just been raised. At the entrance to the Arbát Square an immense expanse of dark starry sky presented itself to his eyes. Almost in the center of it, surrounded and sprinkled on all sides by stars but distinguished from them all by its nearness to the earth, its white light, and its long uplifted tail, shone the enormous and brilliant comet of 1812—the comet which was said to portend all kinds of woes and the end of the world. In Pierre, however, that comet with its long luminous tail aroused no feeling of fear. On the contrary he gazed joyfully, his eyes moist with tears, at this bright comet. It seemed to Pierre that this comet fully responded to what was passing in his own softened and uplifted soul, now blossoming into a new life.

1812

⊟━━⊟⊟━━⊟⊟━━⊟⊟━━⊟⊟━━⊟

BOOK NINE

1

From the close of the year 1811 an intensified arming and concentrating of the forces of Western Europe began, and in 1812 these forces—millions of men, reckoning those transporting and feeding the army—moved from the west eastwards to the Russian frontier, toward which since 1811 Russian forces had been similarly drawn. On the twelfth of June, 1812, the forces of Western Europe crossed the Russian frontier and war began, that is, an event took place opposed to human reason and to human nature. Millions of men perpetrated against one another such innumerable crimes, frauds, treacheries, thefts, forgeries, issues of false money, burglaries, incendiarisms, and murders as in whole centuries are not recorded in the annals of all the law courts of the world, but which those who committed them did not at the time regard as being crimes.

What produced this extraordinary occurrence? What were its causes? The historians tell us with naïve assurance that its causes were the wrongs inflicted on the Duke of Oldenburg, the nonobservance of the Continental System, the ambition of Napoleon, the firmness of Alexander, the mistakes of the diplomatists, and so on.

To us, their descendants, who are not historians and are not carried away by the process of research and can therefore regard the event with unclouded common sense, an incalculable number of causes present themselves. The deeper we delve in search of these causes the more of them we find; and each separate cause or whole series of causes appears to us equally valid in itself and equally false by its insignificance compared to the magnitude of the events, and by its impotence—apart from the cooperation of all the other co-incident causes—to occasion the event.

We are forced to fall back on fatalism as an explanation of irrational events (that is to say, events the reasonableness of of which we do not understand). The more we try to explain such events in history reasonably, the more unreasonable and incomprehensible do they become to us.

Each man lives for himself, using his freedom to attain his personal aims, and feels with his whole being that he can now do or abstain from doing this or that action; but as soon as he has done it, that action performed at a certain moment in time becomes irrevocable and belongs to history, in which it has not a free but a predestined significance.

There are two sides to the life of every man, his individual life, which is the more free the more abstract its interests, and his elemental hive life in which he inevitably obeys laws laid down for him.

Man lives consciously for himself, but is an unconscious instrument in the attainment of the historic, universal, aims of humanity. A deed done is irrevocable, and its result coinciding in time with the actions of millions of other men assumes an historic significance.

In historic events, the so-called great men are labels giving names to events, and like labels they have but the smallest connection with the event itself.

Every act of theirs, which appears to them an act of their own will, is in an historical sense involuntary and is related to the whole course of history and predestined from eternity.

2

Napoleon invades Russia. His men venerate him. He is portrayed as pompous, callous of the lives of his soldiers, and convinced of his own omnipotence.

3

The Emperor of Russia had, meanwhile, been in Vílna for more than a month, reviewing troops and holding maneuvers. Nothing was ready for the war that everyone expected and to prepare for which the Emperor had come from Petersburg. There was no general plan of action.

The very day that Napoleon issued the order to cross the Niemen, and his vanguard, driving off the Cossacks, crossed the Russian frontier, Alexander spent the evening at the entertainment given by his aides-de-camp at Bennigsen's country house.

It was a gay and brilliant fete. Connoisseurs of such matters declared that rarely had so many beautiful women been assembled in one place. Countess Bezúkhova was present among other Russian ladies who had followed the sovereign from Petersburg to Vílna and eclipsed the refined Polish ladies by her massive, so-called Russian type of beauty. The Emperor noticed her and honored her with a dance.

Borís Drubetskóy, having left his wife in Moscow and being for the present *en garçon* (as he phrased it), was also there and, though not an aide-de-camp, had subscribed a large sum toward the expenses. Borís was now a rich man who had risen to high honors and no longer sought patronage but stood on an equal footing with the highest of those of his own age. He was meeting Hélène in Vílna after not having seen her for a long time and did not recall the past, but as Hélène was enjoying the favors of a very important personage and Borís had only recently married, they met as good friends of long standing.

At midnight dancing was still going on. Hélène, not having a suitable partner, herself offered to dance the mazurka with Borís.

As the mazurka began, Borís saw that Adjutant General Balashëv, one of those in closest attendance on the Emperor, went up to him and contrary to court etiquette stood near him while he was talking to a Polish lady. Having finished speaking to her, the Emperor looked inquiringly at Balashëv and, evidently understanding that he only acted thus because there were important reasons for so doing, nodded slightly to the lady and turned to him. Hardly had Balashëv begun to speak before a look of amazement appeared on the Emperor's face. He took Balashëv by the arm and crossed the room with him, unconsciously clearing a path seven yards wide as the people on both sides made way for him.

All the time Borís was going through the figures of the mazurka, he was worried by the question of what news Balashëv had brought and how he could find it out before others.

In the figure in which he had to choose two ladies, he whispered to Hélène that he meant to choose Countess Potocka who, he thought, had gone out onto the veranda, and glided over the parquet to the door opening into the garden, where, seeing Balashëv and the Emperor returning to the veranda, he stood still. They were moving toward the door. Borís, fluttering as if he had not had time to withdraw, respectfully pressed close to the doorpost with bowed head.

The Emperor, with the agitation of one who has been personally affronted, was finishing with these words:

"To enter Russia without declaring war! I will not make peace as long as a single armed enemy remains in my country!"

It seemed to Borís that it gave the Emperor pleasure to utter these words. He was satisfied with the form in which he had expressed his thoughts, but displeased that Borís had overheard it.

"Let no one know of it!" the Emperor added with a frown.

Borís understood that this was meant for him and, closing his eyes, slightly bowed his head. The Emperor re-entered the ballroom and remained there about another half-hour.

Borís was thus the first to learn the news that the French army had crossed the Niemen and, thanks to this, was able to show certain important personages that much that was concealed from others was usually known to him, and by this means he rose higher in their estimation.

4

At two in the morning of the fourteenth of June, the Emperor, having sent for Balashëv and read him his letter to Napoleon, ordered him to take it and hand it personally to the French Emperor. When dispatching Balashëv, the Emperor repeated to him the words that he would not make peace so long as a single armed enemy remained on Russian soil and told him to transmit those words to

Napoleon. Alexander did not insert them in his letter to Napoleon, because with his characteristic tact he felt it would be injudicious to use them at a moment when a last attempt at reconciliation was being made, but he definitely instructed Balashëv to repeat them personally to Napoleon.

Adjutant General Balashëv, bearing a letter from Alexander I to Napoleon, encounters on the way the amusingly vainglorious French General Murat.

5

Balashëv is harshly treated by the French Marshal Davout who delays his appearance before Napoleon for several days. So rapid is the French advance that Balashëv's audience with Napoleon takes place in the headquarters in Vílna which Alexander I has had to abandon.

6

Though Balashëv was used to imperial pomp, he was amazed at the luxury and magnificence of Napoleon's court.

After some minutes, the gentleman-in-waiting who was on duty came into the great reception room and, bowing politely, asked Balashëv to follow him.

Balashëv went into a small reception room, one door of which led into a study, the very one from which the Russian Emperor had dispatched him on his mission. He stood a minute or two, waiting. He heard hurried footsteps beyond the door, both halves of it were opened rapidly; all was silent and then from the study the sound was heard of other steps, firm and resolute—they were those of Napoleon. He had just finished dressing for his ride, and wore a blue uniform, opening in front over a white waistcoat so long that it covered his rotund stomach, white leather breeches tightly fitting the fat thighs of his short legs, and Hessian boots. His short hair had evidently just been brushed, but one lock hung down in the middle of his broad forehead. His plump white neck stood out sharply above the black collar of his uniform, and he smelled of Eau de Cologne. His full face, rather young-looking, with its prominent chin, wore a gracious and majestic expression of imperial welcome.

He entered briskly, with a jerk at every step and his head slightly thrown back. His whole short corpulent figure with broad thick shoulders, and chest and stomach involuntarily protruding, had that imposing and stately appearance one sees in men of forty who live in comfort. It was evident, too, that he was in the best of spirits that day.

He nodded in answer to Balashëv's low and respectful bow, and coming up to him at once began speaking like a man who values every moment of his time and does not condescend to prepare what he has to say but is sure he will always say the right thing and say it well.

"Good day, General!" said he. "I have received the letter you brought from the Emperor Alexander and am very glad to see you." He glanced with his large eyes into Balashëv's face and immediately looked past him.

It was plain that Balashëv's personality did not interest him at all. Evidently only what took place within *his own* mind interested him. Nothing outside himself had any significance for him, because everything in the world, it seemed to him, depended entirely on his will.

"I do not, and did not, desire war," he continued, "but it has been forced on me. Even *now*" (he emphasized the word) "I am ready to receive any explanations you can give me."

And he began clearly and concisely to explain his reasons for dissatisfaction with the Russian government. Judging by the calmly moderate and amicable tone in which the French Emperor spoke, Balashëv was firmly persuaded that he wished for peace and intended to enter into negotiations.

After saying all he had been instructed to say, Balashëv added that the Emperor Alexander wished for peace, but would not enter into negotiations except on condition that . . . Here Balashëv hesitated: he remembered the words the Emperor Alexander had not written in his letter, but had specially inserted in the rescript to Saltykóv and had told Balashëv to repeat to Napoleon. Balashëv remembered these words, "So long as a single armed foe remains on Russian soil," but some complex feeling restrained him. He could not utter them, though he wished to do so. He grew confused and said: "On condition that the French army retires beyond the Niemen."

Napoleon noticed Balashëv's embarrassment when uttering these last words; his face twitched and the calf of his left leg began to quiver rhythmically. Without moving from where he stood he began speaking in a louder tone and more hurriedly than before. During the speech that followed, Balashëv, who more than once lowered his eyes, involuntarily noticed the quivering of Napoleon's left leg which increased the more the more Napoleon raised his voice.

"I desire peace, no less than the Emperor Alexander," he began. "Have I not for eighteen months been doing everything to obtain it? I have waited eighteen months for explanations. But in order to begin negotiations, what is demanded of me?" he said, frowning and making an energetic gesture of inquiry with his small white plump hand.

"The withdrawal of your army beyond the Niemen, sire," replied Balashëv.

"The Niemen?" repeated Napoleon. "So now you want me to retire beyond the Niemen—only the Niemen?" repeated Napoleon, looking straight at Balashëv.

The latter bowed his head respectfully.

During the remainder of the interview with Balashëv, Napoleon in an angry monologue berates Alexander I, pointing out what a great reign he might have had if he had remained friendly with him.

7

After all that Napoleon had said to him Balashëv felt convinced that Napoleon would not wish to see him, and would even avoid another meeting with him— an insulted envoy—especially as he had witnessed his unseemly anger. But, to his surprise, Balashëv received, through Duroc, an invitation to dine with the Emperor that day.

The Emperor was in very good spirits after his ride through

Vílna, where crowds of people had rapturously greeted and followed him.

At dinner, having placed Balashëv beside him, Napoleon not only treated him amiably but behaved as if Balashëv were one of his own courtiers, one of those who sympathized with his plans and ought to rejoice at his success. In the course of conversation he mentioned Moscow and questioned Balashëv about the Russian capital, not merely as an interested traveler asks about a new city he intends to visit, but as if convinced that Balashëv, as a Russian, must be flattered by his curiosity.

After dinner they went to drink coffee in Napoleon's study, which four days previously had been that of the Emperor Alexander. Napoleon sat down, toying with his Sèvres coffee cup, and motioned Balashëv to a chair beside him.

Napoleon was in that well-known after-dinner mood which, more than any reasoned cause, makes a man contented with himself and disposed to consider everyone his friend. It seemed to him that he was surrounded by men who adored him: and he felt convinced that, after his dinner, Balashëv too was his friend and worshiper. Napoleon turned to him with a pleasant, though slightly ironic, smile.

"They tell me this is the room the Emperor Alexander occupied? Strange, isn't it, General?" he said, evidently not doubting that this remark would be agreeable to his hearer since it went to prove his, Napoleon's, superiority to Alexander.

Balashëv bowed his head with an air indicating that he would like to make his bow and leave, and only listened because he could not help hearing what was said to him. Napoleon did not notice this expression; he treated Balashëv not as an envoy from his enemy, but as a man now fully devoted to him and who must rejoice at his former master's humiliation.

"And why has the Emperor Alexander taken command of the armies? What is the good of that? War is my profession, but his business is to reign and not to command armies! Why has he taken on himself such a responsibility?"

Again Napoleon brought out his snuffbox, paced several times up and down the room in silence, and then, suddenly and unexpectedly, went up to Balashëv and with a slight smile, as confidently, quickly, and simply as if he were doing something not merely important but pleasing to Balashëv, he raised his hand to the forty-year-old Russian general's face and, taking him by the ear, pulled it gently, smiling with his lips only.

To have one's ear pulled by the Emperor was considered the greatest honor and mark of favor at the French court.

"Well, adorer and courtier of the Emperor Alexander, why don't you say anything?" said he, as if it was ridiculous, in his presence, to be the adorer and courtier of anyone but himself, Napoleon. "Are the horses ready for the general?" he added, with a slight inclination of his head in reply to Balashëv's bow. "Let him have mine, he has a *long way to go!*"

The letter taken by Balashëv was the last Napoleon sent to Alexander. Every detail of the interview was communicated to the Russian monarch, and the war began. . . .

8

After his interview with Pierre in Moscow, Prince Andrew went to Petersburg, on business as he told his family, but really to meet Anatole Kurágin whom he felt it necessary to encounter. On reaching Petersburg he inquired for Kurágin but the latter had already left the city. Pierre had warned his brother-in-law that Prince Andrew was on his track. Anatole Kurágin promptly obtained an appointment from the Minister of War and went to join the army in Moldavia. While in Petersburg Prince Andrew met Kutúzov, his former commander who was always well disposed toward him, and Kutúzov suggested that he should accompany him to the army in Moldavia, to which the old general had been appointed commander in chief. So Prince Andrew, having received an appointment on the headquarters staff, left for Turkey.

Prince Andrew did not think it proper to write and challenge Kurágin. He thought that if he challenged him without some fresh cause it might compromise the young Countess Rostóva and so he wanted to meet Kurágin personally in order to find a fresh pretext for a duel. But he again failed to meet Kurágin in Turkey, for soon after Prince Andrew arrived, the latter returned to Russia.

Of the activities that presented themselves to him, army service was the simplest and most familiar. As a general on duty on Kutúzov's staff, he applied himself to business with zeal and perseverance and surprised Kutúzov by his willingness and accuracy in work. Not having found Kurágin in Turkey, Prince Andrew did not think it necessary to rush back to Russia after him.

In the year 1812, when news of the war with Napoleon reached Bucharest, Prince Andrew asked Kutúzov to transfer him to the Western Army. Kutúzov, who was already weary of Bolkónski's activity which seemed to reproach his own idleness, very readily let him go and gave him a mission to Barclay de Tolly.

Before joining the Western Army which was then, in May, encamped at Drissa, Prince Andrew visited Bald Hills which was directly on his way, being only two miles off the Smolénsk highroad. On reaching Bald Hills it struck him as strange and unexpected to find the way of life there unchanged and still the same in every detail. But though externally all remained as of old, the inner relations of all these people had changed since Prince Andrew had seen them last. The household was divided into two alien and hostile camps, who changed their habits for his sake and only met because he was there. To the one camp belonged the old prince, Mademoiselle Bourienne, and the architect; to the other Princess Mary, Dessalles, little Nicholas, and all the old nurses and maids.

During his stay at Bald Hills all the family dined together, but they were ill at ease and Prince Andrew felt that he was a visitor for whose sake an exception was being made and that his presence made them all feel awkward. Involuntarily feeling this at dinner on the first day, he was taciturn, and the old prince noticing this also became morosely dumb and retired to his apartments directly after dinner. In the evening, when Prince Andrew went to him and, trying to rouse him, began to tell him of the young Count Kámensky's campaign, the old prince began unexpectedly to talk about Princess Mary, blaming her for her superstitions and her dislike of

Mademoiselle Bourienne, who, he said, was the only person really attached to him.

"Why does Prince Andrew, who sees this, say nothing to me about his sister? Does he think me a scoundrel, or an old fool who, without any reason, keeps his own daughter at a distance and attaches this Frenchwoman to himself? He doesn't understand, so I must explain it, and he must hear me out," thought the old prince. And he began explaining why he could not put up with his daughter's unreasonable character.

"If you ask me," said Prince Andrew, without looking up (he was censuring his father for the first time in his life), "I did not wish to speak about it, but as you ask me I will give you my frank opinion. If there is any misunderstanding and discord between you and Mary, I can't blame her for it at all. I know how she loves and respects you. Since you ask me," continued Prince Andrew, becoming irritable—as he was always liable to do of late—"I can only say that if there are any misunderstandings they are caused by that worthless woman, who is not fit to be my sister's companion."

"What companion, my dear boy? Eh? You've already been talking it over! Eh?"

"Father, I did not want to judge," said Prince Andrew, in a hard and bitter tone, "but you challenged me, and I have said, and always shall say, that Mary is not to blame, but those to blame—the one to blame—is that Frenchwoman."

"Ah, he has passed judgment . . . passed judgment!" said the old man in a low voice and, as it seemed to Prince Andrew, with some embarrassment, but then he suddenly jumped up and cried: "Be off, be off! Let not a trace of you remain here! . . ."

Prince Andrew wished to leave at once, but Princess Mary persuaded him to stay another day. Next day, before leaving, Prince Andrew went to his son's rooms. The boy, curly-headed like his mother and glowing with health, sat on his knee, and Prince Andrew began telling him the story of Bluebeard, but fell into a reverie without finishing the story. He thought not of this pretty child, his son whom he held on his knee, but of himself. He sought in himself either remorse for having angered his father or regret at leaving home for the first time in his life on bad terms with him, and was horrified to find neither. What meant still more to him was that he sought and did not find in himself the former tenderness for his son which he had hoped to reawaken by caressing the boy and taking him on his knee.

As soon as Prince Andrew had given up his daily occupations, and especially on returning to the old conditions of life amid which he had been happy, weariness of life overcame him with its former intensity, and he hastened to escape from these memories and to find some work as soon as possible.

"So you've decided to go, Andrew?" asked his sister.

"Thank God that I can," replied Prince Andrew. "I am very sorry you can't."

"Why do you say that?" replied Princess Mary. "Why do you say that, when you are going to this terrible war, and he is so old? Mademoiselle Bourienne says he has been asking about you. . . ."

As soon as she began to speak of that, her lips trembled and her tears began to fall. Prince Andrew turned away and began pacing the room.

"Ah, my God! my God! When one thinks who and what—what trash—can cause people misery!" he said with a malignity that alarmed Princess Mary.

She understood that when speaking of "trash" he referred not only to Mademoiselle Bourienne, the cause of her misery, but also to the man who had ruined his own happiness.

"Andrew! . . . Don't imagine that sorrow is the work of *men*. Men are His tools . . . If you think someone has wronged you, forget it and forgive! We have no right to punish. And then you will know the happiness of forgiving."

"If Mary is already persuading me to forgive, it means that I ought long ago to have punished him," he thought. And giving her no further reply, he began thinking of the glad vindictive moment when he would meet Kurágin who he knew was now in the army.

Princess Mary begged him to stay one day more, saying that she knew how unhappy her father would be if Andrew left without being reconciled to him, but Prince Andrew replied that he would probably soon be back again from the army and would certainly write to his father, but that the longer he stayed now the more embittered their differences would become.

"Good-by, Andrew! Remember that misfortunes come from God, and men are never to blame," were the last words he heard from his sister when he took leave of her.

9

Prince Andrew reached the general headquarters of the army at the end of June. The first army, with which was the Emperor, occupied the fortified camp at Drissa; the second army was retreating, trying to effect a junction with the first one from which it was said to be cut off by large French forces. Everyone was dissatisfied with the general course of affairs in the Russian army, but no one anticipated any danger of invasion of the Russian provinces, and no one thought the war would extend farther than the western, the Polish, provinces.

Prince Andrew found Barclay de Tolly, to whom he had been assigned, on the bank of the Drissa.

He received Bolkónski stiffly and coldly and told him in his foreign accent that he would mention him to the Emperor for a decision as to his employment, but asked him meanwhile to remain on his staff. Anatole Kurágin, whom Prince Andrew had hoped to find with the army, was not there. He had gone to Petersburg, but Prince Andrew was glad to hear this. His mind was occupied by the interests of the center that was conducting a gigantic war, and he was glad to be free for a while from the distraction caused by the thought of Kurágin. During the first four days, while no duties were required of him, Prince Andrew rode round the whole fortified camp and, by the aid of his own knowledge and by talks with experts, tried to form a definite opinion about it. But the question whether the camp was advantageous or disadvantageous remained for him undecided. Already from his military experience and what he had seen in the Austrian campaign, he had come to the conclusion that in war the most deeply considered plans have no significance and that all depends on the way unexpected movements of the enemy—that cannot be foreseen—are met, and on how and by whom the whole matter is handled. To clear up this last point for himself, Prince Andrew, utilizing his position and acquaintances, tried to fathom the character of the control of the army and of the men and parties engaged in it, and he deduced for himself the following idea of the state of affairs.

In the mass of generals, foreign as well as native, in the Russian army, and among the numerous courtiers surrounding Alexander I, who insists upon remaining with the army although not as commander in chief, Prince Andrew discerns at least eight groups with various conflicting opinions as to the conduct of the war and who should lead the troops. Many are swayed by self-interest.

From among all these parties, just at the time Prince Andrew reached the army, another, a ninth party, was being formed and was beginning to raise its voice. This was the party of the elders, reasonable men experienced and capable in state affairs, who, without sharing any of those conflicting opinions, were able to take a detached view of what was going on at the staff at headquarters and to consider means of escape from this muddle, indecision, intricacy, and weakness.

The men of this party said and thought that what was wrong resulted chiefly from the Emperor's presence in the army with his military court and from the consequent presence there of an indefinite, conditional, and unsteady fluctuation of relations, which is in place at court but harmful in an army; that a sovereign should reign but not command the army, and that the only way out of the position would be for the Emperor and his court to leave the army; that the mere presence of the Emperor paralyzed the action of fifty thousand men required to secure his personal safety, and that the worst commander in chief if independent would be better than the very best one trammeled by the presence and authority of the monarch.

Just at the time Prince Andrew was living unoccupied at Drissa, Shishkóv, the Secretary of State and one of the chief representatives of this party, wrote a letter to the Emperor which Arakchéev and Balashëv agreed to sign. In this letter, availing himself of permission given him by the Emperor to discuss the general course of affairs, he respectfully suggested—on the plea that it was necessary for the sovereign to arouse a warlike spirit in the people of the capital—that the Emperor should leave the army.

That arousing of the people by their sovereign and his call to them to defend their country—the very incitement which was the chief cause of Russia's triumph in so far as it was produced by the Tsar's personal presence in Moscow—was suggested to the Emperor, and accepted by him, as a pretext for quitting the army.

10

Prince Andrew is asked by the Emperor to appear at his headquarters and tell of his experiences with the army in Turkey. There he meets the pedantic German military theoretician Pfuel, who has drawn up the defenses of the Drissa camp.

11

Prince Andrew's eyes were still following Pfuel out of the room when Count Bennigsen entered hurriedly, and nodding to Bolkónski, but not pausing, went into the study, giving instructions to his adjutant as he went. The Emperor was following him, and Bennigsen had hastened on to make some preparations and to be ready to receive the sovereign. Prince Andrew went out into the porch, where the Emperor, who looked fatigued, was dismounting. Marquis Paulucci was talking to him with particular warmth and the Emperor, with his head bent to the left, was listening with a dissatisfied air.

"And as for the man who advised forming this camp—the Drissa camp," said Paulucci, as the Emperor mounted the steps and noticing Prince Andrew scanned his unfamiliar face, "as to that person, sire . . ." continued Paulucci, desperately, apparently unable to restrain himself, "the man who advised the Drissa camp—I see no alternative but the lunatic asylum or the gallows!"

Without heeding the end of the Italian's remarks, and as though not hearing them, the Emperor, recognizing Bolkón-ski, addressed him graciously.

"I am very glad to see you! Go in there where they are meeting, and wait for me."

In the council of war that follows, the generals bit-terly attack and defend Pfuel's plan for the campaign. With contempt for all, Pfuel angrily defends his theory which Prince Andrew regards as ridiculous, simply be-cause of the German's absolute conviction that war is a science.

The discussions continued a long time, and the longer they lasted the more heated became the disputes, culminating in shouts and personalities, and the less was it possible to arrive at any general conclusion from all that had been said. Prince Andrew, listening to this polyglot talk and to these surmises, plans, refutations, and shouts, felt nothing but amazement at what they were saying. A thought that had long since and often occurred to him during his military activities—the idea that there is not and cannot be any science of war, and that therefore there can be no such thing as a military genius—now appeared to him an obvious truth. "What theory and science is possible about a matter the conditions and circumstances of which are unknown and can-not be defined, especially when the strength of the acting forces cannot be ascertained? No one was or is able to foresee in what condition our or the enemy's armies will be in a day's time, and no one can gauge the force of this or that detach-ment. . . . And why do they all speak of a 'military genius'? Is a man a genius who can order bread to be brought up at the right time and say who is to go to the right and who to the left? It is only because military men are invested with pomp and power and crowds of sychophants flatter power, attributing to it qualities of genius it does not possess. The best generals I have known were, on the contrary, stupid or absent-minded men. . . . Not only does a good army com-mander not need any special qualities, on the contrary he

needs the absence of the highest and best human attributes
—love, poetry, tenderness, and philosophic inquiring doubt.
He should be limited, firmly convinced that what he is doing
is very important (otherwise he will not have sufficient patience), and only then will he be a brave leader. God forbid
that he should be humane, should love, or pity, or think of
what is just and unjust. It is understandable that a theory
of their 'genius' was invented for them long ago because they
have power! The success of a military action depends not
on them, but on the man in the ranks who shouts, 'We are
lost!' or who shouts, 'Hurrah!' And only in the ranks can one
serve with assurance of being useful."

At the review next day the Emperor asked Prince Andrew
where he would like to serve, and Prince Andrew lost his
standing in court circles forever by not asking to remain attached to the sovereign's person, but for permission to serve
in the army.

12

Before the beginning of the campaign, Ros-
tóv had received a letter from his parents in which they told
him briefly of Natásha's illness and the breaking off of her
engagement to Prince Andrew (which they explained by
Natásha's having rejected him) and again asked Nicholas
to retire from the army and return home. On receiving this
letter, Nicholas did not even make any attempt to get leave
of absence or to retire from the army, but wrote to his parents
that he was sorry Natásha was ill and her engagement broken
off, and that he would do all he could to meet their wishes.
To Sónya he wrote separately.

"Adored friend of my soul!" he wrote. "Nothing but honor
could keep me from returning to the country. But now, at
the commencement of the campaign, I should feel dishonored,
not only in my comrades' eyes but in my own, if I preferred
my own happiness to my love and duty to the Fatherland. But
this shall be our last separation. Believe me, directly the
war is over, if I am still alive and still loved by you, I will
throw up everything and fly to you, to press you forever to
my ardent breast."

It was, in fact, only the commencement of the campaign that prevented Rostóv from returning home as he had promised and marrying Sónya. The autumn in Otrádnoe with the hunting, and the winter with the Christmas holidays and Sónya's love, had opened out to him a vista of tranquil rural joys and peace such as he had never known before, and which now allured him.

On his return from his furlough Nicholas, having been joyfully welcomed by his comrades, was sent to obtain remounts and brought back from the Ukraine excellent horses which pleased him and earned him commendation from his commanders. During his absence he had been promoted captain, and when the regiment was put on war footing with an increase in numbers, he was again allotted his old squadron.

The campaign began, the regiment was moved into Poland on double pay, new officers arrived, new men and horses, and above all everybody was infected with the merrily excited mood that goes with the commencement of a war, and Rostóv, conscious of his advantageous position in the regiment, devoted himself entirely to the pleasures and interests of military service, though he knew that sooner or later he would have to relinquish them.

On the thirteenth of July the Pávlograds took part in a serious action for the first time.

On the twelfth of July, on the eve of that action, there was a heavy storm of rain and hail. In general, the summer of 1812 was remarkable for its storms.

The two Pávlograd squadrons were bivouacking on a field of rye, which was already in ear but had been completely trodden down by cattle and horses. The rain was descending in torrents, and Rostóv, with a young officer named Ilyín, his protégé, was sitting in a hastily constructed shelter. An officer of their regiment, Zdrzhinski, with long mustaches extending onto his cheeks, who after riding to the staff had been overtaken by the rain, entered Rostóv's shelter.

"I have come from the staff, Count. Have you heard of Raévski's exploit?"

And the officer gave them details of the Saltánov battle, which he had heard at the staff.

Rostóv, smoking his pipe and turning his head about as the water trickled down his neck, listened inattentively, with an occasional glance at Ilyín, who was pressing close to him. This officer, a lad of sixteen who had recently joined the regiment, was now in the same relation to Nicholas that Nicholas had been to Denísov seven years before. Ilyín tried to imitate Rostóv in everything and adored him as a girl might have done.

"I can't stand this any more," said Ilyín, noticing that Rostóv did not relish Zdrzhinski's conversation. "My stockings and shirt . . . and the water is running on my seat! I'll go and look for shelter. The rain seems less heavy."

Five minutes later Ilyín, splashing through the mud, came running back to the shanty.

"Hurrah! Rostóv, come quick! I've found it! About two hundred yards away there's a tavern where *ours* have already gathered. We can at least get dry there, and Mary Hendríkhovna's there."

Mary Hendríkhovna was the wife of the regimental doctor, a pretty young German woman he had married in Poland. The doctor, whether from lack of means or because he did not like to part from his young wife in the early days of their marriage, took her about with him wherever the hussar regiment went and his jealousy had become a standing joke among the hussar officers.

Rostóv threw his cloak over his shoulders, shouted to Lavrúshka to follow with the things, and—now slipping in the mud, now splashing right through it—set off with Ilyín in the lessening rain and the darkness that was occasionally rent by distant lightning.

13

In the tavern, before which stood the doctor's covered cart, there were already some five officers. Mary Hendríkhovna, a plump little blonde German, in a dressing jacket and nightcap, was sitting on a broad bench in the front corner. Her husband, the doctor, lay asleep behind her. Rostóv and Ilyín, on entering the room, were welcomed with merry shouts and laughter.

Rostóv and Ilyín hastened to find a corner where they

could change into dry clothes without offending Mary Hendríkhovna's modesty.

A fire was made up in the dilapidated brick stove. A board was found, fixed on two saddles and covered with a horsecloth, a small samovar was produced and a cellaret and half a bottle of rum, and having asked Mary Hendríkhovna to preside, they all crowded round her. One offered her a clean handkerchief to wipe her charming hands, another spread a jacket under her little feet to keep them from the damp, another hung his coat over the window to keep out the draft, and yet another waved the flies off her husband's face, lest he should wake up.

"Leave him alone," said Mary Hendríkhovna, smiling timidly and happily. "He is sleeping well as it is, after a sleepless night."

"Oh, no, Mary Hendríkhovna," replied the officer, "one must look after the doctor. Perhaps he'll take pity on me someday, when it comes to cutting off a leg or an arm for me."

There were only three tumblers, the water was so muddy that one could not make out whether the tea was strong or weak, and the samovar held only six tumblers of water, but this made it all the pleasanter to take turns in order of seniority to receive one's tumbler from Mary Hendríkhovna's plump little hands with their short and not overclean nails. All the officers appeared to be, and really were, in love with her that evening.

There was only one spoon, sugar was more plentiful than anything else, but it took too long to dissolve, so it was decided that Mary Hendríkhovna should stir the sugar for everyone in turn. Rostóv received his tumbler, and adding some rum to it asked Mary Hendríkhovna to stir it.

"But you take it without sugar?" she said, smiling all the time, as if everything she said and everything the others said was very amusing and had a double meaning.

"It is not the sugar I want, but only that your little hand should stir my tea."

Mary Hendríkhovna assented and began looking for the spoon which someone meanwhile had pounced on.

"Use your finger, Mary Hendríkhovna, it will be still nicer," said Rostóv.

When they had emptied the samovar, Rostóv took a pack

of cards and proposed that they should play "Kings" with Mary Hendríkhovna. They drew lots to settle who should make up her set. At Rostóv's suggestion it was agreed that whoever became "King" should have the right to kiss Mary Hendríkhovna's hand, and that the "Booby" should go to refill and reheat the samovar for the doctor when the latter awoke.

They had hardly begun to play before the doctor's disheveled head suddenly appeared from behind Mary Hendríkhovna. He had been awake for some time, listening to what was being said, and evidently found nothing entertaining or amusing in what was going on. His face was sad and depressed. Without greeting the officers, he scratched himself and asked to be allowed to pass as they were blocking the way. As soon as he had left the room all the officers burst into loud laughter and Mary Hendríkhovna blushed till her eyes filled with tears and thereby became still more attractive to them. Returning from the yard, the doctor told his wife (who had ceased to smile so happily, and looked at him in alarm, awaiting her sentence) that the rain had ceased and they must go to sleep in their covered cart, or everything in it would be stolen.

"But I'll send an orderly. . . . Two of them!" said Rostóv. "What an idea, doctor!"

"I'll stand guard on it myself!" said Ilyín.

"No, gentlemen, you have had your sleep, but I have not slept for two nights," replied the doctor, and he sat down morosely beside his wife, waiting for the game to end.

14

It was nearly three o'clock but no one was yet asleep, when the quartermaster appeared with an order to move on to the little town of Ostróvna.

Half an hour later the squadron was lined up on the road. The command was heard to "mount" and the soldiers crossed themselves and mounted. Rostóv riding in front gave the order "Forward!" and the hussars, with clanking sabers and subdued talk, their horses' hoofs splashing in the mud, defiled in fours and moved along the broad road planted with birch trees on each side, following the infantry and a battery that had gone on in front.

Formerly, when going into action, Rostóv had felt afraid; now he had not the least feeling of fear. He was fearless, not because he had grown used to being under fire (one cannot grow used to danger), but because he had learned how to manage his thoughts when in danger. He had grown accustomed when going into action to think about anything but what would seem most likely to interest him—the impending danger. He glanced with pity at the excited face of Ilyín, who talked much and in great agitation. He knew from experience the tormenting expectation of terror and death the cornet was suffering and knew that only time could help him.

The whole sun appeared on the horizon and disappeared behind a long narrow cloud that hung above it. A few minutes later it reappeared brighter still from behind the top of the cloud, tearing its edge. Everything grew bright and glittered. And with that light, and as if in reply to it, came the sound of guns ahead of them.

Before Rostóv had had time to consider and determine the distance of that firing, Count Ostermann-Tolstóy's adjutant came galloping from Vítebsk with orders to advance at a trot along the road.

And the hussars, passing along the line of troops on the left flank of our position, halted behind our Uhlans who were in the front line.

The hussars remained in the same place for about an hour. A cannonade began. Count Ostermann with his suite rode up behind the squadron, halted, spoke to the commander of the regiment, and rode up the hill to the guns.

After Ostermann had gone, a command rang out to the Uhlans.

"Form column! Prepare to charge!"

The infantry in front of them parted into platoons to allow the cavalry to pass. The Uhlans started, the streamers on their spears fluttering, and trotted downhill toward the French cavalry which was seen below to the left.

They swooped down close to the French dragoons, something confused happened there amid the smoke, and five minutes later our Uhlans were galloping back, not to the place they had occupied but more to the left, and among the orange-colored Uhlans on chestnut horses and behind them, in a large group, blue French dragoons on gray horses could be seen.

15

Rostóv, with his keen sportsman's eye, was one of the first to catch sight of these blue French dragoons pursuing our Uhlans. Nearer and nearer in disorderly crowds came the Uhlans and the French dragoons pursuing them. Rostóv gazed at what was happening before him as at a hunt. He felt instinctively that if the hussars struck at the French dragoons now, the latter could not withstand them, but if a charge was to be made it must be done now, at that very moment, or it would be too late. He looked around. A captain, standing beside him, was gazing like himself with eyes fixed on the cavalry below them.

"Andrew Sevastyánych!" said Rostóv. "You know, we could crush them. . . ."

"A fine thing too!" replied the captain, "and really . . ."

Rostóv, without waiting to hear him out, touched his horse, galloped to the front of his squadron, and before he had time to finish giving the word of command, the whole squadron, sharing his feeling, was following him. Rostóv himself did not know how or why he did it. He acted as he did when hunting, without reflecting or considering. He touched his horse, gave the word of command, and immediately, hearing behind him the tramp of the horses of his deployed squadron, rode at full trot downhill toward the dragoons. Hardly had they reached the bottom of the hill before their pace instinctively changed to a gallop, which grew faster and faster as they drew nearer to our Uhlans and the French dragoons who galloped after them. The dragoons were now close at hand. On seeing the hussars, the foremost began to turn, while those behind began to halt. With the same feeling with which he had galloped across the path of a wolf, Rostóv gave rein to his Donéts horse and galloped to intersect the path of the dragoons' disordered lines. Nearly all the French dragoons were galloping back. Rostóv, picking out one on a gray horse, dashed after him. On the way he came upon a bush, his gallant horse cleared it, and almost before he had righted himself in his saddle he saw that he would immediately overtake the enemy he had selected. That Frenchman, by his uniform an officer, was going at a gallop, crouching on his gray horse and urging it on with his saber. In another moment Rostóv's horse dashed its breast against the hindquarters of the officer's horse, almost knocking it over, and at the same instant Rostóv, without knowing why, raised his saber and struck the Frenchman with it.

The instant he had done this, all Rostóv's animation vanished. The officer fell, not so much from the blow—which had but slightly cut his arm above the elbow—as from the shock to his horse and from fright. Rostóv reined in his horse, and his eyes sought his foe to see whom he had vanquished. The French dragoon officer was hopping with one foot on the ground, the other being caught in the stirrup. His eyes, screwed up with fear as if he every moment expected another blow, gazed up at Rostóv with shrinking terror. His pale and mud-stained face—fair and young, with a dimple in the chin and light-blue eyes—was not an enemy's face at all suited to a battlefield, but a most ordinary, homelike face. Before Rostóv had decided what to do with him, the officer cried, "I surrender!" He hurriedly but vainly tried to get his foot out of the stirrup and did not remove his frightened blue eyes from Rostóv's face. Some hussars who galloped up disengaged his foot and helped him into the saddle. On all sides, the hussars were busy with the dragoons; one was wounded, but though his face was bleeding, he would not give up his horse; another was perched up behind an hussar with his arms round him; a third was being helped by an hussar to mount his horse. In front, the French infantry were firing as they ran. The hussars galloped hastily back with their prisoners.

Count Ostermann-Tolstóy met the returning hussars, sent for Rostóv, thanked him, and said he would report his gallant deed to the Emperor and would recommend him for a St. George's Cross. When sent for by Count Ostermann, Rostóv, remembering that he had charged without orders, felt sure his commander was sending for him to punish him for breach of discipline. Ostermann's flattering words and promise of a reward should therefore have struck him all the more pleasantly, but he still felt that same vaguely disagreeable feeling of moral nausea.

All that day and the next his friends and comrades noticed that Rostóv, without being dull or angry, was silent, thoughtful, and preoccupied. He drank reluctantly, tried to remain alone, and kept turning something over in his mind.

Rostóv was always thinking about that brilliant exploit of his, which to his amazement had gained him the St. George's Cross and even given him a reputation for bravery, and there was something he could not at all understand. "So others are even more afraid than I am!" he thought. "So that's all there is in what is called heroism! And did I do it for my country's sake? And how was he to blame, with his dimple and blue eyes? And how frightened he was! He thought that I should kill him. Why should I kill him? My hand trembled. And they have given me a St. George's Cross. . . . I can't make it out at all."

But while Nicholas was considering these questions and still could reach no clear solution of what puzzled him so, the wheel of fortune in the service, as often happens, turned in his favor. After the affair at Ostróvna he was brought into notice, received command of an hussar battalion, and when a brave officer was needed he was chosen.

16

On receiving news of Natásha's illness, the countess, though not quite well yet and still weak, went to Moscow with Pétya and the rest of the household, and the whole family moved from Márya Dmítrievna's house to their own and settled down in town.

Natásha's illness was so serious that, fortunately for her and for her parents, the consideration of all that had caused the illness, her conduct and the breaking off of her engagement, receded into the background. She was so ill that it was impossible for them to consider in how far she was to blame for what had happened. She could not eat or sleep, grew visibly thinner, coughed, and, as the doctors made them feel, was in danger.

The symptoms of Natásha's illness were that she ate little, slept little, coughed, and was always low-spirited. The doctors said that she could not get on without medical treatment, so they kept her in the stifling atmosphere of the town, and the Rostóvs did not move to the country that summer of 1812.

In spite of the many pills she swallowed and the drops and powders out of the little bottles and boxes of which Madame Schoss who was fond of such things made a large collection, and in spite of being deprived of the country life to which she was accustomed, youth prevailed. Natásha's grief began to be overlaid by the impressions of daily life, it ceased to press so painfully on her heart, it gradually faded into the past, and she began to recover physically.

17

Natásha was calmer but no happier. She not merely avoided all external forms of pleasure—balls, promenades, concerts, and theaters—but she never laughed without a sound of tears in her laughter. She could not sing. As soon as she began to laugh, or tried to sing by herself, tears choked her: tears of remorse, tears at the recollection of those pure times which could never return, tears of vexation that she should so uselessly have ruined her young life which might have been so happy. Yet it was necessary to live on.

It comforted her to reflect that she was not better as she had formerly imagined, but worse, much worse, than anybody else in the world. But this was not enough. She knew that, and asked herself, "What next?" But there was nothing to come. There was no joy in life, yet life was passing. Natásha apparently tried not to be a burden or a hindrance to anyone, but wanted nothing for herself. She kept away from everyone in the house and felt at ease only with her brother Pétya. She liked to be with him better than with the others, and when alone with him she sometimes laughed. She hardly ever left the house and of those who came to see them was glad to see only one person, Pierre. It would have been impossible to treat her with more delicacy, greater care, and at the same time more seriously than did Count Bezúkhov.

Natásha unconsciously felt this delicacy and so found great pleasure in his society. But she was not even grateful to him for it; nothing good on Pierre's part seemed to her to be an effort, it seemed so natural for him to be kind to everyone that there was no merit in his kindness. After those involuntary words—that if he were free he would have asked on his knees for her hand and her love—uttered at a moment when she was so strongly agitated, Pierre never spoke to Natásha of his feelings; and it seemed plain to her that those words, which had then so comforted her, were spoken as all sorts of meaningless words are spoken to comfort a crying child. It was not because Pierre was a married man, but because Natásha felt very strongly with him that moral barrier the absence of which she had experienced with Kurágin that it never entered her head that the relations between him and herself could lead to love on her part, still less on his, or even to the kind of tender, self-conscious, romantic friendship between a man and a woman of which she had known several instances.

Before the end of the fast of St. Peter, Agraféna Ivánovna Belóva, a country neighbor of the Rostóvs, came to Moscow to pay her devotions at the shrines of the Moscow saints. She suggested that Natásha should fast and prepare for Holy Communion, and Natásha gladly welcomed the idea.

The countess was pleased with Natásha's zeal; after the poor results of the medical treatment, in the depths of her heart she hoped that prayer might help her daughter more than medicines and, though not without fear and concealing it from the doctor, she agreed to Natásha's wish and entrusted her to Belóva. Agraféna Ivánovna used to come to wake Natásha at three in the morning, but generally found her already awake. She was afraid of being late for Matins.

The prayers to which she surrendered herself most of all were those of repentance. On her way home at an early hour when she met no one but bricklayers going to work or men sweeping the street, and everybody within the houses was still asleep, Natásha experienced a feeling new to her, a sense of the possibility of correcting her faults, the possibility of a new, clean life, and of happiness.

During the whole week she spent in this way, that feeling grew every day. And the happiness of taking communion, or "communing" as Agraféna Ivánovna, joyously playing with the word, called it, seemed to Natásha so great that she felt she should never live till that blessed Sunday.

But the happy day came, and on that memorable Sunday, when, dressed in white muslin, she returned home after communion, for the first time for many months she felt calm and not oppressed by the thought of the life that lay before her.

18

At the beginning of July more and more disquieting reports about the war began to spread in Moscow; people spoke of an appeal by the Emperor to the people, and of his coming himself from the army to Moscow. And as up to the eleventh of July no manifesto or appeal had been received, exaggerated reports became current about them and about the position of Russia.

On the eleventh of July, which was Saturday, the manifesto was received but was not yet in print, and Pierre, who was at the Rostóvs', promised to come to dinner next day, Sunday, and bring a copy of the manifesto and appeal, which he would obtain from Count Rostopchín.

That Sunday, the Rostóvs went to Mass at the Razumóvskis' private chapel as usual. As Natásha, at her mother's side, passed through the crowd behind a liveried footman who cleared the way for them, she heard a young man speaking about her in too loud a whisper.

"That's Rostóva, the one who . . ."

"She's much thinner, but all the same she's pretty!"

She heard, or thought she heard, the names of Kurágin and Bolkónski. But she was always imagining that. It always seemed to her that everyone who looked at her was thinking only of what had happened to her. With a sinking heart, wretched as she always was now when she found herself in a crowd, Natásha in her lilac silk dress trimmed with black lace walked—as women can walk—with the more repose and stateliness the greater the pain and shame in her soul. She knew for certain that she was pretty, but this no longer gave her satisfaction as it used to. On the contrary it tormented her more than anything else of late, and particularly so on this bright, hot summer day in town. "It's Sunday again—another week past," she thought, recalling that she had been here the Sunday before, "and always the same life that is no life, and the same surroundings in which it used to be so easy to live. I'm pretty, I'm young, and I know that now I am good. I used to be bad, but now I know I am good," she thought, "but yet my best years are slipping by and are no good to anyone."

A comely, fresh-looking old man was conducting the service with that mild solemnity which has so elevating and soothing an effect on the souls of the worshipers. The gates of the sanctuary screen were closed, the curtain was slowly drawn, and from behind it a soft mysterious voice pronounced some words. Tears, the cause of which she herself did not understand, made Natásha's breast heave, and a joyous but oppressive feeling agitated her.

"Teach me what I should do, how to live my life, how I may grow good forever, forever!" she pleaded.

When they prayed for the warriors, she thought of her brother and Denísov. When they prayed for all traveling by land and sea, she remembered Prince Andrew, prayed for him, and asked God to forgive her all the wrongs she had done him. When they prayed for those who love us, she prayed for the members of her own family, her father and mother and Sónya, realizing for the first time how wrongly she had acted toward them, and feeling all the strength of her love for them. Only at prayer did she feel able to think clearly and calmly of Prince Andrew and Anatole, as men for whom her feelings were as nothing compared with her awe and devotion to God.

When he had finished the Litany the deacon crossed the stole over his breast and said, "Let us commit ourselves and our whole lives to Christ the Lord!"

"Commit ourselves to God," Natásha inwardly repeated. "Lord God, I submit myself to Thy will!" she thought. "I want nothing, wish for nothing; teach me what to do and how to use my will! Take me, take me!" prayed Natásha, with impatient emotion in her heart, not crossing herself but letting her slender arms hang down as if expecting some invisible power at any moment to take her and deliver her from herself, from her regrets, desires, remorse, hopes, and sins.

The countess looked round several times at her daughter's softened face and shining eyes and prayed God to help her.

19

From the day when Pierre, after leaving the Rostóvs' with Natásha's grateful look fresh in his mind, had gazed at the comet that seemed to be fixed in the sky and felt that something new was appearing on his own horizon—from that day the problem of the vanity and uselessness of all earthly things, that had incessantly tormented him, no longer presented itself. That terrible question "Why?" "Wherefore?" which had come to him amid every occupation, was now replaced, not by another question or by a reply to the former question, but by *her* image. When he listened to, or himself took part in, trivial conversations, when he read or heard of human baseness or folly, he was not horrified as formerly, and did not ask himself why men struggled so about these things when all is so transient and incomprehensible—but he remembered her as he had last seen her, and all his doubts vanished —not because she had answered the questions that had haunted him, but because his conception of her transferred him instantly to another, a brighter, realm of spiritual activity in which no one could be justified or guilty—a realm of beauty and love which it was worth living for.

But latterly, when more and more disquieting reports came from the seat of war and Natásha's health began to improve and she no longer aroused in him the former feeling of careful pity, an ever-increasing restlessness, which he could not explain, took possession of him. He felt that the condition he was in could not continue long, that a catastrophe was coming which would change his whole life, and he impatiently sought everywhere for signs of that approaching catastrophe.

A brother Mason reveals to Pierre a prophecy concerning Napoleon, drawn from the Revelation of St. John. Through a formula, in which numbers equal letters of the alphabet, Pierre believes that 666, the total of the letters of his name, is the same as the total of the letters of Napoleon's name and thus connects him with the ultimate fate of the leader.

On the eve of the Sunday when the special prayer was read, Pierre had promised the Rostóvs to bring them, from Count Rostopchín whom he knew well, both the appeal to the people and the latest news from the army. In the morning, when he went to call at Rostopchín's he met there a courier fresh from the army, an acquaintance of his own, who often danced at Moscow balls.

"Do, please for heaven's sake, relieve me of something!" said the courier. "I have a sackful of letters to parents."

Among these letters was one from Nicholas Rostóv to his father. Pierre took that letter, and Rostopchín also gave him the Emperor's appeal to Moscow, which had just been printed, the last army orders, and his own most recent bulletin. Glancing through the army orders, Pierre found in one of them, in the lists of killed, wounded, and rewarded, the name of Nicholas Rostóv, awarded a St. George's Cross of the Fourth Class for courage shown in the Ostróvna affair, and in the same order the name of Prince Andrew Bolkónski, appointed to the command of a regiment of Chasseurs. Though he did not want to remind the Rostóvs of Bolkónski, Pierre could not refrain from making them happy by the news of their son's having received a decoration, so he sent that printed army order and Nicholas' letter to the Rostóvs, keeping the appeal, the bulletin, and the other orders to take with him when he went to dinner.

He had long been thinking of entering the army and would have done so had he not been hindered, first, by his membership of the Society of Freemasons to which he was bound by oath and which preached perpetual peace and the abolition of war, and secondly, by the fact that when he saw the great mass of Muscovites who had donned uniform and were talking patriotism, he somehow felt ashamed to take the step. But the chief reason for not carrying out his intention to enter the army lay in the vague idea that he was *L'russe Besuhof* who had the number of the beast, 666; that his part in the great affair of setting a limit to the power of the beast that spoke great and blasphemous things had been predestined from eternity, and that therefore he ought not to undertake anything, but wait for what was bound to come to pass.

20

A few intimate friends were dining with the Rostóvs that day, as usual on Sundays.

Pierre came early so as to find them alone.

He had grown so stout this year that he would have been abnormal had he not been so tall, so broad of limb, and so strong that he carried his bulk with evident ease.

The first person he saw in the house was Natásha. Even before he saw her, while taking off his cloak, he heard her. She was practicing sol-fa exercises in the music room. She had her back to him when he opened the door, but when, turning quickly, she saw his broad, surprised face, she blushed and came rapidly up to him.

"I want to try to sing again," she said, adding as if by way of excuse, "it is, at least, something to do."

"That's capital!"

"Count, is it wrong of me to sing?" she said blushing, and fixing her eyes inquiringly on him.

"No . . . Why should it be? On the contrary . . . But why do you ask me?"

"I don't know myself," Natásha answered quickly, "but I should not like to do anything you disapproved of. I believe in you completely. You don't know how important you are to me, how much you've done for me. . . ." She spoke rapidly and did not notice how Pierre flushed at her words. "I saw in the army order that *he*, Bolkónski" (she whispered the name hastily), "is in Russia, and in the army again. What do you think?"—she was speaking hurriedly, evidently afraid her strength might fail her—"Will he ever forgive me? Will he not always have a bitter feeling toward me? What do you think? What do you think?"

"I think . . ." Pierre replied, "that he has nothing to forgive. . . . If I were in his place . . ."

By association of ideas, Pierre was at once carried back to the day when, trying to comfort her, he had said that if he were not himself but the best man in the world and free, he would ask on his knees for her hand; and the same feeling of pity, tenderness, and love took possession of him and the same words rose to his lips. But she did not give him time to say them.

"Yes, you . . . you . . ." she said, uttering the word *you* rapturously—"that's a different thing. I know no one kinder, more generous, or better than you; nobody could be! Had you not been there then, and now too, I don't know what would have become of me, because . . ."

Tears suddenly rose in her eyes, she turned away, lifted her music before her eyes, began singing again, and again began walking up and down the room.

Just then Pétya came running in from the drawing room.

Pétya was now a handsome rosy lad of fifteen with full red lips and resembled Natásha. He was preparing to enter the university, but he and his friend Obolénski had lately, in secret, agreed to join the hussars.

Pétya had come rushing out to talk to his namesake about this affair. He had asked Pierre to find out whether he would be accepted in the hussars.

Pierre walked up and down the drawing room, not listening to what Pétya was saying.

Pétya pulled him by the arm to attract his attention.

"Well, what about my plan? Peter Kirílych, for heaven's sake! You are my only hope!" said Pétya.

"Oh yes, your plan. To join the hussars? I'll mention it, I'll bring it all up today."

"Well, *mon cher*, have you got the manifesto?" asked the old count.

"Yes, I've got it," said Pierre. "The Emperor is to be here tomorrow . . . there's to be an Extraordinary Meeting of the nobility, and they are talking of a levy of ten men per thousand."

After dinner the count settled himself comfortably in an easy chair and with a serious face asked Sónya, who was considered an excellent reader, to read the appeal.

"To Moscow, our ancient Capital!

"The enemy has entered the borders of Russia with immense forces. He comes to despoil our beloved country," Sónya read painstakingly in her high-pitched voice. The count listened with closed eyes, heaving abrupt sighs at certain passages.

Natásha sat erect, gazing with a searching look now at her father and now at Pierre.

Pierre felt her eyes on him and tried not to look round. The countess shook her head disapprovingly and angrily at every solemn expression in the manifesto. In all these words she saw only that the danger threatening her son would not soon be over.

"May the ruin he hopes to bring upon us recoil on his own head, and may Europe delivered from bondage glorify the name of Russia!"

"Yes, that's it!" cried the count, opening his moist eyes and sniffing repeatedly, as if a strong vinaigrette had been held to his nose; and he added, "Let the Emperor but say the word and we'll sacrifice everything and begrudge nothing."

"What a darling our Papa is!" Natásha cried, kissing him, and she again looked at Pierre with the unconscious coquetry that had returned to her with her better spirits.

At this moment, Pétya, to whom nobody was paying any attention, came up to his father with a very flushed face and said in his breaking voice that was now deep and now shrill:

"Well, Papa, I tell you definitely, and Mamma too, it's as you please, but I say definitely that you must let me enter the army, because I can't . . . that's all. . . ."

The countess, in dismay, looked up to heaven, clasped her hands, and turned angrily to her husband.

"That comes of your talking!" said she.

But the count had already recovered from his excitement.

"Come, come!" said he. "Here's a fine warrior! No! Nonsense! You must study."

"And I tell you—Peter Kirílych here will also tell you . . ."

"Nonsense, I tell you."

"Well, Peter Kirílych, let's go and have a smoke," he said.

Pierre was agitated and undecided. Natásha's unwontedly brilliant eyes, continually glancing at him with a more than cordial look, had reduced him to this condition.

"No, I think I'll go home."

"Home? Why, you meant to spend the evening with us. . . . You don't often come nowadays as it is, and this girl of mine," said the count good-naturedly, pointing to Natásha, "only brightens up when you're here."

"Yes, I had forgotten . . . I really must go home . . . business . . ." said Pierre hurriedly.

"Well, then, *au revoir!*" said the count, and went out of the room.

"Why are you going? Why are you upset?" asked Natásha, and she looked challengingly into Pierre's eyes.

"Because I love you!" was what he wanted to say, but he did not say it, and only blushed till the tears came, and lowered his eyes.

"Because it is better for me to come less often . . . because . . . No, simply I have business. . . ."

"Why? No, tell me!" Natásha began resolutely and suddenly stopped.

They looked at each other with dismayed and embarrassed faces. He tried to smile but could not: his smile expressed suffering, and he silently kissed her hand and went out.

Pierre made up his mind not to go to the Rostóvs' any more.

21

After the definite refusal he had received, Pétya went to his room and there locked himself in and wept bitterly. When he came in to tea, silent, morose, and with tear-stained face, everybody pretended not to notice anything.

Next day the Emperor arrived in Moscow, and several of the Rostóvs' domestic serfs begged permission to go to have a look at him. That morning Pétya was a long time dressing and arranging his hair and collar to look like a grown-up man. He frowned before his looking glass, gesticulated, shrugged his shoulders, and finally, without saying a word to anyone, took his cap and left the house by the back door, trying to avoid notice. Pétya decided to go straight to where the Emperor was and to explain frankly to some gentleman-in-waiting (he imagined the Emperor to be always surrounded by gentlemen-in-waiting) that he, Count Rostóv, in spite of his youth wished to serve his country; that youth could be no hindrance to loyalty, and that he was ready to . . . While dressing, Pétya had prepared many fine things he meant to say to the gentleman-in-waiting.

But the farther he went and the more his attention was diverted by the ever-increasing crowds moving toward the Krémlin, the less he remembered to walk with the sedateness and deliberation of a man. As he approached the Krémlin he even began to avoid being crushed and resolutely stuck out his elbows in a menacing way.

As soon as Pétya found himself in the square he clearly heard the sound of bells and the joyous voices of the crowd that filled the whole Krémlin.

For a while the crowd was less dense, but suddenly all heads were bared, and everyone rushed forward in one direction. Pétya was being pressed so that he could scarcely breathe, and everybody shouted, "Hurrah! hurrah! hurrah!" Pétya stood on tiptoe and pushed and pinched, but could see nothing except the people about him.

Quite beside himself, Pétya, clenching his teeth and rolling his eyes ferociously, pushed forward, elbowing his way and shouting "hurrah!" as if he were prepared that instant to kill himself and everyone else, but on both sides of him other people with similarly ferocious faces pushed forward and everybody shouted "hurrah!"

"You've crushed the young gentleman!" said a clerk. "What are you up to? Gently! . . . They've crushed him, crushed him!"

The Emperor entered the Cathedral of the Assumption. The crowd spread out again more evenly, and the clerk led Pétya—pale and breathless—to the Tsar-cannon.

Pétya soon came to himself, the color returned to his face, the pain had passed, and at the cost of that temporary unpleasantness he had obtained a place by the cannon from where he hoped to see the Emperor who would be returning that way. Pétya no longer thought of presenting his petition. If he could only see the Emperor he would be happy!

At last four men in uniforms and sashes emerged from

the cathedral doors. "Hurrah! hurrah!" shouted the crowd
again.

"Which is he? Which?" asked Pétya in a tearful voice, of
those around him, but no one answered him, everybody was
too excited; and Pétya, fixing on one of those four men,
whom he could not clearly see for the tears of joy that filled
his eyes, concentrated all his enthusiasm on him—though it
happened not to be the Emperor—frantically shouted "Hurrah!" and resolved that tomorrow, come what might, he
would join the army.

While the Emperor was dining, Valúev, looking out of the
window, said:

"The people are still hoping to see Your Majesty again."

The dinner was nearly over, and the Emperor, munching
a biscuit, rose and went out onto the balcony. The people,
with Pétya among them, rushed toward the balcony.

A largish piece of the biscuit the Emperor was holding
in his hand broke off, fell on the balcony parapet, and then
to the ground. A coachman in a jerkin, who stood nearest,
sprang forward and snatched it up. Several people in the
crowd rushed at the coachman. Seeing this the Emperor had
a plateful of biscuits brought him and began throwing them
down from the balcony. Pétya's eyes grew bloodshot, and still
more excited by the danger of being crushed, he rushed
at the biscuits. He did not know why, but he had to have
a biscuit from the Tsar's hand and he felt that he must not
give way. He sprang forward and upset an old woman
who was catching at a biscuit; the old woman did not consider herself defeated though she was lying on the ground—
she grabbed at some biscuits but her hand did not reach
them. Pétya pushed her hand away from his knee, seized a
biscuit, and as if fearing to be too late, again shouted "Hurrah!" with a voice already hoarse.

Happy as Pétya was, he felt sad at having to go home
knowing that all the enjoyment of that day was over. He
did not go straight home from the Krémlin, but called on his
friend Obolénski, who was fifteen and was also entering the
regiment. On returning home Pétya announced resolutely
and firmly that if he was not allowed to enter the service
he would run away. And next day, Count Ilyá Rostóv—

though he had not yet quite yielded—went to inquire how he could arrange for Pétya to serve where there would be least danger.

22

At an assembly of the gentry and merchants called to hear the Emperor's appeal for aid, there is much discussion. The liberal-minded Pierre suggests that the government give a full account of the state of the war and an explanation of needs before aid is offered. The nobles criticize him.

23

At that moment Count Rostopchín entered the room, stepping briskly to the front of the crowd of gentry.

"Our sovereign the Emperor will be here in a moment," said Rostopchín. "I am straight from the palace. Seeing the position we are in, I think there is little need for discussion. The Emperor has deigned to summon us and the merchants. Millions will pour forth from there"—he pointed to the merchants' hall—"but our business is to supply men and not spare ourselves. . . . That is the least we can do!"

A conference took place confined to the magnates sitting at the table.

The secretary was told to write down the resolution of the Moscow nobility and gentry, that they would furnish ten men, fully equipped, out of every thousand serfs, as the Smolénsk gentry had done.

"The Emperor! The Emperor!" a sudden cry resounded through the halls and the whole throng hurried to the entrance.

The Emperor entered the hall through a broad path between two lines of nobles. Every face expressed respectful, awe-struck curiosity. Pierre stood rather far off and could not hear all that the Emperor said. From what he did hear he understood that the Emperor spoke of the danger threatening the empire and of the hopes he placed on the Moscow nobility. He was answered by a voice which informed him of the resolution just arrived at.

"Gentlemen!" said the Emperor with a quivering voice. There was a rustling among the crowd and it again subsided, so that Pierre distinctly heard the pleasantly human voice of the Emperor saying with emotion:

"I never doubted the devotion of the Russian nobles, but today it has surpassed my expectations. I thank you in the name of the Fatherland! Gentlemen, let us act. Time is most precious. . . ."

The Emperor ceased speaking, the crowd began pressing round him, and rapturous exclamations were heard from all sides.

"Yes, most precious . . . a royal word," said Count Rostóv, with a sob. He stood at the back, and, though he had heard hardly anything, understood everything in his own way.

From the hall of the nobility the Emperor went to that of the merchants. There he remained about ten minutes. As became known later, he had scarcely begun to address the merchants before tears gushed from his eyes and he concluded in a trembling voice. When Pierre saw the Emperor he was coming out accompanied by two merchants.

"Our lives and property—take them, Your Majesty!"

Pierre's one feeling at the moment was a desire to show that he was ready to go to all lengths and was prepared to sacrifice everything. He now felt ashamed of his speech with its constitutional tendency and sought an opportunity of effacing it. Having heard that Count Mamónov was furnishing a regiment, Bezúkhov at once informed Rostopchín that he would give a thousand men and their maintenance.

Old Rostóv could not tell his wife of what had passed without tears, and at once consented to Pétya's request and went himself to enter his name.

Next day the Emperor left Moscow. The assembled nobles all took off their uniforms and settled down again in their homes and clubs, and not without some groans gave orders to their stewards about the enrollment, feeling amazed themselves at what they had done.

1812

■──■8──■8■──■8■──■8■──■

BOOK TEN

1

Tolstoy theorizes on the course of history. All people involved in war act in accord with their personal characteristics, habits, circumstances and aims. Though they imagine what they do is done of their own free will, they are really involuntary tools of history.

2

The day after his son had left, Prince Nicholas sent for Princess Mary to come to his study.

"Well? Are you satisfied now?" said he. "You've made me quarrel with my son! Satisfied, are you? That's all you wanted! Satisfied? . . . It hurts me, it hurts. I'm old and weak and this is what you wanted. Well then, gloat over it! Gloat over it!"

After that Princess Mary did not see her father for a whole week. He was ill and did not leave his study.

At the end of the week the prince reappeared and resumed his former way of life, devoting himself with special activity to building operations and the arrangement of the gardens and completely breaking off his relations with Mademoiselle Bourienne. His looks and cold tone to his daughter seemed to say: "There, you see? You plotted against me, you lied to Prince Andrew about my relations with that Frenchwoman and made me quarrel with him, but you see I need neither her nor you!"

Of the war Princess Mary thought as women do think about wars. She feared for her brother who was in it, was horrified

359

by and amazed at the strange cruelty that impels men to kill one another, but she did not understand the significance of this war, which seemed to her like all previous wars.

The chief reason Princess Mary did not realize the full significance of this war was that the old prince never spoke of it, did not recognize it, and laughed at Dessalles when he mentioned it at dinner. The prince's tone was so calm and confident that Princess Mary unhesitatingly believed him.

On August 1, a second letter was received from Prince Andrew. In his first letter which came soon after he had left home, Prince Andrew had dutifully asked his father's forgiveness for what he had allowed himself to say and begged to be restored to his favor. To this letter the old prince had replied affectionately, and from that time had kept the Frenchwoman at a distance. Prince Andrew's second letter, written near Vítebsk after the French had occupied that town, gave a brief account of the whole campaign, enclosed for them a plan he had drawn and forecasts as to the further progress of the war. In this letter Prince Andrew pointed out to his father the danger of staying at Bald Hills, so near the theater of war and on the army's direct line of march, and advised him to move to Moscow.

At dinner that day, on Dessalles' mentioning that the French were said to have already entered Vítebsk, the old prince remembered his son's letter.

On moving to the drawing room he handed the letter to Princess Mary and, spreading out before him the plan of the new building and fixing his eyes upon it, told her to read the letter aloud. When she had done so Princess Mary looked inquiringly at her father. He was examining the plan, evidently engrossed in his own ideas.

"What do you think of it, Prince?" Dessalles ventured to ask.

"I? I? . . ." said the prince as if unpleasantly awakened, and not taking his eyes from the plan of the building.

"Very possibly the theater of war will move so near to us that . . ."

"Ha ha ha! The theater of war!" said the prince. "I have said and still say that the theater of war is Poland and the enemy will never get beyond the Niemen."

Dessalles looked in amazement at the prince, who was

talking of the Niemen when the enemy was already at the Dnieper, but Princess Mary, forgetting the geographical position of the Niemen, thought that what her father was saying was correct.

"When the snow melts they'll sink in the Polish swamps. Only they could fail to see it," the prince continued, evidently thinking of the campaign of 1807 which seemed to him so recent. "Bennigsen should have advanced into Prussia sooner, then things would have taken a different turn . . ."

"But, Prince," Dessalles began timidly, "the letter mentions Vítebsk. . . ."

"Ah, the letter? Yes . . ." replied the prince peevishly, "Yes . . yes . ." His face suddenly took on a morose expression He paused "Yes, he writes that the French were beaten at . at . . what river is it?"

Dessalles dropped his eyes.

"The prince says nothing about that," he remarked gently.

"Doesn't he? But I didn't invent it myself."

No one spoke for a long time.

3

The prince had a list of things to be bought in Smolénsk and, walking up and down the room past Alpátych who stood by the door, he gave his instructions.

Alpátych went out. The prince again went to his bureau, glanced into it, fingered his papers, closed the bureau again, and sat down at the table to write to the governor.

It was already late when he rose after sealing the letter. He wished to sleep, but he knew he would not be able to and that most depressing thoughts came to him in bed.

Frowning with vexation at the effort necessary to divest himself of his coat and trousers, the prince undressed, sat down heavily on the bed, and appeared to be meditating as he looked contemptuously at his withered yellow legs. He was not meditating, but only deferring the moment of making the effort to lift those legs up and turn over on the bed. "Ugh, how hard it is! Oh, that this toil might end and *you* would release me!" thought he.

"Tíkhon, what did we talk about at dinner?"

"About Prince Michael . . ."

"Be quiet, quiet!" The prince slapped his hand on the table. "Yes, I know, Prince Andrew's letter! Princess Mary read it. Dessalles said something about Vítebsk. Now I'll read it."

He had the letter taken from his pocket and the table—on which stood a glass of lemonade and a spiral wax candle—moved close to the bed, and putting on his spectacles he began reading. Only now in the stillness of the night, reading it by the faint light under the green shade, did he grasp its meaning for a moment.

"The French at Vítebsk, in four days' march they may be at Smolénsk; perhaps are already there! Tíkhon!" Tíkhon jumped up. "No, no, I don't want anything!" he shouted.

4

Bald Hills, Prince Nicholas Bolkónski's estate, lay forty miles east from Smolénsk and two miles from the main road to Moscow.

The same evening that the prince gave his instructions to Alpátych, Dessalles, having asked to see Princess Mary, told her that, as the prince was not very well and was taking no steps to secure his safety, though from Prince Andrew's letter it was evident that to remain at Bald Hills might be dangerous, he respectfully advised her to send a letter by Alpátych to the Provincial Governor at Smolénsk, asking him to let her know the state of affairs and the extent of the danger to which Bald Hills was exposed. Dessalles wrote this letter to the Governor for Princess Mary, she signed it, and it was given to Alpátych with instructions to hand it to the Governor and to come back as quickly as possible if there was danger.

Alpátych kept meeting and overtaking baggage trains and troops on the road. As he approached Smolénsk he heard the sounds of distant firing, but these did not impress him.

On reaching Smolénsk on the evening of the fourth of August he put up in the Gáchina suburb across the Dnieper, at the inn kept by Ferapóntov, where he had been in the habit of putting up for the last thirty years.

All night long troops were moving past the inn. Next morning Alpátych donned a jacket he wore only in town and went out on business.

From beyond the town firing had been heard since early morning. At eight o'clock the booming of cannon was added to the sound of musketry. Many people were hurrying through the streets and there were many soldiers, but cabs were still driving about, tradesmen stood at their shops, and service was being held in the churches as usual. Alpátych went to the shops, to government offices, to the post office, and to the Governor's.

"To his Honor Baron Asch, from General in Chief Prince Bolkónski," he announced with such solemnity and significance that the official turned to him and took the letters.

A few minutes later the Governor received Alpátych and hurriedly said to him:

"Inform the prince and princess that I knew nothing: I acted on the highest instructions—here . . ." and he handed a paper to Alpátych. "Still, as the prince is unwell my advice is that they should go to Moscow. I am just starting myself. Inform them . . ."

Alpátych collected his parcels, handed them to the coachman who had come in, and settled up with the innkeeper.

It was by now late in the afternoon. Half the street was in shadow, the other half brightly lit by the sun. Alpátych looked out of the window and went to the door. Suddenly the strange sound of a far-off whistling and thud was heard, followed by a boom of cannon blending into a dull roar that set the windows rattling.

He went out into the street: two men were running past toward the bridge. From different sides came whistling sounds and the thud of cannon balls and bursting shells falling on the town.

Toward dusk the cannonade began to subside. Alpátych left the cellar and stopped in the doorway. The evening sky that had been so clear was clouded with smoke, through which, high up, the sickle of the new moon shone strangely. Now that the terrible din of the guns had ceased a hush seemed to reign over the town, broken only by the rustle of footsteps, the moaning, the distant cries, and the crackle of fires which seemed widespread everywhere. Alpátych went out to the gate. A retreating regiment, thronging and hurrying, blocked the street.

Noticing him, an officer said: "The town is being abandoned. Get away, get away!"

As Alpátych was driving out of the gate he saw some ten soldiers in Ferapóntov's open shop, talking loudly and filling their bags and knapsacks with flour and sunflower seeds.

Night had come. There were stars in the sky and the new moon shone out amid the smoke that screened it. On the sloping descent to the Dnieper Alpátych's cart and that of the innkeeper's wife, which were slowly moving amid the rows of soldiers and of other vehicles, had to stop. In a side street near the crossroads where the vehicles had stopped, a house and some shops were on fire.

"Alpátych!" a familiar voice suddenly hailed the old man.

"Mercy on us! Your excellency!" answered Alpátych, immediately recognizing the voice of his young prince.

Prince Andrew in his riding cloak, mounted on a black horse, was looking at Alpátych from the back of the crowd.

"Why are you here?" he asked.

At that moment the flames flared up and showed his young master's pale worn face. Alpátych told how he had been sent there and how difficult it was to get away.

"Are we really quite lost, your excellency?"

Prince Andrew without replying took out a notebook and raising his knee began writing in pencil on a page he tore out. He wrote to his sister:

"Smolénsk is being abandoned. Bald Hills will be occupied by the enemy within a week. Set off immediately for Moscow. Let me know at once when you will start. Send by special messenger to Usvyázh."

Having written this and given the paper to Alpátych, he told him how to arrange for the departure of the prince, the princess, his son, and the boy's tutor, and how and where to let him know immediately. Before he had had time to finish giving these instructions, a chief of staff followed by a suite galloped up to him.

"You are a colonel?" shouted the chief of staff with a German accent, in a voice familiar to Prince Andrew. "Houses are set on fire in your presence and you stand by! What does this mean? You will answer for it!" shouted Berg, who was now assistant to the chief of staff of the commander of the left flank of the infantry of the first army, a place, as Berg said, "very agreeable and well *en évidence*."

Prince Andrew looked at him and without replying went on speaking to Alpátych.

"So tell them that I shall await a reply till the tenth, and if by the tenth I don't receive news that they have all got away I shall have to throw up everything and come myself to Bald Hills."

"Prince," said Berg, recognizing Prince Andrew, "I only spoke because I have to obey orders, because I always do obey exactly. . . . You must please excuse me," he went on apologetically.

"Well then," continued Prince Andrew to Alpátych, "report to them as I have told you"; and not replying a word to Berg who was now mute beside him, he touched his horse and rode down the side street.

5

From Smolénsk the troops continued to retreat, followed by the enemy. On the tenth of August the regiment Prince Andrew commanded was marching along the highroad past the avenue leading to Bald Hills. Heat and drought had continued for more than three weeks.

The burning of Smolénsk and its abandonment made an epoch in his life. A novel feeling of anger against the foe made him forget his own sorrow. He was entirely devoted to the affairs of his regiment and was considerate and kind to his men and officers. In the regiment they called him "our prince," were proud of him and loved him. But he was kind and gentle only to those of his regiment, to Timókhin and the like—people quite new to him, belonging to a different world and who could not know and understand his past.

Two days previously he had received news that his father, son, and sister had left for Moscow; and though there was nothing for him to do at Bald Hills, Prince Andrew with a characteristic desire to foment his own grief decided that he must ride there.

He ordered his horse to be saddled and, leaving his regiment on the march, rode to his father's estate where he had been born and spent his childhood.

Prince Andrew rode up to the house. Alpátych, having sent his family away, was alone at Bald Hills and was sitting indoors reading the *Lives of the Saints*. On hearing that Prince Andrew had come, he went out with his spectacles on his nose, buttoning his coat, and, hastily stepping up, without a word began weeping and kissing Prince Andrew's knee.

Then, vexed at his own weakness, he turned away and began to report on the position of affairs. Everything precious and valuable had been removed to Boguchárovo.

Without waiting to hear him out, Prince Andrew asked:

"When did my father and sister leave?" meaning when did they leave for Moscow.

Alpátych, understanding the question to refer to their departure for Boguchárovo, replied that they had left on the seventh and again went into details concerning the estate management, asking for instructions.

"Well, and what are you going to do? Will you stay here if the enemy occupies the place?" asked Prince Andrew.

Alpátych turned his face to Prince Andrew, looked at him, and suddenly with a solemn gesture raised his arm.

"He is my refuge! His will be done!" he exclaimed.

"Well, good-by!" said Prince Andrew, bending over to Alpátych. "You must go away too, take away what you can and tell the serfs to go to the Ryazán estate or to the one near Moscow."

Alpátych clung to Prince Andrew's leg and burst into sobs. Gently disengaging himself, the prince spurred his horse and rode down the avenue at a gallop.

Two little girls, running out from the hothouse carrying in their skirts plums they had plucked from the trees there, came upon Prince Andrew. On seeing the young master, the elder one with frightened look clutched her younger companion by the hand and hid with her behind a birch tree, not stopping to pick up some green plums they had dropped.

Prince Andrew turned away with startled haste, unwilling to let them see that they had been observed. A new sensation of comfort and relief came over him when, seeing these girls, he realized the existence of other human interests entirely aloof from his own and just as legitimate as those that occupied him.

Prince Andrew was somewhat refreshed by having ridden off the dusty highroad along which the troops were moving. But not far from Bald Hills he again came out on the road and overtook his regiment at its halting place by the dam of a small pond. As he crossed the dam Prince Andrew smelled the ooze and freshness of the pond. He longed to get into that water, however dirty it might be, and he glanced round at the pool from whence came sounds of shrieks and laughter. The small, muddy, green pond had risen visibly more than a foot, flooding the dam, because it was full of the naked white bodies of soldiers with brick-red hands, necks, and faces, who were splashing about in it. All this naked white human flesh, laughing and shrieking, floundered about in that dirty pool like carp stuffed into a watering can, and the suggestion of merriment in that floundering mass rendered it specially pathetic.

The officer, Timókhin, with his red little nose, standing on the dam wiping himself with a towel, felt confused at seeing the prince, but made up his mind to address him nevertheless.

"It's very nice, your excellency! Wouldn't you like to?" said he.

"It's dirty," replied Prince Andrew, making a grimace.

"We'll clear it out for you in a minute," said Timókhin, and, still undressed, ran off to clear the men out of the pond.

"The prince wants to bathe."

"What prince? Ours?" said many voices, and the men were in such haste to clear out that the prince could hardly stop them. He decided that he would rather souse himself with water in the barn.

"Flesh, bodies, cannon fodder!" he thought, and he looked at his own naked body and shuddered, not from cold but from a sense of disgust and horror he did not himself understand, aroused by the sight of that immense number of bodies splashing about in the dirty pond.

On the seventh of August Prince Bagratión wrote as follows from his quarters at Mikháylovka on the Smolénsk road:

"Dear Count Aléxis Andréevich"—(He was writing to Arakchéev but knew that his letter would be read by the

Emperor, and therefore weighed every word in it to the best of his ability.)

"I expect the Minister" (Barclay de Tolly) "has already reported the abandonment of Smolénsk to the enemy. It is pitiable and sad, and the whole army is in despair that this most important place has been wantonly abandoned. I, for my part, begged him personally most urgently and finally wrote him, but nothing would induce him to consent . . .

"There is a rumor that you are thinking of peace. God forbid that you should make peace after all our sacrifices and such insane retreats! . . .

"One man ought to be in command, and not two. Your Minister may perhaps be good as a Minister, but as a general he is not merely bad but execrable, yet to him is entrusted the fate of our whole country. . . . What are we scared at and of whom are we afraid? I am not to blame that the Minister is vacillating, a coward, dense, dilatory, and has all bad qualities. The whole army bewails it and calls down curses upon him. . . ."

6

Anna Pávlovna's salon is frankly pro-Russian but that of Hélène discreetly praises Napoleon and argues for peace. Prince Vasíli, a link between both salons, sometimes gets his positions mixed. He and Anna Pávlovna, though they detest Kutúzov, applaud his appointment by the Emperor as field marshal and commander of all the Russian armies, displacing Barclay de Tolly.

7

Napoleon's imagination is fired at the thought of reaching Moscow. Tolstoy shows how the historian Thiers misrepresents the questioning of Rostóv's captured orderly by Napoleon.

8

Princess Mary was not in Moscow and out of danger as Prince Andrew supposed.

After the return of Alpátych from Smolénsk the old prince suddenly seemed to awake as from a dream. He ordered the militiamen to be called up from the villages and armed, and wrote a letter to the commander in chief informing him that he had resolved to remain at Bald Hills to the last extremity and to defend it, leaving to the commander in chief's discretion to take measures or not for the defense of Bald Hills, where one of Russia's oldest generals would be captured or killed, and he announced to his household that he would remain at Bald Hills.

But while himself remaining, he gave instructions for the departure of the princess and Dessalles with the little prince to Boguchárovo and thence to Moscow. Princess Mary, alarmed by her father's feverish and sleepless activity after his previous apathy, could not bring herself to leave him alone and for the first time in her life ventured to disobey him. She refused to go away and her father's fury broke over her in a terrible storm.

The morning after little Nicholas had left, the old prince donned his full uniform and prepared to visit the commander in chief. Princess Mary sat by the window listening to his voice which reached her from the garden. Suddenly several men came running up the avenue with frightened faces.

Princess Mary ran out to the porch, down the flower-bordered path, and into the avenue. A large crowd of militiamen and domestics were moving toward her, and in their midst several men were supporting by the armpits and dragging along a little old man in a uniform and decorations.

The doctor, who was fetched that same night, bled him and said that the prince had had a seizure paralyzing his right side.

It was becoming more and more dangerous to remain at Bald Hills, and next day they moved the prince to Boguchárovo, the doctor accompanying him.

By the time they reached Boguchárovo, Dessalles and the little prince had already left for Moscow.

For three weeks the old prince lay stricken by paralysis in the new house.

He was evidently suffering both physically and mentally. There was no hope of recovery. It was impossible for him to travel, it would not do to let him die on the road. "Would it not be better if the end did come, the very end?" Princess Mary sometimes thought. Night and day, hardly sleeping at all, she watched him and, terrible to say, often watched him not with hope of finding signs of improvement but wishing to find symptoms of the approach of the end.

Strange as it was to her to acknowledge this feeling in herself, yet there it was. And what seemed still more terrible to her was that since her father's illness began (perhaps even sooner, when she stayed with him expecting something to happen), all the personal desires and hopes that had been forgotten or sleeping within her had reawakened. Thoughts that had not entered her mind for years—thoughts of a life free from the fear of her father, and even the possibility of love and of family happiness—floated continually in her imagination like temptations of the devil.

It was becoming dangerous to remain in Boguchárovo. News of the approach of the French came from all sides, and in one village, ten miles from Boguchárovo, a homestead had been looted by French marauders.

The princess decided to leave on the fifteenth. The cares of preparation and giving orders, for which everyone came to her, occupied her all day. She spent the night of the fourteenth as usual, without undressing, in the room next to the one where the prince lay. She could not sleep and several times went to the door and listened, wishing to enter but not deciding to do so.

But never had she felt so grieved for him or so much afraid of losing him. She recalled all her life with him and in every word and act of his found an expression of his love of her. Occasionally amid these memories temptations of the devil would surge into her imagination: thoughts of how things would be after his death, and how her new, liberated life would be ordered. But she drove these thoughts away with disgust. Toward morning he became quiet and she fell asleep.

She woke late. It was a warm, gray morning. Princess Mary stopped at the porch, still horrified by her spiritual baseness and trying to arrange her thoughts before going to her father.

The doctor came downstairs and went out to her.

"He is a little better today," said he. "I was looking for you. One can make out something of what he is saying. His head is clearer. Come in, he is asking for you. . . ."

Princess Mary entered her father's room and went up to his bed. He was lying on his back propped up high, and his small bony hands with their knotted purple veins were lying on the quilt; his left eye gazed straight before him, his right eye was awry, and his brows and lips motionless.

She looked at him in dismay trying to guess what he wanted of her. Then his lips and tongue moved, sounds came, and he began to speak, gazing timidly and imploringly at her, evidently afraid that she might not understand.

Princess Mary pressed her head against his hand, trying to hide her sobs and tears.

He moved his hand over her hair.

"I have been calling you all night . . ." he brought out.

"If only I had known . . ." she said through her tears. "I was afraid to come in."

He pressed her hand.

"Dear one . . . Dearest . . ." Princess Mary could not quite make out what he said, but from his look it was clear that he had uttered a tender caressing word such as he had never used to her before. "Why didn't you come in?"

"And I, I was wishing for his death!" thought Princess Mary.

He was silent awhile.

"Thank you . . . daughter dear! . . . for all, for all . . . forgive! . . . thank you! . . . forgive! . . . thank you! . . ." and tears began to flow from his eyes. "Call Andrew!"

"He's with the army, Father, at Smolénsk."

He closed his eyes and remained silent for a long time. Then as if in answer to his doubts and to confirm the fact that now he understood and remembered everything, he nodded his head and reopened his eyes.

"Yes," he said, softly and distinctly. "Russia has perished. They've destroyed her."

She ran out sobbing into the garden and as far as the pond,

along the avenues of young lime trees Prince Andrew had planted.

She did not know how long she had been there when she was aroused by the sound of a woman's footsteps running along the path. She rose and saw Dunyásha her maid, who was evidently looking for her, and who stopped suddenly as if in alarm on seeing her mistress.

"Please come, Princess . . . The Prince . . ." said Dunyásha in a breaking voice.

"Immediately, I'm coming. I'm coming!" replied the princess hurriedly.

In the room were her nurse and other women. They all drew back from the bed, making way for her. He was still lying on the bed as before, but the stern expression of his quiet face made Princess Mary stop short on the threshold.

"No, he's not dead—it's impossible!" she told herself and approached him, and repressing the terror that seized her, she pressed her lips to his cheek. But she stepped back immediately. All the force of the tenderness she had been feeling for him vanished instantly and was replaced by a feeling of horror at what lay there before her. "No, he is no more! He is not, but here where he was is something unfamiliar and hostile, some dreadful, terrifying, and repellent mystery!" And hiding her face in her hands, Princess Mary sank into the arms of the doctor, who held her up.

9

The steward Alpátych fails to persuade Dron, the village elder of Boguchárovo, to provide horses and carts to move themselves and Princess Mary to Moscow. Alpátych goes to the police. A suspicion has sprung up among the peasantry that in moving them the masters have some evil purpose.

10

After her father's funeral Princess Mary shut herself up in her room and did not admit anyone.

The sun had reached the other side of the house, and its

slanting rays shone into the open window. The flow of her thoughts suddenly stopped. Unconsciously she sat up, smoothed her hair, got up, and went to the window, involuntarily inhaling the freshness of the clear but windy evening.

"Yes, you can well enjoy the evening now! He is gone and no one will hinder you," she said to herself, and sinking into a chair she let her head fall on the window sill.

Someone spoke her name in a soft and tender voice from the garden and kissed her head. She looked up. It was Mademoiselle Bourienne.

Princess Mary vividly pictured to herself the position of Mademoiselle Bourienne, whom she had of late kept at a distance, but who yet was dependent on her and living in her house. She felt sorry for her and held out her hand with a glance of gentle inquiry.

Mademoiselle Bourienne took from her reticule a proclamation (not printed on ordinary Russian paper) of General Rameau's, telling people not to leave their homes and that the French authorities would afford them proper protection. She handed this to the princess.

"I think it would be best to appeal to that general," she continued, "and I am sure that all due respect would be shown you."

Princess Mary read the paper, and her face began to quiver with stifled sobs.

Princess Mary, with the paper in her hand, rose from the window and with a pale face went out of the room and into what had been Prince Andrew's study.

"Dunyásha, send Alpátych, or Drónushka, or somebody to me!" she said, "and tell Mademoiselle Bourienne not to come to me," she added. "We must go at once, at once!" she said, appalled at the thought of being left in the hands of the French.

"If Prince Andrew heard that I was in the power of the French! That I, the daughter of Prince Nicholas Bolkónski, asked General Rameau for protection and accepted his favor!" This idea horrified her, made her shudder, blush, and feel such a rush of anger and pride as she had never experienced before.

At length Dron, the village Elder, entered the room and with a deep bow to Princess Mary came to a halt by the door-post.

Princess Mary walked up and down the room and stopped in front of him.

"Drónushka, Alpátych has gone off somewhere and I have no one to turn to. Is it true, as they tell me, that I can't even go away?"

"Why shouldn't you go away, your excellency? You can go," said Dron.

"I was told it would be dangerous because of the enemy. Dear friend, I can do nothing. I understand nothing. I have nobody! I want to go away tonight or early tomorrow morning."

Dron paused. He looked askance at Princess Mary and said: "There are no horses; I told Yákov Alpátych so."

"Why are there none?" asked the princess.

"It's all God's scourge," said Dron. "What horses we had have been taken for the army or have died—this is such a year! It's not a case of feeding horses—we may die of hunger ourselves! As it is, some go three days without eating. We've nothing, we've been ruined."

Princess Mary listened attentively to what he told her.

"But we have grain belonging to my brother?" she said.

"The landlord's grain is all safe," replied Dron proudly. "Our prince did not order it to be sold."

"Give it to the peasants, let them have all they need; I give you leave in my brother's name," said she.

Dron made no answer but sighed deeply.

11

The peasants reject Princess Mary's offer of grain and accuse her of trying to persuade them to desert their village and follow her into bondage.

12

For a long time that night Princess Mary sat by the open window of her room hearing the sound of the peasants' voices that reached her from the village, but it was not of them she was thinking.

After sunset the wind had dropped. The night was calm and fresh. Toward midnight the voices began to subside, a cock crowed. Pictures of the near past—her father's illness and last moments—rose one after another to her memory. With mournful pleasure she now lingered over these images, repelling with horror only the last one, the picture of his death, which she felt she could not contemplate even in imagination at this still and mystic hour of night.

And Princess Mary uttered aloud the caressing word he had said to her on the day of his death. "Dear-est!" she repeated, and began sobbing, with tears that relieved her soul.

"What was he thinking when he uttered that word? What is he thinking now?" This question suddenly presented itself to her, and in answer she saw him before her with the expression that was on his face as he lay in his coffin. She tried to think of something else and to pray, but could do neither. With wide-open eyes she gazed at the moonlight and the shadows, expecting every moment to see his dead face, and she felt that the silence brooding over the house and within it held her fast.

"Dunyásha," she whispered. "Dunyásha!" she screamed wildly, and tearing herself out of this silence she ran to the servants' quarters to meet her old nurse and the maidservants who came running toward her.

13

On the seventeenth of August Rostóv and Ilyín, accompanied by Lavrúshka and by an hussar orderly, left their quarters at Yankóvo, ten miles from Boguchárovo, and went for a ride—to try a new horse Ilyín had bought and to find out whether there was any hay to be had in the villages.

For the last three days Boguchárovo had lain between the two hostile armies, so that it was as easy for the Russian rearguard to get to it as for the French vanguard; Rostóv, as a careful squadron commander, wished to take such provisions as remained at Boguchárovo before the French could get them.

Rostóv had no idea that the village he was entering was the

property of that very Bolkónski who had been engaged to his sister.

They rode at a footpace to the barn, where a large crowd of peasants was standing.

At that moment, on the road leading from the big house, two women and a man in a white hat were seen coming toward the officers.

"The one in pink is mine, so keep off!" said Ilyín on seeing Dunyásha running resolutely toward him.

"She'll be ours!" said Lavrúshka to Ilyín, winking.

"What do you want, my pretty?" said Ilyín with a smile.

"The princess ordered me to ask your regiment and your name."

"This is Count Rostóv, squadron commander, and I am your humble servant."

Following Dunyásha, Alpátych advanced to Rostóv, having bared his head while still at a distance.

"May I make bold to trouble your honor?" said he respectfully, but with a shade of contempt for the youthfulness of this officer and with a hand thrust into his bosom. "My mistress, daughter of General in Chief Prince Nicholas Bolkónski who died on the fifteenth of this month, finding herself in difficulties owing to the boorishness of these people"—he pointed to the peasants—"asks you to come up to the house."

"What's the matter?" Rostóv asked.

"I make bold to inform your honor that the rude peasants here don't wish to let the mistress leave the estate, and threaten to unharness her horses, so that though everything has been packed up since morning, her excellency cannot get away."

"Impossible!" exclaimed Rostóv.

"I have the honor to report to you the actual truth," said Alpátych.

Rostóv dismounted, gave his horse to the orderly, and followed Alpátych to the house, questioning him as to the state of affairs.

"Father! Benefactor! God has sent you!" exclaimed deeply moved voices as Rostóv passed through the anteroom.

Princess Mary was sitting helpless and bewildered in the large sitting room, when Rostóv was shown in. She could not grasp who he was and why he had come, or what was happening to her. When she saw his Russian face, and by his walk and the first words he uttered recognized him as a man of her own class, she glanced at him with her deep radiant look and began speaking in a voice that faltered and trembled with emotion. This meeting immediately struck Rostóv as a romantic event. "A helpless girl overwhelmed with grief, left to the mercy of coarse, rioting peasants! And what a strange fate sent me here! What gentleness and nobility there are in her features and expression!" thought he as he looked at her and listened to her timid story.

When she began to tell him that all this had happened the day after her father's funeral, her voice trembled. She turned away, and then, as if fearing he might take her words as meant to move him to pity, looked at him with an apprehensive glance of inquiry. There were tears in Rostóv's eyes. Princess Mary noticed this and glanced gratefully at him with that radiant look which caused the plainness of her face to be forgotten.

"I cannot express, Princess, how glad I am that I happened to ride here and am able to show my readiness to serve you," said Rostóv, rising. "Go when you please, and I give you my word of honor that no one shall dare to cause you annoyance if only you will allow me to act as your escort." And bowing respectfully, as if to a lady of royal blood, he moved toward the door.

Rostóv's deferential tone seemed to indicate that though he would consider himself happy to be acquainted with her, he did not wish to take advantage of her misfortunes to intrude upon her.

Princess Mary understood this and appreciated his delicacy.

"I am very, very grateful to you," said in French, "but I hope it was all a misunderstanding and that no one is to blame for it." She suddenly began to cry.

"Excuse me!" she said.

Rostóv, knitting his brows, left the room with another low bow.

14

"I'll show them; I'll give it to them, the brigands!" said Rostóv to himself.

Without considering what he would do he moved unconsciously with quick, resolute steps toward the crowd.

After the hussars had come to the village and Rostóv had gone to see the princess, a certain confusion and dissension had arisen among the crowd. Some of the peasants said that these new arrivals were Russians and might take it amiss that the mistress was being detained. Dron was of this opinion, but as soon as he expressed it Karp and others attacked their ex-Elder.

As soon as Rostóv, followed by Ilyín, Lavrúshka, and Alpátych, came up to the crowd, Karp, thrusting his fingers into his belt and smiling a little, walked to the front. Dron on the contrary retired to the rear and the crowd drew closer together.

"Who is your Elder here? Hey?" shouted Rostóv, coming up to the crowd with quick steps.

"The Elder? What do you want with him? . . ." asked Karp.

But before the words were well out of his mouth, his cap flew off and a fierce blow jerked his head to one side.

"Caps off, traitors!" shouted Rostóv in a wrathful voice. "Where's the Elder?" he cried furiously.

"We don't riot, we're following the orders," declared Karp, and at that moment several voices began speaking together.

"It's as the old men have decided—there's too many of you giving orders."

"Arguing? Mutiny! . . . Brigands! Traitors!" cried Rostóv unmeaningly in a voice not his own, gripping Karp by the collar. "Bind him, bind him!" he shouted, though there was no one to bind him but Lavrúshka and Alpátych.

Lavrúshka, however, ran up to Karp and seized him by the arms from behind.

"Shall I call up our men from beyond the hill?" he called out.

Alpátych turned to the peasants and ordered two of them by name to come and bind Karp. The men obediently came out of the crowd and began taking off their belts.

"Where's the Elder?" demanded Rostóv in a loud voice.

With a pale and frowning face Dron stepped out of the crowd.

"Are you the Elder? Bind him, Lavrúshka!" shouted Rostóv, as if that order, too, could not possibly meet with any opposition.

"And you all listen to me!" said Rostóv to the peasants. "Be off to your houses at once, and don't let one of your voices be heard!"

"Why, we've not done any harm! We did it just out of foolishness. It's all nonsense. . . . I said then that it was not in order," voices were heard bickering with one another.

"There! What did I say?" said Alpátych, coming into his own again. "It's wrong, lads!"

"All our stupidity, Yákov Alpátych," came the answers, and the crowd began at once to disperse through the village.

Two hours later the carts were standing in the courtyard of the Boguchárovo house. The peasants were briskly carrying out the proprietor's goods and packing them on the carts, and Dron, liberated at Princess Mary's wish from the cupboard where he had been confined, was standing in the yard directing the men.

Unwilling to obtrude himself on the princess, Rostóv did not go back to the house but remained in the village awaiting her departure. When her carriage drove out of the house, he mounted and accompanied her eight miles from Boguchárovo to where the road was occupied by our troops. At the inn at Yankóvo he respectfully took leave of her, for the first time permitting himself to kiss her hand.

"Good-by, Princess. I wish you happiness and consolation and hope to meet you again in happier circumstances. If you don't want to make me blush, please don't thank me!"

But the princess, if she did not again thank him in words, thanked him with the whole expression of her face, radiant with gratitude and tenderness.

When she had taken leave of him and remained alone she suddenly felt her eyes filling with tears, and then not for the first time the strange question presented itself to her: did she love him?

On the rest of the way to Moscow, though the princess' position was not a cheerful one, Dunyásha, who went with her in the carriage, more than once noticed that her mistress leaned out of the window and smiled at something with an expression of mingled joy and sorrow.

"Well, supposing I do love him?" thought Princess Mary.

Ashamed as she was of acknowledging to herself that she

had fallen in love with a man who would perhaps never love her, she comforted herself with the thought that no one would ever know it and that she would not be to blame if, without ever speaking of it to anyone, she continued to the end of her life to love the man with whom she had fallen in love for the first and last time in her life.

Sometimes when she recalled his looks, his sympathy, and his words, happiness did not appear impossible to her. It was at those moments that Dunyásha noticed her smiling as she looked out of the carriage window.

For himself personally Nicholas could not wish for a better wife: by marrying her he would make the countess his mother happy, would be able to put his father's affairs in order, and would even—he felt it—ensure Princess Mary's happiness.

But Sónya? And his plighted word? That was why Rostóv grew angry when he was rallied about Princess Bolkónskaya.

15

On receiving command of the armies Kutúzov remembered Prince Andrew and sent an order for him to report at headquarters.

Prince Andrew arrived at Tsárevo-Zaymíshche on the very day and at the very hour that Kutúzov was reviewing the troops for the first time. He stopped in the village at the priest's house in front of which stood the commander in chief's carriage, and he sat down on the bench at the gate awaiting his Serene Highness, as everyone now called Kutúzov. A short, swarthy lieutenant colonel of hussars with thick mustaches and whiskers rode up to the gate and, glancing at Prince Andrew, inquired whether his Serene Highness was putting up there and whether he would soon be back.

Prince Andrew replied that he was not on his Serene Highness' staff but was himself a new arrival.

"You're also waiting for the commander in chief?" said he. "They say he weceives evewyone, thank God! . . . Did you take part in the campaign?" he asked.

"I had the pleasure," replied Prince Andrew, "not only of taking part in the retreat but of losing in that retreat all I held dear—not to mention the estate and home of my birth—my father, who died of grief. I belong to the province of Smolénsk."

"Ah? You're Prince Bolkónski? Vewy glad to make your acquaintance! I'm Lieutenant Colonel Denísov, better known as 'Váska,'" said Denísov, pressing Prince Andrew's hand and looking into his face with a particularly kindly attention.

Prince Andrew knew Denísov from what Natásha had told him of her first suitor. This memory carried him sadly and sweetly back to those painful feelings of which he had not thought lately, but which still found place in his soul. For Denísov, too, the memories awakened by the name of Bolkónski belonged to a distant, romantic past, when after supper and after Natásha's singing he had proposed to a little girl of fifteen without realizing what he was doing.

"He's coming! He's coming!" shouted a Cossack standing at the gate.

Bolkónski and Denísov moved to the gate, at which a knot of soldiers (a guard of honor) was standing, and they saw Kutúzov coming down the street mounted on a rather small sorrel horse.

Since Prince Andrew had last seen him Kutúzov had grown still more corpulent, flaccid, and fat. But the bleached eyeball, the scar, and the familiar weariness of his expression were still the same. He sat heavily and swayed limply on his brisk little horse.

"Whew . . . whew . . . whew!" he whistled just audibly as he rode into the yard. His face expressed the relief of relaxed strain felt by a man who means to rest after a ceremony.

As often occurs with old men, it was only after some seconds that the impression produced by Prince Andrew's face linked itself up with Kutúzov's remembrance of his personality.

"Ah, how do you do, my dear prince? How do you do, my dear boy? Come along . . ." said he, glancing wearily round, and he stepped onto the porch which creaked under his weight.

He unbuttoned his coat and sat down on a bench in the porch.

"And how's your father?"

"I received news of his death, yesterday," replied Prince Andrew abruptly.

Kutúzov looked at him with eyes wide open with dismay and then took off his cap and crossed himself:

"May the kingdom of Heaven be his! God's will be done to us all!" He sighed deeply, his whole chest heaving, and was silent for a while. "I loved him and respected him, and sympathize with you with all my heart."

But at that moment Denísov, no more intimidated by his superiors than by the enemy, came with jingling spurs up the steps of the porch, despite the angry whispers of the adjutants who tried to stop him. Denísov, having given his name, announced that he had to communicate to his Serene Highness a matter of great importance for their country's welfare. "For our country's welfare? Well, what is it? Speak!" Denísov blushed like a girl and boldly began to expound his plan of cutting the enemy's lines of communication between Smolénsk and Vyázma. Kutúzov looked down at his own legs, occasionally glancing at the door of the adjoining hut as if expecting something unpleasant to emerge from it.

"All right, all right, friend, stay here at the staff and tomorrow we'll have a talk."

With a nod to Denísov he turned away and put out his hand for the papers Konovnítsyn had brought him.

"Would not your Serene Highness like to come inside?" said the general on duty in a discontented voice, "the plans must be examined and several papers have to be signed."

"No, tell them to bring a small table out here, my dear boy. I'll look at them here," said he. "Don't go away," he added, turning to Prince Andrew, who remained in the porch and listened to the general's report.

While this was being given, Prince Andrew heard the whisper of a woman's voice and the rustle of a silk dress behind the door.

All that Denísov had said was clever and to the point. What the general was saying was even more clever and to the point, but it was evident that Kutúzov despised knowledge and cleverness, and knew of something else that would decide the matter—something independent of cleverness and knowledge. He despised them because of his old age and experience of life.

16

"Well, that's all!" said Kutúzov as he signed the last of the documents, and rising heavily and smoothing out the folds of his fat white neck he moved toward the door with a more cheerful expression.

The priest's wife, flushing rosy red, caught up the dish she had after all not managed to present at the right moment, though she had so long been preparing for it, and with a low bow offered it to Kutúzov.

He screwed up his eyes, smiled, lifted her chin with his hand, and said:

"Ah, what a beauty! Thank you, sweetheart!"

Half an hour later Prince Andrew was again called to Kutúzov. He found him reclining in an armchair, still in the same unbuttoned overcoat.

"Well, sit down, sit down here. Let's have a talk," said Kutúzov.

Prince Andrew told Kutúzov all he knew of his father's death, and what he had seen at Bald Hills when he passed through it.

"What . . . what they have brought us to!" Kutúzov suddenly cried in an agitated voice, evidently picturing vividly to himself from Prince Andrew's story the condition Russia was in. "But give me time, give me time!" he said with a grim look, evidently not wishing to continue this agitating conversation, and added: "I sent for you to keep you with me."

"I thank your Serene Highness, but I fear I am no longer fit for the staff," replied Prince Andrew with a smile which Kutúzov noticed.

Kutúzov glanced inquiringly at him.

"But above all," added Prince Andrew, "I have grown used to my regiment, am fond of the officers, and I fancy the men also like me. I should be sorry to leave the regiment. If I decline the honor of being with you, believe me . . ."

A shrewd, kindly, yet subtly derisive expression lit up Kutúzov's podgy face. He cut Bolkónski short.

"I am sorry, for I need you. But you're right, you're right! It's not here that men are needed. . . . I remember you at Austerlitz. . . . I remember, yes, I remember you with the standard!" said Kutúzov, and a flush of pleasure suffused Prince Andrew's face at this recollection.

"Go your way and God be with you. I know your path is the path of honor!" And changing the subject, Kutúzov began to speak of the Turkish war and the peace that had been concluded. "It is not difficult to capture a fortress but it is difficult to win a campaign. For that, not storming and attacking but *patience and time* are wanted. Kámenski sent soldiers to Rustchuk, but I only employed these two things and took more fortresses than Kámenski and made the Turks eat horseflesh!" He swayed his head. "And the French shall too, believe me," he went on, growing warmer and beating his chest, "I'll make them eat horseflesh!"

"But shan't we have to accept battle?" remarked Prince Andrew.

"We shall if everybody wants it; it can't be helped. . . . But believe me, my dear boy, there is nothing stronger than those two; *patience and time,* they will do it all. . . . Some want a thing—others don't. What's one to do?" he asked, evidently expecting an answer. "Well, what do you want us to do?" he repeated and his eye shone with a deep, shrewd look. "I'll tell you what to do," he continued, as Prince Andrew still did not reply: "When in doubt, my dear fellow, do nothing."

"Well, good-by, my dear fellow; remember that with all my heart I share your sorrow, and that for you I am not a Serene Highness, nor a prince, nor a commander in chief, but a father! If you want anything come straight to me. Good-by, my dear boy."

Prince Andrew could not have explained how or why it was, but after that interview with Kutúzov he went back to his regiment reassured as to the general course of affairs and as to the man to whom it had been entrusted. "He will not bring in any plan of his own. He will not devise or undertake anything," thought Prince Andrew, "but he will hear everything, remember everything, and put everything in its place. He will not hinder anything useful nor allow anything harmful. He understands that there is something stronger and more important than his own will—the inevitable course of events, and he can see them and grasp their significance, and seeing that significance can refrain from meddling and renounce his personal wish directed to something else."

17

After the patriotic excitement of the Emperor's visit to Moscow, life flows on as usual there. It even grows frivolous with the enemy's approach to the city. Julie Drubetskáya, Borís' wife, twits Pierre on becoming Natásha's knight; he is offended at this gossip. Julie also tells him of Princess Mary's arrival in Moscow and of her rescue by Nicholas Rostóv.

18

When Pierre returned home he was handed two of Rostopchín's broadsheets that had been brought that day.

Pierre pondered over these broadsheets. Evidently the terrible stormcloud he had desired with the whole strength of his soul but which yet aroused involuntary horror in him was drawing near.

"Shall I join the army and enter the service, or wait?" he asked himself for the hundredth time. He took a pack of cards that lay on the table and began to lay them out for a game of patience.

"If this patience comes out," he said to himself after shuffling the cards, holding them in his hand, and lifting his head, "if it comes out, it means . . . what does it mean?"

Although that patience did come out, Pierre did not join the army, but remained in deserted Moscow ever in the same state of agitation, irresolution, and alarm, yet at the same time joyfully expecting something terrible.

To distract his thoughts he drove that day to the village of Vorontsóvo to see the great balloon Leppich was constructing to destroy the foe, and a trial balloon that was to go up next day.

On his way home from Vorontsóvo, as he was passing the Bolótnoe Place, Pierre, seeing a large crowd round the Lóbnoe Place, stopped and got out of his trap. A French cook accused of being a spy was being flogged. The flogging was only just over, and the executioner was releasing from the flogging bench a stout man with red whiskers, in blue stockings and a green jacket, who was moaning piteously.

Pierre choked, his face puckered, and he turned hastily away, went back to his trap muttering something to himself as he went, and took his seat.

At the sight of the tortured Frenchman and the crowd surrounding the Lóbnoe Place, Pierre had definitely made up his mind that he could no longer remain in Moscow and would leave for the army that very day.

On the twenty-fourth the weather cleared up after a spell of rain, and after dinner Pierre left Moscow. When changing horses that night in Perkhúshkovo, he learned that there had been a great battle that evening. (This was the battle of Shevardino.) At dawn next day Pierre was approaching Mozháysk.

Everywhere in Mozháysk and beyond it, troops were stationed or on the march. Pierre pushed forward as fast as he could, and the farther he left Moscow behind and the deeper he plunged into that sea of troops the more was he overcome by restless agitation and a new and joyful feeling he had not experienced before. He now experienced a glad consciousness that everything that constitutes men's happiness—the comforts of life, wealth, even life itself—is rubbish it is pleasant to throw away, compared with something . . . With what? Pierre could not say, and he did not try to determine for whom and for what he felt such particular delight in sacrificing everything. He was not occupied with the question of what to sacrifice for; the fact of sacrificing in itself afforded him a new and joyous sensation.

19

Tolstoy maintains that both Napoleon and Kutúzov acted involuntarily and irrationally in accepting battle at Borodinó.

20

On the morning of the twenty-fifth Pierre was leaving Mozháysk. At the descent of the high steep hill, down which a winding road led out of the town past the cathedral on the right, where a service was being held and the bells were ringing, Pierre got out of his vehicle and proceeded on foot. Behind him a cavalry regiment was coming down the hill preceded by its singers. Coming up toward him was a train of carts carrying men who had been wounded in the engagement the day before. The peasant drivers, shouting and lashing their horses, kept crossing from side to side. The carts, in each of which three or four wounded soldiers were lying or sitting, jolted over the stones that had been thrown on the steep incline to make it something like a road. The wounded, bandaged with rags, with pale cheeks, compressed lips, and knitted brows, held on to the sides of the carts as they were jolted against one another. Almost all of them stared with naïve, childlike curiosity at Pierre's white hat and green swallowtail coat.

Having gone nearly three miles he at last met an acquaintance and eagerly addressed him. This was one of the head army doctors. He was driving toward Pierre in a covered gig, sitting beside a young surgeon, and on recognizing Pierre he told the Cossack who occupied the driver's seat to pull up.

"Count! Your excellency, how come you to be here?" asked the doctor.

"Well, you know, I wanted to see . . ."

"Yes, yes, there will be something to see. . . ."

Pierre got out and talked to the doctor, explaining his intention of taking part in a battle.

The doctor advised him to apply direct to Kutúzov.

"Ah, I also wanted to ask you where our position is exactly?" said Pierre.

"The position?" repeated the doctor. "Well, that's not my line. Drive past Tatárinova, a lot of digging is going on there. Go up the hillock and you'll see."

"Can one see from there? . . . It you would . . ."

But the doctor interrupted him and moved toward his gig.

"I would go with you but on my honor I'm up to here"—and he pointed to his throat. "I'm galloping to the commander of the corps. How do matters stand? . . . You know, Count, there'll be a battle tomorrow. Out of an army of a hundred thousand we must expect at least twenty thousand wounded, and we haven't stretchers, or bunks, or dressers, or doctors enough for six thousand. We have ten thousand carts, but we need other things as well—we must manage as best we can!"

The strange thought that of the thousands of men, young and old, who had stared with merry surprise at his hat (perhaps the very men he had noticed), twenty thousand were inevitably doomed to wounds and death amazed Pierre.

In front of a landowner's house to the left of the road stood carriages, wagons, and crowds of orderlies and sentinels. The commander in chief was putting up there, but just when Pierre arrived he was not in and hardly any of the staff were there—they had gone to the church service. Pierre drove on toward Górki.

21

Pierre stepped out of his carriage and, passing the toiling militiamen, ascended the knoll from which, according to the doctor, the battlefield could be seen.

It was about eleven o'clock. The sun shone somewhat to the left and behind him and brightly lit up the enormous panorama which, rising like an amphitheater, extended before him in the clear rarefied atmosphere.

All that Pierre saw was so indefinite that neither the left nor the right side of the field fully satisfied his expectations. Nowhere could he see the battlefield he had expected to find, but only fields, meadows, troops, woods, the smoke of campfires, villages, mounds, and streams; and try as he would he could descry no military "position" in this place which teemed with life, nor could he even distinguish our troops from the enemy's.

A church procession was coming up the hill from Borodinó. First along the dusty road came the infantry in ranks, bareheaded and with arms reversed. From behind them came the sound of church singing.

Soldiers and militiamen ran bareheaded past Pierre toward the procession.

"They are bringing her, our Protectress! . . . The Iberian Mother of God!" someone cried.

"The Smolénsk Mother of God," another corrected him.

Following the battalion that marched along the dusty road came priests in their vestments—one little old man in a hood with attendants and singers. Behind them soldiers and officers bore a large, dark-faced icon with an embossed metal cover. This was the icon that had been brought from Smolénsk and had since accompanied the army. Behind, before, and on both sides, crowds of militiamen with bared heads walked, ran, and bowed to the ground.

At the summit of the hill they stopped with the icon; the men who had been holding it up by the linen bands attached to it were relieved by others, the chanters relit their censers, and service began.

The crowd round the icon suddenly parted and pressed against Pierre. Someone, a very important personage judging by the haste with which way was made for him, was approaching the icon.

It was Kutúzov, who had been riding round the position and on his way back to Tatárinova had stopped where the service was being held. Pierre recognized him at once by his peculiar figure, which distinguished him from everybody else.

With a long overcoat on his exceedingly stout, round-shouldered body, with uncovered white head and puffy face showing the white ball of the eye he had lost, Kutúzov walked with plunging, swaying gait into the crowd and stopped behind the priest. He crossed himself with an accustomed movement, bent till he touched the ground with his hand, and bowed his white head with a deep sigh.

When the service was over, Kutúzov stepped up to the icon, sank heavily to his knees, bowed to the ground, and for a long time tried vainly to rise, but could not do so on account of his weakness and weight. His white head twitched with the effort. At last he rose, kissed the icon as a child does with naïvely pouting lips, and again bowed till he touched the ground with his hand. The other generals followed his example, then the officers, and after them with excited faces, pressing on one another, crowding, panting, and pushing, scrambled the soldiers and militiamen.

22

Staggering amid the crush, Pierre looked about him.

"Count Peter Kirílovich! How did you get here?" said a voice.

Pierre looked round. Borís Drubetskóy, brushing his knees with his hand (he had probably soiled them when he, too, had knelt before the icon), came up to him smiling.

Meanwhile Kutúzov had reached the village and seated himself in the shade of the nearest house, on a bench which one Cossack had run to fetch and another had hastily covered with a rug. An immense and brilliant suite surrounded him.

Pierre stopped some thirty paces from Kutúzov, talking to Borís.

He explained his wish to be present at the battle and to see the position.

"This is what you must do," said Borís. "I will do the honors of the camp to you. You will see everything best from where Count Bennigsen will be. I am in attendance on him, you know; I'll mention it to him."

Though Kutúzov had dismissed all unnecessary men from the staff, Borís had contrived to remain at headquarters after the changes. He had established himself with Count Bennigsen, who, like all on whom Borís had been in attendance, considered young Prince Drubetskóy an invaluable man.

In the higher command there were two sharply defined parties: Kutúzov's party and that of Bennigsen, the chief of staff. Borís belonged to the latter and no one else, while showing servile respect to Kutúzov, could so create an impression that the old fellow was not much good and that Bennigsen managed everything.

Others whom Pierre knew came up to him, and he had not time to reply to all the questions about Moscow that were showered upon him, or to listen to all that was told him. The faces all expressed animation and apprehension, but it seemed to Pierre that the cause of the excitement shown in some of these faces lay chiefly in questions of personal success; his mind, however, was occupied by the different expression he saw on other faces—an expression that spoke not of personal matters but of the universal questions of life and death. Kutúzov noticed Pierre's figure and the group gathered round him.

"Call him to me," said Kutúzov.

An adjutant told Pierre of his Serene Highness' wish, and Pierre went toward Kutúzov's bench. But a militiaman got there before him. It was Dólokhov.

"How did that fellow get here?" asked Pierre.

"He's a creature that wriggles in anywhere!" was the answer. "He has been degraded, you know. Now he wants to bob up again. He's been proposing some scheme or other and has crawled into the enemy's picket line at night. . . . He's a brave fellow."

Pierre took off his hat and bowed respectfully to Kutúzov.

"So you want to smell gunpowder?" he said to Pierre. "Yes, it's a pleasant smell. I have the honor to be one of your wife's adorers. Is she well? My quarters are at your service."

When Pierre had left Kutúzov, Dólokhov came up to him and took his hand.

"I am very glad to meet you here, Count," he said aloud, regardless of the presence of strangers and in a particularly resolute and solemn tone. "On the eve of a day when God alone knows who of us is fated to survive, I am glad of this opportunity to tell you that I regret the misunderstandings that occurred between us and should wish you not to have any ill feeling for me. I beg you to forgive me."

Pierre looked at Dólokhov with a smile, not knowing what to say to him. With tears in his eyes Dólokhov embraced Pierre and kissed him.

Borís said a few words to his general, and Count Bennigsen turned to Pierre and proposed that he should ride with him along the line.

23

Bennigsen shows Pierre the position of the Russian forces before the battle of Borodinó and also alters one of Kutúzov's dispositions without understanding its purpose.

24

On that bright evening of August 25, Prince Andrew lay leaning on his elbow in a broken-down shed in the village of Knyazkóvo at the further end of his regiment's encampment.

Narrow and burdensome and useless to anyone as his life now seemed to him, Prince Andrew on the eve of battle felt agitated and irritable as he had done seven years before at Austerlitz.

He had received and given the orders for next day's battle and had nothing more to do. But his thoughts—the simplest, clearest, and therefore most terrible thoughts—would give him no peace. He knew that tomorrow's battle would be the most terrible of all he had taken part in, and for the first time in his life the possibility of death presented itself to him. The three great sorrows of his life held his attention in particular: his love for a woman, his father's death, and the French invasion which had overrun half Russia. "Love! . . . that little girl who seemed to me brimming over with mystic forces! Yes, indeed, I loved her. I made romantic plans of love and happiness with her! Oh, what a boy I was!" he said aloud bitterly. "Ah me! I believed in some ideal love which was to keep her faithful to me for the whole year of my absence! Like the gentle dove in the fable she was to pine apart from me. . . . But it was much simpler really. . . . It was all very simple and horrible.

"When my father built Bald Hills he thought the place was his: his land, his air, his peasants. But Napoleon came and swept him aside, unconscious of his existence, as he might brush a chip from his path, and his Bald Hills and his whole life fell to pieces."

The red-nosed Captain Timókhin, formerly Dólokhov's squadron commander, but now from lack of officers a battalion commander, shyly entered the shed followed by an adjutant and the regimental paymaster.

Prince Andrew rose hastily, listened to the business they had come about, gave them some further instructions, and was about to dismiss them when he heard a familiar, lisping voice behind the shed.

Prince Andrew looked out of the shed and saw Pierre, who had tripped over a pole on the ground and had nearly fallen, coming his way. It was unpleasant to Prince Andrew to meet people of his own set in general, and Pierre especially, for he reminded him of all the painful moments of his last visit to Moscow.

"You? What a surprise!" said he. "What brings you here? This is unexpected!"

As he said this his eyes and face expressed more than coldness—they expressed hostility, which Pierre noticed at once. He had approached the shed full of animation, but on seeing Prince Andrew's face he felt constrained and ill at ease.

"I have come . . . simply . . . you know . . . come . . . it interests me," said Pierre, who had so often that day senselessly repeated that word "interesting." "I wish to see the battle."

"Well, and how's Moscow? And my people? Have they reached Moscow at last?" he asked seriously.

"Yes, they have. Julie Drubetskáya told me so. I went to see them, but missed them. They have gone to your estate near Moscow."

25

The officers were about to take leave, but Prince Andrew, apparently reluctant to be left alone with his friend, asked them to stay and have tea. The officers gazed with surprise at Pierre's huge stout figure and listened to his talk of Moscow and the position of our army, round which he had ridden.

"So you understand the whole position of our troops?" Prince Andrew interrupted him.

"Yes—that is, how do you mean?" said Pierre.

"Success never depends, and never will depend, on position, or equipment, or even on numbers, and least of all on position."

"But on what then?"

"On the feeling that is in me and in him," he pointed to Timókhin, "and in each soldier."

In contrast to his former reticent taciturnity Prince Andrew now seemed excited. He could apparently not refrain from expressing the thoughts that had suddenly occurred to him.

"A battle is won by those who firmly resolve to win it! . . . You talk about our position, the left flank weak and the right flank too extended," he went on. "That's all nonsense, there's nothing of the kind. But what awaits us tomorrow? A hundred million most diverse chances which will be decided on the instant by the fact that our men or theirs run or do not run, and that this man or that man is killed, but all that is being done at present is only play. The fact is that those men with whom you have ridden round the position not only do not help matters, but hinder. They are only concerned with their own petty interests."

"At such a moment?" said Pierre reproachfully.

"*At such a moment!*" Prince Andrew repeated. "To them it is only a moment affording opportunities to undermine a rival and obtain an extra cross or ribbon. For me tomorrow means this: a Russian army of a hundred thousand and a French army of a hundred thousand have met to fight, and the thing is that these two hundred thousand men *will* fight and the side that fights more fiercely and spares itself least will win. And if you like I will tell you that whatever happens and whatever muddles those at the top may make, we shall win tomorrow's battle. Tomorrow, happen what may, we shall win!"

"There now, your excellency! That's the truth, the real truth," said Timókhin. "Who would spare himself now? The soldiers in my battalion, believe me, wouldn't drink their vodka! 'It's not the day for that!' they say."

"So you think we shall win tomorrow's battle?" asked Pierre.

"Yes, yes," answered Prince Andrew absently. "One thing I would do if I had the power," he began again, "I would not take prisoners. Why take prisoners? It's chivalry! The French have destroyed my home and are on their way to destroy Moscow, they have outraged and are outraging me every moment. They are my enemies. In my opinion they are all criminals. And so thinks Timókhin and the whole army. They should be executed! Since they are my foes they cannot be my friends, whatever may have been said at Tilsit!"

"Yes, yes," muttered Pierre, looking with shining eyes at Prince Andrew. "I quite agree with you!"

The question that had perturbed Pierre on the Mozháysk hill and all that day now seemed to him quite clear and completely solved. He now understood the whole meaning and importance of this war and of the impending battle. All he had seen that day, all the significant and stern expressions on the faces he had seen in passing, were lit up for him by a new light. He understood that latent heat (as they say in physics) of patriotism which was present in all these men he had seen, and this explained to him why they all prepared for death calmly, and as it were lightheartedly.

Prince Andrew, who had thought it was all the same to him whether or not Moscow was taken as Smolénsk had been, was suddenly checked in his speech by an unexpected cramp in his throat. He paced up and down a few times in silence, but his eyes glittered feverishly and his lips quivered as he began to speak again.

"But what is war? What is needed for success in warfare? What are the habits of the military? The aim of war is murder; the methods of war are spying, treachery, and their encouragement, the ruin of a country's inhabitants, robbing them or stealing to provision the army, and fraud and falsehood termed military craft. The habits of the military class are the absence of freedom, that is, discipline, idleness, ignorance, cruelty, debauchery, and drunkenness. And in spite of all this it is the highest class, respected by everyone. . . .

"How does God above look at them and hear them?" exclaimed Prince Andrew in a shrill, piercing voice. "Ah, my friend, it has of late become hard for me to live. I see that I have begun to understand too much. And it doesn't do for

man to taste of the tree of knowledge of good and evil. . . .
Ah, well, it's not for long!" he added.

"However, you're sleepy, and it's time for me to sleep. Go
back to Górki!" said Prince Andrew suddenly.

He came quickly up to Pierre and embraced and kissed
him.

"Good-by, be off!" he shouted. "Whether we meet again
or not . . ." and turning away hurriedly he entered the shed.

He closed his eyes. One picture succeeded another in his
imagination. On one of them he dwelt long and joyfully. He
vividly recalled an evening in Petersburg. Natásha with
animated and excited face was telling him how she had gone
to look for mushrooms the previous summer and had lost her
way in the big forest. She incoherently described the depths
of the forest, her feelings, and a talk with a beekeeper she
met, and constantly interrupted her story to say: "No, I can't!
I'm not telling it right; no, you don't understand."

"I not only understood her, but it was just that inner,
spiritual force, that sincerity, that frankness of soul—that very
soul of hers which seemed to be fettered by her body—it
was that soul I loved in her . . . loved so strongly and happily . . ." and suddenly he remembered how his love had
ended.

Prince Andrew jumped up as if someone had burned him,
and again began pacing up and down in front of the shed.

26

On August 25, the eve of the battle of Boro-
dinó, M. de Beausset, prefect of the French Emperor's palace,
arrived at Napoleon's quarters at Valúevo with Colonel
Fabvier, the former from Paris and the latter from Madrid.

Donning his court uniform, M. de Beausset ordered a
box he had brought for the Emperor to be carried before him
and entered the first compartment of Napoleon's tent, where
he began opening the box while conversing with Napoleon's
aides-de-camp who surrounded him.

The Emperor Napoleon had not yet left his bedroom and
was finishing his toilet. Slightly snorting and grunting, he
presented now his back and now his plump hairy chest to

the brush with which his valet was rubbing him down. Another valet, with his finger over the mouth of a bottle, was sprinkling Eau de Cologne on the Emperor's pampered body with an expression which seemed to say that he alone knew where and how much Eau de Cologne should be sprinkled. Napoleon's short hair was wet and matted on the forehead, but his face, though puffy and yellow, expressed physical satisfaction. "Go on, harder, go on!" he muttered to the valet who was rubbing him, slightly twitching and grunting.

"Let Monsieur de Beausset enter, and Fabvier too," he said, nodding to the aide-de-camp.

Two valets rapidly dressed His Majesty, and wearing the blue uniform of the Guards he went with firm quick steps to the reception room.

De Beausset's hands meanwhile were busily engaged arranging the present he had brought from the Empress, on two chairs directly in front of the entrance.

De Beausset bowed low, with that courtly French bow which only the old retainers of the Bourbons knew how to make, and approached him, presenting an envelope.

Napoleon turned to him gaily and pulled his ear.

"I am very sorry to have made you travel so far," said he.

"Sire, I expected nothing less than to find you at the gates of Moscow," replied de Beausset.

"Ha, what's this?" asked Napoleon, noticing that all the courtiers were looking at something concealed under a cloth.

With courtly adroitness de Beausset half turned and without turning his back to the Emperor retired two steps, twitching off the cloth at the same time, and said:

"A present to Your Majesty from the Empress."

It was a portrait, painted in bright colors by Gérard, of the son borne to Napoleon by the daughter of the Emperor of Austria, the boy whom for some reason everyone called "The King of Rome."

A very pretty curly-headed boy with a look of the Christ in the Sistine Madonna was depicted playing at stick and ball. The ball represented the terrestrial globe and the stick in his other hand a scepter.

"The King of Rome!" he said, pointing to the portrait with a graceful gesture. "Admirable!"

He felt that what he now said and did would be historical. His eyes grew dim, he moved forward, glanced round at a chair (which seemed to place itself under him), and sat down on it before the portrait. At a single gesture from him everyone went out on tiptoe, leaving the great man to himself and his emotion.

Having sat still for a while he recalled de Beausset and the officer on duty. He ordered the portrait to be carried outside his tent, that the Old Guard, stationed round it, might not be deprived of the pleasure of seeing the King of Rome, the son and heir of their adored monarch.

And while he was doing M. de Beausset the honor of breakfasting with him, they heard, as Napoleon had anticipated, the rapturous cries of the officers and men of the Old Guard who had run up to see the portrait.

"*Vive l'Empereur! Vive le roi de Rome! Vive l'Empereur!*" came those ecstatic cries.

After breakfast Napoleon in de Beausset's presence dictated his order of the day to the army.

When Napoleon came out of the tent the shouting of the Guards before his son's portrait grew still louder. Napoleon frowned.

"Take him away!" he said, pointing with a gracefully majestic gesture to the portrait. "It is too soon for him to see a field of battle."

27

Tolstoy summarizes Napoleon's dispositions for the battle of Borodinó and points out why they could not be, and were not, executed.

28

Many historians say that the French did not win the battle of Borodinó because Napoleon had a cold, and that if he had not had a cold the orders he gave before and during the battle would have been still more full of genius and Russia would have been lost and the face of the world have been changed.

If it had depended on Napoleon's will to fight or not to fight the battle of Borodinó, and if this or that other arrangement depended on his will, then evidently a cold affecting the manifestation of his will might have saved Russia, and consequently the valet who omitted to bring Napoleon his waterproof boots on the twenty-fourth would have been the savior of Russia. To the question of what causes historic events another answer presents itself, namely, that the course of human events is predetermined from on high—depends on the coincidence of the wills of all who take part in the events, and that a Napoleon's influence on the course of these events is purely external and fictitious.

And it was not Napoleon who directed the course of the battle, for none of his orders was executed and during the battle he did not know what was going on before him. So the way in which these people killed one another was not decided by Napoleon's will but occurred independently of him, in accord with the will of hundreds of thousands of people who took part in the common action. It *only seemed* to Napoleon that it all took place by his will. And so the question whether he had or had not a cold has no more historic interest than the cold of the least of the transport soldiers.

Moreover, the assertion made by various writers that his cold was the cause of his dispositions not being as well planned as on former occasions, and of his orders during the battle not being as good as previously, is quite baseless, which again shows that Napoleon's cold on the twenty-sixth of August was unimportant.

Napoleon at the battle of Borodinó fulfilled his office as representative of authority as well as, and even better than, at other battles. He did nothing harmful to the progress of the battle; he inclined to the most reasonable opinions, he made no confusion, did not contradict himself, did not get frightened or run away from the field of battle, but with his great tact and military experience carried out his role of appearing to command, calmly and with dignity.

29

Napoleon passes a sleepless night before the battle of Borodinó. He talks with Beausset and his adjutant Rapp.

30

On returning to Górki after having seen Prince Andrew, Pierre ordered his groom to get the horses ready and to call him early in the morning, and then immediately fell asleep behind a partition in a corner Borís had given up to him.

Before he was thoroughly awake next morning everybody had already left the hut. The panes were rattling in the little windows and his groom was shaking him.

"What? Has it begun? Is it time?" Pierre asked, waking up.

"Hear the firing," said the groom, a discharged soldier. "All the gentlemen have gone out, and his Serene Highness himself rode past long ago."

Pierre dressed hastily and ran out to the porch. Outside all was bright, fresh, dewy, and cheerful. The roar of guns sounded more distinct outside. An adjutant accompanied by a Cossack passed by at a sharp trot.

"It's time, Count; it's time!" cried the adjutant.

Telling the groom to follow him with the horses, Pierre went down the street to the knoll from which he had looked at the field of battle the day before. A crowd of military men was assembled there, members of the staff could be heard conversing in French, and Kutúzov's gray head in a white cap with a red band was visible, his gray nape sunk between his shoulders. He was looking through a field glass down the highroad before him.

Mounting the steps to the knoll Pierre looked at the scene before him, spellbound by its beauty. There were troops to be seen everywhere, in front and to the right and left. All this was vivid, majestic, and unexpected; but what impressed Pierre most of all was the view of the battlefield itself, of

Borodinó and the hollows on both sides of the Kolochá. The smoke of the guns mingled with mist, and over the whole expanse and through that mist the rays of the morning sun were reflected, flashing back like lightning from the water, from the dew, and from the bayonets of the troops crowded together by the riverbanks and in Borodinó.

Pierre wished to be there with that smoke, those shining bayonets, that movement, and those sounds. He turned to look at Kutúzov and his suite, to compare his impressions with those of others. They were all looking at the field of battle as he was, and, as it seemed to him, with the same feelings. All their faces were now shining with that latent warmth of feeling Pierre had noticed the day before and had fully understood after his talk with Prince Andrew.

"To the crossing!" said the general coldly and sternly in reply to one of the staff who asked where he was going.

"I'll go there too, I too!" thought Pierre, and followed the general.

31

Having descended the hill the general after whom Pierre was galloping turned sharply to the left, and Pierre, losing sight of him, galloped in among some ranks of infantry marching ahead of him. He tried to pass either in front of them or to the right or left, but there were soldiers everywhere, all with the same preoccupied expression and busy with some unseen but evidently important task. They all gazed with the same dissatisfied and inquiring expression at this stout man in a white hat, who for some unknown reason threatened to trample them under his horse's hoofs.

"Why's that fellow in front of the line?" shouted somebody at him.

"To the left! . . . Keep to the right!" the men shouted to him.

Pierre went to the right, and unexpectedly encountered one of Raévski's adjutants whom he knew.

"Come along with me to our knoll. We can get a view

from there and in our battery it is still bearable," said the adjutant. "Will you come?"

"Yes, I'll come with you," replied Pierre, looking round for his groom.

Pierre did not find his groom and rode along the hollow with the adjutant to Raévski's Redoubt. His horse lagged behind the adjutant's and jolted him at every step.

"Why . . . she's wounded!" said the adjutant. "In the off foreleg above the knee. A bullet, no doubt. I congratulate you, Count, on your baptism of fire!"

The knoll to which Pierre ascended was that famous one afterwards known to the Russians as the Knoll Battery or Raévski's Redoubt, around which tens of thousands fell, and which the French regarded as the key to the whole position.

This redoubt consisted of a knoll, on three sides of which trenches had been dug. Within the entrenchment stood ten guns that were being fired through openings in the earthwork.

In line with the knoll on both sides stood other guns which also fired incessantly. A little behind the guns stood infantry. When ascending that knoll Pierre had no notion that this spot, on which small trenches had been dug and from which a few guns were firing, was the most important point of the battle.

On the contrary, just because he happened to be there he thought it one of the least significant parts of the field.

The guns of that battery were being fired continually one after another with a deafening roar, enveloping the whole neighborhood in powder smoke.

The soldiers shook their heads disapprovingly as they looked at Pierre. But when they had convinced themselves that this man in the white hat was doing no harm, but either sat quietly on the slope of the trench with a shy smile or, politely making way for the soldiers, paced up and down the battery under fire as calmly as if he were on a boulevard, their feeling of hostile distrust gradually began to change into a kindly and bantering sympathy, such as soldiers feel for their dogs, cocks, goats, and in general for the animals that live with the regiment. The men soon accepted Pierre into their family, adopted him, gave him a nickname ("our gentleman"), and made kindly fun of him among themselves.

A shell tore up the earth two paces from Pierre and he looked around with a smile as he brushed from his clothes some earth it had thrown up.

"And how's it you're not afraid, sir, really now?" a red-faced, broad-shouldered soldier asked Pierre, with a grin that disclosed a set of sound, white teeth.

"Are you afraid, then?" said Pierre.

"What else do you expect?" answered the soldier. "She has no mercy, you know! When she comes spluttering down, out go your innards. One can't help being afraid," he said laughing.

By ten o'clock some twenty men had already been carried away from the battery; two guns were smashed and cannon balls fell more and more frequently on the battery and spent bullets buzzed and whistled around. But the men in the battery seemed not to notice this, and merry voices and jokes were heard on all sides.

"A live one!" shouted a man as a whistling shell approached.

"Not this way! To the infantry!" added another with loud laughter, seeing the shell fly past and fall into the ranks of the supports.

Pierre noticed that after every ball that hit the redoubt, and after every loss, the liveliness increased more and more.

As the flames of the fire hidden within come more and more vividly and rapidly from an approaching thundercloud, so, as if in opposition to what was taking place, the lightning of hidden fire growing more and more intense glowed in the faces of these men.

Pierre did not look out at the battlefield and was not concerned to know what was happening there; he was entirely absorbed in watching this fire which burned ever more brightly and which he felt was flaming up in the same way in his own soul.

Projectiles began to fall still more frequently in the battery. Several men were lying about who had not been removed. Around the cannon the men moved still more briskly and busily. No one any longer took notice of Pierre. Once or twice he was shouted at for being in the way. The senior officer moved with big, rapid strides from one gun to another with a frowning face.

The sergeant ran up to the officer and in a frightened whisper informed him (as a butler at dinner informs his master that there is no more of some wine asked for) that there were no more charges.

"The scoundrels! What are they doing?" shouted the officer, turning to Pierre.

The officer's face was red and perspiring and his eyes glittered under his frowning brow.

"Run to the reserves and bring up the ammunition boxes!" he yelled, angrily avoiding Pierre with his eyes and speaking to his men.

"I'll go," said Pierre.

The man who had been ordered to go for ammunition stumbled against Pierre.

"Eh, sir, this is no place for you," said he, and ran down the slope.

Pierre ran down the slope. "Where am I going?" he suddenly asked himself when he was already near the green ammunition wagons. He halted irresolutely, not knowing whether to return or go on. Suddenly a terrible concussion threw him backwards to the ground. At the same instant he was dazzled by a great flash of flame, and immediately a deafening roar, crackling, and whistling made his ears tingle.

When he came to himself he was sitting on the ground leaning on his hands; the ammunition wagons he had been approaching no longer existed, only charred green boards and rags littered the scorched grass, and a horse, dangling fragments of its shaft behind it, galloped past, while another horse lay, like Pierre, on the ground, uttering prolonged and piercing cries.

32

Beside himself with terror Pierre jumped up and ran back to the battery, as to the only refuge from the horrors that surrounded him.

But he had not time to realize that the colonel had been killed, that the soldier shouting "Brothers!" was a prisoner, and that another man had been bayoneted in the back before his eyes, for hardly had he run into the redoubt before a thin, sallow-faced, perspiring man in a blue uniform rushed on him sword in hand, shouting something. Instinctively guarding against the shock—for they had been running together at full speed before they saw one another—Pierre put out his hands and seized the man (a French officer) by the shoulder with one hand and by the throat with the other. The officer, dropping his sword, seized Pierre by his collar.

For some seconds they gazed with frightened eyes at one another's unfamiliar faces and both were perplexed at what they had done and what they were to do next. The Frenchman was about to say something, when just above their heads, terrible and low, a cannon ball whistled, and it seemed to Pierre that the French officer's head had been torn off, so swiftly had he ducked it.

Pierre too bent his head and let his hands fall. Without further thought as to who had taken whom prisoner, the Frenchman ran back to the battery and Pierre ran down the slope stumbling over the dead and wounded who, it seemed to him, caught at his feet. But before he reached the foot of the knoll he was met by a dense crowd of Russian soldiers who, stumbling, tripping up, and shouting, ran merrily and wildly toward the battery.

The French who had occupied the battery fled, and our troops shouting "Hurrah!" pursued them so far beyond the battery that it was difficult to call them back.

Pierre again went up onto the knoll where he had spent over an hour, and of that family circle which had received him as a member he did not find a single one.

Pierre ran down the slope once more.

"Now they will stop it, now they will be horrified at what they have done!" he thought, aimlessly going toward a crowd of stretcher-bearers moving from the battlefield.

33

Tolstoy explains that it was impossible for Napoleon, from where he was standing on the Shevárdino Redoubt, to see what was happening on the field of battle at Borodinó, a mile away, especially as the smoke mingling with the mist hid the whole locality, and that therefore

things took their own course apart from the orders is-
sued.

34

Napoleon refuses frequent demands for reinforce-
ments. Hs is depressed over the failure of his troops to
achieve the expected quick victory.

35

On the rug-covered bench were Pierre had
seen him in the morning sat Kutúzov, his gray head hanging, his heavy body relaxed. He gave no orders, but only
assented to or dissented from what others suggested.

By long years of military experience he knew, and with the
wisdom of age understood, that it is impossible for one man
to direct hundreds of thousands of others struggling with
death, and he knew that the result of a battle is decided not
by the orders of a commander in chief, nor the place where
the troops are stationed, nor by the number of cannon or of
slaughtered men, but by that intangible force called the spirit
of the army, and he watched this force and guided it in as far
as that was in his power.

Kutúzov was in Górki, near the center of the Russian position. The attack directed by Napoleon against our left flank
had been several times repulsed. In the center the French
had not got beyond Borodinó, and on their left flank Uvárov's
cavalry had put the French to flight.

Toward three o'clock the French attacks ceased. On the
faces of all who came from the field of battle, and of those
who stood around him, Kutúzov noticed an expression of extreme tension. He was satisfied with the day's success—a success exceeding his expectations, but the old man's strength
was failing him. Several times his head dropped low as if it
were falling and he dozed off. Dinner was brought him.

Adjutant General Wolzogen had come from Barclay de
Tolly to report on the progress of affairs on the left flank.

"All the points of our position are in the enemy's hands and we cannot dislodge them for lack of troops, the men are running away and it is impossible to stop them," he reported.

"How . . . how dare you! . . ." Kutúzov shouted, choking and making a threatening gesture with his trembling arms: "How dare you, sir, say that to *me*? You know nothing about it. Tell General Barclay from me that his information is incorrect and that the real course of the battle is better known to me, the commander in chief, than to him."

Wolzogen was about to make a rejoinder, but Kutúzov interrupted him.

"The enemy has been repulsed on the left and defeated on the right flank. If you have seen amiss, sir, do not allow yourself to say what you don't know! Be so good as to ride to General Barclay and inform him of my firm intention to attack the enemy tomorrow," said Kutúzov sternly.

All were silent, and the only sound audible was the heavy breathing of the panting old general.

Wolzogen, shrugging his shoulders and curling his lips, stepped silently aside, marveling at "the old gentleman's" conceited stupidity.

"Ah, here he is, my hero!" said Kutúzov to a portly, handsome, dark-haired general who was just ascending the knoll.

This was Raévski, who had spent the whole day at the most important part of the field of Borodinó.

Raévski reported that the troops were firmly holding their ground and that the French no longer ventured to attack.

Kutúzov called to his adjutant. "Sit down and write out the order of the day for tomorrow. And you," he continued, addressing another, "ride along the line and announce that tomorrow we attack."

It was far from being the same words or the same order that reached the farthest links of that chain. The tales passing from mouth to mouth at different ends of the army did not even resemble what Kutúzov had said, but the sense of his words spread everywhere because what he said was not the outcome of cunning calculations, but of a feeling that lay in the commander in chief's soul as in that of every Russian.

And on learning that tomorrow they were to attack the enemy, and hearing from the highest quarters a confirmation of what they wanted to believe, the exhausted, wavering men felt comforted and inspired.

36

Prince Andrew's regiment was among the reserves which till after one o'clock were stationed inactive behind Semënovsk, under heavy artillery fire. Toward two o'clock the regiment, having already lost more than two hundred men, was moved forward into a trampled oatfield in the gap between Semënovsk and the Knoll Battery, where thousands of men perished that day and on which an intense, concentrated fire from several hundred enemy guns was directed between one and two o'clock.

Without moving from that spot or firing a single shot the regiment here lost another third of its men. From in front and especially from the right, in the unlifting smoke the guns boomed, and out of the mysterious domain of smoke that overlay the whole space in front, quick hissing cannon balls and slow whistling shells flew unceasingly.

Prince Andrew, pale and gloomy like everyone in the regiment, paced up and down from the border of one patch to another, at the edge of the meadow beside an oatfield, with head bowed and arms behind his back. There was nothing for him to do and no orders to be given. Everything went on of itself. The killed were dragged from the front, the wounded carried away, and the ranks closed up. At first Prince Andrew, considering it his duty to rouse the courage of the men and to set them an example, walked about among the ranks, but he soon became convinced that this was unnecessary and that there was nothing he could teach them. All the powers of his soul, as of every soldier there, were unconsciously bent on avoiding the contemplation of the horrors of their situation. A whizz and a thud! Five paces from him, a cannon ball tore up the dry earth and disappeared. A chill ran down his back. Again he glanced at the ranks. Probably many had been hit—a large crowd had gathered near the second battalion.

"Adjutant!" he shouted. "Order them not to crowd together."

The adjutant, having obeyed this instruction, approached Prince Andrew. From the other side a battalion commander rode up.

"Look out!" came a frightened cry from a soldier and, like a bird whirring in rapid flight and alighting on the ground, a shell dropped with little noise within two steps of Prince Andrew and close to the battalion commander's horse. The horse first, regardless of whether it was right or wrong to show fear, snorted, reared almost throwing the major, and galloped aside. The horse's terror infected the men.

"Lie down!" cried the adjutant, throwing himself flat on the ground.

Prince Andrew hesitated. The smoking shell spun like a top between him and the prostrate adjutant, near a wormwood plant between the field and the meadow.

"Can this be death?" thought Prince Andrew, looking with a quite new, envious glance at the grass, the wormwood, and the streamlet of smoke that curled up from the rotating black ball. "I cannot, I do not wish to die. I love life—I love this grass, this earth, this air. . . ." He thought this, and at the same time remembered that people were looking at him.

"It's shameful, sir!" he said to the adjutant. "What . . ."

He did not finish speaking. At one and the same moment came the sound of an explosion, a whistle of splinters as from a breaking window frame, a suffocating smell of powder, and Prince Andrew started to one side, raising his arm, and fell on his chest. Several officers ran up to him. From the right side of his abdomen, blood was welling out making a large stain on the grass.

The militiamen with stretchers who were called up stood behind the officers. Prince Andrew lay on his chest with his face in the grass, breathing heavily and noisily.

The militiamen carried Prince Andrew to the dressing station by the wood, where wagons were stationed. The dressing station consisted of three tents with flaps turned back, pitched at the edge of a birch wood. Around the tents, over more than five acres, bloodstained men in various garbs stood, sat, or lay. From the tents came now loud angry cries and now plaintive groans. The wounded men awaiting their turn outside the tents groaned, sighed, wept, screamed, swore, or asked for vodka. Some were delirious. Prince Andrew's bearers, stepping over the wounded who had not yet been bandaged, took him, as a regimental commander, close up to one of the tents and there stopped, awaiting instructions. Prince Andrew opened his eyes and for a long time could not make out what was going on around him. He remembered the meadow, the wormwood, the field, the whirling black ball, and his sudden rush of passionate love of life.

"But isn't it all the same now?" thought he. "And what will be there, and what has there been here? Why was I so reluctant to part with life? There was something in this life I did not and do not understand."

37

One of the doctors came out of the tent in a bloodstained apron, holding a cigar between the thumb and little finger of one of his small bloodstained hands, so as not to smear it.

"All right, immediately," he replied to a dresser who pointed Prince Andrew out to him, and he told them to carry him into the tent.

Prince Andrew was carried in and laid on a table that had only just been cleared and which a dresser was washing down. The pitiful groans from all sides and the torturing pain in his thigh, stomach, and back distracted him. All he saw about him merged into a general impression of naked, bleeding human bodies.

There were three operating tables in the tent. Two were occupied, and on the third they placed Prince Andrew. For a little while he was left alone and involuntarily witnessed what was taking place on the other two tables. On the nearest one sat a Tartar, probably a Cossack, judging by the uniform thrown down beside him.

On the other table, round which many people were crowding, a tall well-fed man lay on his back with his head thrown back. His curly hair, its color, and the shape of his head seemed strangely familiar to Prince Andrew. Several dressers were pressing on his chest to hold him down. One large, white, plump leg twitched rapidly all the time with a feverish tremor. The man was sobbing and choking convulsively. Two doctors—one of whom was pale and trembling—were silently doing something to this man's other, gory leg. When he had finished with the Tartar, whom they covered with an overcoat, the spectacled doctor came up to Prince Andrew, wiping his hands.

He glanced at Prince Andrew's face and quickly turned away.

"Undress him! What are you waiting for?" he cried angrily to the dressers.

His very first, remotest recollections of childhood came back to Prince Andrew's mind when the dresser with sleeves rolled up began hastily to undo the buttons of his clothes and undressed him. The doctor bent down over the wound, felt it, and sighed deeply. Then he made a sign to someone, and the torturing pain in his abdomen caused Prince Andrew to lose consciousness. When he came to himself the splintered portions of his thighbone had been extracted, the torn flesh cut away, and the wound bandaged. Water was being sprinkled on his face. As soon as Prince Andrew opened his eyes, the doctor bent over, kissed him silently on the lips, and hurried away.

After the sufferings he had been enduring, Prince Andrew enjoyed a blissful feeling such as he had not experienced for a long time. All the best and happiest moments of his life—especially his earliest childhood, when he used to be undressed and put to bed, and when leaning over him his nurse sang him to sleep and he, burying his head in the pillow, felt happy in the mere consciousness of life—returned to his memory, not merely as something past but as something present.

The doctors were busily engaged with the wounded man the shape of whose head seemed familiar to Prince Andrew: they were lifting him up and trying to quiet him.

"Show it to me. . . . Oh, ooh . . . Oh! Oh, ooh!" his frightened moans could be heard, subdued by suffering and broken by sobs.

Hearing those moans Prince Andrew wanted to weep. Whether because he was dying without glory, or because he was sorry to part with life, or because of those memories of a childhood that could not return, or because he was suffering and others were suffering and that man near him was groaning so piteously—he felt like weeping childlike, kindly, and almost happy tears.

The wounded man was shown his amputated leg stained with clotted blood and with the boot still on.

"Oh! Oh, ooh!" he sobbed, like a woman.

The doctor who had been standing beside him, preventing Prince Andrew from seeing his face, moved away.

"My God! What is this? Why is he here?" said Prince Andrew to himself.

In the miserable, sobbing, enfeebled man whose leg had just been amputated, he recognized Anatole Kurágin. Men were supporting him in their arms and offering him a glass of water, but his trembling, swollen lips could not grasp its rim. Anatole was sobbing painfully. "Yes, it is he! Yes, that man is somehow closely and painfully connected with me," thought Prince Andrew, not yet clearly grasping what he saw before him. "What is the connection of that man with my childhood and my life?" he asked himself without finding an answer. And suddenly a new unexpected memory from that realm of pure and loving childhood presented itself to him. He remembered Natásha as he had seen her for the first time at the ball in 1810, with her slender neck and arms and with a frightened happy face ready for rapture, and love and tenderness for her, stronger and more vivid than ever, awoke in his soul. He now remembered the connection that existed between himself and this man who was dimly gazing at him through tears that filled his swollen eyes. He remembered everything, and ecstatic pity and love for that man overflowed his happy heart.

Prince Andrew could no longer restrain himself and wept tender loving tears for his fellow men, for himself, and for his own and their errors.

"Compassion, love of our brothers, for those who love us and for those who hate us, love of our enemies; yes, that love which God preached on earth and which Princess Mary taught me and I did not understand—that is what made me sorry to part with life, that is what remained for me had I lived. But now it is too late. I know it!"

38

Napoleon's mind and conscience are troubled over the results of the battle of Borodinó. Later he takes comfort

in the fact that more Russians than French were killed
and that the war was for a great cause—the end of un-
certainties and the beginning of security.

39

Over the whole field, previously so gaily beautiful with the glitter of bayonets and cloudlets of smoke in the morning sun, there now spread a mist of damp and smoke and a strange acid smell of saltpeter and blood. Clouds gathered and drops of rain began to fall on the dead and wounded, on the frightened, exhausted, and hesitating men, as if to say: "Enough, men! Enough! Cease . . . bethink yourselves! What are you doing?"

Anyone looking at the disorganized rear of the Russian army would have said that, if only the French made one more slight effort, it would disappear; and anyone looking at the rear of the French army would have said that the Russians need only make one more slight effort and the French would be destroyed. But neither the French nor the Russians made that effort, and the flame of battle burned slowly out.

The Russians did not make that effort because they were not attacking the French. At the beginning of the battle they stood blocking the way to Moscow and they still did so at the end of the battle as at the beginning.

The French, with the memory of all their former victories during fifteen years, with the assurance of Napoleon's invincibility, with the consciousness that they had captured part of the battlefield and had lost only a quarter of their men and still had their Guards intact, twenty thousand strong, might easily have made that effort.

It was not Napoleon alone who had experienced that nightmare feeling of the mighty arm being stricken powerless, but all the generals and soldiers of his army whether they had taken part in the battle or not, after all their experience of previous battles—when after one tenth of such efforts the enemy had fled—experienced a similar feeling of terror before an enemy who, after losing HALF his men, stood as threateningly at the end as at the beginning of the battle. The moral force of the attacking French army was exhausted. Not that sort of victory which is defined by the capture of pieces of material fastened to sticks, called standards, and of the ground on which the troops had stood and were standing, but a moral victory that convinces the enemy of the moral superiority of his opponent and of his own impotence was gained by the Russians at Borodinó. By the impetus gained, the French army was still able to roll forward to Moscow, but there, without further effort on the part of the Russians, it had to perish, bleeding from the mortal wound it had received at Borodinó. The direct consequence of the battle of Borodinó was Napoleon's senseless flight from Moscow, his retreat along the old Smolénsk road, the destruction of the invading army of five hundred thousand men, and the downfall of Napoleonic France, on which at Borodinó for the first time the hand of an opponent of stronger spirit had been laid.

1812

⊫━━▥▥━━━━▥▥━━━━▥▥━━━━▥▥━━━━▥▥━━━━▥

BOOK ELEVEN

1

Tolstoy repudiates the conventional notion of historians that the actions of some one man—a king or a commander—are equivalent to the sum of many individual wills. On the contrary, Tolstoy declares, the sum of individual wills is never expressed by the activity of a single historic personage.

2

The French army pushed on to Moscow. Behind it were seven hundred miles of hunger-stricken, hostile country; ahead were a few dozen miles separating it from its goal.

At Borodinó a collision took place. Neither army was broken up, but the Russian army retreated immediately after the collision.

The Russians retreated eighty miles—to beyond Moscow—and the French reached Moscow and there came to a standstill. For five weeks after that there was not a single battle. The French did not move. As a bleeding, mortally wounded animal licks its wounds, they remained inert in Moscow for five weeks, and then suddenly, with no fresh reason, fled back.

On the evening of the twenty-sixth of August, Kutúzov and the whole Russian army were convinced that the battle of Borodinó was a victory. Kutúzov reported so to the Emperor. He gave orders to prepare for a fresh conflict to finish the enemy and did this not to deceive anyone, but because he knew that the enemy was beaten, as everyone who had taken part in the battle knew it.

3

The Council of War began to assemble at two in the afternoon in the better and roomier part of Andrew Savostyánov's hut.

Round the peasant's deal table, on which lay maps, plans, pencils, and papers, so many people gathered that the orderlies brought in another bench and put it beside the table.

Bennigsen opened the council with the question: "Are we to abandon Russia's ancient and sacred capital without a struggle, or are we to defend it?" A prolonged and general silence followed. There was a frown on every face and only Kutúzov's angry grunts and occasional cough broke the silence. All eyes were gazing at him.

"Russia's ancient and sacred capital!" Kutúzov suddenly said, repeating Bennigsen's words in an angry voice and thereby drawing attention to the false note in them. "Allow me to tell you, your excellency, that that question has no meaning for a Russian. Such a question cannot be put; it is senseless! The question I have asked these gentlemen to meet to discuss is a military one. The question is that of saving Russia. Is it better to give up Moscow without a battle, or by accepting battle to risk losing the army as well as Moscow? That is the question on which I want your opinion," and he sank back in his chair.

The discussion began. Bennigsen did not yet consider his game lost. Admitting the view of Barclay and others that a defensive battle at Filí was impossible, but imbued with Russian patriotism and the love of Moscow, he proposed to move troops from the right to the left flank during the night and attack the French right flank the following day. Opinions were divided, and arguments were advanced for and against that project.

"Gentlemen," said Kutúzov, "I cannot approve of the count's plan. Moving troops in close proximity to an enemy is always dangerous, and military history supports that view. For instance . . ." Kutúzov seemed to reflect, searching for an example, then with a clear, naïve look at Bennigsen he added: "Oh yes; take the battle of Friedland, which I think the count well remembers, and which was . . . not fully successful, only because our troops were rearranged too near the enemy. . . ."

There followed a momentary pause, which seemed very long to them all.

The discussion recommenced, but pauses frequently occurred and they all felt that there was no more to be said.

During one of these pauses Kutúzov heaved a deep sigh as if preparing to speak. They all looked at him.

"Well, gentlemen, I see that it is I who will have to pay for the broken crockery," said he, and rising slowly he moved to the table. "Gentlemen, I have heard your views. Some of you will not agree with me. But I," he paused, "by the authority entrusted to me by my Sovereign and country, order a retreat."

After that the generals began to disperse with the solemnity and circumspect silence of people who are leaving after a funeral.

When he had dismissed the generals Kutúzov sat a long time with his elbows on the table, thinking always of the same terrible question: "When, when did the abandonment of Moscow become inevitable? When was that done which settled the matter? And who was to blame for it?"

"I did not expect this," said he to his adjutant Schneider when the latter came in late that night. "I did not expect this! I did not think this would happen."

"You should take some rest, your Serene Highness," replied Schneider.

"But no! They shall eat horseflesh yet, like the Turks!" exclaimed Kutúzov without replying, striking the table with his podgy fist. "They shall too, if only . . ."

4

At that very time, in circumstances even more important than retreating without a battle, namely the evacuation and burning of Moscow, Rostopchín, who is usually represented as being the instigator of that event, acted in an altogether different manner from Kutúzov.

After the battle of Borodinó the abandonment and burning of Moscow was as inevitable as the retreat of the army beyond Moscow without fighting.

Every Russian might have predicted it, not by reasoning but by the feeling implanted in each of us and in our fathers.

The same thing that took place in Moscow had happened in all the towns and villages on Russian soil beginning with Smolénsk, without the participation of Count Rostopchín and his broadsheets. The people awaited the enemy unconcernedly, did not riot or become excited or tear anyone to pieces, but faced its fate, feeling within it the strength to find what it should do at that most difficult moment. And as soon as the enemy drew near the wealthy classes went away abandoning their property, while the poorer remained and burned and destroyed what was left.

The consciousness that this would be so and would always be so was and is present in the heart of every Russian. And a consciousness of this, and a foreboding that Moscow would be taken, was present in Russian Moscow society in 1812. Those who had quitted Moscow already in July and at the beginning of August showed that they expected this. Those who went away, taking what they could and abandoning their houses and half their belongings, did so from the latent patriotism which expresses itself not by phrases or by giving one's children to save the fatherland and similar unnatural exploits, but unobtrusively, simply, organically, and therefore in the way that always produces the most powerful results.

5

An old grandee, occupying one of the highest posts in the Empire, and a young foreign prince vie with each other for Hélène's favors. She decides to marry one of them and to this end allows herself to be converted to Catholicism in order to obtain a dispensation from the Pope annulling her marriage. In August she sends a letter to Pierre asking him to carry out the formalities necessary for a divorce.

6

Toward the end of the battle of Borodinó, Pierre, having run down from Raévski's battery a second time, made his way through a gully to Knyazkóvo with a crowd of soldiers, reached the dressing station, and seeing blood and hearing cries and groans hurried on, still entangled in the crowds of soldiers.

The one thing he now desired with his whole soul was to get away quickly from the terrible sensations amid which he had lived that day and return to ordinary conditions of life and sleep quietly in a room in his own bed. He felt that only in the ordinary conditions of life would he be able to understand himself and all he had seen and felt. But such ordinary conditions of life were nowhere to be found.

Having gone a couple of miles along the Mozháysk road, Pierre sat down by the roadside.

Dusk had fallen, and the roar of guns died away. Pierre lay leaning on his elbow for a long time, gazing at the shadows that moved past him in the darkness. He was continually imagining that a cannon ball was flying toward him with a terrific whizz, and then he shuddered and sat up. He had no idea how long he had been there. In the middle of the night three soldiers, having brought some firewood, settled down near him and began lighting a fire.

"Where have you to go to? Tell us!" said one of them.

"To Mozháysk."

"And what's your name?"

"Peter Kirílych."

"Well then, Peter Kirílych, come along with us, we'll take you there."

Pierre went on with the soldiers, quite forgetting that his inn was at the bottom of the hill and that he had already passed it. He would not soon have remembered this, such was his state of forgetfulness, had he not halfway up the hill stumbled upon his groom, who had been to look for him in the town and was returning to the inn. The groom recognized Pierre in the darkness by his white hat.

"Your excellency!" he said. "Why, we were beginning to

despair! How is it you are on foot? And where are you going, please?"

"Oh, yes!" said Pierre.

The soldiers stopped.

"So you've found your folk?" said one of them. "Well, good-by, Peter Kirílych—isn't it?"

"Good-by!" he said and turned with his groom toward the inn.

There was not a room to be had at the inn, they were all occupied. Pierre went out into the yard and, covering himself up head and all, lay down in his carriage.

Pierre sleeps and in his dreams he hears a voice that declares: "Man can be master of nothing while he fears death, but he who does not fear it possesses all."

The groom, the coachman, and the innkeeper told Pierre that an officer had come with news that the French were already near Mozháysk and that our men were leaving it.

Pierre got up and, having told them to harness and overtake him, went on foot through the town.

The troops were moving on, leaving about ten thousand wounded behind them. There were wounded in the yards, at the windows of the houses, and the streets were crowded with them. In the streets, around carts that were to take some of the wounded away, shouts, curses, and blows could be heard. Pierre offered the use of his carriage, which had overtaken him, to a wounded general he knew, and drove with him to Moscow. On the way Pierre was told of the death of his brother-in-law Anatole and of that of Prince Andrew.

7

On the thirtieth of August Pierre reached Moscow. Close to the gates of the city he was met by Count Rostopchín's adjutant.

"We have been looking for you everywhere," said the adjutant. "The count wants to see you particularly. He asks you to come to him at once on a very important matter."

Without going home Pierre took a cab and drove to see the Moscow commander in chief.

Though the news was being concealed from the inhabitants, the officials—the heads of the various government departments—knew that Moscow would soon be in the enemy's hands, just as Count Rostopchín himself knew it, and to escape personal responsibility they had all come to the governor to ask how they were to deal with their various departments.

While waiting in the reception room Pierre with weary eyes watched the various officials, old and young, military and civilian, who were there. They all seemed dissatisfied and uneasy. Pierre went up to a group of men, one of whom he knew. After greeting Pierre they continued their conversation.

"And who is that?" Pierre asked, indicating a short old man in a clean blue peasant overcoat, with a big snow-white beard and eyebrows and a ruddy face.

"He? That's a tradesman, that is to say, he's the restaurant keeper, Vereshchágin. Perhaps you have heard of that affair with the proclamation."

"Oh, so that is Vereshchágin!" said Pierre, looking at the firm, calm face of the old man and seeking any indication of his being a traitor.

"That's not he himself, that's the father of the fellow who wrote the proclamation," said the adjutant. "The young man is in prison and I expect it will go hard with him."

"It's a complicated story, you know," said the adjutant. "That proclamation appeared about two months ago. The count was informed of it. He gave orders to investigate the matter. The proclamation had passed through exactly sixty-three hands. He asked one, 'From whom did you get it?' 'From so-and-so.' He went to the next one. 'From whom did you get it?' and so on till he reached Vereshchágin, a half-educated tradesman, you know, 'a pet of a trader,'" said the adjutant smiling. "They asked him, 'Who gave it you?' He replied: 'From no one; I made it up myself.'"

"And the count wanted him to say it was from Klyucharëv? I understand!" said Pierre.

"Not at all," rejoined the adjutant in dismay. "Klyucharëv had his own sins to answer for without that and that is why he has been banished."

In the middle of this fresh tale Pierre was summoned to the commander in chief.

When he entered the private room Count Rostopchín, puckering his face, was rubbing his forehead and eyes with his hand.

"Ah, how do you do, great warrior?" said Rostopchín. "We have heard of your prowess. But that's not the point. Between ourselves, *mon cher*, do you belong to the Masons?" he went on severely, as though there were something wrong about it which he nevertheless intended to pardon. Pierre remained silent "I am well informed, my friend, but I am aware that there are Masons and Masons and I hope that you are not one of those who on pretense of saving mankind wish to ruin Russia."

"Yes, I am a Mason," Pierre replied.

"There, you see, *mon cher!* I expect you know that Messrs. Speránski and Magnítski have been deported to their proper place. Mr. Klyucharëv has been treated in the same way, and so have others who on the plea of building up the temple of Solomon have tried to destroy the temple of their fatherland. . . . I like you and don't wish you any harm and—as you are only half my age—I advise you, as a father would, to cease all communication with men of that stamp and to leave here as soon as possible."

"But what did Klyucharëv do wrong, Count?" asked Pierre.

"That is for me to know, but not for you to ask," shouted Rostopchín.

"If he is accused of circulating Napoleon's proclamation it is not proved that he did so," said Pierre without looking at Rostopchín, "and Vereshchágin . . ."

"There we are!" Rostopchín shouted at Pierre louder than before, frowning suddenly. "Vereshchágin is a renegade and a traitor who will be punished as he deserves," said he with the vindictive heat with which people speak when recalling an insult. "But I did not summon you to discuss my actions, but to give you advice—or an order if you prefer it. I beg you to leave the town and break off all communication with such men as Klyucharëv. And I will knock the nonsense out of anybody" —but probably realizing that he was shouting at Bezúkhov who so far was not guilty of anything, he added, taking Pierre's hand in a friendly manner, "We are on the eve of a public disaster and I haven't time to be polite to everybody who has business with me. My head is sometimes in a whirl. Well, *mon cher*, what are you doing personally?"

"Why, nothing," answered Pierre without raising his eyes or changing the thoughtful expression of his face.

The count frowned.

"A word of friendly advice, *mon cher*. Be off as soon as you can, that's all I have to tell you. Happy he who has ears to hear. Good-by, my dear fellow. Oh, by the by!" he shouted through the doorway after Pierre, "is it true that the countess has fallen into the clutches of the holy fathers of the Society of Jesus?"

Pierre did not answer and left Rostopchín's room more sullen and angry than he had ever before shown himself.

When he reached home it was already getting dark. Some eight people had come to see him that evening. When left alone at last he opened and read his wife's letter.

"*They*, the soldiers at the battery, Prince Andrew killed . . . that old man . . . Simplicity is submission to God. Suffering is necessary . . . the meaning of all . . . one must harness . . . my wife is getting married . . . One must forget and understand . . ." And going to his bed he threw himself on it without undressing and immediately fell asleep.

When he awoke next morning the major-domo came to inform him that a special messenger, a police officer, had come from Count Rostopchín to know whether Count Bezúkhov had left or was leaving the town.

A dozen persons who had business with Pierre were awaiting him in the drawing room. Pierre dressed hurriedly and, instead of going to see them, went to the back porch and out through the gate.

From that time till the end of the destruction of Moscow no one of Bezúkhov's household, despite all the search they made, saw Pierre again or knew where he was.

8

The Rostóvs remained in Moscow till the first of September, that is, till the eve of the enemy's entry into the city.

After Pétya had joined Obolénski's regiment of Cossacks and left for Bélaya Tsérkov where that regiment was forming, the countess was seized with terror. Nicholas was somewhere with the army and had not sent a word since his last letter, in which he had given a detailed account of his meeting with Princess Mary. The countess did not sleep at night, or when she did fall asleep dreamed that she saw her sons lying dead. After many consultations and conversations, the count at last devised means to tranquilize her. He got Pétya transferred from Obolénski's regiment to Bezúkhov's, which was in training near Moscow. Though Pétya would remain in the service, this transfer would give the countess the consolation of seeing at least one of her sons under her wing, and she hoped to arrange matters for her Pétya so as not to let him go again, but always get him appointed to places where he could not possibly take part in a battle.

Though by the twentieth of August nearly all the Rostóvs' acquaintances had left Moscow, and though everybody tried to persuade the countess to get away as quickly as possible, she would not hear of leaving before her treasure, her adored Pétya, returned. On the twenty-eighth of August he arrived. The passionate tenderness with which his mother received him did not please the sixteen-year-old officer. Though she concealed from him her intention of keeping him under her wing, Pétya guessed her designs, and instinctively fearing that he might give way to emotion when with her—might "become womanish" as he termed it to himself—he treated her coldly, avoided her, and during his stay in Moscow attached himself exclusively to Natásha for whom he had always had a particularly brotherly tenderness, almost lover-like.

During the three days preceding the occupation of Moscow the whole Rostóv family was absorbed in various activities. The head of the family, Count Ilyá Rostóv, continually drove about the city collecting the current rumors from all sides and gave superficial and hasty orders at home about the preparations for their departure.

Sónya alone directed the practical side of matters by getting things packed. But of late Sónya had been particularly sad and silent. Nicholas' letter in which he mentioned Princess Mary had elicited, in her presence, joyous comments from the countess, who saw an intervention of Providence in this meeting of the princess and Nicholas.

Sónya felt that this was true: that the only possibility of retrieving the Rostóvs' affairs was by Nicholas marrying a rich woman, and that the princess was a good match. It was very bitter for her. Pétya and Natásha on the contrary, far from helping their parents, were generally a nuisance and a hindrance to everyone. Almost all day long the house resounded with their running feet, their cries, and their spontaneous laughter. Natásha was gay because she had been sad too long and now nothing reminded her of the cause of her sadness, and because she was feeling well. Above all, they were gay because there was a war near Moscow, there would be fighting at the town gates, arms were being given out, everybody was escaping—going away somewhere, and in general something extraordinary was happening, and that is always exciting, especially to the young.

On Saturday, the thirty-first of August, everything in the Rostóvs' house seemed topsy-turvy. All the doors were open, all the furniture was being carried out or moved about, and the mirrors and pictures had been taken down.

Natásha was ashamed of doing nothing when everyone else was so busy, and several times that morning had tried to set to work, but her heart was not in it, and she could not and did not know how to do anything except with all her heart and all her might. She got up and looked out of the window. An enormously long row of carts full of wounded men had stopped in the street.

Natásha, throwing a clean pocket handkerchief over her hair and holding an end of it in each hand, went out into the street.

The former housekeeper, old Mávra Kuzmínichna, had stepped out of the crowd by the gate, gone up to a cart with a hood constructed of bast mats, and was speaking to a pale young officer who lay inside. Natásha moved a few steps forward and stopped shyly, still holding her handkerchief, and listened to what the housekeeper was saying.

"Then you have nobody in Moscow?" she was saying. "You would be more comfortable somewhere in a house . . . in ours, for instance . . . the family are leaving."

Natásha glanced with frightened eyes at the face of the wounded officer and at once went to meet the major.

"May the wounded men stay in our house?" she asked.

"Oh yes, why not? They may," he said.

With a slight inclination of her head, Natásha stepped back quickly to Mávra Kuzmínichna, who stood talking compassionately to the officer.

"They may. He says they may!" whispered Natásha.

The cart in which the officer lay was turned into the Rostóvs' yard. Natásha was evidently pleased to be dealing with new people outside the ordinary routine of her life. She and Mávra Kuzmínichna tried to get as many of the wounded as possible into their yard.

"Your Papa must be told, though," said Mávra Kuzmínichna.

Natásha ran into the house and went on tiptoe through the half-open door into the sitting room.

"Mamma darling!" said Natásha, "Mávra Kuzmínichna has sent me: they have brought some wounded here—officers. Will you let them come? They have nowhere to go. I knew you'd let them come . . ." she said quickly all in one breath.

"What officers? Whom have they brought? I don't understand anything about it," said the countess.

Natásha laughed, and the countess too smiled slightly.

"I knew you'd give permission . . . so I'll tell them," and, having kissed her mother, Natásha got up and went to the door.

After dinner the whole Rostóv household set to work with enthusiastic haste packing their belongings and preparing for their departure. The servants ran noisily about the house and yard, shouting and disputing. Natásha, with the ardor characteristic of all she did, suddenly set to work too.

But hard as they all worked till quite late that night, they could not get everything packed. The countess had fallen asleep and the count, having put off their departure till next morning, went to bed.

Sónya and Natásha slept in the sitting room without undressing.

That night another wounded man was driven down the Povarskáya, and Mávra Kuzmínichna, who was standing at the gate, had him brought into the Rostóvs' yard. Mávra Kuzmínichna concluded that he was a very important man. He was being conveyed in a *calèche* with a raised hood, and was quite covered by an apron. On the box beside the driver sat a venerable old attendant. A doctor and two soldiers followed the carriage in a cart.

"Do us the honor to come in, there's plenty of everything in the master's house. Come in," said Mávra Kuzmínichna. "Is he very ill?" she asked.

The attendant made a hopeless gesture.

But they had to avoid carrying the man upstairs, and so they took him into the wing and put him in the room that had been Madame Schoss'.

This wounded man was Prince Andrew Bolkónski.

Moscow's last day had come. It was a clear bright autumn day, a Sunday. The church bells everywhere were ringing for service, just as usual on Sundays. Nobody seemed yet to realize what awaited the city.

In the Rostóvs' staid old-fashioned house the dissolution of former conditions of life was but little noticeable. As to the serfs the only indication was that three out of their huge retinue disappeared during the night, but nothing was stolen; and as to the value of their possessions, the thirty peasant carts that had come in from their estates and which many people envied proved to be extremely valuable and they were offered enormous sums of money for them.

On waking up that morning Count Ilyá Rostóv left his bedroom softly, so as not to wake the countess who had fallen asleep only toward morning, and came out to the porch in his lilac silk dressing gown. In the yard stood the carts ready corded. The carriages were at the front porch. The majordomo stood at the porch talking to an elderly orderly and to a pale young officer with a bandaged arm.

The officer came nearer and suddenly his face flushed crimson.

"Count, be so good as to allow me . . . for God's sake, to get into some corner of one of your carts! I have nothing here with me. . . . I should be all right on a loaded cart. . . ."

Before the officer had finished speaking the orderly made the same request on behalf of his master.

"Oh yes, yes, yes!" said the count hastily. "I shall be very pleased, very pleased. Vasílich, you'll see to it. Just unload one or two carts. Well, what of it . . . do what's necessary . . ." said the count, muttering some indefinite order.

The count went into the house with him, repeating his order not to refuse the wounded who asked for a lift.

"Well, never mind, some of the things can be unloaded," he added in a soft, confidential voice, as though afraid of being overheard.

At nine o'clock the countess woke up. The countess learned that Madame Schoss was offended because her trunk had been taken down from its cart, and all the loads were being uncorded and the luggage taken out of the carts to make room for wounded men whom the count in the simplicity of his heart had ordered that they should take with them. The countess sent for her husband.

"What is this, my dear? I hear that the luggage is being unloaded."

"You know, love, I wanted to tell you . . . Countess dear . . . an officer came to me to ask for a few carts for the wounded. After all, ours are things that can be bought but think what being left behind means to them!"

She assumed her dolefully submissive manner and said to her husband: "Listen to me, Count, you have managed matters so that we are getting nothing for the house, and now you wish to throw away all our—all *the children's* property! You said yourself that we have a hundred thousand rubles' worth of things in the house. I don't consent, my dear, I don't! Do as you please! It's the government's business to look after the wounded."

Flourishing his arms in despair the count left the room without replying.

"Papa, what are you doing that for?" asked Natásha, who had followed him into her mother's room.

"Nothing! What business is it of yours?" muttered the count angrily.

Natásha stepped up to the window and pondered.

"Papa! Here's Berg coming to see us," said she, looking out of the window.

Berg, the Rostóvs' son-in-law, was already a colonel wearing the orders of Vladímir and Anna, and he still filled the quiet and agreeable post of assistant to the head of the staff of the assistant commander of the first division of the Second Army.

On the first of September he had come to Moscow from the army.

He had nothing to do in Moscow, but he had noticed that everyone in the army was asking for leave to visit Moscow and had something to do there. So he considered it necessary to ask for leave of absence for family and domestic reasons.

From the anteroom Berg ran with smooth though impatient steps into the drawing room, where he embraced the count, kissed the hands of Natásha and Sónya, and hastened to inquire about "Mamma's" health.

"And I have a great favor to ask of you, Papa," said he.

"I was driving past Yusúpov's house just now," said Berg with a laugh, "when the steward, a man I know, ran out and asked me whether I wouldn't buy something. I went in out of curiosity, you know, and there is a small chiffonier . . . And dear Véra has long wanted one. I wish to give her a surprise, you see. I saw so many of those peasant carts in your yard. Please let me have one, I will pay the man well, and . . ."

The count frowned and coughed.

"Ask the countess, I don't give orders."

"If it's inconvenient, please don't," said Berg. "Only I so wanted it, for dear Véra's sake."

"Oh, go to the devil, all of you! To the devil, the devil, the devil . . . !" cried the old count. "My head's in a whirl!"

Natásha left the room with her father and, as if finding it difficult to reach some decision, first followed him and then ran downstairs.

Pétya was in the porch, engaged in giving out weapons to the servants who were to leave Moscow. The loaded carts were still standing in the yard. Two of them had been uncorded and a wounded officer was climbing into one of them helped by an orderly.

"Do you know what it's about?" Pétya asked Natásha.

She understood that he meant what were their parents quarreling about. She did not answer.

"It's because Papa wanted to give up all the carts to the wounded," said Pétya. "Vasílich told me. I consider . . ."

"I consider," Natásha suddenly almost shouted, turning her

angry face to Pétya, "I consider it so horrid, so abominable, so
. . . I don't know what. Are we despicable Germans?"

Her throat quivered with convulsive sobs and, afraid of
weakening and letting the force of her anger run to waste, she
turned and rushed headlong up the stairs.

Berg was sitting beside the countess consoling her with the
respectful attention of a relative. The count, pipe in hand, was
pacing up and down the room, when Natásha, her face distorted by anger, burst in like a tempest and approached her
mother with rapid steps.

"It's horrid! It's abominable!" she screamed. "You can't possibly have ordered it!"

Berg and the countess looked at her, perplexed and frightened. The count stood still at the window and listened.

"Mamma, it's impossible: see what is going on in the yard!"
she cried. "They will be left! . . ."

"What's the matter with you? Who are 'they'? What do you
want?"

"Why, the wounded! It's impossible, Mamma. It's monstrous! . . . No, Mamma darling, it's not the thing. Please forgive me, darling. . . . Mamma, what does it matter what we
take away? Only look what is going on in the yard . . . Mamma! . . . It's impossible!"

The count stood by the window and listened without turning round. Suddenly he sniffed and put his face closer to the
window.

The countess glanced at her daughter, saw her face full of
shame for her mother, saw her agitation, and understood why
her husband did not turn to look at her now, and she glanced
round quite disconcerted.

"Oh, do as you like! Am I hindering anyone?" she said, not
surrendering at once.

"Mamma, darling, forgive me!"

But the countess pushed her daughter away and went up to
her husband.

"My dear, you order what is right. . . . You know I don't
understand about it," said she, dropping her eyes shamefaced-
ly.

"The eggs . . . the eggs are teaching the hen . . ." muttered
the count through tears of joy, and he embraced his wife who
was glad to hide her look of shame on his breast.

"Papa! Mamma! May I see to it? May I? . . ." asked Natásha. "We will still take all the most necessary things."

The count nodded affirmatively, and Natásha, at the rapid pace at which she used to run when playing at tag, ran through the ballroom to the anteroom and downstairs into the yard.

The servants gathered round Natásha, but could not believe the strange order she brought them until the count himself, in his wife's name, confirmed the order to give up all the carts to the wounded and take the trunks to the storerooms. When they understood that order the servants set to work at this new task with pleasure and zeal. It no longer seemed strange to them but on the contrary it seemed the only thing that could be done, just as a quarter of an hour before it had not seemed strange to anyone that the wounded should be left behind and the goods carted away but that had seemed the only thing to do.

The news that carts were to be had spread to the neighboring houses, from which wounded men began to come into the Rostóvs' yard.

The whole household, servants included, was bright and animated. Natásha was in a state of rapturous excitement such as she had not known for a long time.

Before two o'clock in the afternoon the Rostóvs' four carriages, packed full and with the horses harnessed, stood at the front yard. One by one the carts with the wounded had moved out of the yard.

The *calèche* in which Prince Andrew was being taken attracted Sónya's attention as it passed the front porch.

"Whose *calèche* is that?" she inquired, leaning out of the carriage window.

"Why, didn't you know, Miss?" replied the maid. "The wounded prince: he spent the night in our house and is going with us.

"But who is it? What's his name?"

"It's our intended that was—Prince Bolkónski himself! They say he is dying," replied the maid with a sigh.

Sónya jumped out of the coach and ran to the countess. The countess, tired out and already dressed in shawl and bonnet for her journey, was pacing up and down the drawing room, waiting for the household to assemble for the usual silent prayer with closed doors before starting. Natásha was not in the room.

"Mamma," said Sónya, "Prince Andrew is here, mortally wounded. He is going with us."

The countess opened her eyes in dismay and, seizing Sónya's arm, glanced around.

"Natásha?" she murmured.

At that moment this news had only one significance for both of them. They knew their Natásha, and alarm as to what would happen if she heard this news stifled all sympathy for the man they both liked.

"Natásha does not know yet, but he is going with us," said Sónya.

"You say he is dying?"

Sónya nodded.

The countess put her arms around Sónya and began to cry.

"Well, Mamma? Everything is ready. What's the matter?" asked Natásha, as with animated face she ran into the room.

"Nothing," answered the countess. "If everything is ready let us start."

And the countess bent over her reticule to hide her agitated face. Sónya embraced Natásha and kissed her.

Natásha looked at her inquiringly.

"What is it? What has happened?"

"Nothing . . . No . . ."

"Is it something very bad for me? What is it?" persisted Natásha with her quick intuition.

Sónya sighed and made no reply.

In the porch and in the yard the men whom Pétya had armed with swords and daggers, with trousers tucked inside their high boots and with belts and girdles tightened, were taking leave of those remaining behind.

At last all were seated, the carriage steps were folded and pulled up, the door was shut, somebody was sent for a traveling case, and the countess leaned out and said what she had to say. The footman sprang onto the box of the moving coach which jolted as it passed out of the yard onto the uneven roadway; the other vehicles jolted in their turn, and the procession of carriages moved up the street.

Rarely had Natásha experienced so joyful a feeling as now,

sitting in the carriage beside the countess and gazing at the slowly receding walls of forsaken, agitated Moscow. Occasionally she leaned out of the carriage window and looked back and then forward at the long train of wounded in front of them. Almost at the head of the line she could see the raised hood of Prince Andrew's *calèche*. She did not know who was in it, but each time she looked at the procession her eyes sought that *calèche*. She knew it was right in front.

As they were going round the Súkharev water tower Natásha, who was inquisitively and alertly scrutinizing the people driving or walking past, suddenly cried out in joyful surprise:

"Dear me! Mamma, Sónya, look, it's he!"

"Who? Who?"

"Look! Yes, on my word, it's Bezúkhov!" said Natásha, putting her head out of the carriage and staring at a tall, stout man in a coachman's long coat, who from his manner of walking and moving was evidently a gentleman in disguise, and who was passing under the arch of the Súkharev tower accompanied by a small, sallow-faced, beardless old man in a frieze coat.

"No, it's not he. How can you talk such nonsense?"

"Mamma," screamed Natásha, "I'll stake my head it's he! I assure you! Stop, stop!" she cried to the coachman.

But the coachman could not stop, for from the Meshchánski Street came more carts and carriages, and the Rostóvs were being shouted at to move on and not block the way.

The old man noticed a face thrust out of the carriage window gazing at them, and respectfully touching Pierre's elbow said something to him and pointed to the carriage. Pierre, evidently engrossed in thought, could not at first understand him. At length when he had understood and looked in the direction the old man indicated, he recognized Natásha, and following his first impulse stepped instantly and rapidly toward the coach. But having taken a dozen steps he seemed to remember something and stopped.

Natásha's face, leaning out of the window, beamed with quizzical kindliness.

"Peter Kirílovich, come here! We have recognized you! This is wonderful!" she cried, holding out her hand to him. "What are you doing? Why are you like this?"

Pierre took her outstretched hand and kissed it awkwardly

as he walked along beside her while the coach still moved on.

"What is the matter, Count?" asked the countess in a surprised and commiserating tone.

"What? What? Why? Don't ask me," said Pierre, and looked round at Natásha whose radiant, happy expression—of which he was conscious without looking at her—filled him with enchantment.

"Are you remaining in Moscow, then?"

Pierre hesitated.

"In Moscow?" he said in a questioning tone. "Yes, in Moscow. Good-by!"

"Ah, if only I were a man! I'd certainly stay with you. How splendid!" said Natásha. "Mamma, if you'll let me, I'll stay!"

Pierre glanced absently at Natásha and was about to say something, but the countess interrupted him.

"You were at the battle, we heard."

"Yes, I was," Pierre answered. "There will be another battle tomorrow . . ." he began, but Natásha interrupted him.

"But what is the matter with you, Count? You are not like yourself. . . ."

"Oh, don't ask me, don't ask me! I don't know myself. Tomorrow . . . But no! Good-by, good-by!" he muttered. "It's an awful time!" and dropping behind the carriage he stepped onto the pavement.

Natásha continued to lean out of the window for a long time, beaming at him with her kindly, slightly quizzical, happy smile.

9

For the last two days, ever since leaving home, Pierre had been living in the empty house of his deceased benefactor, Bazdéev. This is how it happened.

When he woke up on the morning after his return to Moscow and his interview with Count Rostopchín, he could not for some time make out where he was and what was expected of him. When he was informed that among others awaiting him in his reception room there was a Frenchman who had brought a letter from his wife, the Countess Hélène, he felt suddenly overcome by that sense of confusion and hopelessness to which he was apt to succumb. His major-domo came in a second time to say that the Frenchman who had brought the letter from the countess was very anxious to see him if only for a minute, and that someone from Bazdéev's widow had called to ask Pierre to take charge of her husband's books, as she herself was leaving for the country.

"Oh, yes, in a minute; wait . . . or no! No, of course . . . go and say I will come directly," Pierre replied to the major-domo.

From the landing where Pierre stood there was a second staircase leading to the back entrance. He went down that staircase and out into the yard. No one had seen him.

Of all the affairs awaiting Pierre that day the sorting of Joseph Bazdéev's books and papers appeared to him the most necessary.

He hired the first cab he met and told the driver to go to the Patriarch's Ponds, where the widow Bazdéev's house was.

Continually turning round to look at the rows of loaded carts that were making their way from all sides out of Moscow, and balancing his bulky body so as not to slip out of the ramshackle old vehicle, Pierre, experiencing the joyful feeling of a boy escaping from school, began to talk to his driver.

Having reached the Patriarch's Ponds Pierre found the Bazdéevs' house, where he had not been for a long time past. He went up to the gate. Gerásim, that sallow beardless old man Pierre had seen at Torzhók five years before with Joseph Bazdéev, came out in answer to his knock.

Pierre went into that gloomy study which he had entered with such trepidation in his benefactor's lifetime. The room, dusty and untouched since the death of Joseph Bazdéev, was now even gloomier.

Gerásim opened one of the shutters and left the room on tiptoe. Pierre went round the study, approached the cupboard in which the manuscripts were kept, and took out what had once been one of the most important, the holy of holies of the order. This was the authentic Scotch Acts with Bazdéev's notes and explanations. He sat down at the dusty writing table, and, having laid the manuscripts before him, opened them out, closed them, finally pushed them away, and resting his head on his hand sank into meditation.

More than two hours passed and Gerásim took the liberty

of making a slight noise at the door to attract his attention, but Pierre did not hear him.

"Is the cabman to be discharged, your honor?"

"Oh yes!" said Pierre, rousing himself and rising hurriedly. "Look here," he added, taking Gerásim by a button of his coat and looking down at the old man with moist, shining, and ecstatic eyes, "I say, do you know that there is going to be a battle tomorrow?"

"We heard so," replied the man.

"I beg you not to tell anyone who I am, and to do what I ask you."

"Yes, your excellency," replied Gerásim. "Will you have something to eat?"

"No, but I want something else. I want peasant clothes and a pistol," said Pierre, unexpectedly blushing.

"Yes, your excellency," said Gerásim after thinking for a moment.

All the rest of that day Pierre spent alone in his benefactor's study, and Gerásim heard him pacing restlessly from one corner to another and talking to himself. And he spent the night on a bed made up for him there.

It was when Pierre (wearing the coachman's coat which Gerásim had procured for him and had disinfected by steam) was on his way with the old man to buy the pistol at the Súkharev market that he met the Rostóvs.

10

Kutúzov's order to retreat through Moscow to the Ryazán road was issued at night on the first of September.

By ten o'clock in the morning of the second of September, only the rearguard remained in the Dorogomílov suburb, where they had ample room. The main army was on the other side of Moscow or beyond it.

At that very time, at ten in the morning of the second of September, Napoleon was standing among his troops on the Poklónny Hill looking at the panorama spread out before him.

The brightness of the morning was magical. Moscow seen from the Poklónny Hill lay spaciously spread out with her river, her gardens, and her churches, and she seemed to be living her usual life, her cupolas glittering like stars in the sunlight.

The view of the strange city with its peculiar architecture, such as he had never seen before, filled Napoleon with the rather envious and uneasy curiosity men feel when they see an alien form of life that has no knowledge of them. This city was evidently living with the full force of its own life. By the indefinite signs which, even at a distance, distinguish a living body from a dead one, Napoleon from the Poklónny Hill perceived the throb of life in the town and felt, as it were, the breathing of that great and beautiful body.

"But could it be otherwise?" he thought. "Here is this capital at my feet. Where is Alexander now, and of what is he thinking? A strange, beautiful, and majestic city; and a strange and majestic moment! In what light must I appear to them!" thought he, thinking of his troops. "Here she is, the reward for all those fainthearted men," he reflected, glancing at those near him and at the troops who were approaching and forming up. "One word from me, one movement of my hand, and that ancient capital of the Tsars would perish. But my clemency is always ready to descend upon the vanquished. I must be magnanimous and truly great. But no, it can't be true that I am in Moscow," he suddenly thought. "Yet here she is lying at my feet, with her golden domes and crosses scintillating and twinkling in the sunshine. But I shall spare her . . . I will tell the deputation that I did not, and do not, desire war, that I have waged war only against the false policy of their court; that I love and respect Alexander and that in Moscow I will accept terms of peace worthy of myself and of my people. . . . But can it be true that I am in Moscow? Yes, there she lies."

A general with a brilliant suite galloped off at once to fetch the boyars.

Two hours passed. Napoleon had lunched and was again standing in the same place on the Poklónny Hill awaiting the deputation. His speech to the boyars had already taken definite shape in his imagination. That speech was full of dignity and greatness as Napoleon understood it.

Meanwhile an agitated consultation was being carried on in whispers among his generals and marshals at the rear of his suite. Those sent to fetch the deputation had returned with the news that Moscow was empty, that everyone had left it.

"He will have to be told, all the same," said some gentlemen of the suite. "But, gentlemen . . ."

The position was the more awkward because the Emperor, meditating upon his magnanimous plans, was pacing patiently up and down before the outspread map, occasionally glancing along the road to Moscow from under his lifted hand with a bright and proud smile.

At last the Emperor, tired of futile expectation, his actor's instinct suggesting to him that the sublime moment having been too long drawn out was beginning to lose its sublimity, gave a sign with his hand. A single report of a signaling gun followed, and the troops, who were already spread out on different sides of Moscow, moved into the city through the Tver, Kalúga, and Dorogomílov gates.

11

Except for some tradesmen, workers, and released criminals, Moscow is deserted. Tolstoy compares the city to a queenless hive. Some of the retreating Russian troops begin looting, and the remaining rabble show signs of mob violence.

12

On the evening of the first of September, after his interview with Kutúzov, Count Rostopchín had returned to Moscow mortified and offended because he had not been invited to attend the council of war, and because Kutúzov had paid no attention to his offer to take part in the defense of the city. After supper he lay down on a sofa without undressing, and was awakened soon after midnight by a courier bringing him a letter from Kutúzov. This letter requested the count to send police officers to guide the troops through the town, as the army was retreating to the Ryazán road beyond Moscow. This was not news to Rostopchín. Yet all the same this information astonished and irritated the count, coming as it did in the form of a simple note with an order from Kutúzov, and received at night, breaking in on his beauty sleep.

When later on in his memoirs Count Rostopchín explained his actions at this time, he repeatedly says that he was then actuated by two important considerations: to maintain tranquillity in Moscow and expedite the departure of the inhabitants. One need only admit that public tranquillity is in danger and any action finds a justification.

All the horrors of the reign of terror were based only on solicitude for public tranquillity.

It is obvious that there would have been even less reason to expect a disturbance among the people if after the battle of Borodinó, when the surrender of Moscow became certain or at least probable, Rostopchín instead of exciting the people by distributing arms and broadsheets had taken steps to remove all the holy relics, the gunpowder, munitions, and money, and had told the population plainly that the town would be abandoned.

Rostopchín, though he had patriotic sentiments, was a sanguine and impulsive man who had always moved in the highest administrative circles and had no understanding at all of the people he supposed himself to be guiding. He was absorbed in the role he had created for himself. As is often the case with those gifted with an ardent imagination, though he had long known that Moscow would be abandoned he knew it only with his intellect, he did not believe it in his heart and did not adapt himself mentally to this new position of affairs.

When, awakened from his sleep, he received that cold, peremptory note from Kutúzov, he felt the more irritated the more he felt himself to blame. All that he had been specially put in charge of, the state property which he should have removed, was still in Moscow and it was no longer possible to take the whole of it away.

"Who is to blame for it? Who has let things come to such a pass?" he ruminated. "Not I, of course. I had everything ready. I had Moscow firmly in hand. And this is what they have let it come to! Villains! Traitors!" he thought, without clearly defining who the villains and traitors were, but feeling it necessary to hate those traitors whoever they might be who were to blame for the false and ridiculous position in which he found himself.

All that night Count Rostopchín issued orders, for which people came to him from all parts of Moscow. Those about him had never seen the count so morose and irritable.

In reply to an inquiry about the convicts in the prison, Count Rostopchín shouted angrily at the governor:

"Do you expect me to give you two battalions—which we have not got—for a convoy? Release them, that's all about it!"

"Your excellency, there are some political prisoners, Meshkóv, Vereshchágin . . ."

"Vereshchágin! Hasn't he been hanged yet?" shouted Rostopchín. "Bring him to me!"

Toward nine o'clock in the morning, when the troops were already moving through Moscow, nobody came to the count any more for instructions.

The count ordered his carriage that he might drive to Sokólniki, and sat in his study with folded hands, morose, sallow, and taciturn.

The superintendent of police, whom the crowd had stopped, went in to see him at the same time as an adjutant who informed the count that the horses were harnessed. They were both pale, and the superintendent of police, after reporting that he had executed the instructions he had received, informed the count that an immense crowd had collected in the courtyard and wished to see him.

"But what do they want?" he asked the superintendent of police.

"Your excellency, they say they have got ready, according to your orders, to go against the French, and they shouted something about treachery. But it is a turbulent crowd, your excellency—I hardly managed to get away from it. Your excellency, I venture to suggest . . ."

"You may go. I don't need you to tell me what to do!" exclaimed Rostopchín angrily.

He stood by the balcony door looking at the crowd.

"This is what they have done with Russia! This is what they have done with me!" thought he, full of an irrepressible fury. "Here is that mob, the dregs of the people," he thought as he gazed at the crowd: "this rabble they have roused by their folly! They want a victim," he thought. And this thought occurred to him just because he himself desired a victim, something on which to vent his rage.

"Is the carriage ready?" he asked again.

"Yes, your excellency. What are your orders about Vereshchágin? He is waiting at the porch," said the adjutant.

"Ah!" exclaimed Rostopchín, as if struck by an unexpected recollection.

And rapidly opening the door he went resolutely out onto the balcony. The talking instantly ceased, hats and caps were doffed, and all eyes were raised to the count.

"Good morning, lads!" said the count briskly and loudly. "Thank you for coming. I'll come out to you in a moment, but we must first settle with the villain. We must punish the villain who has caused the ruin of Moscow. Wait for me!"

And the count stepped as briskly back into the room and slammed the door behind him.

A few minutes later an officer came hurriedly out of the front door, gave an order, and the dragoons formed up in line. The crowd moved eagerly from the balcony toward the porch. Rostopchín, coming out there with quick angry steps, looked hastily around as if seeking someone.

"Where is he?" he inquired. And as he spoke he saw a young man coming round the corner of the house between two dragoons. He had a long thin neck, and his head, that had been half shaved, was again covered by short hair. This young man was dressed in a threadbare blue cloth coat lined with fox fur, that had once been smart, and dirty hempen convict trousers, over which were pulled his thin, dirty, trodden-down boots. On his thin, weak legs were heavy chains which hampered his irresolute movements.

"Ah!" said Rostopchín, hurriedly turning away his eyes from the young man in the fur-lined coat and pointing to the bottom step of the porch. "Put him there."

While waiting for the young man to take his place on the step Rostopchín stood frowning and rubbing his face with his hand.

"Lads!" said he, with a metallic ring in his voice. "This man, Vereshchágin, is the scoundrel by whose doing Moscow is perishing."

The young man in the fur-lined coat, stooping a little, stood in a submissive attitude, his fingers clasped before him.

"He has betrayed his Tsar and his country, he had gone over to Bonaparte. He alone of all the Russians has disgraced the Russian name, he has caused Moscow to perish," said Rostopchín in a sharp, even voice, but suddenly he glanced down at Vereshchágin who continued to stand in the same submissive attitude. As if inflamed by the sight, he raised his arm and addressed the people, almost shouting:

"Deal with him as you think fit! I hand him over to you."

The crowd remained silent and only pressed closer and closer to one another.

"Beat him! . . . Let the traitor perish and not disgrace the Russian name!" shouted Rostopchín. "Cut him down. I command it."

Hearing not so much the words as the angry tone of Rostopchín's voice, the crowd moaned and heaved forward, but again paused.

"Count!" exclaimed the timid yet theatrical voice of Vereshchágin in the midst of the momentary silence that ensued, "Count! One God is above us both. . . ."

He did not finish what he wished to say.

"Cut him down! I command it . . ." shouted Rostopchín, suddenly growing pale like Vereshchágin.

And one of the soldiers, his face all at once distorted with fury, struck Vereshchágin on the head with the blunt side of his saber.

"Ah!" cried Vereshchágin in meek surprise, looking round with a frightened glance as if not understanding why this was done to him. A similar moan of surprise and horror ran through the crowd. "O Lord!" exclaimed a sorrowful voice.

But after the exclamation of surprise that had escaped from Vereshchágin he uttered a plaintive cry of pain, and that cry was fatal. The barrier of human feeling, strained to the utmost, that had held the crowd in check suddenly broke. The crime had begun and must now be completed. The plaintive moan of reproach was drowned by the threatening and angry roar of the crowd. The dragoon was about to repeat his blow. Vereshchágin with a cry of horror, covering his head with his hands, rushed toward the crowd.

Some beat and tore at Vereshchágin. And for a long time, despite the feverish haste with which the mob tried to end the work that had been begun, those who were hitting, throttling, and tearing at Vereshchágin were unable to kill him, for the crowd pressed from all sides, swaying as one mass with them in the center and rendering it impossible for them either to kill him or let him go.

"Hit him with an ax, eh! . . . Crushed? . . . Traitor, he sold Christ . . . Still alive . . . tenacious . . . serve him right! Torture serves a thief right. Use the hatchet! . . . What—still alive?"

Only when the victim ceased to struggle and his cries changed to a long-drawn, measured death rattle did the crowd around his prostrate, bleeding corpse begin rapidly to change places. Each one came up, glanced at what had been done, and with horror, reproach, and astonishment pushed back again.

At the moment when Vereshchágin fell and the crowd closed in with savage yells and swayed about him, Rostopchín suddenly turned pale.

"This way, your excellency . . . Where are you going? . . . This way, please . . ." said a trembling, frightened voice behind him.

Count Rostopchín was unable to reply and, turning obediently, went in the direction indicated. At the back entrance stood his *calèche*. The distant roar of the yelling crowd was audible even there. He hastily took his seat and told the coachman to drive him to his country house in Sokólniki.

Lightly swaying on the flexible springs of his carriage and no longer hearing the terrible sounds of the crowd, Rostopchín grew physically calm and, as always happens, as soon as he became physically tranquil his mind devised reasons why he should be mentally tranquil too. The thought which tranquilized Rostopchín was not a new one. Since the world began and men have killed one another no one has ever committed such a crime against his fellow man without comforting himself with this same idea. This idea is *le bien public*, the hypothetical welfare of other people.

"Vereshchágin was tried and condemned to death," thought Rostopchín (though the Senate had only condemned Vereshchágin to hard labor), "he was a traitor and a spy. I could not let him go unpunished and so I have killed two birds with one stone: to appease the mob I gave them a victim and at the same time punished a miscreant."

Having reached his country house and begun to give orders about domestic arrangements, the count grew quite tranquil.

Half an hour later he was driving with his fast horses across the Sokólniki field, no longer thinking of what had occurred but considering what was to come. He was driving to the Yaúza bridge where he had heard that Kutúzov was. Count Rostopchín was mentally preparing the angry and stinging reproaches he meant to address to Kutúzov for his deception.

Troops were still crowding at the Yaúza bridge. It was hot. Kutúzov, dejected and frowning, sat on a bench by the bridge toying with his whip in the sand when a *calèche* dashed up noisily. It was Count Rostopchín. He told Kutúzov that he had come because Moscow, the capital, was no more and only the army remained.

"Things would have been different if your Serene Highness had not told me that you would not abandon Moscow without another battle; all this would not have happened," he said.

Kutúzov slightly shook his head and not taking his penetrating gaze from Rostopchín's face muttered softly:

"No! I shall not give up Moscow without a battle!"

Whether Kutúzov was thinking of something entirely different when he spoke those words, or uttered them purposely, knowing them to be meaningless, at any rate Rostopchín made no reply and hastily left him. And strange to say, the Governor of Moscow, the proud Count Rostopchín, took up a Cossack whip and went to the bridge where he began with shouts to drive on the carts that blocked the way.

13

Toward four o'clock in the afternoon Murat's troops were entering Moscow. In front rode a detachment of Württemberg hussars and behind them rode the King of Naples himself accompanied by a numerous suite.

Though tattered, hungry, worn out, and reduced to a third of their original number, the French entered Moscow in good marching order. It was a weary and famished, but still a fighting and menacing army. But it remained an army only until its soldiers had dispersed into their different lodgings.

As soon as the men of the various regiments began to disperse among the wealthy and deserted houses, the army was lost forever and there came into being something nondescript, neither citizens nor soldiers but what are known as marauders. When five weeks later these same men left Moscow, they no longer formed an army. They were a mob of marauders, each carrying a quantity of articles which seemed to him valuable or useful. The aim of each man when he left Moscow was no longer, as it had been, to conquer, but merely to keep what he had acquired.

Order after order was issued by the French commanders that day forbidding the men to disperse about the town, sternly forbidding any violence to the inhabitants or any looting, and announcing a roll call for that very evening. But despite all these measures the men, who had till then constituted an army, flowed all over the wealthy, deserted city with its comforts and plentiful supplies.

No residents were left in Moscow, and the soldiers—like water percolating through sand—spread irresistibly through the city in all directions from the Krémlin into which they had first marched. Before they had had time to secure quarters the soldiers ran out into the streets to see the city and, hearing that everything had been abandoned, rushed to places where valuables were to be had for the taking. The officers followed to check the soldiers and were involuntarily drawn into doing the same. When water is spilled on dry ground both the dry ground and the water disappear and mud results; and in the same way the entry of the famished army into the rich and deserted city resulted in fires and looting and the destruction of both the army and the wealthy city.

The French attributed the Fire of Moscow to Rostopchín's ferocious patriotism, the Russians to the barbarity of the French. In reality, however, it was not, and could not be, possible to explain the burning of Moscow by making any individual, or any group of people, responsible for it. Moscow was burned because it found itself in a position in which any town built of wood was bound to burn, quite apart from whether it had, or had not, a hundred and thirty inferior fire engines. Deserted Moscow had to burn as inevitably as a

heap of shavings has to burn on which sparks continually fall
for several days.

However tempting it might be for the French to blame
Rostopchín's ferocity and for Russians to blame the scoundrel
Bonaparte, or later on to place an heroic torch in the hands
of their own people, it is impossible not to see that there
could be no such direct cause of the fire, for Moscow had to
burn as every village, factory, or house must burn which is
left by its owners and in which strangers are allowed to live
and cook their porridge. Moscow was burned by its inhabitants, it is true, but by those who had abandoned it and not
by those who remained in it. Moscow when occupied by the
enemy did not remain intact like Berlin, Vienna, and other
towns, simply because its inhabitants abandoned it and did
not welcome the French with bread and salt, nor bring them
the keys of the city.

14

The absorption of the French by Moscow,
radiating starwise as it did, only reached the quarter where
Pierre was staying by the evening of the second of September.

After the last two days spent in solitude and unusual circumstances, Pierre was in a state bordering on insanity. He
was completely obsessed by one persistent thought. He did
not know how or when this thought had taken such possession
of him, but he remembered nothing of the past, understood
nothing of the present, and all he saw and heard appeared to
him like a dream.

He had left home only to escape the intricate tangle of
life's demands that enmeshed him, and which in his present
condition he was unable to unravel. He sought a quiet refuge,
and in Joseph Alezéevich's study he really found it. When
Gerásim roused him from his reverie the idea occurred to him
of taking part in the popular defense of Moscow which he
knew was projected. And with that object he had asked
Gerásim to get him a peasant's coat and a pistol, confiding to
him his intentions of remaining in Joseph Alexéevich's house
and keeping his name secret. Then during the first day spent
in inaction and solitude the idea that had previously occurred

to him of the cabalistic significance of his name in connection with Bonaparte's more than once vaguely presented itself.

When, having bought the coat merely with the object of taking part among the people in the defense of Moscow, Pierre had met the Rostóvs and Natásha had said to him: "Are you remaining in Moscow? . . . How splendid!" the thought flashed into his mind that it really would be a good thing, even if Moscow were taken, for him to remain there and do what he was predestined to do.

He must remain in Moscow, concealing his name, and must meet Napoleon and kill him, and either perish or put an end to the misery of all Europe—which it seemed to him was solely due to Napoleon.

Two equally strong feelings drew Pierre irresistibly to this purpose. The first was a feeling of the necessity of sacrifice and suffering in view of the common calamity, the same feeling that had caused him to go to Mozháysk on the twenty-fifth and to make his way to the very thick of the battle and had now caused him to run away from his home and, in place of the luxury and comfort to which he was accustomed, to sleep on a hard sofa without undressing and eat the same food as Gerásim. The other was that vague and quite Russian feeling of contempt for everything conventional, artificial, and human—for everything the majority of men regard as the greatest good in the world.

From the very day Pierre had experienced this feeling he had been continuously under its influence, but only now found full satisfaction for it. Moreover, at this moment Pierre was supported in his design and prevented from renouncing it by what he had already done in that direction. If he were now to leave Moscow like everyone else, his flight from home, the peasant coat, the pistol, and his announcement to the Rostóvs that he would remain in Moscow would all become not merely meaningless but contemptible and ridiculous, and to this Pierre was very sensitive.

Pierre's physical condition, as is always the case, corresponded to his mental state. The unaccustomed coarse food, the vodka he drank during those days, the absence of wine and cigars, his dirty unchanged linen, two almost sleepless nights passed on a short sofa without bedding—all this kept him in a state bordering on insanity.

It was two o'clock in the afternoon. The French had already entered Moscow. Pierre knew this, but instead of acting he only thought about his undertaking, going over its minutest details in his mind. In his fancy he did not clearly picture to himself either the striking of the blow or the death of Napoleon, but with extraordinary vividness and melancholy enjoyment imagined his own destruction and heroic endurance.

"Yes, alone, for the sake of all, I must do it or perish!" he thought. "Yes, I will approach . . . and then suddenly . . . with pistol or dagger? But that is all the same! 'It is not I but the hand of Providence that punishes thee,' I shall say," thought he, imagining what he would say when killing Napoleon. "Well then, take me and execute me!" he went on, speaking to himself and bowing his head with a sad but firm expression.

A French officer, Captain Ramballe, seeks to quarter himself in Bazdéev's house. Pierre saves the officer's life when a mad drunken brother of Bazdéev tries to shoot him. Ramballe, filled with sentimental generosity, thrusts his friendship on Pierre. Under the influence of good food, liquor, and pleasant companionship, Pierre's determination to conceal his identity weakens, also his resolve to kill Napoleon. Ramballe tells his life story and of his many conquests of women.

Listening to the captain's tales, Pierre—as often happens late in the evening and under the influence of wine—followed all that was told him, understood it all, and at the same time followed a train of personal memories which, he knew not why, suddenly arose in his mind. While listening to these love stories his own love for Natásha unexpectedly rose to his mind, and going over the pictures of that love in his imagination he mentally compared them with Ramballe's tales. Listening to the story of the struggle between love and duty, Pierre saw before his eyes every minutest detail of his last meeting with the object of his love at the Súkharev water tower. At the time of that meeting it had not produced an effect upon him—he had not even once recalled it. But now it seemed to him that that meeting had had in it something very important and poetic.

"Peter Kirílovich, come here! We have recognized you," he now seemed to hear the words she had uttered and to see before him her eyes, her smile, her traveling hood, and a stray lock of her hair . . . and there seemed to him something pathetic and touching in all this.

Having finished his tale about the enchanting Polish lady, the captain asked Pierre if he had ever experienced a similar impulse to sacrifice himself for love and a feeling of envy of the legitimate husband.

Challenged by this question Pierre raised his head and felt a need to express the thoughts that filled his mind. He began to explain that he understood love for a woman somewhat differently. He said that in all his life he had loved and still loved only one woman, and that she could never be his.

"*Tiens!*" said the captain.

Pierre then explained that he had loved this woman from his earliest years, but that he had not dared to think of her because she was too young, and because he had been an illegitimate son without a name. Afterwards when he had received a name and wealth he dared not think of her because he loved her too well, placing her far above everything in the world, and especially therefore above himself.

When he had reached this point, Pierre asked the captain whether he understood that.

The captain made a gesture signifying that even if he did not understand it he begged Pierre to continue.

"Platonic love, clouds . . ." he muttered.

Whether it was the wine he had drunk, or an impulse of frankness, or the thought that this man did not, and never would, know any of those who played a part in his story, or whether it was all these things together, something loosened Pierre's tongue. Speaking thickly and with a faraway look in his shining eyes, he told the whole story of his life: his marriage, Natásha's love for his best friend, her betrayal of him, and all his own simple relations with her. Urged on by Ramballe's questions he also told what he had at first concealed—his own position and even his name.

More than anything else in Pierre's story the captain was impressed by the fact that Pierre was very rich, had two mansions in Moscow, and that he had abandoned everything and not left the city, but remained there concealing his name and station.

When it was late at night they went out together into the street. The night was warm and light. To the left of the house on the Pokróvka a fire glowed—the first of those that were beginning in Moscow.

There was nothing terrible in the one small, distant fire in the immense city.

Gazing at the high starry sky, and at the glow from the fire, Pierre experienced a joyful emotion. "There now, how good it is, what more does one need?" thought he. And suddenly remembering his intention he grew dizzy and felt so faint that he leaned against the fence to save himself from falling.

Without taking leave of his new friend, Pierre left the gate with unsteady steps and returning to his room lay down on the sofa and immediately fell asleep.

15

The Rostóv party spent the night at Mytíshchi, fourteen miles from Moscow. At ten o'clock that evening they and the wounded traveling with them were all distributed in the yards and huts of that large village. The Rostóvs' servants and coachmen and the orderlies of the wounded officers, after attending to their masters, had supper, fed the horses, and came out into the porches.

In the darkness of the night one of the servants noticed, above the high body of a coach standing before the porch, the small glow of another fire. One glow had long been visible and everybody knew that it was Little Mytíshchi burning—set on fire by Mamónov's Cossacks.

Two of the gazers went round to the other side of the coach and sat down on its steps.

"See how it's flaring," said one. "That's a fire in Moscow: either in the Sushchévski or the Rogózhski quarter."

No one replied to this remark and for some time they all gazed silently at the spreading flames of the second fire in the distance.

And it was as if they had all only waited for this to realize the significance for them of the glow they were watching. Sighs were heard, words of prayer, and the sobbing of the count's old valet.

The valet, returning to the cottage, informed the count that Moscow was burning. The count donned his dressing gown and went out to look. Only Natásha and the countess remained in the room. Pétya was no longer with the family, he had gone on with his regiment which was making for Tróitsa.

The countess, on hearing that Moscow was on fire, began to cry. Natásha, pale, with a fixed look, was sitting on the bench under the icons just where she had sat down on arriving and paid no attention to her father's words.

She had been in this condition of stupor since this morning, when Sónya, to the surprise and annoyance of the countess, had for some unaccountable reason found it necessary to tell Natásha of Prince Andrew's wound and of his being with their party. The countess had seldom been so angry with anyone as she was with Sónya. Sónya had cried and begged to be forgiven and now, as if trying to atone for her fault, paid unceasing attention to her cousin.

"Look, Natásha, how dreadfully it is burning!" said she.

"What's burning?" asked Natásha. "Oh, yes, Moscow."

When Natásha had been told that morning that Prince Andrew was seriously wounded and was traveling with their party, she had at first asked many questions: Where was he going? How was he wounded? Was it serious? And could she see him? But after she had been told that she could not see him, that he was seriously wounded but that his life was not in danger, she ceased to ask questions or to speak at all, evidently disbelieving what they told her, and convinced that say what she might she would still be told the same. All the way she had sat motionless in a corner of the coach with wide-open eyes, and the expression in them which the countess knew so well and feared so much, and now she sat in the same way on the bench where she had seated herself on arriving. She was planning something and either deciding or had already decided something in her mind. The countess knew this, but what it might be she did not know, and this alarmed and tormented her.

"Natásha, undress, darling; lie down on my bed."

A bed had been made on a bedstead for the countess only. Madame Schoss and the two girls were to sleep on some hay on the floor.

"No, Mamma. I will lie down here on the floor," Natásha replied irritably. She knew Prince Andrew was in the same yard as themselves and in a part of the hut across the passage.

"Lie down, darling; lie down, my pet," said the countess, softly touching Natásha's shoulders. "Come, lie down."

"Oh, yes . . . I'll lie down at once," said Natásha, and began hurriedly undressing, tugging at the tapes of her petticoat.

For a long time Natásha listened attentively to the sounds that reached her from inside and outside the room and did not move.

"Sónya, are you asleep? Mamma?" she whispered.

No one replied. Natásha rose slowly and carefully, crossed herself, and stepped cautiously on the cold dirty floor with her slim, supple, bare feet. The boards of the floor creaked. Stepping cautiously from one foot to the other she ran like a kitten the few steps to the door and grasped the cold door handle.

It seemed to her that something heavy was beating rhythmically against all the walls of the room: it was her own heart, sinking with alarm and terror and overflowing with love.

She opened the door and stepped across the threshold and onto the cold, damp earthen floor of the passage. The cold she felt refreshed her. With her bare feet she touched a sleeping man, stepped over him, and opened the door into the part of the hut where Prince Andrew lay. It was dark in there. In the farthest corner, on a bench beside a bed on which someone was lying, stood a tallow candle with a long, thick, and smoldering wick.

From the moment she had been told that morning of Prince Andrew's wound and his presence there, Natásha had resolved to see him. She did not know why she had to, she knew the meeting would be painful, but felt the more convinced that it was necessary.

All day she had lived only in hope of seeing him that night. But now that the moment had come she was filled with dread of what she might see. But an irresistible impulse drew her forward. She cautiously took one step and then another, and found herself in the middle of a small room containing baggage. Another man—Timókhin—was lying in a corner on the benches beneath the icons, and two others— the doctor and a valet—lay on the floor.

The valet sat up and whispered something. Timókhin, kept awake by the pain in his wounded leg, gazed with wide-open eyes at this strange apparition of a girl in a white chemise, dressing jacket, and nightcap. The valet's sleepy, frightened exclamation, "What do you want? What's the matter?" made Natásha approach more swiftly to what was lying in the corner. Horribly unlike a man as that body looked, she must see him. She passed the valet, the snuff fell from the candle wick, and she saw Prince Andrew clearly with his arms outside the quilt, and such as she had always seen him.

He was the same as ever, but the feverish color of his face, his glittering eyes rapturously turned toward her, and especially his neck, delicate as a child's, revealed by the turn-down collar of his shirt, gave him a peculiarly innocent, childlike look, such as she had never seen on him before. She went up to him and with a swift, flexible, youthful movement dropped on her knees.

He smiled and held out his hand to her.

Seven days had passed since Prince Andrew found himself in the ambulance station on the field of Borodinó. His feverish state and the inflammation of his bowels, which were injured, were in the doctor's opinion sure to carry him off. But on the seventh day he ate with pleasure a piece of bread with some tea, and the doctor noticed that his temperature was lower. He had regained consciousness that morning. The first night after they left Moscow had been fairly warm and he had remained in the *calèche*, but at Mytíshchi the wounded man himself asked to be taken out and given some tea.

They gave Prince Andrew some tea. He drank it eagerly, looking with feverish eyes at the door in front of him as if trying to understand and remember something.

"I don't want any more. Is Timókhin here?" he asked.

Timókhin crept along the bench to him.

"I am here, your excellency."

"How's your wound?"

"Mine, sir? All right. But how about you?"

Prince Andrew again pondered as if trying to remember something.

"Couldn't one get a book?" he asked.

"What book?"

"The Gospels. I haven't one."

The doctor promised to procure it for him and began to ask how he was feeling. Prince Andrew answered all his questions reluctantly but reasonably, and then said he wanted a bolster placed under him as he was uncomfortable and in great pain. The doctor and valet lifted the cloak with which he was covered and, making wry faces at the noisome smell of mortifying flesh that came from the wound, began examining that dreadful place. The doctor was very much displeased about something and made a change in the dressings, turning the wounded man over so that he groaned again and grew unconscious and delirious from the agony. He kept asking them to get him the book and put it under him.

After growing confused from pain while being carried into the hut Prince Andrew had again regained consciousness, and while drinking tea once more recalled all that had happened to him, and above all vividly remembered the moment at the ambulance station when, at the sight of the sufferings of a man he disliked, those new thoughts had come to him which promised him happiness. And those thoughts, though now vague and indefinite, again possessed his soul. He remembered that he had now a new source of happiness and that this happiness had something to do with the Gospels. That was why he asked for a copy of them.

His mind was not in a normal state. At times his brain suddenly began to work with a vigor, clearness, and depth it had never reached when he was in health, but suddenly in the midst of its work it would turn to some unexpected idea and he had not the strength to turn it back again.

"Yes, a new happiness was revealed to me of which man cannot be deprived," he thought as he lay in the semidarkness of the quiet hut, gazing fixedly before him with feverish, wide-open eyes. "A happiness lying beyond material forces, outside the material influences that act on man—a happiness of the soul alone, the happiness of loving. Every man can understand it, but to conceive it and enjoin it was possible only for God. But how did God enjoin that law? And why was the Son . . . ?"

And suddenly the sequence of these thoughts broke off, and Prince Andrew heard (without knowing whether it was a delusion or reality) a soft whispering voice incessantly and rhythmically repeating "piti-piti-piti," and then "ti-ti," and then again "piti-piti-piti," and "ti-ti" once more. But besides this there was something else of importance. It was something white by the door—the statue of a sphinx, which also oppressed him.

"Yes—love," he thought again quite clearly. "But not love which loves for something, for some quality, for some purpose, or for some reason, but the love which I—while dying —first experienced when I saw my enemy and yet loved him. I experienced that feeling of love which is the very essence of the soul and does not require an object. Now again I feel that bliss. To love one's neighbors, to love one's enemies, to love everything, to love God in all His manifestations. It is possible to love someone dear to you with human love, but an enemy can only be loved by divine love. That is why I experienced such joy when I felt that I loved that man. What has become of him? Is he alive? . . .

"When loving with human love one may pass from here to hatred, but divine love cannot change. No, neither death nor anything else can destroy it. It is the very essence of the soul. Yet how many people have I hated in my life? And of them all, I loved and hated none as I did her." And he vividly pictured to himself Natásha, not as he had done in the past with nothing but her charms which gave him delight, but for the first time picturing to himself her soul. And he understood her feelings, her sufferings, shame, and remorse. He now understood for the first time all the cruelty of his rejection of her, the cruelty of his rapture with her. "If only it were possible for me to see her once more! Just once, looking into those eyes to say . . ."

"Piti-piti-piti and ti-ti and piti-piti-piti boom!" And his attention was suddenly carried into another world, a world of reality and delirium.

But besides all this something creaked, there was a whiff

of fresh air, and a new white sphinx appeared, standing at the door. And that sphinx had the pale face and shining eyes of the very Natásha of whom he had just been thinking.

"Oh, how oppressive this continual delirium is," thought Prince Andrew, trying to drive that face from his imagination. But the face remained before him with the force of reality and drew nearer. Prince Andrew wished to return to that former world of pure thought, but he could not, and delirium drew him back into its domain. The soft whispering voice continued its rhythmic murmur, something oppressed him and stretched out, and the strange face was before him. Prince Andrew collected all his strength in an effort to recover his senses, he moved a little, and suddenly there was a ringing in his ears, a dimness in his eyes, and like a man plunged into water he lost consciousness. When he came to himself, Natásha, that same living Natásha whom of all people he most longed to love with this new pure divine love that had been revealed to him, was kneeling before him. He realized that it was the real living Natásha, and he was not surprised but quietly happy. Natásha, motionless on her knees (she was unable to stir), with frightened eyes riveted on him, was restraining her sobs. Her face was pale and rigid. Only in the lower part of it something quivered.

Prince Andrew sighed with relief, smiled, and held out his hand.

"You?" he said. "How fortunate!"

With a rapid but careful movement Natásha drew nearer to him on her knees and, taking his hand carefully, bent her face over it and began kissing it, just touching it lightly with her lips.

"Forgive me!" she whispered, raising her head and glancing at him. "Forgive me!"

"I love you," said Prince Andrew.

"Forgive . . . !"

"Forgive what?" he asked.

"Forgive me for what I ha-ve do-ne!" faltered Natásha in a scarcely audible, broken whisper, and began kissing his hand more rapidly, just touching it with her lips.

"I love you more, better than before," said Prince Andrew, lifting her face with his hand so as to look into her eyes.

Those eyes, filled with happy tears, gazed at him timidly,

compassionately and with joyous love. Natásha's thin pale face, with its swollen lips, was more than plain—it was dreadful. But Prince Andrew did not see that, he saw her shining eyes which were beautiful. They heard the sound of voices behind them.

Peter the valet, who was now wide awake, had roused the doctor. Timókhin, who had not slept at all because of the pain in his leg, had long been watching all that was going on, carefully covering his bare body with the sheet as he huddled up on his bench.

"What's this?" said the doctor, rising from his bed. "Please go away, madam!"

At that moment a maid sent by the countess, who had noticed her daughter's absence, knocked at the door.

Like a somnambulist aroused from her sleep Natásha went out of the room and, returning to her hut, fell sobbing on her bed.

From that time, during all the rest of the Rostóvs' journey, at every halting place and wherever they spent a night, Natásha never left the wounded Bolkónski, and the doctor had to admit that he had not expected from a young girl either such firmness or such skill in nursing a wounded man.

Dreadful as the countess imagined it would be should Prince Andrew die in her daughter's arms during the journey —as, judging by what the doctor said, it seemed might easily happen—she could not oppose Natásha. Though with the intimacy now established between the wounded man and Natásha the thought occurred that should he recover their former engagement would be renewed, no one—least of all Natásha and Prince Andrew—spoke of this: the unsettled question of life and death, which hung not only over Bolkónski but over all Russia, shut out all other considerations.

16

On the third of September Pierre awoke late. His head was aching, the clothes in which he had slept without undressing felt uncomfortable on his body, and his mind had a dim consciousness of something shameful he had done the day before. That something shameful was his yesterday's conversation with Captain Ramballe.

Pierre rose, rubbed his eyes, and seeing the pistol with an engraved stock which Gerásim had replaced on the writing table, he remembered where he was and what lay before him that very day.

"Am I not too late?" he thought. "No, probably *he* won't make his entry into Moscow before noon."

Pierre did not allow himself to reflect on what lay before him, but hastened to act.

After arranging his clothes, he took the pistol and was about to go out. It was difficult to hide such a big pistol even under his wide coat. He could not carry it unnoticed in his belt or under his arm. Besides, it had been discharged, and he had not had time to reload it. But as his chief aim consisted not in carrying out his design, but in proving to himself that he would not abandon his intention and was doing all he could to achieve it, Pierre hastily took the blunt jagged dagger in a green sheath which he had bought at the Súkharev market with the pistol, and hid it under his waistcoat.

Having tied a girdle over his coat and pulled his cap low on his head, Pierre went down the corridor, trying to avoid making a noise or meeting the captain, and passed out into the street.

The conflagration, at which he had looked with so much indifference the evening before, had greatly increased during the night. Moscow was on fire in several places.

Pierre's way led through side streets to the Povarskóy and from there to the church of St. Nicholas on the Arbát, where he had long before decided that the deed should be done. The gates of most of the houses were locked and the shutters up. The streets and lanes were deserted. The air was full of smoke and the smell of burning. At the gate of one house three Frenchmen, who were explaining something to some Russian who did not understand them, stopped Pierre asking if he did not know French.

Pierre shook his head and went on. He heard nothing and saw nothing of what went on around him. He carried his resolution within himself in terror and haste, like something dreadful and alien to him, for, after the previous night's experience, he was afraid of losing it. But he was not destined to bring his mood safely to his destination. And even had he not been hindered by anything on the way, his intention could not now have been carried out, for Napoleon had passed the Arbát more than four hours previously on his way from the Dorogomílov suburb to the Krémlin, and was now sitting in a very gloomy frame of mind in a royal study in the Krémlin, giving detailed and exact orders as to measures to be taken immediately to extinguish the fire, to prevent looting, and to reassure the inhabitants. But Pierre did not know this; he was entirely absorbed in what lay before him, and was tortured—as those are who obstinately undertake a task that is impossible for them not because of its difficulty but because of its incompatibility with their natures—by the fear of weakening at the decisive moment and so losing his self-esteem.

Though he heard and saw nothing around him he found his way by instinct and did not go wrong in the side streets that led to the Povarskóy.

As Pierre approached that street the smoke became denser and denser—he even felt the heat of the fire. As he was going along a footpath across a wide-open space adjoining the Povarskóy on one side and the gardens of Prince Gruzínski's house on the other, Pierre suddenly heard the desperate weeping of a woman close to him. He stopped as if awakening from a dream and lifted his head.

Pierre, relieved by a call to action, heeds the plea of the anguished wife of a civil servant to rescue her little daughter from their burning house. He discovers the child unharmed and is taking the girl to her parents when he is distracted by another call for help.

He did not find the civil servant or his wife where he had left them. He walked among the crowd with rapid steps, scanning the various faces he met. Involuntarily he noticed a Georgian or Armenian family consisting of a very handsome old man of Oriental type, wearing a new, cloth-covered, sheepskin coat and new boots, an old woman of similar type, and a young woman. That very young woman seemed to Pierre the perfection of Oriental beauty, with her sharply outlined, arched, black eyebrows and the extraordinarily soft, bright color of her long, beautiful, expressionless face. She was sitting on some bundles a little behind the old woman. Evidently she was aware of her beauty and fearful because of it. Her face struck Pierre and, hurrying along by the fence, he turned several times to look at her. When he had reached the fence, still without finding those he sought, he stopped and looked about him.

With the child in his arms his figure was now more conspicuous than before, and a group of Russians, both men and women, gathered about him.

"Have you lost anyone, my dear fellow? You're of the gentry yourself, aren't you? Whose child is it?" they asked him.

"Why, that must be the Anférovs," said an old deacon, addressing a pockmarked peasant woman. "Lord have mercy, Lord have mercy!" he added in his customary bass.

"The Anférovs? No," said the woman. "They left in the morning. That must be either Mary Nikoláevna's or the Ivánovs'!"

But Pierre was not listening. He had for some seconds been intently watching what was going on a few steps away. He was looking at the Armenian family and at two French soldiers who had gone up to them. One of these, a nimble little man, was wearing a blue coat tied round the waist with a rope. The other, whose appearance particularly struck Pierre, was a long, lank, round-shouldered, fair-haired man, slow in his movements and with an idiotic expression of face. He wore a woman's loose gown of frieze, blue trousers, and large torn Hessian boots.

"Here, take the child!" said Pierre peremptorily and hurriedly to the woman, handing the little girl to her. "Give her back to them, give her back!" he almost shouted, putting the child, who began screaming, on the ground, and again looking at the Frenchman and the Armenian family.

The old man was already sitting barefoot. The little Frenchman had secured his second boot and was slapping one boot against the other. The old man was saying something in a voice broken by sobs, but Pierre caught but a glimpse of this, his whole attention was directed to the Frenchman in the frieze gown who meanwhile, swaying slowly from side to side, had drawn nearer to the young woman and taking his hands from his pockets had seized her by the neck.

While Pierre was running the few steps that separated

him from the Frenchman, the tall marauder in the frieze gown was already tearing from her neck the necklace the young Armenian was wearing, and the young woman, clutching at her neck, screamed piercingly.

"Let that woman alone!" exclaimed Pierre hoarsely in a furious voice, seizing the soldier by his round shoulders and throwing him aside.

The soldier fell, got up, and ran away. But his comrade, throwing down the boots and drawing his sword, moved threateningly toward Pierre.

Pierre was in such a transport of rage that he remembered nothing and his strength increased tenfold. He rushed at the Frenchman and, before the latter had time to draw his sword, knocked him off his feet and hammered him with his fists. Shouts of approval were heard from the crowd around, and at the same moment a mounted patrol of French Uhlans appeared from round the corner. The Uhlans came up at a trot to Pierre and the Frenchman and surrounded them. Pierre remembered nothing of what happened after that. He only remembered beating someone and being beaten and finally feeling that his hands were bound and that a crowd of French soldiers stood around him and were searching him.

"Lieutenant, he has a dagger," were the first words Pierre understood.

"Ah, a weapon?" said the officer and turned to the soldier who had been arrested with Pierre. "All right, you can tell all about it at the court-martial." Then he turned to Pierre. "Do you speak French?"

Pierre looked around him with bloodshot eyes and did not reply. His face probably looked very terrible, for the officer said something in a whisper and four more Uhlans left the ranks and placed themselves on both sides of Pierre.

"Do you speak French?" the officer asked again, keeping at a distance from Pierre. "Call the interpreter."

"Ah, he looks very much like an incendiary," remarked the officer. "And ask him who he is," he added.

"Who are you?" asked the interpreter in poor Russian. "You must answer the chief."

"I will not tell you who I am. I am your prisoner—take me!" Pierre suddenly replied in French.

"Ah, ah!' muttered the officer with a frown. "Well then, march!"

The French patrol was one of those sent out through the various streets of Moscow by Durosnel's order to put a stop to the pillage, and especially to catch the incendiaries who, according to the general opinion which had that day originated among the higher French officers, were the cause of the conflagrations. After marching through a number of streets the patrol arrested five more Russian suspects: a small shopkeeper, two seminary students, a peasant, and a house serf, besides several looters. But of all these various suspected characters, Pierre was considered to be the most suspicious of all. When they had all been brought for the night to a large house on the Zúbov Rampart that was being used as a guardhouse, Pierre was placed apart under strict guard.

1812

■━━■■■━━■■■━━■■■━━■■■━━■

BOOK TWELVE

1

In Petersburg at that time a complicated struggle was being carried on with greater heat than ever in the highest circles, between the parties of Rumyántsev, the French, Márya Fëdorovna, the Tsarévich, and others, drowned as usual by the buzzing of the court drones. But the calm, luxurious life of Petersburg, concerned only about phantoms and reflections of real life, went on in its old way and made it hard, except by a great effort, to realize the danger and the difficult position of the Russian people.

At Anna Pávlovna's on the twenty-sixth of August, the very day of the battle of Borodinó, there was a soirée, the chief feature of which was to be the reading of a letter from His Lordship the Bishop when sending the Emperor an icon of the Venerable Sergius. It was regarded as a model of ecclesiastical, patriotic eloquence. Prince Vasíli himself, famed for his elocution, was to read it.

The news of the day in Petersburg was the illness of Countess Bezúkhova. She had fallen ill unexpectedly a few days previously, had missed several gatherings of which she was usually the ornament, and was said to be receiving no one, and instead of the celebrated Petersburg doctors who usually attended her had entrusted herself to some Italian doctor who was treating her in some new and unusual way.

They all knew very well that the enchanting countess' illness arose from an inconvenience resulting from marrying two husbands at the same time, and that the Italian's cure consisted in removing such inconvenience; but in Anna Pávlovna's presence no one dared to think of this or even appear to know it.

"You are speaking of the poor countess?" said Anna Pávlovna, coming up just then. "I sent to ask for news, and hear that she is a little better. Oh, she is certainly the most charming woman in the world," she went on, with a smile at her own enthusiasm. "We belong to different camps, but that does not prevent my esteeming her as she deserves. She is very unfortunate!" added Anna Pávlovna.

And during the awkward silence that ensued, Anna Pávlovna invited Prince Vasíli to the table and bringing him two candles and the manuscript begged him to begin. Everyone became silent.

"Most Gracious Sovereign and Emperor!" Prince Vasíli sternly declaimed, looking round at his audience as if to inquire whether anyone had anything to say to the contrary. But no one said anything. "Moscow, our ancient capital, the New Jerusalem, receives _her_ Christ"—he placed a sudden emphasis on the word _her_—"as a mother receives her zealous sons into her arms, and through the gathering mists, foreseeing the brilliant glory of thy rule, sings in exultation, 'Hosanna, blessed is he that cometh!' "

Prince Vasíli pronounced these last words in a tearful voice.

"What force! What a style!" was uttered in approval both of reader and of author.

Animated by that address Anna Pávlovna's guests talked for a long time of the state of the fatherland and offered various conjectures as to the result of the battle to be fought in a few days.

"You will see," said Anna Pávlovna, "that tomorrow, on the Emperor's birthday, we shall receive news. I have a favorable presentiment!"

Anna Pávlovna's presentiment was in fact fulfilled. Next day during the service at the palace church in honor of the Emperor's birthday, Prince Volkónski was called out of the church and received a dispatch from Prince Kutúzov. It was Kutúzov's report, written from Tatárinova on the day of the battle. Kutúzov wrote that the Russians had not retreated a step, that the French losses were much heavier than ours, and that he was writing in haste from the field of battle before collecting full information. It followed that there must have been a victory.

And at once, without leaving the church, thanks were rendered to the Creator for His help and for the victory.

"What did I tell you about Kutúzov?" Prince Vasíli now said with a prophet's pride. "I always said he was the only man capable of defeating Napoleon."

But next day no news arrived from the army and the public mood grew anxious. The courtiers suffered because of the suffering the suspense occasioned the Emperor.

Moreover, toward evening, as if everything conspired to make Petersburg society anxious and uneasy, a terrible piece of news was added. Countess Hélène Bezúkhova had suddenly died. Officially, at large gatherings, everyone said that Countess Bezúkhova had died of a terrible attack of angina pectoris, but in intimate circles details were mentioned of how the physician had prescribed small doses of a certain drug to produce a certain effect; but Hélène, tortured by the fact that the old count suspected her and that her husband to whom she had written (that wretched, profligate Pierre) had not replied, had suddenly taken a very large dose of the drug, and had died in agony before assistance could be rendered her. It was said that Prince Vasíli and the old count had turned upon the Italian, but the latter had produced such letters from the unfortunate deceased that they had immediately let the matter drop.

On the third day after Kutúzov's report a country gentleman arrived from Moscow, and news of the surrender of Moscow to the French spread through the whole town. This was terrible! What a position for the Emperor to be in! Kutúzov was a traitor, and Prince Vasíli during the visits of condolence paid to him on the occasion of his daughter's death said of Kutúzov, whom he had formerly praised (it was excusable for him in his grief to forget what he had said), that it was impossible to expect anything else from a blind and depraved old man.

As long as this news remained unofficial it was possible to doubt it, but the next day a communication was received from Count Rostopchín.

On receiving this dispatch the Emperor sent Prince Volkónski to Kutúzov with the following rescript:

"Prince Michael Ilariónovich! Since the twenty-ninth of August I have received no communication from you, yet on the first of September I received from the commander in chief of Moscow, via Yaroslávl, the sad news that you, with the army, have decided to abandon Moscow. You can yourself imagine the effect this news has had on me, and your silence increases my astonishment. I am sending this by Adjutant-General Prince Volkónski, to hear from you the situation of the army and the reasons that have induced you to make this melancholy decision."

Nine days after the abandonment of Moscow, a messenger from Kutúzov reached Petersburg with the official announcement of that event. This messenger was Michaud.

"Have you brought me sad news, Colonel?"

"Very sad, sire," replied Michaud, lowering his eyes with a sigh. "The abandonment of Moscow."

"Have they surrendered my ancient capital without a battle?" asked the Emperor quickly, his face suddenly flushing.

Michaud respectfully delivered the message Kutúzov had entrusted to him, which was that it had been impossible to fight before Moscow, and that as the only remaining choice was between losing the army as well as Moscow, or losing Moscow alone, the field marshal had to choose the latter.

The Emperor listened in silence, not looking at Michaud.

"Has the enemy entered the city?" he asked.

"Yes, sire, and Moscow is now in ashes. I left it all in flames," replied Michaud in a decided tone, but glancing at the Emperor he was frightened by what he had done.

The Emperor began to breathe heavily and rapidly, his lower lip trembled, and tears instantly appeared in his fine blue eyes.

But this lasted only a moment. He suddenly frowned, as if blaming himself for his weakness, and raising his head addressed Michaud in a firm voice:

"I see, Colonel, from all that is happening, that Providence requires great sacrifices of us. . . . I am ready to submit myself in all things to His will; but tell me, Michaud, how did you leave the army when it saw my ancient capital abandoned without a battle? Did you not notice discouragement? . . ."

"Sire, will you allow me to speak frankly as befits a loyal soldier?" he asked to gain time.

"Colonel, I always require it," replied the Emperor. "Conceal nothing from me, I wish to know absolutely how things are."

"Sire!" said Michaud with a subtle, scarcely perceptible smile on his lips, having now prepared a well-phrased reply, "sire, I left the whole army, from its chiefs to the lowest soldier, without exception in desperate and agonized terror . . ."

"How is that?" the Emperor interrupted him, frowning sternly. "Would misfortune make my Russians lose heart? . . . Never!"

Michaud had only waited for this to bring out the phrase he had prepared.

"Sire," he said, with respectful playfulness, "they are only afraid lest Your Majesty, in the goodness of your heart, should allow yourself to be persuaded to make peace. They are burning for the combat," declared this representative of the Russian nation, "and to prove to Your Majesty by the sacrifice of their lives how devoted they are. . . ."

"Ah!" said the Emperor reassured, and with a kindly gleam in his eyes, he patted Michaud on the shoulder. "You set me at ease, Colonel."

He bent his head and was silent for some time.

"Colonel Michaud, do not forget what I say to you here, perhaps we may recall it with pleasure someday . . . Napoleon or I," said the Emperor, touching his breast. "We can no longer both reign together. I have learned to know him, and he will not deceive me any more. . . ."

"Sire!" said he, "Your Majesty is at this moment signing the glory of the nation and the salvation of Europe!"

With an inclination of the head the Emperor dismissed him.

2

The more closely a man was engaged in the events then taking place in Russia the less did he realize their significance. In Petersburg and in the provinces at a distance from Moscow, ladies, and gentlemen in militia uniforms, wept for Russia and its ancient capital and talked of self-sacrifice and so on; but in the army which retired beyond Moscow there was little talk or thought of Moscow, and when they caught sight of its burned ruins no one swore to be avenged on the

French, but they thought about their next pay, their next quarters, of Matrëshka the vivandière, and like matters.

As the war had caught him in the service, Nicholas Rostóv took a close and prolonged part in the defense of his country, but did so casually, without any aim at self-sacrifice, and he therefore looked at what was going on in Russia without despair and without dismally racking his brains over it.

As he looked at the matter in this way, he learned that he was being sent to Vorónezh to buy remounts for his division, not only without regret at being prevented from taking part in the coming battle, but with the greatest pleasure—which he did not conceal and which his comrades fully understood.

A few days before the battle of Borodinó, Nicholas received the necessary money and warrants, and having sent some hussars on in advance, he set out with post horses for Vorónezh.

In the highest spirits Nicholas arrived at night at a hotel in Vorónezh, ordered things he had long been deprived of in camp, and next day, very clean-shaven and in a full-dress uniform he had not worn for a long time, went to present himself to the authorities.

From the commander of the militia he drove to the governor. The governor was a brisk little man, very simple and affable. He indicated the stud farms at which Nicholas might procure horses, recommended to him a horse dealer in the town and a landowner fourteen miles out of town who had the best horses, and promised to assist him in every way.

"You are Count Ilyá Rostóv's son? My wife was a great friend of your mother's. We are at home on Thursdays—today is Thursday, so please come and see us quite informally," said the governor, taking leave of him.

The landowner to whom Nicholas went was a bachelor, an old cavalry man, a horse fancier, a sportsman, the possessor of some century-old brandy and some old Hungarian wine, who had a snuggery where he smoked, and who owned some splendid horses.

In very few words Nicholas bought seventeen picked stallions for six thousand rubles—to serve, as he said, as samples of his remounts. After dining and taking rather too much of the Hungarian wine, Nicholas—having exchanged kisses with the landowner, with whom he was already on the friendliest terms—galloped back over abominable roads, in the brightest frame of mind, continually urging on the driver so as to be in time for the governor's party.

When he had changed, poured water over his head, and scented himself, Nicholas arrived at the governor's rather late, but with the phrase "better late than never" on his lips.

The society gathered together at the governor's was the best in Vorónezh.

As soon as Nicholas entered in his hussar uniform, diffusing around him a fragrance of perfume and wine, and had uttered the words "better late than never" and heard them repeated several times by others, people clustered around him; all eyes turned on him, and he felt at once that he had entered into his proper position in the province—that of a universal favorite: a very pleasant position, and intoxicatingly so after his long privations. At posting stations, at inns, and in the landowner's snuggery, maidservants had been flattered by his notice, and here too at the governor's party there were (as it seemed to Nicholas) an inexhaustible number of pretty young women, married and unmarried, impatiently awaiting his notice. Among these was the governor's wife herself, who welcomed Rostóv as a near relative and called him "Nicholas."

All the evening Nicholas paid attention to a blue-eyed, plump and pleasing little blonde, the wife of one of the provincial officials. Toward the end of the evening, however, as the wife's face grew more flushed and animated, the husband's became more and more melancholy and solemn, as though there were but a given amount of animation between them and as the wife's share increased the husband's diminished.

Nicholas sat leaning slightly forward in an armchair, bending closely over the blonde lady and paying her mythological compliments with a smile that never left his face.

The husband came up and sullenly asked his wife what she was talking about.

"Ah, Nikíta Iványch!" cried Nicholas, rising politely, and as if wishing Nikíta Iványch to share his joke, he began to tell him of his intention to elope with a blonde lady.

The husband smiled gloomily, the wife gaily. The governor's good-natured wife came up with a look of disapproval.

"Anna Ignátyevna wants to see you, Nicholas," said she, pronouncing the name so that Nicholas at once understood that Anna Ignátyevna was a very important person. "Come, Nicholas! You know you let me call you so?"

"Oh, yes, Aunt. Who is she?"

"Anna Ignátyevna Malvíntseva. She has heard from her niece how you rescued her. . . . Can you guess?"

"I rescued such a lot of them!" said Nicholas.

"Her niece, Princess Bolkónskaya. She is here in Vorónezh with her aunt. Oho! How you blush. Why, are . . . ?"

"Not a bit! Please don't, Aunt!"

"Very well, very well! . . . Oh, what a fellow you are!"

The governor's wife led him up to a tall and very stout old lady with a blue headdress, who had just finished her game of cards with the most important personages of the town. This was Malvíntseva, Princess Mary's aunt on her mother's side, a rich, childless widow who always lived in Vorónezh.

"Very pleased, *mon cher*," she said, holding out her hand to Nicholas. "Pray come and see me."

After a few words about Princess Mary and her late father, whom Malvíntseva had evidently not liked, and having asked what Nicholas knew of Prince Andrew, who also was evidently no favorite of hers, the important old lady dismissed Nicholas after repeating her invitation to come to see her.

Nicholas promised to come and blushed again as he bowed. At the mention of Princess Mary he experienced a feeling of shyness and even of fear, which he himself did not understand.

When he had parted from Malvíntseva, Nicholas wished to return to the dancing, but the governor's little wife placed her plump hand on his sleeve and, saying that she wanted to have a talk with him, led him to her sitting room, from which those who were there immediately withdrew so as not to be in her way.

"Do you know, dear boy," began the governor's wife with a serious expression on her kind little face, "that really would be the match for you: would you like me to arrange it?"

"Whom do you mean, Aunt?" asked Nicholas.

"I will make a match for you with the princess. . . . Do you want me to do it? I am sure your mother will be grateful to me. What a charming girl she is, really! And she is not at all so plain, either."

"Not at all," replied Nicholas as if offended at the idea. "As befits a soldier, Aunt, I don't force myself on anyone or refuse anything," he said before he had time to consider what he was saying.

"Well then, remember, this is not a joke!"

"Of course not!"

"But what nonsense I have been saying to the governor's wife!" thought Nicholas suddenly at supper. "She will really begin to arrange a match . . . and Sónya . . . ?" And on taking leave of the governor's wife, when she again smilingly said to him, "Well then, remember!" he drew her aside.

"But see here, to tell you the truth, Aunt . . ."

"What is it, my dear? Come, let's sit down here," said she.

Nicholas suddenly felt a desire and need to tell his most intimate thoughts (which he would not have told to his mother, his sister, or his friend) to this woman who was almost a stranger.

"You see, Aunt, Mamma has long wanted me to marry an heiress, but the very idea of marrying for money is repugnant to me."

"Oh yes, I understand," said the governor's wife.

"But Princess Bolkónskaya—that's another matter. I will tell you the truth. In the first place I like her very much, I feel drawn to her; and then, after I met her under such circumstances—so strangely, the idea often occurred to me: 'This is fate.' Especially if you remember that Mamma had long been thinking of it; but I had never happened to meet her before; somehow it had always happened that we did not meet. And as long as my sister Natásha was engaged to her brother it was of course out of the question for me to think of marrying her. And it must needs happen that I should meet her just when Natásha's engagement had been broken off . . . and then everything . . . So you see . . . I never told this to anyone and never will, only to you."

The governor's wife pressed his elbow gratefully.

"You know Sónya, my cousin? I love her, and promised to marry her, and will do so. . . . So you see there can be no question about—" said Nicholas incoherently and blushing.

"My dear boy, what a way to look at it! You know Sónya has nothing and you yourself say your Papa's affairs are in a very bad way. And what about your mother? It would kill her, that's one thing. And what sort of life would it be for Sónya—if she's a girl with a heart? Your mother in despair, and you all ruined. . . . No, my dear, you and Sónya ought to understand that."

Nicholas remained silent. It comforted him to hear these arguments.

"All the same, Aunt, it is impossible," he rejoined with a sigh, after a short pause. "Besides, would the princess have me? And besides, she is now in mourning. How can one think of it!"

"But you don't suppose I'm going to get you married at once? There is always a right way of doing things," replied the governor's wife.

"What a matchmaker you are, Aunt . . ." said Nicholas, kissing her plump little hand.

On reaching Moscow after her meeting with Rostóv, Princess Mary had found her nephew there with his tutor, and a letter from Prince Andrew giving her instructions how to get to her Aunt Malvíntseva at Vorónezh. She was sad, but in the depths of her soul she felt at peace—a peace arising from consciousness of having stifled those personal dreams and hopes that had been on the point of awaking within her and were related to her meeting with Rostóv.

The day after her party the governor's wife came to see Malvíntseva and, after discussing her plan with the aunt, remarked that though under present circumstances a formal betrothal was, of course, not to be thought of, all the same the young people might be brought together and could get to know one another. Malvíntseva expressed approval, and the governor's wife began to speak of Rostóv in Mary's presence. But Princess Mary experienced a painful rather than a joyful feeling—her mental tranquillity was destroyed, and desires, doubts, self-reproach, and hopes reawoke.

During the two days that elapsed before Rostóv called, Princess Mary continually thought of how she ought to behave to him. More than anything she feared lest the confusion she felt might overwhelm her and betray her as soon as she saw him.

But when on Sunday after church the footman announced in the drawing room that Count Rostóv had called, the princess showed no confusion, only a slight blush suffused her cheeks and her eyes lit up with a new and radiant light.

When Rostóv entered the room, the princess dropped her eyes for an instant, as if to give the visitor time to greet her aunt, and then just as Nicholas turned to her she raised her head and met his look with shining eyes. With a movement full of dignity and grace she half rose with a smile of pleasure, held out her slender, delicate hand to him, and began to speak in a voice in which for the first time new deep womanly notes vibrated.

From the moment she recognized that dear, loved face, a new life force took possession of her and compelled her to speak and act apart from her own will. From the time Rostóv entered, her face became suddenly transformed. All her inward labor, her dissatisfaction with herself, her sufferings, her strivings after goodness, her meekness, love, and self-sacrifice—all this now shone in those radiant eyes, in her delicate smile, and in every trait of her gentle face.

Rostóv saw all this as clearly as if he had known her whole life. He felt that the being before him was quite different from, and better than, anyone he had met before, and above all better than himself.

Their conversation was very simple and unimportant. She did not talk about her brother, diverting the conversation as soon as her aunt mentioned Andrew. Evidently she could speak of Russia's misfortunes with a certain artificiality, but her brother was too near her heart and she neither could nor would speak lightly of him. Nicholas noticed this, as he noticed every shade of Princess Mary's character with an observation unusual to him, and everything confirmed his conviction that she was a quite unusual and extraordinary being.

As at Tilsit Rostóv had not allowed himself to doubt that what everybody considered right was right, so now, after a short but sincere struggle between his effort to arrange his life by his own sense of justice, and in obedient submission to circumstances, he chose the latter and yielded to the power he felt irresistibly carrying him he knew not where. He knew that after his promise to Sónya it would be what he deemed base to declare his feelings to Princess Mary. And he knew that he would never act basely. But he also knew (or rather felt at the bottom of his heart) that by resigning himself now to the force of circumstances and to those who were guiding him, he was not only doing nothing wrong, but was doing something very very important—more important than anything he had ever done in his life.

The dreadful news of the battle of Borodinó, of our losses in killed and wounded, and the still more terrible news of the loss of Moscow reached Vorónezh in the middle of September. Princess Mary, having learned of her brother's wound only from the *Gazette* and having no definite news of him, prepared (so Nicholas heard, he had not seen her again himself) to set off in search of Prince Andrew.

When he received the news of the battle of Borodinó and the abandonment of Moscow, Rostóv was not seized with despair, anger, the desire for vengeance, or any feeling of that kind, but everything in Vorónezh suddenly seemed to him dull and tiresome, and he experienced an indefinite feeling of shame and awkwardness. Only in the regiment would everything again become clear to him. He made haste to finish buying the horses, and often became unreasonably angry with his servant and squadron quartermaster.

A few days before his departure a special thanksgiving, at which Nicholas was present, was held in the cathedral for the Russian victory. When the service was over the governor's wife beckoned him to her.

"Have you seen the princess?" she asked, indicating with a movement of her head a lady standing on the opposite side, beyond the choir.

Nicholas immediately recognized Princess Mary not so much by the profile he saw under her bonnet as by the feeling of solicitude, timidity, and pity that immediately overcame him.

Nicholas looked at her face with surprise. It was the same face he had seen before, there was the same general expression of refined, inner, spiritual labor, but now it was quite differently lit up. There was a pathetic expression of sorrow, prayer, and hope in it. As had occurred before when she was present, Nicholas went up to her and told her he had heard of her trouble and sympathized with his whole soul. As soon as she heard his voice a vivid glow kindled in her face, lighting up both her sorrow and her joy.

"There is one thing I wanted to tell you, Princess," said

Rostóv. "It is that if your brother, Prince Andrew Nikoláevich, were not living, it would have been at once announced in the *Gazette*, as he is a colonel."

The princess looked at him, not grasping what he was saying, but cheered by the expression of regretful sympathy on his face.

"And I have known so many cases of a splinter wound" (the *Gazette* said it was a shell) "either proving fatal at once or being very slight," continued Nicholas. "We must hope for the best, and I am sure . . ."

Princess Mary interrupted him.

"Oh, that would be so dread . . ." she began and, prevented by agitation from finishing, she bent her head with a movement as graceful as everything she did in his presence and, looking up at him gratefully, went out, following her aunt.

That evening Nicholas did not go out, but stayed at home to settle some accounts with the horse dealers. When he had finished that business it was already too late to go anywhere but still too early to go to bed, and for a long time he paced up and down the room, reflecting on his life, a thing he rarely did.

"She must be a wonderful woman. A real angel!" he said to himself. "Why am I not free? Why was I in such a hurry with Sónya?" And he involuntarily compared the two: the lack of spirituality in the one and the abundance of it in the other—a spirituality he himself lacked and therefore valued most highly. He tried to picture what would happen were he free. How he would propose to her and how she would become his wife. But no, he could not imagine that.

"How she prayed!" he thought. "It was plain that her whole soul was in her prayer. Yes, that was the prayer that moves mountains, and I am sure her prayer will be answered. Why don't I pray for what I want?" he suddenly thought. "What do I want? To be free, released from Sónya . . . She was right," he thought, remembering what the governor's wife had said: "Nothing but misfortune can come of marrying Sónya. Besides, I don't love her—not as I should. O, God! release me from this dreadful, inextricable position!" Softened by memories of Princess Mary he began to pray as he had not done for a long time. Tears were in his eyes and in his throat when the door opened and Lavrúshka came in with some papers.

"Blockhead! Why do you come in without being called?" cried Nicholas, quickly changing his attitude.

"From the governor," said Lavrúshka in a sleepy voice. "A courier has arrived and there's a letter for you."

"Well, all right, thanks. You can go!"

Nicholas took the two letters, one of which was from his mother and the other from Sónya. He recognized them by the handwriting and opened Sónya's first. He had read only a few lines when he turned pale and his eyes opened wide with fear and joy.

"No, it's not possible!" he cried aloud.

Unable to sit still he paced up and down the room holding the letter and reading it. He glanced through it, then read it again, and then again, and standing still in the middle of the room he raised his shoulders, stretching out his hands, with his mouth wide open and his eyes fixed. What he had just been praying for with confidence that God would hear him had come to pass.

This unexpected and, as it seemed to Nicholas, quite voluntary letter from Sónya freed him from the knot that fettered him and from which there had seemed no escape. She wrote that the last unfortunate events—the loss of almost the whole of the Rostóvs' Moscow property—and the countess' repeatedly expressed wish that Nicholas should marry Princess Bolkónskaya, together with his silence and coldness of late, had all combined to make her decide to release him from his promise and set him completely free.

"It would be too painful to me to think that I might be a cause of sorrow or discord in the family that has been so good to me," she wrote, "and my love has no aim but the happiness of those I love; so, Nicholas, I beg you to consider yourself free, and to be assured that, in spite of everything, no one can love you more than does

YOUR SÓNYA."

Both letters were written from Tróitsa. The other, from the countess, described their last days in Moscow, their departure, the fire, and the destruction of all their property. In this letter the countess also mentioned that Prince Andrew was among the wounded traveling with them; his state was very critical, but the doctor said there was now more hope. Sónya and Natásha were nursing him.

Next day Nicholas took his mother's letter and went to see Princess Mary. Neither he nor she said a word about what "Natásha nursing him" might mean, but thanks to this letter Nicholas suddenly became almost as intimate with the princess as if they were relations.

The following day he saw Princess Mary off on her journey to Yaroslávl, and a few days later left to rejoin his regiment.

Sónya's letter written from Tróitsa, which had come as an answer to Nicholas' prayer, was prompted by this: the thought of getting Nicholas married to an heiress occupied the old countess' mind more and more. The countess let no occasion slip of making humiliating or cruel allusions to Sónya.

But a few days before they left Moscow, moved and excited by all that was going on, she called Sónya to her and, instead of reproaching and making demands on her, tearfully implored her to sacrifice herself and repay all that the family had done for her by breaking off her engagement with Nicholas.

"I shall not be at peace till you promise me this."

Sónya burst into hysterical tears and replied through her sobs that she would do anything and was prepared for anything, but gave no actual promise and could not bring herself to decide to do what was demanded of her. She must sacrifice herself for the family that had reared and brought her up. To sacrifice herself for others was Sónya's habit. But in all her former acts of self-sacrifice she had been happily conscious that they raised her in her own esteem and in that of others, and so made her more worthy of Nicholas whom she loved more than anything in the world. But now they wanted her to sacrifice the very thing that constituted the whole reward for her self-sacrifice and the whole meaning of her life. And for the first time she felt bitterness against those who had been her benefactors only to torture her the more painfully. And for the first time Sónya felt that out of her pure, quiet love for Nicholas a passionate feeling was beginning to grow up which was stronger than principle, virtue, or religion. Under the influence of this feeling Sónya, whose life of dependence had taught her involuntarily to be secretive, having answered the countess in vague general terms, avoided talking with her and resolved to wait till she should see Nicholas, not in order to set him free but on the contrary at that meeting to bind him to her forever.

The bustle and terror of the Rostóvs' last days in Moscow stifled the gloomy thoughts that oppressed Sónya. She was glad to find escape from them in practical activity. But when she heard of Prince Andrew's presence in their house, despite her sincere pity for him and for Natásha, she was seized by a joyful and superstitious feeling that God did not intend her to be separated from Nicholas. She knew that Natásha loved no one but Prince Andrew and had never ceased to love him. She knew that being thrown together again under such terrible circumstances they would again fall in love with one another, and that Nicholas would then not be able to marry Princess Mary as they would be within the prohibited degrees of affinity.

At the Tróitsa monastery the Rostóvs first broke their journey for a whole day.

Three large rooms were assigned to them in the monastery hostelry, one of which was occupied by Prince Andrew. The wounded man was much better that day and Natásha was sitting with him. Sónya was there too, tormented by curiosity as to what Prince Andrew and Natásha were talking about. She heard the sound of their voices through the door. That door opened and Natásha came out, looking excited. Not noticing the monk, who had risen to greet her and was drawing back the wide sleeve on his right arm, she went up to Sónya and took her hand.

"Sónya, will he live?" she asked. "Sónya, how happy I am, and how unhappy! . . . Sónya, dovey, everything is as it used to be. If only he lives! He cannot . . . because . . . because . . . of . . ." and Natásha burst into tears.

"Yes! I knew it! Thank God!" murmured Sónya. "He will live."

They had an opportunity that day to send letters to the army, and the countess was writing to her son.

"Sónya!" said the countess, raising her eyes from her letter as her niece passed, "Sónya, won't you write to Nicholas?" She

spoke in a soft, tremulous voice, and in the weary eyes that
looked over her spectacles Sónya read all that the countess
meant to convey with these words. Those eyes expressed
entreaty, shame at having to ask, fear of a refusal, and readiness for relentless hatred in case of such refusal.

Sónya went up to the countess and, kneeling down, kissed
her hand.

"Yes, Mamma, I will write," said she.

Now that she knew that the renewal of Natásha's relations
with Prince Andrew would prevent Nicholas from marrying
Princess Mary, she was joyfully conscious of a return of that
self-sacrificing spirit in which she was accustomed to live and
loved to live. So with a joyful consciousness of performing a
magnanimous deed—interrupted several times by the tears
that dimmed her velvety black eyes—she wrote that touching
letter the arrival of which had so amazed Nicholas.

3

*Pierre is tried with others for incendiarism. He wit-
nesses the execution of five of his fellow prisoners by the
French and expects to be shot next, but at the last moment he is pardoned.*

After the execution Pierre was separated from
the rest of the prisoners and placed alone in a small, ruined,
and befouled church.

Toward evening a noncommissioned officer entered with two
soldiers and told him that he had been pardoned and would
now go to the barracks for the prisoners of war. Without understanding what was said to him, Pierre got up and went
with the soldiers. They took him to the upper end of the field,
where there were some sheds built of charred planks, beams,
and battens, and led him into one of them. In the darkness
some twenty different men surrounded Pierre. He looked at
them without understanding who they were, why they were
there, or what they wanted of him.

From the moment Pierre had witnessed those terrible murders committed by men who did not wish to commit them, it
was as if the mainspring of his life, on which everything de-

pended and which made everything appear alive, had suddenly been wrenched out and everything had collapsed into a heap of meaningless rubbish. Though he did not acknowledge it to himself, his faith in the right ordering of the universe, in humanity, in his own soul, and in God, had been destroyed. He felt that it was not in his power to regain faith in the meaning of life.

Sitting silent and motionless on a heap of straw against the wall, Pierre sometimes opened and sometimes closed his eyes. But as soon as he closed them he saw before him the dreadful face of the factory lad—especially dreadful because of its simplicity—and the faces of the murderers, even more dreadful because of their disquiet. And he opened his eyes again and stared vacantly into the darkness around him.

Beside him in a stooping position sat a small man of whose presence he was first made aware by a strong smell of perspiration which came from him every time he moved. This man was doing something to his legs in the darkness, and though Pierre could not see his face he felt that the man continually glanced at him. On growing used to the darkness Pierre saw that the man was taking off his leg bands, and the way he did it aroused Pierre's interest.

"You've seen a lot of trouble, sir, eh?" the little man suddenly said.

And there was so much kindliness and simplicity in his singsong voice that Pierre tried to reply, but his jaw trembled and he felt tears rising to his eyes. The little fellow, giving Pierre no time to betray his confusion, instantly continued in the same pleasant tones:

"Eh, lad, don't fret!" said he, in the tender singsong caressing voice old Russian peasant women employ. "Don't fret, friend—'suffer an hour, live for an age!' that's how it is, my dear fellow. And here we live, thank heaven, without offense. Among these folk, too, there are good men as well as bad," said he, and still speaking, he turned on his knees with a supple movement, got up, coughed, and went off to another part of the shed.

"Eh, you rascal!" Pierre heard the same kind voice saying at the other end of the shed. "So you've come, you rascal? She remembers. . . . Now, now, that'll do!"

And the soldier, pushing away a little dog that was jumping

up at him, returned to his place and sat down. In his hands he had something wrapped in a rag.

"Here, eat a bit, sir," said he, resuming his former respectful tone as he unwrapped and offered Pierre some baked potatoes. "We had soup for dinner and the potatoes are grand!"

Pierre had not eaten all day and the smell of the potatoes seemed extremely pleasant to him. He thanked the soldier and began to eat.

"And how did they arrest you, dear lad? At your house?"

"No, I went to look at the fire, and they arrested me there, and tried me as an incendiary."

"Where there's law there's injustice," put in the little man.

"And have you been here long?" Pierre asked as he munched the last of the potato.

"I? It was last Sunday they took me, out of a hospital in Moscow."

"Why, are you a soldier then?"

"Yes, we are soldiers of the Ápsheron regiment. I was dying of fever. We weren't told anything. There were some twenty of us lying there. We had no idea, never guessed at all."

"And do you feel sad here?" Pierre inquired.

"How can one help it, lad? My name is Platón, and the surname is Karatáev," he added, evidently wishing to make it easier for Pierre to address him. "They call me 'little falcon' in the regiment. How is one to help feeling sad? Moscow— she's the mother of cities. How can one see all this and not feel sad? But 'the maggot gnaws the cabbage, yet dies first'; that's what the old folks used to tell us," he added rapidly.

"What? What did you say?" asked Pierre.

"Who? I?" said Karatáev. "I say things happen not as we plan but as God judges," he replied, thinking that he was repeating what he had said before, and immediately continued:

"Well, and you, have you a family estate, sir? And a house? So you have abundance, then? And a housewife? And your old parents, are they still living?" he asked.

And though it was too dark for Pierre to see, he felt that a suppressed smile of kindliness puckered the soldier's lips as he put these questions. He seemed grieved that Pierre had no parents, especially that he had no mother.

He seated himself more comfortably and coughed, evidently preparing to tell a long story.

"Well, my dear fellow, I was still living at home," he began. "We had a well-to-do homestead, plenty of land, we peasants lived well and our house was one to thank God for. When Father and we went out mowing there were seven of us. We lived well. We were real peasants. It so happened . . ."

And Platón Karatáev told a long story of how he had gone into someone's copse to take wood, how he had been caught by the keeper, had been tried, flogged, and sent to serve as a soldier.

"Well, I think you must be sleepy," said he, and began rapidly crossing himself and repeating:

"Lord Jesus Christ have mercy on us and save us!" He then bowed to the ground, got up, sighed, and sat down again on his heap of straw. "That's the way. Lay me down like a stone, O God, and raise me up like a loaf," he muttered as he lay down, pulling his coat over him.

For a long time Pierre did not sleep, but lay with eyes open in the darkness, listening to the regular snoring of Platón who lay beside him, and he felt that the world that had been shattered was once more stirring in his soul with a new beauty and on new and unshakable foundations.

Twenty-three soldiers, three officers, and two officials were confined in the shed in which Pierre had been placed and where he remained for four weeks.

When Pierre remembered them afterwards they all seemed misty figures to him except Platón Karatáev, who always remained in his mind a most vivid and precious memory and the personification of everything Russian, kindly, and round. When Pierre saw his neighbor next morning at dawn the first impression of him, as of something round, was fully confirmed: Platón's whole figure—in a French overcoat girdled with a cord, a soldier's cap, and bast shoes—was round. His head was quite round, his back, chest, shoulders, and even his arms, which he held as if ever ready to embrace something, were rounded, his pleasant smile and his large, gentle brown eyes were also round.

Platón Karatáev must have been fifty, judging by his stories of campaigns he had been in, told as by an old soldier. He did not himself know his age and was quite unable to determine it. But his brilliantly white, strong teeth which showed in two unbroken semicircles when he laughed—as he often did— were all sound and good, there was not a gray hair in his beard or on his head, and his whole body gave an impression of suppleness and especially of firmness and endurance.

His face, despite its fine, rounded wrinkles, had an expression of innocence and youth, his voice was pleasant and musical. But the chief peculiarity of his speech was its directness and appositeness. It was evident that he never considered what he had said or was going to say, and consequently the rapidity and justice of his intonation had an irresistible persuasiveness.

His physical strength and agility during the first days of his imprisonment were such that he seemed not to know what fatigue and sickness meant. He could do everything, not very well but not badly. He baked, cooked, sewed, planed, and mended boots. He was always busy, and only at night allowed himself conversation—of which he was fond—and songs.

Having been taken prisoner and allowed his beard to grow, he seemed to have thrown off all that had been forced upon him—everything military and alien to himself—and had returned to his former peasant habits.

Karatáev had no attachments, friendships, or love, as Pierre understood them, but loved and lived affectionately with everything life brought him in contact with, particularly with man—not any particular man, but those with whom he happened to be. He loved his dog, his comrades, the French, and Pierre who was his neighbor, but Pierre felt that in spite of Karatáev's affectionate tenderness for him (by which he unconsciously gave Pierre's spiritual life its due) he would not have grieved for a moment at parting from him. And Pierre began to feel in the same way toward Karatáev.

To all the other prisoners Platón Karatáev seemed a most ordinary soldier. They called him "little falcon" or "Platósha," chaffed him good-naturedly, and sent him on errands. But to Pierre he always remained what he had seemed that first night: an unfathomable, rounded, eternal personification of the spirit of simplicity and truth.

4

When Princess Mary heard from Nicholas that her brother was with the Rostóvs at Yaroslávl she at once prepared to go there, in spite of her aunt's efforts to dissuade her —and not merely to go herself but to take her nephew with her. Whether it were difficult or easy, possible or impossible, she did not ask and did not want to know: it was her duty not only herself to be near her brother who was perhaps dying, but to do everything possible to take his son to him, and so she prepared to set off. That she had not heard from Prince Andrew himself, Princess Mary attributed to his being too weak to write or to his considering the long journey too hard and too dangerous for her and his son.

The last days of her stay in Vorónezh had been the happiest of her life. Her love for Rostóv no longer tormented or agitated her. It filled her whole soul, had become an integral part of herself, and she no longer struggled against it. She knew that she loved for the first and only time in her life and felt that she was beloved, and was happy in regard to it.

But this happiness on one side of her spiritual nature did not prevent her feeling grief for her brother with full force; on the contrary, that spiritual tranquillity on the one side made it the more possible for her to give full play to her feeling for her brother.

As always happens when traveling, Princess Mary thought only of the journey itself, forgetting its object. But as she approached Yaroslávl the thought of what might await her there —not after many days, but that very evening—again presented itself to her and her agitation increased to its utmost limit.

The carriage door was opened. On the left there was water —a great river—and on the right a porch. There were people at the entrance: servants, and a rosy girl with a large plait of black hair, smiling as it seemed to Princess Mary in an unpleasantly affected way. (This was Sónya.) Princess Mary ran up the steps. "This way, this way!" said the girl, with the same artificial smile, and the princess found herself in the hall facing an elderly woman of Oriental type, who came rapidly

484

to meet her with a look of emotion. She embraced Princess Mary and kissed her.

Despite her excitement, Princess Mary realized that this was the countess and that it was necessary to say something to her. Hardly knowing how she did it, she contrived to utter a few polite phrases in French in the same tone as those that had been addressed to her, and asked: "How is he?"

"The doctor says that he is not in danger," said the countess, but as she spoke she raised her eyes with a sigh, and her gesture conveyed a contradiction of her words.

"Where is he? Can I see him—can I?" asked the princess.

"One moment, Princess, one moment, my dear! Is this his son?" said the countess, turning to little Nicholas who was coming in with Dessalles. "There will be room for everybody, this is a big house. Oh, what a lovely boy!"

"This is my niece," said the count, introducing Sónya—"You don't know her, Princess?"

Princess Mary turned to Sónya and, trying to stifle the hostile feeling that arose in her toward the girl, she kissed her. But she felt oppressed by the fact that the mood of everyone around her was so far from what was in her own heart.

"Where is he?" she asked again, addressing them all.

"He is downstairs. Natásha is with him," answered Sónya, flushing. "We have sent to ask. I think you must be tired, Princess."

Tears of vexation showed themselves in Princess Mary's eyes. She turned away and was about to ask the countess again how to go to him, when light, impetuous, and seemingly buoyant steps were heard at the door. The princess looked around and saw Natásha coming in, almost running—that Natásha whom she had liked so little at their meeting in Moscow long since.

But hardly had the princess looked at Natásha's face before she realized that here was a real comrade in her grief, and consequently a friend. She ran to meet her, embraced her, and began to cry on her shoulder.

There was only one expression on her agitated face when she ran into the drawing room—that of love—boundless love for him, for her, and for all that was near to the man she loved; and of pity, suffering for others, and passionate desire to give herself entirely to helping them.

Princess Mary, with her acute sensibility, understood all

this at the first glance at Natásha's face, and wept on her shoulder with sorrowful pleasure.

"Come, come to him, Mary," said Natásha, leading her into the other room.

Princess Mary raised her head, dried her eyes, and turned to Natásha. She felt that from her she would be able to understand and learn everything.

"How has his whole illness gone? Is it long since he grew worse? When did this happen?" Princess Mary inquired.

Natásha told her that at first there had been danger from his feverish condition and the pain he suffered, but at Tróitsa that had passed and the doctor had only been afraid of gangrene. That danger had also passed.

"But two days ago *this* suddenly happened," said Natásha, struggling with her sobs. "I don't know why, but you will see what he is like."

"Is he weaker? Thinner?" asked the princess.

"No, it's not that, but worse. You will see. O, Mary, he is too good, he cannot, cannot live, because . . ."

When Natásha opened Prince Andrew's door with a familiar movement and let Princess Mary pass into the room before her, the princess felt the sobs rising in her throat. Hard as she had tried to prepare herself, and now tried to remain tranquil, she knew that she would be unable to look at him without tears.

The princess understood what Natásha had meant by the words: "two days ago *this* suddenly happened." She understood those words to mean that he had suddenly softened and that this softening and gentleness were signs of approaching death.

He was lying in a squirrel-fur dressing gown on a divan, surrounded by pillows. He was thin and pale. In one thin, translucently white hand he held a handkerchief, while with the other he stroked the delicate mustache he had grown, moving his fingers slowly. His eyes gazed at them as they entered.

On seeing his face and meeting his eyes Princess Mary's pace suddenly slackened, she felt her tears dry up and her sobs ceased. She suddenly felt guilty and grew timid on catching the expression of his face and eyes.

"But in what am I to blame?" she asked herself. And his cold, stern look replied: "Because you are alive and thinking of the living, while I . . ."

In the deep gaze that seemed to look not outwards but inwards there was an almost hostile expression as he slowly regarded his sister and Natásha.

He kissed his sister, holding her hand in his as was their wont.

"How are you, Mary? How did you manage to get here?" said he in a voice as calm and aloof as his look.

Had he screamed in agony, that scream would not have struck such horror into Princess Mary's heart as the tone of his voice.

"And have you brought little Nicholas?" he asked in the same slow, quiet manner and with an obvious effort to remember.

In his words, his tone, and especially in that calm, almost antagonistic look could be felt an estrangement from everything belonging to this world, terrible in one who is alive.

"There, you see how strangely fate has brought us together," said he, breaking the silence and pointing to Natásha. "She looks after me all the time."

Princess Mary heard him and did not understand how he could say such a thing. He, the sensitive, tender Prince Andrew, how could he say that, before her whom he loved and who loved him?

The conversation was cold and disconnected and continually broke off.

"And so you have met Count Nicholas, Mary?" Prince Andrew suddenly said, evidently wishing to speak pleasantly to them. "He wrote here that he took a great liking to you," he went on simply and calmly, evidently unable to understand all the complex significance his words had for living people. "If you liked him too, it would be a good thing for you to get married," he added rather more quickly, as if pleased at having found words he had long been seeking.

Princess Mary heard his words but they had no meaning for her, except as a proof of how far away he now was from everything living.

"Andrew, would you like . . ." Princess Mary suddenly said

in a trembling voice, "would you like to see little Nicholas? He is always talking about you!"

Prince Andrew smiled just perceptibly and for the first time, but Princess Mary, who knew his face so well, saw with horror that he did not smile with pleasure or affection for his son, but with quiet, gentle irony because he thought she was trying what she believed to be the last means of arousing him.

"Yes, I shall be very glad to see him. Is he quite well?"

When little Nicholas was brought into Prince Andrew's room he looked at his father with frightened eyes, but did not cry, because no one else was crying. Prince Andrew kissed him and evidently did not know what to say to him.

When Nicholas had been led away, Princess Mary again went up to her brother, kissed him, and unable to restrain her tears any longer began to cry.

He looked at her attentively.

"Is it about Nicholas?" he asked.

Princess Mary nodded her head, weeping.

"Mary, you know the Gosp . . ." but he broke off.

"What did you say?"

"Nothing. You mustn't cry here," he said, looking at her with the same cold expression.

When Princess Mary had left Prince Andrew she fully understood what Natásha's face had told her. She did not speak any more to Natásha of hopes of saving his life. She took turns with her beside his sofa, and did not cry any more, but prayed continually, turning in soul to that Eternal and Unfathomable, whose presence above the dying man was now so evident.

Not only did Prince Andrew know he would die, but he felt that he was dying and was already half dead. He was conscious of an aloofness from everything earthly and a strange and joyous lightness of existence. Without haste or agitation he awaited what was coming. That inexorable, eternal, distant, and unknown—the presence of which he had felt continually all his life—was now near to him and, by the strange lightness he experienced, almost comprehensible and palpable. . . .

But after the night in Mytíshchi when, half delirious, he had seen her for whom he longed appear before him and, having pressed her hand to his lips, had shed gentle, happy tears, love for a particular woman again crept unobserved into his heart and once more bound him to life. And joyful and agitating thoughts began to occupy his mind.

His illness pursued its normal physical course, but what Natásha referred to when she said: *"This* suddenly happened," had occurred two days before Princess Mary arrived. It was the last spiritual struggle between life and death, in which death gained the victory. It was the unexpected realization of the fact that he still valued life as presented to him in the form of his love for Natásha, and a last, though ultimately vanquished, attack of terror before the unknown.

It was evening. As usual after dinner he was slightly feverish, and his thoughts were preternaturally clear. Sónya was sitting by the table. He began to doze. Suddenly a feeling of happiness seized him.

"Ah, she has come!" thought he.

And so it was: in Sónya's place sat Natásha who had just come in noiselessly.

Since she had begun looking after him, he had always experienced this physical consciousness of her nearness. She was sitting in an armchair placed sideways, screening the light of the candle from him, and was knitting a stocking.

At the Tróitsa monastery they had spoken of the past, and he had told her that if he lived he would always thank God for his wound which had brought them together again, but after that they never spoke of the future.

"Can it or can it not be?" he now thought as he looked at her and listened to the light click of the steel needles. "Can fate have brought me to her so strangely only for me to die? . . . Is it possible that the truth of life has been revealed to me only to show me that I have spent my life in falsity? I love her more than anything in the world! But what am I to do if I love her?" he thought, and he involuntarily groaned, from a habit acquired during his sufferings.

On hearing that sound Natásha put down the stocking, leaned nearer to him, and suddenly, noticing his shining eyes, stepped lightly up to him and bent over him.

"You are not asleep?"

"No, I have been looking at you a long time. I felt you come in. No one else gives me that sense of soft tranquillity that you do . . . that light. I want to weep for joy."

Natásha drew closer to him. Her face shone with rapturous joy.

"Natásha, I love you too much! More than anything in the world."

"And I!"—She turned away for an instant. "Why too much?" she asked.

"Why too much? . . . Well, what do you think, what do you feel in your soul, your whole soul—shall I live? What do you think?"

"I am sure of it, sure!" Natásha almost shouted, taking hold of both his hands with a passionate movement.

He remained silent awhile.

"How good it would be!" and taking her hand he kissed it.

Natásha felt happy and agitated, but at once remembered that this would not do and that he had to be quiet.

"But you have not slept," she said, repressing her joy. "Try to sleep . . . please!"

Soon he really shut his eyes and fell asleep. He did not sleep long and suddenly awoke with a start and in a cold perspiration.

As he fell asleep he had still been thinking of the subject that now always occupied his mind—about life and death, and chiefly about death. He felt himself nearer to it.

"Love? What is love?" he thought.

"Love hinders death. Love is life. All, everything that I understand, I understand only because I love. Everything is, everything exists, only because I love. Everything is united by it alone. Love is God, and to die means that I, a particle of love, shall return to the general and eternal source." These thoughts seemed to him comforting. But they were only thoughts. He fell asleep.

He dreamed that he was lying in the room he really was in, but that he was quite well and unwounded. Many various, indifferent, and insignificant people appeared before him. Gradually, unnoticed, all these persons began to disappear and a single question, that of the closed door, superseded all else. He rose and went to the door to bolt and lock it. Everything depended on whether he was, or was not, in time to lock it. He went, and tried to hurry, but his legs refused to move and he knew he would not be in time to lock the door though he painfully strained all his powers. He was seized by an agonizing fear. And that fear was the fear of death. *It* stood behind the door.

His last superhuman efforts were vain and both halves of the door noiselessly opened. *It* entered, and it was *death*, and Prince Andrew died.

But at the instant he died, Prince Andrew remembered that he was asleep, and at the very instant he died, having made an effort, he awoke.

"Yes, it was death! I died—and woke up. Yes, death is an awakening!" And all at once it grew light in his soul and the veil that had till then concealed the unknown was lifted from his spiritual vision. He felt as if powers till then confined within him had been liberated, and that strange lightness did not again leave him.

When, waking in a cold perspiration, he moved on the divan, Natásha went up and asked him what was the matter. He did not answer and looked at her strangely, not understanding.

That was what had happened to him two days before Princess Mary's arrival. From that day, as the doctor expressed it, the wasting fever assumed a malignant character, but what the doctor said did not interest Natásha, she saw the terrible moral symptoms which to her were more convincing.

His last days and hours passed in an ordinary and simple way. Both Princess Mary and Natásha, who did not leave him, felt this.

They both saw that he was sinking slowly and quickly, deeper and deeper, away from them, and they both knew that this had to be so and that it was right.

When the last convulsions of the body, which the spirit was leaving, occurred, Princess Mary and Natásha were present.

"Is it over?" said Princess Mary when his body had for a few minutes lain motionless, growing cold before them. Natásha went up, looked at the dead eyes, and hastened to close them. She closed them but did not kiss them, but clung to that which reminded her most nearly of him—his body.

"Where has he gone? Where is he now? . . ."

When the body, washed and dressed, lay in the coffin on a table, everyone came to take leave of him and they all wept.

Little Nicholas cried because his heart was rent by painful perplexity. The countess and Sónya cried from pity for Natásha and because he was no more. The old count cried because he felt that before long, he, too, must take the same terrible step.

Natásha and Princess Mary also wept now, but not because of their own personal grief; they wept with a reverent and softening emotion which had taken possession of their souls at the consciousness of the simple and solemn mystery of death that had been accomplished in their presence.

1812

※━━━※※━━━━※※━━━━※※━━━━※※━━━━※

BOOK THIRTEEN

1

Tolstoy describes the flanking movement of the Russian forces beyond Moscow to the Kalúga road and the Tarútino battle, where Murat's forces are taken by surprise, and he insists that these two successful actions were, in the nature of things, inevitable and not the results of military foresight and careful planning. These actions, however, expose the weakness of the French and provide the shock which Napoleon's army awaited to begin its flight.

2

Napoleon enters Moscow after the brilliant victory *de la Moskowa;* there can be no doubt about the victory for the battlefield remains in the hands of the French. The Russians retreat and abandon their ancient capital. Moscow, abounding in provisions, arms, munitions, and incalculable wealth, is in Napoleon's hands. The Russian army, only half the strength of the French, does not make a single attempt to attack for a whole month. Napoleon's position is most brilliant. He can either fall on the Russian army with double its strength and destroy it; negotiate an advantageous peace, or in case of a refusal make a menacing move on Petersburg, or even, in the case of a reverse, return to Smolénsk or Vílna; or remain in Moscow; in short, no special genius would seem to be required to retain the brilliant position the French held at that time. For that, only very simple and easy steps were necessary: not to allow the troops to loot, to prepare winter clothing—of which there was sufficient in Moscow for the whole army—and methodically to collect the provisions, of which (according to the French historians) there were enough in Moscow to supply the whole army for six months. Yet Napoleon, that greatest of all geniuses, who the historians declare had control of the army, took none of these steps.

He not merely did nothing of the kind, but on the contrary he used his power to select the most foolish and ruinous of all the courses open to him. Of all that Napoleon might have done: wintering in Moscow, advancing on Petersburg or on Nízhni-Nóvgorod, or retiring by a more northerly or more southerly route (say by the road Kutúzov afterwards took), nothing more stupid or disastrous can be imagined than what he actually did. He remained in Moscow till October, letting the troops plunder the city; then, hesitating whether to leave a garrison behind him, he quitted Moscow, approached Kutúzov without joining battle, turned to the right and reached Málo-Yaroslávets, again without attempting to break through and take the road Kutúzov took, but retiring instead to Mozháysk along the devastated Smolénsk road. Nothing more stupid than that could have been devised, or more disastrous for the army, as the sequel showed. Had Napoleon's aim been to destroy his army, the most skillful strategist could hardly have devised any series of actions that would so completely have accomplished that purpose, independently of anything the Russian army might do.

Napoleon, the man of genius, did this! But to say that he destroyed his army because he wished to, or because he was very stupid, would be as unjust as to say that he had brought his troops to Moscow because he wished to and because he was very clever and a genius.

In both cases his personal activity, having no more force than the personal activity of any soldier, merely coincided with the laws that guided the event.

Tolstoy lists the things Napoleon did to preserve his army and consolidate his victory; such as his message to the inhabitants of Moscow to persuade them to cooperate; his proclamation to artisans, workmen, and peas-

*ants to carry on business as usual; and his messages to
Emperor Alexander to negotiate; and shows how all these
failed.*

But strange to say, all these measures, efforts, and plans—
which were not at all worse than others issued in similar circumstances—did not affect the essence of the matter but, like
the hands of a clock detached from the mechanism, swung
about in an arbitrary and aimless way without engaging the
cogwheels.

With reference to the military side—the pursuit of the
Russian army, about which Napoleon was so concerned, produced an unheard-of result. The French generals lost touch
with the Russian army of sixty thousand men.

With reference to diplomacy, all Napoleon's arguments as
to his magnanimity and justice proved useless; Alexander did
not receive these envoys and did not reply to their embassage.

With regard to legal matters, after the execution of the supposed incendiaries the rest of Moscow burned down.

With regard to administrative matters, the establishment
of a municipality did not stop the robberies and was only of
use to certain people who formed part of that municipality
and under pretext of preserving order looted Moscow or saved
their own property from being looted.

With reference to commerce, the proclamation to industrious workmen and to peasants evoked no response. There
were no industrious workmen, and the peasants caught the
commissaries who ventured too far out of town with the
proclamation and killed them.

Even philanthropy did not have the desired effect. The
French, collecting booty, cared only for gold. Not only was
the paper money valueless which Napoleon so graciously distributed to the unfortunate, but even silver lost its value in
relation to gold.

But the most amazing example of the ineffectiveness of the
orders given by the authorities at that time was Napoleon's
attempt to stop the looting and re-establish discipline.

The army, like a herd of cattle run wild and trampling un-
derfoot the provender which might have saved it from starva-
tion, disintegrated and perished with each additional day it
remained in Moscow. But it did not go away.

It began to run away only when suddenly seized by a panic caused by the capture of transport trains on the Smolénsk road, and by the battle of Tarútino. The news of that battle of Tarútino, unexpectedly received by Napoleon at a review, evoked in him a desire to punish the Russians (Thiers says), and he issued the order for departure which the whole army was demanding.

Fleeing from Moscow the soldiers took with them everything they had stolen. Napoleon gazed at the *calèches* and carriages in which soldiers were riding and remarked that it was a very good thing, as those vehicles could be used to carry provisions, the sick, and the wounded.

The plight of the whole army resembled that of a wounded animal which feels it is perishing and does not know what it is doing. To study the skillful tactics and aims of Napoleon and his army from the time it entered Moscow till it was destroyed is like studying the dying leaps and shudders of a mortally wounded animal.

During the whole of that period Napoleon, who seems to us to have been the leader of all these movements—as the figurehead of a ship may seem to a savage to guide the vessel—acted like a child who, holding a couple of strings inside a carriage, thinks he is driving it.

3

Early in the morning of the sixth of October Pierre went out of the shed, and on returning stopped by the door to play with a little blue-gray dog, with a long body and short bandy legs, that jumped about him. This little dog lived in their shed, sleeping beside Karatáev at night.

Pierre's attire by now consisted of a dirty torn shirt (the only remnant of his former clothing), a pair of soldier's trousers which by Karatáev's advice he tied with string round the ankles for warmth, and a peasant coat and cap. Physically he had changed much during this time. He no longer seemed stout, though he still had the appearance of solidity and strength hereditary in his family. A beard and mustache covered the lower part of his face, and a tangle of hair, infested with lice, curled round his head like a cap. The look of his eyes was resolute, calm, and animatedly alert, as never before. The former slackness which had shown itself even in his eyes was now replaced by an energetic readiness for action and resistance. His feet were bare.

Pierre first looked down the field across which vehicles and horsemen were passing that morning, then into the distance across the river, then at the dog who was pretending to be in earnest about biting him, and then at his bare feet which he placed with pleasure in various positions, moving his dirty thick big toes. Every time he looked at his bare feet a smile of animated self-satisfaction flitted across his face. The sight of them reminded him of all he had experienced and learned during these weeks and this recollection was pleasant to him.

A French corporal, with coat unbuttoned in a homely way, a skullcap on his head, and a short pipe in his mouth, came from behind a corner of the shed and approached Pierre with a friendly wink.

"What sunshine, Monsieur Kirill" (Their name for Pierre.) "Eh? Just like spring!"

And the corporal leaned against the door and offered Pierre his pipe, though whenever he offered it Pierre always declined it.

"To be on the march in such weather . . ." he began.

Pierre inquired what was being said about leaving, and the corporal told him that nearly all the troops were starting and there ought to be an order about the prisoners that day. Sokolóv, one of the soldiers in the shed with Pierre, was dying, and Pierre told the corporal that something should be done about him. The corporal replied that Pierre need not worry about that as they had an ambulance and a permanent hospital and arrangements would be made for the sick, and that in general everything that could happen had been foreseen by the authorities.

"Besides, Monsieur Kiril, you have only to say a word to the captain, you know. He is a man who never forgets anything. Speak to the captain when he makes his round, he will do anything for you."

(The captain of whom the corporal spoke often had long chats with Pierre and showed him all sorts of favors.)

Four weeks had passed since Pierre had been taken prisoner and though the French had offered to move him from the men's to the officers' shed, he had stayed in the shed where he was first put.

In burned and devastated Moscow Pierre experienced almost the extreme limits of privation a man can endure; but thanks to his physical strength and health, of which he had till then been unconscious, and thanks especially to the fact that the privations came so gradually that it was impossible to say when they began, he endured his position not only lightly but joyfully. And just at this time he obtained the tranquillity and ease of mind he had formerly striven in vain to reach. He had long sought in different ways that tranquillity of mind, that inner harmony which had so impressed him in the soldiers at the battle of Borodinó. He had sought it in philanthropy, in Freemasonry, in the dissipations of town life, in wine, in heroic feats of self-sacrifice, and in romantic love for Natásha; he had sought it by reasoning—and all these quests and experiments had failed him. And now without thinking about it he had found that peace and inner harmony only through the horror of death, through privation, and through what he recognized in Karatáev.

Those dreadful moments he had lived through at the executions had as it were forever washed away from his imagination and memory the agitating thoughts and feelings that had formerly seemed so important. It did not now occur to him to think of Russia, or the war, or politics, or Napoleon. It was plain to him that all these things were no business of his, and that he was not called on to judge concerning them and therefore could not do so. "Russia and summer weather are not bound together," he thought, repeating words of Karatáev's which he found strangely consoling. His intention of killing Napoleon and his calculations of the cabalistic number of the beast of the Apocalypse now seemed to him meaningless and even ridiculous. His anger with his wife and anxiety that his name should not be smirched now seemed not merely trivial but even amusing. What concern was it of his that somewhere or other that woman was leading the life she preferred? What did it matter to anybody, and especially to him, whether or not they found out that their prisoner's name was Count Bezúkhov?

All Pierre's daydreams now turned on the time when he would be free. Yet subsequently, and for the rest of his life, he thought and spoke with enthusiasm of that month of captivity, of those irrecoverable, strong, joyful sensations, and chiefly of the complete peace of mind and inner freedom which he experienced only during those weeks.

The French evacuation began on the night between the sixth and seventh of October: kitchens and sheds were dismantled, carts loaded, and troops and baggage trains started.

At seven in the morning a French convoy in marching trim, wearing shakos and carrying muskets, knapsacks, and enormous sacks, stood in front of the sheds, and animated French talk mingled with curses sounded all along the lines.

Pierre, girt with a rope round his waist and wearing shoes Karatáev had made for him from some leather a French soldier had torn off a tea chest and brought to have his boots mended with, went up to the sick man and squatted down beside him.

"You know, Sokolóv, they are not all going away! They have a hospital here. You may be better off than we others," said Pierre.

"O Lord! Oh, it will be the death of me! O Lord!" moaned the man in a louder voice.

"I'll go and ask them again directly," said Pierre, rising and going to the door of the shed.

Just as Pierre reached the door, the corporal who had offered him a pipe the day before came up to it with two soldiers. The corporal and soldiers were in marching kit with knapsacks and shakos that had metal straps, and these changed their familiar faces.

The corporal came, according to orders, to shut the door. The prisoners had to be counted before being let out.

"Corporal, what will they do with the sick man? . . ." Pierre began.

But even as he spoke he began to doubt whether this was the corporal he knew or a stranger, so unlike himself did the corporal seem at that moment. Moreover, just as Pierre was speaking a sharp rattle of drums was suddenly heard from both sides. The corporal frowned at Pierre's words and, uttering some meaningless oaths, slammed the door. The shed became semidark, and the sharp rattle of the drums on two sides drowned the sick man's groans.

"There it is! . . . *It* again! . . ." said Pierre to himself, and an involuntary shudder ran down his spine. In the corporal's changed face, in the sound of his voice, in the stirring and deafening noise of the drums, he recognized that mysterious, callous force which compelled people against their will to kill their fellow men—that force the effect of which he had witnessed during the executions.

When that door was opened and the prisoners, crowding against one another like a flock of sheep, squeezed into the exit, Pierre pushed his way forward and approached that very captain who as the corporal had assured him was ready to do anything for him.

Pierre told him about the sick man.

"He'll manage to walk, devil take him!" said the captain. "Pass on, pass on!" he continued without looking at Pierre.

"But he is dying," Pierre again began.

"Be so good . . ." shouted the captain, frowning angrily.

"*Dram-da-da-dam, dam-dam* . . ." rattled the drums, and Pierre understood that this mysterious force completely controlled these men and that it was now useless to say any more.

The officer prisoners were separated from the soldiers and told to march in front. There were about thirty officers, with Pierre among them, and about three hundred men.

Through the cross streets of the Khamóvniki quarter the prisoners marched, followed only by their escort and the vehicles and wagons belonging to that escort, but when they reached the supply stores they came among a huge and closely packed train of artillery mingled with private vehicles.

At the bridge they all halted, waiting for those in front to get across. From the bridge they had a view of endless lines of moving baggage trains before and behind them.

From all sides, like the roar of the sea, were heard the rattle of wheels, the tramp of feet, and incessant shouts of anger and abuse. Pierre stood pressed against the wall of a charred house, listening to that noise which mingled in his imagination with the roll of the drums.

To get a better view, several officers climbed onto the wall of the half-burned house against which Pierre was leaning.

"What crowds! Just look at the crowds! . . . They've loaded goods even on the cannon! Look there, those are furs!" they exclaimed. "Just see what the blackguards have looted. . . . There! See what that one has behind in the cart. . . . Why, those are settings taken from some icons, by heaven! . . . Oh, the rascals! . . . See how that fellow has loaded himself up, he can hardly walk! Good Lord, they've even grabbed those chaises! . . . See that fellow there sitting on the trunks. . . . Heavens! They're fighting."

From the moment Pierre had recognized the appearance of the mysterious force nothing had seemed to him strange or dreadful. All that he now witnessed scarcely made an impression on him—as if his soul, making ready for a hard struggle, refused to receive impressions that might weaken it.

They marched very quickly, without resting, and halted only when the sun began to set. The baggage carts drew up close together and the men began to prepare for their night's rest. They all appeared angry and dissatisfied. For a long time, oaths, angry shouts, and fighting could be heard from all sides.

During this halt the escort treated the prisoners even worse than they had done at the start. It was here that the prisoners for the first time received horseflesh for their meat ration.

From the officer down to the lowest soldier they all showed what seemed like personal spite against each of the prisoners, in unexpected contrast to their former friendly relations.

This spite increased still more when, on calling over the roll of prisoners, it was found that in the bustle of leaving Moscow one Russian soldier, who had pretended to suffer from colic, had escaped. Pierre saw a Frenchman beat a Russian soldier cruelly for straying too far from the road, and heard his friend the captain reprimand and threaten to court-martial a noncommissioned officer on account of the escape of the Russian. To the noncommissioned officer's excuse that the prisoner was ill and could not walk, the officer replied that the order was to shoot those who lagged behind. Pierre felt that that fatal force which had crushed him during the executions, but which he had not felt during his imprisonment, now again controlled his existence. It was terrible, but he felt that in proportion to the efforts of that fatal force to crush him, there grew and strengthened in his soul a power of life independent of it.

4

In the early days of October another envoy came to Kutúzov with a letter from Napoleon proposing peace and falsely dated from Moscow, though Napoleon was already not far from Kutúzov on the old Kalúga road. Kutúzov replied to this letter as he had done to the one formerly brought by Lauriston, saying that there could be no question of peace.

Soon after that a report was received from Dórokhov's guerrilla detachment operating to the left of Tarútino that troops of Broussier's division had been seen at Formínsk and that being separated from the rest of the French army they might easily be destroyed. The soldiers and officers again demanded action. Generals on the staff, excited by the memory of the easy victory at Tarútino, urged Kutúzov to carry out Dórokhov's suggestion. Kutúzov did not consider any offensive necessary. The result was a compromise which was inevitable: a small detachment was sent to Formínsk to attack Broussier.

By a strange coincidence, this task, which turned out to be a most difficult and important one, was entrusted to Dokhtúrov —that same modest little Dokhtúrov whom no one had described to us as drawing up plans of battles, dashing about in front of regiments, showering crosses on batteries, and so on, and who was thought to be and was spoken of as undecided and undiscerning—but whom we find commanding wherever the position was most difficult all through the Russo-French wars from Austerlitz to the year 1813. Many heroes have been described to us in verse and prose, but of Dokhtúrov scarcely a word has been said.

It was Dokhtúrov again whom they sent to Formínsk and from there to Málo-Yaroslávets, the place where the last battle with the French was fought and where the obvious disintegration of the French army began; and we are told of many geniuses and heroes of that period of the campaign, but of Dokhtúrov nothing or very little is said and that dubiously. And this silence about Dokhtúrov is the clearest testimony to his merit.

On the tenth of October when Dokhtúrov had gone halfway to Formínsk and stopped at the village of Aristóvo, preparing faithfully to execute the orders he had received, the whole French army having, in its convulsive movement, reached Murat's position apparently in order to give battle—suddenly without any reason turned off to the left onto the new Kalúga road and began to enter Formínsk, where only Broussier had been till then. At that time Dokhtúrov had under his command, besides Dórokhov's detachment, the two small guerrilla detachments of Figner and Seslávin.

On the evening of October 11 Seslávin came to the Aristóvo headquarters with a French guardsman he had captured. The prisoner said that the troops that had entered Formínsk that day were the vanguard of the whole army, that Napoleon was there and the whole army had left Moscow four days previously. Dokhtúrov was unwilling to undertake any action, as it was not clear to him now what he ought to do. He had been ordered to attack Formínsk. But only Broussier had been there at that time and now the whole French army was there. Ermólov wished to act on his own judgment, but Dokhtúrov insisted that he must have Kutúzov's instructions. So it was decided to send a dispatch to the staff.

For this purpose a capable officer, Bolkhovítinov, was chosen, who was to explain the whole affair by word of mouth, besides delivering a written report. Toward midnight Bolkhovítinov, having received the dispatch and verbal instructions, galloped off to the General Staff accompanied by a Cossack with spare horses.

It was a warm, dark, autumn night. It had been raining for four days. Having changed horses twice and galloped twenty miles in an hour and a half over a sticky, muddy road, Bolkhovítinov reached Litashëvka after one o'clock at night. Dismounting at a cottage on whose wattle fence hung a signboard, GENERAL STAFF, and throwing down his reins, he entered a dark passage.

"The general on duty, quick! It's very important!" said he to someone who had risen and was sniffing in the dark passage.

While listening to the officer's report Konovnítsyn broke the seal and read the dispatch.

Konovnítsyn had understood at once that the news brought was of great importance and that no time must be lost.

Peter Petróvich Konovnítsyn, like Dokhtúrov, seems to have been included merely for propriety's sake in the list of the so-called heroes of 1812—the Barclays, Raévskis, Ermólovs, Plátovs, and Milorádoviches. Like Dokhtúrov he had the reputation of being a man of very limited capacity and information, and like Dokhtúrov he never made plans of battle but was always found where the situation was most difficult.

Coming out of the hut into the damp, dark night Konovnítsyn frowned—partly from an increased pain in his head and partly at the unpleasant thought that occurred to him, of how all that nest of influential men on the staff would be stirred up by this news, especially Bennigsen, who ever since Tarútino had been at daggers drawn with Kutúzov; and how they would make suggestions, quarrel, issue orders, and rescind them. And this premonition was disagreeable to him though he knew it could not be helped.

And in fact Toll, to whom he went to communicate the news, immediately began to expound his plans to a general sharing his quarters, until Konovnítsyn, who listened in weary silence, reminded him that they must go to see his Highness.

Kutúzov like all old people did not sleep much at night. He often fell asleep unexpectedly in the daytime, but at night, lying on his bed without undressing, he generally remained awake thinking.

So he lay now on his bed, supporting his large, heavy, scarred head on his plump hand, with his one eye open, meditating and peering into the darkness.

"They must understand that we can only lose by taking the offensive. Patience and time are my warriors, my champions," thought Kutúzov. Like an experienced sportsman he knew that the beast was wounded, and wounded as only the whole strength of Russia could have wounded it, but whether it was mortally wounded or not was still an undecided question.

On the night of the eleventh of October he lay leaning on his arm and thinking of that.

There was a stir in the next room and he heard the steps of Toll, Konovnítsyn, and Bolkhovítinov.

"Eh, who's there? Come in, come in! What news?" the field marshal called out to them.

While a footman was lighting a candle, Toll communicated the substance of the news.

"Who brought it?" asked Kutúzov with a look which, when the candle was lit, struck Toll by its cold severity.

"There can be no doubt about it, your Highness."

"Call him in, call him here."

Kutúzov sat up with one leg hanging down from the bed and his big paunch resting against the other which was doubled under him. He screwed up his seeing eye to scrutinize the messenger more carefully, as if wishing to read in his face what preoccupied his own mind.

"Tell me, tell me, friend," said he to Bolkhovítinov in his low, aged voice, as he pulled together the shirt which gaped open on his chest, "come nearer—nearer. What news have you brought me? Eh? That Napoleon has left Moscow? Are you sure? Eh?"

Bolkhovítinov gave a detailed account from the beginning of all he had been told to report.

"Speak quicker, quicker! Don't torture me!" Kutúzov interrupted him.

Bolkhovítinov told him everything and was then silent, awaiting instructions. Toll was beginning to say something but Kutúzov checked him. He tried to say something, but his face suddenly puckered and wrinkled; he waved his arm at Toll and turned to the opposite side of the room, to the corner darkened by the icons that hung there.

"O Lord, my Creator, Thou hast heard our prayer . . ." said he in a tremulous voice with folded hands. "Russia is saved. I thank Thee, O Lord!" and he wept.

From the time he received this news to the end of the campaign all Kutúzov's activity was directed toward restraining his troops, by authority, by guile, and by entreaty, from useless attacks, maneuvers, or encounters with the perishing enemy. Dokhtúrov went to Málo-Yaroslávets, but Kutúzov lingered with the main army and gave orders for the evacuation of Kalúga—a retreat beyond which town seemed to him quite possible.

Everywhere Kutúzov retreated, but the enemy without waiting for his retreat fled in the opposite direction.

Napoleon's historians describe to us his skilled maneuvers at Tarútino and Málo-Yaroslávets, and make conjectures as to what would have happened had Napoleon been in time to penetrate into the rich southern provinces.

But not to speak of the fact that nothing prevented him from advancing into those southern provinces (for the Russian army did not bar his way), the historians forget that nothing could have saved his army, for then already it bore within itself the germs of inevitable ruin.

So it came about that at the council at Málo-Yaroslávets, when the generals pretending to confer together expressed various opinions, all mouths were closed by the opinion uttered by the simple-minded soldier General Mouton who, speaking last, said what they all felt: that the one thing needful was to get away as quickly as possible; and no one, not even Napoleon, could say anything against that truth which they all recognized.

The day after the council at Málo-Yaroslávets Napoleon rode out early in the morning amid the lines of his army with his suite of marshals and an escort, on the pretext of inspecting the army and the scene of the previous and of the impending battle. Some Cossacks on the prowl for booty fell in with the Emperor and very nearly captured him. If the Cossacks did not capture Napoleon then, what saved him was the very thing that was destroying the French army, the booty on which the Cossacks fell. Here as at Tarútino they went after plunder, leaving the men. Disregarding Napoleon they rushed after the plunder and Napoleon managed to escape.

When *les enfants du Don* might so easily have taken the Emperor himself in the midst of his army, it was clear that there was nothing for it but to fly as fast as possible along the nearest, familiar road. Napoleon with his forty-year-old stomach understood that hint, not feeling his former agility and boldness, and under the influence of the fright the Cossacks had given him he at once agreed with Mouton and issued orders—as the historians tell us—to retreat by the Smolénsk road.

Coming out onto the highroad the French fled with surprising energy and unheard-of rapidity toward the goal they had fixed on. Besides the common impulse which bound the whole crowd of French into one mass and supplied them with a certain energy, there was another cause binding them together—their great numbers. As with the physical law of gravity, their enormous mass drew the individual human atoms to itself. In their hundreds of thousands they moved like a whole nation.

Each of them desired nothing more than to give himself up as a prisoner to escape from all this horror and misery; but on the one hand the force of this common attraction to Smolénsk, their goal, drew each of them in the same direction; on the other hand an army corps could not surrender to a company, and though the French availed themselves of every convenient opportunity to detach themselves and to surrender on the slightest decent pretext, such pretexts did not always occur.

When the flight of the French army along the Smolénsk road became well defined, what Konovnítsyn had foreseen on the night of the eleventh of October began to occur. The superior officers all wanted to distinguish themselves, to cut off, to seize, to capture, and to overthrow the French, and all clamored for action.

Kutúzov alone used all his power (and such power is very limited in the case of any commander in chief) to prevent an attack.

He could not tell them what we say now: "Why fight, why block the road, losing our own men and inhumanly slaughtering unfortunate wretches? What is the use of that, when a third of their army has melted away on the road from Moscow to Vyázma without any battle?"

Ermólov, Milorádovich, Plátov, and others in proximity to the French near Vyázma could not resist their desire to cut off and break up two French corps, and by way of reporting their intention to Kutúzov they sent him a blank sheet of paper in an envelope.

And try as Kutúzov might to restrain the troops, our men attacked, trying to bar the road. Infantry regiments, we are told, advanced to the attack with music and with drums beating, and killed and lost thousands of men.

But they did not cut off or overthrow anybody and the French army, closing up more firmly at the danger, continued, while steadily melting away, to pursue its fatal path to Smolénsk.

1812

❙━━❙❙❙━━❙❙━━❙❙❙━━❙❙━━❙

BOOK FOURTEEN

1

The battle of Borodinó, with the occupation of Moscow that followed it and the flight of the French without further conflicts, is one of the most instructive phenomena in history. An army gains a victory, and at once the rights of the conquering nation have increased to the detriment of the defeated. An army has suffered defeat, and at once a people loses its rights in proportion to the severity of the reverse, and if its army suffers a complete defeat the nation is quite subjugated.

So according to history it has been found from the most ancient times, and so it is to our own day. All Napoleon's wars serve to confirm this rule. In proportion to the defeat of the Austrian army Austria loses its rights, and the rights and the strength of France increase. The victories of the French at Jena and Auerstädt destroy the independent existence of Prussia.

But then, in 1812, the French gain a victory near Moscow. Moscow is taken and after that, with no further battles, it is not Russia that ceases to exist, but the French army of six hundred thousand, and then Napoleonic France itself. To strain the facts to fit the rules of history: to say that the field of battle at Borodinó remained in the hands of the Russians, or that after Moscow there were other battles that destroyed Napoleon's army, is impossible.

The period of the campaign of 1812 from the battle of Borodinó to the expulsion of the French proved that the winning of a battle does not produce a conquest and is not even an invariable indication of conquest; it proved that the force

509

which decides the fate of peoples lies not in the conquerors, nor even in armies and battles, but in something else.

That unknown quantity is the spirit of the army, that is to say, the greater or lesser readiness to fight and face danger felt by all the men composing an army, quite independently of whether they are, or are not, fighting under the command of a genius, in two- or three-line formation, with cudgels or with rifles that repeat thirty times a minute. Men who want to fight will always put themselves in the most advantageous conditions for fighting.

The spirit of an army is the factor which multiplied by the mass gives the resulting force. To define and express the significance of this unknown factor—the spirit of an army—is a problem for science.

The tactical rule that an army should act in masses when attacking, and in smaller groups in retreat, unconsciously confirms the truth that the strength of an army depends on its spirit. To lead men forward under fire more discipline (obtainable only by movement in masses) is needed than is needed to resist attacks. But this rule which leaves out of account the spirit of the army continually proves incorrect and is in particularly striking contrast to the facts when some strong rise or fall in the spirit of the troops occurs, as in all national wars.

The French, retreating in 1812—though according to tactics they should have separated into detachments to defend themselves—congregated into a mass because the spirit of the army had so fallen that only the mass held the army together. The Russians, on the contrary, ought according to tactics to have attacked in mass, but in fact they split up into small units, because their spirit had so risen that separate individuals, without orders, dealt blows at the French without needing any compulsion to induce them to expose themselves to hardships and dangers.

2

The so-called partisan war began with the entry of the French into Smolénsk.

Before partisan warfare had been officially recognized by

the government, thousands of enemy stragglers, marauders, and foragers had been destroyed by the Cossacks and the peasants, who killed them off as instinctively as dogs worry a stray mad dog to death. Denís Davýdov, with his Russian instinct, was the first to recognize the value of this terrible cudgel which regardless of the rules of military science destroyed the French, and to him belongs the credit for taking the first step toward regularizing this method of warfare.

On August 24 Davýdov's first partisan detachment was formed and then others were recognized. The further the campaign progressed the more numerous these detachments became.

The irregulars destroyed the great army piecemeal. They gathered the fallen leaves that dropped of themselves from that withered tree—the French army—and sometimes shook that tree itself.

On October 22 Denísov (who was one of the irregulars) was with his group at the height of the guerrilla enthusiasm. Since early morning he and his party had been on the move. All day long he had been watching from the forest that skirted the highroad a large French convoy of cavalry baggage and Russian prisoners separated from the rest of the army, which—as was learned from spies and prisoners—was moving under a strong escort to Smolénsk. Besides Denísov and Dólokhov (who also led a small party and moved in Denísov's vicinity), the commanders of some large divisions with staffs also knew of this convoy and, as Denísov expressed it, were sharpening their teeth for it.

Denísov and Dólokhov intended, without reporting matters to the higher command, to attack and seize that convoy with their own small forces. That morning, Cossacks of Denísov's party had seized and carried off into the forest two wagons loaded with cavalry saddles, which had stuck in the mud not far from Mikúlino where the forest ran close to the road. Since then, and until evening, the party had watched the movements of the French without attacking. It was necessary to let the French reach Shámshevo quietly without alarming them and then, after joining Dólokhov who was to come that evening to a consultation at a watchman's hut in the forest less than a mile from Shámshevo, to surprise the French at dawn, falling like an avalanche on their heads from two sides, and rout and capture them all at one blow.

Beyond Shámshevo, Dólokhov was to observe the road in the same way, to find out at what distance there were other French troops. They reckoned that the convoy had fifteen hundred men. Denísov had two hundred, and Dólokhov might have as many more, but the disparity of numbers did not deter Denísov. All that he now wanted to know was what troops these were and to learn that he had to capture a "tongue"— that is, a man from the enemy column. That morning's attack on the wagons had been made so hastily that the Frenchmen with the wagons had all been killed; only a little drummer boy had been taken alive, and as he was a straggler he could tell them nothing definite about the troops in that column.

It was a warm rainy autumn day. The sky and the horizon were both the color of muddy water. At times a sort of mist descended, and then suddenly heavy slanting rain came down.

Denísov in a felt cloak and a sheepskin cap from which the rain ran down was riding a thin thoroughbred horse with sunken sides. Like his horse, which turned its head and laid its ears back, he shrank from the driving rain and gazed anxiously before him. His thin face with its short, thick black beard looked angry.

Beside Denísov rode an *esaul*, Denísov's fellow worker, also in felt cloak and sheepskin cap, and riding a large sleek Don horse.

Denísov was out of sorts because of the rain and also from hunger (none of them had eaten anything since morning), and yet more because he still had no news from Dólokhov and the man sent to capture a "tongue" had not returned.

On coming to a path in the forest along which he could see far to the right, Denísov stopped.

"There's someone coming," said he.

The *esaul* looked in the direction Denísov indicated.

"There are two, an officer and a Cossack."

The officer, a very young lad with a broad rosy face and keen merry eyes, galloped up to Denísov and handed him a sodden envelope.

"From the general," said the officer. "Please excuse its not being quite dry."

Denísov, frowning, took the envelope and opened it.

"There, they kept telling us: 'It's dangerous, it's dangerous,'" said the officer, addressing the *esaul* while Denísov was reading the dispatch. "But Komaróv and I"—he pointed to the Cossack—"were prepared. We have each of us two pistols. . . . But what's this?" he asked, noticing the French drummer boy. "A prisoner? You've already been in action? May I speak to him?"

"Wostóv! Pétya!" exclaimed Denísov, having run through the dispatch. "Why didn't you say who you were?" and turning with a smile he held out his hand to the lad.

The officer was Pétya Rostóv.

All the way Pétya had been preparing himself to behave with Denísov as befitted a grown-up man and officer—without hinting at their previous acquaintance. But as soon as Denísov smiled at him Pétya brightened up, blushed with pleasure, forgot the official manner he had been rehearsing, and began telling him how he had already been in a battle near Vyázma and how a certain hussar had distinguished himself there.

"Well, I am glad to see you," Denísov interrupted him, and his face again assumed its anxious expression.

"Michael Feoklítych," said he to the *esaul*, "this is again fwom that German, you know. He"—he indicated Pétya—"is serving under him."

And Denísov told the *esaul* that the dispatch just delivered was a repetition of the German general's demand that he should join forces with him for an attack on the transport.

"If we don't take it tomowwow, he'll snatch it fwom under our noses," he added.

"Will there be any orders, your honor?" Pétya asked Denísov, holding his hand at the salute and resuming the game of adjutant and general for which he had prepared himself, "or shall I remain with your honor?"

"Orders?" Denísov repeated thoughtfully. "But can you stay till tomowwow?"

"Oh, please . . . May I stay with you?" cried Pétya.

"But, just what did the general tell you? To wetuwn at once?" asked Denísov.

Pétya blushed.

"He gave me no instructions. I think I could?" he returned, inquiringly.

"Well, all wight," said Denísov.

Denísov, Pétya, and the *esaul*, accompanied by some Cossacks and the hussar who had the prisoner, rode to the left across a ravine to the edge of the forest.

The rain had stopped, and only the mist was falling and drops from the trees. Denísov, the *esaul*, and Pétya rode silently to the edge of the forest.

Immediately beyond the forest, on a downward slope, lay a field of spring rye. To the right, beyond a steep ravine, was a small village and a landowner's house with a broken roof. In the village, in the house, in the garden, by the well, by the pond, over all the rising ground, and all along the road uphill from the bridge leading to the village, not more than five hundred yards away, crowds of men could be seen through the shimmering mist. Their un-Russian shouting at their horses which were straining uphill with the carts, and their calls to one another, could be clearly heard.

Pétya, rapidly turning his head, looked now at the drummer boy, now at Denísov, now at the *esaul*, and now at the French in the village and along the road, trying not to miss anything of importance.

"Whether Dólokhov comes or not, we must seize it, eh?" said Denísov with a merry sparkle in his eyes.

"It is a very suitable spot," said the *esaul*.

"We'll send the infantwy down by the swamps," Denísov continued. "They'll cweep up to the garden; you'll wide up fwom there with the Cossacks"—he pointed to a spot in the forest beyond the village—"and I with my hussars fwom here. And at the signal shot . . ."

After talking for some time with the *esaul* about next day's attack, which now, seeing how near they were to the French, he seemed to have definitely decided on, Denísov turned his horse and rode back.

"Now, my lad, we'll go and get dwy," he said to Pétya.

The officer who had been sent to inquire met Denísov on the way with the news that Dólokhov was soon coming and that all was well with him.

Denísov at once cheered up and, calling Pétya to him, said: "Well, tell me about yourself."

Pétya, having left his people after their departure from Moscow, joined his regiment and was soon taken as orderly by a general commanding a large guerrilla detachment. From the time he received his commission, and especially since he had joined the active army and taken part in the battle of Vyázma, Pétya had been in a constant state of blissful excitement at being grown-up and in a perpetual ecstatic hurry not to miss any chance to do something really heroic. He was highly delighted with what he saw and experienced in the army, but at the same time it always seemed to him that the really heroic exploits were being performed just where he did not happen to be. And he was always in a hurry to get where he was not.

When on the twenty-first of October his general expressed a wish to send somebody to Denísov's detachment, Pétya begged so piteously to be sent that the general could not refuse. But when dispatching him he recalled Pétya's mad action at the battle of Vyázma, where instead of riding by the road to the place to which he had been sent, he had galloped to the advanced line under the fire of the French and had there twice fired his pistol. So now the general explicitly forbade his taking part in any action whatever of Denísov's. That was why Pétya had blushed and grown confused when Denísov asked him whether he could stay. Before they had ridden to the outskirts of the forest Pétya had considered that he must carry out his instructions strictly and return at once. But when he saw the French and learned that there would certainly be an attack that night, he decided, with the rapidity with which young people change their views, that the general, whom he had greatly respected till then, was a rubbishy German, that Denísov was a hero, the *esaul* a hero, and that it would be shameful for him to leave them at a moment of difficulty.

It was already growing dusk when Denísov, Pétya, and the *esaul* rode up to the watchhouse. In the passage of the small watchhouse a Cossack with sleeves rolled up was chopping some mutton. In the room three officers of Denísov's band were converting a door into a tabletop. Pétya took off his wet clothes, gave them to be dried, and at once began helping the officers to fix up the dinner table.

Sitting at table with the officers and tearing the fat savory mutton with his hands, down which the grease trickled, Pétya was in an ecstatic childish state of love for all men, and consequently of confidence that others loved him in the same way.

"So then what do you think, Vasíli Dmítrich?" said he to Denísov. "It's all right my staying a day with you?" And not waiting for a reply he answered his own question: "You see I was told to find out—well, I am finding out. . . . Only do let me into the very . . . into the chief . . . I don't want a reward. . . . But I want . . ."

Pétya clenched his teeth and looked around, throwing back his head and flourishing his arms.

"Into the vewy chief . . ." Denísov repeated with a smile.

"Only, please let me command something, so that I may really command . . ." Pétya went on. "What would it be to you? . . . Oh, you want a knife?" he said, turning to an officer who wished to cut himself a piece of mutton.

And he handed him his clasp knife. The officer admired it.

"Please keep it. I have several like it," said Pétya, blushing. "Heavens! I was quite forgetting!" he suddenly cried. "I have some raisins, fine ones; you know, seedless ones. We have a new sutler and he has such capital things. I bought ten pounds. I am used to something sweet. Would you like some? . . ." and Pétya ran out into the passage to his Cossack and brought back some bags which contained about five pounds of raisins. "Have some, gentlemen, have some!"

Then suddenly, dismayed lest he had said too much, Pétya stopped and blushed.

He tried to remember whether he had not done anything else that was foolish. And running over the events of the day he remembered the French drummer boy. "It's capital for us here, but what of him? Where have they put him? Have they fed him? Haven't they hurt his feelings?" he thought.

"I might ask," he thought, "but they'll say: 'He's a boy himself and so he pities the boy.' I'll show them tomorrow whether I'm a boy. Will it seem odd if I ask?" Pétya thought. "Well, never mind!" and immediately, blushing and looking anxiously at the officers to see if they appeared ironical, he said:

"May I call in that boy who was taken prisoner and give him something to eat? . . . Perhaps . . ."

"Yes, he's a poor little fellow," said Denísov, who evidently saw nothing shameful in this reminder. "Call him in. His name is Vincent Bosse. Have him fetched."

"I'll call him," said Pétya.

"Yes, yes, call him. A poor little fellow," Denísov repeated.

Pétya was standing at the door when Denísov said this. He slipped in between the officers, came close to Denísov, and said:

"Let me kiss you, dear old fellow! Oh, how fine, how splendid!"

And having kissed Denísov he ran out of the hut.

"Bosse! Vincent!" Pétya cried, stopping outside the door.

The sound of bare feet splashing through the mud was heard in the darkness, and the drummer boy came to the door.

"*Ah, c'est vous* [Ah, it's you]!" said Pétya. "*Voulez-vous manger? N'ayez pas peur, on ne vous fera pas de mal* [Do you want something to eat? Don't be afraid, they won't hurt you]," he added shyly and affectionately, touching the boy's hand. "*Entrez, entrez* [Come in, come in]."

"*Merci, monsieur* [Thank you, sir]," said the drummer boy in a trembling almost childish voice, and he began scraping his dirty feet on the threshold.

There were many things Pétya wanted to say to the drummer boy, but did not dare to. He stood irresolutely beside him in the passage. Then in the darkness he took the boy's hand and pressed it.

"Come in, come in!" he repeated in a gentle whisper. "Oh, what can I do for him?" he thought, and opening the door he let the boy pass in first.

When the boy had entered the hut, Pétya sat down at a distance from him, considering it beneath his dignity to pay attention to him. But he fingered the money in his pocket and wondered whether it would seem ridiculous to give some to the drummer boy.

The arrival of Dólokhov diverted Pétya's attention from the drummer boy, to whom Denísov had had some mutton and vodka given, and whom he had had dressed in a Russian coat so that he might be kept with their band and not sent away with the other prisoners. Pétya had heard in the army many stories of Dólokhov's extraordinary bravery and of his cruelty to the French, so from the moment he entered the hut Pétya did not take his eyes from him, but braced himself up more and more and held his head high, that he might not be unworthy even of such company.

Denísov told him of the designs the large detachments had on the transport, of the message Pétya had brought. . . . Then he told him all he knew of the French detachment.

"That's so. But we must know what troops they are and their numbers," said Dólokhov. "It will be necessary to go there. We can't start the affair without knowing for certain how many of them there are. I like to work accurately. Here now—wouldn't one of these gentlemen like to ride over to the French camp with me? I have brought a spare uniform."

"I, I . . . I'll go with you!" cried Pétya.

"There's no need for you to go at all," said Denísov, addressing Dólokhov, "and as for him, I won't let him go on any account."

"I like that!" exclaimed Pétya. "Why shouldn't I go?"

"Because it's useless."

"Well, you must excuse me, because . . . because . . . I shall go, and that's all. You'll take me, won't you?" he said, turning to Dólokhov.

"Why not?" Dólokhov answered absently, scrutinizing the face of the French drummer boy. "Have you had that youngster with you long?" he asked Denísov.

"He was taken today but he knows nothing. I'm keeping him with me."

"Yes, and where do you put the others?" inquired Dólokhov.

"Where? I send them away and take a weceipt for them," shouted Denísov, suddenly flushing. "And I say boldly that I have not a single man's life on my conscience. Would it be difficult for you to send thirty or thwee hundwed men to town under escort, instead of staining—I speak bluntly—staining the honor of a soldier?"

"That kind of amiable talk would be suitable from this young count of sixteen," said Dólokhov with cold irony, "but it's time for you to drop it."

While Dólokhov had been disputing with Denísov what should be done with prisoners, Pétya had once more felt awkward and restless; but again he had no time to grasp fully what they were talking about. "If grown-up, distinguished men think so, it must be necessary and right," thought he. "But above all Denísov must not dare to imagine that I'll obey

him and that he can order me about. I will certainly go to the
French camp with Dólokhov. If he can, so can I!"

And to all Denísov's persuasions, Pétya replied that he too
was accustomed to do everything accurately and not just anyhow, and that he never considered personal danger.

"For you'll admit that if we don't know for sure how many
of them there are . . . hundreds of lives may depend on it,
while there are only two of us. Besides, I want to go very
much and certainly will go, so don't hinder me," said he. "It
will only make things worse. . . ."

Having put on French greatcoats and shakos, Pétya and Dólokhov rode to the clearing from which Denísov had reconnoi-
tered the French camp, and emerging from the forest in pitch
darkness they descended into the hollow. On reaching the bottom, Dólokhov told the Cossacks accompanying him to await
him there and rode on at a quick trot along the road to the
bridge. Pétya, his heart in his mouth with excitement, rode by
his side.

"If we're caught, I won't be taken alive! I have a pistol,"
whispered he.

"Don't talk Russian," said Dólokhov in a hurried whisper,
and at that very moment they heard through the darkness the
challenge: *"Qui vive?* [Who goes there]" and the click of a
musket.

The blood rushed to Pétya's face and he grasped his pistol.

"Lanciers du 6-me [Lancers of the 6th Regiment]," replied
Dólokhov, neither hastening nor slackening his horse's pace.

And without waiting for an answer from the sentinel, who
had stepped aside, Dólokhov rode up the incline at a walk.

Having ridden up the road, on both sides of which French
talk could be heard around the campfires, Dólokhov turned into the courtyard of the landowner's house. Having ridden in,
he dismounted and approached a big blazing campfire, around
which sat several men talking noisily. Something was boiling
in a small cauldron at the edge of the fire and a soldier in a
peaked cap and blue overcoat, lit up by the fire, was kneeling
beside it stirring its contents with a ramrod.

"Bonjour, messieurs [Good day, gentlemen]!" said Dólokhov
loudly and clearly.

There was a stir among the officers in the shadow beyond

the fire, and one tall, long-necked officer, walking round the fire, came up to Dólokhov.

"Is that you, Clément?" he asked. "Where the devil . . . ?" But, noticing his mistake, he broke off short and, with a frown, greeted Dólokhov as a stranger, asking what he could do for him.

Dólokhov said that he and his companion were trying to overtake their regiment, and addressing the company in general asked whether they knew anything of the 6th Regiment. None of them knew anything, and Pétya thought the officers were beginning to look at him and Dólokhov with hostility and suspicion. For some seconds all were silent.

"If you were counting on the evening soup, you have come too late," said a voice from behind the fire with a repressed laugh.

Dólokhov replied that they were not hungry and must push on farther that night.

He handed the horses over to the soldier who was stirring the pot and squatted down on his heels by the fire beside the officer with the long neck. That officer did not take his eyes from Dólokhov and again asked to what regiment he belonged. Dólokhov, as if he had not heard the question, did not reply, but lighting a short French pipe which he took from his pocket began asking the officer how far the road before them was safe from Cossacks.

"Those brigands are everywhere," replied an officer from behind the fire.

Dólokhov remarked that the Cossacks were a danger only to stragglers such as his companion and himself, "but probably they would not dare to attack large detachments?" he added inquiringly. No one replied.

"Well, now he'll come away," Pétya thought every moment as he stood by the campfire listening to the talk.

But Dólokhov restarted the conversation which had dropped and began putting direct questions as to how many men there were in the battalion, how many battalions, and how many prisoners. Asking about the Russian prisoners with that detachment, Dólokhov said:

"A horrid business dragging these corpses about with one! It would be better to shoot such rabble," and burst into loud laughter, so strange that Pétya thought the French would immediately detect their disguise, and involuntarily took a step back from the campfire.

No one replied a word to Dólokhov's laughter, and a French officer whom they could not see (he lay wrapped in a great-coat) rose and whispered something to a companion. Dólokhov got up and called to the soldier who was holding their horses.

"Will they bring our horses or not?" thought Pétya, instinctively drawing nearer to Dólokhov.

The horses were brought.

"Good evening, gentlemen," said Dólokhov.

Pétya wished to say "Good night" but could not utter a word. The officers were whispering together. Dólokhov was a long time mounting his horse which would not stand still, then he rode out of the yard at a footpace. Pétya rode beside him, longing to look round to see whether or no the French were running after them, but not daring to.

Coming out onto the road Dólokhov did not ride back across the open country, but through the village. At one spot he stopped and listened. "Do you hear?" he asked. Pétya recognized the sound of Russian voices and saw the dark figures of Russian prisoners round their campfires. When they had descended to the bridge Pétya and Dólokhov rode past the sentinel, who without saying a word paced morosely up and down it, then they descended into the hollow where the Cossacks awaited them.

"Well now, good-by. Tell Denísov, 'at the first shot at daybreak,'" said Dólokhov and was about to ride away, but Pétya seized hold of him.

"Really!" he cried, "you are such a hero! Oh, how fine, how splendid! How I love you!"

"All right, all right!" said Dólokhov. But Pétya did not let go of him and Dólokhov saw through the gloom that Pétya was bending toward him and wanted to kiss him. Dólokhov kissed him, laughed, turned his horse, and vanished into the darkness.

Having returned to the watchman's hut, Pétya found Denísov in the passage. He was awaiting Pétya's return in a state of agitation, anxiety, and self-reproach for having let him go.

"Thank God!" he exclaimed. "Yes, thank God!" he repeated,

listening to Pétya's rapturous account. "But, devil take you, I haven't slept because of you! Well, thank God. Now lie down. We can still get a nap before morning."

"But . . . no," said Pétya, "I don't want to sleep yet. Besides I know myself, if I fall asleep it's finished. And then I am used to not sleeping before a battle."

He sat awhile in the hut joyfully recalling the details of his expedition and vividly picturing to himself what would happen next day. Then, noticing that Denísov was asleep, he rose and went out of doors.

"Why aren't you asleep, sir?" said a Cossack who was sitting under a wagon.

"No, ah . . . Likhachëv—isn't that your name? Do you know I have only just come back! We've been into the French camp."

And Pétya gave the Cossack a detailed account not only of his ride but also of his object, and why he considered it better to risk his life than to act "just anyhow."

"Well, you should get some sleep now," said the Cossack.

"No, I am used to this," said Pétya.

"Just so," said the Cossack.

"Oh yes, another thing! Please, my dear fellow, will you sharpen my saber for me? It's got bl . . ." (Pétya feared to tell a lie, and the saber never had been sharpened.) "Can you do it?"

"Of course I can."

Likhachëv got up, rummaged in his pack, and soon Pétya heard the warlike sound of steel on whetstone. He climbed onto the wagon and sat on its edge.

Pétya's eyes began to close and he swayed a little.

"*Ozheg-zheg, Ozheg-zheg . . .*" hissed the saber against the whetstone, and suddenly Pétya heard an harmonious orchestra playing some unknown, sweetly solemn hymn.

"Oh—why, that was in a dream!" Pétya said to himself, as he lurched forward. "It's in my ears. But perhaps it's music of my own. Well, go on, my music! Now! . . ."

He closed his eyes, and, from all sides as if from a distance, sounds fluttered, grew into harmonies, separated, blended, and again all mingled into the same sweet and solemn hymn. "Oh, this is delightful! As much as I like and as I like!" said

Pétya to himself. He tried to conduct that enormous orchestra.

He was awakened by Likhachëv's kindly voice.

"It's ready, your honor; you can split a Frenchman in half with it!"

Pétya woke up.

"It's getting light, it's really getting light!" he exclaimed.

Pétya shook himself, jumped up, took a ruble from his pocket and gave it to Likhachëv; then he flourished the saber, tested it, and sheathed it. The Cossacks were untying their horses and tightening their saddle girths.

"And here's the commander," said Likhachëv.

Denísov came out of the watchman's hut and, having called Pétya, gave orders to get ready.

The men rapidly picked out their horses in the semidarkness, tightened their saddle girths, and formed companies. Pétya held his horse by the bridle, impatiently awaiting the order to mount. His face, having been bathed in cold water, was all aglow, and his eyes were particularly brilliant. Cold shivers ran down his spine and his whole body pulsed rhythmically.

"Well, is ev'wything weady?" asked Denísov. "Bwing the horses."

"Vasíli Dmítrich, entrust me with some commission! Please . . . for God's sake . . . !" said Pétya.

Denísov seemed to have forgotten Pétya's very existence. He turned to glance at him.

"I ask one thing of you," he said sternly, "to obey me and not shove you'self fo'ward anywhere."

He did not say another word to Pétya but rode in silence all the way. When they had come to the edge of the forest it was noticeably growing light over the field. Pétya rode beside Denísov, the pulsation of his body constantly increasing. It was getting lighter and lighter, but the mist still hid distant objects. Having reached the valley, Denísov looked back and nodded to a Cossack beside him.

"The signal!" said he.

The Cossack raised his arm and a shot rang out. In an instant the tramp of horses galloping forward was heard, shouts came from various sides, and then more shots.

At the first sound of trampling hoofs and shouting, Pétya lashed his horse and loosening his rein galloped forward, not heeding Denísov who shouted at him. It seemed to Pétya that at the moment the shot was fired it suddenly became as bright as noon. He galloped to the bridge. Cossacks were galloping along the road in front of him.

Cossacks were crowding about a hut, busy with something. From the midst of that crowd terrible screams arose. Pétya galloped up, and the first thing he saw was the pale face and trembling jaw of a Frenchman, clutching the handle of a lance that had been aimed at him.

"Hurrah! . . . Lads! . . . ours!" shouted Pétya, and giving rein to his excited horse he galloped forward along the village street.

He could hear shooting ahead of him. Cossacks, hussars, and ragged Russian prisoners, who had come running from both sides of the road, were shouting something loudly and incoherently. A gallant-looking Frenchman, in a blue overcoat, capless, and with a frowning red face, had been defending himself against the hussars. When Pétya galloped up the Frenchman had already fallen. "Too late again!" flashed through Pétya's mind and he galloped on to the place from which the rapid firing could be heard. The shots came from the yard of the landowner's house he had visited the night before with Dólokhov. The French were making a stand there behind a wattle fence in a garden thickly overgrown with bushes and were firing at the Cossacks who crowded at the gateway. Through the smoke, as he approached the gate, Pétya saw Dólokhov, whose face was of a pale-greenish tint, shouting to his men. "Go round! Wait for the infantry!" he exclaimed as Pétya rode up to him.

"Wait? . . . Hurrah-ah-ah!" shouted Pétya, and without pausing a moment galloped to the place whence came the sounds of firing and where the smoke was thickest.

A volley was heard, and some bullets whistled past, while others plashed against something. The Cossacks and Dólokhov galloped after Pétya into the gateway of the courtyard. In the dense wavering smoke some of the French threw down their arms and ran out of the bushes to meet the Cossacks, while others ran down the hill toward the pond. Pétya was galloping along the courtyard, but instead of holding the reins he waved both his arms about rapidly and strangely, slipping farther and farther to one side in his saddle. His horse, having galloped up to a campfire that was smoldering in the morning light, stopped suddenly, and Pétya fell heavily on to the wet ground. The Cossacks saw that his arms and legs jerked rapidly though his head was quite motionless. A bullet had pierced his skull.

After speaking to the senior French officer, who came out of the house with a white handkerchief tied to his sword and announced that they surrendered, Dólokhov dismounted and went up to Pétya, who lay motionless with outstretched arms.

"Done for!" he said with a frown, and went to the gate to meet Denísov who was riding toward him.

"Killed?" cried Denísov, recognizing from a distance the unmistakably lifeless attitude—very familiar to him—in which Pétya's body was lying.

"Done for!" repeated Dólokhov as if the utterance of these words afforded him pleasure, and he went quickly up to the prisoners, who were surrounded by Cossacks who had hurried up. "We won't take them!" he called out to Denísov.

Denísov did not reply; he rode up to Pétya, dismounted, and with trembling hands turned toward himself the bloodstained, mud-bespattered face which had already gone white.

"I am used to something sweet. Raisins, fine ones . . . take them all!" he recalled Pétya's words. And the Cossacks looked round in surprise at the sound, like the yelp of a dog, with which Denísov turned away, walked to the wattle fence, and seized hold of it.

Among the Russian prisoners rescued by Denísov and Dólokhov was Pierre Bezúkhov.

3

During the whole of their march from Moscow no fresh orders had been issued by the French authorities concerning the party of prisoners among whom was Pierre. On the twenty-second of October that party was no longer with the same troops and baggage trains with which it had left Moscow. The artillery the prisoners had seen in front of them during the first days was now replaced by Marshal Junot's enormous baggage train, convoyed by Westphalians. Behind the prisoners came a cavalry baggage train.

Of the artillery baggage train which had consisted of a hundred and twenty wagons, not more than sixty now remained; the rest had been captured or left behind.

The group of prisoners had melted away most of all. Of the three hundred and thirty men who had set out from Moscow fewer than a hundred now remained. The prisoners were more burdensome to the escort than even the cavalry saddles or Junot's baggage. And the escort, as if afraid, in the grievous condition they themselves were in, of giving way to the pity they felt for the prisoners and so rendering their own plight still worse, treated them with particular moroseness and severity.

The arrangement adopted when they started, that the officer prisoners should be kept separate from the rest, had long since been abandoned. All who could walk went together, and after the third stage Pierre had rejoined Karatáev and the gray-blue bandy-legged dog that had chosen Karatáev for its master.

On the third day after leaving Moscow Karatáev again fell ill with the fever he had suffered from in hospital in Moscow, and as he grew gradually weaker Pierre kept away from him. Pierre did not know why, but since Karatáev had begun to grow weaker it had cost him an effort to go near him. When he did so and heard the subdued moaning with which Karatáev generally lay down at the halting places, and when he smelled the odor emanating from him which was now stronger than before, Pierre moved farther away and did not think about him.

While imprisoned in the shed Pierre had learned not with his intellect but with his whole being, by life itself, that man is created for happiness, that happiness is within him, in the satisfaction of simple human needs, and that all unhappiness arises not from privation but from superfluity. And now during these last three weeks of the march he had learned still another new, consolatory truth—that nothing in this world is terrible. He had learned that as there is no condition in which man can be happy and entirely free, so there is no condition in which he need be unhappy and lack freedom. He learned that suffering and freedom have their limits and that those limits are very near together. Of all that he himself subsequently termed his sufferings, but which at the time he scarcely felt, the worst was the state of his bare, raw, and scab-covered feet.

Only now did Pierre realize the full strength of life in man and the saving power he has of transferring his attention from one thing to another.

He did not see and did not hear how they shot the prisoners who lagged behind, though more than a hundred perished in that way. He did not think of Karatáev who grew weaker every day and evidently would soon have to share that fate. Still less did Pierre think about himself. The harder his position became and the more terrible the future, the more independent of that position in which he found himself were the joyful and comforting thoughts, memories, and imaginings that came to him.

At midday on the twenty-second of October Pierre was going uphill along the muddy, slippery road, looking at his feet and at the roughness of the way.

It seemed to him that he was thinking of nothing, but far down and deep within him his soul was occupied with something important and comforting. This something was a most subtle spiritual deduction from a conversation with Karatáev the day before.

At their yesterday's halting place, feeling chilly by a dying campfire, Pierre had got up and gone to the next one, which was burning better. There Platón Karatáev was sitting covered up—head and all—with his greatcoat as if it were a vestment, telling the soldiers in his effective and pleasant though now feeble voice a story Pierre knew. It was already past midnight, the hour when Karatáev was usually free of his fever and particularly lively. When Pierre reached the fire and heard Platón's voice enfeebled by illness, and saw his pathetic face brightly lit up by the blaze, he felt a painful prick at his heart. His feeling of pity for this man frightened him and he wished to go away, but there was no other fire, and Pierre sat down, trying not to look at Platón.

"Well, how are you?" he asked.

"How am I? If we grumble at sickness, God won't grant us death," replied Platón, and at once resumed the story he had begun.

"And so, brother," he continued, with a smile on his pale emaciated face and a particularly happy light in his eyes, "you see, brother . . ."

Pierre had long been familiar with that story. Karatáev had told it to him alone some half-dozen times and always with a specially joyful emotion. But well as he knew it, Pierre now listened to that tale as to something new, and the quiet rapture Karatáev evidently felt as he told it communicated itself also to Pierre. The story was of an old merchant who lived a good and God-fearing life with his family, and who went once to the Nízhni fair with a companion—a rich merchant.

Karatáev paused, smiling joyously as he gazed into the fire, and he drew the logs together.

"And the old man said, 'God will forgive you, we are all sinners in His sight. I suffer for my own sins,' and he wept bitter tears. Well, and what do you think, dear friends?" Karatáev continued, his face brightening more and more with a rapturous smile as if what he now had to tell contained the chief charm and the whole meaning of his story: "What do you think, dear fellows? That murderer confessed to the authorities. 'I have taken six lives,' he says (he was a great sinner), 'but what I am most sorry for is this old man. Don't let him suffer because of me.' So he confessed and it was all written down and the papers sent off in due form. . . . The affair reached the Tsar. After a while the Tsar's decree came: to set the merchant free and give him a compensation that had been awarded. . . . So they began looking for him," here Karatáev's lower jaw trembled, "but God had already forgiven him— he was dead! That's how it was, dear fellows!" Karatáev concluded and sat for a long time silent, gazing before him with a smile.

And Pierre's soul was dimly but joyfully filled not by the story itself but by its mysterious significance: by the rapturous joy that lit up Karatáev's face as he told it, and the mystic significance of that joy.

From all sides came shouts of command, and from the left came smartly dressed cavalrymen on good horses, passing the prisoners at a trot.

"The Emperor! The Emperor! The Marshal! The Duke!" and hardly had the sleek cavalry passed, before a carriage drawn by six gray horses rattled by. Pierre caught a glimpse of a man in a three-cornered hat with a tranquil look on his handsome, plump, white face. It was one of the marshals.

While the marshal was passing, the prisoners had huddled together in a crowd, and Pierre saw Karatáev whom he had not yet seen that morning. He sat in his short overcoat leaning against a birch tree. On his face, besides the look of joyful emotion it had worn yesterday while telling the tale of the merchant who suffered innocently, there was now an expression of quiet solemnity.

Karatáev looked at Pierre with his kindly round eyes now filled with tears, evidently wishing him to come near that he might say something to him. But Pierre was not sufficiently sure of himself. He made as if he did not notice that look and moved hastily away.

When the prisoners again went forward Pierre looked round. Karatáev was still sitting at the side of the road under the birch tree and two Frenchmen were talking over his head. Pierre did not look round again but went limping up the hill.

From behind, where Karatáev had been sitting, came the sound of a shot. Pierre heard it plainly, but at that moment he remembered that he had not yet finished reckoning up how many stages still remained to Smolénsk—a calculation he had begun before the marshal went by. And he again started reckoning. Two French soldiers ran past Pierre, one of whom carried a lowered and smoking gun.

Behind him, where Karatáev had been sitting, the dog began to howl. "What a stupid beast! Why is it howling?" thought Pierre.

The stores, the prisoners, and the marshal's baggage train stopped at the village of Shámshevo. The men crowded together round the campfires. Pierre went up to the fire, ate some roast horseflesh, lay down with his back to the fire, and immediately fell asleep. He again slept as he had done at Mozháysk after the battle of Borodinó.

Again real events mingled with dreams and again someone, he or another, gave expression to his thoughts, and even to the same thoughts that had been expressed in his dream at Mozháysk.

"Life is everything. Life is God. Everything changes and moves and that movement is God. And while there is life there is joy in consciousness of the divine. To love life is to love

God. Harder and more blessed than all else is to love this life in one's sufferings, in innocent sufferings."

"Karatáev!" came to Pierre's mind.

"How simple and clear it is," thought Pierre. "How is it I did not know it before?"

"God is in the midst, and each drop tries to expand so as to reflect Him to the greatest extent. And it grows, merges, disappears from the surface, sinks to the depths, and again emerges. There now, Karatáev has spread out and disappeared."

Before sunrise he was awakened by shouts and loud and rapid firing. French soldiers were running past him.

"The Cossacks!" one of them shouted, and a moment later a crowd of Russians surrounded Pierre.

For a long time he could not understand what was happening to him. All around he heard his comrades sobbing with joy.

"Brothers! Dear fellows! Darlings!" old soldiers exclaimed, weeping, as they embraced Cossacks and hussars.

The hussars and Cossacks crowded round the prisoners; one offered them clothes, another boots, and a third bread. Pierre sobbed as he sat among them and could not utter a word. He hugged the first soldier who approached him, and kissed him, weeping.

Dólokhov stood at the gate of the ruined house, letting a crowd of disarmed Frenchmen pass by. The French, excited by all that had happened, were talking loudly among themselves, but as they passed Dólokhov who gently switched his boots with his whip and watched them with cold glassy eyes that boded no good, they became silent. On the opposite side stood Dólokhov's Cossack, counting the prisoners and marking off each hundred with a chalk line on the gate.

"How many?" Dólokhov asked the Cossack.

"The second hundred," replied the Cossack.

Denísov, bareheaded and with a gloomy face, walked behind some Cossacks who were carrying the body of Pétya Rostóv to a hole that had been dug in the garden.

4

Tolstoy depicts the headlong retreat and terrible losses of the French, and contends, contrary to the historians, that there was no plan in the flight. In fact, he insists that the one thought of Napoleon and his marshals was to save their own skins.

5

How was it that the Russian army, which when numerically weaker than the French had given battle at Borodinó, did not achieve its purpose when it had surrounded the French on three sides and when its aim was to capture them? Can the French be so enormously superior to us that when we had surrounded them with superior forces we could not beat them? How could that happen?

Why was the Russian army—which with inferior forces had withstood the enemy in full strength at Borodinó—defeated at Krásnoe and the Berëzina by the disorganized crowds of the French when it was numerically superior?

If the aim of the Russians consisted in cutting off and capturing Napoleon and his marshals—and that aim was not merely frustrated but all attempts to attain it were most shamefully baffled—then this last period of the campaign is quite rightly considered by the French to be a series of victories, and quite wrongly considered victorious by Russian historians.

But putting national vanity entirely aside one feels that such a conclusion involves a contradiction, since the series of French victories brought the French complete destruction, while the series of Russian defeats led to the total destruction of their enemy and the liberation of their country.

The source of this contradiction lies in the fact that the historians studying the events from the letters of the sovereigns and the generals, from memoirs, reports, projects, and so forth, have attributed to this last period of the war of 1812 an aim that never existed, namely that of cutting off and capturing Napoleon with his marshals and his army.

There never was or could have been such an aim, for it would have been senseless and its attainment quite impossible.

It would have been senseless, first because Napoleon's disorganized army was flying from Russia with all possible speed, that is to say, was doing just what every Russian desired. So what was the use of performing various operations on the French who were running away as fast as they possibly could?

Secondly, it would have been senseless to block the passage of men whose whole energy was directed to flight.

Thirdly, it would have been senseless to sacrifice one's own troops in order to destroy the French army, which without external interference was destroying itself at such a rate that, though its path was not blocked, it could not carry across the frontier more than it actually did in December, namely, a hundredth part of the original army.

But besides the fact that cutting off Napoleon with his army would have been senseless, it was impossible.

It was impossible first because—as experience shows that a three-mile movement of columns on a battlefield never coincides with the plans—the probability of Chichagóv, Kutúzov, and Wittgenstein effecting a junction on time at an appointed place was so remote as to be tantamount to impossibility, as in fact thought Kutúzov, who when he received the plan remarked that diversions planned over great distances do not yield the desired results.

Secondly, it was impossible because to paralyze the momentum with which Napoleon's army was retiring, incomparably greater forces than the Russians possessed would have been required.

Thirdly, it was impossible because the military term "to cut off" has no meaning. One can cut off a slice of bread, but not an army. To cut off an army—to bar its road—is quite impossible, for there is always plenty of room to avoid capture and there is the night when nothing can be seen.

Fourthly and chiefly, it was impossible because never since the world began has a war been fought under such conditions as those that obtained in 1812, and the Russian army in its pursuit of the French strained its strength to the utmost and could not have done more without destroying itself.

During the movement of the Russian army from Tarútino to Krásnoe it lost fifty thousand sick or stragglers, that is a number equal to the population of a large provincial town. Half the men fell out of the army without a battle.

The Russians, half of whom died, did all that could and should have been done to attain an end worthy of the nation, and they are not to blame because other Russians, sitting in warm rooms, proposed that they should do what was impossible.

The aim of cutting off Napoleon and his army never existed except in the imaginations of a dozen people. It could not exist because it was senseless and unattainable.

The people had a single aim: to free their land from invasion. That aim was attained in the first place of itself, as the French ran away, and so it was only necessary not to stop their flight. Secondly, it was attained by the guerrilla warfare which was destroying the French, and thirdly, by the fact that a large Russian army was following the French, ready to use its strength in case their movement stopped.

The Russian army had to act like a whip to a running animal. And the experienced driver knew it was better to hold the whip raised as a menace than to strike the running animal on the head.

1812-13

━━━━━━━━━━━━━━━━━━━━━━━

BOOK FIFTEEN

1

After Prince Andrew's death Natásha and Princess Mary carefully guarded their open wounds from any rough and painful contact.

Both avoided any allusion to the future. To admit the possibility of a future seemed to them to insult his memory. Still more carefully did they avoid anything relating to him who was dead. It seemed to them that what they had lived through and experienced could not be expressed in words, and that any reference to the details of his life infringed the majesty and sacredness of the mystery that had been accomplished before their eyes.

Continued abstention from speech, and constant avoidance of everything that might lead up to the subject—this halting on all sides at the boundary of what they might not mention—brought before their minds with still greater purity and clearness what they were both feeling.

But pure and complete sorrow is as impossible as pure and complete joy. Princess Mary, in her position as absolute and independent arbiter of her own fate and guardian and instructor of her nephew, was the first to be called back to life from that realm of sorrow in which she had dwelt for the first fortnight. Alpátych came to Yaroslávl with reports on the state of their affairs and with advice and suggestions that they should return to Moscow to the house on the Vozdvízhenka Street, which had remained uninjured and needed only slight repairs. She went through the accounts with Alpátych, conferred with Dessalles about her nephew, and gave orders and made preparations for the journey to Moscow.

Natásha remained alone and, from the time Princess Mary

began making preparations for departure, held aloof from her too.

Princess Mary asked the countess to let Natásha go with her to Moscow, and both parents gladly accepted this offer, for they saw their daughter losing strength every day and thought that a change of scene and the advice of Moscow doctors would be good for her.

"I am not going anywhere," Natásha replied when this was proposed to her. "Do please just leave me alone!" And she ran out of the room, with difficulty refraining from tears of vexation and irritation rather than of sorrow.

One day toward the end of December, Natásha, pale and thin, dressed in a black woolen gown, her plaited hair negligently twisted into a knot, was crouched feet and all in the corner of her sofa, nervously crumpling and smoothing out the end of her sash while she looked at a corner of the door.

She was gazing where she knew him to be; but she could not imagine him otherwise than as he had been here. She now saw him again as he had been at Mytíshchi, at Tróitsa, and at Yaroslávl.

She saw his face, heard his voice, repeated his words and her own, and sometimes devised other words they might have spoken.

"One thing would be terrible," said he: "to bind oneself forever to a suffering man. It would be continual torture." And he looked searchingly at her. Natásha as usual answered before she had time to think what she would say. She said: "This can't go on—it won't. You will get well—quite well."

And now he again seemed to be saying the same words to her, only in her imagination Natásha this time gave him a different answer. She stopped him and said: "Terrible for you, but not for me! You know that for me there is nothing in life but you, and to suffer with you is the greatest happiness for me," and he took her hand and pressed it as he had pressed it that terrible evening four days before his death. And in her imagination she said other tender and loving words which she might have said then but only spoke now: "I love thee! . . . thee! I love, love . . ." she said, convulsively pressing her hands and setting her teeth with a desperate effort. . . .

But at the instant when it seemed that the incomprehensible was revealing itself to her a loud rattle of the door handle struck painfully on her ears. Dunyásha, her maid, entered the room quickly and abruptly with a frightened look on her face and showing no concern for her mistress.

"Come to your Papa at once, please!" said she with a strange, excited look. "A misfortune . . . about Peter Ilýich . . . a letter," she finished with a sob.

Besides a feeling of aloofness from everybody Natásha was feeling a special estrangement from the members of her own family.

"What misfortune? What misfortune can happen to them? They just live their own old, quiet, and commonplace life," thought Natásha.

As she entered the ballroom her father was hurriedly coming out of her mother's room. When he saw Natásha he waved his arms despairingly and burst into convulsively painful sobs that distorted his soft round face.

"Pe . . . Pétya . . . Go, go, she . . . is calling . . ." and weeping like a child and quickly shuffling on his feeble legs to a chair, he almost fell into it, covering his face with his hands.

Suddenly an electric shock seemed to run through Natásha's whole being. Terrible anguish struck her heart, she felt a dreadful ache as if something was being torn inside her and she were dying. But the pain was immediately followed by a feeling of release from the oppressive constraint that had prevented her taking part in life. The sight of her father, the terribly wild cries of her mother that she heard through the door, made her immediately forget herself and her own grief.

The countess was lying in an armchair in a strange and awkward position, stretching out and beating her head against the wall. Sónya and the maids were holding her arms.

"Natásha! Natásha! . . ." cried the countess. "It's not true . . . it's not true . . . He's lying . . . Natásha!" she shrieked, pushing those around her away. "Go away, all of you; it's not true! Killed! . . . ha, ha, ha! . . . It's not true!"

Natásha put one knee on the armchair, stooped over her mother, embraced her, and with unexpected strength raised her, turned her face toward herself, and clung to her.

"Mummy! . . . darling! . . . I am here, my dearest Mummy," she kept on whispering, not pausing an instant.

She did not let go of her mother but struggled tenderly with her, demanded a pillow and hot water, and unfastened and tore open her mother's dress.

"My dearest darling . . . Mummy, my precious! . . ." she whispered incessantly, kissing her head, her hands, her face, and feeling her own irrepressible and streaming tears tickling her nose and cheeks.

During the third night the countess kept very quiet for a few minutes, and Natásha rested her head on the arm of her chair and closed her eyes, but opened them again on hearing the bedstead creak. The countess was sitting up in bed and speaking softly.

"How glad I am you have come. You are tired. Won't you have some tea?" Natásha went up to her. "You have improved in looks and grown more manly," continued the countess, taking her daughter's hand.

"Mamma! What are you saying? . . ."

"Natásha, he is no more, no more!"

And embracing her daughter, the countess began to weep for the first time.

Princess Mary postponed her departure. Sónya and the count tried to replace Natásha but could not. They saw that she alone was able to restrain her mother from unreasoning despair. For three weeks Natásha remained constantly at her mother's side, sleeping on a lounge chair in her room, making her eat and drink, and talking to her incessantly because the mere sound of her tender, caressing tones soothed her mother.

The mother's wounded spirit could not heal. Pétya's death had torn from her half her life. When the news of Pétya's death had come she had been a fresh and vigorous woman of fifty, but a month later she left her room a listless old woman taking no interest in life. But the same blow that almost killed the countess, this second blow, restored Natásha to life. She thought her life was ended, but her love for her mother unexpectedly showed her that the essence of life—love—was still active within her. Love awoke and so did life.

Prince Andrew's last days had bound Princess Mary and Natásha together; this new sorrow brought them still closer to one another.

One afternoon noticing Natásha shivering with fever, Princess Mary took her to her own room and made her lie down on the bed. Natásha lay down, but when Princess Mary had drawn the blinds and was going away she called her back.

"I don't want to sleep, Mary, sit by me a little."

"You are tired—try to sleep."

"No, no. Why did you bring me away? She will be asking for me."

"She is much better. She spoke so well today," said Princess Mary.

Natásha lay on the bed and in the semidarkness of the room scanned Princess Mary's face.

"Is she like him?" thought Natásha. "Yes, like and yet not like. But she is quite original, strange, new, and unknown. And she loves me. What is in her heart? All that is good. But how? What is her mind like? What does she think about me? Yes, she is splendid!"

"Mary," she said timidly, drawing Princess Mary's hand to herself, "Mary, you mustn't think me wicked. No? Mary darling, how I love you! Let us be quite, quite friends."

And Natásha, embracing her, began kissing her face and hands, making Princess Mary feel shy but happy by this demonstration of her feelings.

From that day a tender and passionate friendship such as exists only between women was established between Princess Mary and Natásha. Together they felt more in harmony with one another than either of them felt with herself when alone. A feeling stronger than friendship sprang up between them; an exclusive feeling of life being possible only in each other's presence.

Just as before, they never mentioned *him* so as not to lower (as they thought) their exalted feelings by words; but this silence about him had the effect of making them gradually begin to forget him without being conscious of it.

Natásha had grown thin and pale and physically so weak that they all talked about her health, and this pleased her. But sometimes she was suddenly overcome by fear not only of death but of sickness, weakness, and loss of good looks.

She did not know and would not have believed it, but beneath the layer of slime that covered her soul and seemed to her impenetrable, delicate young shoots of grass were already sprouting, which taking root would so cover with their living verdure the grief that weighed her down that it would soon no longer be seen or noticed. The wound had begun to heal from within.

At the end of January Princess Mary left for Moscow, and the count insisted on Natásha's going with her to consult the doctors.

2

After the encounter at Vyázma, where Kutúzov had been unable to hold back his troops in their anxiety to overwhelm and cut off the enemy and so on, the farther movement of the fleeing French, and of the Russians who pursued them, continued as far as Krásnoe without a battle. The flight was so rapid that the Russian army pursuing the French could not keep up with them; cavalry and artillery horses broke down, and the information received of the movements of the French was never reliable.

The men in the Russian army were so worn out by this continuous marching at the rate of twenty-seven miles a day that they could not go any faster.

To realize the degree of exhaustion of the Russian army it is only necessary to grasp clearly the meaning of the fact that, while not losing more than five thousand killed and wounded after Tarútino and less than a hundred prisoners, the Russian army which left that place a hundred thousand strong reached Krásnoe with only fifty thousand.

The rapidity of the Russian pursuit was just as destructive to our army as the flight of the French was to theirs.

Kutúzov as far as was in his power, instead of trying to check the movement of the French as was desired in Petersburg and by the Russian army generals, directed his whole activity here, as he had done at Tarútino and Vyázma, to hastening it on while easing the movement of our army.

In 1812 and 1813 Kutúzov was openly accused of blundering. The Emperor was dissatisfied with him. And in a history recently written by order of the Highest Authorities it is said that Kutúzov was a cunning court liar, frightened of the name of Napoleon, and that by his blunders at Krásnoe and the

Berëzina he deprived the Russian army of the glory of complete victory over the French.

And yet it is difficult to imagine an historical character whose activity was so unswervingly directed to a single aim; and it would be difficult to imagine any aim more worthy or more consonant with the will of the whole people. Still more difficult would it be to find an instance in history of the aim of an historical personage being so completely accomplished as that to which all Kutúzov's efforts were directed in 1812.

Nor do words alone prove that only he understood the meaning of the events. His actions—without the smallest deviation—were all directed to one and the same threefold end: (1) to brace all his strength for conflict with the French, (2) to defeat them, and (3) to drive them out of Russia, minimizing as far as possible the sufferings of our people and of our army.

This procrastinator Kutúzov, whose motto was "Patience and Time," this enemy of decisive action, gave battle at Borodinó, investing the preparations for it with unparalleled solemnity. This Kutúzov who before the battle of Austerlitz began said that it would be lost, he alone, in contradiction to everyone else, declared till his death that Borodinó was a victory, despite the assurance of generals that the battle was lost and despite the fact that for an army to have to retire after winning a battle was unprecedented. He alone during the whole retreat insisted that battles, which were useless then, should not be fought, and that a new war should not be begun nor the frontiers of Russia crossed.

It is easy now to understand the significance of these events —if only we abstain from attributing to the activity of the mass aims that existed only in the heads of a dozen individuals —for the events and their results now lie before us.

But how did that old man, alone, in opposition to the general opinion, so truly discern the importance of the people's view of the events that in all his activity he was never once untrue to it?

The source of that extraordinary power of penetrating the meaning of the events then occurring lay in the national feeling which he possessed in full purity and strength.

That simple, modest, and therefore truly great, figure could not be cast in the false mold of a European hero—the supposed ruler of men—that history has invented.

To a lackey no man can be great, for a lackey has his own conception of greatness.

3

The fifth of November was the first day of what is called the battle of Krásnoe. Toward evening—after much disputing and many mistakes made by generals who did not go to their proper places, and after adjutants had been sent about with counterorders—when it had become plain that the enemy was everywhere in flight and that there could and would be no battle, Kutúzov left Krásnoe and went to Dóbroe whither his headquarters had that day been transferred.

The day was clear and frosty. Kutúzov rode to Dóbroe on his plump little white horse, followed by an enormous suite of discontented generals who whispered among themselves behind his back. All along the road groups of French prisoners captured that day (there were seven thousand of them) were crowding to warm themselves at campfires. One of the generals was reporting to him where the guns and prisoners had been captured.

Kutúzov seemed preoccupied and did not listen to what the general was saying. He screwed up his eyes with a dissatisfied look as he gazed attentively and fixedly at these prisoners, who presented a specially wretched appearance. Most of them were disfigured by frost-bitten noses and cheeks, and nearly all had red, swollen, and festering eyes.

"What were you saying?" he asked the general, who continuing his report directed the commander in chief's attention to some standards captured from the French and standing in front of the Preobrazhénsk regiment.

"Ah, the standards!" said Kutúzov, evidently detaching himself with difficulty from the thoughts that preoccupied him.

He looked about him absently. Thousands of eyes were looking at him from all sides awaiting a word from him.

"I thank you all!" he said, addressing the soldiers and then again the officers. In the stillness around him his slowly uttered words were distinctly heard. "I thank you all for your hard and faithful service. The victory is complete and Russia will not forget you! Honor to you forever."

He paused and looked round.

"Lower its head, lower it!" he said to a soldier who had accidentally lowered the French eagle he was holding before the Preobrazhénsk standards. "Lower, lower, that's it. Hurrah, lads!" he added, addressing the men with a rapid movement of his chin.

"Hur-r-rah!" roared thousands of voices.

While the soldiers were shouting Kutúzov leaned forward in his saddle and bowed his head, and his eye lit up with a mild and apparently ironic gleam.

"You see, brothers . . ." said he when the shouts had ceased . . . and all at once his voice and the expression of his face changed. It was no longer the commander in chief speaking but an ordinary old man who wanted to tell his comrades something very important.

There was a stir among the throng of officers and in the ranks of the soldiers, who moved that they might hear better what he was going to say.

"You see, brothers, I know it's hard for you, but it can't be helped! Bear up; it won't be for long now! We'll see our visitors off and then we'll rest. The Tsar won't forget your service. It is hard for you, but still you are at home while they—you see what they have come to," said he, pointing to the prisoners. "Worse off than our poorest beggars. While they were strong we didn't spare ourselves, but now we may even pity them. They are human beings too. Isn't it so, lads?"

He looked around, and in the direct, respectful, wondering gaze fixed upon him he read sympathy with what he had said. His face grew brighter and brighter with an old man's mild smile, which drew the corners of his lips and eyes into a cluster of wrinkles. He ceased speaking and bowed his head as if in perplexity.

"But after all who asked them here? Serves them right, the bloody bastards!" he cried, suddenly lifting his head.

And flourishing his whip he rode off at a gallop for the first time during the whole campaign, and left the broken ranks of the soldiers laughing joyfully and shouting "Hurrah!"

When the troops reached their night's halting place on the eighth of November, the last day of the Krásnoe battles, it was already growing dusk. All day it had been calm and frosty with occasional lightly falling snow and toward evening it began to clear. Through the falling snow a purple-black and starry sky showed itself and the frost grew keener.

An infantry regiment which had left Tarútino three thousand strong but now numbered only nine hundred was one of the first to arrive that night at its halting place—a village on the highroad. The quartermasters who met the regiment announced that all huts were full of sick and dead Frenchmen, cavalrymen, and members of the staff. There was only one hut available for the regimental commander.

The commander rode up to his hut. The regiment passed through the village and stacked its arms in front of the last huts.

Like some huge many-limbed animal, the regiment began to prepare its lair and its food. One part of it dispersed and waded knee-deep through the snow into a birch forest to the right of the village, and immediately the sound of axes and swords, the crashing of branches, and merry voices could be heard from there. Another section amid the regimental wagons and horses which were standing in a group was busy getting out cauldrons and rye biscuit, and feeding the horses. A third section scattered through the village arranging quarters for the staff officers, carrying out the French corpses that were in the huts, and dragging away boards, dry wood, and thatch from the roofs, for the campfires, or wattle fences to serve for shelter.

Some fifteen men with merry shouts were shaking down the high wattle wall of a shed, the roof of which had already been removed.

"Now then, all together—shove!" cried the voices, and the huge surface of the wall, sprinkled with snow and creaking with frost, was seen swaying in the gloom of the night. The lower stakes cracked more and more and at last the wall fell, and with it the men who had been pushing it. Loud, coarse laughter and joyous shouts ensued.

"Now then, catch hold in two's! Hand up the lever! That's it. . . . Where are you shoving to?"

"Now, all together! But wait a moment, boys . . . With a song!"

All stood silent, and a soft, pleasant velvety voice began to sing. At the end of the third verse as the last note died away, twenty voices roared out at once: "Oo-oo-oo-oo! That's it. All together! Heave away, boys! . . ." but despite their united efforts the wattle hardly moved, and in the silence that followed the heavy breathing of the men was audible.

"Here, you of the Sixth Company! Devils that you are! Lend a hand . . . will you? You may want us one of these days."

Some twenty men of the Sixth Company who were on their way into the village joined the haulers, and the wattle wall, which was about thirty-five feet long and seven feet high, moved forward along the village street, swaying, pressing upon and cutting the shoulders of the gasping men.

"Get along . . . Falling? What are you stopping for? There now. . . ."

Merry senseless words of abuse flowed freely.

"What are you up to?" suddenly came the authoritative voice of a sergeant major who came upon the men who were hauling their burden. "There are gentry here; the general himself is in that hut, and you foul-mouthed devils, you brutes, I'll give it to you!" shouted he, hitting the first man who came in his way a swinging blow on the back. "Can't you make less noise?"

The men became silent. The soldier who had been struck groaned and wiped his face, which had been scratched till it bled by his falling against the wattle.

"There, how that devil hits out! He's made my face all bloody," said he in a frightened whisper when the sergeant major had passed on.

"Don't you like it?" said a laughing voice, and moderating their tones the men moved forward.

When they were out of the village they began talking again as loud as before, interlarding their talk with the same aimless expletives.

In the hut which the men had passed, the chief officers had gathered and were in animated talk over their tea about the events of the day and the maneuvers suggested for tomorrow. It was proposed to make a flank march to the left, cut off the Vice-King (Murat) and capture him.

By the time the soldiers had dragged the wattle fence to its place the campfires were blazing on all sides ready for cooking, the wood crackled, the snow was melting, and black shadows of soldiers flitted to and fro all over the occupied space where the snow had been trodden down.

Axes and choppers were plied all around. Everything was done without any orders being given. Stores of wood were brought for the night, shelters were rigged up for the officers, cauldrons were being boiled, and muskets and accouterments put in order.

The wattle wall the men had brought was set up in a semicircle by the Eighth Company as a shelter from the north, propped up by musket rests, and a campfire was built before it. They beat the tattoo, called the roll, had supper, and settled down round the fires for the night—some repairing their footgear, some smoking pipes, and some stripping themselves naked to steam the lice out of their shirts.

4

The French Army melted away at the uniform rate of a mathematical progression; and that crossing of the Berëzina about which so much has been written was only one intermediate stage in its destruction, and not at all the decisive episode of the campaign.

The sole importance of the crossing of the Berëzina lies in the fact that it plainly and indubitably proved the fallacy of all the plans for cutting off the enemy's retreat and the soundness of the only possible line of action—the one Kutúzov and the general mass of the army demanded—namely, simply to follow the enemy up. The French crowd fled at a continually increasing speed and all its energy was directed to reaching its goal. It fled like a wounded animal and it was impossible to block its path.

Certain destruction lay behind the French but in front there was hope. Their ships had been burned, there was no salvation save in collective flight, and on that the whole strength of the French was concentrated.

The farther they fled the more wretched became the plight of the remnant, especially after the Berëzina, on which special hopes had been placed by the Russians, and the keener grew the passions of the Russian commanders, who blamed one another and Kutúzov most of all. Anticipation that the failure would be attributed to Kutúzov led to dissatisfaction, contempt, and ridicule, more and more strongly expressed. The ridicule and contempt were of course expressed in a respectful form, making it impossible for him to ask wherein he was to blame.

After the junction with the army of the brilliant admiral and Petersburg hero Wittgenstein, this mood and the gossip of the staff reached their maximum. Kutúzov saw this and merely sighed and shrugged his shoulders. Only once, after the affair of the Berëzina, did he get angry and write to Bennigsen (who reported separately to the Emperor) the following letter:

"On account of your spells of ill health, will your excellency please be so good as to set off for Kalúga on receipt of this, and there await further commands and appointments from His Imperial Majesty."

But after Bennigsen's departure, the Grand Duke Tsarévich Constantine Pávlovich joined the army. He had taken part in the beginning of the campaign but had subsequently been removed from the army by Kutúzov. Now having come to the army, he informed Kutúzov of the Emperor's displeasure at the poor success of our forces and the slowness of their advance. The Emperor intended to join the army personally in a few days' time.

The old man, experienced in court as well as in military affairs—this same Kutúzov who in August had been chosen commander in chief against the sovereign's wishes and who had removed the Grand Duke and heir-apparent from the army—who on his own authority and contrary to the Emperor's will had decided on the abandonment of Moscow, now realized at once that his day was over, that his part was played, and that the power he was supposed to hold was no longer his. And he understood this not merely from the attitude of the court. He saw on the one hand that the military business in which he had played his part was ended and felt that his mission was accomplished; and at the same time he began to be conscious of the physical weariness of his aged body and of the necessity of physical rest.

On the twenty-ninth of November Kutúzov entered Vílna —his "dear Vílna" as he called it. Twice during his career Kutúzov had been governor of Vílna. In that wealthy town, which had not been injured, he found old friends and associations, besides the comforts of life of which he had so long been deprived. And he suddenly turned from the cares of army and state and, as far as the passions that seethed around him allowed, immersed himself in the quiet life to which he had formerly been accustomed, as if all that was taking place and all that had still to be done in the realm of history did not concern him at all.

Contrary to the Emperor's wish Kutúzov detained the greater part of the army at Vílna. Those about him said that he became extraordinarily slack and physically feeble during his stay in that town. He attended to army affairs reluctantly, left everything to his generals, and while awaiting the Emperor's arrival led a dissipated life.

Having left Petersburg on the seventh of December with his suite, the Emperor reached Vílna on the eleventh, and in his traveling sleigh drove straight to the castle. In spite of the severe frost some hundred generals and staff officers in full parade uniform stood in front of the castle, as well as a guard of honor of the Semënov regiment.

A courier who galloped to the castle in advance, in a troika with three foam-flecked horses, shouted "Coming!" and Konovnítsyn rushed into the vestibule to inform Kutúzov, who was waiting in the hall porter's little lodge.

A minute later the old man's large stout figure in full-dress uniform, his chest covered with orders and a scarf drawn round his stomach, waddled out into the porch. He put on his hat with its peaks to the sides and, holding his gloves in his hand and walking with an effort sideways down the steps to the level of the street, took in his hand the report he had prepared for the Emperor.

The Emperor with a rapid glance scanned Kutúzov from head to foot, frowned for an instant, but immediately mastering himself went up to the old man, extended his arms and embraced him. And this embrace too, owing to a long-standing impression related to his innermost feelings, had its usual effect on Kutúzov and he gave a sob.

The Emperor greeted the officers and the Semënov guard,

and again pressing the old man's hand went with him into the castle.

When alone with the field marshal the Emperor expressed his dissatisfaction at the slowness of the pursuit and at the mistakes made at Krásnoe and the Berëzina, and informed him of his intentions for a future campaign abroad. Kutúzov made no rejoinder or remark. The same submissive, expressionless look with which he had listened to the Emperor's commands on the field of Austerliz seven years before settled on his face now.

Next day the field marshal gave a dinner and ball which the Emperor honored by his presence. Kutúzov had received the Order of St. George of the First Class and the Emperor showed him the highest honors, but everyone knew of the imperial dissatisfaction with him.

The Emperor's displeasure with Kutúzov was specially increased at Vílna by the fact that Kutúzov evidently could not or would not understand the importance of the coming campaign.

When on the following morning the Emperor said to the officers assembled about him: "You have not only saved Russia, you have saved Europe!" they all understood that the war was not ended.

Kutúzov alone would not see this and openly expressed his opinion that no fresh war could improve the position or add to the glory of Russia, but could only spoil and lower the glorious position that Russia had gained. He tried to prove to the Emperor the impossibility of levying fresh troops, spoke of the hardships already endured by the people, of the possibility of failure and so forth.

This being the field marshal's frame of mind he was naturally regarded as merely a hindrance and obstacle to the impending war.

To avoid unpleasant encounters with the old man, the natural method was to do what had been done with him at Austerlitz and with Barclay at the beginning of the Russian campaign—to transfer the authority to the Emperor himself, thus cutting the ground from under the commander in chief's feet without upsetting the old man by informing him of the change.

With this object his staff was gradually reconstructed and its real strength removed and transferred to the Emperor. Everyone spoke loudly of the field marshal's great weakness and failing health.

His health had to be bad for his place to be taken away and given to another. And in fact his health was poor.

The war of 1812, besides its national significance dear to every Russian heart, was now to assume another, a European, significance.

Alexander I was as necessary for the movement of the peoples from east to west and for the refixing of national frontiers as Kutúzov had been for the salvation and glory of Russia.

Kutúzov did not understand what Europe, the balance of power, or Napoleon meant. He could not understand it. For the representative of the Russian people, after the enemy had been destroyed and Russia had been liberated and raised to the summit of her glory, there was nothing left to do as a Russian. Nothing remained for the representative of the national war but to die, and Kutúzov died.

5

As generally happens, Pierre did not feel the full effects of the physical privation and strain he had suffered as prisoner until after they were over. After his liberation he reached Orël, and on the third day there, when preparing to go to Kiev, he fell ill and was laid up for three months.

Scarcely any impression was left on Pierre's mind by all that happened to him from the time of his rescue till his illness. On the day of his rescue he had seen the body of Pétya Rostóv. That same day he had learned that Prince Andrew, after surviving the battle of Borodinó for more than a month, had recently died in the Rostóvs' house at Yaroslávl, and Denísov who told him this news also mentioned Hélène's death, supposing that Pierre had heard of it long before. All this at the time seemed merely strange to Pierre: he felt he could not grasp its significance. When he came to himself after his illness he saw in attendance on him two of his servants, Terénty and Váska, who had come from Moscow; and also his cousin the eldest princess.

It was only gradually during his convalescence that Pierre lost the impressions he had become accustomed to during the last few months and got used to the idea that no one would oblige him to go anywhere tomorrow, that no one would deprive him of his warm bed, and that he would be sure to get his dinner, tea, and supper. But for a long time in his dreams he still saw himself in the conditions of captivity. In the same way little by little he came to understand the news he had been told after his rescue, about the death of Prince Andrew, the death of his wife, and the destruction of the French.

A joyous feeling of freedom—that complete inalienable freedom natural to man which he had first experienced at the first halt outside Moscow—filled Pierre's soul during his convalescence. He had all he wanted: the thought of his wife which had been a continual torment to him was no longer there, since she was no more.

The very question that had formerly tormented him, the thing he had continually sought to find—the aim of life—no longer existed for him now. That search for the aim of life had not merely disappeared temporarily—he felt that it no longer existed for him and could not present itself again. And this very absence of an aim gave him the complete, joyous sense of freedom which constituted his happiness at this time.

He could not see an aim, for he now had faith—not faith in any kind of rule, or words, or ideas, but faith in an ever-living, ever-manifest God. Formerly he had sought Him in aims he set himself. In his captivity he had learned that in Karatáev God was greater, more infinite and unfathomable than in the Architect of the Universe recognized by the Freemasons.

That dreadful question, "What for?" which had formerly destroyed all his mental edifices, no longer existed for him. To that question, "What for?" a simple answer was now always ready in his soul: "Because there is a God, that God without whose will not one hair falls from a man's head."

In external ways Pierre had hardly changed at all. In appearance he was just what he used to be. As before he was absent-minded and seemed occupied not with what was before his eyes but with something special of his own. Formerly he had appeared to be a kindhearted but unhappy man, and so people had been inclined to avoid him. Now a smile at the joy of life always played round his lips, and sympathy for others shone in his eyes with a questioning look as to whether they were as contented as he was, and people felt pleased by his presence.

Previously he had talked a great deal, grew excited when he talked, and seldom listened; now he was seldom carried away in conversation and knew how to listen so that people readily told him their most intimate secrets.

The princess, who had never liked Pierre and had been particularly hostile to him since she had felt herself under obligations to him after the old count's death, now after staying a short time in Orël—where she had come intending to show Pierre that in spite of his ingratitude she considered it her duty to nurse him—felt to her surprise and vexation that she had become fond of him.

The most cunning man could not have crept into her confidence more successfully, evoking memories of the best times of her youth and showing sympathy with them. Yet Pierre's cunning consisted simply in finding pleasure in drawing out the human qualities of the embittered, hard, and (in her own way) proud princess.

There was a new feature in Pierre's relations with all the people he now met, which gained for him the general good will. This was his acknowledgment of the impossibility of changing a man's convictions by words, and his recognition of the possibility of everyone thinking, feeling, and seeing things each from his own point of view. This legitimate peculiarity of each individual which used to excite and irritate Pierre now became a basis of the sympathy he felt for, and the interest he took in, other people. The difference, and sometimes complete contradiction, between men's opinions and their lives, and between one man and another, pleased him and drew from him an amused and gentle smile.

In practical matters Pierre unexpectedly felt within himself a center of gravity he had previously lacked. Formerly all pecuniary questions, especially requests for money to which, as an extremely wealthy man, he was very frequently exposed, produced in him a state of hopeless agitation and perplexity.

Now to his surprise he found that he no longer felt either doubt or perplexity about these questions. There was now within him a judge who by some rule unknown to him decided what should or should not be done.

He was as indifferent as heretofore to money matters, but now he felt certain of what ought and what ought not to be done.

His head steward came to him at Orël and Pierre reckoned up with him his diminished income. The burning of Moscow had cost him, according to the head steward's calculation, about two million rubles.

To console Pierre for these losses the head steward gave him an estimate showing that despite these losses his income would not be diminished but would even be increased if he refused to pay his wife's debts which he was under no obligation to meet, and did not rebuild his Moscow house and the country house on his Moscow estate, which had cost him eighty thousand rubles a year and brought in nothing.

"Yes, of course that's true," said Pierre with a cheerful smile. "I don't need all that at all. By being ruined I have become much richer."

But in January Savélich came from Moscow and gave him an account of the state of things there, and spoke of the estimate an architect had made of the cost of rebuilding the town and country houses, speaking of this as of a settled matter. About the same time he received letters from Prince Vasíli and other Petersburg acquaintances speaking of his wife's debts. And Pierre decided that the steward's proposals which had so pleased him were wrong and that he must go to Petersburg and settle his wife's affairs and must rebuild in Moscow. Why this was necessary he did not know, but he knew for certain that it was necessary. His income would be reduced by three fourths, but he felt it must be done.

At the end of January Pierre went to Moscow and stayed in an annex of his house which had not been burned. He called on Count Rostopchín and on some acquaintances who were back in Moscow, and he intended to leave for Petersburg two days later. Everybody was celebrating the victory, everything was bubbling with life in the ruined but reviving city. Everyone was pleased to see Pierre, everyone wished to meet him, and everyone questioned him about what he had seen.

He had heard that the Rostóvs were at Kostromá but the thought of Natásha seldom occurred to him. If it did it was only as a pleasant memory of the distant past. He felt himself not only free from social obligations but also from that feeling which, it seemed to him, he had aroused in himself.

On the third day after his arrival he heard from the Drubetskóys that Princess Mary was in Moscow. The death, sufferings, and last days of Prince Andrew had often occupied Pierre's thoughts and now recurred to him with fresh vividness. Having heard at dinner that Princess Mary was in Moscow and living in her house—which had not been burned—in Vozdvízhenka Street, he drove that same evening to see her.

On his way to the house Pierre kept thinking of Prince Andrew, of their friendship, of his various meetings with him, and especially of the last one at Borodinó.

"Is it possible that he died in the bitter frame of mind he was then in? Is it possible that the meaning of life was not disclosed to him before he died?" thought Pierre. He recalled Karatáev and his death and involuntarily began to compare these two men, so different, and yet so similar in that they had both lived and both died and in the love he felt for both of them.

In a rather low room lit by one candle sat the princess and with her another person dressed in black. Pierre remembered that the princess always had lady companions, but who they were and what they were like he never knew or remembered. "This must be one of her companions," he thought, glancing at the lady in the black dress.

The princess rose quickly to meet him and held out her hand.

"Yes," she said, looking at his altered face after he had kissed her hand, "so this is how we meet again. He often spoke of you even at the very last," she went on, turning her eyes from Pierre to her companion with a shyness that surprised him for an instant.

"I was so glad to hear of your safety. It was the first piece of good news we had received for a long time."

Again the princess glanced round at her companion with even more uneasiness in her manner and was about to add something, but Pierre interrupted her.

"Just imagine—I knew nothing about him!" said he. "I thought he had been killed. All I know I heard at second hand from others. I only know that he fell in with the Rostóvs. . . . What a strange coincidence!"

Pierre spoke rapidly and with animation. He glanced once at the companion's face, saw her attentive and kindly gaze fixed on him, and, as often happens when one is talking, felt somehow that this companion in the black dress was a good, kind, excellent creature who would not hinder his conversing freely with Princess Mary.

But when he mentioned the Rostóvs, Princess Mary's face expressed still greater embarrassment. She again glanced rapidly from Pierre's face to that of the lady in the black dress and said:

"Do you really not recognize her?"

Pierre looked again at the companion's pale, delicate face with its black eyes and peculiar mouth, and something near to him, long forgotten and more than sweet, looked at him from those attentive eyes.

"But no, it can't be!" he thought. "This stern, thin, pale face that looks so much older! It cannot be she. It merely reminds me of her." But at that moment Princess Mary said, "Natásha!" And with difficulty, effort, and stress, like the opening of a door grown rusty on its hinges, a smile appeared on the face with the attentive eyes, and from that opening door came a breath of fragrance which suffused Pierre with a happiness he had long forgotten and of which he had not even been thinking—especially at that moment. It suffused him, seized him, and enveloped him completely. When she smiled doubt was no longer possible, it was Natásha and he loved her.

At that moment Pierre involuntarily betrayed to her, to Princess Mary, and above all to himself, a secret of which he himself had been unaware. He flushed joyfully yet with painful distress. He tried to hide his agitation. But the more he tried to hide it the more clearly—clearer than any words could have done—did he betray to himself, to her, and to Princess Mary that he loved her.

Pierre had failed to notice Natásha because he did not at all expect to see her there, but he had failed to recognize her because the change in her since he last saw her was immense.

Pierre's confusion was not reflected by any confusion on Natásha's part, but only by the pleasure that just perceptibly lit up her whole face.

"She has come to stay with me," said Princess Mary. "The count and countess will be here in a few days. The countess is in a dreadful state; but it was necessary for Natásha herself to see a doctor. They insisted on her coming with me."

"Yes, is there a family free from sorrow now?" said Pierre, addressing Natásha. "You know it happened the very day we were rescued. I saw him. What a delightful boy he was!"

Natásha looked at him, and by way of answer to his words her eyes widened and lit up.

"What can one say or think of as a consolation?" said Pierre. "Nothing! Why had such a splendid boy, so full of life, to die?"

"Yes, in these days it would be hard to live without faith . . ." remarked Princess Mary.

"Yes, yes, that is really true," Pierre hastily interrupted her.

"Why is it true?" Natásha asked, looking attentively into Pierre's eyes.

"How can you ask why?" said Princess Mary. "The thought alone of what awaits . . ."

Natásha without waiting for Princess Mary to finish again looked inquiringly at Pierre.

"And because," Pierre continued, "only one who believes that there is a God ruling us can bear a loss such as hers and . . . yours."

Natásha had already opened her mouth to speak but suddenly stopped. Pierre hurriedly turned away from her and again addressed Princess Mary, asking about his friend's last days.

Princess Mary—reluctantly as is usual in such cases—began telling of the condition in which she had found Prince Andrew. But Pierre's face quivering with emotion, his questions and his eager restless expression, gradually compelled her to go into details which she feared to recall for her own sake.

"What a happy thing that he saw you again," he added,

suddenly turning to Natásha and looking at her with eyes full of tears.

Natásha's face twitched. She frowned and lowered her eyes for a moment. She hesitated for an instant whether to speak or not.

"Yes, that was happiness," she then said in her quiet voice with its deep chest notes. "For me it certainly was happiness." She paused. "And he . . . he . . . he said he was wishing for it at the very moment I entered the room. . . ."

Natásha's voice broke. She blushed, pressed her clasped hands on her knees, and then controlling herself with an evident effort lifted her head and began to speak rapidly.

And not letting them interrupt her she went on to tell what she had never yet mentioned to anyone—all she had lived through during those three weeks of their journey and life at Yaroslávl.

Pierre listened to her with lips parted and eyes fixed upon her full of tears. As he listened he did not think of Prince Andrew, nor of death, nor or what she was telling. He listened to her and felt only pity for her, for what she was suffering now while she was speaking.

Princess Mary, frowning in her effort to hold back her tears, sat beside Natásha, and heard for the first time the story of those last days of her brother's and Natásha's love.

Evidently Natásha needed to tell that painful yet joyful tale.

Dessalles' voice was heard outside the door asking whether little Nicholas might come in to say good night.

"Well, that's all—everything," said Natásha.

She got up quickly just as Nicholas entered, almost ran to the door which was hidden by curtains, struck her head against it, and rushed from the room with a moan either of pain or sorrow.

Pierre gazed at the door through which she had disappeared and did not understand why he suddenly felt all alone in the world. He wished to take leave of Princess Mary, but she would not let him go.

"No, Natásha and I sometimes don't go to sleep till after two, so please don't go. I will order supper. Go downstairs, we will come immediately."

Before Pierre left the room Princess Mary told him: "This is the first time she has talked of him like that."

Pierre was shown into the large, brightly lit dining room; a few minutes later he heard footsteps and Princess Mary entered with Natásha. Natásha was calm, though a severe and grave expression had again settled on her face. They all three of them now experienced that feeling of awkwardness which usually follows after a serious and heartfelt talk.

"Do you take vodka, Count?" asked Princess Mary, and those words suddenly banished the shadows of the past. "Now tell us about yourself," said she. "One hears such improbable wonders about you."

"Yes," replied Pierre with the smile of mild irony now habitual to him. "They even tell me wonders I myself never dreamed of!"

"Tell me, you did not know of the countess' death when you decided to remain in Moscow?" asked Princess Mary and immediately blushed.

"No," answered Pierre. "I heard of it in Orël and you cannot imagine how it shocked me. We were not an exemplary couple," he added quickly, glancing at Natásha and noticing on her face curiosity as to how he would speak of his wife, "but her death shocked me terribly. When two people quarrel they are always both in fault, and one's own guilt suddenly becomes terribly serious when the other is no longer alive. And then such a death . . . without friends and without consolation! I am very, very sorry for her," he concluded, and was pleased to notice a look of glad approval on Natásha's face.

"Yes, and so you are once more an eligible bachelor," said Princess Mary.

Pierre suddenly flushed crimson and for a long time tried not to look at Natásha.

Supper was over, and Pierre who at first declined to speak about his captivity was gradually led on to do so.

Princess Mary with a gentle smile looked now at Pierre and now at Natásha. In the whole narrative she saw only Pierre and his goodness. Natásha, leaning on her elbow, the expression of her face constantly changing with the narrative, watched Pierre with an attention that never wandered—evidently herself experiencing all that he described.

"I am sure you're not telling us everything; I am sure you

did something . . ." said Natásha, and pausing added, "something fine?"

Pierre began to tell about Karatáev, but paused. By this time he had risen from table and was pacing the room, Natásha following him with her eyes. Then he added:

"No, you can't understand what I learned from that illiterate man—that simple fellow."

"Yes, yes, go on!" said Natásha. "Where is he?"

"They killed him almost before my eyes."

And Pierre, his voice trembling continually, went on to tell of the last days of their retreat, of Karatáev's illness and his death.

Pierre finished his story. Natásha continued to look at him intently with bright, attentive, and animated eyes, as if trying to understand something more which he had perhaps left untold. Pierre in shamefaced and happy confusion glanced occasionally at her, and tried to think what to say next to introduce a fresh subject. Princess Mary was silent. It occurred to none of them that it was three o'clock and time to go to bed.

"People speak of misfortunes and sufferings," remarked Pierre, "but if at this moment I were asked: 'Would you rather be what you were before you were taken prisoner, or go through all this again?' then for heaven's sake let me again have captivity and horseflesh! We imagine that when we are thrown out of our usual ruts all is lost, but it is only then that what is new and good begins. While there is life there is happiness. There is much, much before us. I say this to you," he added, turning to Natásha.

"Yes, yes," she said, answering something quite different. "I too should wish nothing but to relive it all from the beginning."

Pierre looked intently at her.

"Yes, and nothing more," said Natásha.

"It's not true, not true!" cried Pierre. "I am not to blame for being alive and wishing to live—nor you either."

Suddenly Natásha bent her head, covered her face with her hands, and began to cry.

"What is it, Natásha?" said Princess Mary.

"Nothing, nothing." She smiled at Pierre through her tears. "Good night! It is time for bed."

Pierre rose and took his leave.

Princess Mary and Natásha met as usual in the bedroom. They talked of what Pierre had told them.

"Do you know, Mary . . ." Natásha suddenly said with a mischievous smile such as Princess Mary had not seen on her face for a long time, "he has somehow grown so clean, smooth, and fresh—as if he had just come out of a Russian bath; do you understand? Out of a moral bath. Isn't it true?"

"I understand why *he*" (Prince Andrew) "liked no one so much as him," said Princess Mary.

"Yes, and yet he is quite different. They say men are friends when they are quite different. That must be true. Really he is quite unlike him—in everything."

"Yes, but he's wonderful."

"Well, good night," said Natásha.

And the same mischievous smile lingered for a long time on her face as if it had been forgotten there.

It was a long time before Pierre could fall asleep that night. He paced up and down his room, now turning his thoughts on a difficult problem and frowning, now suddenly shrugging his shoulders and wincing, and now smiling happily.

He was thinking of Prince Andrew, of Natásha, and of their love, at one moment jealous of her past, then reproaching himself for that feeling. It was already six in the morning and he still paced up and down the room.

"Well, what's to be done if it cannot be avoided? What's to be done? Evidently it has to be so," said he to himself, and hastily undressing he got into bed, happy and agitated but free from hesitation or indecision.

"Strange and impossible as such happiness seems, I must do everything that she and I may be man and wife," he told himself.

A few days previously Pierre had decided to go to Petersburg on the Friday. When he awoke on the Thursday, Savélich came to ask him about packing for the journey.

"What, to Petersburg? What is Petersburg? Who is there in Petersburg?" he asked involuntarily, though only to himself.

Pierre went to Princess Mary's to dinner.

At the entrance to Princess Mary's house Pierre felt doubtful whether he had really been there the night before and had really seen Natásha and talked to her. But he had hardly entered the room before he felt her presence with his whole being by the loss of his sense of freedom.

She was as he had known her almost as a child and later on as Prince Andrew's fiancée. A bright questioning light shone in her eyes, and on her face was a friendly and strangely roguish expression.

Pierre dined with them and would have spent the whole evening there, but Princess Mary was going to vespers and Pierre left the house with her.

Next day he came early, dined, and stayed the whole evening. Princess Mary and Natásha exchanged glances, evidently wondering when he would go. Pierre noticed this but could not go. He felt uneasy and embarrassed, but sat on because he simply could not get up and take his leave.

Princess Mary, foreseeing no end to this, rose first, and complaining of a headache began to say good night.

"So you are going to Petersburg tomorrow?" she asked.

"No, I am not going," Pierre replied hastily, in a surprised tone and as though offended. "Yes . . . no . . . to Petersburg? Tomorrow—but I won't say good-by yet. I will call round in case you have any commissions for me," said he, standing before Princess Mary and turning red, but not taking his departure.

Natásha gave him her hand and went out. Princess Mary on the other hand instead of going away sank into an armchair, and looked sternly and intently at him with her deep, radiant eyes. The weariness she had plainly shown before had now quite passed off. With a deep and long-drawn sigh she seemed to be prepared for a lengthy talk.

When Natásha left the room Pierre's confusion and awkwardness immediately vanished and were replaced by eager excitement. He quickly moved an armchair toward Princess Mary.

"Yes, I wanted to tell you," said he, answering her look as if she had spoken. "Princess, help me! What am I to do? Can I hope? Princess, my dear friend, listen! I know it all. I know I am not worthy of her, I know it's impossible to speak of it now. But I want to be a brother to her. No, not that, I don't, I can't . . ."

He paused and rubbed his face and eyes with his hands.

"Well," he went on with an evident effort at self-control

and coherence. "I don't know when I began to love her, but I have loved her and her alone all my life, and I love her so that I cannot imagine life without her. I cannot propose to her at present, but the thought that perhaps she might someday be my wife and that I may be missing that possibility . . . that possibility . . . is terrible. Tell me, can I hope? Tell me what I am to do, dear princess!" he added after a pause, and touched her hand as she did not reply.

"I am thinking of what you have told me," answered Princess Mary. "This is what I will say. You are right that to speak to her of love at present . . ."

Princess Mary stopped. She was going to say that to speak of love was impossible, but she stopped because she had seen by the sudden change in Natásha two days before that she would not only not be hurt if Pierre spoke of his love, but that it was the very thing she wished for.

"To speak to her now wouldn't do," said the princess all the same.

"But what am I to do?"

"Leave it to me," said Princess Mary. "I know . . ."

Pierre was looking into Princess Mary's eyes.

"Well? . . . Well? . . ." he said.

"I know that she loves . . . will love you," Princess Mary corrected herself.

Before her words were out, Pierre had sprung up and with a frightened expression seized Princess Mary's hand.

"What makes you think so? You think I may hope? You think . . . ?"

"Yes, I think so," said Princess Mary with a smile. "Write to her parents, and leave it to me. I will tell her when I can. I wish it to happen and my heart tells me it will."

"No, it cannot be! How happy I am! But it can't be. . . . How happy I am! No, it can't be!" Pierre kept saying as he kissed Princess Mary's hands.

"Go to Petersburg, that will be best. And I will write to you," she said.

"To Petersburg? Go there? Very well, I'll go. But I may come again tomorrow?"

Next day Pierre came to say good-by. Natásha was less animated than she had been the day before; but that day as he looked at her Pierre sometimes felt as if he was vanishing and that neither he nor she existed any longer, that nothing existed but happiness. "Is it possible? No, it can't be," he told himself at every look, gesture, and word that filled his soul with joy.

When on saying good-by he took her thin, slender hand, he could not help holding it a little longer in his own.

"Is it possible that this hand, that face, those eyes, all this treasure of feminine charm so strange to me now, is it possible that it will one day be mine forever, as familiar to me as I am to myself? . . . No, that's impossible! . . ."

"Good-by, Count," she said aloud. "I shall look forward very much to your return," she added in a whisper.

And these simple words, her look, and the expression on her face which accompanied them, formed for two months the subject of inexhaustible memories, interpretations, and happy meditations for Pierre.

There was nothing in Pierre's soul now at all like what had troubled it during his courtship of Hélène.

There was now not a shadow of doubt in his mind as to whether what he had undertaken was right or wrong. Only one terrible doubt sometimes crossed his mind: "Wasn't it all a dream? Isn't Princess Mary mistaken? Am I not too conceited and self-confident? I believe all this—and suddenly Princess Mary will tell her, and she will be sure to smile and say: 'How strange! He must be deluding himself. Doesn't he know that he is a man, just a man, while I . . . ? I am something altogether different and higher.'"

That was the only doubt often troubling Pierre. He did not now make any plans. The happiness before him appeared so inconceivable that if only he could attain it, it would be the end of all things. Everything ended with that.

Often in afterlife Pierre recalled this period of blissful insanity. All the views he formed of men and circumstances at this time remained true for him always. He not only did not renounce them subsequently, but when he was in doubt or inwardly at variance, he referred to the views he had held at this time of his madness and they always proved correct.

"I may have appeared strange and queer then," he thought, "but I was not so mad as I seemed. On the contrary I was then wiser and had more insight than at any other time, and

understood all that is worth understanding in life, because
. . . because I was happy."

Pierre's insanity consisted in not waiting, as he used to do,
to discover personal attributes which he termed "good qualities" in people before loving them; his heart was now overflowing with love, and by loving people without cause he
discovered indubitable causes for loving them.

After Pierre's departure that first evening, something hidden
and unknown to herself, but irrepressible, awoke in Natásha's
soul.

Everything: her face, walk, look, and voice, was suddenly
altered. To her own surprise a power of life and hope of happiness rose to the surface and demanded satisfaction. From
that evening she seemed to have forgotten all that had happened to her. She no longer complained of her position, did
not say a word about the past, and no longer feared to make
happy plans for the future. She spoke little of Pierre, but
when Princess Mary mentioned him a long-extinguished light
once more kindled in her eyes and her lips curved with a
strange smile.

When Princess Mary returned to her room after her noc-
turnal talk with Pierre, Natásha met her on the threshold.

"He has spoken? Yes? He has spoken?" she repeated.

And a joyful yet pathetic expression which seemed to beg
forgiveness for her joy settled on Natásha's face.

"I wanted to listen at the door, but I knew you would tell
me."

Understandable and touching as the look with which
Natásha gazed at her seemed to Princess Mary, and sorry as
she was to see her agitation, these words pained her for a moment. She remembered her brother and his love.

"But what's to be done? She can't help it," thought the
princess.

And with a sad and rather stern look she told Natásha all
that Pierre had said. On hearing that he was going to Petersburg Natásha was astounded.

"To Petersburg!" she repeated as if unable to understand.

But noticing the grieved expression on Princess Mary's face
she guessed the reason of that sadness and suddenly began
to cry.

"Mary," said she, "tell me what I should do! I am afraid of being bad. Whatever you tell me, I will do. Tell me. . . ."

"You love him?"

"Yes," whispered Natásha.

"Then why are you crying? I am happy for your sake," said Princess Mary, who because of those tears quite forgave Natásha's joy.

"It won't be just yet—someday. Think what fun it will be when I am his wife and you marry Nicholas!"

"Natásha, I have asked you not to speak of that. Let us talk about you."

They were silent awhile.

"But why go to Petersburg?" Natásha suddenly asked, and hastily replied to her own question. "But no, no, he must. . . . Yes, Mary. He must. . . ."

1813-20

EPILOGUE

1

*If we admit that human life can be ruled by reason,
Tolstoy declares, then the possibility of life is destroyed,
and he applies this dictum to the reasoned conclusions
of historians. For if we assume, as historians do, that
great men lead humanity to the attainment of certain
ends, then it is impossible to explain the facts of history
without introducing the conception of chance and genius.
But chance and genius become superfluous as explanations, Tolstoy asserts—in a brief review of the careers of
Napoleon and Alexander I—when we realize that the
events of historic actions are inevitable and their ultimate purpose can never be immediately intelligible.*

2

Natásha's wedding to Bezúkhov, which took
place in 1813, was the last happy event in the family of the
old Rostóvs. Count Ilyá Rostóv died that same year and, as
always happens, after the father's death the family group
broke up.

Nicholas was with the Russian army in Paris when the
news of his father's death reached him. He at once resigned
his commission, and without waiting for it to be accepted
took leave of absence and went to Moscow. The state of the
count's affairs became quite obvious a month after his death,
surprising everyone by the immense total of small debts the
existence of which no one had suspected. The debts amounted
to double the value of the property.

Friends and relations advised Nicholas to decline the inheritance. But he regarded such a refusal as a slur on his father's memory, which he held sacred, and therefore would not hear of refusing and accepted the inheritance together with the obligation to pay the debts.

He could not rejoin the army where he would have been made colonel at the next vacancy, for his mother now clung to him as her one hold on life; and so despite his reluctance to remain in Moscow among people who had known him before, and despite his abhorrence of the civil service, he accepted a post in Moscow in that service, doffed the uniform of which he was so fond, and moved with his mother and Sónya to a small house on the Sívtsev Vrazhëk.

Natásha and Pierre were living in Petersburg at the time and had no clear idea of Nicholas' circumstances. Having borrowed money from his brother-in-law, Nicholas tried to hide his wretched condition from him. His position was the more difficult because with his salary of twelve hundred rubles he had not only to keep himself, his mother, and Sónya, but had to shield his mother from knowledge of their poverty.

Sónya kept house, attended on her aunt, read to her, put up with her whims and secret ill-will, and helped Nicholas to conceal their poverty from the old countess. Nicholas felt himself irredeemably indebted to Sónya for all she was doing for his mother and greatly admired her patience and devotion, but tried to keep aloof from her.

Nicholas' position became worse and worse. The idea of putting something aside out of his salary proved a dream. Not only did he not save anything, but to comply with his mother's demands he even incurred some small debts. He could see no way out of this situation. The idea of marrying some rich woman, which was suggested to him by his female relations, was repugnant to him. He wished for nothing and hoped for nothing, and deep in his heart experienced a gloomy and stern satisfaction in an uncomplaining endurance of his position.

At the beginning of winter Princess Mary came to Moscow. From reports current in town she learned how the Rostóvs were situated, and how "the son has sacrificed himself for his mother," as people were saying.

"I never expected anything else of him," said Princess Mary to herself, feeling a joyous sense of her love for him. Remembering her friendly relations with all the Rostóvs which had made her almost a member of the family, she thought it her duty to go to see them. But remembering her relations with Nicholas in Vorónezh she was shy about doing so. Making a great effort she did however go to call on them a few weeks after her arrival in Moscow.

Nicholas was the first to meet her, as the countess' room could only be reached through his. But instead of being greeted with pleasure as she had expected, at his first glance at her his face assumed a cold, stiff, proud expression she had not seen on it before. He inquired about her health, led the way to his mother, and having sat there for five minutes left the room.

When the princess came out of the countess' room Nicholas met her again, and with marked solemnity and stiffness accompanied her to the anteroom. To her remarks about his mother's health he made no reply. "What's that to you? Leave me in peace," his looks seemed to say.

"Why does she come prowling here? What does she want? I can't bear these ladies and all these civilities!" said he aloud in Sónya's presence, evidently unable to repress his vexation, after the princess' carriage had disappeared.

"Oh, Nicholas, how can you talk like that?" cried Sónya, hardly able to conceal her delight. "She is so kind and Mamma is so fond of her!"

Nicholas did not reply and tried to avoid speaking of the princess any more. But after her visit the old countess spoke of her several times a day.

After her visit to the Rostóvs and her unexpectedly chilly reception by Nicholas, Princess Mary confessed to herself that she had been right in not wishing to be the first to call.

But she could not pacify herself with these reflections; a feeling akin to remorse troubled her when she thought of her visit. Though she had firmly resolved not to call on the Rostóvs again and to forget the whole matter, she felt herself all the time in an awkward position. And when she asked herself what distressed her, she had to admit that it was her relation to Rostóv. His cold, polite manner did not express his feeling for her (she knew that) but it concealed something, and until she could discover what that something was, she felt that she could not be at ease.

One day in midwinter when sitting in the schoolroom attending to her nephew's lessons, she was informed that Rostóv had called. With a firm resolution not to betray herself and not show her agitation, she sent for Mademoiselle Bourienne and went with her to the drawing room.

Her first glance at Nicholas' face told her that he had only come to fulfill the demands of politeness, and she firmly resolved to maintain the tone in which he addressed her.

They spoke of the countess' health, of their mutual friends, of the latest war news, and when the ten minutes required by propriety had elapsed after which a visitor may rise, Nicholas got up to say good-by.

With Mademoiselle Bourienne's help the princess had maintained the conversation very well, but at the very last moment, just when he rose, she was so tired of talking of what did not interest her, and her mind was so full of the question why she alone was granted so little happiness in life, that in a fit of absent-mindedness she sat still, her luminous eyes gazing fixedly before her, not noticing that he had risen.

He suddenly felt sorry for her and was vaguely conscious that he might be the cause of the sadness her face expressed. He wished to help her and say something pleasant, but could think of nothing to say.

"Good-by, Princess!" said he.

She started, flushed, and sighed deeply.

"Oh, I beg your pardon," she said as if waking up. "Are you going already, Count? Well then, good-by! Oh, but the cushion for the countess!"

"Wait a moment, I'll fetch it," said Mademoiselle Bourienne, and she left the room.

They both sat silent, with an occasional glance at one another.

"Yes, Princess," said Nicholas at last with a sad smile, "it doesn't seem long ago since we first met at Boguchárovo, but how much water has flowed since then! In what distress we all seemed to be then, yet I would give much to bring back that time . . . but there's no bringing it back."

Princess Mary gazed intently into his eyes with her own luminous ones as he said this. She seemed to be trying to fathom the hidden meaning of his words which would explain his feeling for her.

"Yes, yes," said she, "but you have no reason to regret the past, Count. As I understand your present life, I think you will always recall it with satisfaction, because the self-sacrifice that fills it now . . ."

"I cannot accept your praise," he interrupted her hurriedly. "On the contrary I continually reproach myself. . . . But this is not at all an interesting or cheerful subject."

His face again resumed its former stiff and cold expression. But the princess had caught a glimpse of the man she had known and loved, and it was to him that she now spoke.

"I thought you would allow me to tell you this," she said. "I had come so near to you . . . and to all your family that I thought you would not consider my sympathy misplaced, but I was mistaken," and suddenly her voice trembled. "I don't know why," she continued, recovering herself, "but you used to be different, and . . ."

"There are a thousand reasons *why*," laying special emphasis on the *why*. "Thank you, Princess," he added softly. "Sometimes it is hard."

"So that's why! That's why!" a voice whispered in Princess Mary's soul. "No, it was not only that gay, kind, and frank look, not only that handsome exterior, that I loved in him. I divined his noble, resolute, self-sacrificing spirit too," she said to herself. "Yes, he is poor now and I am rich. . . . Yes, that's the only reason. . . . Yes, were it not for that . . ." And remembering his former tenderness, and looking now at his kind, sorrowful face, she suddenly understood the cause of his coldness.

"But why, Count, why?" she almost cried, unconsciously moving closer to him. "Why? Tell me. You must tell me!"

He was silent.

"I don't understand your *why*, Count," she continued, "but it's hard for me . . . I confess it. For some reason you wish to deprive me of our former friendship. And that hurts me." There were tears in her eyes and in her voice. "I have had so little happiness in life that every loss is hard for me to bear. . . . Excuse me, good-by!" and suddenly she began to cry and was hurrying from the room.

"Princess, for God's sake!" he exclaimed, trying to stop her. "Princess!"

She turned round. For a few seconds they gazed silently into one another's eyes—and what had seemed impossible and remote suddenly became possible, inevitable, and very near.

In the winter of 1813 Nicholas married Princess Mary and moved to Bald Hills with his wife, his mother, and Sónya.

Within four years he had paid off all his remaining debts without selling any of his wife's property, and having received a small inheritance on the death of a cousin he paid his debt to Pierre as well.

In another three years, by 1820, he had so managed his affairs that he was able to buy a small estate adjoining Bald Hills and was negotiating to buy back Otrádnoe—that being his pet dream.

Having started farming from necessity, he soon grew so devoted to it that it became his favorite and almost his sole occupation. Nicholas was a plain farmer. He always had before his mind's eye the estate as a whole and not any particular part of it. The chief thing in his eyes was not the nitrogen in the soil, nor the oxygen in the air, nor manures, nor special plows, but that most important agent by which nitrogen, oxygen, manure, and plow were made effective—the peasant laborer. When Nicholas first began farming and began to understand its different branches, it was the serf who especially attracted his attention. The peasant seemed to him not merely a tool, but also a judge of farming and an end in himself. At first he watched the serfs, trying to understand their aims and what they considered good and bad, and only pretended to direct them and give orders while in reality learning from them their methods, their manner of speech, and their judgment of what was good and bad. Only when he had understood the peasants' tastes and aspirations, had learned to talk their language, to grasp the hidden meaning of their words, and felt akin to them did he begin boldly to manage his serfs, that is, to perform toward them the duties demanded of him. And Nicholas' management produced very brilliant results.

He was as careful of the sowing and reaping of the peasants' hay and corn as of his own, and few landowners had their crops sown and harvested so early and so well, or got so good a return, as did Nicholas.

Countess Mary was jealous of this passion of her husband's and regretted that she could not share it; but she could not understand the joys and vexations he derived from that world, to her so remote and alien. She could not understand why he was so particularly animated and happy when, after getting up at daybreak and spending the whole morning in the fields or on the threshing floor, he returned from the sowing or mowing or reaping to have tea with her.

Still less did she understand why he, kindhearted and always ready to anticipate her wishes, should become almost desperate when she brought him a petition from some peasant men or women who had appealed to her to be excused some work; why he, that kind Nicholas, should obstinately refuse her, angrily asking her not to interfere in what was not her business. She felt he had a world apart, which he loved passionately and which had laws she had not fathomed.

Sometimes when, trying to understand him, she spoke of the good work he was doing for his serfs, he would be vexed and reply: "Not in the least; it never entered my head and I wouldn't do *that* for their good!"

And all Nicholas did was fruitful—probably just because he refused to allow himself to think that he was doing good to others for virtue's sake. His means increased rapidly; serfs from neighboring estates came to beg him to buy them, and long after his death the memory of his administration was devoutly preserved among the serfs. "He was a master . . . the peasants' affairs first and then his own. Of course he was not to be trifled with either—in a word, he was a real master!"

Among the gentry of the province Nicholas was respected but not liked. He did not concern himself with the interests of his own class, and consequently some thought him proud and others thought him stupid. The whole summer, from spring sowing to harvest, he was busy with the work on his farm. In autumn he gave himself up to hunting with the same businesslike seriousness. In winter he visited his other villages or spent his time reading. The books he read were chiefly historical, and on these he spent a certain sum every year. In winter, except for business excursions, he spent most of his time at home making himself one with his family and

entering into all the details of his children's relations with their
their mother. The harmony between him and his wife grew
closer and closer and he daily discovered fresh spiritual
treasures in her.

From the time of his marriage Sónya had lived in his house.
Before that, Nicholas had told his wife all that had passed
between himself and Sónya, blaming himself and commend-
ing her. He had asked Princess Mary to be gentle and kind to
his cousin. She thoroughly realized the wrong he had done
Sónya, felt herself to blame toward her, and imagined that
her wealth had influenced Nicholas' choice. She could not find
fault with Sónya in any way and tried to be fond of her, but
often felt ill-will toward her which she could not overcome.

Once she had a talk with her friend Natásha about Sónya
and about her own injustice toward her.

"You know," said Natásha, "you have read the Gospels a
great deal—there is a passage in them that just fits Sónya."

"What?" asked Countess Mary, surprised.

" 'To him that hath shall be given, and from him that hath
not shall be taken away.' You remember? She is one that hath
not; why, I don't know. Perhaps she lacks egotism, I don't
know, but from her is taken away, and everything has been
taken away. Sometimes I am dreadfully sorry for her. Formerly I very much wanted Nicholas to marry her, but I always
had a sort of presentiment that it would not come off. She is
a *sterile flower,* you know—like some strawberry blossoms.
Sometimes I am sorry for her, and sometimes I think she
doesn't feel it as you or I would."

It was the eve of St. Nicholas, the fifth of December, 1820.
Natásha had been staying at her brother's with her husband
and children since early autumn. Pierre had gone to Petersburg on business of his own for three weeks as he said, but
had remained there nearly seven weeks and was expected back
every minute.

Besides the Bezúkhov family, Nicholas' old friend the retired General Vasíli Dmítrich Denísov was staying with the
Rostóvs this fifth of December.

Having taken precautions against the general drunkenness
to be expected on the morrow because it was a great saint's
day, Nicholas returned to dinner, and without having time

for a private talk with his wife sat down at the long table laid for twenty persons, at which the whole household had assembled. At the table were his mother, his mother's old lady companion Belóva, his wife, their three children with their governess and tutor, his wife's nephew with his tutor, Sónya, Denísov, Natásha, her three children, their governess, and old Michael Ivánovich, the late prince's architect, who was living on in retirement at Bald Hills.

Countess Mary sat at the other end of the table. When her husband took his place she concluded, from the rapid manner in which after taking up his table napkin he pushed back the tumbler and wineglass standing before him, that he was out of humor, as was sometimes the case when he came in to dinner straight from the farm—especially before the soup. Countess Mary well knew that mood of his, and when she herself was in a good frame of mind quietly waited till he had had his soup and then began to talk to him and make him admit that there was no cause for his ill-humor. But today she quite forgot that and was hurt that he should be angry with her without any reason, and she felt unhappy. She asked him where he had been. He replied. She again inquired whether everything was going well on the farm. Her unnatural tone made him wince unpleasantly and he replied hastily.

"Then I'm not mistaken," thought Countess Mary. "Why is he cross with me?"

Thanks to Denísov the conversation at table soon became general and lively, and she did not talk to her husband. When they left the table Countess Mary held out her hand and kissed her husband, and asked him why he was angry with her.

"You always have such strange fancies! I didn't even think of being angry," he replied.

But the word *always* seemed to her to imply: "Yes, I am angry but I won't tell you why."

Nicholas and his wife lived together so happily that even Sónya and the old countess, who felt jealous and would have liked them to disagree, could find nothing to reproach them with; but even they had their moments of antagonism. Occasionally, and it was always just after they had been happiest together, they suddenly had a feeling of estrangement and hostility, which occurred most frequently during Countess Mary's pregnancies, and this was such a time.

"Well, *messieurs et mesdames*," said Nicholas loudly and with apparent cheerfulness (it seemed to Countess Mary that he did it on purpose to vex her), "I have been on my feet since six this morning. Tomorrow I shall have to suffer, so today I'll go and rest."

Having sat awhile with her visitors without understanding anything of what they were saying, she softly left the room and went to the nursery.

"Perhaps he is not asleep; I'll have an explanation with him," she said to herself. Little Andrew, her eldest boy, imitating his mother, followed her on tiptoe. She did not notice him.

From the room in which Nicholas was sleeping came the sound of his even breathing, every slightest tone of which was familiar to his wife. As she listened to it she saw before her his smooth handsome forehead, his mustache, and his whole face, as she had so often seen it in the stillness of the night when he slept. Nicholas suddenly moved and cleared his throat. And at that moment little Andrew shouted from outside the door: "Papa! Mamma's standing here!" Countess Mary turned pale with fright and made signs to the boy. He grew silent, and quiet ensued for a moment, terrible to Countess Mary. She knew how Nicholas disliked being waked. Then through the door she heard Nicholas clearing his throat again and stirring, and his voice said crossly:

"I can't get a moment's peace. . . . Mary, is that you? Why did you bring him here?"

"I only came in to look and did not notice . . . forgive me. . . ."

Nicholas coughed and said no more. Countess Mary moved away from the door and took the boy back to the nursery. Five minutes later little black-eyed three-year-old Natásha, her father's pet, having learned from her brother that Papa was asleep and Mamma was in the sitting room, ran to her father unobserved by her mother. The dark-eyed little girl boldly opened the creaking door, went up to the sofa with energetic steps of her sturdy little legs, and having examined the position of her father, who was asleep with his back to her, rose on tiptoe and kissed the hand which lay under his head. Nicholas turned with a tender smile on his face.

"Natásha, Natásha!" came Countess Mary's frightened whisper from the door. "Papa wants to sleep."

"No, Mamma, he doesn't want to sleep," said little Natásha with conviction. "He's laughing."

Nicholas lowered his legs, rose, and took his daughter in his arms.

"Come in, Mary," he said to his wife.

She went in and sat down by her husband.

"I did not notice him following me," she said timidly. "I just looked in."

Holding his little girl with one arm, Nicholas glanced at his wife and, seeing her guilty expression, put his other arm around her and kissed her hair.

"May I kiss Mamma?" he asked Natásha.

Natásha smiled bashfully.

"Again!" she commanded, pointing with a peremptory gesture to the spot where Nicholas had placed the kiss.

"I don't know why you think I am cross," said Nicholas, replying to the question he knew was in his wife's mind.

"You have no idea how unhappy, how lonely, I feel when you are like that. It always seems to me . . ."

"Mary, don't talk nonsense. You ought to be ashamed of yourself!" he said gaily.

"It seems to me that you can't love me, that I am so plain . . . always . . . and now . . . in this cond . . ."

"Oh, how absurd you are! It is not beauty that endears, it's love that makes us see beauty. It is only Malvínas and women of that kind who are loved for their beauty. But do I love my wife? I don't love her, but . . . I don't know how to put it. Without you, or when something comes between us like this, I seem lost and can't do anything. Now do I love my finger? I don't love it, but just try to cut it off!"

"I'm not like that myself, but I understand. So you're not angry with me?"

"Awfully angry!" he said, smiling and getting up. And smoothing his hair he began to pace the room.

At that moment they heard the sound of the door pulley and footsteps in the hall and anteroom, as if someone had arrived.

"Somebody has come."

"I am sure it is Pierre. I will go and see," said Countess Mary and left the room.

"It is he, it is he, Nicholas!" said Countess Mary, re-entering the room a few minutes later. "Now our Natásha has come to life. You should have seen her ecstasy, and how he caught it for having stayed away so long. Well, come along now, quick, quick! It's time you two were parted," she added, looking smilingly at the little girl who clung to her father.

Nicholas went out holding the child by the hand.

Countess Mary remained in the sitting room.

"I should never, never have believed that one could be so happy," she whispered to herself. A smile lit up her face but at the same time she sighed, and her deep eyes expressed a quiet sadness as though she felt, through her happiness, that there is another sort of happiness unattainable in this life and of which she involuntarily thought at that instant.

3

Natásha had married in the early spring of 1813, and in 1820 already had three daughters besides a son for whom she had longed and whom she was now nursing. She had grown stouter and broader, so that it was difficult to recognize in this robust, motherly woman the slim, lively Natásha of former days. Her features were more defined and had a calm, soft, and serene expression. In her face there was none of the ever-glowing animation that had formerly burned there and constituted its charm. Now her face and body were often all that one saw, and her soul was not visible at all. All that struck the eye was a strong, handsome, and fertile woman. The old fire very rarely kindled in her face now. That happened only when, as was the case that day, her husband returned home, or a sick child was convalescent, or when she and Countess Mary spoke of Prince Andrew (she never mentioned him to her husband, who she imagined was jealous of Prince Andrew's memory), or on the rare occasions when something happened to induce her to sing, a practice she had quite abandoned since her marriage. At the rare moments when the old fire did kindle in her handsome, fully developed body she was even more attractive than in former days.

Since their marriage Natásha and her husband had lived in
Moscow, in Petersburg, on their estate near Moscow, or with
her mother, that is to say, in Nicholas' house. The young
Countess Bezúkhova was not often seen in society, and those
who met her there were not pleased with her and found her
neither attractive nor amiable. Not that Natásha liked solitude
—she did not know whether she liked it or not, she even
thought that she did not—but with her pregnancies, her con-
finements, the nursing of her children, and sharing every moment of her husband's life, she had demands on her time
which could be satisfied only by renouncing society.

The subject which wholly engrossed Natásha's attention was
her family: that is, her husband whom she had to keep so that
he should belong entirely to her and to the home, and the
children whom she had to bear, bring into the world, nurse,
and bring up.

And the deeper she penetrated, not with her mind only but
with her whole soul, her whole being, into the subject that
absorbed her, the larger did that subject grow and the weaker
and more inadequate did her own powers appear, so that she
concentrated them wholly on that one thing and yet was unable to accomplish all that she considered necessary.

If the purpose of food is nourishment and the purpose of
marriage is the family, the whole question resolves itself into
not eating more than one can digest, and not having more
wives or husbands than are needed for the family—that is, one
wife or one husband. Natásha needed a husband. A husband
was given her and he gave her a family. And she not only saw
no need of any other or better husband, but as all the powers
of her soul were intent on serving that husband and family,
she could not imagine and saw no interest in imagining how it
would be if things were different.

Natásha did not care for society in general, but prized the
more the society of her relatives—Countess Mary, and her
brother, her mother, and Sónya. She valued the company of
those to whom she could come striding disheveled from the
nursery in her dressing gown, and with joyful face show a
yellow instead of a green stain on baby's napkin, and from
whom she could hear reassuring words to the effect that baby
was much better.

Pierre's subjection consisted in the fact that he not only

dared not flirt with, but dared not even speak smilingly to, any other woman; did not dare dine at the Club as a pastime, did not dare spend money on a whim, and did not dare absent himself for any length of time, except on business—in which his wife included his intellectual pursuits, which she did not in the least understand but to which she attributed great importance. To make up for this, at home Pierre had the right to regulate his life and that of the whole family exactly as he chose. At home Natásha placed herself in the position of a slave to her husband, and the whole household went on tiptoe when he was occupied—that is, was reading or writing in his study. Pierre had but to show a partiality for anything to get just what he liked done always. He had only to express a wish and Natásha would jump up and run to fulfill it.

The entire household was governed according to Pierre's supposed orders, that is, by his wishes which Natásha tried to guess. Their way of life and place of residence, their acquaintances and ties, Natásha's occupations, the children's upbringing, were all selected not merely with regard to Pierre's expressed wishes, but to what Natásha from the thoughts he expressed in conversation supposed his wishes to be. And she deduced the essentials of his wishes quite correctly, and having once arrived at them clung to them tenaciously. When Pierre himself wanted to change his mind she would fight him with his own weapons.

After seven years of marriage Pierre had the joyous and firm consciousness that he was not a bad man, and he felt this because he saw himself reflected in his wife. He felt the good and bad within himself inextricably mingled and overlapping. But only what was really good in him was reflected in his wife, all that was not quite good was rejected. And this was not the result of logical reasoning but was a direct and mysterious reflection.

Two months previously when Pierre was already staying with the Rostóvs he had received a letter from Prince Theodore, asking him to come to Petersburg to confer on some important questions that were being discussed there by a society of which Pierre was one of the principal founders.

On reading that letter (she always read her husband's letters) Natásha herself suggested that he should go to Petersburg, though she would feel his absence very acutely. She attributed immense importance to all her husband's intellectual and abstract interests though she did not understand them, and she always dreaded being a hindrance to him in such matters. To Pierre's timid look of inquiry after reading the letter she replied by asking him to go, but to fix a definite date for his return. He was given four week's leave of absence.

Ever since that leave of absence had expired, more than a fortnight before, Natásha had been in a constant state of alarm, depression, and irritability.

Denísov, now a general on the retired list and much dissatisfied with the present state of affairs, had arrived during that fortnight. He looked at Natásha with sorrow and surprise as at a bad likeness of a person once dear. A dull, dejected look, random replies, and talk about the nursery was all he saw and heard from his former enchantress.

Natásha was sad and irritable all that time, especially when her mother, her brother, Sónya, or Countess Mary in their efforts to console her tried to excuse Pierre and suggested reasons for his delay in returning.

"It's all nonsense, all rubbish—those discussions which lead to nothing and all those idiotic societies!" Natásha declared of the very affairs in the immense importance of which she firmly believed.

And she would go to the nursery to nurse Pétya, her only boy. No one else could tell her anything so comforting or so reasonable as this little three-month-old creature when he lay at her breast and she was conscious of the movement of his lips and the snuffling of his little nose. That creature said: "You are angry, you are jealous, you would like to pay him out, you are afraid—but here am I! And I am he . . ." and that was unanswerable. It was more than true.

She was nursing her boy when the sound of Pierre's sleigh was heard at the front door, and the old nurse—knowing how to please her mistress—entered the room inaudibly but hurriedly and with a beaming face.

"Go, ma'am! Don't worry, go!" she whispered, smiling, with the kind of familiarity that grows up between a nurse and her mistress.

Natásha ran with light footsteps to the anteroom.

Denísov, who had come out of the study into the dancing

room with his pipe, now for the first time recognized the old Natásha. A flood of brilliant, joyful light poured from her transfigured face.

"He's come!" she exclaimed as she ran past, and Denísov felt that he too was delighted that Pierre, whom he did not much care for, had returned.

On reaching the vestibule Natásha saw a tall figure in a fur coat unwinding his scarf. "It's he! It's really he! He has come!" she said to herself, and rushing at him embraced him, pressed his head to her breast, and then pushed him back and gazed at his ruddy, happy face, covered with hoar-frost. "Yes, it is he, happy and contented. . . ."

Then all at once she remembered the tortures of suspense she had experienced for the last fortnight, and the joy that had lit up her face vanished; she frowned and overwhelmed Pierre with a torrent of reproaches and angry words.

"Yes, it's all very well for you. You are pleased, you've had a good time. . . . But what about me? You might at least have shown consideration for the children. I am nursing and my milk was spoiled. . . . Pétya was at death's door. But you were enjoying yourself. Yes, enjoying . . ."

Pierre knew he was not to blame, for he could not have come sooner; he knew this outburst was unseemly and would blow over in a minute or two; above all he knew that he himself was bright and happy. He wanted to smile but dared not even think of doing so. He made a piteous, frightened face and bent down.

"I could not, on my honor. But how is Pétya?"

"All right now. Come along! I wonder you're not ashamed! If only you could see what I was like without you, how I suffered!"

"You are well?"

"Come, come!" she said, not letting go of his arm. And they went to their rooms.

When Nicholas and his wife came to look for Pierre he was in the nursery holding his baby son, who was again awake, on his huge right palm and dandling him.

"How sweet!" said Countess Mary, looking at and playing with the baby. "Now, Nicholas," she added, turning to her husband, "I can't understand how it is you don't see the charm of these delicious marvels."

"I don't and can't," replied Nicholas, looking coldly at the baby. "A lump of flesh. Come along, Pierre!"

"And yet he's such an affectionate father," said Countess Mary, vindicating her husband, "but only after they are a year old or so . . ."

"Now, Pierre nurses them splendidly," said Natásha. "He says his hand is just made for a baby's seat. Just look!"

"Only not for this . . ." Pierre suddenly exclaimed with a laugh, and shifting the baby he gave him to the nurse.

As in every large household, there were at Bald Hills several perfectly distinct worlds which merged into one harmonious whole, though each retained its own peculiarities and made concessions to the others. Every event, joyful or sad, that took place in that house was important to all these worlds, but each had its own special reasons to rejoice or grieve over that occurrence independently of the others.

For instance, Pierre's return was a joyful and important event and they all felt it to be so.

Young Nicholas, now a slim lad of fifteen, delicate and intelligent, with curly light-brown hair and beautiful eyes, was delighted because Uncle Pierre as he called him was the object of his rapturous and passionate affection. No one had instilled into him this love for Pierre whom he saw only occasionally. Countess Mary who had brought him up had done her utmost to make him love her husband as she loved him, and little Nicholas did love his uncle, but loved him with just a shade of contempt. Pierre, however, he adored. From broken remarks about Natásha and his father, from the emotion with which Pierre spoke of that dead father, and from the careful, reverent tenderness with which Natásha spoke of him, the boy, who was only just beginning to guess what love is, derived the notion that his father had loved Natásha and when dying had left her to his friend. But the father whom the boy did not remember appeared to him a divinity who could not be pictured, and of whom he never thought without a swelling heart and tears of sadness and rapture. So the boy also was happy that Pierre had arrived.

The guests welcomed Pierre because he always helped to enliven and unite any company he was in.

The grown-up members of the family, not to mention his

wife, were pleased to have back a friend whose presence made life run more smoothly and peacefully.

The old ladies were pleased with the presents he brought them, and especially that Natásha would now be herself again.

Pierre felt the different outlooks of these various worlds and made haste to satisfy all their expectations.

With a merry, smiling face Pierre was sorting his purchases. "What do you think of this?" said he, unrolling a piece of stuff like a shopman.

Natásha, who was sitting opposite to him with her eldest daughter on her lap, turned her sparkling eyes swiftly from her husband to the things he showed her.

"That's for Belóva? Excellent!" She felt the quality of the material. "It was a ruble an arshín, I suppose?"

Pierre told her the price.

"Too dear!" Natásha remarked. "How pleased the children will be and Mamma too! Only you need not have bought me this," she added, unable to suppress a smile as she gazed admiringly at a gold comb set with pearls, of a kind then just coming into fashion.

"When am I to wear it?" and Natásha stuck it in her coil of hair. "When I take little Másha into society? Perhaps they will be fashionable again by then. Well, let's go now."

And collecting the presents they went first to the nursery and then to the old countess' rooms.

The countess was sitting with her companion Belóva, playing grand-patience as usual, when Pierre and Natásha came into the drawing room with parcels under their arms.

The countess was now over sixty, was quite gray, and wore a cap with a frill that surrounded her face. Her face had shriveled, her upper lip had sunk in, and her eyes were dim.

After the deaths of her son and husband in such rapid succession, she felt herself a being accidentally forgotten in this world and left without aim or object for her existence. She ate, drank, slept, or kept awake, but did not *live*. Life gave her no new impressions. She wanted nothing from life but tranquillity, and that tranquillity only death could give her. But until death came she had to go on living, that is, to use her vital forces.

The old lady's condition was understood by the whole household though no one ever spoke of it, and they all made every possible effort to satisfy her needs. Only by a rare glance exchanged with a sad smile between Nicholas, Pierre, Natásha, and Countess Mary was the common understanding of her condition expressed.

When Pierre and his wife entered the drawing room the countess was in one of her customary states in which she needed the mental exertion of playing patience, and so—though by force of habit she greeted him with the words she always used when Pierre or her son returned after an absence: "High time, my dear, high time! We were all weary of waiting for you. Well, thank God!" and received her presents with another customary remark: "It's not the gift that's precious, my dear, but that you give it to me, an old woman . . ."—yet it was evident that she was not pleased by Pierre's arrival at that moment when it diverted her attention from the unfinished game.

Though Pierre, Natásha, Nicholas, Countess Mary, and Denísov had much to talk about that they could not discuss before the old countess—not that anything was hidden from her, but because she had dropped so far behindhand in many things that had they begun to converse in her presence they would have to answer inopportune questions and to repeat what they had already told her many times: that so-and-so was dead and so-and-so was married.

Conversation of this kind, interesting to no one yet unavoidable, continued all through teatime. All the grown-up members of the family were assembled near the round tea table at which Sónya presided beside the samovar. The children with their tutors and governesses had had tea and their voices were audible from the next room. At tea all sat in their accustomed places: Nicholas beside the stove at a small table where his tea was handed to him; Mílka, the old gray borzoi bitch (daughter of the first Mílka), with a quite gray face and large black eyes that seemed more prominent than ever, lay on the armchair beside him; Denísov, whose curly hair, mustache, and whiskers had turned half gray, sat beside Countess Mary with his general's tunic unbuttoned; Pierre sat between his wife and the old countess. He spoke of what he knew might interest the old lady and that she could understand. Natásha saw by Pierre's animation that his visit had been interesting and that he had much to tell them but dare not say it before the old countess. Denísov, not being a member of the family, did not understand Pierre's caution and being, as a malcontent, much interested in what was occurring in Petersburg, kept urging Pierre to tell them about what had happened in the Semënovsk regiment, then about Arakchéev, and then about the Bible Society.

"Is that weally still going on?"

"Going on?" Pierre exclaimed. "Why more than ever! The Bible Society is the whole government now!"

"What is that, *mon cher ami?*" asked the countess, who had finished her tea and evidently needed a pretext for being angry after her meal. "What are you saying about the government? I don't understand."

"Arakchéev and Golítsyn," incautiously remarked Pierre, "are now the whole government! And what a government! They see treason everywhere and are afraid of everything."

"Nowadays everyone finds fault. A Gospel Society! Well, and what harm is there in that?" and she rose (everybody else got up too) and with a severe expression sailed back to her table in the sitting room.

The melancholy silence that followed was broken by the sounds of the children's voices and laughter from the next room. Evidently some jolly excitement was going on there.

"Finished, finished!" little Natásha's gleeful yell rose above them all.

Pierre exchanged glances with Countess Mary and Nicholas (Natásha he never lost sight of) and smiled happily.

"That's delightful music!" said he.

"It means that Anna Makárovna has finished her stocking," said Countess Mary.

"Oh, I'll go and see," said Pierre, jumping up. "You know," he added, stopping at the door, "why I'm especially fond of that music? It is always the first thing that tells me all is well. When I was driving here today, the nearer I got to the house the more anxious I grew. As I entered the anteroom I heard Andrúsha's peals of laughter and that meant that all was well."

Soon after this the children came in to say good night. They kissed everyone, the tutors and governesses made their bows, and they went out. Only young Nicholas and his tutor remained. Dessalles whispered to the boy to come downstairs.

"No, Monsieur Dessalles, I will ask my aunt to let me stay," replied Nicholas Bolkónski also in a whisper.

"*Ma tante,* please let me stay," said he, going up to his aunt. His face expressed entreaty, agitation, and ecstasy. Countess Mary glanced at him and turned to Pierre.

"When you are here he can't tear himself away," she said.

"I will bring him to you directly, Monsieur Dessalles. Good night!" said Pierre, giving his hand to the Swiss tutor, and he turned to young Nicholas with a smile. "You and I haven't seen anything of one another yet. . . . How like he is growing, Mary!" he added, addressing Countess Mary.

"Like my father?" asked the boy, flushing crimson and looking up at Pierre with bright, ecstatic eyes.

Pierre nodded, and went on with what he had been saying when the children had interrupted. Countess Mary sat down doing woolwork; Natásha did not take her eyes off her husband. Nicholas and Denísov rose, asked for their pipes, smoked, went to fetch more tea from Sónya—who sat weary but resolute at the samovar—and questioned Pierre. The curly-headed, delicate boy sat with shining eyes unnoticed in a corner, starting every now and then and muttering something to himself, and evidently experiencing a new and powerful emotion as he turned his curly head, with his thin neck exposed by his turn-down collar, toward the place where Pierre sat.

The conversation turned on the contemporary gossip about those in power, in which most people see the chief interest of home politics. Denísov, dissatisfied with the government on account of his own disappointments in the service, heard with pleasure of the things done in Petersburg which seemed to him stupid, and made forcible and sharp comments on what Pierre told them.

Nicholas, though free from Denísov's readiness to find fault with everything, also thought that discussion of the government was a very serious and weighty matter. The questions put by these two kept the conversation from changing its ordinary character of gossip about the higher government circles.

But Natásha, knowing all her husband's ways and ideas, saw that he had long been wishing but had been unable to divert the conversation to another channel and express his own deeply felt idea for the sake of which he had gone to Petersburg to consult with his new friend Prince Theodore, and she helped him by asking how his affairs with Prince Theodore had gone.

"What was it about?" asked Nicholas.

"Always the same thing," said Pierre, looking round at his listeners. "Everybody sees that things are going so badly that they cannot be allowed to go on so and that it is the duty of all decent men to counteract it as far as they can."

"What can decent men do?" Nicholas inquired, frowning slightly. "What can be done?"

"Why, this . . ."

"Come into my study," said Nicholas.

Natásha, who had long expected to be fetched to nurse her baby, now heard the nurse calling her and went to the nursery. Countess Mary followed her. The men went into the study and little Nicholas Bolkónski followed them unnoticed by his uncle and sat down at the writing table in a shady corner of the window.

"Well, what would you do?" asked Denísov.

"Always some fantastic schemes," said Nicholas.

"Why this," began Pierre, not sitting down but pacing the room, sometimes stopping short, gesticulating, and lisping: "the position in Petersburg is this: the Emperor does not look into anything. He has abandoned himself altogether to this mysticism" (Pierre could not tolerate mysticism in anyone now). "He seeks only for peace, and only these people without faith or law can give it him—people who recklessly hack at and strangle everything."

"Well, what does that lead up to?" said Nicholas.

"Well, everything is going to ruin! Robbery in the law courts, in the army nothing but flogging, drilling; the people are tortured, enlightenment is suppressed. All that is young and honest is crushed! Everyone sees that this cannot go on. Everything is strained to such a degree that it will certainly break," said Pierre(as those who examine the actions of any government have always said since governments began). "I told them just one thing in Petersburg."

"Told whom?"

"Well, you know whom," said Pierre, with a meaning glance from under his brows. "Prince Theodore and all those. To encourage culture and philanthropy is all very well of course. The aim is excellent but in the present circumstances something else is needed."

At that moment Nicholas noticed the presence of his nephew. His face darkened and he went up to the boy.

"Why are you here?"

"Why? Let him be," said Pierre, taking Nicholas by the arm and continuing. "That is not enough, I told them. Something else is needed. When you stand expecting the overstrained string to snap at any moment, when everyone is expecting the inevitable catastrophe, as many as possible must join hands as closely as they can to withstand the general calamity. Everything that is young and strong is being enticed away and depraved. One is lured by women, another by honors, a third by ambition or money, and they go over to that camp. No independent men, such as you or I, are left. What I say is widen the scope of our society, let the *mot d'ordre* be not virtue alone but independence and action as well!"

Nicholas, who had left his nephew, irritably pushed up an armchair, sat down in it, and listened to Pierre, coughing discontentedly and frowning more and more.

"But action with what aim?" he cried. "And what position will you adopt toward the government?"

"Why, the position of assistants. The society need not be secret if the government allows it. Not merely is it not hostile to government, but it is a society of true conservatives—a society of gentlemen in the full meaning of that word."

"Yes, but it's a secret society and therefore a hostile and harmful one which can only cause harm."

"Why? Did the Tugendbund which saved Europe" (they did not then venture to suggest that Russia had saved Europe) "do any harm? The Tugendbund is an alliance of virtue: it is love, mutual help . . . it is what Christ preached on the Cross."

Natásha, who had come in during the conversation, looked joyfully at her husband. It was not what he was saying that pleased her—that did not even interest her, for it seemed to her that it was all extremely simple and that she had known it a long time (it seemed so to her because she knew that it sprang from Pierre's whole soul), but it was his animated and enthusiastic appearance that made her glad.

The boy with the thin neck stretching out from the turn-down collar—whom everyone had forgotten—gazed at Pierre with even greater and more rapturous joy. Every word of Pierre's burned into his heart, and with a nervous movement of his fingers he unconsciously broke the sealing wax and quill pens his hands came upon on his uncle's table.

"It is not at all what you suppose; but that is what the German Tugendbund was, and what I am proposing."

"No, my fwiend; The Tugendbund is all vewy well for the sausage eaters, but I don't understand it and can't even pwo-nounce it," interposed Denísov in a loud and resolute voice.

Pierre smiled, Natásha began to laugh, but Nicholas knitted his brows still more and began proving to Pierre that there was no prospect of any great change and that all the danger he spoke of existed only in his imagination.

"I will tell you this," he said, rising and trying with nervous-ly twitching fingers to prop up his pipe in a corner, but finally abandoning the attempt. "I can't prove it to you. You say that everything here is rotten and that an overthrow is coming: I don't see it. But you also say that our oath of allegiance is a conditional matter, and to that I reply: 'You are my best friend, as you know, but if you formed a secret society and began working against the government—be it what it may—I know it is my duty to obey the government. And if Arakchéev ordered me to lead a squadron against you and cut you down, I should not hesitate an instant, but should do it.' And you may argue about that as you like!"

An awkward silence followed these words. Natásha was the first to speak, defending her husband and attacking her brother. Her defense was weak and inept but she attained her object. The conversation was resumed, and no longer in the unpleasantly hostile tone of Nicholas' last remark.

When they all got up to go in to supper, little Nicholas Bolkónski went up to Pierre, pale and with shining, radiant eyes.

"Uncle Pierre, you . . . no . . . If Papa were alive . . . would he agree with you?" he asked.

And Pierre suddenly realized what a special, independent, complex, and powerful process of thought and feeling must have been going on in this boy during that conversation, and remembering all he had said he regretted that the lad should have heard him. He had, however, to give him an answer.

"Yes, I think so," he said reluctantly, and left the study.

4

The conversation at supper was not about politics or societies, but turned on the subject Nicholas liked best—recollections of 1812. Denísov started these and Pierre was particularly agreeable and amusing about them. The family separated on the most friendly terms.

After supper Nicholas, having undressed in his study and given instructions to the steward who had been waiting for him, went to the bedroom in his dressing gown, where he found his wife still at her table, writing.

"What are you writing, Mary?" Nicholas asked.

Countess Mary blushed. She was afraid that what she was writing would not be understood or approved by her husband.

She had wanted to conceal what she was writing from him, but at the same time was glad he had surprised her at it and that she would now have to tell him.

"A diary, Nicholas," she replied, handing him a blue exercise book filled with her firm, bold writing.

"A diary?" Nicholas repeated with a shade of irony, and he took up the book.

It was in French.

Under the date "5" was entered:

"Mítya was naughty at table. Papa said he was to have no pudding. He had none, but looked so unhappily and greedily at the others while they were eating! I think that punishment by depriving children of sweets only develops their greediness. Must tell Nicholas this."

He was proud of her intelligence and goodness, recognized his own insignificance beside her in the spiritual world, and rejoiced all the more that she with such a soul not only belonged to him but was part of himself.

"I quite, quite approve, my dearest!" said he with a significant look, and after a short pause he added: "And I behaved badly today. You weren't in the study. We began disputing—

Pierre and I—and I lost my temper. But he is impossible: such a child! I don't know what would become of him if Natásha didn't keep him in hand. . . . Have you any idea why he went to Petersburg? They have formed . . ."

"Yes, I know," said Countess Mary. "Natásha told me."

"When I told him that duty and the oath were above everything, he started proving goodness knows what! A pity you were not there—what would you have said?"

"As I see it you were quite right, and I told Natásha so. Pierre says everybody is suffering, tortured, and being corrupted, and that it is our duty to help our neighbor. Of course he is right there," said Countess Mary, "but he forgets that we have other duties nearer to us, duties indicated to us by God Himself, and that though we might expose ourselves to risks we must not risk our children."

"Yes, that's it! That's just what I said to him," put in Nicholas, who fancied he really had said it. "But they insisted on their own view: love of one's neighbor and Christianity—and all this in the presence of young Nicholas, who had gone into my study and broke all my things."

"Ah, Nicholas, do you know I am often troubled about little Nicholas," said Countess Mary. "He is such an exceptional boy. I am afraid I neglect him in favor of my own: we all have children and relations while he has no one. He is constantly alone with his thoughts."

"Well, I don't think you need reproach yourself on his account. All that the fondest mother could do for her son you have done and are doing for him, and of course I am glad of it. He is a fine lad, a fine lad! This evening he listened to Pierre in a sort of trance, and fancy—as we were going in to supper I looked and he had broken everything on my table to bits, and he told me of it himself at once! I never knew him to tell an untruth. A fine lad, a fine lad!" repeated Nicholas, who at heart was not fond of Nicholas Bolkónski but was always anxious to recognize that he was a fine lad.

"Still, I am not the same as his own mother," said Countess Mary. "I feel I am not the same and it troubles me. A wonderful boy, but I am dreadfully afraid for him. It would be good for him to have companions."

"Well it won't be for long. Next summer I'll take him to Petersburg," said Nicholas. "Yes, Pierre always was a dreamer and always will be," he continued, returning to the talk in the study which had evidently disturbed him. "Well, what business is it of mine what goes on there? . . . And then there are you and the children and our affairs. Is it for my own pleasure that I am at the farm or in the office from morning to night? No, but I know I must work to comfort my mother, to repay you, and not to leave the children such beggars as I was."

Countess Mary wanted to tell him that man does not live by bread alone and that he attached too much importance to these matters. But she knew she must not say this and that it would be useless to do so. She only took his hand and kissed it. He took this as a sign of approval and a confirmation of his thoughts, and after a few minutes' reflection continued to think aloud.

"You know, Mary, today Elias Mitrofánych" (this was his overseer) "came back from the Tambóv estate and told me they are already offering eighty thousand rubles for the forest."

Countess Mary listened to her husband and understood all that he told her. She felt a submissive tender love for this man who would never understand all that she understood, and this seemed to make her love for him still stronger and added a touch of passionate tenderness.

Countess Mary's soul always strove toward the infinite, the eternal, and the absolute, and could therefore never be at peace. A stern expression of the lofty, secret suffering of a soul burdened by the body appeared on her face. Nicholas gazed at her. "O God! What will become of us if she dies, as I always fear when her face is like that?" thought he, and placing himself before the icon he began to say his evening prayers.

Natásha and Pierre, left alone, also began to talk as only a husband and wife can talk, that is, with extraordinary clearness and rapidity, understanding and expressing each other's thoughts in ways contrary to all rules of logic, without premises, deductions, or conclusions, and in a quite peculiar way. Natásha was so used to this kind of talk with her husband that for her it was the surest sign of something being wrong between them if Pierre followed a line of logical reasoning.

From the moment they were alone and Natásha came up to him with wide-open happy eyes, and quickly seizing his head pressed it to her bosom, saying: "Now you are all mine, mine! You won't escape!"—from that moment this conversation began, contrary to all the laws of logic and contrary to them because quite different subjects were talked about at one and the same time. This simultaneous discussion of many topics did not prevent a clear understanding but on the contrary was the surest sign that they fully understood one another.

Natásha spoke to Pierre about her brother's life and doings, of how she had suffered and lacked life during his own absence, and of how she was fonder than ever of Mary, and how Mary was in every way better than herself. In saying this Natásha was sincere in acknowledging Mary's superiority, but at the same time by saying it she made a demand on Pierre that he should, all the same, prefer her to Mary and to all other women, and that now, especially after having seen many women in Petersburg, he should tell her so afresh.

Pierre, answering Natásha's words, told her how intolerable it had been for him to meet ladies at dinners and balls in Petersburg.

"I have quite lost the knack of talking to ladies," he said. "It was simply dull. Besides, I was very busy."

Natásha looked intently at him and went on:

"Mary is so splendid," she said. "How she understands children! It is as if she saw straight into their souls. Yesterday, for instance, Mítya was naughty . . ."

"How like his father he is," Pierre interjected.

Natásha knew why he mentioned Mítya's likeness to Nicholas: the recollection of his dispute with his brother-in-law was unpleasant and he wanted to know what Natásha thought of it.

"Nicholas has the weakness of never agreeing with anything not generally accepted. But I understand that you value what opens up a fresh line," said she, repeating words Pierre had once uttered.

"No, the chief point is that to Nicholas ideas and discussions are an amusement—almost a pastime," said Pierre.

"So you say ideas are an amusement to him. . . ."

"Yes, and for me nothing else is serious. All the time in Petersburg I saw everyone as in a dream. When I am taken up by a thought, all else is mere amusement."

Natásha would have had no doubt as to the greatness of Pierre's idea, but one thing disconcerted her. "Can a man so important and necessary to society be also my husband? How did this happen?" She wished to express this doubt to him. "Now who could decide whether he is really cleverer than all the others?" she asked herself, and whom Pierre most respected. Judging by there was no one he had respected so highly all those Karatáev.

"Do you know what I am thinking about?" she asked. "About Platón Karatáev. Would he have approved of you now, do you think?"

Pierre was not at all surprised at this question. He understood his wife's line of thought.

"Platón Karatáev?" he repeated, and pondered, evidently sincerely trying to imagine Karatáev's opinion on the subject. "He would not have understood . . . yet perhaps he would."

"I love you awfully!" Natásha suddenly said. "Awfully, awfully!"

"No, he would not have approved," said Pierre, after reflection. "What he would have approved of is our family life. He was always so anxious to find seemliness, happiness, and peace in everything, and I should have been proud to let him see us. There now—you talk of my absence, but you wouldn't believe what a special feeling I have for you after a separation. . . ."

"Yes, I should think . . ." Natásha began.

"No, it's not that. I never leave off loving you. And one couldn't love more, but this is something special. . . . Yes, of course—" he did not finish because their eyes meeting said the rest.

Meanwhile downstairs in young Nicholas Bolkónski's bedroom a little lamp was burning as usual. (The boy was afraid of the dark and they could not cure him of it.) Dessalles slept propped up on four pillows and his Roman nose emitted sounds of rhythmic snoring. Little Nicholas, who had just waked up in a cold perspiration, sat up in bed and gazed before him with wide-open eyes. He had awaked from a terrible dream. He had dreamed that he and Uncle Pierre, wearing helmets such as were depicted in his Plutarch, were leading a huge army. The army was made up of white slanting lines that filled the air like the cobwebs that float about in autumn and which Dessalles called *les fils de la Vièrge*. In front was Glory, which was similar to those threads but rather thicker. He and Pierre were borne along lightly and joyously, nearer and nearer to their goal. Suddenly the threads that moved them began to slacken and become entangled and it grew difficult to move.

stood before them in a stern and threatening...

...have you done this?" he said, pointing to some broken sealing wax and pens. "I loved you, but I have orders from Arakchéev and will kill the first of you who moves forward." Little Nicholas turned to look at Pierre but Pierre was no longer there. In his place was his father—Prince Andrew—and his father had neither shape nor form, but he existed, and when little Nicholas perceived him he grew faint with love: he felt himself powerless, limp, and formless. His father caressed and pitied him. But Uncle Nicholas came nearer and nearer to them. Terror seized young Nicholas and he awoke.

"My father!" he thought. "My father has been with me and caressed me. He approved of me and of Uncle Pierre. Whatever he may tell me, I will do it . . . I know they want me to learn. And I will learn. But someday I shall have finished learning, and then I will do something. I only pray God that something may happen to me such as happened to Plutarch's men, and I will act as they did. I will do better. Everyone shall know me, love me, and be delighted with me!" And suddenly his bosom heaved with sobs and he began to cry.

"Are you ill?" he heard Dessalles' voice asking.

"No," answered Nicholas, and lay back on his pillow.

"He is good and kind and I am fond of him!" he thought of Dessalles. "But Uncle Pierre! Oh, what a wonderful man he is! And my father? Oh, Father, Father! Yes, I will do something with which even *he* would be satisfied. . . ."

FOLGER LIBRARY GENERAL READER'S
SHAKESPEARE

Twenty-nine of Shakespeare's plays appear in this series edited by Louis B. Wright, Director, and Virginia A. LaMar, Executive Secretary, Folger Shakespeare Library, Washington, D.C., two of the world's foremost Elizabethan authorities. The Folger text of each play is printed on right hand pages only, with notes on the facing left hand pages keyed by line number to the text for easy reference.

If you are unable to obtain these plays from your regular dealer, you may order them by sending 45c each, plus 10c per book for postage and handling, to: Mail Service Department, WASHINGTON SQUARE PRESS, Inc., 1 West 39th Street, New York, N.Y. 10018. Please enclose check or money order—*do not send cash.*